By Faye Kellerman
Published by Fawcett Books:

THE RITUAL BATH
SACRED AND PROFANE
THE QUALITY OF MERCY
MILK AND HONEY
DAY OF ATONEMENT
FALSE PROPHET
GRIEVOUS SIN

The Quality of Mercy

Faye Kellerman

FAWCETT CREST • NEW YORK

A Fawcett Crest Book
Published by Ballantine Books
Copyright © 1989 by Faye Kellerman

http://www.randomhouse.com

Library of Congress Catalog Card Number: 88-29275

ISBN 0-449-21892-9

This edition published by arrangement with William Morrow and Company, Inc.

Manufactured in the United States of America

First Ballantine Books Edition: December 1990

15   14   13

For Jonathan.

And for Barney Karpfinger: Diogenes, stop looking, I found him.

Thanking the translators: Maribel Romero, Phyllis Elliott, and Miriam Lewis.

And a special thanks to John and Mary Jane Hertz—two people worthy of their titles.

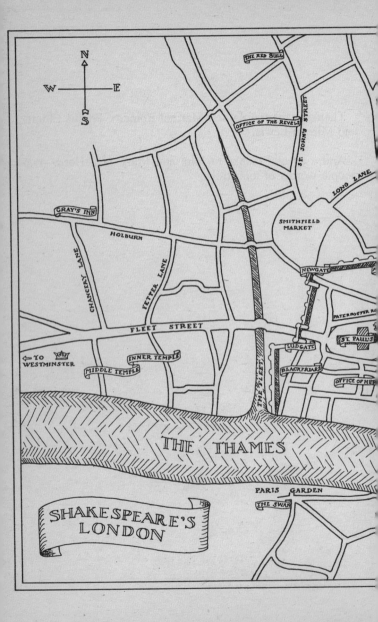

SHAKESPEARE'S
LONDON

FINSBURY
FIELDS

THE CURTAIN

GOLDING LAN

THE FORTUNE

SHOREDITCH

MOORFIELDS

BISHOPSGATE STREET

CRIPPLEGATE

NTJOY HOUSE

LAVE'S

ST. MARYS

MOORGATE

CITY WALL

ALDERMANBURY

COLEMAN STREET

BISHOPSGATE

LOTHBURY STREET

GREENAM COLLEGE

BULL INN

ST. HELEN'S

BISHOPGATE STREET

CROSBY PLACE

MAID TAVERN

CHEAPSIDE

ROYAL EXCHANGE

LEADENHALL STREET

ALDGATE

WATLING STREET

BREAD STREET

BELL INN

CROSS KEYS INN

FENCHURCH STREET

CANNON STREET

GRACE CHURCH STREET

EAST CHEAP

THAMES STREET

TOWER
HILL

LONDON BRIDGE

THE TOWER

ARDEN

THE GLOBE

ROSE

ST. SAVIOR'S

ERTY OF
CLINK

SOUTHWARK

TO NEWINGTON

Lisbon, 1540

1

As I see the first hint of sunlight, the death march begins. We advance toward the Terriero do Paco—the great city square adjacent to the Royal Palace on the seafront.

Leading the processional is Don Henrique—the Inquisitor General of Portugal by appointment of his older brother, His Royal Highness John the Third. Don Henrique is an ugly man—lean, with an avian nose, and black eyes set so deeply that the sockets appear hollow. His thick beard—a weave of bronze, copper, and iron—is meticulously shaped to a dagger point. His dress is appropriately august—official: floor-length black robe and cape, white clerical collar, and black trapezoidal hat. Dangling from his neck is his scallop-edged crucifix of gold, inset with topaz, lapis, aquamarine, sapphire, and topped with a finial of diamonds. A haughty man, Don Henrique always wears jeweled crosses. Gilt bible clutched to his breast, eyes fixed straight ahead, he presses on slowly but inexorably, prepared to carry out the work of his God.

Following the Inquisitor are four rows of black-garbed monks. Around their necks are unadorned crucifixes fashioned from the heavier base metals. Rigid and stone-faced, they carry black-covered bibles and hold aloft crosses and banners. They chant low-pitched dirges as they trudge forward on sandaled feet.

Behind the clergy are the royal officials and the black-hooded executioners—the secular arm of the law. Their ranks advance in taut, military fashion—arms swinging with pendular precision, not a boot out of step.

We are at the rear of the retinue. The victims—the wretches. We are heavily guarded and hold lighted tapers that spit fire into the early morning sky. Some of us endure the ordeal with stoicism—posture erect, gait sure-footed and strong. That is how I walk. Others about me seem stuporous, stumbling off-balance, as if being yanked forward by an invisible harness. The weakest weep openly.

The auto-da-fé—act of faith—is the day of reckoning for us. We've been convicted of violations of the Church. We walk forward, clearly identified for the onlookers; we wear the dreaded *sambenito*—the two-sided apron of shame imprinted with symbols corresponding to our infractions. Serious sinners like myself wear *corazas*—conical miters—as well.

Some are considered penitent and deemed reconcilable to the Church. They will gratefully accept the penalties meted out to them. The pettiest among them will be punished with fines, terms of forced servitude, or imprisonment. More serious transgressors will merit whipping or public shaming—being stripped to the waist and paraded around town to the derision and jeers of their countrymen. Wretches who committed grave infractions will be plunged into poverty, have all their worldly possessions confiscated by the Holy Office. These offenders will be stigmatized for generations, their descendants barred forever from entering the Holy Office, from becoming physicians, tutors, apothecaries, advocates, scriveners, or farmers for revenue. They will be forbidden to dress in cloth woven from gold or silver thread, wear jewelry, or ride on horseback.

But they are fortunate.

I, and others like me, are deemed impenitent. We hapless souls are guilty of the most odious heresies. My specific crime is Judaizing—practicing and professing the ancient laws of Moses rendered obsolete by their Jesus Christ. Once, Spain called me a converso—a *Christian* of Jewish bloodline. I was an overt Catholic, but secretly I practiced the old ways. My transgressions were discovered by a wanton woman. Now I am doomed.

Distinguished from the fortunates by our green tapers and dress, we—the *relapsos*—wear special fiery miters and the *sambenito* of death imprinted with the likeness of the Devil himself. Around his horned visage and pronged fork are leaping flames: the Hell that is to await us.

I spit on their stinking Christian ground. That's what I think of their Hell.

This morning will be my last. Before the night is over, I will be sentenced to die without effusion of blood, their castigation derived from John 15:6—from the teachings of their Savior Himself: *If a man abide not in me, he is cast forth as a branch and is withered and men gather them and cast them into the fire, and they are burned.*

The dank ocean fog begins to melt, yielding to an opaline sky dotted with tufts of woolly cloud. At six in the morning the city bells ring out the signal and I shudder with dread. The cobblestone walkways begin to fill with austere gentlemen somberly wrapped in dark capes. They step with much haste, their servants at their heels. Ten minutes later the veiled women of the households emerge—wives, mothers, sisters, and daughters. Some of the women hold babies and toddlers, others drag older children, chiding them for slowness. The streets soon become a throng of bodies. In the center is this murderous tribunal—as poisonous as an asp. It undulates its way to the city square.

By the time the officials arrive at the Terreiro, most of the spectators have been positioned, either standing, or seated in the gallery benches that form a semicircle around the dais, the garrotes, and the stakes. In the foreground are the white-capped swells of the ocean. In the background stands the great palace, casting a deep shadow over the galleries.

We are ordered to stand up straight. A guard hits the woman next to me. She is eight months pregnant, younger than I, I think. Around seventeen. Her back is stooped from the weight of her fruit. I smile at her. Wet-eyed, she smiles back at me. Our eyes have told each to be strong.

As Don Henrique ascends to the black-draped podium, the noise of idle conversation softens, then finally quiets to silence. The Inquisitor stands immobile, his head bowed in meditation. The sun, now higher in the advanced morning sky, projects a metallic sheen onto the ground, gilding the Inquisitor. Tides yawn rhythmic, lazy growls. An uneasy calm has blanketed the air.

Suddenly, a mourner's wail blasts through the square, reverberating against salty air and harmonizing with the ocean's roar—the baritone summons of a sheep's horn. The pregnant girl next to me jumps. I do nothing. The audience is cleaved in two by a red carpet, unfurled and smoothed by royal attendants.

King John and Queen Catalina—may they rot in Hell—enter the gathering, followed by their entourage. His Majesty's porcine features are embedded in pillowy cheeks that are pink and pockmarked. He's fair-complexioned, with a neatly trimmed but scant beard. His portly frame looks especially obese today, swaddled under layers of clothing. His sable collar, draped over a padded doublet of gold, frames his chin like the mane of a lion. Resting on his shoulders is a blue velvet robe secured by a clasp of jewel-encrusted animals linked together with braided silver. His round hose are pleats of blue and scarlet velvet and puffed out at the hip line. Hanging from his belt is a gold scabbard revealing the gem-studded handle of a broadsword. His stockings, no doubt made of pure silk, are obscured by high-polished black boots that end mid-thigh. On his head is perched the royal crown of the State.

The Queen is the daughter of the Emperor Charles the Fifth of Rome, granddaughter of Ferdinand and Isabella. Her facial features are small and pinched, her complexion tinged with olive. Her slender arms are hidden under full, maroon sleeves, but the bodice and stomacher of her dress reveal her pride, her vanity—a tiny waist that is rumored to be encircled easily by her husband's thick hands. She wears a flowing skirt of black taffety overlaid with gold lace, and is crowned with a diamond and emerald tiara. A staunch Catholic, Catalina is the driving wind behind the Inquisition. She was inspired by the religious fervor of her late confessor, Frai Diogo da Silva—another pig.

The monarchs are led to raised thrones at the top of the galleries. As soon as they are seated, the Inquisitor lifts his head and extends his arms toward the rulers of the land.

"Mighty Sovereigns." Don Henrique bows low. "King and Queen, Protectors of the True Faith. On a throne of velvet you sit most high. Justice and truth in God you preach as well as practice. In the great reign of King John the Third, the Savior shall once again witness purity of blood as we ferret out the foul stench that has infiltrated the rightful Church. Only under fair and impartial rulers such as yourselves, good King and Queen, will Catholicism be purified for true believers. A pure race—of pure, true Christians—to serve the most Holy One, Jesus Christ, the embodiment of the Father, the Son, and the Holy Spirit."

King John and Queen Catalina—the swine—duly nod.

"As for the condemned, the wretched souls," Don Henrique continues, "assuming they *have* souls, so beastly and dung-riddled are their filthy, ghastly undertakings . . ."

The crowd nods in agreement. A baby lets out a sudden shriek.

"Yea," Henrique exclaims. "Yea . . . even an innocent *babe* cries out at the sight of the Devil himself, beseeching the Lord, 'Most holy Savior! Protect my baptized soul!' "

The Inquisitor's voice rings out. "Protect me against the disgusting, putrid pollution that has entered the most holy religion of God, subverting the good into evil."

Don Henrique points to us—those sentenced to death.

"Damned ye be! Damnable are your crimes against man and against God. Ye are to consider the stake a most gentle taste of what awaits you once ye are in the grasp of the Devil. Ye shall drink boiling lead and eat molten brimstone for ale and food. Daily ye shall be skinned and burned, steamed in cauldrons of liquid fire. Your livers shall be fodder for the vulture, your hearts sustenance for the crow. Your entrails shall ye eat, the filth of your bowels shall ye breathe. Your eyes will be plucked out with glowing pokers as the Devil and his servants laugh at your wretched miseries."

The Inquisitor holds his breath until his face is flushed, then lets out a chilling scream directed at the crowd.

"Ye think you are safe from the wiles of the Devil? Think again lest in your airs ye drop your shields and give space for the Devil to come and do his bidding."

He returns his attention to us. I listen, but his words do not affect me. I've heard them many times before. Don Henrique clutches his heart and says,

"Satan—cursed be his name—has entered these filthy souls. But Jesus Christ, in His martyrdom, died for you. Died for your souls—all souls, the filthy with the pure. There remains hope for your souls in the life hereafter. Your earthly life is over. By your own stinking hand ye were sentenced, as God and the Church had tried to enter in life and failed. Perhaps ye shall see His wisdom now that death is upon your wretched bodies.

"Ye still have a chance! Ye still can make restitution to the cross by publicly confessing your errors and admitting them before man as well as God."

Don Henrique lights a torch and hoists it into the air.

"Let the proceedings begin," he says.

The ordeal will last all day. The lightest offenders are dealt with first. One by one they are summoned before the Inquisitor, insulted and cursed, then assigned their punishment by the secular arm. Maria Gomez is fined for appearing unveiled in public against the wishes of her husband. Joao Dias is whipped for theft. Salvador Guterrias is imprisoned for life for unnatural fornication with his wife. They should know the real truth. In the dungeon he told me that he had fornicated with animals, that they were more satisfying to him than his fat, stinking wife. Had that bit of knowledge come to the attention of the Inquisition, he would have been sentenced to die.

Name after name is called. We are forced to stand rigid during the proceedings. I worry about the girl next to me. I fear she will faint and then the guards will beat her. But she proves stronger than I had first thought. Yes, she sways on her feet, but her spine remains upright.

The tribunal continues past the noon hour and chews up the afternoon until dusk spreads over the square. No conversation in the audience is permitted. Children who violate the rule are immediately silenced—first verbally, then with a sharp slap. Roving guards maintain decorum with stern demeanors and, for those who have succumbed to dozing, a rap on the head with a stout staff.

Nightfall begins to darken the landscape, but the Inquisitor shows no signs of tiring. Do murderers ever tire of their lust for blood? As the torches are lit around the edges of the stage, Don Henrique points an accusing finger at the first of us condemned to death.

"Fernando Lopes!" he cries out. "Come forward."

Lopes is an emaciated, hirsute man of thirty. His pale skin stretches over a large bony frame that once had been thick and muscular. I had known him before he was caught. He has degenerated very badly. His eyes, dulled by years of incarceration, seem mad now. They dart about aimlessly. His beard, once dark and handsome, is a gray nest of brambles, caked with spittle and blood. His hands are bound with leather straps, but his feet are untethered and bare. He is pulled forward by two guards.

"Thou miserable, filthy wretch of dung!" the Inquisitor says. "Thou hast been accused of relapsing!"

"No," Lopes protests.

It is useless to deny, but Lopes will do it anyway. He is that kind of man.

"Quiet, sinner!" shouts the Inquisitor. "Thou knowest this to be truth! Thine own daughter confessed thy sins. Because her confessions were made under oath to the Holy Office, her life shall be mercifully spared. But thee . . . thou who wast warned in good faith—"

"But I have done nothing, Most Holy—"

"Still thou deniest what has been observed and verified by thine own daughter!" the Inquisitor screams. "Thou art to be eternally damned if thy confessions are not made before thy death. Make thy confessions, sinner!"

"But I have done nothing—"

Don Henrique addresses the audience, his expression incredulous. "*What* is to be done with this mongrel to save his soul? Must we show him the Devil's way?"

Turning to one of the sentries, he orders, "Shave this *New Christian*!"

As two warders restrain Lopes, a third takes his torch and brings it to the struggling man's beard. The whiskers catch fire and Lopes screams. I cannot watch anymore.

Henrique says, "Confess thy sins, wretched soul, and allow the Savior to take pity on you!"

"I confess! I confess!"

"Thou will confess in earnest?"

"Yes, yes, only please! . . ."

I force myself to glance at the wretched man. Lopes is on fire—a human torch. His shrieks curdle my blood.

"Douse the fire," Don Henrique suddenly commands.

A bucket of water is splashed into Lopes's face. He gasps for air, his face a grotesque melting candle of dripping water, burnt hair, and charred skin.

The Inquisitor accuses, "Thou changest linens on Friday. And thou concealest the treacherous act from thy servants by placing the dirty linens atop the clean, only to remove them before sunset on Friday. Admit it!"

Lopes says nothing.

"Still thou wadest in defiance!"

"No, Your Holiness," Lopes squeaks.

"Speak up, Fernando Lopes!" the Inquisitor thunders. "Did thou change linens on Friday?"

Lopes nods.

"Dost thou admit to thy sin?'

"Yes, Your—" Lopes swallows. "Yes, Your Holiness."

"And to thy sin of refraining from the consumption of pork?"

"But Your Holiness," Lopes protests feebly, "pork makes me ill—"

"Still thou retainest the Devil's obstinence?"

"Truly my stomach is ill-bred for its consumption."

Don Henrique turns to the galleries.

"Must we continue listening to the lies of this filthy Jew? Must we prove our intent to save his soul once again? Light the beard."

"No!" Lopes screams. "Yes, I confess. I did abstain from the consumption of pork."

"Thou art a Judaizer. Admit it, Jew!"

"Yes, yes, it is true!"

"And who else was involved in thy crimes? Thy wife?"

"No! Verily, she is an honest Christian!"

"As thou art an honest Christian," Don Henrique mocks.

"No, no! She knows nothing of my sins—"

"Admit it, dog! Thy wife is also a sinner—"

"But it is not true!"

"Light his beard."

"No," Lopes pleads with anguish. But this time he refuses to speak further. His cries are put to rest when again Don Henrique orders his beard to be drenched.

"Fernando Lopes," says the Inquisitor, "dost thou repent for thy wicked ways?"

"Yes," Lopes whispers.

"Dost thou embrace the cross and pledge an oath of faith that Jesus Christ is thine only chance for salvation in the Hereafter?"

"Yes."

Don Henrique walks over to the condemned man and holds out his crucifix.

"Embrace the cross, Fernando."

Lopes does as ordered.

"Pledge thy faith to Christ the Lord," demands the Inquisitor.

"I pledge my faith to Christ the Lord."

"That He is thy Savior."

"He is my Savior."

"And thy salvation in the Hereafter."

"And my salvation in the Hereafter."

"Thou art a wretched sinner, but thou dost make penitence on this day for all thy previous sins."

"I am a wretched sinner, but I do make penitence on this day for all my previous sins."

"And pray for the mercy of Christ."

"And pray for the mercy of Christ."

"In nomine Patris et Filii et Spiritus Sancti."

"In nomine Patris et Filii et Spiritus Sancti."

"Fernando Lopes," cries the Inquisitor, "for thy *free* confessions, thou warrant mercy. Thou shalt be relaxed to the secular arm for punishment, but shalt be garroted in a swift manner as a reward for thy *free* confessions and thy pledge of oath to the True Faith."

The guards unbound the prisoner's limbs and lead the limp, burnt man over to an open iron collar attached perpendicularly to a metal post. As the collar is clamped shut around his scrawny neck, Lopes begs for his life, but his whines are cut short at the first turn of the screw.

The collar tightens. Lopes gasps and clutches at the metal band constricting his throat.

The screw is turned again.

Lopes's pasty face takes on the blue tinge of strangulation.

The screw makes a final revolution, and Lopes's arms, legs, and bowels relax.

The crowd roars at the sight of the lifeless body.

A few minutes later a warder loosens the screw and removes the collar. Lopes tumbles to the ground, a pile of dead bone and skin. The body is dragged by the hair to a pyre. After securing the corpse to the stake, the sentry notices that the head is dangling precariously from its broken neck. He grabs a handful of Lopes's hair and ties it around the stake. The head is now sufficiently upright, dead eyes gaping at the galleries. Satisfied, the sentry walks away to join his ranks.

The corpse will be burnt at the conclusion of the ceremony— the grand finale that serves as a caveat for those who contemplate straying from the catechisms of the Church.

Don Henrique turns his attention to the woman next to me. She, like me, is a *relapso*—a converso found guilty of Judaizing. She admits her guilt freely. She begs for another chance, not for her, but for her unborn child. Her pleas, though acknowledged, merit her no special favors. She makes a final effort to save her baby. Let her be punished by death, but cannot the tribunal wait until after the baby is born?

The answer is no. She is garroted after reaffirming her faith to the cross.

Three more men are placed in the iron collar—two for Judaizing, one for sodomy with his stableboy. Two more women. Another man. Another woman. Deep into the night until Don Henrique eyes the last victim—me.

I am nineteen, with gray eyes that used to shine like newly pressed coins. Once my hair was beautiful. It is now a cap of untamed dusty curls that fall past my waistline. My face is covered with sores, my lips cracked open, oozing blood. My teeth are gone, having been rooted out with tongs as punishment for biting a jailer. My nude gums are uneven nodules of angry red flesh.

A guard gags me. I fight viciously against leather restraints that bind my arms and legs. Two guards are holding me in place, but the sweat on their faces bespeaks the intensity of my struggles.

"Teresa Roderiguez!" the Inquisitor announces. "Filthy wretch of a daughter. Have thee anything to say in behalf of thy defense?"

I nod.

"Remove the *morgaza*," orders Don Henrique.

As one of the sentries pulls off the gag, I yell,

"A pox on thee!"

Don Henrique stiffens with rage. I am glad. He shouts, "Wretched, filthy dog! Save thy soul!"

I spit in his direction.

The Inquisitor raises his fist and cries, "Thou shalt burn in Hell continuously lest ye make confessions!"

I say, "I *piss* on thy confessions!" I spit again.

"Putrid agent of the Devil—"

"I am a Jew! I shall die a Jew!"

"Aye, the witch dost admit her heresy!" Don Henrique says to the audience. He faces me. "Thy ghastly, bull-dunged body shall be a playmate for the Devil lest thou make thy confessions to Christ—"

"I shit on thy Christ! *Shma Yisroel, Adonai*—"

"Silence! Gag the filth!"

The rag is stuffed back into my mouth.

"Light the dog's feet!"

A torch is held under my soles. The flames tickled, then burned the callused flesh, causing it to blister and wrinkle like roasted chestnuts. I scream. The agony causes me to buck harder than before.

"Have thee something to say now, Teresa Roderiguez?"

I nod.

"Remove the *morgaza*," the Inquisitor says.

A sentry sighs and pulls the rag out of my mouth.

I scream, *"Shma Yisroel, Adonai—"*

"Replace the *morgaza*! For thy obstinance, bitch, shalt thou burnest. To the *quemadero* shalt thou be placed *alive*, and there shalt thou be raped by the Devil for eternity!"

The guard pulls me to the stake. I fight him, attempt to land blows and kicks with my bound arms and legs.

It is useless.

As I thrash, they strap me onto the pyre and the Inquisitor offers his torch to King John. His Royal Highness rises, straightens his cape, then takes the arm of his Queen. Both monarchs step down from their thrones and, heavily guarded, walk to the pyre where I am jerking and twitching. The torch passes from the Inquisitor to the King, then again from the King to the Queen. With the help of her husband, the Queen grazes the torch against the bottom layer of the pyre and the wood erupts into flames.

As the fire creeps upward, toward my feet, the crowd begins to stir. Smoke soon envelops me, the hot breath of the stake erupting into an open conflagration of skipping plumes. I howl in pain, then cry out a single word—*Adonai*.

I hear the crackle of flames, the screams and cheers of the crowd, the bleating of goats. I smell my own burnt flesh. . . .

I am going.

I am gone. . . .

London, 1593

2

As the last bits of dirt were shoveled over the grave, William Shakespeare arose and dusted clots of mud and loose earth from his stockings. He looked down at the fresh soil, still stunned by the sudden loss of his mentor, his best friend, Henry Whitman. What villain had done such a foul deed, slaughtered a man on the open road? Shakespeare shuddered as he pictured Whitman dying in that muddy sheep's cot, his bones cold and stiff from the chilled northern air. The body had been found by a shepherdess, the rapier still embedded in Harry's back. It had pierced his heart.

Dear God have mercy upon his soul and rest be to his ashes.

Harry's demise. A surprise attack from a hidden enemy or a madman? The culminating act of a heated quarrel? Always clever—even when sorely drunk—Harry had been an expert improviser, had talked his way out of many tense situations.

A good player must be creative, Harry had told him once. *If the book is less than perfect, it's up to the man on stage to make amends*.

Poor Harry. Performing his final scene without an audience. The ultimate insult for an actor. In life, periods of solitude were blessings. Dying alone was a bitter curse.

Rubbing his gloved hands together and tightening his cloak, Shakespeare stared off into the gray landscape. The cemetery was four miles from Bishopsgate, an hour's walk from London—a long walk when the heart was heavy with sadness. He turned to his right and spotted an incoming funeral train about two hundred yards to the north—a long line of mourners holding banners, torches, and scutcheons. Squires, bearing the family's coat-of-arms, were followed by blue-gowned servants. Evidence of a man of much means: the deceased had been a gentleman. The casket, draped in black, plodded through the fog as if it had been cast into choppy waters. The funeral party soon came into sharper view. Beyond the staff there were very few mourners. Very few had shown up at Whitman's funeral as well. A day for small funerals.

The incoming party passed to the right of Harry's grave,

steadily crunching wet grass underneath leather soles. Shakespeare returned his eyes to the grave, almost expecting Whitman to pop his head up and claim his entire demise was jest. When that didn't happen, he began to walk away.

He hadn't gone more than ten feet when he felt the presence of eyes upon him—an eerie, intangible touch that crept down his spine and grabbed his legs. He spun to his left, in the direction of the gentleman's funeral, and saw a motionless, veiled woman appearing to stare at him. Transfixed by her image—a black icon enveloped by shimmering air—he stared back. Delicately, she lifted her veil and regarded him further. She was young, Shakespeare noticed immediately, and beautiful. Her eyes were steely gray, yet burned like coals afire. Her complexion was flawless—milky white with a hint of blush on high arches of cheekbone. Her lips were full and slightly parted, emitting small wisps of warm breath. Her brow and most of her hair were shadowed by hat and veil, but several loose tresses streamed alongside her cheeks and gleamed as black and silky as the fur of a witch's cat. Statuesque but hazy, as if chiseled out of the clouds that surrounded her, she seemed but a dream.

"Rebecca," a distant voice said.

The woman didn't respond.

The voice suddenly took the shape of a man. An elderly gentleman with a sizable belly and a comely red beard, dressed in a knee-length physician's gown. The cloths of his vestments were not wool or linen, but silk and velvet, the leather of his boots polished to a high shine.

"Rebecca," he repeated. "Grandmama needs your help."

Immediately, the woman lowered her veil and caught up with the rest of her party.

Shakespeare felt a tap on the shoulder and jumped. It was only Cuthbert. His eyelids drooped with fatigue, his hazel eyes were red and watery. Like his famous brother, Richard Burbage, Cuthbert was well developed, with thick lips, high cheekbones, and a bulbous nose. The main difference between the two was their voices—Richard's was deep and melodious, Cuthbert's thin and tinny. He wasn't much older than Shakespeare, yet he always walked with a stoop reserved for men twice his age. He placed his hand gently on Shakespeare's shoulder.

"Your roving eye shows no respect for the solemnity of the occasion," Cuthbert said kindly.

"Reproach me not," said Shakespeare. "It was she who engaged me."

"Who was she?" asked Cuthbert.

"I know not."

"Save that she is beautiful."

Shakespeare smiled. "My eye isn't alone in its wanderings."

"I admit it to be the truth," Cuthbert said. "She was a lovely spirit amid all this death." He paused, then said, "Harry's death is a great loss for all of us. But I know what Whitman meant to you, Willy. I'm sorry."

Shakespeare said, "Whitman was a drunk, a braggart, and a carouser. He constantly floundered in a sea of mischief, coming periously close to drowning until someone—usually me—had the decency to rescue him. This time I wasn't there. Whitman was a millstone about my neck."

"You don't mean that," Cuthbert said.

"Don't I?"

"You're angry with him."

"How can you be angry at a corpse?"

But he was angry. Enraged! And *guilty*! If only he had been there. In the early days it had been the other way around—Harry the nursemaid, he the baby. Shakespeare had been nineteen at the time, void of any marketable craft. A convicted poacher, he'd been expelled from his native shire of Warwick because he hadn't been able to pay the stiff fine and had been too full of pride to ask his in-laws for help. He packed a bag and bid good-bye to Anne and the children, swearing to send them all his money just as soon as he was hired by a troupe. But after living on the streets for six months, his only income pennies for lyrics he'd written for troubador songs, Shakespeare had become despondent. No one would hire him as a player, no one was interested in reading his playbooks.

It had been desperation that made him seek out Whitman. The famous actor, though known to be moody and drink in excess, had sudden bouts of unexplained generosity. After one of Whitman's productions, Shakespeare approached him, fully expecting to be rebuffed. Though there was no room in the fellowship for another itinerate player, Whitman agreed to read Shakespeare's play.

And read it Harry did, grunting, muttering to himself as he sorted through the uneven scraps of paper on which the lines were written. Shakespeare couldn't afford anything as luxurious as unused paper. When Harry had finished, he calmly handed Shakespeare back his play and asked what he knew about horses. That was it. Not a single comment on his work, just what did he know about horses.

Shakespeare told Harry that he knew much about grooming—a bald lie—and was hired on the spot. His first real work in London—tending the horses of the gentleman playgoers. He'd been so grateful to Harry for the opportunity.

A few days later Shakespeare burned the book. It remained

forgotten until six months later. Harry had been voicing one of his many soliloquies on stage when he started to improvise using lines from Shakespeare's ill-fated play. The rogue had committed the book to *memory* as he read it! Afterward, in a tavern, of course, Harry begrudgingly gave Shakespeare a word or two of credit for the well-received lines he'd orated.

Shakespeare looked back at Harry's grave. Only Whitman's widow and her parish priest remained, the other members of the fellowship having already begun the walk back to London. Cuthbert followed Shakespeare's eyes and said,

"Poor Margaret. What will she do? We'll have to help."

"Such were my intentions," Shakespeare said.

"What have you in savings?"

"Four crowns—two are in my doublet."

"Good luck at the cockfights over the year?"

"Not so," Shakespeare replied. "I've simply been saving my coins. Anne should lack nothing."

"What a liar you be," said Cuthbert, grinning. He quickly added: "A statement made in jest, dear cousin."

"I see you value your ballocks." Shakespeare laughed. "In truth, perhaps a bet or two *did* turn up sweet. Now, how does a gentleman offer the widow money without offending her honor? Margaret's a woman sated in pride."

"Yes, a problem." Cuthbert broke into a series of spasmodic coughs. "Then this is what you do. You must *lie*—in good faith, of course."

"How so?"

"Tell her the money was owed to her husband. He had lent you the pounds when your debts mounted, and had never told her lest he sully your image in her gentle mind. If it pleases her, she may take her just due."

"She won't take my money."

"You approach her with a humbleness of tone, yet insistence in your voice. The hooded eyelid, a grave downturn of the lip. Marry, Will, you're a *player*! Use your skills and convince the poor widow."

"Aye, a player I am," Shakespeare said. "But she was the superior player's wife."

Cuthbert coughed and nodded. "True. But now she's stricken with grief. Her finely honed senses have been dulled." He nudged Shakespeare in the ribs. "The priest is leaving her alone. You have opportunity. Make the most of it."

Shakespeare nodded and approached the grieving widow. She was a tall woman with colorless eyes, the lids red and puffy with sorrow. Because her veil was up, the frosty air had bitten raw her cheeks and nose. She held in her hand a sprig of rosemary which she fingered absently.

Such pain etched on her face, he thought. It served to increase his own.

"William," she said quietly.

"Margaret." He kissed her on the cheek then lowered his head.

"Harry was a good soul, wasn't he?" she asked.

"Yes, he was."

"I loved him, Willy."

"I loved him as well," Shakespeare said softly. "He was my brother in spirit if not in flesh. I'll miss him dearly."

"So will we all," Margaret said. "At least he's not departed in vain. Nine living souls will attest to that."

"How are the children faring?"

Margaret sighed. "Their father's death leans heavily on their legs, but with God's help they shall keep their balance."

"May God shine his love on them."

"Thank you," Margaret whispered.

Shakespeare held her hands. Margaret had always impressed him as being a strong woman. She had to be. Nine children and a husband who was never home. But Shakespeare never heard her complain. Harry had always supported his family quite well.

Shakespeare cleared his throat. "I have something I must give you," he said.

"I'm not in want of anything."

"Nor do I claim you to be. I simply want to pay you back for money I borrowed from Harry." Shakespeare reached into his doublet and took several gold coins. "It's long overdue."

Margaret said, "Harry did not make it a habit to lend money, Will. You, more than anyone, should be aware of that. Ye men! Cuthbert had tried the same tactic and was no more successful."

The scoundrel, Shakespeare thought. Instructing me, knowing all the while I would fail. He sighed to himself.

"I pray you, Margaret," he said. "Take it so I may do honor to my mentor's widow. The favor will be yours." He extended his hand toward her. "Please."

Slowly, Margaret reached for the crowns, then retracted her hand. "If I'm in need, dear Will, I'll call you. For now, let's leave the matter untouched. Agreed?"

"Agreed." Shakespeare stuffed the coins back into his doublet.

"Aye, such times we live in, Will," Margaret said, walking away from the grave. "An honest man cannot traverse the land without fear of the bastard highwaymen."

Shakespeare said, "Were I to find the cutpurse responsible for this act, I'd give him his entitlement. Bait for the unchained bear would be an appropriate death.''

"Aye, make it slow and painful," Margaret added.

"And gruesome."

Margaret laughed hollowly. "We're as bad as heathens. Christians do not engage in this kind of speech."

Shakespeare said nothing.

"Aye, Will, you are as Harry. Incorrigible." Margaret sighed. "How I yearn for more innocent days."

"An illusion, Margaret."

"Not so," she protested. "My grandmother recalls such times."

Shakespeare didn't answer.

"And you think this not so?"

"Memories of the elderly are bathed in sunlight—exceedingly bright yet very indistinct."

Margaret shook her head.

"So I shall remain wistful and labor in my delusion," she said. "It's a terrible lot to be a player. Traveling on the road, dependent on the kindness of the hostler, alert and watchful lest you fall prey to the cozening knave that roams the country's highways. If you were sound of mind, Will, you'd go back to Anne and the children and return to the occupation of your father."

Shakespeare shook his head.

"Go home to your family, Will. Go home and make peace."

"My home is here with the fellowship, Margaret," Shakespeare said. "I'd be one foot in the grave if I gave up the theater. Anne knows that. I cannot live without the stage, and she refuses to uproot. So we both act as we must. The great Guild of Whittawer will have to go on without me." He smiled. "Heaven only knows how it has endured this long in my absence."

They walked a few more feet in silence. The wind shot chilled arrows that pierced their lungs.

Shakespeare said, "Margaret, why did you bury Harry outside of London instead of in his family land up North?"

Margaret turned white. "Harry mentioned his family to you?"

"Very briefly. He claimed he was born of displaced nobility. But then again, he claimed diverse things, many of which were products of a prevaricating mind."

"Harry had kinsmen up North," Margaret said. "But they are not *family*. You see how many have come to his funeral today."

"Yet he was visiting them when he was killed," Shakespeare said.

Margaret didn't respond. She wrapped herself in resentment

and wore it as visibly as her cloak. She bit her thumbnail, then said,

"Who will find my husband's murderer, Willy?"

It was Shakespeare's turn to be silent.

"None of Harry's true brothers have offered to seek vengeance for him," Margaret said. "My husband's soul cannot rest in eternity until the slayer is brought to justice."

"I'm aware of that, Margaret."

"When you had no one to turn to, twas Harry—"

"I know," Shakespeare interrupted. "What would you like me to do?"

"Find this fiend," Margaret announced.

She stated it so simply, as if it were the only agenda open to him.

"I suppose I could take a brief trip up North," Shakespeare said. "Make a few inquiries . . . Although without Harry, the fellowship is sadly lacking competent players. And the theaters have just reopened—"

"If the fellowship can go on without Harry, production can proceed without *you*. Find my husband's *murderer*!"

Shakespeare said he'd try, though his stomach had become knotted at the thought. He would depart in a few days.

Margaret whispered breathlessly, "Hints are that the killer is well versed in the Italianate style of dueling. The rapier's thrust cut deep into Harry's heart."

"Then the murderer must have been very adroit," noted Shakespeare. "Harry was a fine swordsman."

"Yes," Margaret answered in a small voice. "Precaution, Will. Be clever or you'll find your fortune as Harry's."

"I shall step lightly," Shakespeare said. For a moment, he wondered how she had ensnared him to do her bidding. But deep in his heart he knew that she really didn't talk him into anything. Shakespeare wanted to avenge his mentor. He also knew that had the situation been reversed, Harry would have done the same for him. "If I find this Hell-rot scum, I shall be well prepared."

"And I shall love you all the more for my Harry's revenge." Margaret's face had become alive with the desire for retribution. "God bless you, Will Shakespeare. An honorable man, you are." Margaret kissed his cheek and dropped his hand. "I must rejoin my children and friends. You'll keep me informed?"

"Of everything I disclose."

"I wish you luck, William." She let down her veil, tightened her cloak, and hurried away.

Cuthbert waited for Shakespeare at the mouth of the open road. The overcast had started to lift, giving way to the green velvety hillside, a smooth verdant wave speckled with silver brush, ancient oaks, wildflowers, and the white nap of unshorn sheep. Taking a deep breath, he tried to exhale slowly, but instead let out a hacking cough. He cleared his lungs, spat out a large ball of phlegm and flexed his stiffened fingers. His eyes swelled with water and he blew his red, round nose.

Bells from the church tower rang out the time—eleven-thirty by the clock. Burbage was well aware of the hour before it was announced. His stomach had told him it was time to take dinner. So late, he thought. And the sets still needed repairs. With Whitman's funeral and so little time to prepare, the production would be a disaster! The troupe could no longer afford to play half-empty galleries. Not with the new batch of costumes recently purchased—genuine furs for the king's robes. Such extravagance his brother, Richard, insisted upon. And the new swords! Not to mention the two new hired men and another member demanding to be a sharer.

Then there was the constant threat of Black Death. The outbreaks of plague had subsided long enough to allow the Master of the Revels to reopen the theaters. But if this year's epidemic proved to be as deadly as last year's, the theater doors again would be locked. Gods, would that be calamitous financially!

Shakespeare caught up with him and the two of them began their journey back to Southwark just across London Bridge.

"You seem lost in thought, friend," Shakespeare said.

"The business of providing pleasure to others," Cuthbert answered. "No matter. How'd you fare with the widow?"

Shakespeare looked impish. "Margaret will be well provided for."

"Good," sighed Cuthbert. "The lady always did prefer you to me."

"My waifish eyes, dear cousin. They tug at the heartstrings."

"Or leer at the chest," mumbled Cuthbert. "Depending on your mood."

"She refused my crowns, my friend—no surprise, eh? But did agree to take them should there be a time of need."

"Fair enough."

Shakespeare stopped walking, "Cuthbert, who would do this to Harry? Yes, someone might filch Harry's purse as he lay sleeping off one of his drunken states. That has happened before. But murder him? He had not a true enemy this side of the channel."

"Vagabonds knew nothing of his kindness."

"True—if his murderer was a highwayman . . ."

"And you think it might be someone else? Someone he knew?"

"I've no pull to one theory or the other."

Cuthbert said, "There is the possibility that Harry became drunk and a foolish fight ensued after words were spoken in choler. Harry often spoke carelessly when drunk."

"Yet he was equally quick with the apologies," Shakespeare said. "Besides, he died in an open field and not on the floor of a tavern."

Alone, Shakespeare thought.

"He could have been moved to the field," Cuthbert said.

"A lot of bother," Shakespeare said.

Cuthbert agreed. He asked,

"What about the coins he was carrying? Margaret made mention that Harry had pocketed several angels before he left for his trip up North. They were gone when the body was discovered. Harry was robbed, Willy."

"Or Harry spent the money before he was murdered," Shakespeare said.

Cuthbert conceded the point. They resumed walking. It seemed to Shakespeare that Harry could have easily done in an ordinary highwayman itching for a scrap. Whitman was a deft swordsman. But was he caught off guard? Had the attacker been a fiercesome enemy or a madman possessed by an evil spirit? Shakespeare stepped in silence for several minutes, brooding over the fate of his partner and friend. Again Cuthbert placed a hand on his shoulder. He said, softly,

"What's the sense, Will? Harry is dead and gone. But we are still among the living. We've a performance at two and our stomachs are empty."

"I've not an appetite," Shakespeare said. "But a pint of ale would well wet my throat."

Cuthbert coughed.

"And yours, also," added Shakespeare. "Have you seen an apothecary about the cough?"

"Aye."

"And what did he say?"

"Quarter teaspoon dragon water, quarter teaspoon mithridate, followed by a quart of flat warmed ale. If it worsens, perhaps more drastic measures need to be taken."

"What kind of measures?"

"He made mention of leeching."

They were silent for a moment.

"Nothing to be concerned about," Cuthbert said.

"Good." Shakespeare paused, then said, "I must go up North for a few weeks."

Cuthbert stopped walking. "Up North? Alone? Are you mad?"

"Far from it."

"Though I mean no disrespect for the deceased, we are already one player short, Will."

"Margaret asked it of me," Shakespeare said. "And I would have done it anyway. I owe it to Harry."

"A minute ago you called him a millstone around your neck."

"He deserves peace in eternity," Shakespeare said. His eyes suddenly moistened. "He visited me in my dreams last night, lectured me in the proper art of projection. . . ." Shakespeare suddenly covered his eyes with his hands. "His restless soul hangs about me like a nagging wife. The Devil with it! I must avenge him, Cuthbert, or I'll have no peace of mind."

"But—"

"Save your breath."

Cuthbert knew arguing with him was useless. Shakespeare and Whitman—both mules. He said, cautiously, "Perhaps the fellowship can handle your absence financially, *if* it's only for one week—"

"Give me two weeks. The open roads may be poor."

Cuthbert sighed. "Two weeks, then. I pray you, Willy, no more than two weeks."

Shakespeare agreed, then added, "Much can happen in two weeks."

3

Judging from the number of people, the funeral party was an immense success. It was only six in the evening, but scores of sweating bodies had already filled the Great Hall of the Ames's manor house. Most were respected commoners—wealthy business merchants, gold traders, and local statesmen—but some gallants and important nobility had elected to make an appearance. The great ladies gossiped, huddling around the lit wall torches or floor sconces so they could be observed and admired under proper lighting. They fanned themselves, studied the crowds, the dress of those without title, wondering if the commoners were violating any of the sumptuary laws. Other wives stood against the black-draped walls and sneered at their husbands stuffing their mouths with food. Two dozen rows of banqueting tables were piled high with delicacies—milk-fed beef stewed with roots, venison in plum sauce, trays of poultry, platters of pheasants roasted over the open pit in the center of the room. The hall had become stifling, choked with the smell of perspiration and the heat of cooking.

But Rebecca Lopez took no notice. Head down, she spoke to no one, and no one dared address her. She was the fiancée of the deceased, Raphael Nuñoz, and as such, entitled to her grief in solitude. She had chosen a spot under a drafty window at the far end of the Great Hall and remained alone, her aloofness constructing an invisible barrier that kept the guests away. Frosty air blew upon her neck and shoulders, and she was shivering—the only one in the room to do so. Her mother had offered her a blanket, but Rebecca had declined. She made no further effort to become warm.

Yesterday she'd been numbed by what had happened. She hadn't been able to feel cold, heat, or pain. But now all she felt was anger and a fervent wish that all the commotion would end soon. Among all of them—the so-named mourners—not a tear had been shed. Sheer hypocrisy, she thought. They come not to console, but instead to gorge themselves or chat idly about the weather. Let them take a stroll if the chill occupies their thoughts so. Let them leave, so the air inside will clear of their foul odor and overbearing perfume.

Through her long black veil she eyed Hector and Miguel steeped in sadness. They were large men made small by black sorrow. Her heart ached for them—father and brother—so deep was the intensity of their loss. Rebecca remembered the swift death of Raphael's mother, Judith. She'd been no more than a little girl at her mother's side, but nevertheless recalled the ashen face, the bloody legs with a dead child between them. The memory had haunted her for years. Now, ironically, she was thankful that Judith had died and been spared the pain of seeing her firstborn dead.

How she wished she could hold Hector and Miguel in her arms, sing them sweet lullabies and take away the anguish. But to perform such an act of solace was to confess that they were more affected than she by Raphael's death. Even though this was true, she didn't dare admit it.

Raphael. Since she had to marry—and he had been forced to wed as well—their union would have been as good as any. He'd been a sweet, sweet lover with a randy laugh, very adventurous under the sheets. But there had been another side to him, dark and brooding. Unlike Miguel, Raphael had a terrible temper, and though he had never struck her, he'd come close more than once. Rebecca learned early in their relationship to stop asking him questions about the mission. Her betrothed, always burdened by worldly matters.

Though Rebecca mourned his death, she was relieved by the aborted nuptials. Unlike most of the girls her age, it had never been her dream to marry, to become the perfect English gentlewoman. All she could see was young girls turning older than their years, weighted down by pregnancy that turned into obesity. Fat and saggy, disgusting in the eyes of husbands who leered and groped after smooth, supple bodies. And the bairns, crying and wailing, drooling cheesy spit.

And then there was the permanently etched fear of ending up as had Judith—the women and girls staring at *her* corpse.

Rebecca knew her reprieve from wedlock was temporary. It was only a matter of time before Father replaced Raphael with another—Miguel, most likely. Once married, she would have to obey her husband without question. It was her duty. But for now, unexpectedly released from marital obligations, she felt like a wild horse destined for domestication but suddenly let loose instead. Freedom snipping away her feelings of numbness, of sadness. Obscene as it was, she couldn't help herself.

Rebecca adjusted her coif, looked around the room and saw Lady Marlburn stuffing her corpulent body with comfits, licking sticky sugar off of her sausage-shaped fingers. Rebecca had been periodically observing her for an hour. The lady had consumed ample quantities of capon, duck, veal, moorcock, pigeon, and pickled eggs, washing it all down with tankards of ale. She'd be heavily purging herself tonight. The chamberpot would be filled with her putrid stools.

Swine, they were. Keeping their close stools next to their bedposts, smelling the fetid stench as they slept. It was Rebecca's grandam who insisted that the pots be kept away from the bedchambers and the kitchen.

And they have the audacity to call us swine.

Thoughts of her grandam filled Rebecca with warmth. Though Rebecca loved her mother—she was a dutiful daughter—it was the old woman who had always been the main recipient of her affections. The hag, as she was called by everyone else, was a skeletal witch, crippled severely by disfigured feet. Toothless and wrinkled, she rarely talked to anyone, and when she did, it was usually nonsense. People thought her a bit daft, but Rebecca knew she spoke foolishly to keep people from prying into her past life—years that even Rebecca was not privy to. When they were alone, Grandmama revealed a remarkable acumen, a steadfast calm in the face of crisis, and an inexhaustible patience. Grandmama had taught her to read Hebrew, had taught her much about the old religion through tales and stories. Young and old—confidantes—each listening to the dreams of the other.

Rebecca was awakened from her reverie by the harsh cackle emitted from Lady Marlburn. As the great dame laughed, layers of chins slapped against her chest. Her breasts were enormous, tumbling out of a too-tight bodice. Her pomander was entrapped in cleavage—the sickly sweet-smelling orb peeking out of the gorge that separated mountainous mounds of flesh. Lord Marlburn stood dutifully at her side, nodding at the appropriate moments, sneaking sidelong glances at Rebecca.

The "great" lord and lady, her father forced to show them respect because they were nobility.

A pox on them.

Rebecca remembered too clearly Lord Marlburn's heavy arms holding her down, the thick hand clamped tightly over her mouth. His prick, stubby and crusted with scum, pushing deeply into her body. His stench and sweat dripping on her freshly washed skin. When he was done, the previously lust-blinded lupine face had become sheepish. He had cried to her, begging her forgiveness at what he had thought was her deflowering. His weeping had made her even more sick and contemptuous. It had been simply her time of the month; she hadn't been a virgin for two years.

But she had told him nothing.

Gifts soon followed—expensive bolts of cloth, bracelets studded with jewels, rare edibles—citrus from southern Italy, asparagus from Holland, chocolate from Spain. He had tried to speak with her, but she feigned illness, knowing he was mad with worry that she was carrying his bastard child. More gifts. More and more.

What a fool!

Looking at the two piggish bodies, Rebecca wondered how he could possibly mount and penetrate her when their torsos were wrapped in so many layers of fat. She tried to imagine their humping—two mastiffs pawing at each other, huffing and puffing.

She hated them! At the moment she hated everyone.

From the shield of her veil she noticed Dunstan approaching her. Her cousin was handsome. Tall, well built, his muscular thighs bulging under his stockings. His chest seemed massive under his peasecod doublet. His hair was long and sleek, his beard midnight black. A diamond winked from his left earlobe. As he neared, Rebecca picked up her head and nodded an acknowledgment.

"How are you faring?" he asked, standing at her side.

"Worry not for my sake," Rebecca said. "Instead worry for

Hector and Miguel. I fear that Raphael's death will leave them weak with grief.''

Dunstan sighed and nodded.

"And what about your grief?"

"I'll survive."

"Did you love him?" Dunstan asked.

"He was my betrothed, Dunstan. Of course I loved him."

Dunstan touched his earring with his forefinger and thumb. "And did you love him even as he bedded your chambermaid?"

Rebecca faced him. "You're despicable."

"Admit it," Dunstan said with a half smile. "You feel relieved."

Rebecca turned away, blushing at the truth. Carelessly, she said, "Raphael's death leaves us in a ticklish position, does it not?"

Dunstan whipped his head around and whispered, "Quiet. We're among strangers."

"My father talks freely," Rebecca said. "He's often unaware who is listening."

"God's sointes, Rebecca, keep your voice down!" Dunstan reprimanded her. "Your father is *discreet* because he trusts you and speaks unmolested in your presence. Don't make an ass out of him—or us. As comfortable as we live, we're not immune from the whims of our rulers."

Rebecca knew that to be the truth. England's religious tolerance could quickly be replaced by the Queen's sudden death or military mutiny. It wasn't that long ago that peace was threatened by Her Majesty's cousin—Mary Queen of Scots. Staunch Catholics had been slaughtered. If the Papist burns easily, how much hotter burns the unbaptized heretic?

Rebecca said, "Father instructs me to concern myself little in matters of politics, only to do what I'm told. I forge the documents and forget what is being said around the house."

"Sound advice," Dunstan answered.

"He treats me as if I hadn't a brain."

"He's worried for your safety. Uncle has some formidable enemies—"

"Essex—"

"Lower your voice."

"I'm whispering."

"Say no more about the mission." Dunstan scanned the room. Thank God no one was watching them. "Raphael's death is not only a great loss for our people, but a dilemma for you as well. We both know that Miguel is unfit as a husband. Your future is no longer ensured."

"It matters not to me."

"Aye, but it matters much to your father." Dunstan patted her knee. "But God gave you a fair face and a beautiful form."

"And a keen mind as well," she reminded him.

"That is no asset, dear cousin. It's a defect."

She turned her head away.

"Not to worry," he said philosophically. "I overheard your father talking to quite a few lords."

"A waste of time."

"Tis good you are less than anxious to wed." *Very good*, he thought wolfishly. "I approve not of the merchandise available."

Rebecca sighed. "And what does not meet with Sir Dunstan Ames's approval?"

"They're Englishmen . . . *real* Englishmen. Best to stick with kinsmen who understand our ways, even if we have to import a man from the Continent." Dunstan looked at his hand, at his gold ring. "Although there are advantages of marrying peerage . . ."

Such as the weight of their purses, Rebecca thought. She said nothing.

Dunstan stroked her cheek under the veil. "Such a face you have. You could be a countess with the bat of an eyelash. . . . The revenues of an earldom at your command . . . all those golden angels falling at your feet."

"And a tarnished noble as well."

Dunstan smiled. "A comfortable position nonetheless."

"And a grand one for the mission," Rebecca said. "A matter of time before hands dip into my lord husband's pockets."

"We don't use money for personal gain, Rebecca," Dunstan said.

Rebecca said, "Then why do *your* fingers sparkle?"

"I work hard, cousin," Dunstan said. "I go without sleep for nights—"

"Yet you still live, while Raphael is cold," Rebecca snapped. "Need I remind you of that detail, cousin?"

"I offer my services wherever I'm needed."

"Bah," Rebecca said.

"Even at a time such as this, you bait me, Becca," Dunstan said. "What pleasure do you derive from it?"

"The same pleasure you derived when you bespoke of Raphael bedding my chambermaid?"

Dunstan didn't answer, and glanced around the room. All he saw were people preoccupied with themselves and the food. The tables sagged under the weight of platters. And so much more still being prepared in the kitchen. As one tray grew empty, another was brought out by a scullion. Since no one was paying them any mind, Dunstan took her hand, and she didn't resist. "I'm truly sorry for your loss, Rebecca."

For the first time this afternoon her lip quivered. The overflowing lakes that had formed in her eyes became rivers of tears pouring down her cheek.

"It was for no purpose, Dunstan," she whispered. "A barter of Raphael's life for another. Yes, I confess that I wasn't keen to wed, but I grieve for the loss of my betrothed. At times the mission seems like such folly—"

"Shh," Dunstan reprimanded her. "There's much thou knowest not, little one."

"Oh Dunstan!" she implored. "Don't let Father marry me to Miguel, as is his duty. You're a man. Be my lips and plead my case. Though I am so very fond of Miguel, our union would be a mockery!"

In sooth, Dunstan thought. He shook his head, knowing it was his cursed luck to tell his uncle Roderigo the truth about Miguel's preferences in the art of love. Uncle had a vile temper and was bound to become enraged. He had always loved Miguel like a son. Diplomacy would be of the essence.

He turned to Rebecca. "Nonetheless, it's your father's duty to find you a husband."

But in the meantime, . . . he thought.

Rebecca moaned. "Dear God help me. At least I had learned to understand Raphael. I become ill at the thought of marrying anyone else."

"Hush," he said soothingly. "Keep your ideas to yourself, Rebecca. The more obstinate you become, the more your father feels a need to tame you by marrying you off to the proper gentleman."

"Yes." She dabbed her eyes with a lace kerchief. "You're correct . . . for once."

Dunstan ignored the barb. They'd become so frequent of late. He said, "Until an appropriate suitor is found, your hand shall remain free."

"I don't want a suitor."

"You are young and foolish. You don't know what you want."

"Had I the skills of a surgeon, I'd rip my womb from my body—"

"Quiet!" Dunstan said. "You're too young to know the power of the bush between your legs. It will not be plump forever, Rebecca. One day it will dry up and no one shall be enamored of it—or you. You must learn to use the graces God has given you. It guarantees a life of leisure for your old age. A man will endow much upon you if in your youth you serve him well."

"The stars cast upon me ill hap when they formed me woman," Rebecca mumbled to herself.

"You speak nonsense." Dunstan held her hands and looked into her veiled eyes. "But these are trying times for all of us, and you especially are confused. Angry one moment, sullen or grief-stricken the next. It's best if you say nothing until you're of stronger mind."

Rebecca knew he was right. She was exhausted by her contradicting emotions.

Dunstan gave the room another cursory glance. They were still talking unnoticed. Lifting her veil, he kissed her quickly on the lips. "And pray, my sweet, speak not of the mission. You must learn to silence your thoughts, Rebecca. Lips should be shields, not sieves through which excess words do escape."

Rebecca nodded and Dunstan kissed her again. This time it was with a passion she had experienced long ago in the darkness of a hayloft, and she immediately pulled away. She felt Dunstan's disappointment and almost felt sorry for him.

Almost.

He had been her first tutor, her mentor. It was he who taught her about freedom, filling her mind with tales of his travel to the Continent, to North Africa and the East. He taught her Arabic, Italian, French, Flemish. With each language she acquired, books in the original editions soon followed. Her head became dizzy with ideas that displeased her father immensely. But Dunstan disregarded him and continued her education—in *body* as well as mind. Rebecca knew he was after the body all along, but he, amongst all the others, was the only one willing to take the time to teach her. So she ceded to his wishes. And he was a gentle one for the first time—calm and slow—coaching with unusual patience the clumsiness out of a twelve-year-old girl.

Rebecca smoothed her cousin's mustache with the tip of her finger. "How are the bairns?" she asked.

"A lively brood. Grace is ready to drop another son for me. She's a healthy woman." A cow, he thought, but God be praised, a good one for breeding—three sons and a daughter, all thriving. Dunstan lowered her veil. "Grace is a good woman also. I thank God for the day I married her. You could learn a great deal from her, cousin."

Surreptitiously, Dunstan placed in Rebecca's hand a folded piece of paper.

"What is this?" she said.

"Your *proper* mourning prayers for your betrothed. Say them in silence before you sleep tonight. God will hear them."

Rebecca started to unfold the paper. Dunstan placed his hand on hers. He whispered, "Not here, Becca, in private. They are written in the old language."

Rebecca paled and quickly stuffed the paper up her sleeve.

Dunstan caught the eye of the fat Lady Marlburn and nodded. He whispered to Rebecca, "When alone, you must sit on the floor, even take your meals while sitting on the floor. You may sleep in your bed, however."

"What happens when my chambermaid comes in my closet," Rebecca whispered back.

"When she knocks, you get up. She mustn't see what you are doing—ever. Our money is to be used for the mission, not for paying off suspicious maids. After she leaves, you must sit back on the floor."

"For just seven days or the whole month?"

"Just the seven days, starting tonight. Then comes the month of lesser mourning." Dunstan squeezed his cousin's hand. "We cannot speak anymore. The grand dame Lady Marlburn has espied our conversation and is coming our way. Soon you'll be besieged with ghouls. Unless you wish to converse with them, I suggest you feign exhaustion."

Rebecca slumped in her chair. It wasn't a hard scene to play. She closed her eyes. Blessed darkness.

4

By midnight only the converso men remained—six tonight because Hector and Miguel had gone home early with the women to grieve in private. The men sat around the table and waited for the servants to finish tidying the mess that the visitors had made. The wooden plank tables upon which the massive feast had rested were barren. With the fifty-foot walls covered in black cloth and a strong wind whistling through mullion-glass windows, the room seemed as desolate as a crypt. Dunstan Ames suggested that the men retire to a smaller closet, but his father shook his head, feeling too tired to move. Servants and scullions scurried about the hall, their footsteps muffled by the rushes that blanketed the stone floor. Eventually Dunstan grew impatient with their presence and shooed his father's lackeys away.

Roderigo Lopez was nearly sick with exhaustion and worry.

Thank God Rebecca had proved herself to be a strong girl. Not an easy chore. The funeral had been a long ordeal, the church service full of pomp and prayer that left the conversos noticeably uncomfortable. As professed Protestants but secret Jews, they were members of the local parish and attended sabbath services as required by the law of the land. But they tried to be as late for church as possible, sometimes not arriving until the conclusion of the service. Roderigo knew that the other parishoners noticed their tardiness. But the congregants never voiced a word of protest because the parish priest always greeted the conversos warmly. The secret Jews were paying him well. Though they breathed easier in England than in their native land of Portugal— there was no Inquisition here, praise God—they were still forced to hide their worship from prying eyes. An extremely difficult task. Like most landed gentry, Roderigo's household—and that of his brother-in-law—contained many servants. Discovery of their secret religious services would brand them as Jews, which would mean deportation.

Now, with the servants gone—privacy at last—the conversos could begin the true service of mourning. Dunstan closed the massive doors to the room and the assembled men stood up from the bench, retrieved black skullcaps from their pockets and covered their heads. Roderigo looked at the men—his son, two nephews, a brother-in-law, and a distant cousin. Five grim faces, worn but visibly relieved to be away from the Gentiles. He nodded for his cousin, Solomon Aben Ayesh, to lead the services.

Lopez envied Aben Ayesh. Solomon was the only one amongst them who was an openly professed Jew—a luxury he was now afforded since he no longer lived in Europe. Solomon was short and as thin as a reed, with midnight-blue eyes which appeared black at a distance. As a diamond farmer in India, Aben Ayesh had become rich and *powerful*—so formidable a man that the Turkish court had rewarded him with the title of Duke of Mytilene. His network of spies was well known throughout the Continent by monarchs who ignored his religious beliefs in order to secure his confidence and, by extension, his privied information. Even though Lopez, as the Queen's physician, held an enviable position in England, he had none of Aben Ayesh's religious freedom and independence.

Roderigo listened to Aben Ayesh's prayers said in Hebrew, then repeated the words out loud. Aching, he felt all of his sixty-eight years. He sucked in his overhanging belly—his stamp of wealth—and straightened his spine. When praying to God, one should stand erect. The Almighty had been kind to him—a good wife and two living, healthy children, one of them a son. God had been good to him physically as well. The hair atop his head was still plentiful, and his skin was nearly wrinkle free, as if Father Time had aged him in leap years. His beard remained as dense as moss and youthfully colored—deep burgundy mixed with rust and wisps of silver.

Roderigo thought back to his first *shiva*—the official ceremony of Jewish mourning. It had been a clandestine affair in Toledo, held for a cousin burnt as a heretic. Roderigo had just turned thirteen, the age of Jewish manhood, and had been told only recently of his converso bloodline by his parents. Marry, what a revelation that had been! Despite the shock, and danger, that lay ahead, Roderigo decided to remain faithful to his forefathers. He wanted to be a healer of mankind and chose to study medicine—the learned art of the Jewish people. He entered the Universidad Literaria de Salamanca in Spain, graduating with high honors and a medical degree.

Desiring more liberty for his secret practices, Roderigo moved to England during the first years of Elizabeth's reign, hoping to find relief from the Inquisition; the Virgin Queen was known for a tolerant monarch. As long as her subjects openly supported her and her Church, she chose not to ferret out those who worshiped differently in private. She did this to retain the support of the thousands of secret Papists who still resided in the northern region of the country. But it had a secondary beneficial effect for Roderigo as a secret Jew. As long as he went to the local church, he could practice his religion in the privacy of his own home.

When it was time to marry, Lopez stayed dutiful and chose a wife from the old country—a Portuguese conversa girl twenty years his junior, a cousin of Solomon Aben Ayesh. The doctor brought her over to England, and they settled down to daily life.

Lopez rose to prominence in his field, becoming a member of the College of Physicians and the first house physician at St. Bartholomew's Hospital. His reputation merited him the appointed physician to the Earl of Leicester. This led to the coveted position of Physician-in-Ordinary to Her Majesty, Queen Elizabeth, seven years ago, a position he still held.

But for all his honors, Roderigo couldn't save Raphael. Teary-eyed, he averted his gaze downward. He'd lost not only a dear friend, but a son-to-be. Such a sorrowful death.

Aben Ayesh finished the prayers and instructed the men to rip the stitching of their doublets then sit on the floor. Roderigo noticed Dunstan wincing. His nephew had been foolish enough to wear a gold-threaded doublet—vain peacock that he was. Roderigo glanced at his son, placed his hand upon his shoulder. Benjamin had just finished Oxford and was planning to go abroad to Venice when the news of Raphael's death came tumbling upon the family. Roderigo had insisted his son stay for the funeral, but instructed him to leave afterward. Benjamin was kind and generous, thanks be to God the boy was not an ingrate, but unlike his sister, he was slow of wit. A plodder, Roderigo had told his wife Sarah. Roderigo hoped that travel would teach him more successfully than had the university.

Lopez sat on the sweet-smelling rushes next to Benjamin. Across from him were Dunstan and his brother Thomas—a smooth-faced fair man of nineteen. Thomas was built lanky, with long, thin, effeminate fingers. The boy cursed his body often and lashed out frequently at anyone who suggested he was anything less than a man. His quick temper had necessitated early in life an expertise of swordplay. Thomas was renowned for his skill of the fence—much to Dunstan's displeasure. Thomas could easily best his older brother with a few quick strokes.

Roderigo faced his brother-in-law, Jorge Añoz—Sir George Ames outside the converso community. Jorge had married Sarah's sister. Good women, thought Roderigo, gentle and dutiful wives. Roderigo thought of his and Jorge's mistresses and mentally added, tolerant women as well. He said to Jorge, "Raphael needs a replacement as soon as possible."

Dunstan twisted a braided gold chain around his first finger, then let it fall back against his chest. Surely they didn't mean him.

Jorge said, "We must find out who told the Spanish captain that Raphael was on board."

"What makes you think that someone told the captain?" Roderigo said. "He could have simply been found by one of the crew, hiding with the stowaways."

"Not in a galleon," Jorge said. "The vessel is so big, twould be an incredible bit of luck to find someone well hidden. So many hatches and compartments."

"Well, *someone* found Raphael and the stowaways," Aben Ayesh said. "Someone handed them over to the Inquisition. But that must not deter us. Too many lives depend on us, on this mission. When was the last time you communicated with the Spanish king, Ruy?"

"I've yet to receive word from King Philip," answered Roderigo.

But Roderigo knew he would hear from His Majesty soon. Another payment was due.

"Do you think he knows what happened?" Jorge asked him.

"I don't know," Roderigo said. "But if he is aware of this mishap, we'll have to increase the payments greatly."

All the men groaned. They were already paying the Spanish King a fortune in bribe money.

"Can you discreetly get word to His Majesty, Ruy?" Aben Ayesh asked. "Find out what he expects from us?"

Roderigo shook his head. "Transactions such as this one may only be made under the most private of conditions. If, God forbid, our correspondence is discovered, Philip will be angered—beyond repair this time."

Everyone knew what Roderigo meant. Four years ago, at Roderigo's and Jorge's prodding, Queen Elizabeth had abetted the revolt of Don Antonio against King Philip. Don Antonio was an illegitimate descendant from the royal house of Portugal. With English forces at his side, Antonio had rallied his people to revolt against the tyrannical yoke of Spain. It had been a well-placed scheme at the time, and had Don Antonio been of stabler character, it would have worked. The Queen hoped to set up Don Antonio as King of Portugal and gain a formidable ally against Spain in the Iberian peninsula. The conversos wanted Don Antonio as monarch because he was of Jewish descent. Perhaps, as king, Don Antonio would do away with the Inquisition in Portugal—if not abolish the tribunal, at least restrict its powers.

Unfortunately Her Majesty's fleet, commanded by Sir John Norris and Sir Francis Drake, failed miserably, their attacks easily repelled by King Philip's Armada. All were left with much to explain. To restore faith with King Philip, appease his wrath, and prevent repercussions against the Spanish conversos, Aben Ayesh paid Philip the enormous sum of fifty thousand ducats. Philip's anger abated and he allowed their mission to progress without interference. To mollify the irate Elizabeth, Jorge opened the coffers of his lucrative spice business—chartered as the Ames Levantine Trade Company—and stuffed the royal treasury with as much gold as his purses would allow. Her Majesty was forgiving. As a token of her merciful nature, she kept Lopez on as her personal physician and knighted Jorge and his two sons.

"We need another man quickly," Aben Ayesh stated. "I've yet to speak with Hector, but it seems that Miguel, being Raphael's brother, is the logical replacement for the mission."

"For Rebecca's husband as well," Roderigo added.

Dunstan cleared his throat, flicked away the rushes about him. It was as good as any chance to tell him. Perhaps, with the other men around, Roderigo would exercise some control over his temper. Again the chain was entwined around Dunstan's finger. He asked permission to speak freely from his father. Jorge nodded.

"Dear Uncle," Dunstan started off, "Miguel would be an ill-advised husband for Rebecca."

Roderigo stared at his nephew. "Ill-advised?"

Dunstan nodded.

"Whatever do you mean?" Roderigo stated. "It is Miguel's religious duty to his brother. He must marry Rebecca and produce a son in his brother's name."

Dunstan hesitated, then said, "Such a union would be doomed, Uncle."

"Where do you come to assert such a statement?" Roderigo asked. "Miguel and Rebecca have known each other for years, they are very fond of each other. She was only promised to Raphael because he was the elder of the two boys. One's as suitable as the other for a husband. Besides, Miguel has no choice. It's our law."

Dunstan looked to his brother for help.

"Uncle," Thomas said gently. "Miguel is Italian in his practices of love."

Roderigo's eyes widened.

"What?" he said. It came out a whisper.

"Where did you hear such twaddle?" Jorge demanded of Thomas.

"From Miguel himself," Thomas answered, rubbing his naked chin.

"He told us, Father, as soon as he was sure that it was Raphael who'd perished," Dunstan said.

"Why wasn't I told?" asked Jorge.

"He begged for no one to know until Uncle had been informed," Dunstan answered his father. "I thought it best not to contest his wish, seeing the emotional state he was in."

"Miguel is a buggerer of *men*?" Roderigo said, horrified.

Thomas nodded.

"'Tis not that uncommon, Uncle," Dunstan said. "Quite the fashion in Venice."

Roderigo looked at his son.

"No worry, Father," Ben reassured. "I find the thought very distasteful."

"We must get back to business," Aben Ayesh said uncomfortably. "Ruy will deal with his matters as he sees fit—"

"I refuse to believe it," Roderigo interrupted.

"Ruy—" Aben Ayesh said.

Roderigo stood up and began to pace. "I *cannot* believe it!"

"Perhaps it's simply a ruse," Jorge suggested. "Perhaps the thought of sudden marriage has left Miguel with cold feet."

Thomas shook his head. "Dunstan and I have known long before Raphael perished. Many times we've seen Miguel roaming St. Paul's Marketplace, frequenting places that specialize in . . . Italian taste. He fancies himself quite a wit, accompanying the likes of Marlowe—"

"Miguel with Marlowe?" Roderigo gasped. "That godless heretic, that hater of Jews? Impossible!"

"Love is strange," Dunstan snickered.

Roderigo slapped him soundly across the cheek. Dunstan's hand went to his face. His eyes burned with fury.

Roderigo said, "How dare you mock your cousin?"

Dunstan spoke slowly, "I mock him not. I simply tell you the truth, whether it be acceptable to you or not, Uncle. I pray you, do not kill the messenger."

Roderigo sank down onto the floor. Thomas took out a poniard and, without thinking, began to scrape the mortar between the stones.

"Marry, Thomas, put that away," said Jorge. "You'll loosen the blocks."

"Your pardon, Father." Thomas returned the dagger to his belt. "I meant no harm."

Dear God, such a horrendous predicament, Roderigo thought. Raphael gone. The mission in jeopardy. And my dear Becca. He said, "How can I marry my daughter to a buggerer?"

Dunstan asked if he could speak. Roderigo nodded wearily.

"Uncle," Dunstan said. "It's best if Rebecca remains available until an appropriate suitor is found."

"The Baron of Herdford seemed interested in her," Thomas remarked. "At least, he inquired about her quite extensively."

"Bah," Dunstan answered, brushing him off. "He's an old bag of wind whose sword lost his thrust many summers ago."

"'Tis not only rutting that makes a good husband," Benjamin argued. "He's rich."

"Tut, Benjamin," Dunstan replied. "Have pity on your sister. The Baron of Herdford!"

"The old lord will die soon," Benjamin persisted. "As a wealthy widow with title, Rebecca could have her pick of suitors."

"She has her pick anyway," Dunstan said. "Beautiful, young—"

"Mulish," Ben said.

"Say rather she's . . . an independent thinker," Dunstan said, smiling.

Roderigo suddenly turned on him. "With quite a bit of help from you, Dunstan. You've filled her brain with unfortunate ideas, nephew. Twas not helpful to her or me."

"Uncle," said Dunstan, "if knowledge be port, Rebecca be a drunkard. The girl soaks it up. Better she be tutored by a kinsman than a stranger who will lure her away from family—"

"Enough of my family matters," Roderigo suddenly announced. "It's my problem and *I'll* do what's best for my daughter. . . . We must concentrate on the problem at hand. There are lives to be saved.''

"Here, here," said Aben Ayesh. "People are dying! We must save them. As Raphael's brother, Miguel still is the logical choice.''

"Miguel? Bah!" Dunstan exclaimed. "Better to send Rebecca.''

"Miguel has always been trustworthy," answered Jorge. "I'm sure he'd be willing to continue his brother's missions. To suggest him a coward, Dunstan, because of his . . . his peculiar passions, is ill-advised.''

"Very well," Dunstan said. "If you think him able—''

"He *is* able," Jorge said. "Do you agree, Solomon?''

"We are in complete accord," said Aben Ayesh. "It is settled. We shall talk to Hector and Miguel immediately.''

"At least Miguel will have something in which to prove his manhood," Dunstan snickered.

Thomas said, "Need I remind you that Miguel is tall and strong. He excels at hawking. He relishes the thrill of the hunt!''

"Aye," Dunstan laughed. "As long as the hunt is for boys.''

"Men," Thomas corrected.

"There's a difference?" Dunstan said.

"A boy is your five-year-old son, brother," Thomas said. "Miguel fancies men. Always has. Tis hard to fathom why God fashioned him as such. One would think him weak and timid. Yet Miguel's grip is as strong as the peregrine's.''

"Miguel is weak in the art of swordplay," Dunstan said.

"So are you," Thomas stated.

"Quiet," Jorge said to his sons. "Both of you are like jackals at each other's throats.''

Roderigo said, "Dunstan raised a good point. Miguel is weak in his swordsmanship. Considerably weaker than had been Raphael, God rest his soul. And many were better than he had been.''

Jorge agreed. He said, "Thomas, it's up to you to teach him your expertise.''

"I'll set up regular times to spar with him," Thomas said.

"Instruct the woman to act the man," Dunstan said with a smile.

"Does jealousy talk?" Thomas asked his brother.

"I? Jealous of Miguel? Absurd!''

"You have yet to forgive him for the pouncing he bestowed upon you at our last wrestling bout.''

"Wrestling for sport is one thing, Thomas," Dunstan retorted hotly. "Braving peril is quite another and is reserved for only true men.''

Jorge wagged an angry finger at Dunstan. "Keep your thoughts to yourself, my elder son. Sport with Miguel as well. He needs much practice if he is to be prepared for the ordeals that await him."

"As you wish, Father."

Jorge faced Aben Ayesh. "How much time do we have to teach Miguel?"

"Never enough," Aben Ayesh said. "A merchant galleon is due here in twenty days, docked at Portsmouth for only a week."

Not much time at all, Roderigo thought. So much to be done. Twenty days to teach Miguel to ride the treacherous road to the port, how to defend himself against the ruthless highwaymen, how to sneak aboard the ship, find the stowaways, and present them with the forged papers that would give them freedom at last.

"How many conversos are we to provide papers for?" Roderigo asked.

"De Gama wrote at least a dozen," Aben Ayesh answered.

Esteban Ferreira de Gama was their Iberian contact, the man responsible for concealing the Spanish conversos on the galleons. King Philip knew about him. As long as the English conversos continued to pay His Majesty, Ferreira de Gama was safe from harassment by the Spanish sentries guarding the docks. But once on board, the stowaways were on their own.

"How many men, women, and children?" Roderigo asked. "I have to tell the women what kind of papers to prepare."

"I know not," Aben Ayesh answered. "De Gama has promised another note letting me know the details of the cargo."

Unusual cargo. But when writing to Philip, the Ames Levantine Trade Company had to refer to the stowaways as something. Roderigo was the intermediary representative acting for the company, requesting in writing the purchase of "cargo" from His Majesty. Sometimes the company acquired "pepper." Other correspondences spoke of the company's desire to buy cargo of musk, amber, pearls, rubies, diamonds. Much "trade" he had with the Spanish king. Perhaps too much trade for the Queen's tolerance. Unofficially, England and Spain were still at war. They had to act as fast as possible.

Aben Ayesh continued, "The stowaways should be docked in Spanish Brussels by the end of June. Our agent there is still David. He will bring them to Amsterdam and integrate them."

Jorge said, "The whole mission will be harder than ever. The galleon ship flies the flag of Sicily—Philip's dominion. There are bound to be Spaniards aboard, and since Raphael was caught, they'll be looking out for more stowaways—as well as Miguel."

"Ferreira de Gama wrote of another possibility," Aben Ayesh

said. "It may be possible to transfer the conversos to an inbound vessel—a ship headed for the Thames. If this is the situation, Miguel has only to sneak aboard a local ship—a much simpler task. The English will not be as suspicious or as vicious as the Spanish. And, God forbid, if Miguel is captured, at least he'll be under the arm of Her Majesty instead of His Majesty and the Inquisition—as was Raphael." He sighed. "Dearest, poor Raphael . . ."

Aben Ayesh lowered his head for a moment. Then it was back to business. He said, "If Ferreira de Gama can arrange such a task, so be it."

"How inconspicuously does Esteban Ferreira de Gama move under the watchful eye of the Inquisition?" Dunstan asked.

"He grows increasingly concerned for his safety," Aben Ayesh said. "But, praise be to God, so far the Holy See has no suspicions that he is one of us."

"What's the name of the galleon that holds the conversos?" Benjamin asked.

"El Don Carlos," said Aben Ayesh. "Would that Philip's son were as mighty as his namesake of a ship."

"We must begin Miguel's training at once. He must be skilled enough to fight off anyone who challenges him on the road to Portsmouth."

All eyes went to Thomas.

"I'll teach him what I'm able." Thomas patted the hilt of his sword. "But only Miguel can execute the moves." He paused, then blurted out, "Of course, I'd be happy to accompany him—"

"You're needed in the business," Jorge said firmly. "I need someone trustworthy with the money and inventory at home."

"What about Dunstan?" Thomas retorted.

"Dunstan travels much," Jorge said.

Benjamin said, "Uncle, I could cancel my overseas travel if I am needed."

"Nonsense," Jorge said. "Go to Venice."

Thomas said, "But—"

"Enough," answered Jorge.

"Father, there is not a man alive who has my skill in swordplay, my swiftness, my strength—"

"Quiet," Jorge yelled. "I've heard your pleas before and again I reject them. Thomas, my son, if we have not the funds with which to bribe, *all* our efforts are for naught. Besides, Tommy, I want you whole until Leah is healthy enough to deliver to you a fine son."

Biting his lip, Thomas sank back in his chair. Dunstan grinned. "By the way, Tommy," he said. "Where *is* your wife?"

Thomas reddened with anger. As if the bastard didn't know.

"Leah has taken rest with her parents in Turkey," Aben Ayesh answered for Thomas. "She's due back in England during autumn."

Dunstan said, "Tut, tut. The lass was sorely worn out by the birth of another *daughter!*"

Thomas bolted up and drew his sword.

"Stow thy peace, Thomas," shouted Jorge. "And quit thy baiting words, Dunstan. Such animosity between brothers! Tis ungodly! Learn a lesson from Miguel and Raphael—God rest his soul. Now there were *true* brothers."

Shamefaced, Thomas returned to the floor. The men sat in silence for a moment. Aben Ayesh asked wearily,

"Any questions about the operation?"

Again, shakes of the head.

Aben Ayesh said, "We need many more citizen's papers. We have left only six official sets."

"Grace is completing a set as we speak," said Dunstan.

"Maria had done two," Jorge said.

"We still are short," Aben Ayesh said.

"I shall tell Sarah to get to work," said Roderigo. "Becca can work as well. The task shall occupy her thoughts, keep her mind off her woes."

"Uncle," Dunstan said, "I pray you, remind Rebecca to speak with discretion."

"Has she been indiscreet?" Roderigo asked.

Dunstan hesitated, then said, "She's a woman. All women have loose tongues. And that can be fatal, especially since you house that worm, de Andrada."

Roderigo grimaced at the mention of the name. De Andrada, Don Antonio's former "trusted" spy, wanted by Don Antonio for being a traitor. A snake Lopez was forced to feed and shelter because de Andrada had managed to learn too much about their operations. Though de Andrada had acted grateful for the help, Lopez knew he could never be trusted.

"I shall remind Becca of the virtue of silence," Roderigo said.

"We must pray," Aben Ayesh said, rising. "Instead of our individual meditations, let us say our morning prayers together— as if we were a minyan."

"Morning prayers?" Dunstan said. "It's still night."

"Would you rather say them when the servants are awake and their ears are open to our chanting?" Roderigo said.

Dunstan turned red.

"Excuse my impertinence, Father," Benjamin said, "but do not we need ten to be a minyan?"

Roderigo said, "We are only six in number but thousands in spirit. God will forgive us."

The men stood and faced the eastern side of the chamber. Jorge extinguished the torches, leaving only the faint, orange flame of candlelight. Silhouettes of faces projected onto the walls. Head down, Aben Ayesh began the prayer of kaddish over Raphael's soul—a supplication praising God's infinite power and wisdom. He whispered the blessing so the servants could not hear. But in truth, he knew he needn't have vocalized the blessing at all. God hears everything.

5

Manuel de Andrada knew they were plotting his demise. He could feel evil vapors swirling about his room. It was the same aura he had sensed before his defection from Don Antonio's service, and it filled him with dread.

Twas only a matter of time.

He shivered under his counterpane, his winter nightshirt itchy, sewn from frieze cloth—a pauper's garment. Marry, how it irritated his skin! Dr. Lopez had not the decency to give him one woven from flax, the miserable wight. Throwing the blanket atop his head, de Andrada bunched himself into a tight knot and began his ritual curses.

Curse Don Antonio—his former master. A man he had fought for, spied for, a man whom he had almost given his life for . . . Almost.

Curse King Philip—a weak old wretch whose generosities were as shriveled as his face. De Andrada remembered his last visit with His Majesty, kissing the bony hand, sitting at the side of the black, velvet wheelchair. The royal features had been as hard as stone, the eyes as small as a rat's. Cold, calculating, and stingy. Did the King not recognize the service that he—Manuel de Andrada—had performed for him?

He had spied against Don Antonio for Philip, had even bribed a helmsman to deliver the Pretender to the Throne of Portugal into the hands of the Spanish king. But the note had been found. Though written in special ink, it had been deciphered. His treason against Don Antonio—who was now in exile, somewhere in

Eton, de Andrada had last heard—had landed him six months in the Tower.

Had *that* been part of Lopez's plan to do him in? Had Lopez only rescued him because he had known about the doctor's mission? Had Lopez been afraid that he—de Andrada—would be of loose lips?

He thought a moment.

No, de Andrada thought, decidedly not. Lopez had been a true healer back then—kind and true-hearted. It was Lopez who'd secured his release from prison. The doctor had taken him into his own home, fed him fresh meats, clothed him in vestments that didn't itch. Had Roderigo not intervened in his behalf, he would have been behalved.

But curse Lopez now. He had dealt deceptively with his faithful servant—Manuel de Andrada—just like the rest. Though Lopez professed that he was a guest in his house, without any funds, de Andrada was completely at Lopez's mercy. Aye, the doctor had turned into a *witch* doctor. Roderigo Lopez had beguiled him, forced him to act as a go-between with the King of Spain, inveigled him into his Jew-saving intrigues. And now, after months of dedicated work, de Andrada was being discarded, tossed out the window like shit in a chamberpot.

He sighed. In his life he'd been employed by so many, turned traitor to so many. It was hard to keep them all sorted.

How would the doctor arrange the death—*his* death? An accidental fall from a horse? Did not the groom look at him with naughty eyes? When had that been? A week ago? Two weeks? Aye, when Saturn had been in Pisces, the sun sign of his birth. A bad omen!

He rolled over onto his back and groaned.

Poison perhaps? Aye, poison was a favorite pastime of the physician to the Queen. De Andrada remembered too clearly Lopez's verbal offer to poison Don Antonio. Aye, Lopez denied it to the world, and nothing in writing could prove otherwise, but de Andrada had heard the words uttered from the witch doctor's lips. Bottles of potions were stored in Lopez's still room. Jugs of Indian acacia. Barrels of distilled hemlock, ripening, aging like kegs of fine wine!

De Andrada trembled.

Suddenly all was clear. Why was he always the first to be served at dinnertime, at suppertime as well? It was not as they claimed—that he was a guest, and as such, honored with the first fruits of the kitchen. Nay, his portion of food had been tainted. Slow and painful poisoning!

The realization of why he'd been so ill of late.

Marry, it was so logical now. They hated him. Had he been invited to the house of the doctor's brother-in-law?

No.

The reason for the exclusion?

It could only be treachery against him. He was wasting away on a stiff straw pallet, racked with fever and pain brought on by poison, while they laughed at his impending death.

He gasped and coughed, trying to bring up his supper. After a minute of retching, he gave up. The juices of his stomach had eaten up the stew hours ago.

The stew, he thought. He recollected tiny pieces of fleshy vegetable mixed with roots, leeks, and mutton.

Mad apple!

He shuddered. Had the stew contained eggplant as well as rat's bane? Poison was not enough for the doctor's delight. He was trying to drive him mad as well!

He'd take no more meals with the evil ones!

Suddenly he smiled. He was safe—at least temporarily. How much he had overheard! How many ''secret'' letters he had read! How much he knew! Lopez had disregarded his own rules—destroy anything written, talk softly, trust no one.

And then there was Nan Humbert—the Ames's chambermaid. All he had to do was pray with the withered, Puritan biddy and she'd sing much about the family whispers. She had bigger and better ears than he did.

De Andrada started to plan his defense.

Who was Lopez pitted against? Who loathed Lopez as much as Don Antonio. . . . No, that wasn't it. Who loathed *Lopez* more than *he* detested the doctor himself—*and* had the power to turn his hatred into action? Certainly not Lord Burghley. He and Lopez had become friends of late. Not his crookback son Robert Cecil either.

Who?

Why, the ambitious red-haired youth with the fair face and the choleric temperament.

Essex!

He would ingratiate himself with Essex. Offer to spy against Lopez in order to secure the lord's favor.

The smile widened to a grin.

Essex. Such an impetuous cock. He'd do anything to advance his War Party. It was no secret that the lord longed for war—for an astounding military victory over Spain, with him at the head of the troops. How Essex hungered for power, the cheers and adulation of his countrymen, the admiration of his peers. How he ached to win the hand of Eliza. Oh yes, it was the crown of

England that the lord desired. It was no secret at all. Even Her Majesty knew his wants.

But the High Treasurer, Lord Burghley, and Lopez were obstacles, both secretly advocating peace with the King of Spain to Her Majesty. Lord Essex was bound to welcome his help, would receive Manuel de Andrada with much cheer, heaping angels upon him as payment for well-executed spying.

Of course, there was the small matter of Antony Bacon, Essex's spy master. De Andrada would have to convince him that he was trustworthy. Bacon was a clever man, exceedingly wary. But hadn't he, Manuel de Andrada, fooled other equally clever men? Bacon was but one small obstacle to overcome.

De Andrada felt confident and congratulated himself for a scheme so brilliant.

He hugged himself harder, tighter, squeezing his knees against his chest.

Eat no food. Not even the fruit in the bowl.

But he was hungry.

One bite of apple?

Nay, do not succumb. It is all vile.

A half bite?

Not even a lick.

He would not give up without a fight! He would scrape and bite and claw and kick, but he would not give up without a fight. If he would lose his head, so would a witch doctor.

Rebecca lay atop her feather mattress, wondering how her father was planning her future. She had no idea how late it was as she couldn't see the sand glass on the mantel opposite her bed. Yet she refused to light her candle, consuming solace once again from the darkness. Her chamber walls, like those in her uncle's Great Hall, had been draped in black cloth, hiding the arras work and tapestries. She felt as though she were sleeping in a bat's cave. The sole illumination came from moonbeams streaking through her bedchamber's window. They fell upon the table next to her bed, highlighting the pitcher and washbasin on the tabletop. Outside, the winds whistled through the shutters, swayed the boughs of the newly budded trees, kicking up eddies of dirt and dust, a moving sketch done in charcoal and framed by the window sash.

Her future. If only she had some control over her destiny. Her life, always in the hands of another—her elders, her cousins, her brother, God—in any hands but hers. Were her hands any less capable than Benjamin's, than Dunstan's or Thomas's? But her hands had the misfortune to be attached to the body of a woman.

She swallowed back tears, cursed her lot in life. A moment

later she broke into sobs, feeling sudden shame at her rantings. Why had she been allowed to live and her betrothed taken in his prime?

Poor Raphael, how did you meet your end?

Rebecca had loved him because it had been her duty. She had addressed him with a modulated tone of voice, greeted him with smiles, suffered his dark moods in silence. She knew it was his work, not she, that had been his true passion. Life was a mysterious animal. In the end it was his passion that did him in. She worried that the passion might also destroy her dear Miguel.

Miguel was her distant cousin but her brother in spirit. He'd never been a lover of women. Yet he was also a dutiful son. If their fathers wished them to wed, they would wed. And what a mockery that would be.

There was a knock on her door, her mother's whisperings. Rebecca forced herself upright, unlocked the door, then fell back atop her counterpane. Sarah Lopez, clad in her bedclothes, entered the bedchamber and sat on her daughter's mattress. A moonbeam fell across her face, turned her cheeks ghostly white. Her eyes looked so sad, but Rebecca had never remembered a day when they had looked happy. Sarah brushed her waist-length gray hair off her shoulders and touched Rebecca's hand. It was rigid and cold.

"Under the covers, Becca," Sarah ordered gently. "I'll not allow you to grow ill from the frigid air. Tis a tomb inside here— dark and wintry. I'll call the chambermaid and have her rekindle the hearth immediately."

Rebecca squeezed her mother's hand. "How can I allow myself warmth and comfort when Raphael sits for eternity in an icy bed?"

Sarah pulled back the bedcovers. "Inside, little one, I prithee."

Rebecca slithered underneath the down blanket. Sarah drew the spread up to her daughter's chin.

"I'm not half the clever wordsmith that you are, Becca," spoke Sarah. "I've stayed up for hours trying to find proper words of solace, yet my mind is as empty as a newborn babe's. Tell me what to do to comfort you."

Rebecca didn't answer. Her mother's voice, though soothing, sounded so weary. It saddened Rebecca to think that she'd brought any more woes to her mother. She embraced her mother and told her she loved her.

Sarah said, "You are my joy, Becca. All I desire is happiness for you and Benjamin."

Rebecca knew this to be the truth. She'd never seen her mother engaged in idle play. Sarah's life revolved around Father and his activities, around her and Ben.

Rebecca asked, "Has Father made mention to you of my future?"

"He has yet to return home from Uncle Jorge's." She sighed. "I suspect he'll spend the night there. By and by you'll know of Father's intention. He's never been one to hide from you his plans."

"I wish he'd leave me in solitude."

"That is impossible, dear Becca," Sarah said. "While you're still somewhat young, the years do pass by quickly. Best to have children while your womb is strong."

"I wish—" Rebecca realized how quiet was the night and dropped her voice. "I wish our religion allowed us nunneries."

"Black is a color ill-suited for your complexion," Sarah said. She kissed her daughter's cheek. "Have you said your proper prayers for . . . for Raphael?"

Rebecca nodded.

Sarah said, "God will hear them."

Rebecca asked, "Have you told Grandmama about Raphael?"

"*I* didn't tell her, yet she knew," Sarah said. "Sometimes I think my mother a witch rather than an addled old woman."

"She is neither," Rebecca said. "She is a marvelous woman."

"'Tis most inappropriate for you to doubt my love and affection for my mother, Becca."

Sarah's voice held a wounded note. Rebecca picked up her hand and kissed it.

"I apologize, my gentle mother."

Sarah squeezed her daughter's hand and said,

"Grandmama shows no fretting over the news. She keeps her tears inside. Yet we both know she feels deeply. Raphael had been kind to her."

"May I spend my mourning in Grandmama's room?"

Sarah thought for a moment. "Father would never permit it. Guests will come to comfort you—"

"They come to eat."

"Nonetheless, you must be visible and behave appropriately. Accept their platitudes of sorrow as if they meant something to you."

"Playact, aye?"

Sarah sighed. "Yes," she said. "Playact."

"At least may I pass my nights with her?"

Her mother lowered her head and said, "Father prefers to keep you away—"

"Father errs," Rebecca interrupted. "Father thinks Grandmama's an old harpy with a head full of mush. You know that's not so.''

"Rebecca, my obligations come first to my master, second to my mother and children. You must learn that else you'll make a poor English gentlewoman and wife.''

"I'd rather become not an English wife but an English spinster,'' Rebecca blurted out. "I've no desire to marry!''

She expected to hear reproachment from her mother. Instead Sarah patted her hand in sympathy.

"Time will alter your desires,'' she said.

Rebecca noticed for the first time how her mother trembled from cold. She held open her cover for her, bade her to come inside. Sarah shook her head.

"I must get back to my chambers. Father will be furious if he finds me sleeping with you. He thinks I've spoiled you beyond redemption.''

"In sooth, his assessment is not far from wrong.''

Sarah smiled. "Do try to sleep.''

"Mother?''

"Aye.''

"Can you request of Father to allow me to sleep with Grandmama? I'd find it most comforting.''

"I'll pose the question to him. But I think you'll mislike the response.''

"Plead with him.''

"I'll do what I can, Becca.''

Rebecca hesitated, then said, "I'm being selfish, Mother. Plead not with him. Ask him most noncommitally. Don't risk his wrath for my sake.''

Sarah kissed her daughter. "I'll do what I can,'' she repeated. "Should I call the chambermaid to rekindle the fire?''

"Not necessary,'' Rebecca said. "I'm very sleepy.''

"Well then,'' Sarah said. "Good night, Becca. Things will be better come the morning light.''

Rebecca nodded, watched her mother's shadow disappear from the room. Her mother, the hours of her life divvied up by Father and his work, by her and Ben, by Grandmama. But never a moment for herself. Sarah had once told her that she thought of herself as an extra arm for the members of her family. Rebecca also remembered when her mother had confided her reveries as a young girl—how one day she'd live in the clouds made of spun sugar, fly upon the back of a golden eagle and touch the sun. Where did those dreams go? Her mother—her heart in the sky, her muscles saddled with duty.

6

Shakespeare knew he was lost. He'd passed the same bridge-shaped rock an hour ago. Madness to come up North alone, trying to retrace a dead man's last steps, chasing revenge as elusive as the wind. He should have insisted to Margaret that the trip would accomplish nothing. But something had propelled him forward, something more than a widow's pleas.

Past images. A costume and a scroll being shoved under his nose as he tended the horses of the playgoers. Harry slapping him on the back . . .

Fiacre Nits, who plays the watchman in the second act, has just turned ill. Vomited all over the ground. Good hap that he wore not his costume.

Harry had turned nearly purple from laughter.

You want me on stage? was all that Shakespeare had been able to say.

You're the only one who's sober enough to memorize the lines on such short notice.

More laughter. Whitman's laughter. It played in Shakespeare's head. A painful reminder, the sound so hollow now.

Shakespeare kicked the haunches of his horse, sending it into a gallop. He cursed, wondered where the hell he was.

So far he'd managed to follow Harry's path quite closely. But this particular route, although the most direct to the burg of Hemsdale, was full of nature's detours—hilly rocks and sudden dales, steep crags and crevices that plunged raggedly into the ground, circumscribing the knolls like a moat around a castle.

He pulled the horse to the left, hoping he'd find a decent inn before dusk. Polished, windswept ledges of sandstone erupted out of rocks and grassland abloom with clumps of purple heather. The summits of the hills reflected the gold of the sun, setting them on fire like a flame on a candle. At least this terrain allowed easy riding—soft, gritty soil that yielded under each beat of the hoof—far more comfortable on the body than the hard slate rock he'd experienced in the extreme northern regions.

He'd been fortunate. The weather had been accommodating, allowing him to cover much ground in a short time; barely a

week since he's left the walls of London. He'd fallen prey to
only a few days of hard rain, and this morning just a thin blanket
of haze covered the sky—that already burning away in the afternoon sun. His horse trampled over a heather bush plump with
baby grouse. They scampered off in all directions—a delicious
feast of tender meat dissipating before his eyes. He groaned,
suddenly, realizing how long it had been since he'd taken a stomach. He would eat, but not while the sun was out. No time to
be wasted.

Days of riding with nothing but a sore bum to show for it. So
far the trip had illuminated nothing about Harry. Questions had
been asked and answered by protestations of ignorance. Shakespeare had spoken to at least two dozen innkeepers. Three hos-
tlers told him that the great actor had indeed blessed their modest
hostel with his drunken but amusing presence. They smiled as
they told Shakespeare that Harry had entertained the guests with
a (cough, cough) randy soliloquy. But beyond that, Whitman had
been a gentleman. He had stayed the night, paid his bills, and
left early the following morning in fine health. One hostler did
recall Harry speaking with excitement about his impending visit
to his relatives up North.

Anything else, Shakespeare asked.

The innkeeper shook his head no.

. His friend's last days of life seemed ordinary. What could
Harry have possibly done to instill murder in a man's heart?
What nefarious creature had done him in? And the ever nagging
question of why.

Shakespeare had been determined to find answers—for Margaret's sake as well as his own. But now, after much wasted
time, the ardor for truth had cooled. He missed London, his
cell, his poetry writings and books.

But he'd come this far. Might as well finish his task. From the
inns Shakespeare learned that Harry had visited his relatives—a
first cousin, Viscount Henley and his family.

And, as Whitman had once mentioned in passing, Lord Henley *was* genuine peerage. He'd been granted a township in
Northumberland. Brithall was the name of his castle, and an
impressive pile of bricks it was. Before Shakespeare left, Margaret had told him that *all* of her husband's kinsmen were secret
Papists, followers of Rome, like many of the northerners. She
said that Harry had once confided to her that Brithall held a
secret underground chapel where votive candles were kept along
with icons of the Virgin. But the boldest act of outrage was a
fugitive priest in their hire—a Jesuit who narrowly escaped capture from the authorities by hiding in one of the castle's priest
holes. Harry later recanted his story about the priest, saying it

had been a tale told in jest—to scare her. But Margaret felt his denial had been a lie.

Margaret had always been nervous about Harry's excursions— the length of the trip, the dangers of the highways—but after the execution of Mary Queen of Scots, with anti-Catholic sentiment running high, she'd actively protested his visit.

What if that *priest were discovered?*

Harry had always taken pains to reassure her. Queen Eliza was a tolerant woman, God sing her praises. Hadn't it been rumored that Eliza's private chapel mimicked those of the High Church despite her excommunication from Rome?

But Margaret hadn't been easily consoled.

Who could say that Eliza will always be tolerant, she'd told Harry. *Is not the Queen older, more eccentric? Did not she hang six hundred northerners for treason? Papist northerners? Priests—and their followers—had been burned before. They could be burned again.*

But Harry had continued his visits.

Harry as a Catholic: that had surprised Shakespeare. His friend and mentor had always been irreverent, and religion was his favorite topic of scorn. How he's mocked the Puritan, ridiculed the pious parish priest. And now to discover that it wasn't the institution that had offended his sensibilities, but rather the method of worship.

A side of Harry Shakespeare knew little about.

Yet he had known a side of Harry that he loved. He knew him as the man who had coached his voice, had taught him how to project over the shouts of the groundlings and the boos of the twopenny rowdies. He knew Harry as the man who instructed him in dance, as the man who had insisted that the fellowship take Shakespeare on as a sharer. He knew Harry as a money lender, the one who paid the enormous sharer's fee of twenty pounds for his 'prentice, Willy.

Yes, once Harry had taken care of him. But Shakespeare had loved him deeply even when the roles had reversed. Shakespeare, apologizing to an irate tapster for Harry's big mouth; Shakespeare, pulling him out of brabbles with younger men ready to kill them both; Shakespeare, patting the back of a stuporous man, hugging him as he cried.

His love for Harry flowed through his veins as sure as blood. Shakespeare's quest for Harry's murderer, for his mentor's eternal peace, was strong and potent—like the sting in the loins.

He'd ridden farther, thinking about the different side of Harry—the one which he'd not been privy to know.

A secret Catholic. Yet Harry had left Brithall alive and well. Or so had said Viscount Henley. Shakespeare had spoken to

Henley briefly as they strolled the Brithall's formal gardens. Shakespeare had asked the lord as many questions as manners would allow, but Henley knew nothing about Harry's murder. Shakespeare hadn't broached the subject of the priest. It hadn't seemed necessary. By the time Shakespeare had departed from Brithall, he was satisfied that Henley had nothing to do with his kinsman's death.

Perhaps the murder was as reported. Harry'd been victimized by the scurrilous highwayman and dumped in the sheep's pen. But perhaps someone—a secret member of some anti-Papist guild—had found out about Harry's Catholic sentiments, stalked him, and had taken his life in the open countryside, away from alert eyes.

Guesswork.

Endless hours of riding, endless hours of nothing.

The sun was bowing low, readying itself for final exit. Clouds were coalescing into thick gray foam. The ground had become wetter; sparse shrubbery had thickened into wooded copses of cotton grass and bilberry bushes and newly budded gnarled oak.

Shakespeare realized he was famished. Another night under a coverlet of stars. He found a pocket of fresh water, not much bigger than a puddle but enough to satisfy the thirst of a tired animal. After the horse had drunk his fill, Shakespeare dismounted and tied him to a tree. The winds were gentle, redolent with the pungent aroma of fermenting bilberries. He opened up his leather bag and pulled out a slab of ham, eating it in three bites. His supper was followed by sips of ale from his drinking gourd and fresh bilberries. He lay undisturbed except for the occasional scurry of fleeing woodland creatures—red deer, grouse, squirrel, hedgehogs. The thought of fresh game aroused his belly—meat crackling over an open fire. A lover of hunting, he reminisced of his days as a boy, hare coursing . . . deer poaching. Though plagued with an unsatisfied stomach, he drifted off to sleep.

Shakespeare was awakened by trampling in the brush. Clay-cold and rigid, his clothes damp with morning dew, he opened his eyes but didn't move. Dawn was waging battle against a metallic sky. He reached for his falchion, grasping the handle tightly, and waited.

Sounds of footsteps. He sprung upward. A startled gasp and a shower of bilberries. Then he saw her.

She was a plump girl, no more than sixteen, with dark, loose hair and alabaster skin—a perfect white except for smidges of rosy pink on her nose and cheeks. Some of her front teeth were missing.

"Ho, wench," Shakespeare said. "What are you doing here alone at this hour?"

The girl cowered in the brush, fear etched in her black eyes.

"Met your lover, did you?" Shakespeare said.

She said nothing. Just quivered in the bushes. An idiot to be sure, he thought.

"Be gone," he said testily.

She didn't move. It was then that he noticed the empty basket stained a deep plum. He bent down, picked it up and tossed it over. It hit her on the left leg, but she didn't react.

"Picking berries, were you?"

Nothing.

"Go on," he said. "I'll not be bothering you."

She smiled. Despite the toothless gaps, she was pretty. Shakespeare felt a tug under his breeches.

"Off with you," he said. "Lest you be enticing the man to act the animal."

She smiled again and hiked up her skirt.

Dumb, he thought. But not deaf.

She was as warm as fresh milk, as sweet as cream and as soft as butter.

She was also not a mute. As she lay, nestled in his arms, she told him her story.

She was the bastard daughter of a whore, orphaned at eleven when her mother died of sweating sickness. Left destitute, she continued her mother's profession of providing aid and comfort to the village men. A year ago, six months pregnant, she'd been inflicted with ague. The baby had died in her belly. Vividly she described to him her fits and fevers, her bloody vomit and stools.

But somehow she had survived, nursed her ills with poppy water, the juice of red nettles, juniper berries, and flat ale with dragon water. She was still weak, she claimed, but at least she was alive. And yes, she was still a punk servicing the local men as well as the foreigner. She lived in a village not far away from this spot.

When she wasn't whoring, she was busy in her still room, preparing remedies and potions. Rising early, three or four in the morn, she'd come to the heather moors to pick bilberries and herbs for her medicines. They were well received throughout the countryside, and often in the plague-infested summertimes, her special mixtures made her more money than her stewing. The only thing that worried her was talk that she was a witch.

Nay, tis not so, she had said. *Simply flapping tongues of the gossip mongers.*

As she told her tale, her hands moved over Shakespeare's body, reawakening his lust once again. He stroked her pillowy thighs, parted them and boarded her. Afterward he offered her money, but she had refused.

Your kindness, good sir. Tis 'nough.

He stood up and brushed dirt off his hose.

"Where is your village?" he asked.

"Yonder," she said, pointing to her left.

"Will you accompany me there?"

She smiled. "Me whorin' is free, but me guidin' will be costin' ye."

"A survivor you are."

"Aye. Ten shillings."

Shakespeare gasped. "That's robbery!"

The toothless smile widened to a grin.

"Ifin it be too much, you be findin' it yourself."

"Blood of a Jew, you have," Shakespeare said. "I shall simply wait for you to return, idiotic wench. Then I shall follow you."

"Aye, and wait all of the day for me to pick me herbs. Whatever pleases you, sir."

Again the smile. It had become venal.

"A penny's more the cost," he said.

"You insult me, sir. Five shillings."

"A penny."

"A shilling."

"Tuppence."

"A sixpence."

"A tuppence," Shakespeare repeated. He mounted his steed. "Keep kicking a jade, wench, and you'll have a dead horse at your feet."

"A tuppence it is," she said, hopping up behind him.

Her knowledge of the terrain was flawless, her senses keen, her skills swift. A large ground squirrel darted in front of their pathway. A moment later it lay dead, impaled to the ground, her dagger through its belly. She dismounted his horse, pulled out the knife and flung the bloodied carcass over her shoulder.

The animal would give her money and food for the week, she explained.

"I shall keep the meat for me meals, sir. The innards will be stuffed with rye and oats, boiled, sliced, then sold to the Fishhead to be eaten cold. The pelt and tail will be a hat, the spleen and liver will be roasted in an open pit and sold at the marketplace, the blood will be mixed with ale and sold to the apothecary as a remedy for virility problems. The brains, heart, lungs, and kidneys shall be minced and made into pies. The teeth shall be ground into powder and mixed with cinnamon and mint.

When stirred with warm ale and a teaspoon of dragon water, tis good for the brain.''

"What about the eyes?" Shakespeare asked.

"Pickled in vinegar," she answered. "When swallowed whole, they are also good for the brain."

He thought about that along the way—a supper of pickled eyes.

The burg of Hemsdale was under the jurisdiction of Henton Hall. It was a poor town eroded by bitter cold and strong winds. The first houses that came into view were built from clay, colored red, white, or blue, and ceiled with straw, reeds, and mud. Little protection from the rain, Shakespeare thought.

As they reached the main thoroughfare, the hamlet awoke from its dormancy. Here were the townspeople busy with activity— wives and daughters buying fruits from the costermongers, or red, fresh beef from the butchers. Laborers and citizens staggered out of red-sashed taverns, children chased one another. There were the merchants shouting from the windows of their houses, "What de ye lack, today?" trying to ensnare buyers to purchase their wares. Aproned men pushing carts loaded with edibles sang out their selections—fresh cucumbers or melons, oatbread and barley cakes, and sweet marchpane and comfits. A lute player strummed out a tune as maidens giggled and danced. Shakespeare dismounted and led the whore and his horse through the tumult. Not as festive as Paul's, but the noise did seem to liven up the weary little village.

He stopped to buy a pear. A big one. He bit into the skin and let the sweet juices dribble down his chin, then wiped them up using his sleeve. As he chewed, his thoughts turned back to Harry, until he was interrupted by a hoarse voice.

"Ye shall burn in hell lest ye repent for your wicked ways."

Shakespeare turned around and saw hard, black eyes. A blasted Puritan as bleak in character as he was in dress. Serious and sour, glutted with scorn. His voice was raw, his features small and pinched. He held out an ungloved hand—red as if burnt by fire. He pointed a gnarled finger at Shakespeare and said,

"Taker of the flesh of a whore. Repent before it's too late!"

Shakespeare and the whore said nothing.

"Repent!" he shouted with urgency in his voice. "You must repent!"

Shakespeare raised his eyebrows. "Why must you wear black all the time? Surely the Lord didn't create colors to be disregarded as such."

"Colors are sinful!" he blasted out. "They cause the eye to see false beauty." He curled his finger into his fist and shook it at them. "Only repentance can bring pure truth, pure beauty. Look around." The Puritan swept his arm across the town. "All is filled with the Devil's biding. Satanic mummeries held not more than a week ago. Spring is here and soon our souls shall be assaulted once again by hedonistic orgies and rituals."

"Beg your pardon, sir?" Shakespeare asked.

"Poles bedecked with flowers—icons of paganism."

"He means the maypole," the whore said.

"Such pastime is merely amusement," Shakespeare said. "Frivolous, but not unseemly godless."

The Puritan's eyes burned with fury.

"Frivolity is the Devil's meat. Thou must repent, sinner! Rid thyself of all foul beasts, *that* foul beast." Out came the finger. He pointed to the whore, and she smiled at him.

"Filth," his raspy voice uttered. He pulled a hood atop his head.

Shakespeare rolled his eyes and led the horse around him. "I thank you for your counsel, good sir."

"Ye still have time to repent, sinner," said the Puritan. "Repent! Repent, I say! Before the gloaming! Before it's too late!"

On the outskirts of town lay the bigger, wooden houses. Four of them. He asked her who lived there.

"The first one over there with gardens, that belongs to Alderman Fottingham," she replied. "He's one of me best sporters. The two over there belongs to citizens—one's a merchant, the other an apothecary. The biggest house—other than Henton—belongs to a yeoman."

"Where is Henton House?" Shakespeare asked.

"Twenty minutes out that way," she said, pointing her finger.

"Is the Earl of Henton in residence?"

"I know not, sir."

"Do you know if Fottingham is home?" Shakespeare asked.

"No, sir."

Shakespeare stopped the horse in front of the alderman's house and then helped her down.

"This is as far as I take you."

She nodded and gave him a small curtsy.

Clearing his throat, he asked, "Is it your habit to entertain the stranger?"

"Ifin he can pay, tis all well with me."

"Have you had occasion to see a man here maybe three weeks ago? His name was Henry Whitman."

"I know not the name."

"Tall fellow, thick brown curls and a woolly brown beard. Full of muscle and grit."

"He sounds like a bear."

"Aye, a bear he was. Deep voice that carried like the roar of thunder."

His own voice had become loud and dramatic. She smiled.

"And hands as big as mutton chops," he went on. "And eyes as wide as the Channel and as dark as a witch's hat. And he loved to attack pretty little maidens," he added, tickling her ribs.

She burst into laughter. He hooked his arms around her waist and spun her around in the air.

"Seen him, you have?" he asked.

She shook her head no.

"He never crossed your bed."

"Sorry, no."

Shakespeare sighed and put her down. "Who was the Puritan who accosted me on the road?"

"That'd be Edward Mann. He's a bit mad in the head. He's been married three times; and all three times his wives died in childbirth. He claims he's possessed, a witch has cast a spell on him and the spell won't be lifted unless all of England repents."

"Had he ever had dealings with a witch?" Shakespeare asked.

The strumpet grinned wickedly and whispered, "I know not a witch exactly, sir, but mayhap I said an evil word or two about him." Her eyes widened with sudden fright. "You'll not be telling anyone what I said, eh?"

"No."

"Good." She leaned over and kissed his cheeks. "Me coins, now."

"Many thanks for your help, little one." He slapped coins into her palm and pinched her bottom. She gave him a coy, closed-lip smile and skipped away.

7

Food before conversation, the portly alderman had insisted. Talk grows irksome on an empty stomach. Fottingham was a man of good height but even more impressive girth. But his smile was welcoming, his voice cheerful, his blue eyes clear and friendly. His servants brought out plates of boiled beef, rabbit, grouse, quail, and venison. The meat was hot and fresh, and Shakespeare ate until his doublet bulged uncomfortably. After the trenchers had been cleared, Fottingham gathered up his fur-trimmed black robe, stood and stretched. Lumbering over to the hearth, he snatched two tankards from the mantel and filled them with ale. He gave one to Shakespeare, then settled back into his chair.

Shakespeare sipped the foam contentedly. The room was cool but dry, the floors covered with fresh straw, the plastered walls adorned with painted cloth. The windows were open, and a healthy wind stirred up air that had been thick with the smell of grease.

"You say that Cat brought you into town?" Fottingham asked. His black beard, spangled with droplets of ale, spread over his chest like a bib.

"Cat?" Shakespeare asked.

"The stew."

"She told me not her name."

Fottingham's eyes brightened. "Flesh of a woman who has no name. How lusty."

Shakespeare smiled. "Why do they call her Cat?"

"Because she purrs like a kitten during the rutting. Her Christian name is also Catherine."

"She tells an interesting story."

"Marry," the alderman said, dismissing him with a wave of his hand. "She's a notorious liar. Her mother lives, as does her father. He's a whoremonger. Cat is his best moneymaker."

"I've been gulled," Shakespeare said dryly.

Fottingham laughed. "Fell for her pathetic tale, did you? Paid her twice as much as necessary?"

"I think so."

"Not to worry," Fottingham said. "Others have been her co-ney. Besides, your face would be pleasing to the young girl. I'm sure she was quite enthusiastic with her favors."

"Quite," Shakespeare said. "Though she did remark that the hair on my head was scant . . . the hair on my chin as well."

"Tact is not the whore's forte," the alderman said. "She chides me constantly for my growing belly." He patted his stomach. "Once I was as trim as you. Once I was as young as you also. The luxury of aging. One may grow fat and content and sport with merry young wenches without bitter tears from the wife. Mine has served her purpose. Fifteen children, ten which still live. She is grateful for the punks. They give her much rest." Fottingham belched out loud, spied a leftover piece of meat on the floor and popped it in his mouth. Rabbit. Delicious.

"And now I have the pleasure of asking what has brought the player and bookwriter William Shakespeare to Hemsdale."

"I'm looking for acquaintances of a man—one Henry Whitman—Harry, as he liked to be called."

"The famous player Harry Whitman?"

"Yes."

"Are you his friend or his enemy?"

"His friend," Shakespeare replied.

"His company played here six years ago," Fottingham said. "The troupe was very well received. Whitman was particularly impressive. He and that other one, who was quite a bit younger."

"Richard Burbage."

"Yes, that was the name," said the alderman. "But you weren't with them."

"I wasn't in London at the time."

"Where is your birthplace?"

"Warwick."

"Never made it this far north before?"

"Not until this day," Shakespeare said. "Mayhap Harry passed through here recently?"

"Harry passed through here yearly," Fottingham said. "On his way down from his visits with his cousin, Lord Henley."

"You knew Harry well?" Shakespeare asked.

"Hardly at all," said Fottingham. "But Harry is hard to miss. He's a noticeable man physically—big and hairy. But as big as Harry is, tis his voice that is most memorable."

Shakespeare said, "He played it as if it were a viol—deep and beautiful. His soliloquies could bring one to tears."

Fottingham saw moisture in the younger man's eyes. He stared at Shakespeare and said, "What happened to Harry?"

Shakespeare whispered, "He was murdered."

"God's blood, that's horrible!" Fottingham seemed genuinely surprised. "Henley never said a word. When did this happen?"

"About two weeks ago."

"Where was he done in?"

"In the open countryside about fifteen miles from here. He was found dead, stabbed, left to rot in a sheep's cot."

"Good heavens!"

Neither one spoke. Fottingham suddenly squinted his eyes with suspicion and asked Shakespeare,

"And why are *you* here?"

Shakespeare replied, "I'm trying to find out what happened to him during his last days. Perhaps you know of someone who had talked to him as he passed through Hemsdale?"

"Not I." The alderman lifted a thigh and passed wind. "I

don't even recall seeing him two weeks ago, although I know he passed through Hemsdale every year right before Mayday.''

"But you had spoken to him in the past?" Shakespeare asked.

"A word or two," the alderman said. "Harry never resided at our local inn—The Grouse. He literally passed through the town."

Fottingham paused. Shakespeare knew there was more but like the line well-acted, timing was of crucial importance. He waited for the alderman to continue. A minute later, Fottingham said, "It might be wise if you let the dead rest in peace, my friend. It's possible you'll discover things about Harry that are best left buried."

"Such as?"

"Things."

"Specifically."

"Just things." The alderman closed his mouth stubbornly.

Shakespeare chose not to push him further. He said, "A poor outcome is a consequence of gambling. I'll chance the game."

"Why is this bit of intrigue important to you?" the alderman asked. "It won't restore breath to Harry's nostrils."

"I have reasons."

"Revenge on his murderer?"

"Perhaps."

"It will eat you alive, Shakespeare. Rot the flesh off the bones. The fiend could be anyone—a man with a personal grudge, a hot-headed drunk, a madman. Leave revenge to the hands of God."

Shakespeare said nothing.

"Revenge is a wily bastard, goodman," said Fottingham. "Be careful or you'll suffer the same fate as your friend." The alderman paused, then said, "Go to the Fishhead Inn and talk to the innkeeper—Edgar Chambers. Harry often stayed there. I've even heard him recite some of his bawdy poetry there. It was quite clever and very randy. I shall write you a letter of reference for Chambers."

"Thank you, sir, for your sound counsel and help." Shakespeare stood up. "Is Lord Henton in his residence?"

Fottingham stood and let out a rakish laugh. "Aye. But he won't be telling you anything important. He's weak in the head." The alderman tapped his temples. "And old and feeble. His quill has been quite dry for years now, though it doesn't bother his young, pretty wife. Her parchment is well-saturated."

Shakespeare smiled, noticed the gleam in the alderman's eye.

"You'll get nothing from the old lord," Fottingham said, scribbling out a letter on a scrap of paper. "Speak with Chambers at the Fishhead. He's a slippery man, Shakespeare. Selectively quiet. You may need to expend a tuppence or two before the innkeeper grows loquacious.''

''Rare is the man who dances not to the tune of jingling coins.''

''True words, my boy,'' said the alderman. He closed the letter with his seal and handed it to Shakespeare. In return, Shakespeare drew his poniard from its hilt.

''A gift for your kindness,'' he said, extending the dagger.

''Nay, insult me not, goodman.''

''But the insult will be mine, sir, if you accept it not.''

''If I come to London, treat me as I treated you.''

''But I cannot hope to entertain you in such a splendid manor.''

''Then invite me to witness you on stage.''

''Done a thousand times.''

The Fishhead Inn lay on the rocky banks of Loch Gelder, a small shadow of the steely, blue water. From time to time the smooth surface of the looking glass would crack open and up would jump an industrious gilded-scaled gudgeon or a silvery loach sided with streaks of pastel pinks and blues. Long seasons of heavy rainfall were common, and flooding of the inn from the lake was warded off by a barrier of piled boulders.

The hostel was modest in size, holding one hundred fifty able-bodied men. The architecture was simple—two stories of plastered walls, roofed with rifts of oak timber. A fine brick chimney puffed out clouds of muddy brown smoke.

The welcome sign—the hallmark of a quality inn—was fashioned from a solid block of walnut. Carved out of the center was a loach painted in bright reds and greens, with its tail curved under its belly. FISHHEAD INN was carved about the loach in bold, blue letters. The rest of the block was smooth, finished wood, sanded and varnished to a high gloss. Three feet in length, six inches in depth, the sign was too large and heavy to hang. Instead it was propped up by two oak posts.

Excessive and costly, thought Shakespeare.

He went inside, sat down at a small, round table and ordered a bottle of the cheapest port on the fareboard—two shillings six-pence. His money was draining, and he hoped his luck at the hare races would continue as it had the past year. He drank half the bottle then, fueled by the warm glow of the spirits, asked the tapster if he might have a word or two with Edgar Chambers. Shakespeare handed him his letter of reference. Minutes later a man sat down at his table and introduced himself as Chambers.

Young, Shakespeare noticed. Perhaps as much as ten years younger than himself. At the most twenty. Ruddy red cheeks and a fleece of strawberry-blond wool for hair. Shakespeare extended his hand and Chambers took it.

"I thank you, kind innkeeper, for permitting me the pleasure of your company," Shakespeare said.

"The honor is mine, goodman," Chambers replied. "Welcome to my humble little hostel."

"Nay, it is a splendid hostel," Shakespeare argued. Such deprecation was not expected to pass without comment. "Full of scrumptious food, fine wines, and company fit for the Queen. Tis truly *English*, goodman."

"You are too kind," Chambers said. "How can I be of service to you?"

"Did not Alderman Fottingham's letter explain the purpose of my visit?"

"Nay. He wrote simply that you wish an audience with me."

"Then I shall tell you the purpose," Shakespeare said. "I'm trying to find out if a friend of mine passed through this town—Harry Whitman."

Chambers paled. Shakespeare leaned forward.

"What do you know about him?" Shakespeare asked.

"Yes, well . . . He's a great player, of course," Chambers stammered.

Shakespeare said, "He lodged here often—"

"No!" cried Chambers. "Who told you that?"

"He stayed overnight—"

"No," Chambers insisted.

Shakespeare took out a shilling.

"No," Chambers said, hitting it out of his hands. "Not for love or money did he lodge here. Good day, sirrah!"

Chambers stalked away, but Shakespeare followed him. He grabbed the hostler's arm.

"Are you challenging me?" Chambers said with sudden viciousness. His hand was clenched around the hilt of his rapier.

"I pray you," Shakespeare said, "understand that I loved Harry, that he was most dear to me. If the tendrils of compassion wrap around your heart, let them squeeze it to remind you of the pain of untimely loss—of murder mòst fell."

"Murder?"

Shakespeare nodded. Chambers had turned ashen.

"We cannot talk here in public," Chambers whispered. "Too many open ears. Come with me."

Shakespeare followed the hostler down a dim hallway dotted with rushlights housed in rusty wall sconces. At the end of the hall was a small, almost hidden door. Chambers took out a large, brass skeleton key and opened the lock.

Chambers's private closet was spacious and brimming over

with natural light. The walls were wainscoted with walnut panels below, forest-green silk cloth above the wood. Framed pictures of fish—all kinds of fish—abounded. A large mounted whitefish rested on a wooded mantel. Chambers pulled out a chair from a round table, offered it to Shakespeare, then sank wearily into his own chair, positioned across the table.

Shakespeare said, "Tell me what happened to Whitman."

"I don't know anything about a murder!" insisted Chambers. "As God is my witness, I speak the truth."

"Then what do you know?"

"He lodged here."

"For how long?" Shakespeare asked.

"Three . . . no, four . . . four days."

"A long time," Shakespeare commented. "Was that his usual length of stay?"

Chambers shook his head rapidly. "His longest visit ever. In the past he had stayed only a night. Last year he stayed two days. This time four."

"Then why did you deny knowing him?" Shakespeare asked.

"I had my reasons," Chambers said.

"And they were?"

Chambers didn't answer. Shakespeare let it go and asked,

"How did Whitman pass the hours here?"

"In pursuit of pleasure," Chambers said. "Your friend was fond of dicing."

Shakespeare frowned. *"Dicing?"*

"Aye."

Shakespeare said, "Harry enjoyed drinking, making merry. But *dicing*? You've mistaken him for someone else."

"No mistake. Whitman diced, gambled. And lost a great deal of money."

"Tell me."

Chambers became animated. "The first night his hap was sweet, his winnings large. But the last days of his stay—he was here for five days—"

"I thought you said four."

"Four days then. Yes, it was four days. On the fourth night, when Harry became involved with a group of rogues—unscrupulous men—his luck suddenly changed."

Shakespeare felt suddenly ired, frustrated. "He became someone's coney—a dupe."

Chambers nodded.

"You didn't stop the rogues from cheating?"

Chambers said, "In my business one never interferes with gentlemen dicing. They become most resentful."

Shakespeare asked him to continue.

"The stakes grew higher," Chambers said. His eyes darted from side to side, "I know not exactly what happened, sir. It was said that Harry's luck took a sudden turn for the better. *Then* it was discovered that Harry held in his pockets several pairs of false dice."

Shakespeare cursed inwardly. *Uncover things best left buried.* He said, "Harry was many things—a philanderer and a carouser—but always an honest man."

"Then it grieves me to tell you this, goodman, but in his possession were a flat carter-treys, a flat cinque-deuces, a barred carter-treys, and high fullam."

"High fullam?"

"Dice weighed toward high numbers."

"I don't believe it," Shakespeare said. "He was duped."

"I was not there when the accusations were made, sir."

"Where were you?" Shakespeare asked.

"I have a brother," Chambers said. "He was in charge of the inn's business that evening."

"May I speak with him?" Shakespeare asked.

"He's in Kent, sir."

"Had you ever seen Harry dice on any previous visit here?" Shakespeare asked.

"Yes sir, I have."

"You have?"

"Yes." Chambers began to shake his left leg.

Shakespeare told him to complete the dreadful tale.

Chambers said, "The next morning *I* saw Harry paying off these men with big coins—angels, nobles, *sovereigns.*"

Where had Harry come to so much money? Shakespeare wondered. He asked, "The name of these rogues?"

"I divulge their identities only because you say he was a kindred spirit with your soul."

"I speak honestly."

"I only know two names. The leader—a vicious uprightman who's quick with the sword—and his doxy."

"His name?"

"Have respect for my soul. Do not breathe the name I'm about to utter."

"On my honor."

"And be careful for your hide," Chambers warned. "He's ruthless and evil."

"I shall be wary," Shakespeare said. "Pray, his name?"

"Mackering—George Mackering."

Shakespeare groaned.

"You know him?" asked Chambers, frightened.

"By reputation only," Shakespeare answered. "An atheist— a foul, cunning man. And deadly with a sword."

Chambers swallowed back a dry heave.

Shakespeare said, "His woman is still Mary Biddle?"

Chambers nodded.

"Are they still here?" Shakespeare asked.

"No."

"Back in London?"

"It seems likely. London is Mackering's favorite place of operation." Chambers paused, then said, "Pray, leave now."

Shakespeare stood up and placed a shilling atop the table. Chambers snatched it up, bit it, and placed it in his purse before Shakespeare was out the door.

8

*A*ll was not well with Roderigo Lopez. Raphael's death had been a black cloud, a storm that had left no one in the family untouched. Rebecca was once again a single woman, and Miguel's peculiarities were keeping her that way for the moment.

But now Lopez was preoccupied with a single thought—it had been nearly a month since he'd been called to court. Though it could not be proven, he knew in his heart that the Queen was deliberately shunning his counsel, her avoidance no doubt fueled by evil words from the damnable Essex. Royal blood ran thick through the earl's veins—another stubborn redhead with a fiery temperament.

Roderigo spewed out curses as he paced, his heavy bootsteps stomping through the straw and echoing against the stone pavers. Normally the East Cell of his home was his favorite place of refuge—a closet where he could work or relax unmolested. Warmed by the fires burning in an exceptionally large hearth, Roderigo often sat at his desk in his favorite chair, admiring his pewter inkstand or unfolding and studying his recently charted maps. Once a week he counted his assets on his calculating board. The chamber was *his* retreat from the outside world. But this afternoon its magical spell of tranquility had been broken by the presence of his nephews—Thomas and Dunstan—and Miguel Nuñoz, sitting around his personal writing table.

May we meet, they had asked. *Details of the mission must be discussed at length. . . . And other things.*

He knew what they meant by other things, what they dared not say in public. He had lost favor with the Queen. Only a temporary condition, he assured himself as he marched to and fro. Essex's doing today would be his undoing in the future. He'd see to that! And to think that he had once trusted the bloodlusting dog.

He had to reach the Queen. But how? As of late Her Grace had no need of his services. The woman was in perfect health, sound in both body and mind—as strong as a bull and as crafty as a witch.

"A pox on him," Roderigo swore out loud once again. "Curse Essex and everything he holds dear."

"Do cool your choler, Uncle," Dunstan said, playing with his diamond earring. Good heavens, the old man was full of spleen tonight. "It does us no good if you mutter and strut."

Roderigo cursed again, but this time the heat of his words was directed against his nephew. "Show respect to your elder, you arrogant little maggot." He slapped Dunstan soundly across the face with the back of his hand.

Stung more by the insult than by injury, Dunstan stammered out words of apology. With an unsteady hand he removed a red silk kerchief from his doublet and wiped a bead of sweat off his forehead, his eyes beseeching his brother for help.

"Do sit, Uncle," Thomas urged. Reflexively, he rubbed his naked chin, and thought angrily of his smooth skin. Why had he been hexed—to exist without manly fur? Why him and not Dunstan? He was star-crossed, pulled too early from the womb under the wrong configuration of planets. He glanced at Roderigo, who hadn't appeared to hear him. "Pray, do not tire yourself unnecessarily, Uncle. Better to save your energy for more noble a purpose."

Roderigo considered the suggestion, and upon deciding it to be a good one, sat down in his favorite oak armchair. Sarah had sewn the pillow used for a backrest—a portrait of Deborah, the blind prophetess, holding the scales of justice. He tilted his head backward and regarded the fresco painted upon the ceiling— Samson breaking down the pillars of the Philistine temple, curly hair cascading down to his loincloth, eye sockets vacant and white. On the walls hung tapestry panels that told the story of David and Bathsheba. When he stared straight ahead, he saw three pairs of anxious eyes. Roderigo longed to look at something that didn't look back at him. Grumpily, he rang for Martino, his blackamoor servant.

"Where is your father?" Roderigo asked Dunstan.

"His trade took him down to Dover," Dunstan answered quietly. "A new shipment of anise."

Martino entered the closet and Roderigo barked out an order for superior port. After the servant departed, Lopez's eyes rested upon Miguel, almost daring him to speak. The young man pushed a ringlet of black hair off his forehead and squirmed under the scrutiny, crossing and recrossing his legs, unsure of how to proceed. Miguel knew he had disappointed Roderigo immensely, but what could he have done differently? Would it have been better to say nothing? Miguel had told Rebecca about his vices years ago. Now, at last, Roderigo knew the truth as well.

After much deliberation, when it had been verified that Raphael indeed had perished, he'd confessed his preferences in the art of love to Dunstan and Thomas, suspecting that they had known about his practices all the while. He'd asked them to deliver the news to their uncle, thus sparing him the initial pain and embarrassment. He held so much admiration and love for the doctor, a man who had treated him as kindly as his own son, Benjamin. And Sarah was the mother he had never known. Though the families were distant relations, they had always been inseparable.

But Roderigo, sorely impatient with anything that upset his plans, had been furious with him—as if Miguel had failed him out of spite. Much as Miguel tried, he couldn't seem to make Roderigo understand: that he loved Rebecca dearly as a sister, that his own welfare was secondary to hers. Rebecca deserved more than he could hope to give her. God knew he had tried to explain it, but the doctor hadn't seemed any more consoled. Such contempt in his eyes as he spoke:

Surely you can tolerate her as a diversion. At least you can hold your nose long enough, until there is a legitimate heir.

Miguel held his own flaring temper and said nothing. Roderigo continued,

Out of my sight, you fop, you woman! Play with your boys until it falls off and rots, for all I care.

Miguel had stalked away, angry and *guilty*. He cursed God for afflicting him with so wretched a perversion made so sweet by his lovers' arms. If only Raphael hadn't died!

But then there came his reprieve. The mission. The family men had approached *him*. Would he volunteer to continue his brother's efforts?

Miguel had offered to work for the mission many times, but

the suggestion always had been met with hesitancy by his father and Raphael. Aye, Raphi had loved him, always tried to protect him against the evil forces that be. And in the end it was Raphi, not he, who'd been murdered by Satan's agents.

After Raphael's death, Miguel was determined to go on with his brother's work. He was thinking about how to approach the other men when they came to him. Would he continue where Raphael had left off? *By God, he would*, he'd replied. It would be an honor! If God were with him, he would save lives, revenge his brother's death and earn back the doctor's respect. Despite the mounting adversity—the Earl of Essex's hatred of Roderigo, the rise in popularity of the lord and his War Party—the secret Jews decided they must carry on.

"The Queen," Miguel began. "Her Grace has yet to send for you, Ruy."

Roderigo continued to stare at him. The tip of his beard was tightly wound around his fool's finger and was turning it purple. Slowly he liberated the finger and clenched his hands into fists. "No," he whispered tensely. "Essex has seen to that. Only war with Spain will satisfy his insatiable love of blood."

"A pity the Queen was inflicted with smallpox so long ago," Dunstan said. "More so a pity that the illness seems only to strike once in a life."

"Dunstan!" Miguel said.

"Harsh, but true," Dunstan retorted. "Surely she couldn't avoid Uncle if she were gravely ill."

Roderigo glared at his nephew. "You repulsive worm!" He raised his hand, then seeing Dunstan flinch, slowly lowered his arm. Why bother? The boy had only stated in words what he himself had wished all along.

"There are servants here with big ears, Dunstan," Roderigo said softly. "And the gutter rat de Andrada as well. Be mindful of that."

Dunstan buried his head in his hands. When he looked up, there were tears in his eyes. "A thousand apologies, Uncle. Raphael's death has affected my nerves, my manners as well."

Miguel placed his hand on Dunstan's shoulder, cheeks wet with sorrow. "His untimely demise is painful to all of us. But we must go on—"

"At what costs, my friend?" Dunstan replied. "Our intrigues are becoming too dangerous."

Miguel pulled his hand away, laced his fingers together. "Dunstan, I'm the one in peril, yet I'm willing to continue."

Because you're young and *rash*, Dunstan thought. He said, "Essex is powerful, Miguel. If he should find out—"

"He will not find out," Roderigo stated.

"But—"

"He knows nothing," Roderigo insisted.

"What we do may be falsely interpreted as *treason*, Uncle," Dunstan said. "Traitors, Uncle, are quartered at Tyburn!"

"You speak absurdities," Roderigo said.

"Does he?" Thomas asked.

"We're loyal subjects of Her Majesty," Miguel exclaimed. "No one could doubt our unswerving allegiance to the crown."

Dunstan said, "We're negotiating with the Queen's bitterest enemy without benefit of her counsel. And before you object, Uncle, pray, hear me out."

Roderigo waved a hand in the air. "Speak."

"The mission was dangerous enough before Raphael had died. Any of our previous correspondence with King Philip could have been—and still could be—enough evidence to hang us—"

"Yes, yes," Roderigo said. "Make your point, Dunstan."

Dunstan said, "Think about this, Uncle. Raphael was murdered a month ago. King Philip was furious at our carelessness because it put His Majesty in a most awkward position. If the Pope or the Holy See found out—"

"Neither did," interrupted Miguel.

"Let me finish," Dunstan insisted. "Suppose either one did. Philip is supposed to be the staunch defender of Catholicism. Imagine what would happen to his standing in Rome if he had been caught dealing with conversos. If it were known publicly that he was allowing Jews to escape from his dominions—"

"Summarize, nephew," Roderigo said.

"If that were to happen, Philip would have to restore his credibility to Rome," Dunstan said. "One way to win back his image as *the* Catholic king would be to burn more conversos. Thus, by our actions, we could be exposing our brethren to more danger—"

Roderigo said, "Since Philip himself is still dealing with us, even after Raphael's death, I don't think he's worried about being censured by Rome."

Dunstan said, "Yet his latest communications with us have been livid in tone, aye? And after Raphael's death, Philip has asked us for much more money per head of Jew smuggled out as compensation for his troubles."

Roderigo's eyes widened. Rebecca had been eavesdropping, her tongue flapping to her cousin. He said, "Where did you come to that knowledge—"

Dunstan turned red. "I hear things."

"Rebecca hears things, you mean." Roderigo was enraged. How could she show so little sense? But he'd deal with her later.

He said, "Go on with your point . . . or her point. I hear my daughter's words coming from your mouth."

Dunstan said, "My thoughts are my own, Uncle." *Almost my own.* "We've had many communications with Philip this past month—letters of reproach, notes of negotiation for the right price of 'pearls, musk, and amber.' Is it *possible* that maybe one note fell into the wrong hands—into *Essex's* hands? Is it possible that the earl has shown the note to Her Majesty and that's why you've not been called to court?"

"Nonsense," Roderigo said.

"You worry too much," said Miguel. "The Queen has been well and has no need for her doctor's services."

Roderigo regarded Miguel and nodded with appreciation. Miguel held a smile in check. Was there not a glint of moisture in the doctor's eyes? Perhaps hatred's cold heart was beginning to thaw.

"Forget Essex," Roderigo said. "His spies are amateurs. He knows nothing about missions. If he did, I would have been dead by now. As for Her Grace, Elizabeth's a keen politician—very adroit indeed. Though Essex be her favorite, she has no use for Essex's desire of war with Spain. Battle is very costly to the treasury."

"It's not the Queen's opinion of Spain I fear," Thomas said, encircling his fingers around the hilt of his sword. So comforting was the chill of metal in his hand. "It's the sentiment of the populace that worries me. Just walk down Paul's at noon. Our countrymen cursed the Spaniard with a vengeance. If we were discovered dealing with Spain, the masses would tear us apart before the courts could try us."

"Essex owns the heart of the Englishman," Dunstan said.

"Essex is a fool," Roderigo said, stroking his beard.

How Thomas envied that mannerism.

"Aye, but the fool is well loved by Her Grace," he said.

"So was Tarletan," Roderigo said. "He had no say in foreign policy."

"She uses Essex for her purposes," Miguel said.

"And he uses her," Dunstan said. "It is only a matter of time before Essex finds out. We must stop these intrigues—"

Roderigo turned to Dunstan, eyes smoldering with rage. "Are you giving me orders, nephew?" he asked softly.

Dunstan paled and quickly answered no.

"Good," said Roderigo. "You've been most helpful to us, Dunstan. Your sound mercantile practices have gained us much revenue. But remember your manners when you're among elders."

Even if the elder was lower class, Dunstan thought. But he apologized anyway. This was not the time for confrontation.

Roderigo said, "Neither Philip nor Elizabeth desire war. Philip is too old, and Essex notwithstanding, Elizabeth is no fool. The Queen does not fight in battles she cannot win."

Thomas said, "Uncle, it was Queen Elizabeth who embraced war with Spain and our Don Antonio in his bid for the throne of Portugal. Certainly that was a battle she didn't win."

The door to the room opened and the conversation quieted to icy silence. Martino entered the closet clad in a blue gown over white broadcloth hose. The blackamoor carried a tray on which rested a jug of port and four goblets fashioned of Venice glass— a gift to Roderigo from Solomon Aben Ayesh. Roderigo was proud that such royal items were in his possession.

Martino placed the tray on the table and lifted the goblets with special care. Despite his Levantine ancestry—the black eyes, the hook of the nose—Martino insisted he was brought up in the Protestant faith, and was a staunch supporter of the Church of England. Roderigo, knowing well the abuse that the converted Moors—the Moroscos—had suffered at the hands of the Spanish Church, immediately hired him. His kindness had been paid off by Martino's loyalty.

As the blackamoor poured the spirits, Roderigo thought of Don Antonio. God in heaven, the ass had had the perfect opportunity. Damn his incompetence! If only he'd been of stabler and stronger character. The conversos would have had one of their own on the throne. Now it seemed that the bastard had taken refuge in Eton, under Essex's protection, and both of them hated his guts.

Martino finished his duties and left the chamber.

Roderigo said, "Don't mention Don Antonio in my presence again. The monster still plagues us. He's under Essex's wing, and de Andrada has told me that he and Essex will stop at nothing to ruin us."

"Uncle, de Andrada is Don Antonio's former spy," Dunstan said. "He is also a perjurer, a noted liar, and a traitor. And before you unharness your anger against me, realize that you've said those very words many times in the past."

Roderigo said nothing.

"Why do you continue to shelter de Andrada in your home?" Dunstan asked.

Roderigo sat back down. "Dunstan, my nephew, you are indeed an idiot. De Andrada is a poisonous snake. He knows too much and is dangerous out of my watch. . . . And yes, I admit he's dangerous inside my house as well. He is a damnable nuisance."

The room fell quiet. Damn them all, Roderigo thought, Don Antonio, de Andrada, Essex, Philip, Elizabeth. If he had the power and guts, he'd poison them all with a healthy dose of Indian acacia.

Roderigo said to Dunstan, "You've asked to speak with me, to discuss the mission, express your worries about our safety. I contend we are safe—for now. But that doesn't mean we haven't become careless. Who knows how Raphael was exposed? We must use extreme caution in the future."

"Uncle," Dunstan said. "I ask you if it's worth it to continue at the expense of our own lives."

Roderigo said, "As long as we keep the monarchs happy with gold, the mission is on safe grounds . . . provided that Miguel is not caught, of course."

The comment reverberated in the quiet of the room. Thomas pulled a dagger from his belt and examined its fine-honed edge. Roderigo took a sip of port, smoothed his beard, then flicked a speck of imaginary dust off his round hose. Dunstan adjusted the cuff on his sleeve and glanced at Miguel, who finally spoke up.

"I'm not worried," he said. "Things are proceeding smoothly. Just a week ago I was able to carry out my first assignment and present papers to six stowaways. They're now residing safely in the Low Countries."

"How did you contact them?" Thomas asked.

Miguel explained how Esteban Ferreira de Gama had sneaked out the stowaways from a Spanish cutter late at night. It had been pouring rain and all of them were soaked and chilled, but no one could dare utter a sound, even a sneeze. The Almighty was merciful, Miguel said. The ship docked safely at Portsmouth. De Gama was the first to venture off the boat, and was elated to see England shrouded in mist. Good cover! He found some empty crates, packed the stowaways inside, then loaded them on an inbound ship as supplies. Miguel described how he was able to board the local ship, docked at the wharf on the Thames, and hand the stowaways their citizen's papers.

"They left the same night for Spanish Brussels," Miguel said. "Father received word that they were successfully met by 'David,' who escorted them into Amsterdam."

"Well executed!" Roderigo cried with pride.

"I thank you," Miguel said. His eyes shifted back and forth between Dunstan and Thomas. "My friends, my *brothers*, if you could have seen the look of gratitude etched upon their faces, you would know that we've no choice but to continue our efforts—increase them if necessary. We're saving *lives*!"

Roderigo said, "And how do *Sir* Thomas and *Sir* Dunstan respond to that?"

Thomas was the first to speak.

"So be it," he said.

Dunstan didn't answer.

Miguel said, "Dunstan, my good man. There's more to life than life itself."

"Miguel," Roderigo said. "I've just received word from de Gama that another ship could be due in Plymouth a month from now. Do you feel able to meet the challenge?"

"Aye."

"Good man!" Roderigo said. "Any comment from the knighted ones?"

Thomas's hand went to his dagger, then slipped by his side. He shook his head no. Dunstan rolled his eyes backward. Roderigo caught the gesture of contempt but said nothing. The boy knew he had been outvoted. No sense in pushing his nose into his failure.

Roderigo rose from his chair—a signal for the others to stand as well. "Let us say our evening prayers. Lord knows how much we need guidance and forebearance."

After the men had finished the "Shemona Esreh," the eighteen verses of Hebraic silent meditation, Miguel said,

"If you have no more need of me, I shall be off. Thomas, be so good as to sport with me this week. Much of the art of fence I have yet to learn."

Thomas answered, "I have time now, if it is convenient for you."

"Good," Miguel replied.

"I shall take my leave as well," Dunstan said.

"Good day, Uncle," Thomas said.

"The three of you shall sup with us tonight," Roderigo announced magnanimously.

"If it pleases you," Dunstan answered for the group.

"I as well?" Miguel asked Roderigo.

The doctor walked over to Miguel and hugged him tightly.

"Yes," he said. "You as well . . . my son."

With Miguel in the lead, the three young men left Lopez's private cell and descended the spiral stairway. Miguel ran down the long hallway, into Lopez's library, and threw open the doors to the formal gardens. The Ames brothers followed at a slower pace. Miguel took a deep breath and let it out slowly. An iron bar had been lifted from his shoulders. He had been forgiven! He felt as swift as a hawk, as bold as a lion. Invincible. He saw

Rebecca resting on a stone bench in the almond orchard and called out to her.

Thomas caught up with Miguel and glared at him.

"Do you want to gossip or sport," he asked irritatedly.

"Shall I ignore the bereaved?" Miguel was just as irritated.

"Bereaved?" Dunstan whispered to his brother. "Never has she been more joyous."

Rebecca waved to the men, and Miguel ran ahead to her. She stood, held out her arms, and they embraced.

"He has made amends?" she asked, but did not wait for the reply. "I knew he would. Father is a sheep in wolf's clothing." She mussed his hair. "And you're continuing the intrigue?"

"Dunstan has told you his doubts about the mission?"

"No, Miguel," Rebecca said. "I disclosed to him my doubts."

"His words were your idea, then," Miguel said.

She pulled away from him.

Miguel said, "Becca, I must continue the work of Raphael—"

"No!"

"We're saving *lives*."

"It isn't enough that I mourn for Raphael?" she asked. "Must I mourn for you, also?"

"I'm cautious—"

"Your brother used caution. He's dead."

Thomas and Dunstan approached, greeting their cousin with a customary kiss.

"You're upset," Dunstan said to her.

"How astute," she answered. "You couldn't talk him out of this?"

"Miguel is stubborn," Dunstan answered.

"You'll not be happy until you die a martyr," she said to Miguel.

"That's not so."

She leaned her face against Miguel's chest and held him. "I'm so worried. We are all so vulnerable."

"Nothing will happen to me—or you—or any of us," Miguel insisted. He broke away from her grasp. "I must practice my swordplay, Becca. My skill is my accursed weakness. Pray, don't worry about me."

"Teach him well, Thomas," she whispered to her cousin.

Thomas whispered he would, then he and Miguel left. Rebecca waited until the both of them were out of sight, then wrapped her cloak snugly around her body.

"The mission turns Miguel's mind to marchpane," she said to Dunstan. "He's drunk from a single sip of success, but it's not pride that motivates him. It's acceptance by my father, by you as well, cousin. Raphael used to call Miguel the eternal puppy, so eager to please and trusting he is.''

''At seventeen I, too, was eager,'' Dunstan said. ''Life shall polish his senses.''

''If he lasts long enough to benefit from experience.'' Her eyes hardened. ''And age has nothing to do with idealism. I'm no older than he, yet I'm as cynical as an old man of forty. Cannot you stop him, Dunstan?''

''No.''

''Then may God bless and help him.''

''How do you feel, Becca?''

''I've been confined here for weeks,'' she answered. ''Much time I've spent in prayer, but it has provided me with little solace. Just lethargy. Grandmama says that idleness has made me slow-witted.''

''Perhaps she compares you to me,'' Dunstan said.

Rebecca laughed. ''Dear cousin, an intelligence of wit assumes a whit of intelligence. One must have the latter to have the former.''

Dunstan frowned.

''Idleness has not made you less clever,'' he said. ''But it has made you more vicious than ever.''

Rebecca cocked her head and pouted. Marry, she was lovely, Dunstan thought.

''Shall I take you to Cheapside?'' he asked.

''Mayhap you mean to bed?''

Dunstan bit his lip to hold back a smile.

''If that be your desire.''

''Go home to your wife.''

Dunstan sat down and cradled his chin in the palms of his hands. He looked so troubled, Rebecca thought, but in a rather childish way. As if his mother had taken away his sweetmeats.

''What is it?'' Rebecca asked.

Dunstan sighed. ''Grace has been so unresponsive since she has foaled. I don't understand it. I give her gifts, I've hired for her more servants than wait upon the King of Scotland. I've indulged her every whim.''

''You might consider giving her attention.''

''I'm *very* attentive.''

''Aye, to the scullery maid, the milkmaid, the chandleress—''

''I'm not a monk, Rebecca. Do not lecture me.''

She became silent at the tone of his voice.

''Come, cousin,'' he said. ''Let us take a ride to the country.''

She shook her head. It would be disastrous to fill him with false hopes. The sparks she'd once felt for him had died years ago. She'd been just a little girl, and Dunstan had been her porthole to the world. Things were different now. She was no longer dependent on him to teach her things. Still, Dunstan persisted in trying to revive the past.

"The country would do your nerves well," he begged.

"I thank you, but no."

"You're a stubborn twit of a wench," Dunstan said angrily.

"Or a wit of a wench," she smirked.

He grabbed her. "Remember, it was I who broke you in."

"I remember it well," she said.

"Then why have you turned so cold to me?"

Not wanting another exhausting confrontation, she smiled and stroked his cheek.

"You look handsome, Dunstan." She tugged the corners of his mustache. "The color red suits you well."

"You taunt me, Becca."

"Not at all."

"Then bed me."

"Impossible." She straightened out his ruff.

"Why do you treat me as thus—the tongue of a kitten one moment, the bite of an asp the next?"

"Blame it on the stars."

"You toy with my emotions."

"Dunstan," she answered, "listen to me. Your cap houses one head, your codpiece the other. Think with the proper one. I've grown into a marriageable woman now. You must stop your ridiculous flirting."

"I love you."

"Would your ardor remain hot if I wore the battle scars that decorate Grace's belly?"

Slowly he released her from his grip. "I cannot stop thinking about you. You must marry before I do something . . . very foolish."

"You mean I must become pregnant, fat, and complacent. Then I will no longer be desirable."

Dunstan smiled sadly. "That is exactly what I mean."

"At the least, you're truthful, if not honest." She pushed him away. "Go home to Grace. Perhaps she's not the wildest between the sheets, but indeed she's served you well."

Rebuffed again, he stood, bowed, and doffed his hat, showing her the inside of his cap—a gesture of scorn. As he left, he turned to see her gathering almond blossoms in her skirt. Her black hair was loose and long, her ungloved hands so delicate and slender. He felt the sting and cursed what he once had, what he finally realized he had lost forever.

9

olitics, politics, and more politics. It made Roderigo weary, and he almost wished himself a simple country doctor again. Putting down his quill, he reread the letter to Ferreira de Gama, admiring the strokes of his Italian hand, so rich with flourishes yet far easier to pen than the traditional secretary hand. Satisfied with the correspondence, he folded and sealed the letter, removed his spectacles and leaned back in his chair. Surrounded by solitude in his private closet, he tried to forget the discouraging words of his nephews. But they buzzed through the air like gnats.

What *if* Essex were to intercept their correspondence with Philip? What would it mean?

Disaster!

Blank failure from your mind, Roderigo told himself. Just use caution and worry not. There would always be naysayers. Let them say nay, he would say yea.

The fire needed to be stoked. Rather than call a servant, he got up and poked the logs himself. The embers erupted into flames, and the gust of heat warmed his stiff hands.

Roderigo regarded the hearth in his closet. The Great Hall was outdated, being warmed by only a central pit. It was time to mason a fireplace there. One that would hold a majestic mantel . . . a mantel carved from the finest walnut. And the hearth should be chiseled from Sicilian marble—deep green preferably, to match the view of the orchards from the leaded-glass windows. And a magnificent chimney puffing out big bellows of smoke so that all of London—and Essex—would know that the Great Hall of Dr. Roderigo Lopez was royally warmed, suitable for entertaining the most revered prince of state. He'd talk to Sarah. A dutiful wife, she'd arrange the details quickly. He had but to speak and Sarah would carry out his wishes.

Lopez heard a knock upon the door. He asked who it was and his daughter identified herself. He allowed her to enter.

Rebecca stood for a moment underneath the frame of the door. Roderigo was surprised to find her still dressed in black. He would have thought she would abandon the dark clothing as soon as her *shiva*—her first period of mourning—had finished.

Mourning. It had only intensified her beauty, and that worried Roderigo. She had become as jumpy as a kenneled hound, and God only knew what would happen when she was freed from her obligatory month of grieving. An appropriate suitor had to be found lest he find himself the grandfather of a bastard. In his mind, Miguel was still the preferred son-in-law, despite his . . . whatever it was. He couldn't imagine marrying her off to anyone but kinsmen. Perhaps there existed an appropriate suitor in the Low Countries or the Levant. He'd speak at length with Solomon and Sarah. They would know who the available men were. Another detail to arrange. He sank down into a padded armchair and called to Rebecca.

"Come to me, daughter."

Approaching with a coy smile, Rebecca took a soft velvet pillow and sat at her father's feet, her overskirt and petticoat billowing over the floor. She curled up against his leg. He reached down and entangled his fingers in her thick, black hair, then stroked it as he would the fur of a lapdog.

"Has the Queen summoned you yet, Father?"

"You can answer your own question," Roderigo said. "You seem to know much about my affairs."

"You're angry at me for telling Dunstan the words of Philip's letters to you," Rebecca said. "So be it. Punish me if you desire, but I did it out of love. I'm worried for Miguel's safety. For yours as well. Essex is clever and vicious."

Roderigo stroked his daughter's cheek. He felt saddened by the burden that the mission had imposed upon her.

"Don't worry about me, Becca. Worry instead about your lack of husband."

"I need not a husband."

"Bah."

She said, "There's none suitable who bids my calling."

"Lord Holderoy?"

"You can't be serious, Father. He's too fat and too old. His seed is no doubt less than copious."

"The Earl of Nottingham?"

"A pompous snot."

"Marquis of Cumberland?"

"Father! He is a Papist!"

"He is also rich and mad for you, daughter."

"I will not marry a Papist!"

"Aye, you truly are your father's daughter," Roderigo said. "Filthy swine are the Catholics. They burn relapsed conversos as readily as firewood. And the Protestants are no more gentle.

Luther, who openly courted the Jews at first, became angered by their refusal to convert. The serpent recanted his praise and went on to blame all the ills of the Continent on the recalcitrant Semites. They all disgust me, the Gentiles. And yet we are completely dependent on their mercy. As much as I plot and plan, it all comes down to the good graces of a tolerant monarch. As of this moment I sit here powerless. I can do nothing until Her Grace beckons me to court.''

"Poor Father," she cooed. "Chafing at the bit while the evil Essex schemes.''

Roderigo said, "I scold you for repeating my words, and still I talk too freely to you. Don't mind my affairs.''

"But I care for you. As you care for me. That's why you'll not insist that I marry just for marriage's sake. Besides, I'm still young—''

"Not so young anymore. Your mother had borne me three children afore she was twenty.''

"And the Lord took them all before their majority—God rest their souls. A young womb yields unripe fruit. Better to wait until the tree grows strong.''

"Bah," he sneered once again. "Don't prattle about unripe fruit. You desire freedom.''

"No," Rebecca protested. "Only the proper bridegroom.''

"Which means no husband at all," Roderigo said. "You're true to your stars, my child. A Scorpio with the moon in Gemini—a fatal sting that's mercurial in nature.''

"Nonsense," Rebecca said, giving him a playful slap.

"A bellyful of children should calm you down.''

"Again nonsense. A bellyful of children will only make me fat and contemptuous to my husband. You wish not that for me, do you, Father?''

"I wish you to be happy. And a gentlewoman cannot be happy without a husband.''

"But—''

"What would you do without a husband?" Roderigo asked.

"I'd have much to do just being your daughter.''

Roderigo smiled. "That is not a sufficient position in life.''

"It is all the position I need.''

"You need to be a gentleman's wife.''

"*I* should like to continue to help you with your patients. Spend valuable time ministering to the ill. Haven't you said that I am your extra set of hands—skilled hands?''

Roderigo kissed those hands. "I cannot reason with you on this issue of marriage. You distract me with silly talk about your hands. If you force me to become a tyrant, I will, Becca. You will marry when I see fit, and now I'll hear nothing more to the contrary.''

Rebecca said nothing. Silence was her best weapon against her father's obstinacy. It had worked in the past, and it seemed to be working now. Roderigo's face softened. He asked her how she spent the last days of her second period of mourning.

Rebecca replied, ''The hours are long when one is weighted down with boredom.''

''I asked you not whether you spent your hours contentedly,'' Roderigo replied. ''Answer my question.''

''I sew and read.''

''And do you do what your mother requests?''

Rebecca paused a moment, puzzled. ''I do all that Mother asks of me.''

''And you've almost completed your tasks?''

Rebecca's face lit up with understanding.

''Marry, you mean the forged papers—''

''Quiet,'' Roderigo interrupted. ''Keep your voice low.''

Rebecca whispered, ''I've finished one set and am busy penning another.''

Roderigo smiled and stroked her cheek. ''Well, then. And your music?''

Rebecca replied that Grandmama said she wasn't allowed to play music until the thirty days of her second period of mourning were over. She told her father she only had six days left, trying to sound casual, but the relief in her voice was too evident. Her father had noticed it and arched his eyebrows in disapproval.

She added, ''Aye, Father, a month of mourning officially for Raphael, but for years he will live in the heart.''

Rebecca sensed that she had said the wrong thing. Her father tensed.

''Raphael was a wonderful man,'' he said.

''Aye.''

''He deserves a true mourning, not simply an official one.''

''I understand,'' Rebecca answered.

''I think not.'' Roderigo pushed her away. ''Leave now.''

''Father, I've always been a dutiful daughter to you,'' Rebecca said. ''I would have been a dutiful wife to Raphael. But I was not passionately in love with him.''

''You would have learned to love him.''

''I'm not denying that,'' Rebecca said. ''Some note in my voice has offended you. I pray you to pardon me.''

''I don't want apologies, Becca. I simply want you to wed for *your* own sake. Find a suitable man that pleases you. Because if no man is to your liking, you'll simply have to marry one you dislike.''

"Father—"

"No more said about it!"

Roderigo curled the tip of his beard with his finger, cleared his throat, then said, "I've received word that Uncle Solomon has safely arrived in Turkey."

"Thanks be to God," Rebecca answered quietly.

He sighed and tried again. "Did I tell you about the letter that your brother sent me?"

"Two times. Ben is well and is enjoying Venice. He eats a great deal—less meat, more bread."

"Did I tell you about their eating geegaw—a fork they call it. They spear their food—"

"Aye, you told me."

"Ben said they eat using these toys for fingers because their hands aren't clean." Roderigo laughed.

Rebecca was not amused. "Shall I go now?"

"No. Your beauty warms my bones," said Roderigo. "Stay. And do not sulk."

"As you wish."

"Stubborn girl," Roderigo muttered.

Before Rebecca could reply, Martino walked in the room, panting with excitement. A gentleman wearing royal livery had arrived with a message to deliver to Dr. Lopez. Rebecca stood up and looked at her father. His face held an expression of concern mixed with excitement. At last. Some word from the Queen. It was, of course, a double-edged sword. Father had been summoned, but for what purpose? Rebecca's heart started hammering, her head suddenly felt light. Please God, let all be well.

Roderigo commanded Martino, "Let him in. But give me some minutes to make myself acceptable." To Rebecca he said, "Dress me quickly."

Immediately she began to truss his points, lacing firmly the ribbons of his gown.

"Where are your shoes?" she asked.

"My boots are—"

"Nay, Father, not your boots. Your velvet shoes—the ones topped with roses."

"Need I my velvet shoes?"

"Father!"

"They are in my bedchamber."

"I will retrieve them along with your garters. And a new ruff as well. The one you wear sags pathetically under the weight of your beard."

She was off. He was elated. The Queen had sent for him. Was Essex out of favor? Did she desire to use his secret contact in Spain? Did she need news from Solomon Aben Ayesh's well-connected band of Levantine spies? Did she simply desire his counsel?

Suddenly he stopped and felt a cold shiver run through his body.

Could the Queen be actually *ill*?

Perish the thought! If her life ended, so would go all his power.

He picked up his bag and checked its contents. A few elixirs, a few powders. He was lacking the necessary medicines—the purges, leeches, potions, poultices. Thank God Rebecca and Sarah were so meticulous in stocking the stillroom.

Rebecca was back with a new ruff and his shoes. Quickly she placed multiple layers of lace and wire around his neck. Her father seemed calm, he wasn't trembling or breathing hard, but his color seemed unusually flushed. Her own fingers were stiff. God give him strength, give *her* strength. Let this be a portent of good things to come.

"My medicine bag is nearly empty," Roderigo told her.

"Tell me what you need."

Roderigo listed the medicines: a jug of leeches, trefoil, thistle, walnut shells, cheese mold, fungus on rye—women of that age are known to have bleeding of the privates.

"Perhaps a sprig or two of parsley mixed with dragon water," Rebecca suggested. "The condition of Her Grace's teeth is quite poor."

"Aye, parsley with water, and dried mint as well. And my special purge."

"Done," said Rebecca. "Shall I ask Martino to show in the messenger?"

"Aye . . . wait."

Rebecca stopped.

"Am I presentable?" Roderigo asked.

"More than presentable, Father. Comely."

Roderigo smiled and blew her a kiss as she left.

The messenger entered—a young man wearing the royal arms. He was just a boy, Roderigo thought, with hardly more than fuzz for a beard. Yet Roderigo quaked before him as if he were the Queen herself.

"Does Her Grace find herself is good health, sir?" Roderigo asked.

"I know not," the gentleman answered.

"Come, sir," Roderigo insisted. "Surely you were informed—"

"I was told to call you to court," the boy said. "One does not inquire about the Queen's business if one wishes to keep his head."

Roderigo swallowed dryly.

"I shall prepare to leave at once."

"A steed shall be waiting for you." The messenger turned on his heels and left.

Revolting little roach, Roderigo thought. Unbecoming for a Queen to use such young rats as messengers. The little worm had a voice as cold as snow. It had sent a shiver through Roderigo's spine. He looked up and saw Rebecca carrying an armful of vials.

"Come, daughter," he said. "Tarry not. Place the medicines in my bag."

She did as instructed, then looped an amulet around his neck. This one was arsenic paste sewed in dog skin, she explained. "It will guard you against Black Death should the Queen be inflicted." She pulled out a white crystal pebble from a jug. "Open up."

Roderigo stared at the crystal. His mother-in-law had always insisted that the salts protected better than any charm the "wisemen" wore. Its taste was bitter, though not as bitter as the plague, Roderigo thought. He'd treated many patients steeped in Black Death, and not once had he or a member of his family been cursed with the disease. The hag might be a wretched old thing, but her potions were strong and effective. There were already mutterings that the false Protestants were not only secret Jews, but agents of Satan as well. How else could they circumvent the ubiquitous plague?

Marry, Roderigo thought, let them mutter. I shall live. He plucked the salt out of Rebecca's hand and swallowed it.

"I shall take one also," Rebecca announced.

"For what purpose?" Roderigo asked.

"Oh Father," she blurted out. "Let me come to court."

"Impossible," Roderigo answered, not unkindly.

"The Queen was very fond of me," Rebecca reminded him. "She brought me comfits and jellied quince. She loved my singing. My virginal playing made her weep."

"Another time, Becca," he said. "Once my favor has been firmly restored in her eyes."

"If she is ill, I can assist you. I've come with you diverse times to visit the ill at St. Bartholomew's."

"This is the Queen."

"How often did I stand by your side when Lord Leicester was ill?"

"He was not the Queen."

"Her body is still human. If she is ill, I can help—"

"Go away, daughter. I have no time for your foolishness."

Rebecca knew she should respect his wishes, but the last twenty-four days had been so confining. She envied her brother,

off in Venice, her cousins gallivanting about. Only she and Uncle Hector had shown any respect for Raphael. True, she had
been his betrothed, but it didn't seem fair that only she should
be cloistered. Rebecca argued,

"Had you not told me I should have been born a man so I
could have practiced your chosen profession?"

"But you're not a man." Roderigo shook his head. "Aye, not
a man at all."

"I'm better equipped than Ben," Rebecca said.

Roderigo glared at his daughter, angry at being confronted
with the truth. Ben was an open wound in Roderigo's heart. A
wonderful boy, kind and good-hearted, but not as clever as Roderigo had wished. A curse to have a quick-witted daughter and
a dull-witted son.

"Even if I would have permitted you to accompany me under
ordinary circumstances, I would not allow it now," he said
sternly. "You're in mourning, Rebecca."

"I pray you, Father." She sunk down on her knees and
grabbed his hands, kissing his jeweled fingers. "I must leave
here. I feel as if I'm being enveloped by the blackness I wear. I
must escape or I'll go mad. I beg of you."

Roderigo withdrew his hands and said, "Your playacting may
have its desired effects on young hearts, Becca, but my ears are
deaf to your antics."

Rebecca's despair looked honest. Roderigo helped her to her
feet and kissed her cheek. He said, "The Queen may have summoned me for reasons other than illness, little one. There is no
place for women in politics."

"Then what is the Queen? A bear? A goose? Aye, she must
be a dog because oft you call her a bitch—"

Roderigo slapped her across the face. "Your tongue needs a
knotting."

The slap was a light one—a warning that she'd gone too far.
But she remained undeterred. "The Queen's a woman. Does *she*
not involve herself in politics?"

"Bah," Roderigo said. "You refuse to give up. Go away, silly
Becca. You irritate me and I'm in no mood to be irritated."

"Please, Father," she implored. "If you have no need of me,
I shall parade my wares around the galleries. Handsome and
rich courtiers abound. Many are single, many are very well regarded. Who knows who may buy the merchandise? How am I
to find a husband if you keep me locked up in these walls? I ask
you so little, Father. Cosset me this one time."

"You are the most pampered, spoiled, self-indulged young
lady I have ever met!" Roderigo said harshly.

But his eyes were smiling. She knew she had won.

"Have your maids prepare you quickly," he said. "If you're not done by the time I depart, you shall be left behind."

Rebecca's heart took off in wild anticipation. To visit London-town. What a glorious place it was in springtime. Full of excitement and bustle. Stalls packed with the latest wares, ladies on the arms of their lords, bedecked in the most fashionable of dress. New sights and smells. New faces. She wanted to throw herself at her father's feet and kiss his shoes in gratitude. He was taking her away from these walls, this *prison*. She should have vowed never to anger him again, should have showered him with obsequious words of praise. Instead all she said was thank you, her voice surprisingly cool and detached.

10

The Queen was in a foul mood, made even fouler the moment Dr. Lopez walked inside her bedchambers. Her Majesty's personal sleeping closet, though modest in size, was opulent in style. The walls of the chamber were covered with silk cloth embroidered with the royal coat-of-arms. Velvet drapes sewn with silver and gold thread hung over two arched windows that provided the Queen with a view of the rose gardens. Her Majesty's poster bed was carved from walnut, its mattress topped with down-filled counterpanes, and velvet and taffety pillows. Elizabeth sat on a throne, positioned to the left of her bed. Next to the royal chair stood a table upon which sat a porcelain water basin and pitcher, both leafed with gold.

Lopez gave the obeisance of reverence—the customary bow given to a monarch—and started to advance, but the Queen commanded him to stop.

"Who called him!" she demanded of the High Treasurer, Lord Burghley.

"But madam, you are ill—"

"You whale!" she screamed at Burghley. "You swine in black. You Puritan! Get him out of here!"

Burghley shrugged haplessly at Roderigo and their eyes met. Not a true friend, Roderigo knew. Impossible to keep one's neck whole and trust anyone in power. But at the moment he was an ally, their connection the hatred of Essex.

"Go!" the Queen commanded Roderigo.

Her nightdress was soaked with perspiration. Yet her teeth chattered. She adjusted her wig—locks of flaming red hair knotted formally and entwined with diamonds and sapphires—then threw her sable-trimmed robe over her chest.

"You are flushed, madam," Roderigo said. He dropped to his knees. "You are short of breath—"

"I didn't ask for your opinion on my state of health," Elizabeth snapped. "Did not I order you to leave? Do you disobey—" She stopped her outburst and stared at Rebecca. "You brought your *daughter* to my bedchamber? *Here? Now?* Are you *mad*?"

"Your Grace—" Roderigo stammered.

"*Why* did you bring her?" the Queen demanded.

"To aid—"

"So you need *assistance*, Dr. Lopez?"

"Why no, but—"

"Stow it!" The Queen smiled, exposing blackened teeth. She tottered over to her bed and collapsed onto the mattress, allowing Burghley to draw her coverlets up to her chin. Her amber eyes danced playfully as she stared at Lopez's daughter.

"I will receive you now, dear girl," she intoned sweetly.

Rebecca felt dizzy. As she approached the Queen she realized that she was trembling from head to foot. Unsteady on her legs, she managed three deep curtsies.

"You may rise," Elizabeth announced as she held out her hand for Rebecca to kiss. "Don't just stand there, Burghley, have someone bring the maiden a pillow so she may sit."

"Yes, madam." Burghley bowed and left.

"And *you*," she said, turning to Roderigo. "What good can *you* do me?"

"Whatever is in my power."

"Which isn't much, is it?"

"Too meager for Your Grace."

She coughed up a ball of sputum and spit it into a laced handkerchief. "Your flattery is revolting," Elizabeth said. She gestured Lopez upward. "You may rise."

Roderigo stood but said nothing. A lady-in-waiting brought in a red pillow. She curtsied before the Queen, lay the cushion down.

A fair little wench, Roderigo thought. Rosy and round . . . no more than Rebecca's age? He had stiffened with lust that now repulsed him. God's blood, where did the time go?

He barked at the maiden, "Prepare for your Queen a posset of milk, honey, and ale immediately."

She nodded stupidly.

"Go," the Queen commanded her.

She curtsied and scurried out the door.

"Shake not like a cornered deer," she told Roderigo. "Prance over here and do something." To Rebecca she said, "Sit at my feet, my sweet. Your face is pleasing to gaze upon."

Rebecca took the pillow and sat on the floor.

"No, no, no, you silly goose," Elizabeth chided, then winked at Rebecca. "Though I hope you not be a Winchester goose." She laughed at her pun. "Now tell me, dear thing: Have you been touched by the Great Pox?"

Rebecca blushed. "No, Your Grace."

"The filthy French do give the English such lifelong gifts," Elizabeth cackled. "Are you certain you're clean?"

"Yes, Your Grace."

"You must have hordes of men competing for your maidenhead." Elizabeth smiled wickedly. "Or should I speak in the past tense?"

Rebecca turned a deep shade of scarlet.

"Come, come," the Queen said abruptly. "Off the floor. You may sit at the foot of my mattress."

Rebecca did as told, then asked, "May I speak?"

"I wish you would," Elizabeth said. "Your voice is so much more palatable than the others that surround me."

"May I rub Your Grace's feet with ointment? I fear they are cold."

"A fine idea," the Queen said, exposing her legs. The skin was pale and loose, webbed with thin blue lines. She pulled off her sable slippers and slapped her feet into Rebecca's lap—two blocks of ice.

"Rub, dear girl," Elizabeth commanded.

Roderigo gave Rebecca a sympathetic look, then handed her a rag, a tin of sweet-smelling herbs, and a vial of ointment from his bag. The woman's feet had become encrusted with flecks of dirt and scaly skin. Rebecca slowly eased away the dead skin and methodically picked off the dirt with her fingernails. After the royal feet were cleaned, she began her rubbing and perfuming. The toes turned from white to pink, from pink to red. As they did, Elizabeth almost purred with contentment. Then, still playing the feline, she turned to Roderigo, arched her back and snarled,

"I feel awful."

"The demands placed upon Your Grace are endless—"

"I know the enormities of my duties, you drooling dolt. Quit fawning me. Instead, tell me what ails me."

"You have a fever, madam. You need honeysuckle leaves steeped in water."

"My throat hurts." She rubbed her neck. Her eyes suddenly beseeched Roderigo's. "Quimsy?"

"Open your mouth, madam," Roderigo said.

The Queen obeyed.

Roderigo raised a lit candlestick and peered down the royal throat. A moment later he shook his head no. "Your gullet is merely raw and red. No telltale signs of quimsy."

The Queen smiled and pushed the candle away. "Get that away from my face, you jack. The light irritates my eyes."

"As you wish." Roderigo tried to remain calm. "The posset that I have requested shall soothe your throat. Also, I will give Your Grace something to help the fever." Roderigo took out a small jug sealed with wax. "A spoonful every hour until the royal forehead feels cool to the touch."

"Your little girl has grown up, Ruy," the Queen said, wiggling her newly warmed toes. "My, how she has grown up! Why didn't you ever do this for me?"

"Why . . . Your Grace never asked," he sputtered.

"And you never volunteered, you plant. The girl has brains under her coif. You must have been away from home the night she was conceived." The Queen prodded Rebecca in the ribs with her toes. "When you are done with my feet, you may proceed with my hands."

"Thank you, Your Grace."

Elizabeth picked up the jug, poked through the wax seal with her finger, and sniffed the contents. "What's in here?" she asked suspiciously.

"Four spoonfuls of the juice of red nettles, eight of ale, thirty grains of nicra picra, and a half pint of aqua vitae."

She handed the container to Rebecca. "Taste it for me, my dear."

"It would be my honor, Your Grace."

Rebecca took a healthy swallow and passed it back to the Queen, who looked at Roderigo with a sly smile.

"It has been rumored that you have a special penchant for ratsbane and Indian acacia, Ruy."

Roderigo turned white and coughed.

"Madam, I've—"

"Oh, stow your mouth!" Elizabeth laughed. She took a gulp of the medicine. "No matter," she said. "I trust you. For your daughter's welfare if not for mine. Tell me, what do your spies in Iberia say about His Majesty, King of Spain?"

"His treasury lessens daily, his navy is in ruins, the sailors poorly paid and mutinous. He has no means for war. He knows when he has been bested."

"Go on, go on," Elizabeth commanded.

"His Majesty is much bothered by the French Protestant Henry of Navarre and continues to stare wistfully to the north. So does the Duke of Parma."

"Tell me something I know not."

Roderigo hoped his voice was steady. He said, "They comprise a stronger team than either one individually."

"Do you think it wise for England to continue to aid France and the two-faced Navarre?" The Queen smiled wickedly. "Speak, man! Give me your opinion."

"It is costly," Roderigo said cautiously.

"Your ancestry shows itself," Elizabeth said, raising her eyes. "But tis true. Our involvement on the Continent is slowly bankrupting the treasury. Not that Essex is concerned. He spends as if I were magical rains always filling the wells he calls his pockets." She shook her head in disgust.

Roderigo said nothing. The Queen knew of his rivalry with Essex, and her comments were meant to incite a reaction from him. She was a master of playing people against each other, thus neutralizing all forces against her. When it was clear that Roderigo refused to enter a game he could not win, the Queen said,

"What does the King of Spain conspire?"

Dark circles of sweat stained Lopez's armpits. Praise God Rebecca had remembered to add the sweating salts to the sleeves. He would be wet, but at least his body odor would offend no one.

"It is rumored that though His Majesty wars with the French king, they meet covertly—"

"The bastards!" the Queen screamed. "When?"

"I've heard the gossip a few days ago."

"And *why* was I not informed?"

"I had not been summoned to court, madam."

Elizabeth winced. "Damn Essex," she muttered.

This time Roderigo smiled. It had been just as he thought. Essex had been keeping him away. And in his absence, the Queen had lost a valuable piece of gossip.

"Damn him!" she repeated. "What are we to do about this?" She was trying to trap him again.

"Your Grace," Lopez began, "England is the Jeweled Maiden of the Sea, the mightiest and swiftest power in centuries. All because on the throne sits a just and fair monarch who governs by divine inheritance—"

"Oh bother! You speak a lot and say little. . . . But you have worthy spies." She thought a moment, then said, "I hear you have a fine falconer."

"I do, madam," Roderigo answered.

"I have a sick bird in my mew, a fine female peregrine. See

if your falconer can restore her to health. If he can, you may have your pick of her eggs.''

"Twould be my honor, Your Grace.''

"Of course it would be your honor.'' She waved him away. "Go and leave me with my medicines.''

"As you wish, madam,'' Roderigo said. "Shall I come by tomorrow and see how Your Grace is faring?''

"Yes, yes,'' the Queen answered. "Away.''

"My most humble gratitude for allowing me the pleasure of serving Your Most Holy—''

"Good, good, enough blather,'' the Queen interrupted. "Now go.''

"Come, Rebecca.''

"The girl stays.''

"Madam, I—''

"The girl stays,'' repeated the Queen. "Did you not hear me the first time, Dr. Lopez?''

"Absolutely, madam. It's just that such an honor you have bestowed upon her . . . I am speechless.''

"Would it were so.'' The Queen pointed to the door. "Be gone!''

Roderigo bowed and tried to meet Rebecca's eyes. But hers were fixed on the brown-spotted flesh topping the Queen's hands. He had no choice but to leave. As he stepped out into the Privy Chambers, his body was shaking uncontrollably.

Rebecca proceeded from rubbing hands to rubbing the neck and face. Though Her Majesty's body had been prey to the ravages of time, her face still retained remarkable smoothness of skin, wrinkle-free except for small lines around the eyes and lips. Her cheeks were dry and rosy, a deeper blush than usual due to fever. She moaned softly under Rebecca's touch.

"What say you of my condition?''

"Excuse a lowly girl's ignorance, Your Grace, but I am not qualified to answer your question lest I err in my appraisal and cause ill to come to you. I'd rather die myself.''

"Answer it anyway,'' Elizabeth commanded.

"If Your Grace insists, I'd say that madam is heavy with choler. Your skin is hot and dry. The phlegm that Your Grace spits is a sign of recovery being moist and cool. Madam must drink. Pints and pints of clear cistern water mixed with aqua vitae. It will bring on more phlegm and keep the humors in balance.''

"Your hands are so young.'' Elizabeth held them to her cheek.

"Do they cool you, madam?''

"Indeed they do.''

"Then I shall keep them on your face all night whilst you sleep."

Elizabeth smiled. "If thy hands are cool and bring relief to thy Queen, how much more so thy body." She rang for one of her ladies-in-waiting. The girl who entered the chamber this time was young, thin, and pockmarked from recent disease.

"Undress the girl," the Queen ordered.

Rebecca froze.

"Go on, little goose." Elizabeth pushed Rebecca upward. "Stand up and allow yourself to be served."

On wobbly feet, Rebecca rose. She felt the points of her sleeve being loosened, her bodice coming undone. Off they dropped to the floor, followed by her skirt—a velvet puddle around her ankles. Trembling, she stood in her chemise and stockings.

Elizabeth smacked her dry lips. "Continue," she said to her attendant.

Rebecca felt her knees nearly cave in.

Off came her undergarments until she was naked, her body lithe and silky, a feast for Elizabeth's gleaming eye. The woman looked as lecherous as Dunstan. Bile rose in Rebecca's throat.

"You may go," the Queen said, dismissing her maid. "Come here, Rebecca. The raw air causes you to shiver."

With no other alternative, Rebecca forced a smile and obeyed the command.

"Such lovely teeth," Elizabeth remarked. She held open her coverlets, and Rebecca slid under them. "Smile for me again."

Rebecca smiled. The old woman's breath smelled of ale and garlic.

"Lovely, lovely teeth."

"I would give them to madam, if I could," Rebecca said softly.

"You really are a dear girl, aren't you." Elizabeth ordered Rebecca to turn over, then pressed her sagging belly against the smooth arch of the young girl's back, grinding her hipbone into a firm buttock. Her arms embraced Rebecca, her hands cupped full, soft breasts. She lowered her left hand and tucked it between Rebecca's legs, a finger poking up into the internal folds of her womb. Ah, to be young again. The girl's body was so lovely, so cool. She closed her eyes. "Are you comfortable?"

"If it is so for madam."

"Madam is quite content."

"Then I am as well," Rebecca replied.

"Go to sleep," Elizabeth said.

Rebecca squeezed her eyes shut and prayed she wouldn't cry out her revulsion in the night.

* * *

The coach bounced slowly as it maneuvered through London's streets, thick with people. Multitudes of human bodies, Roderigo thought, clogging up the roads, scaring the horses. In this traffic it would take at least an hour to reach his home in Holborn. And the noise was fierce. The shouts of the mongers, the banging of hammers, the clang of clashing swords, and the bells ringing endlessly, announcing births, deaths, christenings. He was getting a headache and was out of extract of thistle. Such was his luck of late.

He glanced at Rebecca, head down, sitting stoically, not saying a word since they'd left the great palace of Whitehall. He was waiting for her to speak, to confide in him about what had happened, but the girl remained fixed in her silence. And her silence only made the horrible noises outside seem louder.

"Enough of your game of handy-dandy, Becca. Open your hands and expose me your nut."

"Pardon?"

"What *happened* with the Queen? What did Her Grace say to you? She *did* speak to you, did she not?"

"Aye."

"What did she *say*?"

"Did she not tell you?" Rebecca asked.

"Would I be *asking* you if Her Majesty were loquacious?" Roderigo snapped. "The Queen said nothing to me, except to complain about her health." Roderigo kept his voice very low. With all the street noise, it was unlikely that the coachman could catch even a wisp of their conversation. But one could not be too careful in these troubled times. "Tell me what transpired."

Rebecca hesitated, then whispered, "Her Grace extended me an invitation to become a maid of honor."

Roderigo smiled. "This is better than I could have hoped for." The smile widened into an open grin. "How much information you'll be privy to, daughter. How much you'll be able to tell me! What a weapon you shall be. Essex's lust for war is well tempered by his lust for the fairer sex. A coy smile in his direction, Becca, and he'll be mush. You'll pierce his nose with your feminine wiles and lead him anywhere. He'll confide in you, tell you things. And then you can tell me things!" He hugged her tightly. "My daughter, words can't express how proud I feel."

Rebecca said nothing.

"Becca, do your ears shut to your father's words?"

"I heard them."

"Even in our moment of triumph you're infuriating." Roderigo shook his head, fought off creeping anger. "If you remain as immobile as stone, so be it. When are you to leave for court?"

She remained silent.

"Becca, when are you to arrive at court?"

"I refused the offer." Rebecca turned to face her father and blanched at the anger she saw. He was scarlet with fury. Her body began to tremble.

"I . . ." She swallowed, tried to bring moisture into her parched throat. "I told Her Grace how pleased I was that such a proposal was bestowed to me. But I spoke to the Queen of my grandam, how much the old woman relies on my care—"

Roderigo slapped her hard across the face. Rebecca brought her hand to her cheek, eyes burning with tears of rage and fear.

"You let a stupid, old turd of a woman stand in the way of such an opportunity?" He spat at her. "You *stupid bitch*!"

"I love her."

"She is a doddering old fool, strictly your mother's mother!"

"Father, I—"

Again Roderigo hit her. "Say nothing unless I command you to speak."

Rebecca bit her lip and fought back more tears.

"How could you have done such an idiotic thing?" he whispered, squeezing her arm. She gave out a small cry. Roderigo took a deep breath and loosened his hold. "Tis so unlike you."

"May I speak?" she choked out.

"You may *not*!"

They continued riding without speaking, the coach suffused with the sound of daily life. Roderigo clenched his fingers around his thighs until they ached. He released his grip on himself and clasped his hands tightly.

Of all the daft things that Rebecca had ever done! She was a lunatic, just like his lunatic mother-in-law. A girl carved out of the same mad nature, built with the same will of iron. He cursed his stars—a shrew for a daughter, a shrew for a mother-in-law. And a wife who mollycoddled them both.

Enough of Rebecca's defiance! She had to *marry* as soon as possible. He thought of Miguel—the preferred choice. Despite his proclivities in the Italian ways, he had shown himself to be brave and loyal. Better he be a man of substance in battle and a woman in bed than the other way around. As for Rebecca, once she was fat with child, nothing else would matter. And at least the two of them were fond of each other. He'd speak with Hector, and damn what the children thought!

Roderigo looked at Rebecca, who was staring ahead, gazing at nothing. He felt his anger abate, replaced by confusion. What possibly could have possessed her to refuse such a splendid opportunity—for herself, if not just for him. Was she a witch? He shuddered and pushed away the thought.

"Explain yourself," he whispered. "And keep the level of your voice to a hush."

She opened her mouth but no words came out, only small, muffled cries.

Roderigo sighed, put his arm around his daughter and pulled her near as she sobbed silently, shoulders heaving against his chest.

"Calm, Becca," he said. "Dear girl, at the least you should have consulted with me before you offered a reason of refusal to Her Grace. I know it's hard to leave family, but such a chance we had, daughter—both of us. Tis too much for me to fathom! I would rather you had told me nothing."

Rebecca continued to cry against her father's doublet.

"What did Her Grace say when you mentioned your grandam?" Roderigo asked, still hugging her.

"She said she understood my plight. In sooth, she was excessively pleased at my devotion. A young lady caring not about herself, but for an old woman's health."

"I'm sure it touched her heart," Roderigo said.

"Aye." Rebecca dried her tears on her sleeve. "She gave me a ring. It's in my bag."

Roderigo snatched her bag, ripped it open and pulled out the piece of jewelry—a large round ruby surrounded by stars of cut diamonds. He gaped at the ring as if it were an evil talisman and felt his hands grow cold.

Twas the exact ring, he said to himself. The very one he'd presented to Elizabeth not too long ago—a peace offering given to him by King Philip for Her Grace, demonstrating His Majesty's sincerity toward harmony of the two nations. And now the ring had been returned to the messenger.

A shiver ran down his spine. An old jewel of Spain he needed not, especially in view of England's current climate of hatred toward Iberia. Why had the Queen restored it to him? And why through Rebecca? Did it mean anything significant? Perhaps Elizabeth in her advancing years had forgotten that he'd given it to her in the first place.

Or perhaps, Roderigo thought, Essex had wanted the ring back in his hands.

"Father, are you well?" Rebecca asked.

Roderigo awoke from his nightmare and stared at her. "I'm quite well," he answered.

"You've turned ashen!" Rebecca gasped. She dabbed his forehead with her handkerchief. "Shall I stop the coach?"

"No!" Roderigo shouted. He immediately dropped his voice to a whisper. "I'm well, Becca . . . I'm simply shocked by the sight of such exquisiteness. The ring must be worth over a hundred pounds.''

''Take it, Father.''

''Marry, no!'' he said. ''I wouldn't think of such a thing, Becca.''

She was taken aback by the vehemence of his refusal.

''I'm flattered by your offer, Rebecca,'' he explained. ''Tis simply to say that the ring is yours.''

''It would do me pleasure if I could give it to you.''

''No, daughter, I cannot take it,'' he said. ''But I see your heart is pure with kindness toward me. The next time we minister to the Queen, you must wear it.'' He slipped it back in Rebecca's bag and kissed her red, wet cheek. ''Such a splendid piece of jewelry. Then you've still much favor with the Queen.''

''She said I may come to court anytime.''

''Then her invitation is still—''

''Father,'' Rebecca implored in a whisper, ''do not force me! I pray you with all my heart, Father, please do not compel me to go.''

She began to sob again.

''Becca, my love . . .'' Roderigo cleared his throat, touched by her emotional cries. ''No one will force you to leave the family you hold so dear. But you must tell me why. You've always been so headstrong, so independent, having shown in the past no need of my advice or assistance. Explain yourself to me.''

Rebecca was silent. How could she begin to tell him? Of the Queen and her perverted ways. Of her foul breath, slimy hands, and serpentine tongue. Her father wouldn't believe her, no matter how she'd insist it to be the truth. The worst insult under heaven—to be called a liar.

''I cannot express it into words.'' She wiped her tears with her handkerchief and sniffed the spicy aroma of her pomander. Would that it could remove the stench of the old woman from her nostrils. And Rebecca knew that odor was not a condition of advanced age. Grandmama smelled as sweet as the rosewater she bathed in.

Roderigo hugged her again. ''Never mind. As long as the Queen bears no ill will toward you.''

Or to me.

''None whatsoever, Father. I assure you.''

Rebecca had made certain of that. She'd accommodated the Queen's every whim, quenched her every desire. The memories made her weak in the stomach.

Roderigo put his mouth against his daughter's ear and whispered, ''She really is a wretched old harpie, is she not?''

For the first time in twenty-four hours, Rebecca smiled sincerely.

11

Christopher Mudd had caught his coney—an old windbag of a knight sorely drunk on cheap booze. The dupe was fat with a honey-tipped beard and surprisingly spindly legs. Wearing a scarlet doublet and brown hose, the gallant looked like an apple perched atop two wooden sticks.

A bene gull he'd be, thought Mudd. He thanked the stars for his good hap and prayed that there were many coins in the coney's purse—enough to please the master. Ye Gods, Mackering had been in a fierce mood of late, constantly cursing, smacking him for bringing in too little money. Waving the sharp dagger in front of his nose and threatening to cut it off.

Mudd shuddered at the thought.

He'd worked for Mackering for five years, his specialty tricks of falling: the spoon drop, the madman, the drunk, the one inflicted with falling sickness. The master had been a decent jack in the past, but now he'd turned into a rabid dog—biting without cause.

All because of that player, Harry Whitman. Tush, was Mudd sorry that he'd come with the master on the high roads up North. Mackering had changed for the worse since that fateful day, the day they'd cheated Whitman at dice. He'd become fretful with a temper that exploded like rain clouds.

Mudd sighed and rubbed his nose, appreciating its wholeness. May his hap stay good, may the coney's purse be heavy tonight.

It wasn't too long before the gull stumbled out of the tavern, his arms looped around a clubfooted jack, the two of them singing loudly about a whore of Greenwich. The dupe's companion was thin and seemed to be having a hard time keeping the lardish knight afoot.

Mudd wondered how much he could cheat out of the sod. Two shillings? Maybe three, if luck be a sweet wench. He had watched the knight for at least an hour, and the gallant had spent freely, buying sack for all those interested in being bored by his tales. The night might prove very good indeed. Maybe, then, with his hands filled with shillings, Master Mackering would be satisfied.

The two dolts stopped. A moment later the knight undid his codpiece and pissed against the side of the alehouse. Now was Mudd's chance. He approached the fat man with an unsteady gait, swaying markedly as if he, too, were inebriated. At the correct moment he bumped into the gallant, bounced to his right and stumbled to the ground.

"A thousand pardons, good sir." Mudd spoke loudly, slurring his words.

The gallant looked at Mudd's torn clothes and dirty face and sneered.

"Watch where you're going, cur!" he yelled, trying to re-attach his dangling codpiece.

"A thousand and thousand pardons, my good sir," Mudd answered. He attempted to upright himself and again fell to the ground.

"Nothing so repulsive as one who cannot hold his drink," remarked the dupe's crippled companion.

"Where are the constables when they are needed?" the gallant boomed. He was fully dressed now, tripping over his feet but not falling. "Constable! Constable!"

"Try the watchmen," suggested the man with the clubfoot.

"Tis a bonny idea," agreed the knight. "Watchman! Watchman!" He leaned against the cripple and his weight knocked both of them over.

"Stupid sot," the knight said to Mudd. "Now see what you've done!" He managed to stand up, and pulled Clubfoot to his feet. "Are you well, sir?" the knight asked his companion, brushing dust off his sleeves.

"Aye, quite well," Clubfoot said. He hobbled around in a circle. "No thanks to this churl!"

"Out of my sight before I step on you, beggar," the gallant said, nudging Mudd's stomach with the tip of his boot. "Watchman! Constable! Watchtable!"

"Now, a God's will," Mudd said, "what have I found?" He picked up a piece of paper and unwrapped it. A gilt spoon spilled to the ground.

The gallant's eyes widened.

Mudd stared stuporously at the item, then picked it up. "What shall I do with such a geegaw?" he asked.

"Sir," the cripple said. "I marvel at your good luck!"

"Good luck?" Mudd acted confused. "What good is this?"

The gallant smiled. "Let me help you to your feet, dear man."

Mudd was yanked upward. He recoiled from the fat knight's breath, reeking of garlic and cheap sack.

Clubfoot said, "Sir, that geegaw is worth—"

The gallant said, "Sir, you have found a trinket worth nothing."

"My luck," Mudd pouted. "Marry, I wish someone else would have found this. What shall I do with such trumpery?"

The knight brushed the dirt off Mudd's shredded jerkin. "I shall take it off your hands."

"Nay, perhaps I shall give it to my mother!" Mudd swayed on his feet. "Perhaps I shall give it to my sister." He stared at it and examined it closely. "Perhaps I shall throw it away. Would I have a crown instead of such a silly toy?"

"A crown, nay," said the cripple. "But I'll trade you a shilling for it."

"You said it is but a toy," Mudd said, confused. "Yet you offer me a shilling?"

"Aye . . . It strikes my fancy," the cripple replied.

"I shall give you two shillings," the gallant countered, shaking off the arm of the cripple.

Clubfoot became angry.

"He tries to cheat you," he said. "I shall give you four shillings."

"This lame jack is a scoundrel," the gallant retorted. "Five."

Mudd stared at Clubfoot. It was now his turn to up the auction.

"Five is too grand a price for me," the cripple said. "I have only four shillings, twopence in my doublet."

"I will give you five shillings for that trinket, sir," the gallant cried.

"Aye, take it for five shillings." Mudd shrugged, giving him a vacant smile. He held out the spoon, then swiftly retracted it. "You'd not be cheatin', would you?"

"Nay, good sir, never!" the gallant insisted. "The trinket is . . . for my wife. She is fond of such toys."

The cripple said, "Sir, I suggest you take it to a goldsmith. I suspect it could be valuable."

The knight glared at him.

Mudd pondered the suggestion, then threw up his arms. "Who has the time for such tomfoolery?" he said. "'Tis but a toy to me, and five shillings is five shillings. If you want it for five shillings, I'll strike a bargain with you."

"Done," the gallant said. He quickly handed Mudd the coins and snatched the spoon from his hands.

"He has cozened you," the clubfoot announced.

"Out of here, you lame fool," the knight yelled.

"Bah!" said the cripple. "Drunken dolt."

"Pay him no attention," the gallant said after Clubfoot left.

"Perhaps this chance meeting, dear sir, will bring us sweet fortune."

"Aye, good luck indeed, indeed," Mudd said. He smiled an idiot's grin.

He tottered away. When safely out of sight, he laughed. Five shillings! So much more than he had hoped for. He opened his jerkin and felt inside his pockets. There were four of them left—four small, wrapped packages of "valuables"—dross metal spoons covered with gold paint. At five shillings apiece, he'd walk away with a goodly bung—a purse full of gold. A sweet evening it was proving itself to be.

Aye, plenty of coins for Master Mackering, and perhaps a groat or two for dicing—ifin he could filch the money without the master knowing it. Marry, Mackering had eyes in the back of his head—always seemed to know which of his men was stealing from him. Dangerous it was to cheat the master.

Mudd felt in his other pocket for the pint of spirits. A necessity—a goodly bribe that caused the head of the watchman to turn in the other direction. Whittled cows, the watchmen were—all of them. In case the booze was less than persuasive, the dagger hidden in the waistband of his galley slops would convince the most mulish of constables to get him hence.

Walking a few more blocks, Mudd heard raucous laughter coming from the inside of another alehouse—the Greenhouse Inn. He stopped. Hidden by shadows, he peered through the red lattice of the inn's window. Twas a bonny tavern that would serve his purposes well, populated with a merry crowd sated to the gills. It wouldn't take long before another coney was caught. Aye, lots of money to be made this night. Mudd leaned against the building, a smirk on his lips.

And he waited.

12

The stink of tallow.

Shakespeare's head felt leaden, his body thick with sleep. Unsure of the hour, he wondered if dawn had awakened from her cyclical slumber. Was he dreaming?

He drifted back into sleep, dreamt of demons prancing around the maypole. They had piggish bodies, forked tails, black eyes, and wore black hoods. Fire sparked from their mouths and nostrils as they hissed like snakes.

But Mayday had passed a week ago with no such demons at all. Bonfires all night. London's revels lasting until dawn.

No black demons.

Or had they been there without him noticing?

Again the stench of burning fat assaulted Shakespeare's nostrils.

He opened his eyes.

Dark, damp, and cold.

Slumped over his writing table, his folded arms a pillow for his cheeks, he realized he had fallen asleep while working, as he had so many times in the past. Had he been asleep for a minute? An hour?

He raised his head, saw sparkling points of golden light. He stared at the flickering wick, at the shadows leaping off of the walls as if engaged in his dream's ritual maypole dance. Nocturnal creatures. His quill lay atop the foul papers of his latest playbook, bleeding ink over the stage directions.

Damn his carelessness! Now he'd have to rewrite the page.

The garlic mutton he'd eaten for supper that night lay like stone in his stomach. His mouth felt dry and numb. He ran his tongue over his lips and stared at the goblet of sack resting a foot away from his hand. Slowly, he extended his arm and clasped the stem of the cup. Raising his lips to the edge of the vessel, he took a small sip; the act of drinking seemed to tire him further. He lowered his head back into the cradle of his arms, but kept his eyes open.

The room suddenly became dark. But not dark.

Shakespeare felt his heart beat rapidly, his body wet with icy sweat.

Another shadow—much bigger and darker. It seemed to blacken the room. It loomed over him, then was silhouetted by the glow of candlelight in witches' colors.

Shakespeare's mind was a swarm of loose thoughts.

> *Black and orange. Orange and black.*
> *Incarnate of evil from doggish pack.*
> *What wolfish scheme hast thou conspired*
> *that pricks my skin and sets it afire?*

"Who are you?" he asked.

No answer.

"Are you touchable?" He extended his hand outward and

sliced through air. "Surely I am dreaming. My eyes deceive my wits."

"We have met," said a voice. Deep, guttural. A voice like none he'd ever heard. Or had he?

Shakespeare began to tremble.

"I ask you again, sir. Who are you?"

The voice answered:

> *"The specter that is to thee nearest*
> *is one thou holds so very dearest.*
> *He comes to give thee counsel wise*
> *to rid thee of the filthy lies*
> *that thou hast heard with thine own ears,*
> *inflicting wounds unto thy peer."*

"Harry?" Shakespeare asked in a whisper.

The apparition said:

> *"My love for thee was never ending,*
> *not as a sapling, ever bending*
> *in a tempest of rumors thick and deep*
> *that makest me moan, alas, cry and weep."*

"Harry," Shakespeare repeated. "Thou art an illusion. I hear, yet I hear nothing. Thou art whirls of imagination brought upon by overwrought nights of too much toil."

"Nay, tis not so," the voice protested. "I am the ghost of thy mentor—thy fellow—Harry Whitman."

Shakespeare shook fiercely.

"Tis true," the apparition insisted.

Shakespeare shivered violently. His closet had turned so cold. He asked, "What counsel doth thou offer me?"

"Let the buried rest in peace."

"My inquiries into thy death—"

"They are false! Lies! They cut me savagely!"

"The innkeeper Chambers spake that—"

"Chambers! A sinner! A cozener! A rogue! Believe him not."

"Dear Harry," Shakespeare said. "If thou desireth me to stop my inquiries, thou must confess to me. Who murdered thee? And why?"

The voice answered:

> *"It matters not the way I leave,*
> *tis 'nough that thy pure heart doth grieve*
> *for a hapless life ended, etched in blood.*
> *And chewed and spat like vomitous cud.*

Be kind, dear Will, spare me sorrow,
Erase thy revenge come the morrow.''

The waning flame began to sputter.

"Don't leave me, Harry," Shakespeare whispered.

The light dimmed, then finally died. Shakespeare felt a sharp rap on the back of his neck, then found himself floating in total blackness.

A serpent had wrapped around his arm, squeezing the blood from the limb. Shakespeare tried to cry out but no sound issued from his throat. As he attempted further cries, he felt his windpipe tighten, constricting his breath. He began to panic. The snake winked at him, an evil look glowing in its eyes. It hissed and clamped more tightly around his arm, its slithery body taut with muscular ripples.

The snake began to speak, but the words were unintelligible. Louder and louder, until it screamed.

"Wake up, Willy!"

At last Shakespeare understood.

Still panting, he barely opened his eyes, opened them enough to see Cuthbert Burbage yanking on his lifeless arms.

"It's already past daybreak, Willy! There's work to be done!" Cuthbert tugged at him mercilessly. "Wake up, you besotted swine!"

"I'm up," Shakespeare croaked.

"You speak but you've not awakened."

In sooth, Shakespeare thought. He said nothing, and suddenly realized that his head was throbbing with pain. Too much drink? Impossible. He'd drunk very little last night. Or so it had seemed to him. His mind was a gale of confusion. He wished that Cuthbert would let go of his arm.

"My apologies in advance," Cuthbert said, releasing him at last.

Shakespeare began to doze off. A minute later he was drenched with water. He bolted upward.

"For God's sake!" he screamed.

Cuthbert placed the empty water pitcher on the floor, found a dry rag and offered it to Shakespeare. "Dry your face."

Shakespeare was seized with the shakes.

"Marry," Cuthbert said. "You're ill."

"No," Shakespeare insisted. "I'm well. Just wet and cold." He stood up on quivering legs and dried his face. "I was having a beast of a nightmare. I thought a serpent was upon me."

"Let me help you dress—"

"I'm able to dress myself, thank you," Shakespeare snarled.

He managed to change his soaked chemise, but it took a great deal of effort. His head throbbed. A bad attack of fever, he thought. No worse, he hoped.

"You're flushed, Willy," Cuthbert said. "Go back to sleep. And for the love of heaven, sleep on your pallet. No one can get a proper night's rest slackened over on a desktop."

"The voice is the voice of Cuthbert, but the words are words of Anne." Shakespeare slipped on his hose.

"You have *need* of your wife." Cuthbert looked around the room. It was covered in dust. "Or at the very least, a wench with a broom."

Shakespeare picked up his doublet and looped his hands through the armholes, straining with each movement. He heard Cuthbert gasp, and looked up.

"What is it?" he asked.

"Your head." Cuthbert reached out to touch the back of his friend's skull, but quickly withdrew his hand.

Shakespeare felt it immediately—a large, crusty lump at the base of his head. He picked off a piece of the scabrous wound and regarded the dried blood.

"Someone attacked me last night," he announced.

"Bigod! *Who?*"

"Harry's ghost."

"What?" Cuthbert whispered.

"Harry's ghost," Shakespeare repeated. "At least that's who it said it was. I never did see its face. Nor was its voice tuned as Harry's." He held up a loose sleeve. "Help me put this on."

Cuthbert sank down onto the straw pallet in the corner of the room. His face was white.

"Whatever it was knocked me over the head," Shakespeare said. "Why Harry's ghost would desire me harm, I know not."

He noticed that Cuthbert had begun to tremble, and sat down next to him. Shakespeare prodded his friend's arm.

"Get hold of your wits, man. We have a performance this afternoon. Best we get in as many as we can while the theaters are still open. In the last few weeks Black Death has stalked the city like a fiend gone mad."

Cuthbert took the sleeve absently.

"Do you think you were *actually* visited by Harry's spirit?" he asked.

Shakespeare shrugged. "I know not."

"What counsel did it offer you?"

"We didn't talk too long. I do remember asking myself this— why was I falling back asleep when there still remained so much more to say? Now I realize that the ghost—or whatever it was— blunted my senses lest I question it too keenly."

They sat in silence. Shakespeare pulled the sleeve away from Cuthbert and, with a heavy sigh, drew it over his arm.

"At least truss up the points for me," he said.

"Merciful Jesu," Cuthbert said, tying the sleeve to the doublet. "If it were Harry's ghost, then the dead shall not rest in peace until the murder has been avenged."

"On the contrary," Shakespeare said. "The voice told me to cease my inquiry in Harry's murder. Which makes me think that it was indeed a man and not a spirit."

"Or maybe it was nothing at all, Willy." Cuthbert stood and began to pace. "Perhaps you drank too much sack last night."

"Only a sip or two."

"Are you sure—"

"A God sointes, Cuthbert, do you honestly think I bashed in my own head? My imagination may be fanciful, but this bump isn't a product of conceit. Nay, I wasn't overpowered by sack last night, but something in the sack overpowered me— nightshade, or perhaps foxglove or Indian acacia. I'm sleepy from potion, my friend. I can barely stand without toddling."

"And you think a spirit did this to you?" Cuthbert asked.

"Either a specter or an imposter. Throw me my other sleeve. It's on the desktop."

"Are you going to listen to its caveats?"

"No."

Cuthbert tossed Shakespeare the sleeve.

"You're not?"

"Not at all. Had it been polite, I would have considered its admonitions. But since it has shown itself to be a rude animal, I will disregard it totally."

"And you will continue to look for Harry's slayer?"

"I shall . . . though it may take me years to find him." Shakespeare finished tying his sleeve and stood up. "It's not the first time it has taken me years to achieve my goals."

It had taken Shakespeare three years to go from horse tender to stagehand, another three years until he'd been made an equal sharer in the fellowship. Whitman had been Shakespeare's staunchest supporter. Richard Burbage, the fellowship's lead actor after Harry, had been vehemently opposed to the idea. Their argument had been overheard by the entire troupe.

Shakespeare is strictly mediocre as a tragedian, Burbage had boomed.

Agreed, orated Whitman in a louder voice than Burbage.

His voice barely projects over the shouts of the groundlings, Burbage argued.

Agreed, said Harry.

He has little presence on stage.

He had a good comic presence in his last performance, Harry said, defending his charge.

Burbage cried, *He almost upstaged me! No, no, I refuse to have equal billing with an upstart.*

Harry said, *If he is not part of the fellowship, then the fellowship will have to do without Whitman.* He added slyly, *See how you do playing against me instead of with me, Burbage.*

Richard Burbage paled. Whitman was the biggest draw in London.

Burbage said, *Divine Jesu, Harry, Shakespeare is a good bookwriter. But why do you insist that he be part of the fellowship?*

Because I love that boy, Harry said. *He's a dreamer . . . as I once was . . . .*

The next day Shakespeare had been voted in as a sharer.

Yes, Shakespeare had had patience then, he would have patience now. He said to Cuthbert, "I shall know Harry's murderer and he shall know me."

"Some things are better put to rest, Willy."

"Harry was cut down before his time. The rogue responsible must pay. Harry's soul must be put to rest." Shakespeare held back his grief. "Enough said. Where did I put my shoes?"

"They're in front of the window."

Shakespeare walked over and picked them up. "They're frozen." He looked at Cuthbert. "I make it not a habit to work in front of an open window in such weather. The cold freezes the ink."

"The spirit—or the imposter—must have come in through the window," Cuthbert said. "Obviously it neglected to secure the latch when it departed."

"Now that's a curious thing indeed," said Shakespeare. "I was always made to understand that ghosts could pass through solid matter."

"Well, your spirit may not have passed through the brick wall, but it must have been an accomplished climber. Your room is at least twenty feet up from the street. Why didn't the apparition simply climb the stairway and jiggle the door?"

"It was bolted shut. Prying it open would have been difficult even for the most experienced of thieves. Twould have created much mess and racket."

"Is your window bolted shut as well?"

"Closed, but not locked. The latch had broken off during the last windstorm. My current preoccupation with Harry has not afforded me time to repair it."

"So there's no other way to come in except through the window?"

Shakespeare nodded. "A practical fellow, this ghost of Harry's."

"Harry was practical," Cuthbert said.

Shakespeare smiled and held up an icy shoe by the toe. "What am I to do? I haven't another pair."

"Use mine."

"Be not absurd. Are my feet more valuable than yours?"

"I've another pair. We'll stop by my closet on the way to the theater."

"Than I shall wear these until we reach your room."

Cuthbert grabbed the shoe from Shakespeare's hand. "Admit it or not, my friend, you are ill. You're red from fever and you're shivering."

"And you've just bested a miserable cough."

"Stop jousting, Shakespeare, and listen to me for once. Wear my shoes, I'll wear these." Cuthbert squeezed the leather pumps and small trickles of water splashed to the ground. "See. They're melting already."

"Such cheer," Shakespeare said. "It makes me sick."

"How does your head feel, Will?"

"As if it were visited by the Scavenger's Daughter."

Papers tucked under his arms, Shakespeare strolled with Cuthbert in silence down Gracechurch Street. With his feet dry, ensconced in warm woolen socks and cracked-leather boots, he felt much better. The sting of the cold was chasing away his lethargy, and his mind began to revitalize, racing with thoughts of one book or another.

He loved the walk from his room in the city of London to the new theater in Southwark, just over the Thames. In the quiet of the predawn dark ideas would come to him, often starting off as no more than a wisp of reflection—a line or two, perhaps taken from bits of overheard conversation or gossip. London was an early riser, waking not as a man who stretches and bellows and farts, but as a woman who slowly wipes sleep from her eyes and smiles, seducing all that surrounds her with innocence and beauty. He loved her all the time, but more deeply in the mornings.

By the time they reached London Bridge, Shakespeare noticed how truly late it was, his oversleeping an outcome of the potion slipped into his sack, no doubt. The shops and houses that lined the bridge were bustling with activity. The sun had risen hours ago and was desperately trying to break through a sheet of steely clouds. A week ago it had been hot. Last night, freezing, unusual for May. Daft weather, daft times.

They passed St. Thomas of the Bridge, with its stately col-

umns and pointed, arched windows—architecture of the old
Church. His mind, filled with the image of Christ, suddenly
juxtaposed against the dark memories of last night.

Who had visited him? Though he believed in ghosts, he was
skeptical that he'd witnessed a genuine apparition. A phantom
from the netherworld would be ethereal—of no form or definite
shape. It needn't have used a physical blow on the back of the
head as an admonition. Yet what visited him last night did pre-
cisely that.

Shakespeare cleared his thoughts. Walking steadily, he and
Cuthbert crossed over the gray waters of the Thames until reaching St. Saviour's in Southwark. As they continued west, Shakespeare could hear the snorts and cries of the bulls, bears, and
dogs caged in Paris Gardens. So far the theaters and baiting
arenas had been allowed to remain open for public viewing, but
if the toll of the dead from plague climbed further, all forms of
amusement would be shut down to prevent further spreading of
disease. Compared to last year, it seemed to Shakespeare that
Black Death was striking earlier in the season and deadlier than
ever.

Shakespeare had been lucky since arriving in London ten years
ago. Rarely had the theaters been forced to close for more than
a month at a time. The last time they had bolted their doors had
been last summer—in July, when London had been choked with
disease. The company had taken its productions on tour. Shakespeare remembered that travel had been exhausting. The country
roads, often flooded, had been small or nonexistent, and the
company's accommodations had been cheap. Frequently they had
passed the night in the stable with the horses, using only loose
straw for a blanket. But, marry, the countryside had been in full
blossom that year, a palette of color, the air scented sweeter than
perfume.

Shakespeare inhaled deeply, and a waft of dung assaulted his
nostrils. A bear's roar filled his ears. A devil it was to project
the lines over the blast of animal noises. But the theater's new
location was amid a lot more traffic, and the more traffic, the
more money.

They reached the Unicorn. The theater was not yet completed,
only half built, and preparations for the play seemed as chaotic
as ever. The recent move from Shoreditch to Southwark was
simply one more complication in a never-ending series of problems. Stagekeepers attempted to clean the standing pit and the
galleries, sweeping away the remains of rotted food served during yesterday's performance. Hired men wielded hammers and
calipers, building scaffolds and fixing warped boards on the platform stage. A boy apprentice, gowned in full costume, raced

THE QUALITY OF MERCY   109

back and forth, toting faggots of wood needed for repairs. Robin Hart paced furiously, the 'tire man shouting complaints to no one in specific about the condition of the players' wardrobe. The clothes were being treated carelessly, and he was tired of mending unnecessary tears.

William Dale grabbed Shakespeare as soon as he saw him enter, pulling him away from Cuthbert.

"Where were you?" he asked. "Don't you realize the time?"

Shakespeare debated giving him an explanation but thought better of it. He shrugged helplessly.

"We've a problem," said the keeper of the books. "The Master of the Revels has taken umbrage to your Richard."

"Which Richard?"

"The Third."

"What's wrong with the book?" Shakespeare asked.

"Willy," shouted the 'tire man from afar. He was upstairs in the second gallery, holding a bundle of clothing. "Come get fitted."

"In a minute, Robin," Shakespeare shouted back. He returned his attention to Dale. "What's wrong with the play?"

"Master Tilney objects to your portrayal of Richard. He claims you've made the Duke of Gloucester too human."

Shakespeare sighed. "Too human?"

"The original book—which you've rewritten—showed Gloucester to be an evil, scheming—"

"I've continued to write him with much evil—"

"He has too much doubt, Will," Dale said. "Aye, he does evil, but he *anguishes* about it."

"Without the anguish," Shakespeare said, "he becomes a flat figure of a man with no thoughts other than those of the Devil. If I'd wanted to write a passion play, where good is named good, evil is named evil, chastity is a boy wearing white and gluttony a fat man with a pomaded beard, I would have done so without using the pretense of Richard."

"Will," Dale explained patiently, "the Duke of Gloucester was usurper of the throne. The Queen will not be pleased if such a man is played for sympathy. The Tudors are claimants from the House of Lancaster."

"Harry the Eighth was more York than Lancaster," Shakespeare countered.

"Owen Tudor came from the House of Lancaster."

"Not a drop of true Lancaster blood had ever flowed in the Welshman's veins—"

"Let us not quibble with bloodline, Will, and address the problem in our hands," said Dale. "Master Tilney feels the play is subversive, and we dare not displease Her Grace." He gently pushed the book against Shakespeare's chest. "Evil up old Richard. And quickly. We'd like to perform the book by the summer."

"Shakespeare!"

Shakespeare turned around. That rich, booming baritone could only belong to one person. Richard Burbage was in fine form today—erect posture, as stately as nobility. His nose wasn't nearly as swollen as it had been the last couple of weeks, and his complexion had returned once again to its rosy hue. His eyes, always dark and secretive, came alive differently with each character he portrayed. This morning they seemed to smolder.

"I see my brother has managed to drag you in before the dinner hour," he said. His voice was piqued.

Shakespeare smiled. He said, "What do you think of my Richard the Third? You're the one who's to play him. Do you think he's evil enough?"

"I've been meaning to speak with you about that very book," Burbage articulated. "I have concerns about Gloucester's opening words."

"What kind of concerns?"

"My entrance speech is much too short."

"It's forty lines."

"Bah," Burbage scoffed. "Hardly a word is out of my mouth before I'm interrupted by Clarence. I need to *expound*—set forth my plans, my wishes, my desires, my *ruthlessness*. Add at least another twenty lines."

"Twenty lines?"

"Or even an addition of thirty would not be excessive."

Back to his desktop tonight, Shakespeare thought. "Do you like the book as written, Burbage?"

"Aside from the opening speech?"

"Aside from the opening speech."

"Richard's part is too small."

"Do you think Richard is played too sympathetically?"

"No," Burbage said. "He just isn't given enough opportunity to speak." He smiled and added, "I like that touch you added about old Gloucester being a crookback. It shall play magnificently on stage. All eyes will be upon me."

The 'tire man shouted again. He was now up on the third level. "You must get fitted at once."

"Five more minutes, please, Robin," Shakespeare screamed back.

"By the way," Robin yelled. "Your new sword just snapped in two. That's what you get for ordering cheap!"

Splendid, thought Shakespeare.

"So you don't think the play is treasonous?" Shakespeare asked Burbage.

"Heavens, I'm in no position to judge such an accusation!" Burbage answered. "I'm a tragedian, not a censor." He patted Shakespeare on the back. "Another forty lines, even fifty if it's going well." Without another word, Burbage walked away. Robin Hart came forward carrying some pins and a costume.

"Since you persist in ignoring my pleas, I've come to you."

"It's not possible to dismiss Richard Burbage in mid-sentence," Shakespeare said.

"Hold still." The 'tire man placed a cook's hat atop Shakespeare's head. The rim was much too large and slipped over his face.

"What is this?" Shakespeare protested, lifting off the hat.

"You are to play the cook this afternoon," Hart said. "By the way, I've found you a sword."

"Whose?"

"Mine."

"Tut, Robin. I can walk home and get my own sword."

"Too late for that. Just be careful with it."

"I shall."

"The blade is imported from—dare I say it—Toledo. Such a fine point it has. The slightest poke could cause a nasty wound. But I trust you with it."

"Many thanks," Shakespeare said. "I thought Augustine was going to play the cook."

"Augustine broke his leg. He fell off a horse, the stupid jack!" Hart plopped the hat back on Shakespeare's head and began to pin the rim. "You're also to play the guard, the night watchman, the constable—"

"How am I to play the constable if I'm to play the drunkard, when the drunkard and the constable are on stage at the same time? Must I talk to myself?"

"You shall simply shift from one position to another."

"That's absurd. I will be laughed off the platform and pelted with slop."

"Nonsense," Hart insisted. "You may play the fool as well, if you'd like."

"I'm already doing that."

The 'tire man pulled the hat off and pounded Shakespeare on the back. "We have confidence in you, Willy."

"Where is the book?" Shakespeare asked. "If I am to be an ass in front of hundreds of people, I may as well learn the lines."

Hart handed him scrolls of the various parts. "The lines are simple enough. If you don't like what's there, write your own.

Only do be careful of the cues. Keep them consistent with the rest of the book.''

Shakespeare groaned as he read. ''Who's doing the prompting this afternoon?'' he asked.

''Willy Dale.''

''Then it seems I should have great need of his services. There are over three hundred lines to commit to memory.''

''I've no worry,'' Hart said. ''You've done it before. But a little suggestion, Willy.'' He smiled and patted his cheek. ''Go gently with the garlics at dinner.''

13

Rebecca placed the mustache over her lip and pressed it down. Picking up the looking glass, she blew warm air onto its surface and buffed it with the hem of her chemise. It was an old mirror, dull and distorted, and she had to squint to keep her eyes in focus. But once she made out her reflection, she smiled. The mustache and beard she'd chosen were perfect—full with reddish tones. With her face disguised in manly pelt, she realized how much she resembled her brother—their features were the same, only their coloring differed.

She stroked the beard and decided it would be a nuisance to have facial hair, something else to be washed, combed, trimmed, and pomaded. Ah, but what it signified! The hair on her chin and above her lip meant she was no longer artwork—a thing of beauty to be courted, wooed, and won. Nor was she required to remain homebound until a proper escort was found. She wasn't obliged to act flirtatious or coy. Or keep her hands busy. (The true English gentlewoman was always industrious, her aunt had lectured.) The beard and mustache allowed her the luxury of idleness, the sudden freedom to come and go and *do* as she pleased.

To be a man, she thought wistfully.

Picking up her brother's hose, Rebecca pulled them over her coltish legs. Although Ben was taller than she, he wasn't particularly tall for a man, not like their father. And she had the fortune—or *mis*fortune, her brother had informed her—of being

well sized for a woman. His hose were too long for her, but the
excess material was easily hidden inside his boots.

Her brother had enormous feet. Even the surplus of stocking
failed to fill up the empty space. No matter, she thought. Grandmama would stuff them with rags until they fit snugly. Marry,
the boots were old. They'd been redyed a sickly brown, the toes
were scuffed beyond repair, and the left sole sported a penny-
sized hole. But a starving man didn't scoff at scraps. They were
the only shoes Ben had left behind, and they would suffice. A
pity he'd taken all his good ones to Venice, Rebecca thought.
She especially liked his red velvet shoes with the gold buckles.
They would have looked splendid with the yellow and black
round hose she'd chosen to wear today.

Her chest would look much too womanly under a doublet. She
needed help. She gathered up a set of gold sleeves, a slashed
gold and red doublet, a pair of gloves, and a brown cap with a
peacock feather. Stuffing the clothes under her arms, she opened
the door to her brother's bedchambers and peered down the hallway: a chambermaid, carrying fresh sheets. She disappeared
into the left guest closet.

Her mother was not due back from her visit with Aunt Maria
until suppertime. Her father was God knew where, discussing
God knew what with God knew whom. He'd taken with him the
new houseguest, Esteban Ferreira de Gama. De Gama had been
most cordial to Rebecca since his arrival a week ago. She thought
him quite witty, if not handsome—thickly set, with enormously
powerful legs, like those of a draft horse. A warm smile, but
not lecherous. Not like Manuel de Andrada.

Only *he* remained inside the house with her, alone with
Grandmama and the servants, the door to his cell shut.

What would that *weasel* say if he saw her like this—false beard
and dressed as a man. Would he laugh at her, tease her, or
threaten to tell her father? She decided most definitely he'd
threaten to expose her game—unless, of course, she capitulated
to him. How many times he had pawed her or worse, tried to
corner her and pry open her legs. She dared not tell the men in
her family about it. She'd implied de Andrada's improprieties to
Ben once before, and her impulsive brother had been ready to
kill the weasel on the spot. She had to use all her feminine wiles
to restrain his rage. The last thing in the world the family needed
was an unexplained murder in their house, the law poking its
nose into the family's personal affairs. So she held her peace
about de Andrada and kept the door to her bedchamber locked.

Manuel de Andrada had to be a very important man for Father
to keep him around. Or at the very least, a man who knew too
much. She spat on the floor and cursed his name. How much

longer would her father have to support that maggot? Give him clothes, food, and shelter? Several of her kinsmen had spoken of poison and de Andrada in the same sentence. She wished the talk would convert to action.

Tiptoeing out of her brother's bower—all the sleeping quarters were on the upper level—she scampered down the hallway, then ran down the spiral staircase, hurrying into the library. She hid behind a walnut bookcase overflowing with her father's medical tomes and surveyed the room.

No one around.

She rushed out of the library to the door of her grandma's closet. Roderigo had built the chamber to suit the old woman's needs. Since the hag was severely crippled, her cell was on the first floor—no steps to maneuver—and right off the kitchen. It made serving her meals easier.

Rebecca threw open the door and the toothless woman looked up from her poster bed and smiled. She was reading, her emaciated body propped up with a half-dozen pillows.

"I need some help," Rebecca said, closing the door.

"You disguise yourself again?" the hag croaked out. "You're the Devil!"

"Hurry, Grandmama. I must leave before that slimy worm de Andrada sees me."

The old woman put down the book, slowly swung her legs off the mattress, and rested her bandaged feet on the floor. Rebecca stood to help her, but her grandmother motioned her down with the palm of her hand.

Her feeble movements were painful for Rebecca to watch—withered, spotted hands pushing up a frail body hanging from a bent spine, bony fingers reaching for her walking sticks. When the hag was finally upright—or as upright as she could be—she extended the sticks out and dragged her legs toward them. Her hands trembled horribly, but Rebecca knew there was yet so much the old woman could do with them. The young girl forced herself to act impatient and short-tempered with the hag. Anything less would seem as if she pitied her grandmama, and as sure as poison, pity would kill her.

"Hurry up, you old sot," she chided. "Father should have put you away years ago."

"Hush your foul mouth, Devil."

"Have I all day to watch a cripple walk?"

"Whore."

Rebecca smiled.

"Daughter of Jezebel," the hag scolded.

"Tell me about Jezebel," said Rebecca.

"Your learning of the scriptures is an abomination." The old

THE QUALITY OF MERCY 115

woman reached her and kissed her bearded cheek. Rebecca threw
her arms around the skeletal frame.

"You'll break me in two," Grandmama screamed.

"I hope so."

The old woman pushed her away, bent down on the floor and
opened the lid to a box. She pulled out swatches of rags, a twine
of string, and a knife. Rebecca stripped naked from the waist
up.

"You've such lovely, large mounds, granddaughter," the old
woman said, wrapping the girl's breasts in rags. "You'll flatten
them out if you keep this up."

"Would I could lop them off."

"Oh hush up." After Grandmama encircled Rebecca's chest
with rags, she pulled the ends tightly from behind and secured
them with string.

"I can't breathe," Rebecca gasped.

"Hush. You'll grow used to it."

"It's too tight."

Her grandmother responded by pulling the twine tighter.

"I'm being crushed," Rebecca pleaded.

The old woman ignored her. "So you know nothing of Jezebel?"

"I know something of her," Rebecca said. "I greatly like
hearing your versions of the stories."

"Not my versions!" the hag said, knocking Rebecca's head.

"Ow."

"These are stories as written by our prophets," the old woman
lectured. "Written for us with God's guiding hand! Now, *what*
do you know of Jezebel?"

"She was enticing . . . and wicked."

"Aye, very wicked. She was the wife of the King of Israel—
King Ahab. She turned him wicked as well."

"Wasn't Jezebel a whore?"

"Much worse, Becca. Jezebel was a murderess who used her
womanly powers for evil—to lead the righteous to do evil. As
she did with King Ahab."

"Yet she was successful in her design, Grandmama," said
Rebecca.

"Why do you say that!"

"Because her scheming gave her the title of Queen."

"And that is your definition of success?"

"Not a bad definition, I should think."

"Ah Becca, it pleases you to rile me." Grandmama tugged
on the twine. Hard. "Aye, most of the time Jezebel was successful. But one man did not succumb to her designs. The

prophet Elijah. He escaped her powers because he was strong in the mind and believed in God."

"Our God," Rebecca clarified.

"When I speak of God, I only speak of one God," the old woman whispered. "The God of Moses—Adonai. *Lo yeheya le'ha elohim a'herim al panai.* 'There shall be no other God before me.' Jesu was an invention of a demented, embittered bastard named Saul. Because of Elijah's faith in Adonai, his mind proved impenetrable to evil."

"Elijah was a very dour prophet."

"All the prophets were dour. They were forecasting doom. It would have been blasphemous to act otherwise. But Elijah did have one distinction. Do you remember what that was?"

"No."

"God took Elijah whilst he was alive."

"Ah, the chariot of fire across the sky," Rebecca said. "What a spectacle that would have been. Twould have bested any fireworks ever performed for the Queen."

The hag knocked Rebecca's head again.

Rebecca laughed. "What finally happened to Jezebel?"

"You remember not?"

"No."

"She was pushed out of a window and was devoured by mad dogs."

"God's sointes, what a horrible death!"

"She was evil."

"Even so, Grandmama."

"All that remained were the soles of her feet and the palms of her hands."

Rebecca laughed and her grandmother slapped her on the back. "It's the truth, you heretic! Read your bible."

"I've lost my new English copy, and the Latin version has half the pages missing."

"I must get you a bible scripted in the old language," Grandmama said. "I have one, but the pages are as yellow as saffron and turn to dust at a finger's touch." The hag paused. "Perhaps Uncle Solomon can find one in his country. How much of the Hebrew you read do you understand?"

"About half."

"If I come upon an old 'Naviim,' I'll translate the entire story for you."

"I would enjoy that," Rebecca said. "Grandmama, why *would* mad dogs leave such strange spoils behind?"

"It wasn't the dogs, silly girl. *God* left such spoils behind." She turned Rebecca around to face her. "You're as flat as a boy now."

Rebecca kissed her cheeks. "Why did God leave such spoils?"

"In our old religion there is a custom of dancing in front of a bride, to gladden her heart and make her wedding day most joyous. It's a righteous thing, to dance before a bride." The old woman hobbled back over to her bed and sat down on the straw-covered mattress. "The sight of a maiden in her wedding dress held spellbound the wicked Jezebel, and she danced with love of Adonai in her heart for the bride. She clapped with her hands and stamped with her feet. So God spared them as a reminder for the one good deed she had done."

The old woman paused, then said, "I have endured many terrible things in my life, Becca, but faith has kept me alive. And clear drinking water can sometimes come from the rottenest of wells. Remember that. It could save your life."

Rebecca looked at her, puzzled.

"Never mind," Grandmama said. "An old woman is loose in her thoughts, as you are loose in your boots."

She began cramming small bits of cloth around Rebecca's feet, tickling them whenever she could. How she loved the sound of her granddaughter's laughter, the echo of her own girlish joy. When the boots were sufficiently tight, Rebecca slipped on the doublet. The old woman tied up the sleeves, and meticulously pinned the young girl's hair under the cap.

"Step away from me," Grandmama commanded Rebecca. She admired the form. "The fairest man I've ever seen."

Rebecca smiled.

"And where is your belt, sword, and dagger, young man?"

"I've 'borrowed' some of Thomas's. He shan't miss them for a few hours. They're hidden in one of the hedges outside."

The old woman reached out for Rebecca's hands and kissed them. "Be careful among those ruffians."

"I will."

"Where will you go today, Becca?"

"Since the theaters remain open, I think I'll go to South-wark." Rebecca slipped on her gloves. "To that new theater, the Unicorn."

De Andrada saw the young man leave through the window and smiled wickedly. So, the beautiful Rebecca had entertained a lover while her parents were away. If she were warmed from one man, how fiery she would be after two.

He grew hard between his legs as he opened the door to his closet. He tiptoed down the stairs, eager with excitement. He could feel himself upon her, smooth skin squirming under his body. She would protest—aye, maybe even pinch and bite. He liked it that way. Then he'd tell her he'd seen her young man—a skinny runt in yellow and black round hose, a fancy slashed doublet, and the cap with the feather—and the fighting would stop.

He snickered. What would she say when he threatened to tell her father? Would she plead with him, beg him to silence? Aye, he would be silent, but he had to get something in return. Having no choice, she'd have to capitulate.

He'd be rough with her, he decided, slap her around, bite the inside of her white thighs—bruise her well, the snobbish wench. Then as she wept, he'd thrust himself into her insides, already well wetted from her previous encounter. Aye, he'd replace the young man's spare seed with a raging river of his own.

He grinned at the thought. Ruy Lopez had betrayed him, had made Ferreira de Gama the new Iberian contact for the mission, taking de Gama instead of him. Though the doctor had tried to downplay the significance of de Gama's visit, he—Manuel de Andrada—had overheard the men speaking about de Gama. He had powerful ears, thanks be to Providence. A good piece of information to be used against Lopez when the time was right!

What flimsy excuses the witch doctor had offered when he and the snake, de Gama, were about to leave this morning.

Esteban is simply accompanying me to St. Bartholomew's, Manuel. Nothing more. He wants to bring a bit of cheer to those hospitalized.

When de Andrada asked if he, too, could go with them, Lopez flatly refused. And the witch doctor had the gall to tell him it was for his own protection.

You've been quite weak the past few days with fever and water loss, Manuel. Better to convalesce away from the breath of the ill.

Aye, he'd been ill, but that wasn't the reason he'd been deserted. Bartholomew's had been a ruse. According to the stable boy, the horses hadn't been pointed in the direction of the hospital.

Scheming behind his back again! Rebecca was *owed* to him as payment for his unappreciated service.

He placed his hand under his hose and stroked his throbbing erection. Shaking with lust, he touched the doorknob of Rebecca's bedchamber, then turned it quickly and stormed his way inside.

His first reaction was one of confusion; the sheets were folded, properly made up. He searched the room, but there was no sight of her, no musky smells from a recent dalliance.

He closed the door and searched other rooms, only to find nothing suspect.

Where had they met?

Maybe the hag knew.

He walked down the stairs and opened the door to the old woman's chambers. She looked up quizzically.

"Where is she?" demanded de Andrada.

The old woman smiled benignly. De Andrada went over to the poster bed and shook her violently.

"Where is Rebecca?" he screamed at her.

"Rebecca?" she said.

"Your granddaughter, you stupid sow!"

"Oh . . . aye, my granddaughter *is* named Rebecca."

"Where is she?" de Andrada bellowed.

"She went with her mother . . . to visit my daughter, Maria. I have two daughters. One married Jorge Añoz, the other married—"

"Stow it, you old fart!" De Andrada paced. "She didn't leave with her mother, hag. Where is she?"

"Ah, I remember now," the hag muttered. "I do, I do, I do. She went riding with my grandson, Dunstan. Or was it Thomas? Or was it Ben?"

"You piece of brown turd." De Andrada covered her face with the sheet. The little bitch had slipped through his fingers. "Who was that man?"

"Which man?" asked the old woman in a muffled voice.

De Andrada uncovered her face and said calmly, "The one with the feather in his brown cap. He just left the house not more than a quarter hour ago."

"Which man?"

"Oh, never mind. You're a blot on the Isle. I'd be doing everyone a service if I murdered you on the spot."

The old woman cracked her thin lips into a smile.

"Aye, I would do it," de Andrada said. "But why should I do any favors for a devil of a doctor?"

He turned around and stomped out of her bower, slamming the door behind him.

14

Shakespeare saw the black shadow pass and felt a sudden chill. His mind was playing tricks again. Had not the sun been darting in and out of the clouds all afternoon? He was seeing ethereal things, hearing voices that were nothing more than the whistle of the wind. Harry's ghost, or whoever it was, had shaken him more than he was willing to admit.

If the midnight visitor had been Harry's ghost, then there lay a very serious state of affairs. A spirit would haunt only if the soul was unclean. And if it hadn't been a specter, then some man had broken into his room, infused his drink with a potion, and clubbed him on the head. Either alternative remained unattractive.

Standing behind the backdrop of the stage platform, Shakespeare readjusted his chef's hat and waited for Burbage to finish up his "Oath of Loyalty" speech. The play they were performing was one of the worst in their repertoire, written by a rakish clod named Dubbin who was inflicted with falling sickness. He claimed his fits were messages from angels. The jack was a false prophet to be sure, but no one dared dispute him. Burbage loved the book because it had many long, solo passages. Shakespeare considered the writing dull and ponderous. The humor was so dry that the groundlings didn't understand it, and the gentlemen who did catch the puns seemed not to like them. Dubbin might have been touched by the divine, but his writings were anything but inspirational.

What the fellowship wouldn't do to please Master Burbage.

Burbage, with his broad, sweeping gestures, exaggerated facial expressions, and deep moaning voices—all of his mannerisms stolen from Harry Whitman. But even Shakespeare had to admit that Burbage had learned his lessons well. He'd become the consummate actor—the only legitimate heir to Harry's throne.

Robin Hart came up to Shakespeare and placed a hand on his shoulder.

"Old Rich is at it again." The 'tire man frowned. "You should see him on stage, stomping over the hem of the robe. He's going to rip the fabric! I just know it!"

Shakespeare smiled.

"Someone came around asking for you," Hart said. "While you were taking dinner."

"Who?"

"He didn't say his name."

Shakespeare felt a sudden prickling on the back of his neck. "What did this nameless someone want?"

"He sends greetings to you from a mutual friend—a gentleman."

"What was the gentleman's name?"

"I don't remember his name, either, save that he called him Master so-and-so. Hence, he had to be a gentleman."

"You're most helpful, Robin," said Shakespeare.

"I'm simply a worn-out 'tire man, not a player, and I make no pretense of having an exceptionally sound memory, as the rest of you do."

Shakespeare turned to him and patted his shoulder. "Did the nameless messenger *mention* the mutual gentleman's name?"

"Aye, he did. It simply slipped my mind." Hart thought a moment. "The name sounded like a fish," he said.

"Master Herring?" Shakespeare asked.

"No, that wasn't it."

"Master Halibut?"

"Nay."

"Master Gudgeon? Master Roach?"

"No, no. It wasn't that at all."

Shakespeare shrugged. His outward appearance was calm, but inside he was very taut.

"Mackerel," Hart announced with a note of pride in his voice. "His name sounded like Mackerel." He looked at Shakespeare and gasped, "Good God, Willy, you're white."

"Mackering," Shakespeare whispered to Hart. "Was the gentleman's name Master Mackering?"

"The very one," Hart said. "What is it?" Hart gasped. "Heavens, do you think he meant the ruffian George Mackering?"

Shakespeare ignored the question and asked, "What did this 'messenger' look like?"

The color had suddenly drained from Hart's face. "Look like?"

"Aye."

"I . . . I know not how to describe him. I know it seems preposterous, but it was as though he had no face."

"Did he have a beard?"

"I recall a beard. At least, I think I would have noticed had he been smooth-faced."

"Tall? Short? Portly? Reedy?"

Hart closed his eyes and said, "I cannot picture his stature."

"A big nose? Fat lips? The color of his eyes?"

"Nothing, Willy." Hart sighed. "I'm sorry."

"What did he sound like?" Shakespeare questioned.

"His voice sounded . . . unnatural. Deep, but hoarse."

"An accent?"

"I remember not. He spoke so little."

"Describe the clothes he was wearing," Shakespeare pressed. "Surely you noticed them."

Hart brightened. "I did. A thick woolen hooded cape, old boots caked with mud at the toes and heels. His doublet was much out of date, its skirt way below the waistline."

"The colors of the garments, Robin?" Shakespeare asked.

Suddenly Hart felt cold. "His entire dress was colored black."

Rebecca took a last bite of apple and dropped the core to the ground. A fat woman pushed against her—no doubt to get a better look at Burbage—and Rebecca pushed her back. In deference to Rebecca's fine dress and beard, the woman retreated.

Rebecca smoothed out an imaginary wrinkle in her doublet. Surrounded by swine, she thought. Yet they were pure of heart, these vulgar groundlings. They laughed, cried, cheered the hero and booed the fiend, and if the play was wretched, the actors would know about it. The nobility in the upper seats were very well-mannered, but not an honest emotion passed through their bodies, not a true passion pierced their hearts. Twas better to stand with the groundlings, smell their foul breath, their sweat, piss, and vomit. Better to be shoved and pushed in their drunken stupor than to sit as a lady, escorted by a lord as beautiful as chiseled marble and equally cold to the touch.

What a lovely voice Burbage has, she thought. So commanding, it soared above the belches, coughs, and rude laughter and boomed out like cannon fire. She loved to listen to him, to look at him. He could be as graceful as if he danced the pavane, as forceful as if he marched to war. Often she would daydream of playing with him on stage, how it would be if he were Hero and she Leander, to be Thisbe to his Pyramus.

She raised her pipe, inhaled a whiff of tobacco and coughed. Heavens, the smoke was strong, and the odor stank like a dung heap. A filthy vice. But she loved the look of disdain elicited from the Puritans as she blissfully puffed away while walking down Paul's. They thought she was doomed to Hell. Would they could know that, as a woman, she was cursed by her own private hell.

Burbage finished, and the setting was immediately switched.

A boy came in carrying a sign that said KITCHEN. On the left side of the stage was a table on which rested a pot housing a squawking chicken, a butcher's cleaver, and a plate full of entrails, the blood dripping to the floor.

The chef entered the platform through a door in the backdrop marked ENTRANCE. Today he was played by William Shakespeare. Rebecca always was drawn to Shakespeare's comic performances. He hadn't half the acting skill of Burbage, his voice being higher and more easily strained, losing projection when he shouted. But his eyes held her as none she'd ever seen. They were the palest blue, like fresh snow awash with sky, imbued with an unmistakable intelligence. She remembered them clearly at the burial grounds, staring back at her, questioning her own eyes. His countenance that day had been so somber, suffused with much pain, completely out of character with the doltish parts he usually played. She hadn't been able to reconcile that man with the player, and so she'd stared at him. Of course, everything that day had been blurry, so very unreal. . . .

She shooed the dark thoughts from her mind and returned her attention to the platform. Shakespeare was wearing a hat much too large, staggering around, trying to bring the bottle he carried to his lips. The crowd began to laugh. When the hat fell over his forehead and eyes, he stumbled about, then danced an exaggerated trip.

Rebecca found herself laughing along with the others.

Shakespeare raised the brim of the hat from his eyes and slowly, in drunkenly fashion, swaggered his way over to the table. Setting the bottle down, he grabbed the chicken, lifting the hapless bird up by the neck, and raised the cleaver. He swung the cleaver at the bird's scrawny throat but cut only air instead. The audience howled with laughter.

Shakespeare stared at the crowd, wearing a look of confusion, then gaped at the chicken.

"Why are you still whole?" he cried. The bird was flapping its wings with distress, fluttering feathers in his face. Shakespeare trapped them in his mouth, then blew them at the crowd like a gust of snow. "You should be very much dead," he explained to the bird. "Pouring out blood as freely as I piss out ale. Like thus."

He picked up a handful of bloody innards and smeared it over the chicken.

"There," he said. "Hold still, and by my will, I shall instill you to nil."

He held up the cleaver, swung it forcefully, but again cut nothing. Again and again he whipped the cleaver through the air, each time barely missing the chicken's throat. Finally he plunged the cleaver down onto the table and split a piece of sanguineous entrail in two, splattering blood all over his costume.

Not written in the book, Shakespeare groaned inwardly. Robin Hart was going to reproach him severely for the mess. Off to the left of the stage Shakespeare could see the 'tire man's face fall.

The crowd cheered.

He was about to speak but stopped cold when he saw them. Eyes! Those gray, fiery eyes! They had awed him once before, but now they didn't match the face.

Or had he really seen *those* eyes on a different face? Or were his memories part of a dream—like Harry's ghost?

Older had the face been, on a much taller man with an over-hanging belly. This face was young, the body slender.

He forced himself to turn away and was about to continue.

The line! What was his next line?

He glanced to the right at Willy Dale, who was mouthing something to him.

Shakespeare's eyes drifted back to the red-bearded boy.

Harry's funeral. He had been a *she*! A she dressed *in black*.

He felt himself slipping. Was he going mad? Seeing ghosts? Seeing men in women?

He heard Willy Dale shouting to him and felt a sharp rap on his chest. Someone had thrown an apple core at him. Another followed.

"A stew," Shakespeare improvised. "I shall make a chicken and apple-core stew." He picked up the apple core and plunked them into the pot. "Would I had more of these things."

He was pelted with a shower of apple cores.

He stared back at the boy whom he'd recollected to be a girl. He/she had turned pale and was leaving. Quickly he collected the cores, threw them in the pot, tossed in the live chicken, limp with exertion, and topped off the concoction with the bloody guts.

He ran off stage like a coursed hare.

"In the name of God, Will!" Robin Hart shouted after him.

"What the devil has possessed Shakespeare?" Richard Burbage demanded, stomping over to Hart.

"I don't know."

"Go on with the next scene, idiot," Willy Dale screamed to a boy apprentice. "On stage, you witless jack!" He walked over to Burbage. "For the love of God, what happened with Will?"

"Should I know?"

"Stage fright?" Hart suggested.

Richard shook his head. "Not Shakespeare."

Cuthbert Burbage approached his brother. "In God's name—"

"I know not what happened with Shakespeare," said Richard.

"Did you have words with him?" Dale asked him.

"No," Richard answered. "And even if we had—which we hadn't—we are both too much the ultimate actor to let offenses impede our duties on stage."

"Aren't you going after him?" Cuthbert inquired.

"My presence is *required* in the next scene," his brother said. "As was Shakespeare's. And he's quite unavailable at the moment. Cuthbert, we need you."

"I'm not going on stage, Richard," Cuthbert answered. "My legs turn to jelly in front of a crowd."

"Someone has to read Shakespeare's parts!" Richard bellowed.

"What about Nicholas Tooly?" suggested Cuthbert.

"He is on stage with me."

"I'll read Will's parts," Willy Dale said. "I've committed the book to memory."

"You can't act," noted Hart.

"Do you have a better suggestion?" Dale snarled back.

"Come, come, gentlemen," insisted Richard Burbage. "Please let's put out of our mind Shakespeare's eerie actions until the play is over. I've a performance to complete." He heard his cue and walked back on stage.

"It's Whitman's death," Hart said to Cuthbert. "Willy's become glutted with vengeance for his murderer."

Cuthbert nodded.

"Harry was an unusual man," said Hart. "A troubled man, oft besotted, but an actor of the utmost grace. He's sorely missed by all."

Cuthbert agreed. "By Shakespeare especially."

"They were close," Hart said.

"Amazingly so," Cuthbert said, "considering how different they were."

"Aye," Hart agreed. "Whitman was wild, unspoiled land. Shakespeare's a knot garden . . . poor Willy. He ran off as if chased by Harry's spirit."

Cuthbert raised his eyebrows and said, "Perhaps he was."

15

It was he—or she—who'd been following him! Of that Shakespeare was certain. A being of many disguises. A witch who had been watching his every move—at the theater, at the burial grounds, in his room last night. Weren't sorceresses known to change shape and form as easily as men changed horses?

He raced past St. Saviour's and over to London Bridge, ran a few yards up the plank and was immersed in a storm of bright colors. Swarms of people wearing brilliant golds, purples, reds, and blues. He shoved his way through the crowds, trying to catch sight of the young man with the feathered cap. But his quarry had vanished.

The witch/boy/girl could have gone anywhere—reversed its steps and slipped into the Bear Garden, ducked into a tavern on the bridge, hidden behind a building, dived into the icy waters of the Thames. Was any feat beyond a witch's supernatural powers?

Or was he simply going mad? Shakespeare wondered. Imagining men to be women, women to be witches? Perhaps the lad had remembered an obligation that required his sudden departure. Perhaps he'd frightened the boy off with his fearsome stare.

If only he could find him!

Suddenly, out of breath and faint, he stopped running. His friends had to think him moonstruck, sick in the brain to bolt off stage like that. Perhaps it was true, that his mind was indeed unwell. Seeing an apparition, hearing it speak. It was daft. *He* was daft. Mayhap he should stop all thoughts of revenge and listen to the ghost's counsel in earnest.

He felt himself ravaged with thirst. Walking another half block, he spotted a red bar over a doorpost—the sign of a tavern. He went inside, seated himself at a table, and had the tapster bring him a pint of ale. Sipping his drink slowly, Shakespeare tried to erase thoughts of insanity.

But images kept darting through his mind.

Mad Willy! Himself a year from now—with a matted beard, skin crusted with sores, drool oozing from the corner of his mouth, confined to the wards of Bedlam or some other back-street bridewell, the sole light of day squeezing through small bars mounted on the ceiling.

He thought, *Tell Margaret to leave the dead in peace.*

But Harry's soul would have no peace until his slayer was caught.

Go back to the theater and forget Harry's murderer. It has caused you naught but grief.

But Shakespeare knew he would not stop until the fiend was caught. Memories of Harry were haunting him as surely as the ghost last night.

Whitman kneeling before a wall. Shakespeare running to his side.

Shakespeare asking what happened as he helped a red-faced Whitman to his feet.

I was rehearsing my dance solo for tomorrow's performance and slipped. But not to worry. Harry stood and brushed off his hose. *My knees are still sound.*

Whitman, the supreme player. He had carried off a virtuoso performance. Down to the hobble in his walk to prove he had fallen.

Bravo! Bravo!

That night had been Christmas Eve—an hour before midnight services. Shakespeare now realized that Harry had stolen some time alone to pray as a Catholic. His blush came not from embarrassment from falling, but from fear of being discovered—even by his star pupil.

Still thinking of things past, Shakespeare looked out the tavern window.

And the witch appeared before his eyes.

Rebecca was panting, frantic with worry. Her heart beat loudly against her chest, her lungs sent out short stabs of pain with each breath. She turned her head over her shoulder, then spun around to make sure he was nowhere in sight.

She lowered her head and let her arms dangle loosely at her sides. *Why* had he stared at her? At first she'd thought it had been the dress—clothing of the well-off amid the tatters of the groundlings. But no, it was more. He'd recognized her from the burial grounds and knew she was a woman. He was going to expose her.

For what purpose? Why?

God knew what would happen if it became known to certain nobles that Roderigo Lopez's daughter had dressed as a man. Essex would make her father an object of derision. Her father would denounce her as a disgrace and demand an immediate marriage to the bridegroom of his choice. And he'd be in his rights.

Why? Why had Shakespeare persecuted her? Curiosity? Humor? Let us laugh at this ridiculous creature and her follies. A woman who thinks herself a man.

She was a stupid jack. Now the jack had played her childish game, and all she wanted to do was catch her wind and go home. Her legs were weak from running, her feet sore from Ben's ill-fitting boots. Her father's house, in the fashionable section of Holborn, was yet an hour away by foot. She dropped from weariness against a building and drew her knees up to her chin. The sheath of her sword dangled awkwardly at her side, its point resting in a pit between cobblestones.

All around her were people, stepping over her as if she were a rock. The sun had finally made an appearance, though the skies were still gray. Hawkers screamed out their wares. To her left was a spike implanted in the ground and topped with the head of a convicted rogue. He'd been skewered on the pike for a while, judging from the gray color of the skin and the plucked-out eye sockets. A crusted brown slab of muscle that had once been a tongue hung out of its mouth. Though many heads decorated the gate of London Bridge, this one, so close to where she sat, made her stomach weak. At least it didn't ruin her mood. She was already full of gloom.

Lost and forlorn, a self-loathing dolt who had to bite her lip so she wouldn't cry. It was well that God made her a woman. She hadn't the strength of mind, and would have been pitiful had she been born a man. The stars knew of what they spoke.

After a few minutes of reflection, she stood up, still breathless, and peered over the side of the bridge. A furious eddy of water swirled beneath the pilings—the only spot of the river that raged continuously regardless of how calmly flowed the Thames. Rebecca had once asked her mother about it, why in that one place the waters always ranted and raved, but her mother had ignored the question and hurried her along to Cheapside.

Rebecca regarded the angry seawater, its ire filling her with unexplained sorrow. She watched the whitecaps explode to spray for a minute, then began her walk home. She hadn't gone more than five steps when her arm was suddenly seized from behind. She spun around.

"You've been following me," Shakespeare said.

She felt light-headed. Her free hand grasped the handle of her sword.

"You're mistaken, sir."

"Why are you following me?" Shakespeare felt her arm, her wrist, her hand through her gloves. "Are you of this earth?"

A smile spread across Rebecca's lips. His eyes were feral—wild but confused. He hadn't wished her any harm specifically. The man was simply crazed.

"I think you unwell, goodman," she said, yanking her arm away.

The voice, Shakespeare noticed immediately. It was not the same one he'd heard last night. This one was thin, barely beyond the stage of its mannish crack.

"I've seen you before, sir," he said. "As a woman." He raised his hand toward her beard but Rebecca swatted it away.

"You've been touched by the moon, sirrah," she said.

"By the blood of Jesu, you were a woman," he said. "Will your conjury next turn you into a black cat? Or is that your natural form? Then I shall tell you get thee to Gehenna."

Rebecca felt a chill down her spine. Far better to be a mere woman dressing as a man than a witch.

"Again you're mistaken, man," she said, frightened. "It is apparent that you're in much need of rest, so I will excuse your molestation. You'd do well if you'd accept your error and be off. Being a proper gallant, I'm willing to forget this mishap."

"You were at Henry Whitman's funeral."

Rebecca felt her skin go hot.

"I know the great player by reputation only," she said. "I was most certainly not at *his* burial."

"But you were, sir," Shakespeare insisted.

"A wise man leaveth in peace, sir," Rebecca answered.

"You were at Harry's funeral. Those same gray orbs that do mock me now did stare at me then as pinpoint daggers."

"Your mind is playing tricks upon your eyes."

"Nay, tis your beard that is playing tricks upon my eyes."

"Do you say I was there when I say I wasn't there?"

"I say you were there."

"Then whoever claims I was there lies in his throat," Rebecca said, then gasped. The words had come out as if catapulted by their own power.

They stared at each other in silence.

A witch indeed, Shakespeare thought. Beguiling him to a duel, knowing full well her mystical powers were no match for his mortal skills. But the wheels of the cosmos halted for no man. The die had been cast and it was too late to alter the events. He was undone.

"Do you call me a liar, sir?" he asked.

Rebecca swallowed dryly. As a proper gentleman she had no choice but to continue the pretense.

"I say, goodman, that whoever claims me to be at Henry Whitman's funeral does lie in his throat."

"I claim you there," he whispered. "You were there dressed as a woman. But now I know that you are a witch."

"You lie in your throat," Rebecca said.

Shakespeare removed a glove from his belt and tossed it on the ground.

The fates were dancing merry tonight, she thought. She bent down and picked up the glove.

The sight of the glove in Rebecca's hand immediately drew a crowd—from gallants and rogues, the lords with the drunkards. They began to place wagers with one another on the outcome of the impending duel. Citizens' wives passing the scene scoffed at the tomfoolery and waste of money. Pickpockets and cutpurses flexed their fingers with gleeful anticipation. A sour-faced Puritan shouted from the back that they were all sinners, all damned to eternal Hell, as betting and dueling were agents of the Devil.

Rebecca looked around. By Divine command the performance had begun. All in the stars. She backed up from Shakespeare and drew her sword, snapping her wrist several times, hearing the whoosh of the blade slice through air.

She had often sparred with Thomas when they were children. He had bested her easily by the time they had reached eight but continued to taunt and tease her with his weapons. He'd loved to see her burst into a fit of temper and charge him with all her might. How swiftly he had riposted her advances, leaving her on her arse, cursing fiercely. Then one day, in a moment of kindness, he had taken her aside and had taught her discipline—how to hold back as well as how to charge. The lessons were repeated several times a month for about a year.

Aye, Thomas had been a valuable tutor. She hoped she'd learned his teachings well. Her life depended on it.

She hefted Thomas's sword several times. It was the newest of weaponry—a superb rapier, the blade imported from the Continent and perfectly balanced, the point deadly. It was not at all like the clumsy broadswords she'd played with as a child. She drew her dagger, brought the blade of her rapier to her forehead and snapped it downward. Her opponent did the same. She positioned herself for the onslaught.

The duel began.

Rebecca knew by Shakespeare's size and musculature that she was no match for him. His strength could topple her in a moment. Her footwork would be her only savior—perhaps she could dance with him to a passageway fifty yards away. It was a maze she'd known well, having lived on the bridge seven years ago. The passageway led to a sinuous conduit that meandered between buildings, houses, and shops—turning sharply at two places, forking at three. Ben and she had often played hide-and-seek in the labyrinth. If she could duck in at the crucial moment, she could escape—disappear and never more be a man. Save her and her father extreme embarrassment.

If only . . .

Shakespeare seemed hesitant, as if he sensed something was wrong. Perhaps he was frightened to duel with a "witch." He kept staring at her with those impenetrable eyes. So be it. If he thought her a witch, she'd use it to her advantage.

She thrust her sword outward, lunged, and felt the clash of metal upon metal.

Shouts and cheers filled the air.

Shakespeare parried her stoccata to his right shoulder with his dagger, and Rebecca immediately took a couple of steps backward to free her sword. She lunged to his left. He parried, flipped his rapier under hers, and charged toward her leg. His sword was arrested by a parry with her rapier, and she riposted with a punta reversa. He blocked the blow with his dagger, then pushed the point of his rapier toward her throat, narrowly missing it by inches. Only quick reactions had saved her neck.

The crowd roared with delight.

She danced backward, assumed a neutral position, then lunged at his heart. He parried the attack, then riposted with an imbroccata to her stomach, his chef's hat falling off with the sudden jolt. She parried, crossed the top of his blade with her own, feigned a stoccata to his left shoulder, then charged to his right. He was too quick with his dagger. He blocked her attack, tried to land a cut on her arm, but she stepped backward, out of his reach.

And backward again.

How many yards remained to the mouth of the passageway? Twenty, thirty at most. Lead him over. She backed up another two yards.

They circled each other like gaming cocks. He lunged, she retreated. She feigned a move, her only purpose to keep him at bay until she could get to the tunnel.

The crowd became impatient with their galliard, crying for them to duel, not dance, demanding to see blood or twas no duel of honor.

But Shakespeare seemed to be ignoring their pleas. Abruptly, his countenance had changed. His eyes were no longer wild. Aye, still troubled they were, but not mad. Rebecca was confused. She knew he wasn't charging her as fiercely as he should. Something was holding him back.

In a blinding moment Shakespeare realized that he wasn't fighting a witch. He was fighting a mortal—and worse still, he was fighting a lad, or a *woman*. It was the lack of strength in the parry, truly not the defense of a swordsman with magical powers. And the voice. Pitched as one who had recently undergone his manhood. But a woman could lower her voice as well.

Truly he'd been moonstruck. And his madness had entered him into a duel with a poor woman who for some reason had dressed as a man. He'd frightened her at the theater, caused her to flee. Then he had terrorized her further with his sword! Shamed-faced, he longed to call off the mockery.

Fiendish miasma in the air. First Whitman's death, now this poor child whose life was in his hands.

She lunged at him. He parried easily with his dagger, then tried to knock the rapier out of her hands with a swift stramazorm. But she was too rapid in her retreat, and he was left flailing at air, stumbling over his feet.

A swell of laughter arose from the crowd. As in the theater, they were laughing at his clumsiness. Only this play was not staged.

He cursed under his breath. He didn't want to hurt this woman—this *girl*—but she was determined to do him harm, her intentions ignited by the fear he'd instilled in her.

And there stood yet another problem. He couldn't disarm her readily. It was clear enough that she'd been trained in the Italian method of fencing—the school of Vincentio or Caranza. Their pupils mastered swift swordplay—thrusts, instead of slashes and cuts, which were perfectly timed, well-aimed, and *deadly*. What she lacked in force she made up in agility. Her footwork was superb, as fast as a greyhound. Nor had he ever seen a woman of such valor. Mars and Mercury ran strong in her star map.

Again he charged with a stoccata to her right, but she averted the thrust. She riposted quickly and the tip of her rapier caught him on his arm.

Immediately his white sleeve became saturated with a spreading circle of crimson.

He could scarcely think about the shouts. Bigod, she meant to kill him if she could, and it was his own cursed fault. He advanced as she retreated.

He slapped his sword broadside against her wrist, hoping to knock out the sword from her hand, but she held it firmly. The slash cut through her sleeve and left a red line drawn across her arm. Immediately she dropped her dagger and clutched the wound with her hand, turning her glove red and sticky.

The noise of the crowd was deafening.

Suddenly Shakespeare was seized with anger directed at himself. The duel was a total mockery. The rogues that had gathered wanted not avenged *honor* but blood. He was but a moment's worth of amusement for those who made it not to the baiting rings. He'd be damned before he'd allow this poor thing to end up as a chained bear with a mastiff at her throat.

Shakespeare swung his rapier as if it were a broadsword and knocked her rapier loose, sending it spinning through the air. He thrust the point of his sword against the bob of her throat and backed her up against the wall of a skinner's stall. The putrid smell from the curing hides penetrated his nose and caused his eyes to water. He felt his head go numb, swimming with cheers of "Kill him! Kill him!"

Their eyes locked. Not a trace of fear lived in hers. She meant to die valiantly.

Slowly he withdrew his sword from her neck and backed away from the wall. When he had retreated several yards, he turned his back on her and went to retrieve her sword. The fine steel blade was still sharp and in one piece. Picking up the rapier, he regarded the handle—gold ring guards etched with the initials T.A. in the Italian hand. The steel was Austrian made, Innsbruck temper. He stashed her sword, as well as his own, in his sling and slipped his dagger into its sheath.

When he looked back at the wall, she was gone.

The crowd jeered his performance.

It wasn't the first time.

To the Devil with all of them, he thought.

He walked over to his fallen chef's hat and bent down to retrieve it. He felt a wind flying past his head and heard the clink of steel upon plaster. He spun around and saw a dagger lying on the cobblestones.

Had he not been kneeling, the dagger would have punctured his heart.

He picked it up and immediately noticed that the poniard's handle had not the same insignia as the handle of his newly vanquished sword. The blade seemed to be northern English or Scottish in origin, clumsily thick and brittle, poorly annealed, clearly a different quality than the imported blade she had thrust at him. Shakespeare turned about, then saw *her* dagger lying where she'd dropped it.

Either he'd gone completely daft or there was yet a witch after him.

16

The hag had been born with the hearing of a bat, her God-given gift heightened long ago by years of solitude in a pitch-black cell. Crying was her specialty. She was supremely adroit at distinguishing between tears of sorrow, torture, joy, and death. The crying she now heard was a mixture—a pinch of pain blended with heavy sobs of shame—Rebecca's voice, and it was strange to hear her weep. Even as a babe in arms, rarely had Rebecca cried. As a woman she was quick with fits of temper but slow to moisten her eyes. The hag was curious as to what had caused her such humiliation, but knew she'd find out soon enough.

Five minutes later the door to her bedchamber flew open.

Rebecca had gained her composure, but her eyes were still red and wet. The old woman plucked a whole cucumber out of a vegetable bowl and threw it at the girl. Rebecca caught it with her right hand still sticky with blood.

"Slice it," Grandmama ordered.

"I have no knife."

"What happened to your sword and dagger, young man?"

Rebecca bit her trembling lip and held back tears. "They're not in my possession at the moment," she said.

"No matter," the old woman said. "Take one of the knives from my box. Slice the cucumbers thinly, then undress and lie on my bed."

Rebecca began cutting the vegetable. Her hands were shaky, her arm throbbing from the slash she'd received an hour ago. The wound was no longer bleeding, but her arm had swelled and was tender to the touch. Carefully she cut six uneven slices, almost nicking her thumb on the blade.

"That's enough," the hag told her. "Come here and let me undress you."

"Pray, Grandmama, why the sudden desire for cucumber?" Rebecca asked in a small voice.

"They're not for me." The old woman clucked her tongue when she saw Rebecca's wound. "You've been making merry, child?"

134

Rebecca let out a small laugh. Despite the fire burning in the hearth, she shivered.

Grandmama said, "Lie down and tell me what happened while I tend your arm."

"It's a rather ridiculous story." Rebecca sank down onto the mattress.

"Close your eyes, Becca." The old woman covered her granddaughter with a warm blanket, then placed cucumber slices on top of her eyelids. "These will soothe your tired eyes."

Yes, they will indeed, Rebecca thought. She said, "I love you, Grandmama."

"Bah! You speak sentimental tripe only because you're weakened."

Rebecca smiled and said, "In sooth, you're a burden and of no use to anyone. Do the family a service and die soon, old cow. But first, patch my wound."

"Better I should bandage your mouth!"

"Is anyone home yet, Grandmama?"

"Only the servants."

"And de Andrada?"

"The worm left the house about two hours ago. He noticed you dressed as a young man, Becca. Use more caution in the future." The old woman pulled out Rebecca's arm. "Now I'm ready for your words. Give me your sad recital."

"I fought a duel."

The hag burst into laughter. "A *duel*?"

"Aye."

"With a *man*?"

"Aye."

"And you were *victorious*?"

Rebecca shook her head. "The point of his rapier was held at my throat. At the last moment he was overcome with mercy and spared my life. But you can see by the sore on my arm that he desired me fierce and great harm."

"Bah, Becca, the sore is but a scratch!"

"Simple for you to say. The scratch is not on your flesh!"

"Tush! Had the gentleman desired you true pain, he wouldn't have released you with such a wee nick." The old woman hobbled over to a shelf and pulled down a vial of clear liquid. "This shall sizzle the skin for a moment, child."

She poured eight drops from the bottle onto a rag and dabbed the skin. Tears swelled up in Rebecca's eyes and ran down her cheeks.

"Your cucumbers are crying," remarked the old woman. She removed the slices, now salted with tears, and placed fresh ones atop the girl's lids.

"Who are you to say that my opponent meant me no real harm, Grandmama," said Rebecca. "After all, you didn't witness the duel."

"I have met many gentlemen who inflict pain on people for their livelihood. They would not have permitted you to walk away on your own two feet. Nay, Rebecca, the cut looks to me like a warning, or mayhap an attempt by your opponent to dislodge the sword from your grasp, not even a true dueling scar, I regret to say."

"I was magnificent in my swordplay!" Rebecca said. "My opponent had no need to show me pity!"

"I'm certain you were a sight to behold," Grandmama answered.

Rebecca said, "Tell me about those gentlemen."

"Which gentlemen?"

"The ones who inflicted pain for livelihood."

Grandmama pursed her lips. It was so long ago, a tedious and painful story. Those "gentlemen." So vicious, yet so ordinary. And they had the gall to call themselves religious men. . . .

Rebecca interrupted the old woman's thoughts.

". . . met them while you languished in the old country's prison, didn't you?"

"Yes."

"Tell me more."

"The memories are hard for me, girl."

"I need to know, Grandmama," said Rebecca. "I need to know everything about you."

The old woman hesitated. Roderigo had requested—no, demanded—her silence about the horrors of the Inquisition. But the hag felt otherwise. Rebecca, though sheltered, was a girl of strong constitution, a woman who'd benefit from her history, the history of her people. Grandmama said,

"What do *you* know about our people, the Jews?"

Rebecca laughed. "You desire me to recite the Bible starting from the Creation?"

Grandmama laughed. "No. I realize you have a scant knowledge of bible—Mother and I have taught it to you. But what do you know about our history after the destruction of the Second Temple—our history in Galut?"

"I regret to say not too much," Rebecca admitted. "You and Mother always emphasized our biblical history. Tell me the history I lack."

"First, what do *you* know?"

Rebecca regurgitated what she was taught. That her people lived a hundred years ago as Jews in Portugal. Her ancestors had converted to the Roman Church under the threat of death. That the Spanish labeled them swine—Marranos—once they did convert. Rebecca stopped talking and the hag urged her to continue.

She shrugged, "Father came to England to get away from the inquisitions . . . I know not what else to add."

"You sadly lack knowledge of your forefathers."

"My ears are open," Rebecca said.

"Very well," said the hag. "But listen carefully for I'll not repeat it. I grow tired just thinking about it."

"Tell me whatever your strength allows," Rebecca said.

The old woman sighed. It was hard to exhume such memories. Slowly she explained to Rebecca how their history had started over a thousand years ago with the fall of the Temple, with the fall of the empire of Pagan Rome. The Jews had settled all over the world—Egypt, Turkey, Cathay. And the Continent—the Italian states, the Rhineland, Gaul. Some traveled as far as the Isle.

The old woman began to wrap Rebecca's arm with rags, noticing her narrative was distracting Rebecca from the pain of her injury. The crone continued,

"The Continent was a violent home for those still clinging to the Jewish faith. The Christians were brutal. The English Christians were no better to their Jews than their sister countries on the mainland."

"England had *real* Jews?" Rebecca asked.

"Aye," the hag said.

"*Overt* Jews?" Rebecca asked incredulously.

"Hundreds of years ago, Becca," the old woman said. "Know you not a whit of history?"

"A whit of Iberian history," Rebecca said. "Father has made it clear that although we live on the Isle, our bloodline is that of true Portuguese."

Grandmama thought for a moment, then said, "Then let me tell you about the Jews of England. They had flourishing communities here. They had been successful. And, as always, they incited the jealously of the bastard uncircumcised peons—I spit on them!"

"Do not excite yourself unduly, Grandmama," Rebecca said.

The old woman smiled. "I fare well, granddaughter. Now hush up before I forget my words." She cleared her throat. "The Christian jealousy peaked at the coronation of Richard the First. As the English Jews carried priceless gifts for their king, unruly mobs of brawlers attacked them at the doors of Westminster Hall. The bastards ended up sacking London's Jewry. Then the barbarism repeated itself at Lynn, at Stamford, at Norwich—the worst being the great riot of York. Thousands of Jews died by their own hands rather than suffer the same fate at the hands of the Catholics. Finally, the Jews were expelled from England on

All Saints' Day in 1290—by decree of Edward the First, may he rot in Hell. Tis the reason we feign illness on the holiday. It's a day of mourning for our people.''

''Father told Ben and me that we celebrated not the holiday of the Saints because we don't believe in the Saints and it is against our laws to glorify witches.''

''Aye, those are sound reasons as well.''

The hag had a pained expression on her face. Rebecca asked, ''What is it, Grandmama?''

''There is a story—an old tale about the departure of the Jews from England,'' the old woman said. ''A troubling story which you should know.''

''Tell me.''

As the hag spoke, her eyes became lost in faraway times. ''When the Jews were expelled from England, they were brought to the Continent by the boatloads and dumped upon the shores of France and Spain, which still allowed Jews to live in their country. There was one nefarious English master mariner who knew the vagaries of the sea better than the face of his wife. With a group of Jews on his vessel, he steered out to sea, waited until the tide of the Thames was low, then steered back onto a dry bank where the ship became grounded.''

''Why?''

''Patience. Once on dry land the master mariner—using guile—enticed the Jews off the ship and told them to come forth with him on the dry bank and wait for the tide to return. The Jews did as told. Finally, when the master mariner saw the tide coming in, he went with haste back onto his ship and pulled up anchor, leaving the Jews stranded as the river waters suddenly rushed upon them. The Jews cried out for succor, but the master mariner laughed and told them to ask their God to split the waters for them as He did the Red Sea for Moses—''

''My God,'' Rebecca said, covering her mouth. Grandmama looked at her. Rebecca's skin had turned white. Perhaps Roderigo knew his daughter better than she. But it was too late to undo what had been started. The crone continued:

''The Jews prayed as the tide rose over them, but alas, their prayers were not answered and they drowned most terribly beneath the Thames.''

Rebecca asked, ''Is the tale true?''

''Methinks it must be, Becca,'' said Grandmama. ''But God remembers his faithful. He has marked their grave site. Beneath London Bridge there is one place that rages forth with boundless wrath even if the rest of the Thames is becalmed.''

''I know the spot,'' Rebecca whispered. She thought how her

own death was nearly met above the very place. Fate. She kissed her grandmother's cheek, squeezed her hand.

"Do my incessant questions tire you?" Rebecca asked.

"No, Becca." Grandmama straightened the bandage around Becca's arm. Her granddaughter's skin, as smooth as marble, as rich as ermine. If only Rebecca could be protected from harm forever. The old woman said, "Hush up and let me finish."

The hag continued to explain that the Jews had been scattered across the world in accordance with the wishes of God. In almost all the countries they inhabited, they were molested—harassed and often murdered.

"But in Iberia"—the old woman raised her finger into the air—"in Toledo, under the rule of the black Levantines—the Moroscos—the Jews were left in peace . . . and we prospered."

"Nonetheless, Grandmama, their worship was not open. They were forced to hide their prayers to God, worshiping in private as we do now."

"So there's more of your mother's feeding that you remember tasting," the old woman said.

"I said I knew a whit of Iberian history. Spain is part of Iberia, is it not?"

The hag knocked Rebecca in the head. "Respect!"

"Ow."

The hag said, "Aye, our people kept their prayers hidden from the Moroscos and appeared in public as if they worshiped the false god, Allah. But like our great Queen Eliza, the Morosco rulers peeked not through windows of their homes." The old woman frowned. "Then Toledo went the way of the rest of Iberia—Roman Christian."

"Under the Catholics, Ferdinand and Isabella," Rebecca said.

"Aye, the twin demons, may they bake in Hell's oven forever!" The old woman spat into the fresh straw covering the floor.

"It was in their reign that the land of Spain was finally united under Christian rule. Jews and Moors alike were given a choice—become Catholic or relinquish all their worldy trinkets to the treasury of Spain and suffer expulsion from the country.

"Understand, Becca, that the demons had need of much money to finance their explorations into the New World. When taxes brought in insufficient revenue, thievery was the only logical option. I shit on Spain—and her explorations."

The old woman sighed. "A few more words, then it's time for my nap."

Rebecca nodded.

"So the Jews converted," said the hag. "Aye, they fell over

each other's feet racing to the font, the dolts, so happy were they to live as Gentiles."

But not equal Gentiles, thought Grandmama bitterly. The Converted Jews were called *Nuevo* or New Christians—to distinguish them from the *Viejo* or Old Christians—Catholics from birth. The Jews were branded as converts, inferiors. Only old Christians had true purity of "bloodline"—*limpieza de sangre*. A pox on their *limpieza*, Grandmama thought. She bent Rebecca's elbow to ensure that the bandage allowed enough movement of her arm.

"Our capitulation was for no purpose, Becca," she continued. "We were considered offspring of tainted blood—second class. Many trials were held against the new converts, confiscating their money and honor. All was lost—our goods and our God."

"You are bitter."

"Bitterness is an evil crab that claws hard at the gut. I'll have none of it in my belly." The hag suddenly smiled, kissed her granddaughter's cheek, and removed the cucumbers from her eyes. "Your arm has been well tended. You must dress quickly, before your father returns home."

"Grandmama, what about *your* history? The priests who inflicted pain upon you?"

"For another time," said the hag. "I grow weary now. I must have my nap."

Rebecca knew there'd be no more lessons today. She had heard that tone of finality hundreds of times in the past. Such was the way her grandam taught. A story here, a tale there. By and by, Rebecca absorbed what the old woman wanted her to know.

Rebecca stood and said, "I have need of your counsel. I'm in a predicament."

"Aye?"

"I've lost Thomas's sword and dagger—the special ones that Uncle Solomon gave to him. Thomas shall know they are gone as soon as he returns home from his day at Paul's. What am I to do?"

"How did you lose them?"

"Tush, Grandmama, they were the spoils of the victor of the duel."

The old woman shrugged. "You must tell Thomas."

"He shall *kill* me!" Rebecca bit her thumbnail. "Those were his *finest* weapons. He dared not carry them in public for fear they'd become marked or abraded."

"Aye, you've a problem, Becca." Grandmama slid onto the mattress. Rebecca pulled the covers over her bony shoulders. The old woman gave her a toothless smile. "Pretty yourself up and talk to Thomas. Your cousin has a weak spot for a fair face.''

"Nay, Grandmama, you realize not the gravity of what I've done. My face won't matter to him, save to scar it with his fingernails.''

Grandmama closed her eyes. "You're a clever girl. You'll think of something.''

Within minutes the old woman was snoring.

Nan Humbert, the Ames's chambermaid, winced at the crash. Sir George's rash son had just smashed another piece of pottery. A God's sointes, she didn't think there was so much in the house that could be destroyed. The crash was followed by a string of curses—unchristian curses. Nan readjusted her bonnet as if it were a battle helmet, and was about to climb the stairs to Sir Thomas's quarters when she heard a knock at the front door. She waited to see who it was. Perhaps it was Sir George Ames, and hopefully, he could calm down his irate son. She frowned when she opened the door, disappointed to find it was only Sir George's punk niece, Rebecca.

And punk she looked indeed—fancied up with painted eyes and lips, carrying in her hand a silly little fan. Such toys were not only vanity, but agents of the Devil. Nan smiled to herself. One day the girl would go the way of the rest of the stews—her skin scalded off by Satan himself, burning forever in a pit of brimstone. One day she'd scream for eternity, rot for the evil she and her father had done to that poor Señor de Andrada—a sinner in the past but a true repenter. One day . . .

''. . . my mother I'm here to see her,'' Rebecca was saying.

Nan snapped herself to attention.

"Your mother left thirty minutes ago, Mistress Rebecca.''

"Is my aunt here?''

"She left with your mother. I believe they meant to sup at your home tonight.''

"Is Sir Thomas in his old quarters?''

"I wouldn't be bothering him now, mistress. He's full of spit and fury.''

"Oh? And why is that?''

"He claims his swords were stolen, mistress. He's torn up the house looking for them, but alas, they've disappeared. Would you be knowing anything about that, Mistress Rebecca?''

"No,'' Rebecca said curtly. *Evil Puritan bitch.* "Why would I, Nan?''

"No reason why you should, Mistress Rebecca. It was merely a question.''

"Tell Sir Thomas I wish to speak with him immediately.''

"I beg your pardon, mistress, but I'm afeared to go up to his room, so spleenful is his choler."

"A woman who fears man can never fear God."

The maid turned crimson.

"No matter," Rebecca said. "I shall see him without being announced."

Nose in the air, she walked past the chambermaid, up the stairs, and knocked on Thomas's door—the chamber he had had as a child. He had his own house, but with his wife away in Turkey, he found it easier to live with his parents than alone with servants. Thomas allowed Rebecca to enter, then slammed the door shut.

"Bother me not, Becca. I've no time for your silly trifles."

"I must talk with you, cousin."

"Speak then with much haste."

Rebecca looked around. The room was in complete disarray. Thomas was disheveled in his dress, his smooth, fair face coated with a sweaty blush.

"What happened to your bedchambers?" Rebecca asked.

"Tis none of your affair. State your business and leave me in peace. My mood is very dark."

"You have lost your swords," she said quietly.

"The bitch Nan has told you?" Thomas cried. "By God's grace that woman has a mouth as big as a cave."

"Aye, she told me."

"My weapons were not misplaced, Becca. They were stolen."

"And I know the thief."

Thomas's eyes widened. He grabbed her shoulders and shook her. "Who is the scoundrel?"

Rebecca said, "Me."

His mouth dropped open. "You?"

She nodded.

"Where are they?" Thomas asked, stunned.

Rebecca dropped to her knees. "I shall try to return your possessions as soon as possible. But in the meantime they are unavailable to me. I beg your forgiveness."

"You took my sword and my dagger?" Thomas whispered.

"I shall pay you every penny of their cost—"

"They were irreplaceable! They were *unique*!"

"They can be remade—"

"Impossible! The blades were cold-steel tempered. Two times the process was repeated, the metal annealed thrice, making it as hard as granite without a trace of brittleness. The cross and ring guards were gilt and personally engraved. They were *gifts* from Uncle Solomon upon my knighthood. What should I tell him if he should ask to see them the next time he visits England? I . . ." He looked down at Rebecca kneeling before him and stopped himself from lunging at her throat. "Get *out* of my sight!"

"Tommy, let me explain—"

"Get out of here *now*, stupid bitch. Before I take a dagger to your heart!"

She grabbed his legs. "I beg of you, cousin, let me explain myself. I disgrace myself before you and plead for your most gracious mercy. I pray you, hear me out."

Thomas pushed her away and walked over to the window. "Get off your knees, Becca. You're truly pathetic when you beg. The princess who always scoffed at me should now beg for my mercy?" He let out a bitter laugh. "What did you do with my weapons, cousin? Give them to one of your drunken lovers?"

Rebecca stood shakily. "I . . . I have no drunken lover," she said. "I have no lover at all."

"Aye, mayhap this is true now, but many a besotted cocksman you've had in the past. History plays as a true seer of the present."

"I have never, never mocked you, either to your face or behind your back! Never!" Rebecca hesitated, then added, "And very few lovers I've had, Thomas. As God is my witness, that is the truth. From whom have you heard differently?"

"What have you done with my weapons? Given them to my brother?"

"Given them to *Dunstan*?"

"Aye, Dunstan. You recall him, do you not? He is the Ames brother with the beard, the swain who oft you meet in a hayloft."

"Thomas, I—"

"Get out of my sight!"

Rebecca clenched her hands and walked over to Thomas. She whispered, "Dunstan was years ago, Thomas."

"Not according to him," Thomas said. "But it matters not to me. Where are my weapons?" He grabbed her arm.

She gasped in pain. "My arm has been injured, Thomas. Let go."

He loosened his grip. "What happened to it?"

She buried her face in her hands, then looked up and said, "I beg you not to breathe a word of this."

"I shall decide that later. First, tell me your tale."

Rebecca regained her composure and cleared her throat.

"My arm was wounded—*slightly* wounded—in a duel which I fought with your swords."

Thomas stared at her.

"I became embroiled in a fight of honor, cousin."

He continued gaping at her.

"Sometimes, I dress up like a man—"

"What?"

She took a deep breath and said, "Upon occasion I dress in Ben's clothing and roam the marketplaces posing as the gallant. I did so today and a certain person took offense to me. I'm not certain what led to the quarrel. Perhaps I offended him in a manner of speech, or perhaps he was simply mad—"

"You are mad."

"Tommy, I swear, I speak with the truth in my throat. A challenge of swords ensued and I was forced to duel with a Tom O'Bedlam lest I shame myself—and you by extension—as a knight."

"Your imagination knows no limits, Becca. I give you high praise for invention."

"All I say is true."

Thomas paused a moment, his countenance softened. He asked, "Where did this duel take place?"

"On the bridge . . . around three by the clock."

"On the bridge, you say."

"Yes."

"Who was your opponent?"

"By my father's blood I swear this to be the truth. I dueled with William Shakespeare, the writer of the pamphlet *Venus and Adonis*. He's also a player—"

"I know who he is," Thomas interrupted. "Oft he plays the fool."

"The very one."

"And you fought a duel with him?"

"Aye."

"And you swear in your throat what you say to be the truth?"

"A thousand times I swear," Rebecca said. "We attracted a large crowd. Ask any gentleman who passed his time about the bridge and he would confirm my story."

"What were you doing on the bridge?"

"I went to Southwark, to the theater to see the great player Burbage. I do so love to look at him."

"What was the name of the theater?"

"The new one—the Unicorn. It is still incomplete—"

Thomas waved her to silence. He said, "I believe you."

Rebecca smiled. "You do?"

"Yes. I was at the Unicorn this afternoon."

"You were?" She burst into laughter. "Then with certainty you saw Shakespeare bolt off the stage in pursuit of me."

"I saw him run off the platform," Thomas said. "I didn't

know he was chasing you specifically. Afterward many a gentleman spoke of a duel between the clownish actor and a slight man with fancy footwork. I'm pleased that you've retained the steps that I had taught you in our childhood.''

"Oh, Thomas! I could not have survived had I any other teacher but you." She hugged him, but he broke her hold and stepped away.

"I want my weapons back," he said.

"I swear on my honor that I will do whatever possible to get them—"

"I will go to Shakespeare—"

"No, you mustn't—"

"Tell me *not* what to do, cousin.''

"Please, Thomas. There were unspoken words between me and Shakespeare that need to be clarified. I know that if I explain the situation to him, he will be kind and return your weapons. Let me try—"

"Why did you do such a knavish thing, Becca? Borrowing my weapons without my permission. You took what was not yours for the taking. Why?''

"Would you have lent them to me had I asked?''

"No. But you had no right—"

"Aye, I had no right. But I took them because I wanted them. They're symbols of power, and as a lowly woman, I have no power. Furthermore, I took the *best* of your swords. I'm nothing, Thomas. Simply a future receptacle for some man's seed. For a brief moment I just wanted *more*. It was knavish to take your weapons, but I don't regret it. I felt so mighty as I dueled. Exhilarated! For once my life rested in my hands.''

Thomas said nothing.

Rebecca said, "I swear the weapons will be returned to you. I'll give you whatever I own as compensation if they are damaged.''

He spun around and looked at her.

"Why did you go to him?''

"To whom?''

"To *Dunstan*," Thomas said. "You must have known the way he spoke about you. The way he speaks about you still.''

Rebecca stiffened. "I know.''

"He laughs at you, Becca. Describes your body to sodden swine he calls his drinking friends. He tells me what he does to you, what he makes you do to him—so open and careless he is in his gossip. Tis a miracle that neither your father nor Grace has ever found out.''

"Dunstan is dreaming in the past," Rebecca said tightly. "I have not been with him in years. He begs me constantly to bed him and I refuse over and over. His gossip is spiteful.'' She clenched her hands until the knuckles turned white. ''Why are you telling me this?''

''Because I'm still *furious* at you. Thou wast *mine*, Becca. Mine and Miguel's. *We* treated you as a peer while Dunstan spat in your face and mocked you to the world. Yet you kissed his arse and became his whore.'' Thomas lowered his head. His voice softened to a whisper: ''Dunstan is a callous braggart and an insufferable fop. I want to kill him when he laughs at you. To defend your honor. But more so, I want to kill you for allowing such abasement.''

''There is no more abasement.''

''Or so you say.''

''Tis the truth!'' Rebecca insisted. ''Yet I seem not to convince you otherwise. How dim is the surface of a tarnished image.'' She turned her back to him and stared out the window.

Thomas said, ''I still goad Dunstan into sparring with me. Though Lord knows he couldn't fence his way out of a chicken coop. I play with the churl, then spring upon him, cutting him down until I hold my dagger at his chest. But it seems not to bother Dunstan. He smiles at me with a well-sated smile that said, 'Aye, you've got the sword, but I've got Becca.' ''

Thomas looked at Rebecca gazing outward. She was hugging herself, kneading her forearms with thin, delicate fingers. He started to speak again, then faltered. Finally he said, ''Even if it is over, as you say, why *did* you allow him to humiliate you?''

''He gave me things,'' Rebecca said without hesitation.

''You played the strumpet for *trinkets*?''

''For *books*, Thomas.'' She whirled around, her face suffused with rage. ''For lessons in Latin, Greek, Arabic, French . . . I *hungered* for knowledge, to know the world about me, and no one else was willing to tutor me except Dunstan. As I grew older, you went off with your fellows and I was left behind with the women. So I paid the piper and became Dunstan's whore. I'm sorry it hurt you, Thomas. I never preferred him to you. It wasn't with pride that I did what I did.''

She bit her lip. ''Tis so cruel of you to recut old wounds. So unlike the gentle man that you are. You act as indecent as your brother.''

Thomas's blush deepened to scarlet. ''I apologize,'' he said.

Rebecca didn't respond. She couldn't. A lump was clogging her throat.

''Truly, I'm sorry for my indiscretion, Becca,'' Thomas said.

She straightened her posture and looked him in the eye, forcing up a tearful smile. ''I know you are a good soul, Tommy.

That your harsh words come from care rather than scorn. I have no need of your apology."

Thomas lifted Rebecca's hand to his lips.

"I love thee," he whispered.

"I know."

Her fingertips touched his lips, stroked his beardless face. He closed his eyes, then abruptly pulled away from her. Shyly, he asked,

"Did you love my brother—as a lover?"

"Sometimes. Despite his rough talk now, he was gentle back then. I ended our dalliances when he had nothing more to teach me—with his mind as well as his body. As you've stated, he was not the swordsman that you were. I'd wanted *you* to continue to school me in the art of the fence. But you pushed me aside and ignored my constant requests."

"I was ired by your betrayal."

"I understand," Rebecca said. "Pray, Tommy, you try to understand me as well."

Thomas brushed the floor with the sole of his shoe and said, "Did you ever think of me as you loved Dunstan?"

"Many times, Thomas," Rebecca answered in earnest. "Many times."

17

Hamor Lowe kept guard from a muck heap. The smell was foul, but the vantage point was splendid. He could easily espy Mary Biddle trying to urge the coney to bed. The doxy had removed her bodice and sleeve and had unpinned her hair—golden tresses resting on smooth skin twinkling with candle-light. Gods, she was lovely. Just as she'd been that night.

Lowe sighed as he reminisced. Mary had been such a bene mort, full of energy and moaning like a birthing cow. He'd only niggled with her the one time. A gift from Mackering for successfully cheating a gentleman—four crowns he'd walked away with. Mackering had laughed, slapped him on the shoulder, kissed him on the cheek, but kept all the money. When Lowe had complained, Mary was tossed his way, a toy to appease his anger. And what a toy she'd been! But when the night ended, so did affection for Lowe. Now the doxy cursed and teased him whenever they worked together.

The Devil take her, he should.

Spitting, Lowe returned his attention to the lit window. Mary was stroking the gentleman's cheek with her left hand and work-. ing on his clothes with her right, the nimble fingers unfastening the ties of his doublet. The gull was ogling the whore, face filled with lust. His mouth was open, his eyes sweeping over her body like a maid's broom. He smiled stupidly and said something to the doxy. She laughed and licked his upper lip. He gave her back another fool's grin. She winked and whispered something in his ear. The man's eyes widened and his tongue fell out of his mouth.

A God's blood, do all men look that idiotic when the sting hits them fierce?

The gentleman's doublet and sleeves were off now. Mary laid them by the open window, then began to untie the points of his hose.

The coney pushed her head toward the floor, and she disappeared from sight for a moment.

She came back into view and shook her head no.

The dupe became angry and tried to push her down again.

She resisted, cocked her head to one side and said something to the dupe.

He nodded, clumsily undid his points and tugged his hose from his legs while remaining upright. For a moment his stockings were bunched around his left foot and he hopped around the room, trying to maintain his balance as he yanked them free. Finally the stockings were off and he lunged at Mary.

She sidestepped him, and Lowe saw him disappear from the window. Mary laughed wildly.

Quickly, she placed the gentleman's stockings, hose, and shoes by the window, and baited her would-be lover to come hither.

He was standing again, his two fool fingers erect and placed behind his head as if they were the horns of Pan.

She laughed, mimed mock fright and brought her hand to her mouth.

The coney chased her around the room. Then they both disappeared from view.

Lowe saw a skirt fly up in the air, followed by her chemise. Then nothing.

Ten minutes later she stood bare-chested, her nipples hard and erect. She peered out the window and shook her head gently.

Lowe sighed and settled back down into the pile of shit.

The gentleman was still not sated.

She disappeared again.

The crier called out three in the morning.

Lowe sighed. He hoped the booty tonight would be enough to please Master George. As of late the master had been smoking in a beastly mood, and no amount of money was ever enough.

Mackering's moodiness had started after the trip up North, Lowe thought; after he and Christopher Mudd had gulled that coney named Whitman at the Fishhead. Lowe had had an evil feeling about it from the start. Aye, an angel they cheated out of him, but the master hadn't been pleased about their winnings. Maybe the master had expected more, who knew with him? And there'd been something strange about Whitman, something troubling. He'd accepted his loss without ever demanding to see the dice.

And then Whitman turned up dead. The master had been furious. Though Mackering enjoyed announcing his cheats to all the world, he wasn't pleased to be associated with a dead man. He cursed his men, swore that he'd cut off the tips of their things if the authorities found out they'd been the last to see the dead man alive. And the master always kept his promises.

Lowe realized he'd been squeezing his crotch and released his grip.

Fifteen minutes had gone by.

And now that fool-player Shakespeare had been asking questions about Mackering on the bridge this afternoon. After his duel with the skinny runt with the fancy sword. Lowe also had heard Shakespeare asking about the Whitman cove. The talk bothered him more than the stink of the dung. The gossip must be reported to Master George, and tush, that would stoke his fire. Though he was not a follower of God—condemned to Hell he was—Lowe prayed that Mackering wouldn't settle his fury on the messenger.

Finally, a half hour later, Mary stood up fully dressed. She placed several articles of clothing by the window, tucked a doublet under her arm, wrapped herself in a sheet, then hoisted herself outward. She fell into the soft underbrush, then trotted over to the muck heap.

"The shit smells ripe," Mary said. "The perfume of a Jake-farmer suits you well, Master Lowe."

"Shut your mouth, you stinkin' whore."

"Do your hookin' and let's be gone," Mary said. "The jack sleeps lightly."

"Nip his purse?" Lowe asked.

"Aye, lots of coins in it. George will be buying big at the taverns."

"How much did you lift?"

"None of your affairs!"

"Shut your mouth!"

She lifted up her skirt.

"Look but don't touch, Hammy. Or I'll tell the master and he'll cut yours off."

"Get your tongue a-tying, you stupid stew," Lowe said. "All you'd be ever giving me is the King's Evil."

"The great pox, eh?" Mary laughed, pinning up her hair. "You wouldn't know the difference. Yours is about to fall off from rot anyway."

"Piss off, stew."

"G'wan," she snickered. "Do yer anglin' and let's begone from the hill of shit."

"I still dunno why you dinna throw the booty out the window and let me catch it."

"That'd be smartass, jack." Mary sneered. "What if me gentleman roused and caught me tossing out his clothes?"

"You coulda thought up a pretty tale."

"Like what?"

"I dunno." Lowe shrugged, then said, "You coulda told him you were hanging them up to dry."

"Yer stupider then you look." Mary laughed. "No wonder you never made it past a hooker. And speakin' of hookin', do some anglin' instead of complainin'."

"I'm waitin' for the master to come with the horses."

"Don't wait too long or me coney'll be wakin'."

Lowe said, "I can pilfer the clothes now, but what ifin he spies us? We can't go far without the horses."

Mary said, "Just do it. The master'll be comin' afore long."

"Then stand aside while I do my labor."

"Piss off. I'm not in your way, jack."

"Piss off yourself, punk." Lowe pulled out two iron staffs and fitted them together into a crome—a pole topped with a large steel hook. Deftly he brought it to the open window and caught the doublet onto the hook. A moment later the doublet was in Lowe's possession.

"Go fer the sleeves," Mary said. "They're sewn with gold thread. The fabric'll go for two pounds a yard."

"Aye." Lowe fished in three pairs of sleeves.

"Here's the master with the horses," Mary said, waving him over. "He's pulling one fer you, Hammy."

Mackering rode up to the dung heap, dismounted, then fed both horses a cube of sugar. He glared at Lowe and said, "You couldn't have found a better place than this stinkpot?"

"Was the only place where I could see Mary clearly," Lowe said.

"You're a dolt, Lowe," Mackering said. "A jackass with shit

where brains should be. You must feel quite at home in this muck pile.''

''Master George, I—''

''Shut up and keep on with your angling before the gentleman wakes up.'' Mackering picked up a doublet and smiled at Mary. ''Bene clothes he wears, my sweet little thing. You chose your sap well tonight.''

Mary smiled and curtsied.

''And how much was in his bung?''

Mary handed Mackering the gentleman's purse. Mackering took out the coins, bit them, then slipped them into his doublet.

''Tis good,'' Mackering said. His expression suddenly hardened. ''You wouldn't be filching a bit off the top, would you, Mary?''

''Oh no, Master George. Never!''

''Open your mouth, girl.''

Mary obeyed and Mackering searched it, then her anus and vagina. Finding them empty, he smiled and patted her bum. He asked,

''Did you lay out the man's sheets, Mary?''

''He only had but one, Master George,'' Mary said nervously. ''I wrapped it around me body and took it myself when I jumped out the window.''

Mackering picked up the sheet, felt the cloth between his thumb and middle finger and shook his head.

''Cheap,'' he sneered. ''Won't bring in more than a tuppence.''

''Aye, but look at his sleeves, Master George. . . .''

Mary held her breath.

''Ah, these are beneship indeed,'' said Mackering. ''Thick velvet, full of gold-threaded embroidery.''

The whore smiled with relief. Mackering asked, ''What else have you hooked, Hamor?''

''I just pulled in four sets of hose,'' the angler answered. ''And two pairs of shoes.''

''Did you leave him what to wear, Mary?''

She shook her head no.

Mackering laughed. ''Let the jack parade in his chemise.''

''Finished,'' Lowe said, taking apart the pole.

''Then pack up the goods and let's be gone.''

''Master George?'' said the hooker.

''Aye?''

''I heard your name being gossiped about on the bridge today.''

Mackering went rigid. ''Go on.''

''A player was asking about you. He goes by the name—''

152   *Faye Kellerman*

"William Shakespeare."

"Aye," said Lowe. "Twas Shakespeare."

"And?" Mackering asked.

"He asked many a gentleman about where you supped and drank," Lowe said, beginning to shake. "Though they heard of you, Master George—who hasn't heard of your great reputation—no one claimed to know where you did your boozing."

"Lo be the one to suffer my sword, eh?"

"Aye," said Lowe. His hands felt numb, and he dropped a shoe into the pile of muck.

"Clod," Mackering said. In a motion as swift as lightning he whipped Lowe across the face with the handle of his dagger. Mary gasped out loud as Lowe clutched his cheekbone.

"Shut up, you wailing whore," snapped Mackering, putting the point to her throat.

Wetting her chemise, Mary clasped her hand over her mouth and trembled.

Mackering laughed and withdrew the dagger. "Tarry not, Lowe. Let's get on with it. Mary, as soon as we're safe, tend to Lowe's small sore, will you?"

"Aye, Master George."

"And Hamor, my good man, worry not about William Shakespeare," Mackering said. "I'll take fine care of him."

"Aye, Master George," Lowe said, holding the side of his face and biting back pain. "Surely you will."

"Surely I will." Mackering gave a lopsided smile. When Lowe had finished packing the clothes, Mackering picked up a rock and flung it into the gentleman's open window. A minute later a face still heavy with sleep looked down upon them.

"Ho, scoundrel!" the gentleman cried. "Who tossed that rock into my chambers?"

"I did," Mackering yelled.

"Who are you?" the gentleman hollered.

"You may tell the world that you were pilfered by the highest uprightman Mackering." George turned to Lowe and said, "Upon your horse."

"Mackering, you cozener!" the gentleman screamed. "Twas your doxy whom I had?"

"The very one, jack." Mackering swung Mary onto his horse. "You've been had by the best, and that in itself is an honor. Spread my name to all who test me and try to best me. Let them beware, for they will be left as naked as thee. Never will they win. Chase us if you can. But you'd better be getting dressed afore you do."

Mackering mounted his horse, yanked on the reins until the

horse reared upward, then left the gentleman spilling his curses into the cold night air.

18

The gyrfalcon spread her wings of pure white, then soared upward until she was bleached from the sky by sunlight. Roderigo tried to track the bird visually, but the blinding rays caused his eyes to water until his vision was a blur. Every time the doctor cast the bird, he became tense, so fine a hunter she was and so rare was her color. He had told no one about her except Francis, his trusted falconer, but somehow the word had escaped. The creature was the envy of many a high-ranking noble and had to be kept in a separate mew under armed guard twenty-four hours a day. Lopez hawked with her under utmost secrecy, and took with him a large staff of trained swordsmen to fend off any wanton attackers.

A raven darted into the sky, and in a finger snap the falcon swooped upon it—a tapestry of black and white against a cerulean canvas. A moment later the raven was nothing more than a burst of pitch-colored feathers and a bloody carcass plummeting to the ground. Lopez ordered his retriever to fetch the pickings, and held out his arm ramrod straight. The gyrfalcon landed on his hawking glove, an ebony plume trapped in her beak, the back of her claws stained with blood. Bending his arm at the elbow, Roderigo took out a piece of raw heron's heart from a leather pouch and fed it to the bird. It was unusually fair weather for mid-May, the mist burned away by unseasonable heat, perfect air for birding.

Roderigo looked at Rebecca. She was dressed in a kelly-green bodice and skirt overlaid with black lace. Her gloves were new— black velvet embroidered with gold and green thread. She was truly a sight to admire, of beautiful form and face. A woman much wanted, but soon to be wasted if no husband was soon found. He said, "Snowbird is truly a magnificent specimen. Kissed by God with a keen acumen, sharp vision, talons of remarkable strength, and a heavenly beauty so rare it would make an angel weep. But all of her attributes are worth nothing unless she's made suitable for her purpose. A stunning but wild bird is a sacrilege, daughter. An upset in God's divine order.''

Rebecca looked at her father, then stared at the rolling hillocks around her. They were hawking on the common property—land owned equally by her father, her uncle Jorge, her uncle Solomon, and Miguel's father Hector. The conversos were indeed landed gentry. The vast acreage held not only wooded area for hawking, but fields for their livestock—cows, goats, and sheep. Each family owned its own manor house and stable which fronted the huge parcel. Dunstan and Thomas, being married men with families, lived on the back side of the land in modest twelve-room houses owned by their father. Next to her cousins' homes lay the skeletal frame of another house, one meant for her and Raphael. Rebecca had not passed by it since the day her betrothed had died.

Some day all the houses and land would pass to Benjamin, Dunstan, Miguel, and Jacob—Uncle Solomon's eldest son. Rebecca often wondered where Thomas fit in, but the thought of being without property never seemed to bother him.

Roderigo gently raised Rebecca's face until her eyes met his. "We mustn't upset the order, eh, Becca?"

Rebecca remained silent.

"Bah." Roderigo released her chin. "You've begged me to take you hawking with Snowbird ever since she was a wee eyas, and yet you watch her possess the sky and remain as stone. I should have thought you'd have been thrilled by the display of her hunt."

The retriever sprinted over to Roderigo and dropped the raven at his feet. The bird was still alive, gasping its last breaths. Roderigo picked up the blackbird by its talons and held it before Rebecca's eyes.

"Does the sight of blood weaken your stomach, daughter?"

Rebecca said, "Only if it's my own."

Roderigo laughed heartily, then said, "Here, here."

He pulled out a knife, and without flinching, bent the bird's neck backward and slit its throat. Immediately he turned the decapitated body upside down and let the blood run off. The dog went wild, lapping up the stream of fresh blood as it splashed to the ground.

Ritual slaughtering—the blessing over the animal to be butchered, the slitting of the throat. The conversos performed their religious duties with each bird caught by the hawks, be it alive or dead. Of course, slaughtering *live* birds was preferable, more in keeping with the customs of the old ways. Her father and uncles killed the domestic fowl in the same manner. The younger men were in charge of the big beasts—the cows and sheep.

Raphael and Benjamin would constrain the animal with ropes.
Miguel would pull back the head and Thomas would sever the
vessels of the neck in a single pass. Rebecca had once witnessed
the butchery of a sheep when she was a girl. The dumb thing
had thrashed about, bleated pathetically. The racket had been
horrifying. Thomas's hand never wavered. Afterward she vomited. Rebecca had been partially relieved when she learned that
Dunstan had no stomach for blood either. As an adult she out-
grew her squeamishness. Dunstan never did.

"My compliments on a job neatly done," Rebecca said.

Roderigo tossed the bird's head a distance of twenty feet. The
retriever darted after the scrap, his mouth drooling with hunger.

Rebecca said, "Why have you brought me out here, Father?"

"As I've stated, you've asked to accompany me and Snowbird
hawking."

"And that is the only reason? To satisfy my desires?"

"You're clever." Roderigo stroked her cheek. "You tell me."

"May I hold Snowbird?" she asked, slipping on a thick leather
glove.

"Can I trust you?"

"Yes."

Roderigo hesitated, then brought the falcon to Rebecca's extended arm. She pushed on the bird's chest. The falcon flapped
her wings, then hopped onto her glove. She giggled with delight.

"Father, she's splendid! Such strength! In the female species,
nonetheless. My heart is beating so rapidly, I'm so excited to
hold her." She turned to Roderigo. "Do you ever worry that
you'll not be able to reclaim her?"

"Every time I cast her aloft I worry that she'll fly away, or
become entangled in a tree and lose her plumage." Roderigo
paused. "But hawks must hawk . . . and women must marry.
The order of life."

Rebecca handed the falcon back to Roderigo and lowered her
head. Dressing as a man had been nothing more than a diversion—something done for excitement. When she'd stripped herself of male dress, all her freedom had fallen off. Gently she
touched her dueling scratch hidden under a velvet sleeve. She
said, "You've found me a husband, have you not?"

"Aye, in a manner of speaking." Roderigo called to his falconer. "Francis, take Snowbird back to the mew and hood her."
The doctor handed him the gyrfalcon and the dead raven. "I fear
the bright sun has made her exhausted," he said. "Make sure
you reward Snowbird with the kidneys and the heart of the
raven."

"As you say, Dr. Lopez," said Francis, smoothing Snowbird's feathers. He was a young, wiry man of nineteen with

feathery blond hair, a long nose, and close-set cornflower-blue eyes. Rebecca often wondered if the falconer was part hawk himself—a creation of a bird and some Olympic god in a moment of drunken stupor. She smiled at Francis, but he didn't notice.

"Snowbird seemed a bit unsteady on her left side," said the falconer.

"Aye?" said Roderigo.

"Ever so slightly, especially when she swoops north by northeast. I think her right ala should be cropped back a wee bit to aid her balance."

"Whatever you say," Roderigo said.

"And we're almost out of herbs necessary for her eyedrops, Dr. Lopez."

"Ask Martino for whatever you need," Roderigo said. "How fares the Queen's goshawk?"

"She is ready to be returned to the royal mew."

"Splendid, Francis," Roderigo exclaimed. "Well done."

"Thank you, Doctor." Francis kissed the bird's beak, closed her eyes, and hooded the falcon. "We've got a sweet treat for you, my beautiful lover," he cooed as he walked away.

Alone with Rebecca, Roderigo said, "Snowbird could well mint me hundreds of pounds if I sold her on the open market. But, alas, it is rumored that the Queen would take much pleasure in adding her to the royal yard."

"What are you going to do?" Rebecca asked.

"I shall offer the bird to Her Grace, of course. We all do things that we like not, eh, daughter?"

"Who is my husband to be?"

"I give you choices, Becca. I cosset you excessively. A weakness of mine that I should overcome!"

"What are my choices?"

"They are thus. You may become a maid of honor at court, or you may marry Miguel. Personally, I hope you select the latter. Better to have a legitimate heir with a woman than to have a bastard with a swain of noble birth."

Rebecca paused, confused. "I know not—"

"Don't *lie* to me, Becca! I know what you do when you're alone in the house."

Rebecca stared at him. Roderigo pulled out a brown cap decorated by a bent peacock feather from his doublet.

"Does this look familiar?" he asked. "It was found yesterday, snagged on one of the hedges."

"By whom?"

"Does it matter?"

"Aye, to me it does."

"By de Andrada, if you must know." Roderigo grabbed her shoulders. "Who does it belong to, Becca? Who are you dallying with behind my back?"

"Father, this cap belongs—" She stopped. If she admitted she had no lover and that the cap was Ben's, it would lead to many questions—reveal her preoccupation with dressing as a man. She knew her father would become more enraged by her games than by normal female desires.

"Go on," Roderigo said.

"I have nothing to say," Rebecca answered.

"Rebecca, how could you act so carelessly!" Roderigo cried. "You could be carrying a bastard in your belly this moment! Then, despite that face, who decent would want you, girl? No one!"

"Father—"

"Listen to me," Roderigo interrupted. "If you should decide to go to court, I would be much pleased if you'd flatter Essex, but keep your legs crossed—that is, if your womb is empty as I pray it should be. The last thing I need is a bastard grandchild by a bastard."

"May I—"

"Quiet! Interrupt not my thoughts." Roderigo began to pace. "If you're already with child, Becca, you must attract a man of noble lineage and much money, and bed him no matter how repulsive he be to you. Then, at least, if your bastard is a son, he should be well cared for. Just make sure he's well-stocked with land *and* gold."

"May I speak?"

"Not yet. If your womb is empty and you marry Miguel, I shall insist upon one *pure*-blooded male heir. Surely that's not too much to ask. After that I'm sure the boy would be happy to claim as his own any bastard that you'd produce and live the rest of his life contentedly with you in separate beds. After all, you two are fond of each other, are you not?"

"Yes, but—"

"Marriage to Miguel would serve thrice its purpose, Becca. The first would be a proper male heir, the second would be congenial companionship for life—that's not to be scoffed at. The third purpose, my dear daughter, would be a boon for you. You could sport with whomever you'd want without incurring the wrath of a jealous husband . . . as long as you were discreet."

There was a moment of silence.

"Well?" Roderigo asked.

"I'm not with child, Father."

"How can you be certain—"

"I'm certain because I have no lover. Furthermore, I find this conversation most distasteful."

"Aye, well . . ." Roderigo cleared his throat. "Becca—"

"Did de Andrada tell you I entertained a lover in your absence?"

"He made mention that he saw a certain fellow with this cap leaving the house."

"And you believed him, Father? A traitor? A known perjurer and thief? A man as slimy as an eel!"

The doctor reddened behind his ears. He said, "Was he lying, Becca? You tell me and I'll believe you."

"De Andrada lied if he told you that the fellow was my amour."

"Then who was he?"

"A friend, nothing more."

"His name?"

Rebecca cocked her head, thought, then said, "I cannot divulge his identity."

"Rebecca, I will not tolerate—"

"I've tolerated your intrigues, Father. And their consequences could bring much harm to me and Mother. Aye, they've already done their damage to your *true* servant, Raphael. Yet Mother and I say nothing, and we live in constant fear of exposure. We do as told with no questions asked. I guarantee you, Father, my friend is of no concern to you nor to your schemes."

"You must tell me his name."

"And if I refuse?"

Roderigo stared at her, then threw up his hands. "Do you see him often?"

"Not at all. Seldomly he shows up at my doorstep."

"Best to keep it that way."

"Yes," agreed Rebecca. "I swear to you with the truth in my throat that the man is not nor has ever been my lover."

Roderigo thought a minute, then said, "I believe you." He hugged her tightly. "I believe you. My God, I'm relieved! I stayed up half the night thinking about your future if you were with child. Thanks be to God you are not. You swear, aye?"

"I swear."

"God is merciful."

"So may we drop these ultimatums and carry on as if we've never had this conversation?"

Roderigo frowned. "No, Becca. Your choices still stand."

"But why? I have done nothing to dishonor you—"

"You are nearly eighteen and *unmarried*, Becca. That is enough to dishonor me! You show no interest in settling down to a proper life as an English gentlewoman. Your sewing is abysmal, your music teacher tells me you spend little time on your virginal lessons, rarely do you converse with your mother or your aunt—"

"I care not to gossip."

"You spend endless hours absorbed in books . . . or worse, dueling with your shadow in the orchard! You are not a man, Becca. You have no need of the skills of the fence! Learn what is *expected* of you!"

"I shall be more diligent in my proper studies," Rebecca said softly.

"No, daughter, your promises are no longer sufficient. You've sung that tune too often. You must marry or go to court. I have a responsibility toward your well-being, Becca, because I am your father and because I love you. I must stop allowing you to bend me to your will with your eyes and your pouts."

Keep calm, Rebecca told herself.

"I shall think about the choices, Father." She gathered up her skirt. "If you have nothing more to tell me, I should like to ride home now."

"I have something more to tell you."

Rebecca waited.

"I want your decision now," Roderigo said.

"This moment?"

"Aye."

"But that's not *fair*!" she protested.

Roderigo shrugged and said, "I care *not* what you think is fair, daughter."

"Why?" she yelled. "Why do you *molest* me with your incessant talk of marriage—"

Roderigo slapped her across the face. "You must learn to modulate the pitch of your voice, daughter. A shrew makes not a gentle wife."

Rebecca held her cheek and said nothing.

"I'm waiting," said Roderigo patiently.

"Apologies, Father."

"Accepted. Girl, if you had been *listening* to me for the past two months, if you'd been thinking of *me* instead of yourself, you'd have known that your betrothal—or lack thereof—had been a constant wound for me. If you care not to abet me, I shall dress the sore in *my* own way. Furthermore, daughter, I do not *molest* you with my talk. You molest *me* with your insolence."

Rebecca started to speak, then nodded instead.

"Give me an answer," Roderigo demanded.

Rebecca sighed. Court would allow her little freedom as long as the Queen desired her attention. Miguel, though far from perfect, would not question her comings and goings. And at least she was fond of him, finding him goodly company and an amusing storyteller. Their union would also get Dunstan off her back.

She could resist, plead, beg with tears to remain free. But the matter would just come up another time. She had no other alternatives, no position outside being a daughter or a wife. She was weary of fighting the inevitable.

"If it pleases you," she said, "I shall tell Mother to start the arrangement for my nuptials to Miguel." Thinking: the planning and trousseau would allow at least six months of freedom.

Roderigo smiled and kissed her cheek, then hugged her once again.

"Birth for me a healthy grandson," he said.

Rebecca smiled, her eyes gazing at the endless acres of wild land. One day the forests would be gone, plowed under for fields, thousands of years of nature done in by mankind's incessant need to tame. She felt her father's hand on her shoulder, felt his strong fingers massaging her flesh. She couldn't be angry with him. He was only doing what he thought was in her best interest. Still, a pity that the domesticated hawk never contemplated flying to freedom, a pity she was so trained as well.

19

The blade plunged into the ground. Rebecca gasped, dropped her book and brought her hand to her chest. Paralyzed, she watched the handle of the embedded sword quiver from the force of the stab, then slowly allowed her eyes to move sideways. At her left was a pair of legs housed in brown stockings. The thighs were thick and strong, ringed with yellow garters—rather ragged ones—resting slightly above the knees.

Her eyes climbed farther.

The round hose were paned in brown and yellow and badly frayed. Rebecca looked past the doublet and old-fashioned small ruff and examined the face.

Shakespeare.

It was the first time she'd seen him up close, and though he appeared close to middle age—in his late twenties—there was something boyish about him. His complexion was smooth and fair with a spot of blush on each cheek. He was round-faced with a straight sloping nose, curled red lips, and small ears, the left lobe adorned with a gold hoop. His hair was becoming sparse, but what tresses remained were colored as the leaves of autumn. But it was his eyes—ah, those eyes!—that muted her speech: full moons of bright blue that smiled as they stared back at her.

"Methinks you've misplaced that which trembles before you, gentlewoman," he said.

"Aye, my goodman," said Rebecca. "In the wrong shoulder."

Shakespeare laughed. "And for whose shoulder was it intended?"

"I know not, except twas not meant for you." Rebecca moved to the side of the bench and bade him to sit.

Shakespeare's eyes scanned over the grounds: ten acres of magnificent gardens bleeding into miles of pasture and uncultivated scrub. He wondered how much of the wild land was owned by her family, then directed his eyes back to the tended grounds. The gardens were by no means the biggest he'd ever seen, but they were among the most beautiful and unusual. To his right were orchards wealthy in foliage and fruit—clouds of emerald green dotted with shimmering sunlit jewels of fiery reds, deep plums, and golden apricots. Splitting the files of trees were rose-lined walkways, the stone pavers inset with hand-hewn diamonds of black marble that interlocked into sunburst patterns. To his left were formal gardens constructed around a reflection pool in the Venetian style—a long rectangular body of sparkling sapphire dappled with white water lilies. The hedges were a waist-high maze of yew, meticulously trimmed and crenellated, interspersed with columns of Italian cyprus and marble statuary.

They sat on a marble bench under a domed pergola fashioned from whitewashed planks of intricate oak latticework and shaded by the giant arms of a maple. Bordering the floor and hanging from the rafters were baskets of lilies, violets, and daffodils mixing their perfume with spring's sweet vapors. Fronting the gazebo were a pair of heart-shaped gardens rimmed with gillyflowers, hyssops, lavender, and cowslips—the knot gardens. Usually they were walled, but these were so splendid they remained open for all visitors to see. One plot hosted serpentine vines of melons, peppers, and cucumbers, the other was sown with neatly labeled rows of medicinal and cooking herbs.

But what amazed Shakespeare most were the plantings in between the hearts: a grove of miniature trees potted in shallow, brass trays filled with dirt, moss, and rock, the tallest of the arbors with a span of not more than two feet. Their tiny boughs sported the smallest leaves he'd ever laid eyes upon. Some of the branches sagged with pearl-sized fruit, others defied the forces of nature and drooped with full-sized cherries and apples. Shakespeare couldn't stop staring.

"Fascinating, eh?" Rebecca said. "They're stunted trees grown in Cipango, gifts to my parents from one of my relatives—a spice dealer who used to trade extensively with the Portuguese Jesuits on that continent."

"Are they living flora?"

"Aye. In autumn the leaves fall. In springtime they bloom and fruit. They are quite strong despite their reduced size, kept small by constant clipping and wires. My grandam cares for them exclusively and they thrive beautifully under her touch. The pines and maples are over fifty years old, the cherry and apple trees are much younger."

"The branches hold such heavy fruit—it's contrary to the laws of God."

"It is," Rebecca said.

"But," Shakespeare added with a twinkle in his eye, "the heathens of the East know not of the divine order."

"Then the English will have to educate them," Rebecca said, smiling.

"A pity if we do," said Shakespeare. "Once the heathens are learned, their trees will realize they're in error of nature and drop their oversized fruit."

"Then mayhap it's best to let the East remain in its spiritual ignorance."

"Aye, for the sake of the trees."

Rebecca nodded, lowered her eyes and said, "I thank you for returning the weapon, sir."

"I'm no knight."

"In title, this is true. But one who spares a life, risking his honor *and* the displeasure of his audience, is more than a knight to me."

"Then your conceited knight shall dub you his lady."

Rebecca blushed, cocked her head to her shoulder. Shakespeare glanced at her, smiled quickly, then returned his eyes to the midget trees. Two weeks ago he'd been locked in combat with this woman. What an ass he'd been. Instead of fighting with her, he should have been bedding her. An exquisite creature— one that defied description. Everything about her was delectable. Had Venus been fashioned after her, Adonis would have been groveling at her feet.

Rebecca ran her fingertips across the handle of the rapier. "The weapon's owner shall be very pleased to see it again. He has been most spleenish since it was discovered missing. You see, the sword wasn't mine to sport with in the first place."

"It belongs to your first cousin. Sir Thomas Ames, a well-sized man of nineteen with a complexion the color of a peach and textured equally as such . . . the younger son of your uncle, Sir George Ames."

Rebecca stared at him. At last she said, "Aye."

"Sir Thomas's reputation in the art of the fence precedes him greatly. Whenever I spoke of him, eyes would widen, and ere long I'd be pelted with diverse tales of his swordsmanship."

"How did you come to know the sword as his?"

"The handle is distinctively engraved with his initials and the Ames coat-of-arms."

"And you recognized the weapon from the heraldry?"

Shakespeare smiled. "I didn't recognize the coat-of-arms. However, there is an ever-so-slight solder line fusing the two halves of the cross guard—a repair, one done with much precision. I took it to the best bladesmith in all of London, Master John Cutlass, and he identified it immediately as his work and the sword as your cousin's. I have in my belt his dagger as well."

Shakespeare pulled the smaller weapon from its sheath and lay it on the palm of his hand. "Perfect balance."

"It's imported," said Rebecca. "From the city of Innsbruck in Austria."

"I knew as much." He offered her the handle. "How does your arm fare?"

"A scratch, sir. And how is your shoulder?"

"It mends very well, thank you."

"Does it impede your duties on the stage?"

"I have no duties on stage. The Master of the Revels ordered the theaters bolted shut a week ago."

Rebecca stared at him. She said,

"I've not ventured from my house since our duel two weeks ago . . . save to go abirding. The plague is back, then?"

"Aye. June has just arrived, with it the warmer weather. The trench diggers work all day, and still not enough pits have been dug. The bodies lay exposed, decomposing faster in the mild air—an assault upon the nose as well as the eyes. Only the maggots benefit."

Rebecca should have known something was amiss. Lately her father had spent little time at home, rising well before dawn and not returning until late at night. The wards of Bartholomew's must be overflowing with the ill, she thought. Nothing could be done for them, may God have pity on their souls. She felt her stomach sink. May God protect her father from their noxious air.

"You're troubled," Shakespeare stated.

Rebecca stated, "My father is a physician. I worry about his health."

"Does your father have a country home?"

"He does."

"Cannot your family take up the summer months there?"

"My father will never abandon the sick who depend on him for succor."

"What about you?"

She shook her head. Shakespeare asked why.

Rebecca said, "My father often has need of my services. I prepare his medicines, run the stillroom."

"Surely a servant can—"

"Where will *you* go?" Rebecca asked, changing the subject. Then she covered her mouth. "I mean not to pry."

"I take no offense," said Shakespeare. "I have several options. My wife's family has a gentle English home in Wilmcote, in my native shire of Warwick. If necessary I can return there, though I, too, prefer to remain in London even in these troubled times. I have business here that requires my attention."

There was a moment of silence.

"Your *wife*?" Rebecca asked.

Shakespeare felt his cheeks go hot and cursed himself. With one slip of the tongue she now knew he was married. Any plans he had for seduction were ruined. As if such a fair woman would have ever considered him worthy of her attention. Still, it had been a beautiful fantasy, had turned his innards warm. Now it had dissolved like sugar in boiling water. He smiled weakly and said, "Yes, m'lady, I have a wife."

Rebecca said nothing.

Shakespeare shrugged. As long as his marriage was known, he might as well tell her everything. "I have three children as well."

Rebecca hesitated, then asked, "Do they reside in London?"

"No."

"No?"

"No."

"Do you miss your wife greatly?"

"At times."

"And is this one of those times?"

Shakespeare's response was laughter. Rebecca felt herself go hot. She said,

"I've overstepped the boundaries of decency, sir. Please forgive—"

"No forgiveness is necessary."

"You are too kind," Rebecca said, smoothing her skirt.

Shakespeare glanced at the fallen book and picked it up. He asked, "In what tongue is this written?"

"Arabic. It's a book of verse."

"What other languages do you read?"

"Latin, Greek, Spanish, Portuguese, Italian, French . . . German after a fashion, though I cannot read it with fluency." Rebecca gave him a shy smile.

"You impress me, mistress," Shakespeare said. "Where were you schooled?"

"In a hayloft."

"Pardon?"

"I was taught by my kinsmen."

"And a liquid-tongued group they must be."

"We have many relatives all over the Continent. My uncle is a duke in North Africa."

"Than I shall call you lady in earnest."

"No. We're not nobility on the Isle."

"Yet it is said that your father sees Her Majesty more often than most of the peers."

"The 'Spanish' upstart!" Rebecca mocked.

Shakespeare said, "I didn't mean offense."

"None taken." Rebecca laughed. "I have ears as well. Let the gossip mongers nurse their wounds of jealousy. My father has studied arduously for the honor of being Her Majesty's physician. Their viciousness doesn't affect him or me."

She turned and faced him. His eyes were playful, flirtatious. All he needed was a pittance of encouragement and he'd be on his knees, kissing her hand. Not that she minded the thought. He was attractive in the way older men sometimes are—as men of experience. But at the moment she was more interested in answers. She asked,

"Shakespeare, why did you stare at me so unrelentingly as I stood in the pit?"

"My error."

"What was it about me that captivated you?"

"Forgive me for what I say. I don't mean to malign the purity of your soul, but I thought you were a witch."

"I?"

"Aye," echoed Shakespeare.

She laughed. "And why did you think me a mistress of black magic?"

Shakespeare took a deep breath. "I owe you an explanation, and I hope you think this one not too daft, but the night before the fateful day of our duel, I was visited by a spirit that claimed to be my deceased mentor. He hit me on the head and laced my sack with sleeping potion."

"God's blood, what did the spirit want?"

"It's a long, long tale," Shakespeare said, waving his hand into the air. "When I woke up in the morning, my ordinarily rational thoughts were tumbled. Then I saw you standing in the pit . . . as a man. I swore I remembered you as a woman at the funeral of my mentor. Illogically, methought you must have been a witch, the evil spirit that had visited me the previous night."

She folded her hands in her lap. "I assure you I am no witch."

"I am assured."

"But I confess to my prevarication. You did see me at the cemetery that day."

"Who died?" Shakespeare asked. "Or is it I who now overstep the bounds of decency?"

Rebecca shook her head. "Twas my intended, may God be with him."

"Rest be to his ashes," whispered Shakespeare. "How did he succumb to his demise?"

"He was mur—" Rebecca stopped herself. "He . . . fell ill to Black Death. I must be gone—"

Shakespeare grabbed her arm. "He was *murdered*?"

"No," Rebecca protested.

But Shakespeare knew it was a lie, and it excited him. Maybe their meeting at the cemetery wasn't a coincidence. As unlikely as it appeared, maybe there was some kind of connection between the two murders. He said, "Tell me the truth, fair one. How he was slain?"

"*Now*, good man, you've crossed the line marked decency."

"Now bad manners have reason. I buried my friend, but someone else nailed the coffin. Harry was murdered."

"Many murders happen in this city. It's a haven for the lawless."

"So you admit your intended was murdered."

Rebecca said nothing.

"Your secret is safe with me," Shakespeare said.

She remained silent.

"What if the murders were done with the *same* hand?" asked Shakespeare.

"My intended was not killed in London."

"Neither was Harry . . . my friend whom I buried," said Shakespeare excitedly.

"My intended was not killed in this country."

Shakespeare said nothing, felt his stomach drop. Two separate, unrelated murders. Nothing unusual. He wasn't sure why he was disappointed, but he was. Maybe he longed to be connected to this woman by something tangential. Any excuse to see such a face again.

"My lips are loose today," sighed Rebecca. "My father shall inter me if he finds out what I've told you."

"You've no worry about that. I'm honorable."

A moment of silence passed.

Rebecca asked, "Where was Harry murdered?"

"On the open road . . . up North."

Rebecca noticed his face had become mournful. "You loved him dearly."

Shakespeare said, "Yes, I loved him dearly. I'd been trying to discover his slayer."

"Any thoughts as to whom he may be?"

"A highwayman has been suggested," Shakespeare said.

Rebecca heard doubt in his voice. "And you think not?"

Shakespeare said, "I think it could be anyone, from the most insignificant to the most sublime." He smiled. "Even you are not above suspect."

Rebecca returned his smile, but Shakespeare became suddenly grave.

"I *need* to find Harry's slayer, so his soul may be put to rest. Yet the ghost that visited my closet warned me to arrest my inquiry."

"The same one that hit you."

"Yes."

"It spoke to you first?"

"Aye."

"Then it hit you."

"Exactly."

"Then perhaps you were not visited by a ghost. Rather, you were visited by Harry's killer disguised as a ghost."

"My thoughts, fair lady."

"Couldn't you distinguish between a ghost and a man dressed as a ghost?"

"In daylight it would have been easy. But remember that my mind had been made sleepy."

"Poor man."

Shakespeare regarded her face. Her eyes were teasing. A small smile was upon her lips. He felt a sting in his loins.

She said, "And has the spirit dampened your spirit?"

"Not a whit. I intend to resume my inquiries with much vigor. And now that the theaters are closed I haven't the former constraints of time."

"Have you had any hap in your search for your friend's murderer?"

"I visited the North. Harry was last seen in a small burg called Hemsdale."

"I've never heard of it."

"Neither had I until this whole thing happened. It's an ordinary hamlet with its array of colorful people. None seemed like murderers. Harry had last been seen there. But instead of mingling with Hemsdale's inhabitants, he'd been seen quarreling with London's most feared uprightman—"

"George Mackering."

"The very one," said Shakespeare.

Rebecca nodded. "He's an expert with the rapier, Shakespeare. Almost as good as my cousin, Thomas. In fact, twas Thomas who first spoke of him. They used to sport together years ago when Thomas was fifteen. My cousin bested him easily even then."

"Mayhap your cousin would like to go after Harry's slayer," said Shakespeare.

"You think Mackering killed Harry?"

"I don't know. But I'd like to find the ruffian. He's the only one who can tell me of Harry's last days."

"Shall I ask my cousin about Mackering for you?" Rebecca said.

Shakespeare said, "No, I pray you don't. Best if you keep your distance from the unclean affair."

"It's no bother, Shakespeare," Rebecca said. "Besides, I owe you for my life which was once in your hands."

"Your life was never in my hands, Mistress Rebecca Lopez. It was my error in the first place that caused us both so much grief." He brushed his fingers against her arm. "Yet I am glad it happened and we've had a chance to meet."

Rebecca blushed, then said, "The alchemy of turning bad hap to good. Had you not found me, I would have searched for you." She added quickly, "For my cousin's weapons, I mean."

"Speaking of weapons . . ." Shakespeare pulled out another dagger. "Do you recognize this? It was thrown at my chest after our duel."

Rebecca inspected the poniard. "It's not one of mine—my cousin's, I mean."

"I thought as much," Shakespeare said. "But it was worth a try."

"Then someone is still after you."

"I think so."

"The midnight ghost?"

Shakespeare shrugged.

"At least allow me to give the dagger to my cousin for you?" she asked. "If anyone can identify it, Thomas can."

Shakespeare thought a moment. "Only if you promise me not to mention Mackering. The name will arouse too much curiosity. It's not good for you or me."

"Agreed." Rebecca looked at the blade again. "It's an old weapon."

Shakespeare said, "Tempered during the first years of the Tudor reign . . . see the wear and the rust . . . at least one hundred years old. And it's not the craftsmanship of a true sword maker—the blade is too imbalanced, the honing too crude."

Rebecca regarded the dagger, gripped the handle and held the blade to the sunlight. "I shall take this to Thomas and report back to you."

Another chance to see her. Shakespeare felt the sting again. He knew he should be ashamed of himself—a middle-aged man with a wife and children, panting like a dog over his bitch. But he couldn't help what his head was feeling.

He tried to speak calmly. "Where shall we meet?"

"Not in my garden," Rebecca said. "How did you sneak in here?"

"I climbed the fence. All my leaps on stage have sculpted me strong legs."

"Well, we can't meet here anymore," Rebecca said. "I'm to be betrothed to another. Your presence alone with me in my father's garden would impugn the honor of my newly intended."

It was Shakespeare's turn to stare. He asked, "And who had the good fortune to ensnare such a woman?"

"The brother of my first beloved."

"Is it not a sin?" Shakespeare asked.

"Not among my—" Rebecca cursed her mouth. "My father thinks not."

"I wish you much good fortune."

"Thank you."

Silence. Eventually Rebecca said,

"Shall we meet at Paul's?"

"You may go out in public unescorted?"

She smiled. "If I am dressed as a man."

"Your father allows you to do such things?"

Rebecca said nothing.

"I thought not," Shakespeare said. "Yet I remember well your footwork. You can defend yourself. So Paul's it will be Saturday at the noon hour."

"Not Saturday," Rebecca said. She dare not profane her sabbath, especially for such a whimsical tryst.

"Is Monday more suitable?" Shakespeare asked.

"Yes."

"Monday, then. At Paul's. I'll buy you fare and drink."

"I shall be there." Rebecca studied the blade again. "Shakespeare, this is not only rust on the blade. It's *blood* as well. See how easily this spot peels off. And these spots over here. They've not eaten into the metal as rust does.''

Shakespeare grabbed the dagger. ''You've the eyes of a hawk, mistress, and a keen mind to match. I pity anything you desire as prey.''

Rebecca felt herself go hot again, chided herself for blushing like an unschooled milkmaid.

''Simply my eye has seen dried blood diverse times,'' she said. ''I often clean my father's surgery knives.''

''Aye, it's blood,'' Shakespeare said. ''*Whose* blood, is the question.''

''What kind of man does not keep his weapons clean?'' Rebecca asked.

''A man who cares not if his weapons are lost in his victims' hearts.''

20

June fifteenth, a fortuitous day according to the stars, marked the official engagement of Miguel Pedro Nuñoz and Rebecca Anne Lopez. The feast and festivities were held in the Lopez's Great Hall of Holborn. Course upon course was laid on long wooden tables—beef and mutton stewed with figs and walnuts, capons and grouse stuffed with barley, oats, and wildflowers, red deer roasted in an open pit, kid boiled in spirits, garlic duck baked with apples and apricots, veal and venison braised with honey, and whole white-fleshed cod poached in cider.

A notable absence of pork, one nobleman pointed out.

Platters of vegetables accompanied the meats—cucumbers, wild greens and flowers, cabbage, turnips, radishes, and potatoes imported from Portugal. After the flesh and roots came dessert plates heaped with sweets. There were flowers of marchpane, castles of sugar bread, confits, and fruit suckets, and gingerbread men topped with caps of sugared violets. A center table held gold trays of gellifs molded into diverse mythical shapes—dragons, minotaurs, centaurs, and the virginal unicorn. Side tables were weighted down with huge silver washing bowls filled with nut-brown ale for dunking roasted crabs—apples singed in fire until they sizzled with sugary juices.

And how copiously flowed the spirits. Sack, port, and the finest wines—premium vintage theologicum, clergy wine, as well as the heavier Italian and lighter French varieties—sloshed in tankards and heavy pewter pots. The women imbibed lighter drink—beer, ale, cider, perry, and for the especially delicate stomach, dulcet mead of honeycomb and water.

Fifty extra servants, hired to accommodate the hundreds of guests, carried away silver trays and wooden trenchers of untouched food and flung it at the huddles of beggars gathered outside the kitchen door. The poor pounced upon the remains, ripping flesh off bones like vultures ravishing a carcass, stuffing their mouths until their cheeks grew to pouches.

The banqueting lasted late into the evening. Torches were lit, and armfuls of seasoned logs were dumped into the central pit. The wood was consumed in a blaze of God's wrath, and the crowd cheered each sudden crack of wood, each exploding plume of smoke.

At the conclusion of the meal began the entertainment. The first act consisted of jugglers tossing into the air knives and axes, catching them as easily as a child does a tennis ball. The final feat had them balancing halberds and pikes upon their chins and feet while dancing on their hands. Next were the contortionists, squeezing their bodies into foot-diameter barrels. Then came the tumblers and fire eaters.

The crowd grew restless from lengthy sitting; a quintet of musicians was summoned for dancing. They played upon viole da gambas, soft recorders and hautbois, pipes and tabors, and the ear-piercing fife. The night was culminated by the performance of Augusto Toon—the finest balladeer in the Isle. Strumming on his lute, the contratenor sung treacle-sweet songs of love, his compositions written specifically for the intended couple.

Rebecca bowed her head demurely as the balladeer sang. *Gods, to endure such an ordeal!* Her father was drunk, her mother nearly overcome with exhaustion. Her cousins, who had been feuding vocally all evening, sat opposite one another cooling the heat of their fierce words. Marry, a duel betwixt the Añoz brothers had nearly been challenged, and when Dunstan's wife—poor, fat Grace—tried to intercede in the name of family peace, she was immediately slapped in the face by Dunstan. Finally Jorge insisted the men end their childish spat, lest the power of the spirits change knight into knave.

And then there was *Benjamin*. Rebecca's brother had come in from Venice sprouting healthy color and much confidence. The reason for his merry countenance was on his arm—the Countess of Pinario, a widow twelve years his senior, a woman of much lineage and little money. She was beautiful, Rebecca thought, in that special way that drove young men daft and their mothers equally as mad. Piles of blond hair topped a smooth, fair face. Peeking from heavy lashes were flashing blue eyes, wide and innocent from afar, hard and cold from up close. Her lips formed an eternal pout and were colored like cranberries. The stomacher of her dress framed a tiny waist, but the bodice of the gown supported white melons that gently shook as she walked.

Rebecca's mother was horrified by Ben's choice, her father was initially appalled as well, until the countess smiled at him in a certain ill-advised manner. Roderigo had danced a galliard with her, and Benjamin was most pleased that Father had found his woman friend charming. During a pavane, Rebecca's mother had pulled her aside and wept openly in her arms. Roderigo had sinned with diverse wenches over their years of marriage, Mother had confessed, but this one—this *countess*—would cause an open scandal. Could not Rebecca speak some proper words to Father in order to avert such an event?

It was a worn story. Each time Father found a new mistress, Mother was sure that *this* one would cause much dishonor and shame to the family. Once, Rebecca had suggested that her mother stop concerning herself with her father's lovers and find one of her own.

Mother had been aghast!

Rebecca sighed, answered that Father was inclined not to listen to her lowly advice, but she'd do what she was able.

Her mother bathed her face in kisses.

As Toon began another ballad, Rebecca regarded her father leering at the countess's bosom. He lifted his eyes, caught Rebecca staring at him, reddened, then smiled.

Rebecca smiled back and blew him a kiss.

Dear Lord, she prayed, *allow me strength to disguise my true feelings until the mockery is over.* She glanced at Miguel. They hadn't exchanged more than a dozen words the entire day. He sat so rigid, with that sickly smile frozen on his face. His complexion had turned even greener the last hour. He had sopped up excessive port for fortification, but the drink had overtaken him, wreaking havoc on his muscular body. Rebecca touched his hand and gave him a smile of sympathy. Miguel nodded, then took a deep breath and held his stomach.

Toon was about to begin another love song when the unmistakable sound of heaving reverberated in the hall. A servant immediately rushed to the stricken one with rags and a bowl. Roderigo stood and with a wave of his hand commanded Toon to begin the ballad.

"At least I was not the first," Miguel whispered to Rebecca.

Rebecca smiled and whispered back, "How art thou faring?"

Miguel saw his father beaming at him. Through tightly drawn, smiling lips he said, "As well as can be expected."

"I love thee," Rebecca said, squeezing his hand.

Miguel said, "I love thee too. There isn't anything I wouldn't do for thee, my Becca. I'll apologize for my shortcomings—my limitations—and promise to make thee a fine husband within my capacity."

He kissed her hand with soft lips and returned his attention back to Toon. Rebecca looked at her betrothed. A very handsome man he was—strong, fearless, God-fearing, and imbued with valor. Perhaps her father had been correct in insisting that they marry. Miguel would make the perfect father of her children. Aye, he would be her children's *father*. Though Miguel would never question her, she'd not force him to claim her bastards as his own.

She had found a good man to marry. A kind man, well-formed, with a pleasing face.

Rebecca sighed.

If only . . .

21

This time Rebecca was careful. Disguised and clothed in her brother's garb, she opened the door to her bedchamber and peeked down the hall. De Andrada was nowhere to be seen. She tiptoed down the stairs, sneaked into the kitchen, and exited the house through the door to the pantry, the side opposite Grandmama's closet. Once free, she ran through the garden and turned onto Holborn Road.

Shakespeare leaped in front of her. She gasped, then said,

"You've become your midnight spirit, good fellow. You seem to appear out of air."

"Did I cause you fright?" he asked.

Rebecca took a deep breath, tried to calm her galloping heart. She shook her head no, her eyes affixed to his. There it was—that twinkle.

Lowering her lashes, she said, "Good morrow."

"And a good morrow to you, my most *beautiful* fellow," he said.

"I thank you for your kind words, honorable man."

"Kind words that you repay in kind. And so this most honorable man does offer this gentlewoman his honor."

She said, "And gentlewoman does honor his offer."

He said,

> *"A woman once offered her honor*
> *to a man who honored her offer*
> *So passed a night*
> *of heavenly delight*
> *Sporting much on-er and off-er."*

Rebecca burst into laughter. "You're playing the piper Pan this morning."

"A beguiling woman dressed as a man makes me daft."

"I thank you for accompanying me to Paul's."

"The pleasure is mine, mistress."

Rebecca smiled, then gazed at her feet. She felt light-headed and warm. After that horrible event called her betrothal feast, she longed for something airy and impulsive, something that would bring out the child rather than the matron in her. Ugh, the thought of marriage and pregnancy. Her eyes climbed upward to his face, then back to the ground. In her brother's boots her feet looked enormous.

They walked down Holborn past four estate homes—three- and four-story houses layered with brick and ornamented with embrasured parapets, turrets emblazoned with balustrades, multiple-peaked roofs, and mullion windows where once were simple holes covered with wood lattice. Great structures of many rooms and landscaped demesne.

The sun shone brightly in the midday sky; no fog, no damp air that seeped into the marrow, only sweet vapors that warmed the lungs. A mild spring day, summer still three weeks away. They stepped in silence, exchanging sidelong looks and occasional shy smiles. A half hour later, as they approached Grey's Inn, the estates suddenly disappeared, replaced by modest wooden houses resting on dirt patches and fronted by beds of flowers. Shakespeare led Rebecca first to Fetter Lane, then twenty minutes later onto Fleet Street—the eastern road leading to the entrance of Londontown. The private homes were gone. Instead stood crumbling, abutted buildings, overcrowded with people and overtaken by rats.

Shakespeare asked, "Have you word from your cousin about the dagger I'd given you?"

Rebecca stopped, pulled out the dagger from her belt and handed it to him. "The metal is old, and the bladesmith was not a man of much skill."

"And?"

"Sir Thomas is of the opinion that the blade was crafted in the northern region. He remembered many Scottish daggers having a similar edge angulation in relationship to the shaft of the blade itself. Sir Thomas thinks that whoever fashioned this dagger found an old discarded Scottish weapon in a scrap pile and personalized it for his use."

"His use being *murder*."

"It would seem thus."

They resumed walking.

"Who would desire you murdered, Shakespeare?"

"The one who murdered Harry."

"And if I may be so bold to ask, who would want Harry murdered?"

"Mackering holds the key to that lock."

"Why would Mackering want to murder Harry?"

Shakespeare shrugged. "I don't know for certain. Harry was found dicing with this ruffian. I think my friend had gambled his soul into heavy debt."

"So why would Mackering murder Harry? Surely the rogue would never recover the money owed to him if his dupe—no offense meant to your mentor—were . . . not among the living."

"You may say dead."

"Dead, then."

Shakespeare said nothing.

Rebecca asked, "Was your friend a man of much means?"

"Modest means," Shakespeare answered. "But he had enough money to pay off an occasional gambling debt."

"And many resources from which to borrow?"

"Yes. There was not a player in our fellowship who would not have sold the shirt off his back for Harry. Gods, how many times we've picked up the tab for his drink."

"Had you ever seen Harry dice in London?" Rebecca asked.

"No."

"Gamble at the baiting arenas?"

"Not at all."

"Bet on a duel?"

"Never."

"So it appears that Harry gambled only when he traveled to the North."

"If he gambled at all."

"And Mackering?" Rebecca said. "It is known that the uprightman spends most of his time in London."

"Yes."

"So what was the ruffian doing up North?" Rebecca asked.

"I know not."

"I would think the riddle would best be solved by another trip to the North, the home of the dagger."

"Perhaps," Shakespeare said. "But first I set my sights on Mackering. He was the last known person to see Harry alive. As long as Mackering is in London—and I believe he is—I should like to speak with him first. Then, if his information necessitates another trip up North, so be it."

"You don't seem the least bit worried about dealing with Mackering."

"I'll be careful."

"He holds a ruthless reputation."

"I'll be *most* careful."

Rebecca rolled her eyes. Shakespeare definitely wasn't stupid. Which meant he had to be either fearless or naive. It was obvious that he'd never met Mackering. Rebecca had. Once. Once had been enough. Thomas had arranged a contest of swords in the middle of the common property with Mackering and had allowed her to tag along. Mackering had been flawlessly polite to her, but the eyes had been deadly. Mucoid green. Evil. Thomas had noticed Mackering's unhealthy gaze. Her cousin had reddened with anger, bested the ruffian in only a half hour. Afterward Thomas had told her to stay away from Mackering.

Exactly what I had in mind, Tommy.

Rebecca sighed, allowed her fingers to rest on his arm. "Pray, do be cautious. Please."

Shakespeare nodded, touched by her concern. Though she was costumed like a lad, her beauty was still evident. Nothing could hide it. As a woman, she excited him. But dressed in manly garb, she evoked in him a feeling of warmth, feelings of friendship.

The people on the street began to thicken into crowds, and along with the throng came the sounds of the city—the cries of the mongers, the banging of the builders, and the ever-present bells.

They passed the Fleet, trodding over the Thames, then entered the walled city through Ludgate.

The stench was immediate.

Piles of bodies lay on the open streets, some of them putrefied, nothing more than skeletal frames under black taut skin. The eyes had been hollowed out by rats and maggots, the mouths open cavities in which nested hordes of vermin, beetles, and flies; skin textured by blotches and buboes of the plague; intact brown tongues hung over blue, mottled lips. A blond girl of no more than ten lay atop the mound of corpses, her muscles still twitching, eyelids fluttering. A beggar was yanking off her skirt, another pulling off her sleeves. Around the bodies burned pyres of fragrant wood. The aromatic scent did little to mask the stink.

Adjacent to the human heaps were shallow pits, some half filled with bodies, some still being dug deeper by laborers sweating in the noon-hour sun. One of the workers, a dwarf, rested on the handle of his spade, the top of the blade buried in the stomach of a corpse. He spat, bit off a piece of dried meat, and chewed as the innards of the dead man coated his tool with blood.

Rebecca had witnessed death countless times at her father's side as he attended the wretches stuffed into the wards at St. Bartholomew's, aiding him again while he ministered to the most famous lords in London. She had seen her own parents bury her four brothers and sisters, her kinsmen stricken with each new outbreak of disease and pestilence. But never had she seen such quantity of dead concentrated in one small area. She averted her eyes and covered her mouth.

"Are you ill?" Shakespeare asked.

She shook her head no.

"Are you certain?"

"Quite certain."

"Come," said Shakespeare. "We'll run by Paul's and go down Thames Street. The air smells not so rotten there."

Rebecca followed. She said, "I had no idea that London had become so foul."

"You father is quite the man to brave this daily," Shakespeare said.

"He calls Bartholomew's the cemetery of the living," Rebecca said. "Yet I've seen him dispense his medical duties diverse times. He greets the sick with a smile on his face and much cheer in his heart. He treats the stricken as if they were his kinsmen."

"Your father has a strong stomach," Shakespeare said. "This way, mis—sir."

They hadn't walked more than a minute when they were espied by a group of beggars. The poor rushed to their side, grabbing ankles and thighs, stretching bony hands upward in desperate supplication. Rebecca knew that few were officially licensed for begging; they had no authority to request alms and should be arrested immediately and placed in the stocks. She also knew that among the helpless were sturdy beggars— able-bodied men who could work a day of honest labor if they were so inclined. She tried to ignore the wretches, but her eyes refused to harden her heart. A pockmarked hand grabbed her arm, a solitary eye beseeched her face; the eye's mate was nothing more than an empty socket.

"A groat, good sir, for a wretched soldier tossed overseas by the accursed Spanish—"

Shakespeare pushed her forward. "If you show pity to one, the rest shall become as leeches."

Rebecca said, "I—"

"A farthing, good sir," interrupted a legless man. He moved his truncated body forward by swinging it between his arms. "I was once a whole-bodied man as yourself, sir, but the evil Spanish blew off my legs in battle in eighty-nine. Under Sir Francis Drake I did serve, amongst his fleet I did sail, but alas the conditions of the sea were treacherous, and the poxed men of Philip, may they rot in Gehenna, took advantage of the good and honest English."

Rebecca pulled out a farthing. The man pushed on his palms and jumped upward on his stumps, snatching the coin between his teeth. Within seconds a score of beggars began to shove open palms into Rebecca's face. Shakespeare took her hand, jerked her away from the black cloud of the destitution, and ran. They slowed their pace a minute later.

"Such misery they endure," Rebecca said, breathing hard. "They are nothing more than today's gladiators, marking their days before they're devoured by lions called Black Death and starvation."

"Death would be sweet sleep for them, so pathetic is their lot." Shakespeare gently nudged her shoulder and said, "Come, sir, erase from the canvas of your mind so pitiable a painting."

Rebecca raised her eyes to his, finding comfort in them. It was strange to find warmth in such light eyes, yet they were welcoming. Her body suddenly became aware of him, how close they were to one another, her right shoulder grazing his left upper arm. She lowered her head and walked in silence, thinking it immoral to feel such sudden physical excitement amid such ugly squalor.

A body, dropped from above, landed in front of their path— a dehydrated boy covered with boils.

Rebecca muttered a dear God.

"This way," Shakespeare said, trying to push her away from the corpse. "The tavern's not far."

"I've no appetite for dinner," she said.

"You must harden your stomach," Shakespeare said tightly. "Contemptible is a man who is able not to quaff ale freely while looking death in the eye."

Rebecca sighed. "Then tis good that the beard is removable. Much as I try, I'm a slave of my emotions."

"God created women different from men, sir. You would not be true to your sex if you walked through these streets unaffected."

"Aye."

They hurried through Paul's. Shakespeare gave her a gentle pat. "How long has it been since you've seen the city?"

"Since our duel. It has become a muck heap."

"And the muck increases by the hour."

"Gardy loo," shouted a voice from an upper window. Shakespeare yanked Rebecca to his right as the contents from a chamberpot splattered on the cobblestones just a yard to their left.

"As if to prove the prophecy of my words," Shakespeare muttered. He swept his arm across the fouled streets and boomed in a theatrical voice, "Cousin and foreigner alike, a goodly welcome from the jeweled scepter of the sea called England!"

A Puritan pointed an angry finger at him and growled, "Until the Devil has been purged, sin shall clog the bowels of this land."

"Then we'd better give the land a purging," Shakespeare said.

"Sinners!" the Puritan shouted. "I know ye all, know ye evil ways."

Rebecca interrupted the fanatic's speech by laughing in his stern face—not a laugh of derision but one of released tension from Shakespeare's awful joke. The Puritan's black eyes became hot with outrage, and Rebecca would have offered her apologies to the black-garbed mountebank, but Shakespeare pulled her along.

A moment later Rebecca said, "The abbeys on the continent situate themselves on mountains. One reason is an earnest desire to be in isolation, that one may become closer to the Almighty when few distractions present themselves. The other stems from the ability to strategically place their jakes on downhill streams and runoffs. The cities below receive such gifts from the men of God."

"And from where did you learn that juicy bit of knowledge?" Shakespeare asked.

"My kinsmen have their fingers in many men's pies."

Shakespeare said, "Among your diverse relations are monks?"

"Not at all." Rebecca smiled cryptically. "As false an assumption as saying I've had relations with diverse monks."

It was Shakespeare's turn to laugh.

A man crusted with sores blocked their path. He was naked from the waist up, a filthy sheet tied around his middle. His hose were torn and blackened with mud, his toes sticking out of holes in his shoes, and his arm inked with the initials F.R. His wrists were red and raw, as if recently manacled, and his hands flapped at his sides. He shouted,

"Now, good sir, what will you give this poor Tom this morrow, wisely and well?" He let go with a high-pitched squeal. "Please, sir, a pound of sheet feathers to make poor Tom a blanket, or a cross of silver to buy poor Tom a shirt and breeches, wisely and well."

"We'll be giving you a leaky heart if you'll not leave our sight," Shakespeare said.

Poor Tom rolled his head, hiccuped, then spat. To Shakespeare he said, "Good sir. A farthing for a drink, wisely and well." He attempted to dance a jig but tripped instead. He shouted, "God save the Queen and her council."

"The man is besotted or daft," Rebecca said to Shakespeare.

"Or desires us to think him so."

"A groat for a pair of shoes to cover poor Tom's aching feet, wisely and well," Poor Tom screamed out.

"Away," Shakespeare commanded. Poor Tom laughed and started to speak, but immediately silenced his wisely and wells when Shakespeare's hand held the hilt of his sword.

"Away," Shakespeare repeated, drawing his sword.

Poor Tom fled.

They resumed their walk, turning onto Bread Street, elbowing their way through the crowds. After they'd walked a mile, Rebecca asked,

"How far is your alehouse?"

"Another ten minutes from here."

A lord bumped into Rebecca, looked at her clothes, said nothing and walked away.

"Unmannered churl," she muttered.

"He's whittled," said Shakespeare.

"But through drunken eyes he was still able to determine I was of lower rank."

"Tis your clothes. Next time, don the dress of a lord. As long as you playact, you may as well receive honor and title." Shakespeare paused, then said, "But enough blather about rank. All stomachs empty. Come, good sir, let us dine."

"I've yet a stomach," she said.

"Still come with me hence," Shakespeare persisted. "If for no other reason than to remove ourselves from the streets."

The Mermaid was a small tavern between Watling and Cheapside, a comfortable place where many bookwriters came to quench their thirst as well as joust in bouts of wordplay. It seemed to Shakespeare that as soon as they stepped upon its threshold, a black shadow momentarily blocked the sun. Rebecca said nothing, so he remained silent. But his reflexes were immediately on their guard, his muscles taut and ready for action.

They took a table at the far side of the room. Shakespeare rubbed his stomach and ordered mutton and cabbage without a glance at the fareboard. Rebecca requested the same dinner, although her belly was still tightly knotted.

Two overflowing tankards of ale were placed before them. Rebecca took a sip, then healthy gulps, allowing the liquid to coat her parched throat.

"Don't drink so fast," Shakespeare said. "You'll become light-headed."

"So much the better after the London I've seen."

Shakespeare smiled. Rebecca looked across the table and felt herself growing timid, aware that she was with a man whom she found desirable. She quickly lowered her head. Picking up the tankard, she brought it to her lips and sipped the ale, her eyes peeking over the rim, observing his well-formed face deep in thought. On the streets conversation with him had been so natural, but now, seeing him like this, she was tongue-tied.

Not like her to be the shy maiden. She started to speak at the moment he uttered a word.

"After you, sir," Shakespeare said.

"Pray, continue in your thought," she said.

"After you have completed yours."

"Upon the completion of yours."

"Better to be unmannerly than to delay you further," Shakespeare said. "I will begin."

Rebecca nodded. Shakespeare paused, then laughed nervously.

"And what does strike Shakespeare with humor?" Rebecca asked.

"I forgot the subject on which I was about to speak." He swallowed a gulp of ale. "Spare me embarrassment, sir, and say your words."

Rebecca took another sip of ale, her head feeling pleasantly hazy. She leaned over the table and said, "How do you propose to sneak into Mackering's ranks?"

"In my duties as a player I have been a lord, a gallant, a soldier of fortune, a ghost, a fairy, a fool, a cook, a laborer, and diverse women of all walks of life. I have lived in many centuries and died numerous times in duels, and of injuries and diseases. Once, my life was taken by my own hand, what a sorrowful scene that was." Shakespeare grinned with the recollection. "I'll have no trouble playing the scoundrel, slipping into Mackering's netherworld as smoothly as melted wax upon a newly dipped candle, viewing it as simply another part.''

"Mackering is clever. The uprightman must know you desire his audience. He has thus avoided you. He'll be looking out for your disguises and will no doubt have a few masks of his own.''

"Then we'll have to see who's the more convincing player.''

"And if he ensnares you? Traps you? Threatens you with bodily harm? How are you to protect yourself?''

"Let it happen first, sir.'' Shakespeare clenched his fists.

"He's dangerous.'' Rebecca placed her hand upon his arm, then remembered that she was dressed as a man and quickly withdrew her hand. "I present to you another option—an addendum to your original plan.''

"Speak.''

Rebecca fortified herself with a gulp of ale. She said, "Let me come with you—''

"Never!''

"I'll be your doxy! I can fence. Four armed hands are better than two.''

"Then give me Thomas's hands. At the least, Thomas's arms.''

"Stop the puns and listen to me. Thomas would not defend you. But I would. I owe it to you after what you did—''

"Out of the question.''

"But—''

"No!''

"Shakespeare, you saw my skill at the fence. True my strength could easily be bested by any man of substance, but my *footwork*! Find me a nobleman as light on the toes as I . . . save my cousin, of course.''

Shakespeare didn't answer her.

Rebecca thought back to their duel. Yes, it had been chilling to look death in the face. But oh how exciting it had been! It had turned her blood truly sanguine, hot with expectation, her heart pumping at full strength. And now was the chance to do something bold and outrageous before the chains of marriage bound her permanently. A last bout of freedom before turning fat and matronly. What memories it would etch into her brain. "Pray, let me help you, Shakespeare,'' Rebecca pleaded. Her voice had raised in pitch. She lowered it and added, "The thrill would be *mine*.''

"Tis a solo battle I fight, sir.''

"But it needn't be that way.''

Shakespeare whispered, "As I recall from conversations past, you have a future husband. Would he give his blessing to your plan?''

Rebecca was silent.

"I thought not," said Shakespeare. "And when is the knight who sits before me due to take his vows?"

"Answer my question first," said Rebecca, undeterred.

"First, ask one."

"May I play your doxy?"

"A most definite no, sir."

"Then give to me sufficient reason."

"Your safety."

"I can care for myself."

"You've just admitted any man of substance can best you. And you've warned me that Mackering is much more than any substantial man. You cannot impose upon me the responsibility of your welfare. It's too big a burden for me. If anything should happen to you, I'd be consumed in guilt."

Rebecca fell back in her chair and folded her arms across her chest.

"Show the manners of your rank, sir," Shakespeare chided. There was a twinkle in his eye. "We're in public."

Rebecca didn't answer, but her expression softened. If she couldn't win her way by the power of her words, perhaps feminine smiles would woo him. She would try again later.

Shakespeare asked, "When are your nuptials?"

"We marry in February—a week after Candlemas."

Shakespeare raised his tankard. "I wish you much cheer and good hap."

Rebecca raised her tankard, then sipped her ale.

"Will your future husband allow you to continue masking as a man?" asked Shakespeare.

"I know not," Rebecca said. "He's unaware of my peculiarities." She added, "Though I am well aware of his."

"Peculiarities?"

Rebecca took another swallow of ale and nodded.

"What peculiarities?" Shakespeare asked.

Rebecca thought a moment, her brain spinning from drink. "A tragedy about Marlowe," she said.

"Horrible," Shakespeare said with feeling. Though he wasn't a close friend of Marlowe's, Shakespeare had been a great admirer of the poet. To die such a wretched death, stabbed in the back during a heated—and no doubt drunken—argument in a dark tavern at Deptford.

Too many deaths in too short a time.

Glumly, Shakespeare said, "What made you think of Marlowe? Did you know him?"

"My betrothed did. He told me of his death yesterday. It had quite an effect on him."

Shakespeare asked, "How well did your fiancé know Marlowe?"

"At one point I believe he knew him intimately."

"Intimately?"

"*Very* intimately."

"I see . . ." Shakespeare said, wondering: What kind of marriage would that be? Perhaps the man was a satyr, interested in anyone and anything. He hesitated, then asked, "If I may be so bold to ask, have you and your betrothed . . ."

She stared at him, then shook her head. "We've yet to discuss what we both know."

"But you intend to live with him as man and wife," Shakespeare said.

"We will be man and wife, yes," Rebecca said. "Though I'm sure he prefers me dressed as a knight than dressed as a bride."

Shakespeare didn't answer. He didn't know what to say.

Rebecca shrugged and ordered another tankard of ale. "The marriage was arranged by my father."

"And the agreement is satisfactory to you?"

"My opinion is of no consequence," Rebecca said. "I know Miguel well if not intimately. I love him greatly, and in his own way he loves me."

There was silence.

"One could say the arrangement differs little from *your* own lawful wedlock," she said.

"Not at all," Shakespeare protested. "Not at all! I'm on most cordial—and intimate—terms with my wife."

"But you see her little."

"Not as often as I desire."

"And no doubt you desire her often."

Shakespeare laughed, sipped his ale. "Aye. Tis true."

Rebecca cocked her head. A very ungallant gesture, but one that brought a blush to his cheeks. She asked, "So what do you do when you feel the sting?"

"Tis none of your affair," Shakespeare snapped.

"Sorry."

The tapster placed a full tankard of ale in front of Rebecca. She raised it in the air and drank. Shakespeare drummed his fingers on the table. He asked,

"Why did your father arrange for you such an unusual marriage? For title?"

"No."

"Money?"

"Nay."

Shakespeare waited.

Rebecca took a huge gulp and coughed. Shakespeare patted on her back. After she dried her watering eyes, she said,

"You'll not breathe a word of this?"

"Not a peep."

"He's my kinsman," she said.

"The marriage is *incestuous*?"

"God forbid such an abomination! He's a *distant* relation."

"And?"

Rebecca touched her cheek. It was hot and moist. The drink was making her dizzy. Or perhaps she was dizzy because she'd drunk not enough. She swallowed more ale and said, "We marry amongst each other because we have family secrets."

"Such as?"

"Our practices—" Rebecca stopped herself. She was sailing in troubled waters. "I cannot tell you."

"You practice the art of witchcraft?" Shakespeare asked, wide-eyed.

"Shh . . . Nay! Not a whit of black arts have I or my kinsmen ever known . . . Simply put, we retain some practices . . . Oh, why am I confessing this to you?"

"I assure you your secrets are safe with me."

Two plates of mutton and cabbage were placed before them. Rebecca finished her tankard of ale and signaled the tapster for a third.

"What is your secret?" Shakespeare asked.

"I cannot—"

"Aye, you can," he whispered. "I see by your eyes that you desire to rid the recesses of your heart of its heavy load. I've confessed to you my demons, tell me *yours*."

Rebecca said nothing. This time, instead of refilling her tankard, a full pitcher of ale was brought to the table. Rebecca poured, then took a full swallow.

"Tell me," prodded Shakespeare.

"Our ancestors . . . We are still influenced by them. We practice some customs of the old religion."

"I knew it!" Shakespeare said, pounding his fist on the table.

"Shh."

"You're Spanish—"

"Portuguese."

"The same thing."

"*Not* at all!"

"You're secret Papist, aye?" Shakespeare whispered. "A Jesuit, mayhap. Did not you mention your kinsmen trade with them?"

"Yes—I mean no! I mean—"

"Not to fear, sir. Harry was also a secret Papist and it matters not to me. I still love him dearly. Do you have icons of the virgin and candles stashed away in some hidden nest?''

"You don't understand—"

"Have you also relatives in the North?"

"Nay! None." Rebecca gulped some ale. "My mouth stretches so wide, it's cavernous. Erase this conversation from your memory."

"Done," Shakespeare said. "But if ever you want to speak of personal matters, you may speak with me as confidently as you talk to yourself.''

"I thank you." Rebecca touched her temples with her fingertips. "My head aches."

"You drink much on an empty stomach," Shakespeare said. He cut up pieces of mutton and fed her one with his fingers. "You must eat. Later we shall resume our conversation."

"Not this one."

"As you wish, sir." Shakespeare handed her another piece of mutton. "Eat."

Rebecca took the meat and chewed it indifferently, washing it down with ale. She picked up a cooked leaf of cabbage, wrapped it around her finger, then placed it daintily into her mouth. She repeated the gesture and noticed Shakespeare staring at her.

"Is my beard slipping from my face?" she whispered.

"No. Simply, I've never seen a gallant eat his victuals in such a manner."

She straightened up in her chair, belched, then bit a chunk of mutton off the leg bone.

"Now do I play better the knight?"

"More believable," said Shakespeare, "though your belch was womanly."

Rebecca smiled. The food in her stomach eased the pain in her head. She felt light once again, as if she were floating. She opened her mouth and tried to burp, but nothing came out.

"Finish your dinner," Shakespeare said. "Then tell me your story, sir.''

Rebecca smiled again, then giggled. "My cousins were always able to emit such loud and resonant belches. Of course, they'd never do it in front of our elders, but alone in the stables . . . or in the hayloft." She laughed and picked up her tankard, but Shakespeare placed his hand atop hers and lowered the vessel.

"Have some more mutton," he said.

"My stomach feels the heat of the flesh," Rebecca said, patting her doublet. "It desires a bath of ale."

"Methinks it will drown if you pour any more down your gullet."

"My innards, Shakespeare, are solely my responsibility," she said, taking a sip of ale.

Shakespeare sighed.

"If I belch womanish," she said with a sly smile, "how does Shakespeare belch in a manly fashion?"

"Shakespeare desires not to belch."

"Ah, but his company desires it. And being the good man that he is, he has no option but to oblige his companion of superior title."

Shakespeare whispered, "We are in public, sir."

"Belches abound in places of drinking, and your fine tavern, Shakespeare, is no exception. Many a burp has punctuated the air like the stab of a quill at the end of a sentence."

"We must exhibit knightly behavior if we are dressed as a knight, sir."

"And how many sober gallants do you see in the room, good man?" Rebecca pouted. "Do show me how to belch."

Shakespeare felt as if he were melting before her eyes. He was burning for her, and the beard and mustache did little to quench his fire. It was her eyes, her voice, her lips, her pout. She touched his hand and he felt himself go numb.

"I pray you, good man," she said. "Instruct me in the finer points of belching."

"Mis—Sir. For the sake of your honor, show restraint."

Rebecca lowered her lashes and squeezed his hand. A flash of heat burst into his loins.

She said, "I pray you . . . Please?"

"Very well, if you insist."

Rebecca clapped her hands with satisfaction. "Very good, my dear fellow. Now tell me."

"The key to a manly belch is the ingestion of ale. It must be done all at once. That way air is trapped inside the gullet and can be easily expelled."

"Pray, continue."

Shakespeare raised his eyebrows, picked up his tankard, downed it in five consecutive swallows, then sat back in his chair. The burp that came out was deep and resonant.

Rebecca burst into laughter. She filled her tankard from the pitcher and said, "To your health and may God bless, good sir." After the fifth swallow, she surfaced coughing, ale spewing from her nose and mouth.

Shakespeare slapped her on the back.

"Too fast," he remarked.

"Aye?" she said, sputtering with laughter.

"You've sated the lungs."

She cleared her throat, dried her eyes on her shirt-sleeve. "Mayhap I need another demonstration."

"No," Shakespeare said. "You need a walk."

"Again, sir, I beg of you."

Shakespeare sighed. It was useless to resist. She'd erode away his will like the tides to the cliffs. "For your pleasure, sir."

His belch this time was louder than the first. Rebecca held her stomach and howled.

"I noticed the tempo with which you gulped," she choked out between chortles. "As perfect as a drummer's. And your pace . . . as steady as a plow horse."

"Many thanks." He stood up. "By your leave now, sir?"

"Nay," Rebecca said, motioning him down. She brought the mug to her face and tilted the cup. Ale poured over her beard. She giggled, her head swimming in a gray fog.

"You've missed your mouth, sir," said Shakespeare.

"Then I shall try again, good fellow." She drank half the tankard in a series of rapid gulps, feeling afterward as bloated as an unmilked cow. She opened her mouth but nothing came out.

"You look ill, sir," Shakespeare said.

Rebecca couldn't answer.

"You're awash in green hues," he said.

"I need air," she croaked out. Her stomach had started to buck. "Very quickly."

Shakespeare stood. "A walk, then."

Rebecca tried to stand, but her knees buckled. Shakespeare caught her by the arm, left some coins on the table, and managed to get her outside. Gods, how heavy she'd become.

"Do you feel the need to empty your stomach?" Shakespeare asked her.

"Death is upon me," she groaned.

"Breathe slowly."

"Nay, tis too late." She gulped, tried to hold down the contents of her stomach. "The otherworld is imminent."

"You shall live to curse your waking, sir."

"This is the end."

Shakespeare jerked Rebecca onto her feet. "Try to walk."

"All my dreams, squashed as an overripe plum—"

"Walk, sir."

She fell against him.

"Come." He hoisted her upright. "Look up at the trees."

"My eyes see nothing but haze as life's precious vapors are sucked from my weary body."

"Open your eyes as wide as you're able. Try to fix them to a sight in front of you."

"I see only black," Rebecca muttered.

"Aye. I said *open* your eyes."

"I cannot."

Shakespeare slapped her cheeks.

"I feel nothing," she moaned. "This is it."

"You're thoroughly boozed."

"At your behest," Rebecca said, swooning. "You ply me with drink to extract the family secrets. But you succeeded not!"

"The room that I let is not far from here. You may sleep off your stupor there."

"While you act the lewd one."

"Base thoughts are far from my mind."

"And *why* is that?" Rebecca burst into newfound giggles. She tripped and crashed into Shakespeare, nearly knocking him over. He shook his head, then hoisted her over his shoulder.

"What're you doing?" Rebecca asked. Her words had come out a slur.

"Trying to remove you from harm's way."

"Down with me, sir!"

"In a minute."

"Down," she shouted. "I demand to be released to my own powers!"

"As you wish."

He placed Rebecca on her feet and she immediately crumpled on the ground, contorting with laughter as if she were inflicted with falling sickness.

"As a man, you're pathetic," Shakespeare said. "But as a woman, you're simply pitiable. Come. Let me help you . . . sir."

Rebecca rolled onto her back and raised her arms. He yanked her to her feet and she threw her arms around his neck. Together they meandered their way to his closet, weaving in and out of the throngs, not a single person taking notice of another drunken knight.

Once inside his room she stumbled to the floor, pulling him down on top of her.

"Kiss me," she said.

"You're drunk."

"Yes. But do it anyway."

He pulled the beard and mustache from her face and gently kissed her cheek.

"You," she said, "*are* an honest man!" She burst into guffaws. "A saint."

"You overstate my worth."

"Then love me, you worthless jack."

"Sleep."

"You find me not to your liking?"

He closed her eyelids, kissed her forehead and said, "Ask of me anything, m'lady, and I shall serve you slavishly. But you must make your requests when you're of sound mind. Then we'll both know tis you and not the ale that does speak."

"I love thee," she said to him.

"Sleep," Shakespeare said. "Dream sweetly."

Rebecca smiled and drifted off.

When she was in deep slumber, Shakespeare lay beside her, watching her sleep, her mouth as rich and red as poinsettia, her chest moving rhythmically with each breath. Like a tune affixed in the brain, Rebecca's laughter rang through Shakespeare's head. The feel of her hand, the smell of her intoxicated breath. Feeling raged inside of him, an intensity of passion as explosive as the first time he'd ever loved a woman. One side of him screamed to possess her; she was willing, he was drowning in desire. His other side begged restraint.

An hour later restraint was victorious. He rose from his pallet and sat at his desk, quill in hand, attempting to pen another verse of the poem he'd promised Lord Southampton; the nobleman was his benefactor. In the past he'd been more than generous with monetary support.

But Shakespeare was distracted by Rebecca's breathing. Like a siren's song, it beckoned him closer.

Restraint.

Harry had used that word to describe him, a depiction that had puzzled Shakespeare then, confused him even more in memory.

I love you, Shakespeare, he had cried out one night as they walked home from a tavern. Harry had been weeping buckets. *You're the man I had always wanted to be. But I failed. My father failed me. My God failed me.*

Sweating, Shakespeare had pulled him onto his feet. *Come, Harry. Walk. Your closet is only five doors away.*

The man I wanted to be, Harry had reiterated. *A man of modesty, a man of restraint, a man of integrity, a man of honesty!*

Shakespeare the fool.

Ever the honest man.

He picked up his quill and dipped it in the inkpot.

22

Sunlight was turning to twilight. Shakespeare squinted, the words in front of him a blur. His closet had become stifling, and he threw open the window, filling his lungs with the scented air of spring's dusk. The city below played its music, a swell of sound ringing between his ears where silence had resided only a moment ago. He capped his inkwell and cleaned his quills, then, savoring the moment, allowed his eyes to focus on his pallet.

Sleep was still heavy upon the girl. Shakespeare wanted to touch her, stroke her, hold her, but he restrained himself lest he'd startle her. She must be wakened soon, he thought. The supper hour grew near and her absence was bound to be noticed. But he wanted to keep her in his possession for yet another day, another hour, at the least another minute. She lay so tranquil, so beautiful . . . Let her sleep a while longer.

He'd take a brief walk. Shake some life into his legs and relieve his mind of the windstorm of swirling images; his head always ached after an afternoon of writing. By the time he returned, she'd be awake, maybe even gone. . . .

He closed the door softly.

The streets were still congested with traffic, people scurrying about in a frantic attempt to complete unfinished business before dark. Mongers were pulling in the wares that hung from their upstairs windows, merchants were closing their booths, fruit peddlers shouted loudly, trying to rid their baskets of overripe edibles that would spoil come the morning. A mile into his walk Shakespeare stopped in front of the stall of a costermonger.

"What do you lack before the night?" the seller asked. He was as bald as a melon. His hands were callused but scrubbed clean, his fingers long and tapered. "Me figs are as sweet as honeycomb and as plump as a milkmaid, me apricots are juicy and taste like the nectar of the gods. Me fruits are better than anything you'll be finding at the Cheape."

Shakespeare bought some figs and apricots.

"A fine evenin' it looks to be, bless be to God for that."

"Beautiful," Shakespeare agreed.

"A fine day it was. May God give us another like it tomorrow. The sellin' was good, the buyers were many. Look how little remains in me baskets."

The costermonger proudly showed them to Shakespeare.

"The goodwife and me'll be making merry tonight," the seller said, laughing. "A goodly day it was indeed. Only some plunky bairns causin' me mischief behind me back. Stole me apples when I turned me eyes. Ifin I catch those boys, I'll give 'em a beatin' they won't forget. They'll be thinkin it was Whitsunday."

Shakespeare nodded.

"Those plunky bairns," the monger repeated. "God save the Queen."

"God save the Queen." Shakespeare bit into a fig. Sweet. Delicious. He tipped his cap to the peddler and walked away.

The golden sunlit streets had tarnished to a dull gray, the tenements casting spectered shadows over the people and on the roads, against the plaster walls of closed shops.

Shadows.

Dark shadows.

They had become objects of fear as of late—something Shakespeare couldn't feel or grasp.

How do you fight a duel of retribution with a spirit that has no form, no body?

A dark cloud passed over his head, and the same eerie aura that had enveloped him at the Mermaid earlier in the day now wrapped its evil arms around him, invisible fingers squeezing his flesh.

He became wary. Felt for his sword, realizing how little protection it offered against a ghost.

He pivoted to his left and caught a glimpse of black. Then appeared a gentleman in a midnight cape.

Was evil in his eyes? Did not they shine and reflect like those of an ebony cat?

The master waved to a trio of gentlemen on the opposite side of the street, crossed the road to join them, his steps slow and calm.

Shakespeare continued his walk on Bishopsgate Street, past Bull's Inn. Though not yet dark, the tavern was crowded. People awaiting their drink, speaking loudly of better times soon to come.

Shakespeare strolled past the gnarled trunk of a hundred-year-old oak. Nothing appeared out of order. Everything was in its place according to the laws of God. Only his mind was confused.

He kept walking. Even at dusk Black Death announced its

presence—soft moans in distant breezes, wafts of burning wood and decayed flesh. Shakespeare's thoughts turned to the clean air of the countryside. Warwickshire. Images of Anne and the children, of his last visit back home. It had been hard to leave, the little ones crying, tugging on his cape. Especially Susannah. The girl was nine now, with a finely honed mind. She had sat on his lap every day after supper, playing with his beard, twirling curls in his hair with delicate fingers. And the twins chasing each other around the house, competing for his laughter and attention.

How they carried on the morning of his departure. Anne stood at the threshold, wishing him well, watching him go. But he sensed her ever-so-slight annoyance at the children for putting up such a fuss.

Anne was calm, always calm. When calamity struck—illness, death, fire—she was calm. When he was accused of poaching on Sir Thomas Lucy's estate, she was calm. When they made love (she was always willing but never seemed anxious), she was calm. Her steadfast nature never seemed to waver. She greeted him with a smile and a kiss when he returned home and sent him back to London in the same fashion.

In the beginning Shakespeare had begged her to come with him. She patted his cheek and told him London was not healthy for the children, that her parents were now older and depended on her company. For two years he pleaded. Then he stopped asking.

He settled into a daily routine in London with the fellowship and, thanks to Harry, finally made enough money to pay off his poaching fine. A burden lifted from his back, Shakespeare was now free to return home. And he would have left London and the fellowship forever had Anne pleaded with him to come back to Warwick. Marry, she needn't have even pleaded. A simple request would have sent him home. But the request never came.

Shakespeare had loved Anne the moment he met her—a woman six years his senior. She'd been so reassuring, a balm for his nerves. He had heard the whisperings when he married this older woman. More speculation abounded when Susannah was born six months later. He didn't care. He had his Anne to stroke his cheek, to wash his laundry, to cook his meals and serve them with a smile on her face.

His own household had been chaotic, his father's burning ambition at the root of it all. John Shakespeare had married *above* him, but his rise in stature after the wedding of Mary Arden did little to satisfy his need for more. He wasn't happy being just a farmer and the town's best glovemaker. He wanted more— always scurrying off to meetings, running for local positions in the town, leaving his mother in a pool of loneliness. She was ill-suited to raise a brood of crying, whining bairns who demanded so much attention, and at the end of many a day, Shakespeare would find his mother collapsed in a chair, weeping with nervous exhaustion.

Anne was such a departure from his own mother—a sensible woman of steady nature. But her calmness converted to apathy not long after they married. It mattered not to her who he was, where he was, or what he was doing. Just as long as the house was neat and there was plenty of food on the table. Shakespeare was frugal by nature, not one to indulge in clothes and trinkets. His home in Warwick lacked for nothing.

Nothing except passion.

Shakespeare thought of the girl sleeping in his closet. Young and beautiful, but more than that. Volatile, passionate, emotional, witty. Her eyes sparkled when she spoke, her lips pouted when she was displeased. No doubt the damsel had a vile temper, but that excited him. Someone unpredictable and stormy. Someone spontaneous.

A love affair.

An adulterous love affair.

She was not his wife, he was not her husband.

As if that meant anything.

He turned down Leadenhall Street.

How many bastards are born in a year? Thousands? Yet his vows still meant something to him. Yes, he'd had diverse tumbles with stews, an occasional roll with a lady whose lord had lost interest. But none of them were like her.

What would Anne say if she knew?

Probably nothing.

He turned back at Aldgate, hugging the wall of the city for his route home.

He sang, his voice full of woe:

> *If my complaints could passions move*
> *Or make love see wherein I suffer wrong:*
> *My passions were enough to prove*
> *That my despairs had governed me too long,*
> *O love I live and die in thee*
> *Thy grief in my deep sighs still speaks*
> *Thy wounds do freshly bleed in me*
> *My heart for thy unkindness breaks*
> *Yet thou dost hope when I despair*
> *And when I hope thou makst me hope in vain*
> *Thou saist thou canst my harms repair*
> *Yet for redress thou lets me still complain*

Can love be rich and yet I want
Is love my judge and yet am I condemned?
Thou plenty hast yet me dost scant
Thou made a god, and yet thy power condemned
That I do live it is thy power
That I desire it is thy worth
If love doth make men's lives too sour
Let me not love, nor live henceforth
Die shall my hopes, but not my faith
That you that of my fall may hearers be
May here despair, which truly saith
I was more true to love than love to me.

He passed the chandleress's shop, the launderess's, the shoe-maker's, the stall of the hide monger. A crescent of moon had peaked over the rooftops, stars sprinkling silver onto a charcoal canvas. Night was upon the city. Shakespeare couldn't believe he'd walked so far and long. He thought of Rebecca. He'd have to accompany her home lest she fall prey to some scurrilous thief. No doubt she'd protest, insisting she was well able to take care of herself, but he'd be adamant. Picking up his pace, he trotted home, wondering: If she still slept, what would she say to him upon awakening? Would she repeat her words of love now that the spirits had fled from her body?

The thrill of uncertainty!

He reached his tenement, climbed the stairs and opened the door to his closet.

He paused a moment to allow his eyes to adjust.

And then he saw it—a hulking form, its head swathed in an inky hood, poised over Rebecca's sleeping frame. A dagger gleamed above its head, waiting for its master to make its malicious arc downward. The shadow saw Shakespeare, laughed sinister, gravelly sounds!

"Noooooo!" Shakespeare shouted.

Rebecca jerked open her eyes and screamed.

The dagger plummeted to the ground as Rebecca rolled to her side, the point of the stylus missing her throat by a fraction of an inch. Shakespeare leaped forward, but the shadow was too quick. Shakespeare caught only air and stumbled. Recovering his balance a second later, he saw the shadow hoisting itself through the window. Shakespeare lunged and grabbed the hem of the shadow's cloak. A glint of moonlight highlighted another dagger now aimed at Shakespeare's face. He ducked, and by the time he lifted his head, the specter had flown away.

Shakespeare stood motionless, breathing heavily as he stared out his window to the empty streets below.

Nothing except the howling of the wind. No, there was no wind. Just . . . screams. *Rebecca's* screams.

He rushed to her, hugging her fiercely as she sobbed, stroking her back, whispering words of comfort. She finally quieted, leaving a night so still, it smoldered in silence.

"He's gone," he said, his words seeming unnaturally loud. "No more harm can he cause you."

She nodded, her head buried in his arms.

"You're safe."

Rebecca threw her arms around his neck and squeezed him tightly. "I was so frightened."

"You're safe."

"So frightened."

"Blame me for what happened."

"What . . . what *did* happen?" she managed to say.

He swallowed, shamefully told her that he'd left her sleeping— unguarded—while he took a walk.

"No doubt the fiend—the one that visited me the night before our fateful duel—thought you were me," he said. "I forgot to close the window when I left the room. That's how he came in the first time. May you and God forgive my stupidity. I should have never left you alone. Unpardonable idiocy—"

She placed her fingers over his lips.

"Speak not," she said. "I owe you my life."

"No. It is I who almost cost you your neck." He brushed the delicate bones of her gullet. To think that once he had aimed his rapier at that beautiful arch of almond-colored flesh.

Rebecca said suddenly, "I feel sick, Shakespeare,"

"Your stomach?"

"My head. It vibrates like the clapper of a bell."

"You imbibed too much this afternoon." He helped her sit up. "Wait."

He quickly fixed a posset of milk and honey and wet a rag.

"Lay this upon your forehead," he said to Rebecca. "And drink slowly."

"The hour is late?"

"Very late."

"My father . . ."

"I'll speak with him. Explain—"

"No!" Rebecca said. "Do not go near him! He angers easily, and this time I've given him much cause for ire."

"Twould be dishonorable and cowardly if I'd allow you to face your father alone. I've had many a confrontation with diverse angry men—"

"Not my father!" Suddenly she grabbed her head and moaned.

"Drink." Shakespeare raised the goblet to her lips.

After she drank half the cup, she said, "I pray you, Shakespeare, let me deal with my father in my own way. I'll think you not a coward and no less honorable if you cede to my judgment in this matter."

Shakespeare said nothing.

"Do not be offended," Rebecca implored. "I trust your manner and speech. Aye, beautiful words you pen. They could move mountains. But I know my father's ways and can play upon them. Walk me to my home, then let me deal with my father. Please trust *me* as I have trusted *you* with certain delicate confidences."

Shakespeare paused, then said, "At your insistence, mistress."

"You'd do me honor if you'd call me by my forename."

"Only if you'll return the honor."

"I thank you much, William."

Shakespeare reddened. The melody in her voice as she spoke his name . . .

He glanced to his right and his eyes fixed upon the dagger that had almost severed that lovely throat. He picked it up and held it to the moonlight.

"Smithed like the first one used against you?" Rebecca asked.

"Seems to be."

"And the other one? The one that this devil threw as he escaped through the window?"

"I've not had opportunity to look at it yet," said Shakespeare, "but methinks it must be fashioned as the other two."

"How many daggers does this vile creature have in his possession?"

"As many as he needs."

"Who is he?"

"I know not, save that he's no ghost." Shakespeare unfolded his fist and showed her a scrap of black cloth. "I tore this from his cape. I felt his body, felt the pull of his muscles as he escaped."

"Mackering?"

"I know not. Only that he was a man. Mayhap an extraordinary man, a madman, but a man nonetheless."

"I think it's better to have a man as your enemy than a ghost."

"Much better." Shakespeare turned to Rebecca and embraced her with relief. "How fares your head?"

"It aches still, but it's better. Your posset was very soothing."

"Good."

"A fiendish wight is your man of black," Rebecca said, snuggling in his arms. "Reconsidering, perhaps a specter would be more fallible a foe. The ghost merely tried to warn you. This *man* desires to murder you.''

Shakespeare gripped the handle of the dagger until his knuckles turned white. ''Ah, but this *man*—made of piss and blood—can be murdered as well.''

''Hug me tightly,'' Rebecca suddenly begged of Shakespeare. ''I feel as if I'm going to fall.''

He placed the dagger on the ground and embraced her.

''I'm so frightened,'' she said.

''He's gone.''

''What if he comes back?''

''You'll not be here. He wants nothing of you. He doesn't even know who you are.''

''And yourself?''

''Aye. He'll come back for me. I'll be prepared.''

''I pray you, William, leave the city.''

Shakespeare said nothing.

''If not for your own welfare, do it for those who care about you,'' Rebecca said. ''Make not a widow of your wife, don't leave your children fatherless.''

Rebecca began to cry. ''I was made a widow . . . of sorts. If I were your wife . . . I would weep sorely for your death. . . . I'm so confused. . . .''

Shakespeare gently rocked her in his arms.

''Nothing will happen to me,'' he said.

''Swear it.''

''I swear it.''

''I'm so scared.''

''He's gone.''

''I feel so alive in your arms. Even as I cry, I feel your strength. Hold me forever.''

''Twould be my heaven.''

''Kiss me,'' Rebecca whispered.

He did.

23

The illusion of youth fell upon Shakespeare like a dazzling ray of sunlight. He was giddy, silly, as prankish as an errant schoolboy. His senses were heightened to extremes, smelling perfume wherever he walked, hearing sweet music in the cacophony of street songs. Never had food tasted so luscious. His fingertips no longer touched, but instead *caressed* everything within their grasp. Gods, what a glory was love!

He hadn't expected it. Yes, Rebecca was exquisite, her kisses as sweet as nectar. But after all was done, he *had* wanted to forget about her and concentrate on finding peace for Harry's soul. Aye, maybe he'd call upon her once or twice . . . or trice. But that was all the distraction he had meant to allow himself. *Meant.* But fate had deemed it otherwise.

Shakespeare had decided to visit her the day after the attack, convincing himself that he'd only wanted to see how she was faring. He stood outside her father's estate, waiting for her to emerge, not daring to enter the grounds. What could he say to her father that would explain his presence? I'm the man in whose company your daughter had become sorely whittled. Or I'm William Shakespeare, a man enthralled with your daughter. Though I be married with three children *and* without means of support at the moment, I am nonetheless a trustworthy fellow.

No, he could *not* come to the door. So he waited, hidden in the brush at the side of the gatehouse.

Lopez's house was built with one central tower dividing two rectangular buildings of stone. The left wall of the manor was partially covered by a scaffold, the men upon it constructing a chimney. Judging by the arch of the windows, the house seemed to be about forty years old—built at the start of the Queen's reign.

Large for a doctor's home—even if the doctor was the Queen's physician. Lopez undoubtedly had found favor in Her Majesty's eyes or had money from other means.

Shakespeare waited and waited, but Rebecca never came out. He left his post at dusk, not so much tired as extremely disappointed. It was as if she were dangling him on purpose.

The devil with her!

The next day he tried unsuccessfully to write in the morning. By noon he was in front of her house again. By nightfall he returned home a discouraged man.

The following morrow he was at his watch at dawn, hoping that she'd at least leave the manor to stroll the outside grounds. At last his patience was rewarded. But she was with a man—a handsome gentlemen, though his face seemed brittle with anger. He stood slightly taller than she.

Her betrothed, no doubt.

Jealousy gripped his body like a cramp. Then he suddenly panicked. How could he justify his being there to her . . . to him?

He crouched behind a tree until they passed the gatehouse. Carefully he shadowed them into town.

They started by visiting the stalls at the Cheape. Rebecca carefully eyed the crafted goods displayed; the man carelessly picked them up and tossed them aside without a glance. He seemed bored and irritated. Rebecca ignored him and spent the next fifteen minutes in front of a broom stall. They began to argue and five minutes later the man left in a huff.

Rebecca seemed relieved.

Shakespeare watched her as she examined the rushes of the broom, the wood of the handle. It was as if she were evaluating a crown jewel. Even the monger became impatient. Buy or begone was his look. But she went about her business and overlooked his hostile stares.

Go up to her, Shakespeare told himself. But his legs felt wobbly. Inhaling deeply, he forced himself to proceed as Shakespeare the *actor*. He feigned an air of casualness and waited until she noticed him first. When she did, she broke into a glittering smile and held out her hands to him. He grabbed them, squeezing them gently. They were velvet. He was a cloud, she the wind. Poof and she'd blow him away.

"I was about to call upon you after I'd finished my errands," Rebecca said.

"Really?"

"Aye." She lowered her head. "I behaved in an unseemly, ill-bred manner the last time we met—"

"Not at all."

"But I did."

Pain pinched Shakespeare's heart. She was apologizing for her intimacy with him. He thought back to the evening of the madman's attack. She had been his newborn fawn, lithe and sleek, trembling with fear, her eyes wide and innocent, beseeching him for guidance and comfort. Her cheeks had been as smooth as windswept sand, marred only by narrow tracks of tears. After he had kissed and hugged her a thousand times, assured her they were both safe, he had walked her home. He'd honored her request and hadn't accompanied her past the gatehouse.

Those kisses, those embraces. For three days Shakespeare had clung to them. Had they meant nothing at all to her?

He said, "That night was unseemly strange."

"That it was." Rebecca shuddered. "Have you found out—"

"Who the villain was?" he interrupted. "No."

"Has he molested you again?"

Without thinking, Shakespeare glanced over his shoulder. "No," he said.

"Are you frightened?" she asked, then added, "Of course you aren't. You weren't frightened that night, were you?"

"I was worried about you."

"But not about yourself."

Shakespeare smiled and said, "I was concerned about my own neck as well."

"Tis a wonderful neck," Rebecca said. "It holds a marvelous head."

"Aye, a strong neck I have. Yet it is neither as long nor graceful as thine—" He corrected himself. "As *yours*. As far as the head is concerned, I've been told I have a head for words, yet not much of one for numbers and none for science and languages, as you have. So as far as heads go, you are heads above me. Which explains why your neck is longer than mine."

Rebecca stared at him, then laughed. Shakespeare laughed as well.

"I'm a brook," he said. "I wander without direction and babble greatly."

"Is it yer intention to buy the broom, m'lady?" interrupted the broom monger irritatedly.

Rebecca dropped Shakespeare's hands and picked up a broom. She said, "The rushes are loosely bound together, my goodfellow, and the wood of the handle is already warped. I fully intend to buy a broom, but I want one that won't fall apart in a fortnight."

The monger curled his lip into a sneer.

Rebecca stopped him before he let out his string of insults. "Are you going to defend poorly crafted items or are you going to let me see what you've hidden in the back of the stall only to be shown to those who are particular enough to ask?"

With a grunt, the broom monger reached under a black piece

of cloth hung over the right side of his stall and pulled out another broom.

"It be costing you more," he grumbled.

"Nonsense," Rebecca said, examining the broom and finding it to her liking. "What you've displayed isn't good for anything but kindling. I'll pay you a tuppence for this broom, however, and not a penny more."

"Get out of here," the broom monger grumped.

"Very well," Rebecca said. She handed him the broom and turned her back.

"Four pence," the broom monger yelled out.

"I said not a penny more," Rebecca said.

The broom monger swore, then said, "A deal."

Rebecca dropped the coin in an open palm and grabbed the broom. She and Shakespeare walked about two hundred feet in silence, then he said, "Wonderfully executed."

"It's in my blood," she said, then gasped. How could she have said *that*! Did she have suet for brains?

"What is it?" Shakespeare asked.

Calm, she told herself. He thinks you mean it metaphorically. She said, "Nothing . . . Nothing at all. It's just that . . . that I forgot, uh . . . when I was supposed to meet my brother. I can't remember whether he said ten or eleven of the clock."

"Your brother was the gentleman who accompanied you into town?" Shakespeare asked.

"Aye," Rebecca said. She fixed her eyes upon him. Then he realized his error and turned red.

"Been following me, Willy?" she said playfully.

"I feel like an ass." He paused, then said, "I haven't been able to stop thinking about you."

"Have you tried?" Rebecca asked.

"Lord knows I've tried," Shakespeare answered.

Rebecca looked perturbed.

"You're interfering with my writings," he explained. "I think of you and can only write love sonnets. I'm supposed to be writing about hapless Lucrece."

"Recite me one of your love sonnets," she said suddenly.

"Now?"

"Aye."

"Here?"

"Yes. Oh, do it."

He felt his face go hot.

Rebecca poked him in the ribs gently. "Your written words may be sweet, but your tongue is false. You haven't written any poems in my honor."

"But I have," he said. "I've written thousands of them in my marvelous brain . . . just not on parchment."

"So if thoughts of love for me clog your head like an over-stocked pond, fish one out for my pleasure."

"Now?" he repeated.

"Yes! Now! This second!" She slipped her arm into his. "Do dedicate soft words to me. Or does it embarrass you when they come from your mouth instead of your quill?"

"One can only describe perfection with perfection. What I say would be too crude for thine . . . for *your* ears."

"Tell me a poem and then thou may thou me."

Dear Almighty, he thought, thou art a bookwriter! Improvise! He cleared his throat and said,

> *"Tempest beats its fury fierce*
> *Upon my hapless soul.*
> *With angry waves it doth pierce*
> *and fill my blackest hole.*
> *Woe desperation! It is vast,*
> *my loneliness so deep.*
> *In endless night I am cast,*
> *Shadowed head to feet*
> *Yet thy love lights me as glowing ember . . ."*

He paused a moment, then thought the devil with it. He recited,

> *"Pray, play thy fingers upon my member."*

Rebecca stared at him, then burst into laughter.

"At least thou spokest from the heart," she said. "Or another part of thy anatomy."

"It was all I could think of on such short notice," he said. "The next time I see thee, I'll come with more polished words."

She stopped walking and frowned. He felt his stomach churn.

"I can't see you?" he asked.

"You?" she said.

"You . . . Thee . . . Can I see thee again?"

She slowly nodded. He exhaled with relief.

"I . . ." She hesitated. "I don't know where we can meet."

"Why not the city?"

"I'm not allowed to come here unaccompanied."

"But thy brother left thee alone." Shakespeare felt sudden anger. "Why did he do that? It's dangerous for thee to be roaming the street without male protection."

"He's in an extremely foul mood," Rebecca said. "He received a letter from his former mistress—some scheming woman of imaginary title. It seems she just ran off and married some very old but wealthy Venetian nobleman. Benjamin comforts himself by saying the man is very close to death and he will again have his savvy mistress in his bed shortly.'' She paused, then said, ''My brother is a fool.''

Shakespeare didn't care a groat about her brother. He said, ''Where can I see thee then?''

''Not in the city, not at my house either.''

''Then *where*?'' Shakespeare said.

''Not in the city,'' she repeated. ''Not at my house . . . during the daylight.''

Shakespeare smiled.

''Come at night. Throw something soft upon my window. Second story, left side, third one from the tower in the back of the house. I'll meet thee outside.''

''By thy will, mistress. *When* may I come to thee?''

''Is tonight too soon?''

''Tonight shall be an eternity,'' he said.

''Beware of the guards that roam the grounds, Willy.''

He nodded. Rebecca gently kissed his lips. Shakespeare grabbed her and mashed his mouth against hers. A mangy street boy hooted. Rebecca pulled away, laughing as she swatted her broom in the boy's direction.

Shakespeare came and tapped upon Rebecca's window that very evening. They met nightly for three weeks. Then they were caught.

24

Standing in the Ames's rose garden, Nan, the chambermaid, was shocked by de Andrada's rapid deterioration. In a month's time señor's eyes had become dull, his face slack with weight loss. He was out of breath, his muscles barely able to hoist him over the estate wall. He tumbled to the ground, rested a few minutes, then stood up and dragged his withered frame over to her.

"Dear Lord," Nan cried, touching her cheek. "What do those heretics do to you?"

"Too cruel . . ." de Andrada gasped out. "Too cruel for your ears, goodwoman."

"You poor man," she said. "I was so worried that you'd not come for our weekly prayer reading. Oh, señor, how much you need the Lord's help in a time of such destitution!"

De Andrada hung his head low and sighed deeply.

Nan swallowed back tears, straightened her spine and regained her composure. "We mustn't dawdle, señor," she said. "The family is gone for the day, but the hours pass quickly when the mind is steeped in the words of our Lord. Come this way. There are victuals for you in the kitchen. Afterward, we'll begin to work toward our salvation."

"Why do you pray for me?" de Andrada asked. He'd recovered his wind but feigned a weakened voice. "I don't deserve such a goddess to speak on my behalf."

"They *starve* you, those blasted dogs!" She hissed as she spoke. "Christian kindness shall not tolerate such atrocities. I know what they think of God." She lifted her eyes to the heavens and clasped her hands. "Most merciful Jesu, forgive me for my lack of compassion, but may they burn in Hell for refusing Thee as king!"

She returned her attention to de Andrada.

"They think I have not ears, but I do indeed hear. Sir George and Sir Thomas muttering their heretical prayers! And I know for fact that Lady Grace—Sir Dunstan's wife—brought not her lastest bairn for holy baptism."

"No!" exclaimed de Andrada.

"Aye, tis true." Nan leaned over and whispered, "And I have eyes as well, señor. I've seen their hidden horns nestled in their hair."

"Aye?"

"Aye. It's in the blood! All of those born of an unbaptized womb grow horns."

De Andrada felt the crown of his head, then quickly withdrew his hand.

"My goodwoman," he croaked out. "Dr. Lopez would never be so overt as to starve me in front of open eyes. Nay, he's much too clever a schemer for that."

"Then how is it that you grow so wretched week to week?" asked Nan.

De Andrada clenched his neck. "The doctor tries to poison me."

The maid gasped.

"Tis the reason for the pathetic state of my body," he said.

"My Lord, señor. Lopez is more devil than man!" Nan exclaimed. "But let God execute judgment on him. Come, come, señor. To the kitchen."

She grabbed his hand. De Andrada went cold at her touch—her bony hand scaly and dry. But he smiled at the sour woman as if she were a madonna.

"My angel," he whispered.

"This way."

Nan led him to the door of the kitchen.

Inside the air was hot and heavy and smelled of flesh and fat. Droplets of grease sprang from sizzling pans and boiling caldrons, a gray rolling fog of steam and soot hovering over the room. The master cook was an obese man of forty named Wort. His face was red and doughy, his nose oversized and dotted with black pores. He wore a tall white hat now limp with moisture, a white apron, and chose to cook without the hindrance of sleeves. His bare arms were as wide as hamhocks, hairy and coated with a layer of oil and sweat. He dropped a chicken into a pot of bubbling water, then cursed his helper, a boy of twelve.

"You worthless dolt!" Wort screamed. "I said three cups of claret, not four!" He backhanded the boy across the room, looked up and saw Nan with her señor both staring at him. "Me son," he explained.

Nan ignored him. "Sit down at this table, señor. Wort will be fixing you some flesh for your stomach."

Wort glared at Nan.

Nan glowered back and said, "That is, Wort will be cooking for you if we want to keep Kate the buttery maid in the household."

"You wretched witch!" he whispered.

"You fat bull!" she countered.

"A bull I am," Wort said, grabbing his crotch.

"You know what happens to bulls." Nan sliced through air with her finger. "Castration!"

De Andrada closed his legs involuntarily.

"Get the good señor some food now!" she ordered.

"Stupid bitch," Wort muttered. He turned around and backhanded another boy across the face. "You turd! Go bring me another dozen quail. And two dozen moorhens. The Lady Mary takes a fancy to its flesh." He faced de Andrada and said, "Me other son."

"The man is like a weed," Nan sneered. "He drops seed wherever he blows."

"Not in your dried-up womb!"

"I'd cut your thing off myself if you tried."

A plump girl of fourteen entered the kitchen with a vat of butter.

"Put it over there, Amy," Wort instructed. "No. Not next to the mutton, you cow. Next to the white flesh, the fish. You know the Lady Mary don'na like butter on her meat." He started to say something to de Andrada but changed his mind.

"Your daughter?" de Andrada asked.

Wort nodded. A sly smile spread over his face. "The good señor is interested?"

"No, the good señor is *not* interested!" Nan barked.

"Ah, shut up," Wort said. He spat and placed a trencher of lamb and beef in front of de Andrada.

It had been three days since de Andrada had tasted succulent flesh. He ripped the meat apart and stuffed it into his mouth. Within minutes the wooden plate was empty.

"More?" asked Nan.

"Aye, my beautiful lady. If it's no bother to your saintly soul."

"Nothing is a bother for you, señor," said Nan, her thin lips becoming invisible as she smiled.

"Give him more, Wort," Nan commanded. "The good señor is starved!"

Wort gave him a tray of chicken and duck and a bowl of boiled turnips. De Andrada finished every last morsel. Nan could see his color return to his cheeks, his eyes glow. She offered him sweets to top off his dinner.

"Go to the Devil," Wort said to Nan. "The sweets take much time to prepare. I need every bit of marchpane for me castle and turrets. I need the sugar bread for the walls, the comfits and fruits for the cannons and doors, the syrups for the moat."

"Give him a dish of candied violets," Nan commanded. "I know you dip hundreds of them because your punk wench fancies them."

"You know everything, you buswife."

"I make it my business to know everything, you lout!"

A bowl of candied violets was angrily shoved in de Andrada's face. He smiled and thanked the ruddy cook for the delicacies. Ah, how he savored each petal, sucking the sticky sugar off his fingers when he was done. Such a meal was especially delicious after three days of self-imposed starvation—almost starvation. In between the three-day visits, he'd sneak food from the Lopez gardens and orchards. He patted his full stomach and suggested to Nan that they return to the gardens where they were less likely to be seen by nosy servants.

Once outside, they sat on a bench by the lily pond. De Andrada said, "My good woman, I cannot thank you enough—"

"Your prayers for your soul are enough, señor. To think that

I was responsible for saving it . . .'' She handed him a book. ''Come. Let us pray together.''

''Good woman, I must ask you first—''

''*First* let us give *thanks* to *God*, señor,'' Nan said firmly.

''Of course,'' de Andrada said. He hung his face in shame.

Stupid dried-up prune of a bitch, he thought. She probably still had her maidenhead, but who would want it?

De Andrada smiled and muttered amen.

Didn't she ever tire of reading those prayer books, those blasted psalms? Didn't she ever long for merriment and drink, for a stiff prick rammed up her insides?

He looked at her again, nose buried in holy words as she muttered. As if you could fill a womb with spiritual salvation. No, the woman craved not joy, only obedience.

''Amen,'' he said.

He couldn't last much longer in Lopez's household. They were becoming suspicious of his eating habits, asked him why he picked at his food, watched his every move. The defection would have to come soon—a month at the earliest, six months at the latest. But first things first. He must get money. His dress must convince Essex and his finicky spymaster, Bacon, that he was a man of much means and wit. To get coins he must have something to sell.

''Amen,'' he responded as Nan paused.

Nan heard much from careless lips, he knew. Perhaps she had heard the name of the ship that was laden with the latest stowaways from Iberia. Perhaps she knew where the galleon was due to dock—and when. Information like that could be sold to the Spanish at a dear price.

He thought of Miguel Nuñoz. De Andrada had nothing against the man save he was allied with Lopez, but it was useless to let a drop of maudlin sentiment stand in the way of a sweet business proposition. So Miguel would follow the same path as his brother Raphael—perish at the hands of the Spanish . . . tortured . . . burned at the stake.

De Andrada erased foul images from his mind, thought instead of how Miguel's death would affect the witch doctor. The old man would cry out with pain, bemoaning his foul luck, a cursed man who had lost two sons-in-law. He'd blame Rebecca for his misfortune, as she had been attached to both men when they had died. He'd call her an agent of the Devil, and, anxious to rid himself of her evil presence, he'd sell her to a vaulting school of common whores. De Andrada would find her years later, riddled with pox and as thin and scrawny as an underfed chicken, begging him to rescue her from the horrid life she led.

Rebecca. How she held him in contempt. But one day it would

be he who despised her . . . after he boarded her, of course.
Ah, such joy is revenge, he thought gleefully.

Nan poked him in the ribs.

"Amen," he said.

"Now let us turn to page—"

"My good woman," de Andrada beseeched her. "I have reason to think that the family you work for is involved with nefarious activities."

"I *know* that!" Nan said.

"Then perhaps you can tell me something. Ordinarily I'd dare not interrupt such a spiritual moment as the one that just passed, knowing that God listens to the righteous, but as this information is most crucial to my well-being—"

"Stop being so winded, señor, and ask me the question."

"Had the heretics recently spoken with extraordinary interest of a certain ship? A Spanish galleon, perhaps?"

"They've mentioned many Spanish ships. The Spanish! Idol-worshiping Papists! Did you know that Mistress Rebecca, Sir George's harlot niece, has in her possession a ring from the Spanish king? I've seen her wear it, I've heard her cousins whispering about it. She is not only a heretic, but a secret spy. May she rot in Hell. May all the Spanish rot in Hell. Not you of course, señor. You've been saved."

"Blessed be to your guidance, good woman. . . . Have they spoken with interest about a specific ship—a galleon or mayhap a Portuguese carrack?"

Though irked by diversion from prayer, Nan nonetheless replied, "Let me think . . . I believe they made mention of an Italian merchant ship that is to travel through the Straits of Gibraltar."

"And that ship has a name?"

"The *Sao Paulo* or *San Pedro*." Nan wrinkled her forehead and closed her eyes. "The *San Pedro* it was. I remember because it had a Spanish name, may God curse it. Its final destination is to be Spanish Brussels."

"And the *San Pedro* has a scheduled stop in England?"

"Yes, I believe it's to stop in England."

"When is it due to dock here?"

"Let me think. They spoke of it on Tuesday two weeks ago, and today is Thursday . . ." Nan began to count on her fingers. "Two, three, four . . . oh, and add eleven days because the Continent follows the Papist Gregorian calendar. . . ." She looked up at de Andrada. "I believe the ship is due to dock in England in autumn. On a Wednesday . . . or maybe Thursday."

"Thank you, good woman, thank you!" De Andrada leaned over and whispered, "Do you know *where* it's due to dock?"

210   *Faye Kellerman*

"Portsmouth, did they say?" Nan bit her thumbnail in concentration. "Plymouth, mayhap Dover. I don't remember." She said to de Andrada sternly, "We must go on with our prayers, señor. The hour grows late."

"I shan't delay us any longer."

Nan said, "Let us begin."

De Andrada smiled and turned to the instructed page. As she read, he thought of women, of their womanhood. Some had big, slobby, wet holes, others were tight and dry—perennial virgins. That's the kind he liked best. Board 'em till their insides were dry, rub yourself raw.

He felt himself go hard.

"Amen."

De Andrada sneaked a sidelong glance at Nan. If her hair were loosened, her lips painted, she could strike a decent pose. Her womb was bound to be tight. Maybe some night he'd sneak into the house and ravish her. Tush, would she put up a fight!

He felt himself about to explode and forced himself to listen to the words Nan read to regain his control. May the Most Merciful One shine His light somewhere. He turned the page.

If he could only sleep away such boredom without the bitch noticing it. He tried to hide his face in the pages, but she looked at him queerly and he lowered the book.

He could feign illness. Nay, the prune-faced woman would only nurse him with more prayers.

No choice but to wait it out. She was much too valuable an ally to alienate, feeding him food and gossip.

An hour passed—a horrid hour—until Nan finally raised her head.

"Much pardons, señor, but I am forced to stop now."

"So soon?"

"Indeed, yes. The family will be back shortly and I have work left to do."

"Such a pity!"

"Yes."

"May I stay here an hour longer and pray?"

Nan grinned. "Aye, my good señor, you may. And feel free to ask Wort for more food if you're hungry. I'll leave firm instructions for him to give you what you desire."

"You're too kind."

"You may do me kindness in return, señor."

"Speak."

"If you know of sinners, as you yourself once were, bring them to me. And with God's help and blessing, I may clear a path of salvation for them."

"Twould be my pleasure, good woman," de Andrada said.

"Though I fear the English have become very lax about being saved."

"Aye," Nan said sour-faced. "All these rich lords ever care about is the rampant pursuit of pleasure." She added quickly, "But God save the Queen."

"God save the Queen," de Andrada answered.

"I must be gone," Nan said. "Pray for me as well, señor."

"You need not my prayers, but always I have included you in them."

Nan bowed her head, then stood up and left. De Andrada waited a few minutes, until he was sure Nan was busy with work, then headed for the kitchen.

Wort grumbled, cursed, then handed him a tankard of beer.

"Thanks, my good man."

Wort spat and returned his attention to a roasted goose.

De Andrada wiped the foam from his mouth and his shirt-sleeve and said to Wort, "Your daughter has left the kitchen?"

Wort turned around and smiled. "I knew you were more of a man than she'd have you out to be. What're you doin' with that hag?"

"She tells me things."

"Aye? Like what?"

"Like none of your business."

"Go to the Devil," Wort mumbled under his breath.

"Where's your daughter?"

"She'll cost you plenty."

"Is she a virgin?"

Wort sneered. "She gave her maidenhead to a twiddle of a chimney sweep, the stupid wench."

"She isn't fair in face or form, she isn't a virgin. . . . Your sow isn't worth more than a groat."

"But her ruttin' is full of spirit. Or so they say, those who've had her."

"Who's had her?"

"Sir George's sons and their fellows. They take her for free, the thieves. Once in a while the younger son, Sir Thomas, throws her a farthing or two to keep her happy. But me daughter's more the clever one than they suspect. She filches a pence or two behind their backs. Gives it all to me."

"Such honor your daughter doth bestow upon you."

"Aye," Wort said, wiping his face on his apron. "I've got much to cook. Either show me some silver or go."

De Andrada flipped him a sovereign. Wort's eye widened as he caught the coin.

"Take me not for an idiot, you churl," said de Andrada. "I pay you much to take the wench whenever I want."

"Aye, señor, certainly," Wort fawned. "Anytime you want her, señor, she's available. I'll call her for you now, señor. Ameeeeee!"

The girl appeared a moment later.

"Go with this man," Wort instructed. "And be very nice to him."

Amy looked at de Andrada's cold eyes, his lupine smile. She gulped and nodded. De Andrada lifted her onto the counter, raised her skirt, undid his codpiece and shoved deep inside of her. Wort gaped as de Andrada tore at his daughter's dress and squeezed her large breasts. De Andrada copulated quickly, withdrew a minute later, then turned to Wort.

"I wanted to make sure she was worth what I paid you."

Wort said nothing, staring at his ravished daughter. Her eyes were blank, void of tears.

"I'm talking to you, you filth," de Andrada said.

"Aye," Wort said, returning his attention to de Andrada. "Was she . . . Was it good?"

"I overpaid," de Andrada announced. "But twas not the first time I've been cozened, and shall let it pass."

He lowered Amy's skirt, pulled her off the counter and held her hand. "To the buttery, girl. There we may be alone and can continue our merriment at a much slower pace. You'll be needing a lesson or two on how to truly please a man." De Andrada slapped her arse. "But we have much time—hours of it, wench—and I'm a patient teacher."

As they left, the girl gazed over shoulder, into her father's eyes.

25

The hag poked Rebecca in the ribs with one of her walking sticks. The young girl looked up from her book, slid to the side of the gazebo bench and said nothing. The old woman sat down.

"Absorbed in your own thought of late," she said. "You've not said much to me this past month, girl. Nor have you visited with me."

"I spent Midsummer's Eve with you."

"That was what? Two weeks ago? It's now the second week in July."

Rebecca ignored her grandam's scolding, though she knew it was well deserved. She had been keeping to herself. Ever since that dreadful night when Father caught her and Shakespeare dallying in the garden. They'd been locked in an embrace when her father had appeared and a terrible scene had resulted—one too freshly painful for her to dwell upon. Her father had forbidden her to see him again, forbidden her to leave the common ground, even had the audacity to hire a man to keep watch over her movements. She'd become a prisoner in her own home, and told Grandmama what she thought of the arrangement and her father.

"He's revolting!" she announced.

"You speak harshly without reason, Becca," the hag said.

"Has he turned you against me as well, Grandmama? Have I lost my only ally?"

"You insult me," the old woman said.

"Why do you defend Father?"

"Because his punishment against you was just."

"Bah!" Rebecca angrily picked up her book.

"Becca, freedom carries with it responsibility—"

"Dunstan carouses often!" Rebecca interrupted. She knew she was being disrespectful, but she pressed on anyway. "Benjamin and Thomas as well. Why are their oh-so-lovestruck spells tolerated with bemused chuckles whilst mine are subjected to scorn and severe punishment!"

"They are discreet and you are not. Your brother—whom you snobbishly consider beneath you in wit—is more clever than you in many respects."

"I happen to fall in love with a man not to my family's liking and I am branded indiscreet by *you*, of all people," Rebecca said.

"I brand you as indiscreet not for falling in love but for indiscretion—"

"And what terrible things did I tell Shakespeare?" Rebecca cried.

"Are you going to listen to me or is my breath going to fall upon deaf ears?"

Rebecca bit her lip and said nothing.

Grandmama touched her granddaughter's hand, feeling sympathy for Rebecca's doomed love. In a kind voice the old woman explained that she'd overheard everything that terrible night: Roderigo's cursing, Rebecca's crying, Shakespeare's shouting.

She said, "Becca, I heard your Shakespeare shout about Miguel's peculiar habits. How did he become aware of Miguellito's preferences if you didn't tell him?"

Rebecca reddened with shame. Yes, she'd been tipsy at the time it had slipped out. But what of it? It was the truth. She said, "I merely mentioned, once, in passing that Miguel was . . . peculiar. Everybody who knows Miguel is aware of his nocturnal visits to *those* kind of taverns."

"Miguel's father doesn't know about his son's visits to *those* kind of taverns."

"Uncle Hector wasn't there that horrible night."

"And if he would have been, would your Shakespeare in his fit of fury have stopped himself?"

"Shakespeare was heated. Father said atrocious things to us. He never gave us a chance to explain."

"Suppose Miguel had heard what Shakespeare proclaimed loudly to your father?" the hag suggested. "How do you imagine Miguel would have felt?"

Rebecca lowered her eyes. How would he have felt? Devastated. Miguel trusted her, and she had gossiped behind his back. It was inexcusable and she knew it.

"But I love my Willy!" was all she could answer.

"Is love a sufficient reason to embarrass Miguel?"

Rebecca was silent.

The hag studied Rebecca. She had that *same* look in her eyes that the old woman's sister had once held—stubborn, willful. Love was all that mattered. Piss on that. The crone said angrily, "What else did you tell your *Willy*?"

Rebecca was taken aback by the venom in the old woman's voice. "I don't know what you mean."

"Did you happen to leak out any other family secrets?"

Rebecca blushed and said, "No."

"You lie in your throat, girl. What did you tell him?"

"Nothing of any significance."

"By God's sointes, Rebecca, what *insignificant* trifles flowed from the cracked dam of your lips?"

Rebecca suddenly threw down her book and buried her face in her hands.

"You told him, eh?" the hag said coldly.

"No!" Rebecca started to cry. "Yes . . . I mean no. I told him nothing that would do us in. I swear to you, Grandmama, we mostly bespoke soft words of love."

"What did you *tell* him, for God's sake?"

"I . . . once I told him . . . twas the first time we were together in the city. I was drunk and spoke foolishly, I admit it. He . . . he thinks we're secret Papists."

"Good Lord—"

"It doesn't matter to him." Rebecca pulled a lace handkerchief from her purse and dried her tears. "Grandmama, the North is full of secret Papists. No one concerns themselves with the Catholics."

"No one?" the hag said, tapping her stick against Rebecca's leg. "Only scarecrows were hung in 'sixty-nine?"

"That was different," Rebecca stammered. "The North . . . those northerners were in open rebellion against the Queen."

"So you did no harm by telling your Willy that we're Papists, eh, Becca?"

"I didn't say that," Rebecca said, frustrated. "I didn't *tell* him we're Papist. He assumed it because—" She stopped herself. The hag grabbed her shoulders and yelled,

"Why did he assume it, girl!"

"Calm yourself, Grandmama," Rebecca begged. "Your face is flushed. My God, you're trembling."

The old woman released Rebecca's shoulders. She folded her skeletal hands into fists, tears streaming from her eyes. Rebecca held the old woman, feeling such deep love for her. She knew how much her grandam had suffered for her religious beliefs, how she'd been imprisoned in the Old Country. Rebecca could understand how such circumstances could permanently cloud her trust in the Gentile. But England was not Portugal, and she told the old woman this.

"No one is going to burst into our house and arrest us because of our silent prayers!" Rebecca said.

The hag pushed her granddaughter away.

"And you believe that?"

"Yes." Rebecca kept her patience. No sense in becoming overwrought. "Our queen wouldn't allow it."

"You think the English would show sympathy to the Jew?"

"You're twisting my words."

"At best, we would be deported, Becca. As Jews are not allowed in this country. At worst—"

"The nobility knows our bloodline. They know that Solomon Aben Ayesh—the Jewish duke—is our uncle. The Queen entertains him royally. Many a lord has passed him in court and has wished him—and Father and Uncle Jorge—a good morrow. They don't care what we do in private."

"Not yet."

"Your fear—this family fear—about being discovered is unfounded."

The hag's eyes hardened. "Is that so?" she said. "And how do you know that our fear is unfounded?"

Rebecca didn't answer her.

The hag said, "Mayhap it's unfounded because you wish it so?"

"Grandmama," Rebecca said. "I pray you to believe me. Shakespeare can keep a secret."

"Let me tell you something about secrets, Becca," Grandmama said angrily. "I spent eight years of my life in a Portuguese dungeon because my sister could not keep secrets. It happened Yom Kippur, of all days, and my spoiled sister did not desire to fast as ordained by God. In a tearful fit of anger at my parents, she informed her Viejo Christian lover that her family was forcing her to starve. She went on to explain our old customs to him. On our fast days we greased our utensils and trenchers to make it appear as though we'd eaten. That we secretly changed the bed linens on Friday day. Small things they were, eh? But it was enough to mark us as heretics—Judaizers. And you know what her drunken scum lover did? He went and reported us to his priest. We were all arrested, including my sister, who was shown leniency only because she'd borne witness against her parents. Ah, but God wrought a final revenge on her soul. She was forced to watch her parents sizzle on the stake—roasted and blackened like lambs on a spit. She spent the rest of her life living with that horrid image. All because she could not keep secrets!"

Rebecca covered her mouth. Never had Grandmama spoken so openly about her wretched experiences in the Old Country.

"Shall I tell you about my life in a dungeon, Becca?" the hag continued in a hoarse whisper. "What your father—whom you dismiss as revolting—had insisted I keep from you."

Rebecca said nothing. Her body began to shake. She knew she was about to hear something horrible.

Grandmama said, "You're a woman who has yearned to be a man. Now act like one and listen. I'll tell you what your father and Uncle Jorge have told your brother and cousins."

Rebecca put her arm around the old woman and stroked the wrinkled cheek. Her grandam, so old and tired. "I never, never wanted to be spared for my own sake. I do want to hear your story. I *need* to hear it. It's my history as well"

Grandmama nodded. She spoke softly as Rebecca rocked her. She explained that after her entire family was arrested, the men of the Holy Office tried to extract a confession of Judaizing from her. When she refused, they resorted to their torture. The old woman felt Rebecca tense. She took her granddaughter's hand and kissed it. Rebecca had to know . . . she *had* to know. Otherwise, how could she learn the mind of a Gentile? Grandmama said,

"First they tied my wrists behind my back, attached my bound hands to a *strappado*—a pulley—and hoisted me off the floor. Left me dangling like a cobweb on the ceiling for hours, Becca, for *days*, it seemed. Finally the men of the tribunal felt me ready to confess. They lowered me to the ground and brought over a scribe, urged me to admit my guilt before them and God. I spat in their faces and resisted. The Inquisitor—not the Grand Inquisitor himself, but a subordinate anxious to prove himself holy—grew very angry. He attached weights to my ankles and once again raised me to the ceiling. I hung there for . . . I don't remember how long it was. Then a henchman lowered me to the ground with sudden jerks that uprooted my arms from their sockets, and pulled me up again.''

Rebecca felt her stomach turn sour. She kissed her grandam's frail little hand and begged her to stop. It was too hard on her. But the hag waved her quiet and continued her story. Again and again the torture was repeated but never to the point of death. A doctor closely guarded her life.

''If I should faint, they'd lower me until the doctor brought me back to earth. His name was Dr. Sanchez and I remember him well. A fair-complexioned man with cold, cold eyes and a wet, fleshy mouth. He never smiled, never winced. Only did his job, Rebecca. His work was to revive the wretches so the Holy See could continue its torture. Often the men would wait a day or two before continuing their evil procedures. That way our arms would swell and the *strappado* would be all the more painful. Then they'd start over again.''

The old woman rubbed her shoulder, swaying as she talked; her voice had become high and strained.

''They got what they wanted—my confession that I was a secret Jewess—but it wasn't enough, Becca. They wanted me to implicate others as well—my cousins, my friends. I refused—unlike my witch sister.''

The old woman began crying. Rebecca hugged her, her own face wet from tears. She was so proud of her grandam's defiance, but the recollection was too much for the old woman. Grandmama had turned a ghostly gray.

Rebecca said, ''I pray you to stop.''

But the old woman refused.

''Your father did you much harm when he insisted we protect you. Aye, after losing your two sisters, he could bear not the thought of his precious little girl's tears and sadness. But it was an error. You're not a rose, child, and you'll not drop your petals at the horrors I tell you.''

''But this talk makes *you* weak,'' Rebecca exclaimed. ''Oh, Grandmama, I'm worried about *your* health.''

''I'm not as weak as you think,'' the old woman said. ''I want to continue.''

Rebecca nodded, feeling utterly helpless to stop her grandmother's pain. The old woman resumed her narrative. Her voice had turned low-pitched and flat.

"When the *strappado* could not bring out from me the evidence against my friends, the Holy Office tried the *aselli*. I was laid naked upon a trestle table that had running across it sharp-edged rungs. . . . Not rapier-sharp blades, but the metal was . . . sharp. They cut slowly, first into the shoulders, then the arse, then the thighs and calves, finally the back almost to the spine. I still bear the scars, girl. . . . My head . . . It was bound in place by an iron bar. My ankles and wrists were clamped to the table with metal cuffs and tightened until my fingers and toes first tingled, then went numb.''

Rebecca covered her face and trembled. The hag lay her bony hand atop her granddaughter's shoulder.

"They forced open my mouth—one of the men was named Marcos, I still remember that. He had a very curly beard and never stopped smiling. I see him now when I close my eyes.'' The old woman shivered. "A group of them . . . they stuffed a rag down my throat. I gagged, coughed, felt my head go black, but the doctor adjusted the rag until it was in my windpipe yet I could still breathe—though with much labor. Marcos picked up a *jug* full of water and poured water slowly into the rag until it became soggy, saturated. It expanded with water and I could feel myself drowning. Of course, I blacked out, then I was revived—by the doctor, it must have been.''

She turned to Rebecca.

"They used four jugs of water on me, Becca. With each jug they poured, they simultaneously tightened the bands that held my wrists and ankles. My body felt like a cow's udder filled to utmost capacity—remember how you and Thomas and Miguel used to play with udders, fill them with air or water, then prick them with a pin until they burst?''

Rebecca nodded.

"My body was that cow's udder. I thought they would cut me with a knife and my innards would explode.''

"Merciful God!''

"They chose not to do that, of course. Twould have killed me.'' The hag broke into a spasm of coughs.

"I beg you to stop now,'' Rebecca pleaded. She patted the old woman's back.

"Aye,'' the hag said, clearing her throat. "I feel very weakened.''

"I'll help you back to your room, Grandmama.''

But the old woman refused to get up. She grabbed Rebecca's shoulder with incredible strength. "Eight hundred years our people lived in Iberia, Becca! Eight hundred years! The great

Maimonides was born in Cordoba! And now our ways, our houses of prayer, are gone! Destroyed! And those who try to secretly practice our old ways are ferreted out and burnt. *Our* mission is one of the few hopes they have left. We provide them a route of escape, with papers and a country willing to accept them. And even once they settle elsewhere, they, as secret or open Jews, are never safe.

"Oh Becca, you are so naive! To think *we* are safe in England, that you can speak freely to anyone! Iberia has the Inquisition, tis true. But England has its Star Chamber. The Queen's henchmen have nothing to learn from the Spanish about torture."

Rebecca nodded solemnly.

"We reside here in England and live as secret Jews only to help those in Iberia escape from the jaws of the Holy See," the hag continued. "The men in our family work continuously, put their lives in great peril, sneaking on ships, working countless hours to accumulate gold that is given to the monarchs to keep them fat and satisfied—and quiet. You must do your part and cause your father no more pain."

"As God is my witness, I'll be a dutiful daughter."

"It's amusing to dress as a man, to come and go at liberty. Go with Miguel if you want to dress as a man. Enjoy the plays, the bear and bull fights. Take pleasure in hawking and hunting. Drink at the fashionable alehouses. But do them with your family—with Miguel. He'll cosset you. His heart is molded from solid gold."

"It is," Rebecca said.

"And this Shakespeare. I believe him to be a honest man, very much taken with you—aye, he's foolish enough to get himself killed for your honor. But you belong to another and so does he. More important, he's an *outsider*. You must swear off of him."

Rebecca was silent, tears falling down her cheeks.

"I . . . can't."

The hag raised her eyebrows. "You've convinced yourself that you love him."

"I *do* love him."

"What you feel, girl, is what my sister felt for her lover—lust, excitement, passion at what is forbidden."

"It is love!"

"My sister loved her man as well. Only a matter of time before Shakespeare betrays us."

"I'll tell him *nothing* about our ways."

"Bah!"

"We speak love to each other, not the mission."

"No doubt," the old woman said disgustedly. "I'm sure you

two have passed your nights in blissful harmony, swearing worthless vows beneath the inconstant moon.''

Tears welled up in Rebecca's eyes. ''You mock me.''

The hag softened her expression. ''I don't mock you, girl. But you must stop thinking about your heart and think about what I've told you. Otherwise you'll end up like my sister and cause harm to your family.''

''Never would I do what your sister had done!'' Rebecca said.

''Then prove to me your iron will and bid Shakespeare goodbye.''

''Ask of me anything save what you ask now.''

''Tis no test of strength to fight a dove, Becca. Your feelings for Shakespeare are strong. Because they are so powerful, I'm now able to examine the fortitude of your convictions.''

''And if I refuse to stop seeing Shakespeare?''

''Then you refuse.''

''Would you tell Father if I continued to dally with Shakespeare?''

''Never.'' The old woman stood up, feeling unburdened. She'd told Becca everything. Now it was up to her granddaughter. ''You're no longer a child, girl. But know this. You have choices to make, Becca. Important choices that have *consequences*. Then—as with my sister—I'll know where *your* loyalties lay.''

The hag patted the young girl's hand, then left.

26

The proper art of knavery was best conducted in packs, Shakespeare discovered. So many good cons could be done with an accomplice, and Rebecca, being clever and fleet-footed, would have made the perfect one had she been a man. But she was a woman—aye, most definitely a woman—a black-hearted fiendish creature more unpredictable than the specter who stalked him.

Shakespeare sat at his desk and cringed as he thought of her.

She had bid him adieu without apologies. Her voice had been steady, her words carefully and painfully well chosen. The night they were caught was regrettable, she said. Most regrettable.

But now she had no choice but to obey her father's orders and never see him again.

Shakespeare understood her need to be a dutiful daughter. But what he didn't understand, what he couldn't *forgive*, was her aloof attitude toward him as she said her farewell. No tearful kisses, no final words of love. Only a simple good-bye. How Rebecca had changed from the girl he'd brought home the night of the attack, her stomach and head still sick from drink, her nerves loosened and raw with fright.

That fateful evening was followed by three weeks of bliss. Then they were caught. Gods, what a monster her father had been. But then again, hadn't Shakespeare—the interloper—also allowed anger to helm his senses? Choleric words had been blown forth by wind-driven tongues, and for a while tragedy had seemed inevitable—a most spleenful night.

Yet even in the wake of anger and distrust, Rebecca still managed to sneak into town and see him. She swore her love for him.

Then that sudden, icy good-bye.

The Devil with her.

Shakespeare sighed and pushed the memories out of his brain. He dipped his quill in his inkpot and planned his future.

Perhaps Rebecca's sudden change of heart was a sign from Providence. During the last month he had made no effort to find Harry's murderer. Though he had spent his waking hours flying on love's wings, his hours asleep were tortured images of a soul exiled to eternal unrest. While his love for Becca blossomed, his conscience wept with despair.

Harry. Always on his mind.

Help me, Whitman's ghost had pleaded in Shakespeare's dreams. The images. A wispy specter with no face standing before the crucifix, a candle in its diaphanous hand. Blood from its eyes. The stigmata.

Help me, Willy.

Ghastly images.

Perhaps it was all for the best. With time a plentiful crop, Shakespeare renewed his efforts to find his mentor's slayer. Now was the moment to blot Rebecca from his mind.

As if it were possible.

Concentrate on that plaintive voice.

Help me.

Shakespeare tapped his quill against his desktop and thought how he could get to Mackering.

Whatever thievery he dared would have to be executed alone. Petty cheating would merit him no reputation among the rogues and might well earn him a month in the stocks at Tyburn. If he wanted to attract Mackering's attention, he'd have to be known

as a cheat of much wit. The easiest way to procure such a dubious title was to cozen in grand fashion—con the *thief* instead
of the coney. Take from the cheats who worked for Mackering,
thereby filching from the uprightman himself.

Shakespeare stood and peered out his window, hoping to snag
a glimpse of the man skulking about the streets as a shadow—
the only real proof of his existence a swatch of black cloth torn
from his cape.

A month had passed and the demon had yet to return. An
elusive shadow, but he would be found.

That gravelly voice. Fading to Harry's voice.

Help me.

Shakespeare had heard the cry many times during Harry's life.
Mostly when Whitman was drunk. But not always. Once the plea
belched forth from Harry's throat as the dust of melancholia
settled upon his distressed soul.

How Harry had cried, cried for his father.

I was his disappointment, he moaned. *I failed to reach my
destiny.*

Harry had never mentioned his father before, and Shakespeare
had been confused by the outburst. He asked if reconciliation
were possible.

Never, Harry cried out. Then in a calm voice he announced,
My father is dead. Suddenly, Harry clutched Shakespeare's hands
and pleaded,

Oh Willy, help me!

Shakespeare had to rock him to sleep.

Sleep was what Shakespeare needed now. But love had already
lost him too much time. No hours left for rest. He slipped his
cloak across his shoulders and closed the door behind him.

It was well known that Mackering had diverse cheats in his
employ—cutpurses, hookers, unlicensed beggars, highwaymen,
and a host of bawds—and a decent amount of money they could
collect. Enough to supply their uprightman with pots of good
port, a feather mattress, and money to waste at dicing. But
Mackering had a reputation for extravagance—the finest clothes,
imported weapons, and purebred steeds. That amount of coins
only came from sacking the houses of the rich, robbing the goldsmith at knifepoint, or dealing in horse tricks. Shakespeare opted
for horse tricks. A properly doctored animal could bring in many
pounds if the disease or handicap was masked especially well.
Many an unsuspecting gentleman had fallen prey to the jiggler's
game.

It was off to Smithfield Market. Shakespeare walked a few
blocks west, then turned south onto Bishopsgate, deciding to
travel by way of the Cheape.

Shakespeare had learned about horses while tending them for the gentlemen playgoers during his early days in London. He had seen thousands of animals in his day, could tell at a glance which horses were swift by nature, which ones foundered and halted out of stubbornness. More than once it had been Shakespeare, not the groomers, who'd first recognized the telltale signs of glanders or other equine disease. Equally as important, Shakespeare learned how defects were hidden by unscrupulous horse traders who had tried to trap him into a partnership of crime. The rogues had showed him how they turned jades into jewels, nags into the horses of nobility. Often these cheats played upon the men as they exited the theater, offering to find them steeds at a laughingly low cost.

Shakespeare had become so clever at detecting imperfections that the Fates and crossed stars might have made him a jiggler instead of a player. But God and Harry had kept him an honest man.

Now the Fates had given him his most challenging role: that of a thief who'd swindle from the villainous Mackering. If Shakespeare's scheme worked as planned, Mackering would have to feel his purse lighter of weight and could no longer ignore Shakespeare's presence.

Shakespeare walked steadily, unable to go for more than a mile without Rebecca entering his thoughts. He imagined her slender hands holding his face, her arms engulfing his waist. Why did she bid him good-bye so coldly? Why? Why? If only she had been as upset as he, then perhaps the open wound in his heart would scab and scar. No, the center of his love would never be virginal again, but at least the ever-present aching that rubbed him sore would heal.

Varium et mutabile semper femina—a woman is an inconstant creature.

For three glorious weeks they had dallied—ah, sweet hours of night they had been, Becca shivering in her nightdress, his cloak draped over her willowy shoulders, her face beautifully framed by creeping mist and wisps of raven hair. How they had kissed, embraced, pledged troths of undying love.

Then that disastrous night. The full moon was deadly, spewing forth outrageous fury. Rebecca's father, driven mad with rage, stormed into the gardens and found them embracing. The doctor was consumed with ire, screaming at her, at him, not giving either of them a chance to explain that nothing unholy had ever passed between them. Finished, Lopez then stalked into the house, Rebecca holding tightly to the hem of his doublet, being pulled along. She had begged her father to listen, but to no avail. Shakespeare had no choice but to follow her indoors.

Inside, her father had renewed his attacks.

This is how you do homage to your father! You liar! You whore! Manuel de Andrada was right about you! Oh, my foul hap! My star-crossed luck! How deep goes the knife that cuts my heart! How it stabs sharply into the man cursed with a willful daughter!

Father, let me explain.

It was at that moment when the doctor had slapped her. Shakespeare stood, holding his tongue and shaking fists, trying to defend Rebecca when the doctor redirected his ire against him, screaming him a drunkard, a knave, a seducer of men's wives, and swearing by God to see him in the stocks. Shakespeare exploded and told the doctor what he thought of him, of the nuptials he had arranged for his daughter, calling him—Gods, had he really uttered such vile words?—a whoremonger who'd thought nothing of selling his own daughter to a buggerer. Rebecca's cousins, witnessing the scene from afar, gasped in horror as Shakespeare spoke. Rebecca's mother, who had been dressed for bed, rushed down the stairs as the shouting increased in volume. She clutched her heart and declared herself ill. Her brother in a moment of hot bluster intervened on his father's behalf and challenged him to a duel.

Shakespeare accepted and drew his sword.

The doctor blanched.

Ben made a few preliminary attacks. It was then obvious to Shakespeare that the brother wasn't the swordsman his sister was.

Rebecca threw herself at Shakespeare's feet and begged him to stop.

He complied.

Benjamin cursed his sister, kicked her out of the way, and lunged at Shakespeare.

Rebecca pleaded with her cousins to intercede for her sake, for *Ben's* sake. The older, dark-complexioned one called Dunstan approached his cousin but was repelled instantly by the tip of Ben's sword at his throat. The doltish brother began shouting curses at both his cousins, calling them cowards and worse, rebuking them for not supporting their uncle's honor.

Suddenly appeared another man in the room—Rebecca's uncle, Shakespeare had learned later—who demanded the duel halt immediately. But Benjamin appeared not to have heard. He lunged at Shakespeare once again. Shakespeare parried the attack and slashed the tip of his sword across Ben's doublet, cutting layers of clothing, but blessed be God, no skin.

The doctor, his color even whiter, shouted for the violence to end. Shakespeare lowered his rapier, but Benjamin charged. Rebecca screamed, stuck out her foot and tripped her brother. Ben stumbled across the room and bashed his head against the wall. Blood dripped from a wide gash across his forehead, crimson rivulets flowing over his eyes, nose, and lips.

Rebecca's mother fainted. Becca rushed to her side and pleaded for everyone to hold their peace.

Ben stood up and wiped the blood from his face. Shakespeare thought at last the fighting was over. But Ben's mind had gone daft. He rushed Shakespeare, rapier thrust outward. Her other cousin—the swordsman, Sir Thomas—interceded and blocked Ben's lunge. With a single blow Thomas knocked the sword out of Ben's hand. Ben frothed with anger. He charged bare-handed at his cousin and finally had to be restrained by his father and uncle. Only then, thanks be to the Merciful One, was the duel called off.

Mercury and Mars—a mortal duo. How brightly they shone that night. With the full moon shining, the planets held the earth spellbound in cursed configuration.

But the planets changed—and so had his luck, he thought. She had showed up at his closet several times, pledging eternal love for him. Despite the wretched evening, she'd come back to him. But her words proved false. The final time was so different. Agonizingly different. She was cool—cold—frosty with composure. Her cousin was waiting for her outside, she said. Then the simple good-bye.

Never see me again.

Marry, how he had tried to change her mind, pleaded with her, cried to her face. She remained unmoved. He sneaked over the wall that very night and tapped at her window, repeated the effort for a week. Never had she given him a response. His only good fortune had been avoiding the estate guards.

How stupidly naive he was! And to think he'd yearned for a passionate, unpredictable woman. Rebecca had sworn her love for him constant and never ending. Aye—as constant as snow in summer, as never ending as youth. She was as mercurial in love as she was in life.

Gods, he was a dolt. A valuable lesson he had learned—the price paid by impetuousness. With Mackering the stakes were higher, and moving rashly might well land him a severed heart instead of merely a broken one. He would have to act with his brain and not with emotions. He would become a Stoic.

Smithfield was open land steeped in a history of ashes and blood. North of Newgate, the undeveloped acreage sat outside London wall, bordered by newly built tenement housing on the west and the massive St. Bartholomew's Church and Hospital to the east, the landmarks having been erected during the reign of

King Henry the First. Smithfield had once been jousting ground—a stage upon which many a mail-armored knight had battled to his death. The site—the Tyburn of its day—had also lived through centuries of executions. Thousands of thieves, murderers, and traitors had been hung, quartered, burned, or beheaded at Smithfield, their humors and remains forever mixed with soil from which sprouted a carpet of velvety, rippling grass. The land still played host to an occasional burning of a witch, but was mostly used for benign purposes like fairgrounds for St. Bartholomew's Day. Today the land had been turned into an open market for buying and selling livestock.

The bright sun illuminated the crowds milling about, people shouting at each other, at the animals, scanning placid horses that occasionally kicked up clouds of dust and hay. Cows mewed and swished their tails lazily, turned circles in their cramped pens. Dung mongers reached between the bars of the stalls, scooped out excrement and slopped it into wooden wheelbarrows.

Shakespeare knew there were but a few priggers among the many honest, and they blended inconspicuously. But with his keen eyes and sharp ears, he felt he could glean them from the masses. He walked among the people, listening, looking, always alert.

An hour later he thought he found a cheat—an unctuous man with a well-formed face and a deep laugh. Shakespeare observed him for another quarter hour, noticing that his eyes never rested on any one spot. The rogue was jumpy, with shaky hands. He hesitated when he walked, taking but a few steps at any one time, paused, pivoted around, then glanced over his shoulder. Shakespeare watched him straighten his back, smooth his doublet, turn around, and follow a gentleman. The cheat sneaked up behind him and covered his eyes with his hands.

The gentleman stood still, appearing to play the cheat's game of guess who.

After a moment or two the gentleman turned around and looked puzzled.

The cheat reddened and appeared to offer bountiful apologies for his error.

Shakespeare elbowed his way through a pile of merchants and eased over to them, managing to catch snatches of speech. ". . . Methought you were my cousin, sir . . . remarkable resemblance, sir . . . twin."

The gentleman responded that no harm was done.

They walked away from Shakespeare, still engaged in conversation. Shakespeare followed, trying to overhear their words. They stopped walking but continued talking.

The gentleman's name was Thomas Grey, and he and the cheat seemed to be conversing about horses. The jiggler spoke to Grey in deferential tones, mentioning ". . . a gray-dabble for sale . . . overpriced . . . older than the owner admitted . . . lower cost . . ."

The gentleman's smile grew with each passing word the jiggler spoke.

Shakespeare edged even closer, his back to Grey's.

"Meet me in the south corner, Master Grey," the jiggler said. "Near the enclosure holding ten spotted sheep. I'll show you a value of a horse. The animal's worth more than anything penned here."

A half hour passed, then the jiggler reemerged on horseback at the designated spot. The animal he rode was a beauty—a coal-black mare with a startling white blaze—and no doubt diseased.

"She's magnificent," the gentleman said.

"Aye," said the cheat, dismounting.

"Simply magnificent," repeated Master Grey. "The noble carriage of a horse of much breeding. Proud and pretty. Why do you offer it to me for so little money, my good man?"

"Alas, goodmaster," said the jiggler. "I dare not burden you with my problems, but once I was a man of much means. Not gentry like you, Master Grey, of course—dare I be so impudent as to imply such a thing! But I was a well-heeled merchant, Master Grey, not this pathetic man which stands before you. I had much in the way of coinage, which I had invested overseas. But the Fates, the winds, and the sea were unkind to me. I was left with piles of bond notes, forced to sell everything to my creditors. Only Midnight . . ." He patted the mare gently. "She is the last reminder of my former days."

"Then why do you sell her, good man?"

"My creditors leave me no choice. And no peace shall I have until all my debts are paid. Alas, I am an honest man."

"But why do you ask so little for her?" asked Grey. "Anyone would be willing to pay you double the price you ask of me."

"My gentle master," the jiggler said, "more important to me than money is the purchaser of Midnight. That's why I offer her to you at a mockery of a price. I see by your eyes that you are good and just and will be a gentle and patient man with my prize steed. I'd rather you own her and receive less compensation than to sell her to a tyrant for more coins. Take her for a ride, Master Grey. See how easily she obeys the slightest pull of the reins."

Master Grey mounted the horse. Twenty minutes later the transaction was completed, the jiggler watching his coney ride off and snickering as he stuffed the coins in his doublet. Shakespeare sneaked up behind him.

"What news have you, good man?" Shakespeare asked him.

Startled, the jiggler whirled around. "Naught," he said quickly. "No news at all."

Suddenly Shakespeare grabbed the jiggler's arm and twisted it behind his back. "I challenge you to call for help, thief," he whispered.

The jiggler gasped.

"Do we understand one another?" Shakespeare asked.

The thief nodded.

"Well it is, then." Shakespeare maintained his grip.

"What is it you want?" asked the jiggler.

"Your name."

"George—"

"Bah," interrupted Shakespeare. "The name that the society calls you."

"Good man, I understand not—"

Shakespeare increased the pressure on the man's arm. "The magnificent horse you'd just sold was infected with glanders. Nay, not a sign of the vile illness did she show. Her head was held high and mighty only because you blew sneezing powder up her nostrils, washing her mouth out with garlic, mustard, and ale. . . . Whew, all but an idiot like your coney could smell the wind of the animal's breath a mile away."

"You err, good man," insisted the jiggler.

"*Do* I? Together we shall ride back to your purchaser and play a simple game. I shall grab the nag by the throat until she coughs. Know what will pass, thief? The mare's jaw will shake—a certain sign of the foul disease. Tush, man, how your gull will raise a hue and a cry."

The jiggler said nothing.

"What is your society name?" Shakespeare repeated.

The cheat paused, then said, "Picker."

"Ah, my good man, Picker, how good it is to make your acquaintance. And who do you work for?"

"Myself."

"And?"

"Just myself."

Shakespeare pulled out his dagger and placed the point against the cheat's ribs. "Who is your uprightman?"

Picker said nothing.

Shakespeare nudged the dagger a little deeper. A small red circle leaked around the dagger point. The cheat bit his lip.

"Pardons, Picker, I heard not your answer. Who is your uprightman?"

Picker remained silent.

Shakespeare pushed the jiggler's arm up his back.

"Aaaaaaaah." Picker's eyes rolled back and he moaned. "Mackering."

"And you give your money to him?"

"Aye," he whispered. "My arm . . ."

Shakespeare lowered the arm. "And you keep none of it?"

"It all goes to Mackering."

"The horse was his?"

"Aye. He buys the sick and the lame out of town. We doctor them and sell them at Smithfield."

"Who is *we*?"

"Me and Teeth."

"And Teeth is here now?"

"I know not, good man." The jiggler pleaded, "For mercy's sake, let go of my arm."

"Not yet. Describe this man Teeth to me."

"He has none."

"Has none of what?"

"Teeth. His mouth is as barren as the womb of a nun."

"Tell me more."

"He's goodly sized in height but very slight in weight. He wears today a black cloak, a green doublet, and brown hose and stockings. He rides upon a milk-white jade."

"Your craw is choked with lies, Picker," said Shakespeare. "In one breath you say you know not if Teeth is even here and in the next you describe him perfectly to me—down to the clothes he wears this morrow."

"Aye, I lie, sir," Picker said, struggling under Shakespeare's grip.

"Yes, you lie, Picker, out of habit. None of that. We must have a meeting of the minds. Teeth is here in Smithfield today?"

"Aye."

"Who else?"

"Only Teeth."

Shakespeare raised his arm upward until the cheat's wrist rested against the crown of his scruffy head.

"One good shove and the bone is broken."

"I swear on my mother's grave that only Teeth and I work the field today!"

"No doubt your mother is very much alive, eh? Know you, scoundrel, what God does to those who swear falsely?"

Picker didn't answer.

"Aye, soon enough you'll find out. But worry not, as you'll not be done in by my hand." Shakespeare walked Picker over to a large, conical haystack, near a pen of horses but away from the crowd. "Of course, I'll still have to rob you and tie you up lest you tell your cousin Teeth that I'm after him. Nothing personal. What transpired betwixt you and me was naught but business. And since the money stays not in your purse anyway, consider me a thief of Mackering, not of you."

"Who are you?" asked Picker in a whisper.

"You may tell your supreme ruffler that he was lifted by William Shakespeare, who most urgently desires an audience with him. I regret the inconvenience I've caused you, Picker, but your master is an impossible man to locate. Like the wood beetle, you never really see him, only the damage he's done. Now scream if you will, man, but know that I've learned the name of the man you gulled. I'm sure Master Grey would love dearly to know yours in a day or two."

Picker was silent.

"Good," Shakespeare said, pulling some leather thongs from his belt. He bound Picker's hands and feet securely, and when he was done, he smiled at the jiggler and took his money. Wishing him a good morrow, Shakespeare buried him lightly in the pile of hay and went off in search of Teeth.

The crowd was packed, people pressed upon one another until it seemed that the penned livestock had more room to move than those who inspected the pens. Wary of the cutpurse, Shakespeare untied his purse from his belt and clutched it in his hand. He passed a fat sow rolling in the cool mud of her sty, squealing and snuffling with delight. Her tiny eyes met his and her thick-whiskered snout seemed to turn upward in a tease of a smile.

Who's mocking whom?

A hopeless task it was to locate Teeth.

Shakespeare swam through the sea of buyers, searching in vain for a tall, thin man with a black cloak, green doublet, and brown round hose and stockings. He found a tall, fat man wearing a green doublet and black hose who turned out to be a German count. He spied a small, thin man wearing a brown cloak, a green doublet, and brown hose who was a clerk from the Chancery.

An hour passed. No sign of Teeth. Shakespeare pressed on, searching for Teeth while witnessing the free entertainment about him. He saw numerous pickpockets perform their trade, overheard heated words between two drunken knights which eventually led to a slow-footed brawl. He received numerous bawdy looks from stews and debated boarding a sweet-looking wench with chestnut curls. After a moment of thought, he declined her lewd offers of pleasure and forced himself to think of Harry. He doubled his efforts—pushed his way through the crowd, looking for Teeth, for a shadow as well.

Two hours into the search he felt a sudden heat on the back of his neck, an invisible force that filled his body with fire.

He spun around.

Rebecca!

Quickly she lowered her eyes, and a second later was lost in the crowd.

He charged in her direction, parting a pathway through the mob as if he were clearing overgrown woodlands.

She was gone.

Damn his luck!

He walked a few more steps, then turned to his right.

Her eyes again, staring at him from afar.

History repeated.

Where can we meet? he mouthed to her.

She shook her head no and turned her back to him.

At Rebecca's side was a tall, muscular man. His face was strong and God had blessed him with a hat of ebony ringlets. She placed her hand gently on his arm, leaned over and whispered something to him. He laughed.

Was this her sodomite fiancé, this handsome man who stood erect, muscles that seemed to be sculpted from stone? Had she mocked him with a tale that was no more than a bundle of lies, gleefully laughing as she versed away his love?

Shakespeare felt his heart go slack, his fingers go numb. An immediate chill doused a fire that only a moment ago had burned uncontrollably, leaving in its wake smoke and ashes.

Rebecca's father—the doctor—appeared. He led the couple over to a splendid white mare and hoisted Rebecca atop the horse. There she sat, the cold queen upon a throne of white velvet, subjugating his heart without a tear of mercy. Shakespeare felt himself weak with desire to hold her. She met his eyes, her bottom lip trembling slightly.

Meet me, he mouthed in desperation.

Again she shook her head no and lowered her gaze to her feet.

Damn her to the Devil!

Shakespeare turned and walked away, his weakened knees barely able to hold his weight. He tried to erase her face from his mind. To concentrate on Teeth.

It was useless. His brain, like a homing pigeon, returned to her—her vows of love, the satin touch of her lips, the taste of her tears. After thirty minutes of aimless wandering, he found himself near the sow who had taunted him earlier. He sank down on the ground next to her.

Move over, pig. Willy's coming in to join you.

He covered his face, hot tears of shame burning his eyes. He felt a tap on his shoulder and jumped upward.

"Stop following me," Rebecca said angrily. "I'm not to see you ever again. If my father catches me talking to you, I'll never have his trust again."

"I didn't *follow* you," Shakespeare said.

"Aye, you're here by coincidence," she said. Her voice was caustic. "I hear well-rhythmed knocks on my window at night, Willy. Are those coincidences as well?"

Such cruel words. Shakespeare felt a sudden burst of anger explode inside of him.

"I fully confess that the knocking was mine, Becca. But I did *not* follow you here."

"You just *happened* to pick today to shop for a horse?"

"I have my reasons for being here. They don't concern you, mistress."

"You lie, Will."

"It's *Shakespeare* to you, and not a word of falsehood have I spoken."

"You followed me here," Rebecca insisted. "Just as you pursued me the day of our duel."

Shakespeare looked at her, her cheeks red and moist. There was no point in exhuming what was dead. He started to walk away. Rebecca grabbed his sleeve.

"Then *what* are you doing here?" she asked.

Shakespeare regarded her hand clutching his sleeve. Embarrassed, she pulled her hand away. They stared at each other. Shakespeare finally asked,

"What are *you* doing here?"

"My betrothed and I met my father at St. Bartholomew's at the noon hour. He had finished his daily ministrations on the wards and suggested a walk about Smithfield. I think Father intends to buy us a horse as an engagement gift. My God, Willy, if he sees you here—talking to me—I can't see you anymore."

"You've made that clear . . . in actions as well as words."

"Oh, stop being so calm," she said. She started to cry. "My God, if he catches me with you—"

Shakespeare pulled her to his breast. She threw her arms around his neck. They hugged, kissed with newfound passion.

"No," Rebecca said, breaking away from his embrace. "I must go."

"Come away with me," Shakespeare said, holding her arms. Rebecca looked at him. "What?"

Shakespeare suddenly realized what he had blurted out, realized what it entailed. The winds of love were pushing him into uncharted lands. But oh how sweet was the sailing.

"I can't do that," Rebecca said.

"Aye, thou canst," he insisted. "Together we'll build what neither can attain alone."

"I can't come with thee . . . My God, my father—"

"Where are he and . . ." Shakespeare rotated his hand in the air.

"Miguel," said Rebecca.

"Yes, Miguel. Where are they?"

"I've supposedly lost them in the crowd. I must go and search for them. Please don't ever try to see me again."

Shakespeare said, "And those are your parting words? You sought me out to crush my heart?"

"I erred to seek you out from the start."

Shakespeare exclaimed, "You swore undying love for me. Was it just empty flattery?"

"No," Rebecca said. She clutched his hands. "No. Not at all. I loved thee, love thee still. But what hope have we for lifelong love, me with my betrothed, thee with a wife. Is it thy intention to divorce her, disown thy children?"

Shakespeare felt a lump form in his throat. He kissed her hands, brought them to his face. "If God had given me the power to foretell the future, I would have reserved my heart for thee. But He keeps it his private possession. I'd sell my soul to Lord Satan himself if he would reverse the passage of passed moons!"

"Don't say that!"

Shakespeare said, "I love thee."

"I love thee as well," Rebecca said. "But love as we do, there's no future for us."

Shakespeare knew she was right. There was an order to life. To upset God's plans could only bring upon them dire tragedy. He hugged her fiercely, smothered her face with kisses.

"Nothing I'd say could change thy mind, eh?"

"Nothing," Rebecca said.

"Pray, just think about it—"

"No, Willy. It is not ordained." She kissed him. "Yet I know I will always love thee. And I wish thee happiness. Pray, give me *thy* blessing. It would mean so much to me."

Shakespeare waited a moment, then said softly, "Go to Miguel. Make for him a good and dutiful wife. I wish thee a long . . . and fruitful . . . and happy life."

"I shall never forget thee," Rebecca said.

"Nor will I forget thee." He released her from his arms. "Much hap I wish you, friend."

"You as well," Rebecca said.

Her voice was steady. Shakespeare turned his back on her. He waited a moment then glanced over his shoulder. She was gone. She never saw his tears.

27

It appeared to Cuthbert Burbage that the beggar was approaching him. Quickly, he turned aside. Had times been plentiful, he would have been generous with his coins. But Black Death had emptied not only his purse, but the pockets of the fellowship as well. Gods, what a terrible spring it had been. The great Harry Whitman dead, the theaters again bolted shut, his brother Richard waxing on about the foul breath of London's air. Cuthbert couldn't wait to get out of the city. Take the books and the fellows on the roads and enjoy some clear vapors.

He looked up and found himself face to face with the beggar.

"Be gone," Cuthbert said. It came out "be god." His high-pitched, whiny voice had become muffled due to a stuffed nose. "I haven't anything in my purse." As if to illustrate the point, he opened his velvet sack and showed the empty lining to the pauper.

"A pity," said the vagabond. "I've an abundance of metal. Twas a fruitful day." He reversed the pockets of his jerkin and out spilled two dozen silver coins. "Need you a groat?"

The voice, Cuthbert thought.

"Shakespeare?"

"Waiting for me, Burbage?"

"What— What are you doing in tatters? And where did you get all this money?"

Shakespeare pointed to the ground and said,

> *"I give you reason for this rhyme.*
> *I present to you offsprings of mother*
> *crime."*

He bent down, picked up the coins from the road and glanced over his shoulder. Jerking his head toward his room, he said. "Upstairs . . . Nasty cold you have, my good man."

Burbage said, "Why in God's name are you dressed—"

"In private, my friend. All will be explained . . . of sorts."

They entered the tenement and climbed the stairs in silence. Shakespeare gave another quick look behind his back and unlocked the door. Cuthbert was about to enter, but Shakespeare held him back.

"A moment," he said. The player swung open the door and slowly let his eyes drift across his room. Satisfied that nothing was out of order, he stepped aside and allowed Cuthbert to cross the threshold. Burbage's eyes rested on a peach sitting solo on the trestle table. Shakespeare picked it up and tossed it to him.

"You look wan, Cuthbert," he said. "Sit."

"It's this blasted nose of mine. And I haven't had much opportunity to eat today."

"I've fresh apricots as well," Shakespeare said. "And some boiled beef from last night's supper." He placed a frothy mug of ale on the table and a trencher of meat. "Eat and drink. We've much time to exchange pleasantries and news."

"Let us forego the pleasantries," Cuthbert said between bites of beef. He wiped his nose on his shirt-sleeve. "What news, Shakespeare? What mean you by attiring yourself in such garb?"

Shakespeare placed the coins on the table then stripped himself naked to the waist, tossing his clothes onto his pallet. "I'm a player bereft of a stage," he said. "So I practice my craft whenever I can on whomever I can. And a very convincing beggar I must have been, as even you did not recognize me until I spoke."

Cuthbert took three successive gulps of ale. "Aye, your ragged costume, your face embellished with sores, the pathetic limp in your walk . . . And what shall you say when the Queen's men arrest you for vagrancy and put your head in the stocks? I was only playacting?"

"Such lack of trust I'd expect from others, Cuthbert . . . but you? If I am to play the beggar, would not I be equipped with a beggar's license?"

"Where'd you get the license?"

Shakespeare smiled cryptically.

"You forged it, aye?" Cuthbert said.

"A wizard never reveals the secrets of his arts."

"Willy, what in God's name are you doing?"

Shakespeare kicked off his toeless shoes. "First tell me what magical bell summoned you to my humble abode."

Cuthbert said, "I've fair news, my cousin."

"The Master of the Revels has reopened the theaters?"

"No . . . not at all. How could he with London so riddled with death?"

"Good news you say?" Shakespeare sat down opposite Cuthbert. "You must have arranged to take the fellowship on the road this summer."

"Fresh air, Willy. Open highways, the summer's greenery in full blossom. And mayhap even a stop at Warwick to see the wife and the bairns." Cuthbert smiled and poked Shakespeare in the ribs with his elbow. "Remove ourselves from the rancid stench of the city."

Shakespeare ran his finger through the coins. "My apologies, but fate dictates that I not join you."

Cuthbert frowned. "And why is that?"

"I fall behind on my promised poem to Lord Southampton," Shakespeare said. "I must poise myself, quill in hand, and finish the work for my benefactor. Since Black Death has been London's constant companion for the last year, methinks Southampton will be buying my bread come the winter. I dare not peeve the young lord with tardiness."

"Then why do you playact a beggar instead of write?" Cuthbert challenged.

Shakespeare thought a moment. "Atmosphere," he said. "A good writer must sate himself with atmosphere."

"I must be missing something," Cuthbert answered. "I see no connection between a beggar and Lucrece. She is the subject of your latest poem, is she not? Had you playacted the raped virgin, then I—being the simpleton—might have understood your point."

"And that is why God has made me the bookwriter and you the housekeeper. You see things much too literally."

"Are we to continue this mockery, Willy, or are you to tell me the truth?"

Shakespeare spun a groat, watched it sparkle as it twirled until it fell flat on its face. "Had the theaters remained opened this past year, I wouldn't have accepted Lord Southampton's endowment. I would have made do as a player. But being greedy, in want of bread and meat, I took his money and owe him the best of my ability."

"You've always acted and written simultaneously . . . well, not simultaneously, but—"

"A poem is different."

"Yet last year you wrote *Venus and Adonis* as we toured."

"*Venus and Adonis* was simplistic compared to Lucrece. The poem I pen now demands more commitment. More concentration."

"And your decision has nothing to do with Harry's death?"

"Why should it?"

"I'm concerned for your welfare, Shakespeare. Everyone

knows you seek out George Mackering, and he's as sly and sharp-toothed a wolverine as ever there lived.''

Shakespeare scooped up a handful of coins, let them fall like a silvery cascade onto the table. "He's my only connection to Harry."

"What makes you think Mackering was involved? Because some jack innkeeper said it was such. How do you know this innkeeper— What was his name?''

"Chambers.''

"How do you know Chambers was speaking to you in earnest?''

"Tis possible he lied in his throat.''

"And his lie could lead you to unmentionable consequences at Mackering's hands.''

"I desire only a word with the ruffian. Surely there's no harm in that.'' But Shakespeare's voice lacked conviction. "The very fact that Mackering has thus avoided my attempts for conversation leads me to believe that he was involved in Harry's death.''

"So your death will somehow avenge Harry's?''

Shakespeare pounded his fist on the table. "I've no room in my gut for fear or doubt, Cuthbert. I owe Henry Whitman his murderer's head on the bridge!''

"I, more than anyone, knew what Harry had done for you. After all, twas I who was the recipient of his words on your behalf.'' He lowered his voice an octave and orated, " 'Cuthbert! I demand that the number of Shakespeare's lines be increased twofold. He's wasted as a groom! . . . Cuthbert, Shakespeare has to live. He needs more money per book! . . . Cuthbert, Shakespeare must become a shareholder else you'll find yourself looking for a replacement this afternoon.' Gods, the man was as insufferable as Richard.''

"Remember how your brother and Harry went at it?'' Shakespeare said wistfully. "How the two of them could blow—like Joshua's horn, their voices could bring down walls.''

Cuthbert smiled. "Harry was the only person I knew whose voice could drown out Richard's.''

"Twas close.''

"Very close.''

Shakespeare sighed. "So you see why I have to follow my heart.''

"Harry would not have approved of your quest,'' Cuthbert said. "His ghost told you to let the dead rest in peace. Perhaps he was protecting you, warding you off of something dangerous. Listen to him.''

"That was no ghost,'' Shakespeare said. "Harry's ghost would not have needed a blow to my head to stun my inquiries.''

"Marry, then who was it?"

"That I don't know."

"It could be anyone," Cuthbert said.

"Anyone who *knew* my connection with Harry, yes," Shakespeare said.

"Have you talked to Margaret about this?"

"What for? I've found out nothing new. And why worry her? It was at her behest that I started looking into Harry's death. If anything were to happen to me, she'd drown in a pool of remorse. As if her request is the reason I continue my quest. It is my will, not hers, that keeps me going."

"But as Harry's wife, tis possible she could illuminate her husband's relationship with this Chambers fellow."

"Margaret and I had already conversed upon the topic of Chambers when I arrived back in town from my first trek up North. She never heard of the innkeeper."

"So there you have it. Chambers is a prevaricator."

"All it means to me is that Harry, like most men, kept secrets from his wife."

"Did you ask Margaret why Harry had upon him so much money?"

"Yes. She knows not the reason for that either."

"I state that Chambers was lying."

"Perhaps."

"I state that Chambers was lying about Mackering as well."

Shakespeare shrugged. "A possibility. But I'll know more about that after I've spoken with the rogue, which I *mean* to do. More ale, Cuthbert?"

28

The coins were neatly stacked and categorized, a piece of vellum attached to each pile stating from which trick the coins had been attained and from whom they'd been filched. Shakespeare's own purse had grown light of late and his eyes couldn't resist the pull of the glittering columns of silver and gold. Aye, the money was tainted, obtained by connivery, yet stolen metal purchased goods as easily as the coins he'd earned from writing or acting.

Pity the good and just. Let no man state that thievery didn't pay. What amazed him was how simple the lifting had been. You wanted it, it was yours for the taking. Twas surprising that there remained any honest men when the rewards from knavery so greatly outweighed the risks of being caught.

He'd done it all—cheated Mackering's cutpurses, stolen coins from his beggars' baskets, outfoxed his stews who had tried to rob him. He even sampled a few of the fairer ones, including Mackering's own doxy, Mary Biddle. Shakespeare had smiled when he filched the clothes off of the hooker's crome and cheated Mackering's horse thieves. He even robbed merchandise from Mackering's barn of stolen wares. Shakespeare had found out where Mackering hid his goods from a whore who was less than enamored of her master. And he had performed all his cheating in the light of day!

Yes, the thieving had been easy, even humorous at times, but always he sensed hidden danger. Not from the constables or the watchmen—they didn't bother him—but from a lurking black shadow waiting for him to lower his guard. His thoughts were not allowed to wander in public—a mixed blessing. He had to push aside images useful for future books and poetry, but at least his mind had been focused away from *her*!

His tired eyes shifted from the coins to the book in front of him. Gods, he'd spent the entire night scribbling away, finishing two pages of verse for Lord Southampton and six hundred lines of prose—two and one-half scenes. The ideas had poured out—a gush of creativity that had been dammed back by daytime vigilance. He could barely decipher his own writing.

All night he'd written, persevering past sunrise, past the breakfast hour. Like most of the men he knew, he never ate in the morning, the early repast being a sign of the weak or the infirm. Now the dinner hour was approaching, but his stomach would have to wait.

Yawning, he rose from his desk and sank onto his pallet. He'd changed the straw yesterday, and the sweet, fresh aroma filled nostrils previously clogged by the smell of tallow. He closed his eyes. Sleep came swiftly but lasted not long enough. His heart was jolted awake by a rude banging at his door.

"Patience," Shakespeare shouted. He arose groggily. "Who comes?"

The reply was muffled.

Shakespeare grabbed his dagger, stepped to the side, and threw open the door.

A boy walked in, a stylus held tightly in his hand. He was no more than fourteen, dressed in rags, dirty and thin. His eyes were wide with fright, his hands and bare arms caked with mud.

"Sir?" he inquired.

Shakespeare grasped him from behind and held a dagger at his neck.

"Drop the skene, my bene cove. You've no need for it here."

The boy's knife fell to the floor.

"That's good," Shakespeare said. "You're a messenger, a tumbler in your language."

The boy nodded.

"For whom?"

"Mackering."

"Your name?"

"Pigsfeet."

Shakespeare looked down at the boy's feet. His exposed toes rested on the soles of his open shoes like sausages on a platter. The fourth and fifth digits had been fused together. Shakespeare kicked the boy's fallen dagger to the opposite side of the room, shut the door with his foot, then released the boy from his grip.

"Sit on that chair."

Pigsfeet backed into the seat, unwilling to turn his back on Shakespeare. His saucer eyes crept around the room and landed on the pile of money. Shakespeare pulled up a chair and sat in front of him.

"State your business."

"Me uprightman be wantin' you to bing a wast with me."

"When?"

"Now."

"Where?"

"Somewhere in London."

"London is a large city. You'll have to be more specific."

The boy said nothing.

"You have parents?" Shakespeare asked.

"Taken by the plague," said Pigsfeet. "Me aunt had me for a summer and a half till I ran away with a wench. She and I filched what we could in the day—and niggled greatly in the night." He smiled with blackened teeth. "Then she dallied with Mackering. Now she's *his* special doxy and I break into houses for the master—steal for him bread, milk, or bacon. Other things ifin I see them well."

He pointed to Shakespeare's door.

"I jiggled many a door, but the lock on yours is harder than rock," he said with admiration. "Can I see the latch?"

"No."

The boy sat back and sulked.

"Hungry?" Shakespeare asked. He got up and threw the boy a piece of stale rye bread.

Pigsfeet caught it. Gobbled it up in two bites.

"Master doesn't feed you too well, does he?" said Shake-speare.

"He's done good by me," Pigsfeet answered warily.

"Did he tell you to break into my closet?"

The boy nodded.

"Aye, the money you found here was his to begin with," said Shakespeare.

"That's what the master said," Pigsfeet answered.

"Where are you to take me?"

"Have you any mess for me storming belly?"

"I've a plum," Shakespeare answered.

"Where?"

"Next to my pallet."

"Can I steal it?"

"You can have it."

Shakespeare watched as the boy slowly rose. He took two steps in the direction of the pallet, then made a sudden dive for his dagger. Shakespeare was too quick. He grabbed the boy by his waist and flung him to the other side of the room. Pigsfeet crashed against the wall and crumpled.

"You wound me, boy," said Shakespeare.

Pigsfeet groaned.

"I offer you food and hospitality and you repay my kindness by trying to knife me. Such thanklessness. Tis most ungrateful."

The boy rolled over on his side, brought his knees to his chest and moaned. Shakespeare walked over, grabbed his collar and pulled him to his feet.

"I'm a player, boy," Shakespeare said. "Easily, I recognize a bad performance."

Pigsfeet frowned, straightened up and smirked.

"In sooth, I'm insulted," Shakespeare said. "You are who your master sends for an assassin? A boy as weak as a woman—"

"I can knock you to the stars."

Shakespeare laughed and waved him away. "Be gone, boy. Out! Away! Bing a wast, as you might say. And don't give me a surly frown. Be glad that I find you comical instead of men-acing. Count your hap as good that you've escaped my ire as well as the ward at Newgate and the noose at Tyburn. Tell your master he'll not see a groat of his money until he meets with me face to face. And tell him I'm keeping your dagger as a present, as we both know it was meant for me in the first place."

"I got some word to be saying," Pigsfeet said.

"Speak."

"If you want to view master Mackering face to face, then go to Cripplegate."

"When?"

"Twelve of the clock in the heart of night," Pigsfeet replied.

"If your master doesn't kill me, the constable will arrest me. Is that the scheme?"

"The constable's not a bother. He boozes at my master's tavern. We give him lots of toys and a pisspot full of ale. It keeps his mouth from canting amok. He won't be bothering you."

"Is that all Mackering has to say to me?"

"Aye."

"Then get you gone," Shakespeare said. "Tell your master I'll see him hence. And Pigsfeet . . ."

"Aye?"

"Tell Mackering you've seen his money, his mint. Tell him you've seen piles and piles of coins sparkling in all their golden glory. Tell him also that I intend to stow his bits in a place most blind. If he wants his due payments, no harm's to come to me. Understand?"

"Aye, sir," the boy answered, nodding his head. "I understand."

Shakespeare carried a dagger, though he knew it did him no good. He was a kite against a peregrine; the only thing that spoke in his behalf was hidden gold. The north side of the city was dusted coal black and vented with pinholes of starry light. Thus far he'd avoided the night watchman, two or three constables as well. He'd wrapped his boots in rags to muffle the sound of his steps.

Shakespeare had always enjoyed this part of the city. The old monastic houses and cottages were set into gardens of fruit trees and flower beds—a rural oasis in a town of tenements. But tonight the buildings looked foreboding. He passed Moorgate silently, walking around the great wall built to protect the city from foreign invaders. The stone edifice had done little to save London from the Visigoths within.

A flurry of movement up in the distance? No, only the whirls of summer's wind. It was a gentle evening, perfect for a lover's stroll. He imagined himself with Rebecca, her body resting under his arm like a hatchling nestled under its mother's wing. He wished her well wherever she was, prayed to the Almighty to guard her from plague and strife, his wife and children as well.

While he had the Great One's attention, he added a word or two for his own keep. Alone he was, a small cog waiting for the impending tempest. He was being watched, stalked, decoyed for death.

He continued toward Aldermanbury Street, past the Old Church of the Papy, the Church of All Hallows. Receding in the breeze was a drunken shout, the flicker of a muck-heap bonfire, the sound of hoofbeats.

Then nothing.

A few steps more before he was forced to stop.

They were upon him like locusts descending from the skies. One grabbed his arm, another took his dagger, still another slipped off his boots—all at the same time. Without shoes he wasn't going anywhere. It took a few minutes for his eyes to adjust, and when they did, he counted about ten of them. They were garbed in tatters and covered with sores. A few were missing limbs, some lacked ears—state punishment given to those convicted of thievery. Tall ones, some bent. One was a dwarf; his neck bulged hideously. The knave who stood directly in front of him was a woman.

She was too bony in the shoulders, but her loose bodice revealed an ample bosom. Her hair was loose, falling midway down her back. Her facial features would have been bonny had her eyes been softer. She smiled at him close-mouthed. Nay, it wasn't a smile, but an evil smirk.

"What news, Mary Biddle?" Shakespeare said. "Though I knew you well, I knew you not with your clothes on."

She spat in his face.

"Such distemperament!" Shakespeare said.

She punched him in the groin.

He gasped out, "Hell has no fury—"

She kicked him in the shins. Tears stung his eyes.

"Done with him, Mary?" asked the man who held Shakespeare's arms. The man's own left arm was amputated to the elbow, his forearm and hand replaced by an iron rod and hook. The other man who held Shakespeare was tall and fat. He wore a patch over his eye. His vision was goodly, thought Shakespeare. No doubt the patch was part of the livery of a sturdy beggar—a "reacher," as they called themselves.

"Nay, Hook," Mary answered the amputee. "Not done with him yet." She began to slip metal rings over her knuckles.

Shakespeare saw the look in her eye—the gleam of the moonstruck. He knew she meant to break him. But he'd rather be damned than show fear before a whore. He said, "The doxy remembers a man not easily sated, eh? Yet you moaned quite pleasantly during the rutting."

"I woulda said nothing ifin you only fucked me for free," Mary said. "But you stole my purse, you scum! Caused me evil with the master."

"That was justice speaking, wench," Shakespeare answered. "You filched *my* purse when you thought I was sleeping. In sooth, I took back what was mine . . . and a few bits more from yours for the inconvenience suffered at your hands.''

"Know what Master Mackering *did* to me because of you?'' she screamed.

"I warrant it wasn't pleasant.''

She gave him a full smile this time. Both front teeth were missing now.

"Regard it with humor,'' said Shakespeare. "Never shall those teeth inflict thee with pain.''

She grinned menacingly. Shakespeare's instinct was to try and jerk free, but he forced himself to remain still. He winced slightly as she pulled back her fist, now shining with silver. She smacked him in the mouth. His head vibrated with pain, his eyes rolled backward. His vision burst into thousands of droplets of light. A warm, wet stream gushed from his nose and mouth. The night blackened into nothingness.

"Speak pretty words now, you malapert patch,'' Mary said, blowing on her stinging hand.

"He's out,'' said Hook.

But Shakespeare wasn't. He could hear them speak even as his head throbbed.

The voice of the patch-eyed man said, "The master'll not be in good humor over this. He wanted no marks on the cove's body.''

Mary said, "Stow it, Patch. I'll say that Shakespeare was asking for the bobbing. And none of ye will say nothing against me, eh?''

They all agreed.

"Looks like you killed him,'' said Hook.

"Bah,'' Mary answered. "He breathes. Bring the cove some booze and pour it in his mouth. Ifin that doesn't do the trick, nothing's able.''

Shakespeare smelled something medicinal and pungent. A moment later he felt his mouth being pried open, something vile being poured down his gullet. He sputtered and coughed.

"Hit his back, Little Dickie,'' Mary ordered the dwarf. She added with a chuckle, "Ifin you can reach it.''

Little Dickie jumped up and pounded him between the shoulder blades. Shakespeare moaned.

"Open your eyes, lout,'' said Mary. "Yer still among the living.''

Shakespeare felt his knees buckling under his weight.

"Hold him up,'' Mary barked. She held up her fist, still decked with metal rings, and slowly extended it toward Shakespeare's bloody mouth. He jerked back, wrestling in the iron grip of the knaves.

"Where'd you hide the master's bits?" she asked.

Shakespeare said nothing.

Mary withdrew her hand.

"Where's the money, Willy boy?"

Again Shakespeare remained silent. Mary clucked her tongue.

"We're not learning you proper, I can see that." She shrugged, pulled back her studded hand and fisted Shakespeare hard in the stomach.

This time his brain went black.

"Yer gonna kill him, Mary," said Hook.

"The master'll not be pleased," warned Little Dickie.

Mary splashed the spirits in Shakespeare's face. "Arise, jack."

Shakespeare opened his eyes. His face felt puffy, his nose seared with pain.

"Anything to say, dolt?" Mary asked.

Shakespeare smiled groggily—a lopsided smile. He slurred out: "The stew thinks herself Huffing Kate."

Mary spat at him.

"Hit . . . me again," gasped Shakespeare, "and . . . no . . . money shall Mackering see."

"I hear the steps of a watchman," Patch said.

"It's nothing," Mary said, brushing him off.

"No," Little Dickie said. "He comes. Get us to the master's hideaway afore we're hung on the gallows at Tyburn."

"Mary," said Hook. "His feet are draggin'."

"Then pick him up and stow him over your shoulder."

"He's heavy," complained Hook.

"Awwww," Mary crooned. She slapped the amputee across the face with her bare hand and held up her fist, still encased in rings. "Another frown, Hook, and my metal hand is in your mouth."

Shakespeare emitted a hazy laugh. "Heed her words, my bene cove."

"Stow you," Mary mumbled. "To the master's hideaway."

"Where's . . . Mackering?" Shakespeare managed to say.

"You'll find him soon enough," Mary said with a smile—an open-mouthed one.

Shakespeare smiled back, then passed out.

29

𝕊hakespeare awoke submerged in pain, his eyes crusted over and swollen shut. He cried out a muffled bleat and a moment later felt his mouth being opened, a sticky syrup being poured down his throat. He coughed weakly, moaned, then drifted back into fitful sleep.

Some time later he was roused from his sleep by fingers playing upon his face. Voices echoed inside his head, the syllables of each word ringing over and over, as if orated by someone with a stammer.

He fell back asleep.

The third time he was able to open his eyes. He was in the corner of a barn, his head resting on a pile of straw. Milling about were eerie outlines—human beings sculpted from unhardened wax, their eyes dripping into their noses, their noses running and melding with their mouths and chins. Distorted, disassembled.

He closed his eyes and felt the contents of his stomach coming out of his mouth.

Dear God, he thought. *She did me in. Killed me. I've gone to Hell.*

He heard Mary's voice swearing at him.

She's gone to Hell with me.

His eternity. To be tortured by the bawd forever.

"The Devil take thee," she cursed at Shakespeare. "Patch, help me lift him up. Little Dickie, move your arse and clean up the straw. He heaved all over it."

"A minute," the dwarf shouted back.

"Come *now*!" Mary screamed. *"Giant!"*

"He hasn't returned yet, Mary," said Patch.

Mary spewed out a string of obscenities then shouted, "Little Dickie! Now!"

"I'm coming, I'm coming," Little Dickie said. He muttered under his breath, "The Devil take her."

Shakespeare groaned.

"More poppy syrup, Angel!" Mary yelled. "Shakespeare ups from the dead."

"Here," said a small voice. Shakespeare opened his eyes. Crouching over him were Mary, Patch, and a small wench with the biggest eyes he'd ever seen.

"A good morrow, Willy cove," Mary said, sneering. "Here. Take this. It'll make you merry."

"Go to Hell," Shakespeare gasped out.

"You'd better not be saying queer words to me, eh?"

"Go to Hell," Shakespeare repeated.

"Take a booze," Mary said, holding a cup to his lips. "G'wan. Drink, man."

Shakespeare turned his head away.

"I'll be forcing it down your gullet if you keep acting queer."

Shakespeare said nothing. Mary sighed. She opened his mouth—he had no strength—and forced him to drink.

He fell back asleep.

He woke up again as fuzzy as wool. His mouth was stuffed with rags. His entire head was swaddled in cloth. He tried to speak but couldn't emit a sound. He opened his eyes. The dwarf was sitting by his side.

"He's up, Mary," Little Dickie said.

"Beneship," Mary announced, coming over to him. She took the rags off his head and out of his mouth, then gave him a sip of aqua vitae with poppy syrup. Gently, she began bathing his face and neck in warm water.

"I bobbed your nose good."

Shakespeare grunted.

"Broke it in three places."

She was smiling! *Laughing!*

"Bobbed out one of your teeth too."

"Which one?" Shakespeare asked. Or did he? She didn't answer him. "Which one?" he repeated, raising his voice.

"Huh?" Mary replied. "I donna understand what you say."

"Which tooth?" Shakespeare said, desperately trying to articulate the words.

Mary sighed. "Don't understand you."

Raising his hand very slowly, Shakespeare pointed to his teeth.

"Which tooth did I bob?" Mary asked.

Shakespeare nodded.

"Your front left one next to the eye tooth. Chipped a little off of the lower teeth too. I cut your left eye up beneship as well, man." She laughed again. "You're ugly now. You could be one of us."

She slapped him on the shoulder.

He moaned. His head began to spin—swirling eddies of sights and sounds—and he knew the poppy syrup was taking effect on his body. He felt her wrap his nose with swatches of medicated cloth that cooled his burning skin.

Mary was next to him, her hands stroking his chest, slipping under his hose.

"No," he felt himself saying. But he never got the words out. Her hand continued down onto his prick.

"Like it, Willy?" she teased. "Remember back to that night. Me and you niggling under the sheets. Aye, you were good back then. Big and strong. More fierce than a harnessed lion. Huh? Remember how you played with my titties. How you sucked 'em, pinched me bull eyes? Wanna pinch 'em again?"

He felt trapped in the eye of a gale.

"G'wan," she said, placing his hand upon her breasts. "Pinch em. I like it. I'll give it all to you. For free now."

She continued stroking him. He felt himself go hard. Weakly, he squeezed her nipples with his fingertips.

"I'll give you more, Willy. For free. Do merry things to your thing. Like this."

She kneeled over his groin and took him in her mouth.

The storm raged throughout his entire body. Tighter and tighter she sucked, then abruptly pulled away.

"Like it?" Mary cooed. "I'll give you more. More and more."

She lowered her mouth to his prick once again. His stomach turned over. He felt himself floating, twisting in torrential winds. About to burst open.

Again she pulled away, mocking him. But her fingers continued to play upon him, rub him lightly.

"You can shoot in my mouth, Willy," Mary said. "I like it when a strong man spends in my throat. All you've got to do is sing to me sweet words, my darling."

She sucked him again, then asked, "Where's the mint, Willy?"

Shakespeare didn't answer.

"The bits, Willy man," she said, "the money you filched from the master. Where'd you hide it?"

"No," he whispered.

"Tell me where it is, my sweet."

He shook his head.

"You can trust me." She began sucking him again. "Tell me," she cooed between mouthfuls. "Tell me."

Shakespeare said nothing. He panted like a raced dog and bit his sore lip, about to spend. She jerked her head away.

"Tell me," she whispered. "Where'd you blind the money, Willy, my sweet?"

"I . . ." he started to say.

"Aye . . ." she encouraged him. "Go on."

"I . . ."

"Tell me."

"No."

Mary wrapped her finger around the shaft of his penis and squeezed as hard as she could. Shakespeare felt himself about to burst.

"Tell me," Mary said, red-faced from squeezing.

Shakespeare groaned.

With an evil smile, Mary held up her fool's finger, the nail honed to a razor-sharp point. All at once she let go of his prick and rammed her fingernail up his anus.

The pain was excruciating, but mixed oddly with an ecstasy Shakespeare had never experienced. He gasped, screamed, then involuntarily spent—all over Mary's face.

"You son of a bitch!" she yelled, jerking her finger out of his bum.

Shakespeare gave her a bruised smile.

Mary wiped her stinging eyes and began to choke him. He didn't care even as he slipped back into darkness. A moment later he felt himself breathing again. He opened his eyes. An ogre as big as a tower was restraining Mary; she was kicking and fighting in his arms.

"Stow you, Mary." The giant tightened his hold upon her. The bawd went slack. "Stow you, I say. You dinna get what you want . . . the master'll get it."

"He's gonna *kill* me."

"Nay."

"Aye. You don't know the master like I know him."

"Let Shakespeare sleep till dawn. Then ply him with more syrup. Keep doing it till the master's ready to see him. The master'll get what he wants."

The next time Shakespeare awoke, he made sure that no one heard him rouse. How many hours, how many *days* had passed, he knew not. Very carefully he opened an eye and saw that no one was tending to him. He allowed himself to look around the barn.

The place was covered with used straw full of dirt and grease—and shit and piss. The north wall was piled high with heaps of stolen clothing. In front of the rags were clouds of feathers, and he heard noise caused by chickens penned in a half-dozen coops.

In the center of the room Poor Tom—the very same madman he'd seen the day he'd walked the streets of London with Rebecca—was dicing with Patch. Little Dickie was pissing in a bowl. A moment later the dwarf blended the urine with brown powder—gunpowder probably. He took a batch of the mixture on a piece of brown paper and rubbed it over Poor Tom's left arm. Within minutes the skin burst open and began to ooze out clear liquid.

Bringing up the crabs, the rogues called it. Beggars crusted with scabs evoked the pity of the tender-hearted Englishwoman. Shakespeare knew the sores would heal over in twenty-four hours.

"Put another dab on me nose," Poor Tom said. He rolled the dice, shouted as his number came up and grabbed a handful of coins. "Me hap's a sweet wench tonight."

Patch swore. Little Dickie returned and placed a spoonful of sore paste on Poor Tom's fleshy nose. The tip instantly broke into a weal of angry red flesh.

"How much bit did you nab yesterday?" Little Dickie asked Tom.

"Not much mint, but a fair lady took pity on me wretched body and gave me a ring that's beneship indeed." Poor Tom pulled it out of his purse and showed it to the dwarf.

"Where's can I get soap?" called a voice at Shakespeare's left—a voice he'd heard before.

Very slowly, Shakespeare turned his head in its direction. There stood Pigsfeet. Nightmares coming to life. He was so tired, needed sleep. But he refused to close his eyes. Must know what's going on. He strained to listen. Pigsfeet was talking . . . needing soap.

". . . and the master wants me down with falling sickness. He says I need the froth and I should eat bits of soap."

"Don't eat 'em," said Little Dickie. "Swish 'em around your mouth. Then fall down on the ground and let the suds fall out."

"Act like a mad dog," said Poor Tom. "Howl and growl." He broke into animal noises. "Like that."

Little Dickie said, "Talk with Christopher Mudd. He'd be at Paul's by now, pickpocketing the gentlemen. You and him can filch some soap from a stall at the Cheape."

Pigsfeet nodded and left. A moment later Poor Tom shouted with glee, leaped up and clapped his hands.

"Me hap is sweeter than a honeyed pear tonight," he said, dropping more coins in his purse.

"You use stopped dice," said Patch.

"Aye," Poor Tom said, admitting the cheat. "But so did you."

Shakespeare heard Patch swear, saw Poor Tom looking at him. Asking how long they had to watch him.

Tom said, "I've got to be gone. Me fans await me playing. 'What'll ye give this Poor Tom, today, wisely and well.' " He laughed. "I say we kill the jack. Slit his throat."

Shakespeare's stomach lurched.

"The master donna want him killed," Patch said. "See, this is the ass that's been filching from the master's purse."

"He's the ass?"

"Yes."

"Then we should kill him."

"The master wants the money that Shakespeare lifted from him," Little Dickie explained. "Mackering told Mary to niggle him. Get him all hot and moaning from a pelting prick. Then he'd tell her where he blinded the coins."

"Did he tell her?"

"Nay," Patch snickered. "Only soaked her eyes with a whirlpool of his stuff."

Tom broke into gales of laughter.

"She does her toil not wisely but too well," he said.

"She does her toil especially well now that she's missing her front teeth," said Patch. "She can't bite it."

They both spasmed with guffaws.

Poor Tom dried his eyes on a sheet wrapped around his waist. "What's the master gonna do with him?" he asked.

"Shakespeare?" asked Patch.

"Aye. Shakespeare."

"I know not," Patch said. "Giant's gonna take him to the master in the dark."

The master, Shakespeare thought. Finally they meet.

"Better give Shakespeare more poppy syrup," said Little Dickie. "Mary said every four hours. It's been four hours."

Shakespeare closed his eyes.

"He's still sleeping," Poor Tom said.

"Give it to him anyway," Patch insisted. "Don't want to dance with Mary's pelting temper, man."

"Aye," Poor Tom said.

Shakespeare felt his mouth being opened. He swallowed the syrup and went back to sleep.

Giant was the biggest man Shakespeare had ever seen. Even though his mind was foggy from poppy syrup, he could discern the lout's enormous jaw, his oversized head. His brow was a knobby shelf topped with black fur, his eyes piggish—one colored muddy brown, the other emerald green. His hands were as wide as spades. One of those hands gripped Shakespeare's shoulder, sending a bolt of pain throughout his body.

"On your feet," the big man ordered, his voice deeper than a blowhole.

Shakespeare stood, rocked on his feet, then fell.

"Get up," Giant ordered, pulling Shakespeare to his feet.

At last he was able to stand erect. Giant slapped a blindfold over Shakespeare's eyes, bound his hands behind his back, and tied his ankles together. Shakespeare felt himself being hoisted into the air, carried, then placed prone onto a hard, cold slab of metal. He sensed himself moving, being rolled along on wheels.

A wagon . . . No, a wheelbarrow.

The cold air bit his face. He began to shiver.

Must be night.

He felt the bumps along the dirt, his body stinging with each jolting movement. A sackcloth was thrown atop his body. The coarse wool itched his face. He thought of more pleasant times, the stolen hours of night he'd shared with Rebecca.

Another bump rocked his body with pain.

Get used to it, he thought. After all, it's time to meet the master.

30

The motion of the wheelbarrow rocked Shakespeare to sleep, and he didn't bother rousing until he'd come to a complete halt. Someone uncovered him, stood him on his feet, cut the ties around his ankles, and jabbed the tip of a blade in his back.

"Walk straight ahead."

Giant's voice.

"With my eyes hooded?" asked Shakespeare.

"Walk."

Shakespeare moved slowly, aware of the dagger behind him.

"Stop," Giant said. "In front of you are stairs. Climb them."

Shakespeare obeyed. They reached a landing. He heard a door open and was suddenly pushed forward. The door closed.

He didn't know where he was, but at least the knife no longer nicked his flesh.

Was he alone?

He walked about, blind, stumbling, straining his ears. Frantically, he began to twist his hands against the binds, abrading them red and raw. The ropes held fast. He cursed, dropped to the ground. He crept like a snake upon its belly, dragging his forehead against the rush-strewn floor. The blindfold remained in place, a nasty scrape above his brow the only result of his efforts. He swore vengeance and turned onto his back. Swinging his knees to his forehead, he wedged the edge of the blindfold between his knees and brow and pushed upward.

Nothing.

Sweating, he tried it again, repeated it a third, fourth, and fifth time. He grunted and once again attempted to loosen the veil that covered his eyes, pulling the rag upward as hard as he was able. After what seemed like an eternity, the cloth began to slip upward, yielding to his tugs. Finally the back knot of the blindfold loosened sufficiently and the cloth slipped over his head.

Though it was still night—he knew not the exact hour—the closet's dim illumination seemed as brilliant as daylight. Lights flickered from wall sconces filled with rush candles. Trying to catch his breath, he lay his head back and watched the shadows leap upon the beamed ceiling. But his moment of solitude was interrupted by heavy clapping. Shakespeare bolted upward, focused his eyes upon the south corner of the near-empty room.

Under a lit sconce stood a man applauding, his face as leathery as a sun-dried hide. Wrinkles, crevices, and creases eroded pathways through nutmeg-colored flesh. His eyes were storming seas of green-gray, his nose surprisingly small and round. He sported no beard at all, but the hair atop his head was coarse and hued yellow—a flat yellow without a hint of gold—a pile of windblown straw. His neck was as wide as his cheeks, giving the illusion of a long, thick face attached directly to his shoulders. He wore a leather jerkin over a white linen shirt and from his belt dangled a gleaming rapier. His teeth were large and whole and sparkled as he smiled.

Shakespeare felt small in his presence. There was a frightening demeanor about him. Here was a clever but evil man as comfortable with power as a monarch, someone who manipulated his inferiors like men on a chessboard.

The man said, " 'Man and a blindfold.' What a scene! As bonny as any you've ever performed on the platform." He threw a chair in Shakespeare's direction. "Sit."

Shakespeare uprighted the chair with his foot and sat down, keeping his eyes fixed upon the rapier. The man stroked his naked chin, then sauntered over to Shakespeare and stood in front of him, his body heavy with bulging muscles. He drew a poniard from his jerkin and said,

"You're a damned nuisance."

Shakespeare said nothing.

"I've tried to ignore you, but you're a persistent bugger. You'd try the patience of the Savior.'' He grazed the tip of the stylus across Shakespeare's throat. ''Where'd you hide my money?''

''Tell me about Harry Whitman, Mackering.''

Mackering said, ''Obviously you still delude yourself that you have power over me.''

Shakespeare looked upward, saw those evil eyes. He said, ''Power, not a whit. Money . . .''

The gray-green orbs compressed to steely balls. ''Where are my bits?''

Shakespeare said, ''Tell me about Harry.''

Mackering brought the blade against the bob of Shakespeare's throat. He said, ''Who is this man, Harry, that he is so important to you?''

''He was my friend,'' Shakespeare whispered. ''I mean to find out who murdered him.''

''So you are Harry's avenging angel, eh?'' Mackering said. ''Not in much of a position to avenge.''

''Did you kill Harry?'' Shakespeare asked.

Mackering gave off a low sinister laugh. ''As a matter of fact, I didn't.'' He flicked the blade against Shakespeare's face and shaved him in three deft strokes. Gliding his fingers across Shakespeare's jawline, Mackering chucked his chin, then soundly slapped Shakespeare's newly shaved cheeks.

''Were I, my good man, at this moment of the inclination, I'd say you look good enough to eat.''

Shakespeare said, ''Though the skin is smooth, the flesh is poisonous.''

Mackering widened his eyes and brought his hand to his chest. ''A remark of intimidation,'' he said. ''I quake.''

''An honest caveat, Mackering. I've partaken of the flesh you sell on the streets. Some of your doxies serve good meat, others only Winchester geese.''

Mackering's face darkened. ''I've had all my doxies inside and out and found them clean. Which have you found infected?''

''All your doxies seem as one in the dark—foul breath, stringy meat, and sloppy, wet holes.''

Mackering laughed. He picked up his dagger and one by one sliced off the buttons of Shakespeare's shirt. The open garment revealed a pink wedge of bare chest.

''You bluff poorly, Willyboy.'' Mackering parted the shirt with his dagger, then ran the tip of his blade around Shakespeare's nipple. ''You lie in your throat as I do stand.'' He grinned, brought the dagger down to Shakespeare's round hose and cut the string of a point. ''I'd say you are very much free from the King's Evil. But for the sake of clever talk, assume you speak the truth. That maybe you are infected. I'm a gambler. I enjoy taking risks."

There was a series of long and short knocks at the door. Mackering snapped his fingers.

"I'd almost forgotten," he said. "Our playtime shall have to be temporarily postponed." He gently drew the stylus across Shakespeare's chest. Immediately a thin line of red appeared.

"Come in, come in," Mackering shouted.

In walked Giant, Little Dickie, Patch, Pigsfeet, Picker, two knaves he'd never seen, Mary Biddle, and the young girl with the wide eyes.

"Ah," said Mackering. "Arrives the entertainment in your honor, Shakespeare. Giant, move the player against the wall."

The ogre picked up the chair with Shakespeare in it and placed him at the far side of the chamber.

"Good, good!" Mackering grinned. "Let me introduce you, Willyboy, to a very small part of my merry family. Little Dickie, Picker, Patch, Pigsfeet, and Mary you undoubtedly know. This young wench with the moon-shaped eyes is called Angel. Maybe you remember her. She ministered you with poppy syrup."

Shakespeare vaguely recalled the face, the eyes staring at him as he fell into a fuzzy sleep.

Mackering went on with the introductions. "These two honored men, coves most beneship, call themselves Hamor Lowe and Christopher Mudd. They, more than I, were the last ones to see your Harry alive. They diced with him extensively and found him a most amenable gull." Mackering laughed. "And what a coney he was! Very greedy. And greedy men are big losers. A pity about his death, and I mean that sincerely, sweet man. Who am I to kill Harry? He was the perfect stooge, feeding my coffers most generously."

Mackering laughed again.

"Enough about Harry," he said. "He's as stiff as a starched ruff and is of no consequence." He clasped his hands together. "My dear coves, get ye down and see what our fair and able-bodied wenches have planned to make our night most merry."

Mary Biddle regarded Mackering with hatred. Angel's eyes darted between Mary's and Mackering's. Slowly, she clenched her fists.

Mackering slapped Shakespeare on the back and sat next to him. Giant stood at his master's side, the rest of the men sat at the uprightman's feet.

"Two bonny stews," Mackering began. "I have fucked them both and found them lacking nothing—spirited young morts, they are. But alas, I have arrived on hard times, as some unknown wight has been filching my money.'' He mussed Shakespeare's hair. ''Now what kind of jack would steal from *me*?''

''A jackass,'' shouted Hamor Lowe.

The men laughed, Shakespeare didn't move. He was frightened, but not as scared as the girls. They seemed terrified.

Mackering said, ''Anyway, my dearth of funds has allotted me only enough food to feed but one of these fine wenches. And I dare say that having two women around is not a good situation. Each one competes for my attention and I find that bothersome. So, which one shall be strong enough to remain, my goodmen? Wager, if you will. Though Angel is younger, still full of piss and vinegar, I'll place my money on Mary, as the Devil has made her as mean as a harpy.''

Something horrible was going to happen. Shakespeare felt it. Though his mind was confused, laden with feelings of dread, the knaves acted as if this were a common event. They were clamoring at one another, shouting odds, throwing coins into a pile. Picker licked his lips, farted, and sat back with a grin on his face. Patch removed his eye covering to get a better view. As Shakespeare thought, the newly exposed eye, though a bit smaller than its unshielded mate, was healthy.

Mackering said, ''Willyboy, you may wager if you'd like. Borrow my coins! An honest man you are! You'll make good on your bets.''

Shakespeare didn't answer.

''Bah,'' Mackering said. ''Remain as sour as a Puritan.'' He raised his sword. ''To the better girl—the most bene mort.''

The cheering began as Mary and Angel began to circle each other. Mary struck first, grabbing Angel's skirt. In response, Angel attempted to yank it out of Mary's hands and a tug of war ensued. A moment later the skirt tore from Angel's bodice, exposing her chemise and stocking-covered legs. Ripped skirt in hand, Mary stumbled backward and fell on her backside.

The men hooted and cheered. New odds were announced, more coins piled onto the floor.

Angel charged, fell atop Mary and straddled her supine body, holding down Mary's arms with her left hand while ripping Mary's bodice with her right. Within seconds the bodice was rent to shreds and Mary's breasts popped out. Angel clawed at the naked skin, raking deep gouges into Mary's chest. Mary screamed, managed to free a hand and jabbed a finger in Angel's eye.

The men cheered Mary's spirit.

Angel covered her throbbing orb, leaving opportunity for Mary's attack. She dug clawish fingernails into Angel's cheek and grated the younger girl's face as if she were skinning roots. Angel shrieked and tried desperately to protect her wounded face.

Mary bucked upward and threw Angel off her stomach. Still on the floor, the women grabbed each other in hostile embrace and rolled along the floor, the rushes flying about as they kicked, bit and scratched.

Nauseated, Shakespeare looked at Mackering, the upright-man's eyes gleaming with pleasure.

Caligula. These were his gladiators.

Mackering noticed Shakespeare's eyes upon him and his lips formed a smile. He said,

"Better than bear baiting, aye?"

Shakespeare didn't answer.

Burn in Hell.

Shakespeare returned his attention to the women. Both were on their feet, naked, their flesh bathed in crimson. From Angel's nose oozed plugs of red mucus; Mary's chest had become two lumps of meaty pulp.

Foul toad.

The women panted and stared at each other. Again it was Mary who attacked, her fingers arched into talons. The deadly nails sprang forward and pierced deep into Angel's throat. Mary screamed, then yanked her claws from Angel's windpipe, exposing the young girl's neck-turned-sieve squirting rills of blood. Angel clutched her throat, fell to the ground and gurgled out cries for mercy.

Mary looked at Mackering.

The master turned his head upward to Giant. "Hold Angel upright," he commanded.

The enormous ogre went over to Angel, writhing in the now crimson-stained rushes. He hoisted the near-dead girl to her feet and held her soundly. Mackering took out his dagger and flicked his wrist with utmost calm. The blade landed right in the center of Angel's heart. The girl gave a sudden jerk. Her eyes rolled upward and her lids fluttered. Then she lay completely slack—lifeless yet still leaking small rivulets of blood.

Rising slowly, Mackering walked over to the dead girl, whose head was draped over Giant's mammoth forearm, pulled the dagger out of her chest and wiped it on Giant's hose.

"Never let it be said that Master isn't merciful." He slipped the dagger into his belt and turned to Biddle. "Mary, dearest—my sweet little doxy. Wash up and meet me in my bedchambers. Together we shall celebrate your victory." He threw her Angel's torn skirt. "Cover yourself with the spoils. My men will accompany you back to my closet so you'll not fall prey to the scurrilous vagabond that roams the darkened streets of London."

Mary said nothing, her eyes red pools of tears. Mackering

kissed her cheek and regarded the pile of bloody flesh on the floor.

"Angel," he whispered. "My dear little girl. Let us pray that you've reached a better world than the one you've just left. If not . . ."

Mackering smiled and shrugged. To Picker he said, "Wrap the body up in sackcloth and dump it in the Thames. The fishermen of the river shall not go empty tonight."

Mackering bade good-bye to Mary and shooed away all his men save Giant. When the three were alone, Mackering placed a thick hand upon Shakespeare's shoulder. His fingers began to knead the muscles gently.

"Are you going to be an ass, Willyboy, or are you going to tell me where you hid my money?"

Shakespeare didn't answer.

"You see what kind of powers I have," Mackering said. "People do whatever I command them to do. Even if it means a fight to their death." He stroked Shakespeare's cheek again. "Now, if you tell me where you hid my money, I might let you leave unmolested, Willyboy. But only if you show proper respect."

Shakespeare remained silent.

"Go on, then," Mackering said, offended. "Be an ass. And a mule as well. But I am a clever man, Willyboy. I figured you to be closed-lipped and knew I'd have to pry the information about my bits out of you. Originally I had envisioned a test of strength for you, Willyboy. Similar to the one you'd just witnessed, save that the contest was to be betwixt you and my bene cove, Giant."

Giant smiled.

"But alas," Mackering sighed. "My desire for sport has been quenched. One grows tired of the color red."

Mackering dug his nails into Shakespeare's skin. Shakespeare felt his eyes water, but didn't react.

Mackering frowned, then brightened. "Not to worry, my good player. I've other challenges for you to meet. Of course, you could avoid all my Herculean tasks and simply tell me where my coins are placed."

"Go to Hell," Shakespeare said.

"So foul a mouth on so fair a face," Mackering said.

There was a knock on the door.

"Ah," Mackering said, skipping about. "And here it comes. Enter, enter."

In came Christopher Mudd, tottering under the weight of a wooden crate. He stumbled and dropped the box on the floor with a thud. Mackering glowered at the dirty knave.

"Dolt," he said, backhanding Mudd across the room. "Show finesse when you handle my goods. Now get out."

Mudd scrambled to his feet and left.

Mackering opened the top of the crate and said, "Willy, my fair boy, come see your new chambers."

During the first part of confinement, the hours passed as quickly as minutes yet as slowly as days, for Shakespeare had lost all concept of time. Naked, bound and blindfolded, his ears stuffed with swatches of wool, he saw nothing, heard nothing. There had been minutes when the wool had been removed from his ears, the gag untied. A hazy voice demanding to know where he had hidden the money. Even though he was in constant pain, he said nothing. The coins were his only bargaining tool. Once Mackering had his money, Shakespeare's life would be useless. So the wool was stuffed back in his ears, the gag tightened firmly across his cheeks.

There was food. Sour, rotten, decayed. For feedings only the gag was removed, the sustenance then forced down his throat in five or six spoonfuls. He had gagged at first, retched a time or two, but soon grew accustomed to the mealy taste of spoiled board.

Sometimes the food was mixed with poppy syrup. His thoughts would become suddenly unclear, his stomach nauseated. Then feedings of undrugged meat. He'd suffer from sniffles and chills, shivering as he slept in his own excrement, smelling his own stench. Mercifully, there wasn't much waste, as he ate very little.

Then the voice—Mackering—ordering him to tell where he'd stowed the money.

Shakespeare remained steadfast in his refusal to talk. He'd once overheard Mackering say it was only a matter of time. How long could Shakespeare last, buried alive in Hell?

In Hell, Shakespeare was physically, but in his brain, ah it was always heaven. The one thing that Mackering had never realized—the power of the fantastic cells.

On the vellum of his mind Shakespeare penned incantations of love, the comic words of the buffoon, grievous orations that wailed out injustices manacled to hapless souls. His eyes didn't need light to see the lines that burned brightly in his head. Often he'd work until exhaustion blackened the paper of his imagination and forced him to sleep.

He wrote tragedies of love and greed, comedies of mishap and mistaken identity. His fools made him laugh, his misfortuned lovers made him cry, his villains made him hiss with rage. He was visited by ghosts of kings, witches steeped in potions, fairies and elves who made magic and mischief on Midsummer eve. His fingers, numbed by leather straps wound about the wrist, intertwined and stroked the palms of his hands. It was not he who touched himself, but the gentle kiss from a lover's velvet lips. The sweet tongue that played upon his lips was rooted not in his mouth but in another's so fair. He learned how to position himself, how to squeeze his legs together to bring himself to pleasure. By rubbing his cheek against his shoulder, he could feel the growth of his beard. He began to measure roughly the days of his captivity.

Occasionally he fell to despair, his mind unable to reach beyond his wretched circumstances. When this happened, he became a soldier—nay, not a soldier, the lord general of a mythical army—and developed a plan of battle. He'd wiggle his fingers and toes until they ached, rotate his bound wrists and ankles, his neck as well, and blink thousands of times under his blindfold. He'd hum, sing, shout, scream until he tired his muscles and was overcome with sleep. Upon awaking, his mind was refreshed and he eagerly awaited his thoughts as a baby does its mother's breast.

As long as he could think, he would live.

It was Mackering who broke.

The top of the crate was opened and Shakespeare lifted his head upward, expecting his spoonfuls of slop. Instead heavy arms hoisted him out of the box and dropped him on a floor covered with fresh-smelling straw. Shakespeare stretched his rusted legs and arms—oh, how they ached!

A bucket of cold water was dumped upon his body. His skin tingled, shivered. How glorious it was to feel! More water followed, washing him clean of shit and stench. His binds were removed, his blindfold as well. Dry straw and rushes were dumped over his wet skin. Shakespeare buried himself in reeds, luxuriating in the straw as if it were a down-filled counterpane.

Heavy footsteps receding. The closing of a door.

Slowly, Shakespeare brushed the straw from his eyes, the movement so exquisitely painful. The room was darkened, the sole illumination a rush candle from one wall sconce.

He was alone and the crate was gone.

What fiendish scheme would Mackering think up next?

One thing at a time.

Shakespeare's eyes turned upward to the heavens and he prayed, offering words of thanks to God, beseeching His infinite mercy for his worthless soul. Shakespeare prayed and prayed and prayed until sweet slumber dusted his brow then covered his body.

31

He awoke abruptly. A foot was on his stomach, the tip of a rapier at his throat. Mackering looming over him, sneering.

"Who art thou?" he said in a booming voice.

Slowly, Shakespeare brought his hand to his neck and gently pushed away the point of the sword.

"William Shakespeare," he whispered. It was so hard to find his voice after all this time. "You're George Mackering. I robbed you blind and you've avenged your loss by having me beaten, fucked, and finally incarcerated in a box for . . ." He rubbed his cheeks. "I'd say by the growth of my beard, perhaps three, maybe four weeks."

Mackering frowned. "Seven and a half," he corrected.

Shakespeare said hoarsely, "Time races when hours are merrily spent." He paused to take a deep breath. "You are no closer to finding your money than you were seven and a half weeks ago."

"The man grows bold," Mackering said. He brought the tip of his boot under Shakespeare's ballocks and gave them a gentle prod. "Your manhood is pathetic," he said.

At least it's intact, Shakespeare thought. He said nothing.

Mackering threw him a pile of clean clothes and his boots and ordered Shakespeare to dress.

He couldn't stand because his legs were too weak. He had to dress himself flat on his back, his movements slow and painful, his joints creaking whenever he bent. With great effort he slipped his hose over his legs, his round hose over his hips. Next the shirt and sleeves, his fingers clumsily tying up his points, an aglet jabbing his fingertip causing it to leak thin, watery blood. When he was garbed as best as he could, he pushed his body up into a sitting position, his legs extended in front of him.

Mackering continued standing. He said, "There is a tavern called the Topmast. It is one of my many alehouses. Gather my coins and go hence. Give them to a tapster there named Ignatius Plant within five days. If you do as I say, you may walk out of here and I guarantee you freedom to come and go unmolested by me and my men. But if you agree then disobey me—become the Welshman—you will be killed most grievously."

Shakespeare was silent.

Mackering said, "What say you, Willyboy?"

"I'm wondering why you're letting me go. Why you didn't kill me."

"For one thing, you have a great deal of my money."

"You knew I was looking for you. You could have killed me before I began to steal from you."

"True."

"Why didn't you?"

"Because despite what you think, I am a merciful god." Mackering grinned. "You've provided me with much sport these past weeks, hearing you mumble and cry and shout like a Tom O'Bedlam. Yet I see you've remained sound of mind. I admire that, Shakespeare. The bull who gorges the master is allowed to go free."

"Your word is my liberty?"

"Aye."

"The honor of Judas."

Mackering pouted. "You wound me with your jabs."

"Would my words be lethal weapons."

"I pay you no heed, petulant child," Mackering said. "The bellman cries it three of the clock. You should make it to your chambers before the crow of the cock—even if weakness dictates you crawling home on your belly."

"What happened to Harry Whitman?"

"Still back on dear Henry, eh?" Mackering laughed. "I've told you, Willyboy. We did not kill your Harry. And I don't know who did."

"You were one of the last people to see him alive."

"But I wasn't *the* last."

Shakespeare believed him for one simple reason. If Mackering had killed Harry, the uprightman would have killed him a long time ago. Shakespeare said, "So you didn't kill him, Mackering. But you cheated him."

Mackering laughed. "In sooth, we did. Mudd and Lowe gulled him out of a few shillings. But your Harry was worth far more to me than what I could cozen from him with tricks."

"In what way?"

"He had secrets, my friend," Mackering said. "Dark secrets that he paid most handsomely for me to keep."

"What kind of secrets?"

Mackering smiled wickedly and crossed himself. "Secrets between him—and a clandestine priest."

So Mackering had found out that Harry had been a secret

Papist. And Harry had been paying the uprightman extortion money to keep the secret. Shakespeare knew there had to be more. But what?

"How did you find out Whitman was a Papist?" he asked.

"He became whittled one evening at an inn called Fishhead's, and the owner is a churl—a man claiming to be honest while selling his mother's soul to the Devil for a groat."

"Edgar Chambers."

"You know the woodcock?"

"I've met him."

"Then you know that he's an idiot. He overheard Harry flaunting his . . . *secret* practices and traded me information for a dappled mare I rode." Mackering grinned. "Poor animal. She turned sickly and died a month later."

"Twas Chambers who forwarded me to you."

"The boy is clever in a stupid sort of way," Mackering said. "Something in the stars told him that you'd pester me, and he knew how much I misliked pestering. No doubt he thought I'd kill you."

Shakespeare was silent a moment, his brain desperately trying to sort out the information Mackering had given him. He thought back to the beginning. His first encounter with the demon in black. The following day at the theater, Robin Hart told him that Mackering had tried to contact him. Shakespeare asked Mackering about the incident. The uprightman denied it was he.

"*My* first communication with you was through Pigsfeet," Mackering said. "Someone wanted to lead you to me. It sounds like Chambers's sort of scheme. If I were you, I'd go up North and find out what the jack has against you."

Shakespeare said, "You've never crawled through my window and plied my drink with drug?"

"No."

"Never threw a dagger at me as I dueled on the bridge?"

"Only madmen waste good weapons."

"You never attacked my companion as sh—, he lay sleeping in my rented cell?"

"How cowardly!"

But someone did all those things. Someone wanted to stop his inquiry. He asked Mackering if Chambers had any reason to kill Whitman.

"None that I know of," Mackering said. "I, for one, seriously doubt that Chambers killed Harry. Why incur my wrath? Harry paid me well to keep secrets. And Chambers knew that Harry was paying me well, as he told me the secret in the first place. I would have been quite piqued had Chambers killed your friend and suffered me financial loss. As you well know, my money is dear to my heart.''

Mackering held the tip of the sword in one hand, its handle in the other. He bent the blade into an arch.

''I *questioned* Chambers after your dear friend died,'' Mackering said. He let go of the tip and the blade sprang upward. ''Though the man is an inveterate liar, I am of the opinion that he spake honestly when he said he did not kill Whitman.''

''Then who killed him?''

Mackering smiled. ''I told you, Willy. I know not. Now go you hence before my generosity withers.''

It took Shakespeare ten minutes before he could stand. Another ten minutes before he could walk solidly. Mackering threw him his dagger and a gourd of ale. Twenty minutes later Shakespeare felt almost whole—still weak and shaky, but well enough to make it on his own.

''You'll remember my coins, eh?'' Mackering said.

Shakespeare said, ''As soon as I give up the money, one of your men will kill me.''

''Such distrust,'' Mackering said, clicking his tongue. ''What are your options, Willyboy?''

''I have none.''

''Then trust me.''

''Trust an asp at my heart.''

''Not always do the fangs bear poison.''

Shakespeare paused, then said, ''I'll do as you've requested.''

''*Commanded.*''

''Commanded, then.'' Shakespeare turned to leave.

''Willyboy,'' Mackering said.

''Aye,'' said Shakespeare, not bothering to face him.

Mackering said, ''Whoever killed your Harry has dried up one of my best springs. I am most displeased about that.''

Shakespeare was puzzled. Mackering's voice held much wrath and a pinch of sorrow as well.

''I know you will continue to look for your friend's murderer,'' Mackering went on. ''If you find the jackass—this fiend—bring him to me. Together, we'll do him in.''

32

Blessed be Almighty God who fashioned man in His image. The body was a truly divine creation, capable of recovery from even the most torturous ordeals. Imbued with gratitude, Shakespeare spent his first few days of freedom in rest and prayer. Within a week his appetite had returned, grown; aye, he'd been ravenous, devouring platters of meat and drinking pots of ale. At last he'd felt well enough to resume his walks.

He'd lost half a season—or, rather, had spent it in endless hours. Summer had yielded gracefully to the cool nip of autumn's air. The greens had withered and died, replaced by flora of gold and copper that glittered atop gnarled and splindly boughs and sailed through seas of soft wind. Gentle breezes rippled through canary fields of hay and alfalfa. Harvest time, the days filled with birthing what spring had conceived.

Michaelmas was but two weeks away.

Lady Summer gone.

Shakespeare had missed the gardens abloom with rainbow flowers, the perfume of the warm nights. He missed St. Peter's Day and its barrels of fish, the bonfires, the summer dances and country fairs.

Though Shakespeare had filched coins from Mackering, the ruffian had stolen from him irreplaceable time.

But there was no sense dwelling in ruined castles. He praised God for his freedom, and when he was able to take long walks on two stable feet, he basked in the fireworks the sun performed for him twice a day. The dawn was cinders in a pit of charcoal sky that ignited into streaks of rose, lavender, and rust. Each morning a different painting, each time heaven's palette faded, early hour colors forced to give obeisance to a great honeyed orb of fire that gilded the city wall. The spectacle was inversely repeated at dusk. God's autumn—a world of angels, a world of gold.

Margaret Whitman poured Shakespeare another pot of ale, then sat down across from him. She ran knotted fingers through gray strands of unwashed hair. Gods, the woman had changed.

As Harry's wife she'd always seemed so strong and independent. But as his widow she seemed weak—beaten down by age and poverty. Shakespeare wondered how she was supporting herself and the children, but he wasn't close enough to her to ask.

Her eyes searched his for comfort. God in heaven, Willy help me, they said. Give me something to live for. As much as Shakespeare felt her desperate need, beyond words of comfort, there was nothing he could do. He wasn't Lazarus: he couldn't raise the dead.

"I haven't been much help, have I?" Margaret said.

"You've been wonderful, Margaret," Shakespeare said. "Just seeing your face infuses me with spirit." He paused, then said, "I pray you, indulge me a few more questions."

"As many as you want, William," Margaret said.

"This . . ." Shakespeare lowered his voice. "This Jesuit priest that Brithall hides—"

"Fra Silvera."

"Aye, Silvera. How long had Harry known him?"

"I think Harry knew him all his life. He used to summer with his uncle quite frequently as a boy."

"Yet Harry was not raised a Papist."

"No. *His* parents were strict followers of the English Church. His uncle and aunt were obviously secret Papists."

"And Harry's parents didn't mind their son associating with a Jesuit priest?"

"William, I don't think they ever knew what Harry did at Brithall. His mother had eleven other children to worry about. I'm certain she was delirious with joy that there was one less mouth to feed."

Shakespeare regarded her haggard face. The woman spoke beyond empathy, her mouth spoke from experience.

"Yet," he said, "Harry told you about Fra Silvera."

"Twas not out of choice," Margaret said. "Several times I begged Harry to take me and the children up North, where the air was cleaner, cooler in the summer. Just for a week. I pleaded, cajoled, pouted, cried, yet Harry remained adamant in his refusal to take us to Brithall. I thought maybe he was ashamed of me, as I had come from lower stock than he. He assured me that wasn't the reason for wanting us home in London. Finally he admitted his concern for my safety and confessed that his relatives up North harbored a Jesuit priest. He wanted not to endanger his family. He never thought by endangering himself, he also put the welfare of his family at risk. Of course, later he denied the priest. Claimed it was a joke."

Bitterness had crept into her voice, turning it ugly.

"So you never ventured up there?" Shakespeare said.

"My husband said no. I did not go."

"How often did Harry go up North?"

"Once a year, two weeks during the spring right before May-day. You could construct a calendar by the regularity of his visits."

"Why did he go, Margaret?"

"I never asked, he never said."

"Did he ever mention Fra Silvera when he returned?"

"No, never. He just mentioned him that one time. Harry spoke much about the foliage at Brithall, little about the people."

"And the burg of Hemsdale?"

"I never knew of its existence until you asked me questions about this innkeeper, Chambers."

"Do you think it was possible that Harry was confessing his demons to this priest?"

"I know nothing about Harry's demons. I never knew Harry very well. After speaking to you, I realize I knew him even less than I had thought. Harry and I lived as most husbands and wives—separate duties, seeing little of each other except at night." She dropped her voice to a whisper. "My God, how long ago those nights seem."

She started to cry.

Shakespeare stood up, pulling Margaret to her feet and into an embrace.

"It will be a better day tomorrow," he said.

"No," she said. "Tomorrow will be as rotten as today." She squeezed Shakespeare tightly. "Kiss me, Will. I need to feel something." She threw her arms around his neck and pulled his mouth hungrily to hers. What followed next was frantic—fingers undoing points and buttons, hands exploring hot flesh, animalistic coupling. When the moment had passed, Margaret clawed at the rushes on the floor and sobbed. Shakespeare tried to hold her, but she recoiled at his touch. Nothing he could do or say would take away the pain or change the fact that she was an old widow with seven children to support.

He stood, dressed quickly, and took out a sovereign from his purse. Her eyes were upon him as he placed the coin upon the table. This time she didn't refuse the money.

The bells of midnight had long since tolled, but Shakespeare lay wide-eyed on his pallet. So much to plan, so much to do. The North was bleak in winter—the wind furious, the chill its frosted companion. Harry's dark secrets lay in the region like a corpse in a steel coffin. If Shakespeare was to make the journey, he'd best start out soon, before ice crystallized the air and tempests unleashed their howling rage.

Harry had paid money to Mackering, ostensibly to keep silent about Harry's practices of worship. There *had* to be more to the story.

Shakespeare thought of Edgar Chambers in his well-lit room, merrily adding up his money, boastful, a self-satisfied smile on the young, snot-nosed face. The bastard had meant to lead Shakespeare to Mackering—to death—and God only knew why Mackering had saved him.

Why *had* he been freed?

Mackering's last words rang in Shakespeare's ears. His tone of voice. The ruffian had seemed *glad* that Shakespeare was continuing on his quest to find Harry's murderer—as if Shakespeare's vengeance were almost his own. He could only conclude that Mackering wanted Harry's slayer found in order to enact his own punishment and that he, Shakespeare, was to be the guide to the killer.

Then why had Mackering imprisoned him, tried to break him? True, Shakespeare had in his possession money filched from Mackering's men, but it was his impression that Mackering never intended to kill him, coins notwithstanding.

Mackering wanted to find out how much he *knew* about Harry's murder.

Or Mackering just desired to toy with him, to exert his power, weaken his manhood.

Caligula.

Shakespeare sighed. He wanted nothing more to do with the monstrous uprightman, had kept his word and given Mackering back his money. Mackering seemed to be keeping his promise as well. Since his release, Shakespeare had experienced no troubles from Mackering, and that was all that mattered to him. Would his liberty continue unbothered as he made new inquiries—possibly indicting inquiries?

Maybe, maybe not.

Many questions, few answers. In several days he'd leave for the North. His recovery had taken up most of fall and there was but a month left before God's fury made travel impossible.

He closed his eyes, but sleep evaded him. Slowly, he rose and lit the wick of his candle. His neglected papers and quill lay upon his worktable like scorned lovers. It had been so long since he'd written. He sat down at his desk and uncapped his inkpot, but was interrupted by a frantic knock on his door.

Grabbing his dagger, he was astounded to hear Rebecca's voice on the other side. Quickly, he unbolted the latch and opened the door.

She was dressed as a man, but the masculine garb did little to hide a thin face pale and frightened. Her hands were clasped together, but still they shook visibly. She entered his closet and Shakespeare shut the door behind her.

Immediately she hugged him, laid her cheeks wet with tears against his nightshirt. He seemed startled by the intensity of her embrace, but a moment later he was hugging her just as tightly. She wanted to melt inside his body, find refuge under his skin, be rocked to the rhythmic beat of his heart.

She knew that after what she'd done to him it was sheer gall to come like this. But there was no one else to turn to.

"What news, Becca?" Shakespeare whispered. "What evil portent has driven you to me?"

"I'm so scared," was all she could answer. How should she begin? She felt Shakespeare trying to ease her into a chair, but she was too taut to sit. She sprang up and clutched him again. She spoke in clipped, rapid sentences.

"You must think me horrid! To come to you. Wretched and frightened. I discard you. Like muck. Then leech your skin when I'm in need." She looked at him with red, swollen eyes. "I should have never bid you adieu. I should have defied the wishes of my elders. . . . I'm weak, William. If you'll help me, I promise—"

"Hand me not the gift of love wrapped in conditions, Becca. I gave you my blessings at our last encounter and I meant them truly. You had my pardon then, you have my help now. What frightens you so?"

Rebecca took a deep breath, then forcibly exhaled. She unfurled her fists and dropped her hands to her sides, leaving wet wrinkles in Shakespeare's nightshirt. For the first time tonight, she studied Shakespeare's face. It was so worn, so haggard. His eyes were tired and troubled. His tooth had been chipped.

"What misfortune has come to you, Willy?" Rebecca asked.

"What do you mean?"

"Your face . . ." She touched his cheek. "It's so thin—"

"It's nothing—"

"Not so," Rebecca insisted. She grabbed his hands. "Tell me!"

"Your problem first, Becca," Shakespeare said.

Rebecca didn't answer him, continued to look at his eyes.

"Pray," Shakespeare said, kissing her fingers. "Speak."

"Very well." Rebecca was drawn back to her present woes. She forced her voice to be calm. "The news concerns my father." She tucked a loose strand of hair under her brother's cap. "He's . . . oh merciful God! He's been arrested!"

There was a long moment of silence. Rebecca began to pace. Shakespeare asked, "What are the charges?"

"I'm not certain. I overheard the words 'conspiracy and sedition' against the crown. *None* of it is true!"

Her face had turned even whiter. Shakespeare had never seen her so terrified. He asked, "When was he arrested?"

"Three hours ago. My uncles and brother left with him to plead his case to Sessions come the morning. We've dispatched word to my other uncle, the Duke of Mytilene— Oh Will, I'm terrified! Yet I shudder to burden you with my troubles after the way I've treated you."

"I embrace your woes happily."

"Oh my dearest, never would I have imposed upon you like this, but lives are at stake—not just my father's, but another's as well. Dear God, I have so much to tell you and the time passes too quickly. . . . Willy, my love, remember back to the day of our drinking?"

"Yes."

"I told you I was of the old religion."

"A Papist, aye."

"I'm not a Papist. I . . ." She put her hand to her mouth, then removed it. "I follow older customs."

Shakespeare looked at her quizzically.

"I'm a converso, Will. I am of Jewish blood. Though my family is outwardly Christian, we secretly retain many of our old Mosaic customs. If our practices were discovered and properly exploited by some wicked nobleman, we could be branded as Jews and deported according to the laws of the land."

Shakespeare stared at her. "You're a *Jewess*?"

Rebecca paused before she answered. "Yes," she said. "I consider myself a Jewess."

"But you were baptized into the Church of England, Becca," Shakespeare said. "That makes you as Christian as I."

She didn't answer him.

Shakespeare said, "You were baptized, were you not?"

"It doesn't matter—"

"It doesn't *matter*?" cried Shakespeare. "God save your soul, for you know not what you say!"

Rebecca looked at him, seeing a different man. A Gentile loathing a Jew. Tears formed in her eyes. Her grandam had been right after all.

She said, "I was wrong to come here. Forgive my intrusion."

Shakespeare grabbed her arm. "I pray you, tell me why you came?"

"What's the use? I see in your eyes that you think me unclean and venal."

"No, Becca," Shakespeare said. "You misread me. I'm confused. I've never seen a Jew before, much less . . . loved one.

Yet I did love thee, love thee still . . ." He sighed. "But now is not the time to sew the seams of a ripped heart. Tell me about your father."

She broke away from his grip and began to walk in circles. "My father is a true prince among men." She stopped, then said, "He was dreadful to you that day, Will. But he's not really fashioned with so hot a temper."

"I understand," Shakespeare said.

"How do I make these confessions without you thinking him a traitor? I falter to find the proper words."

"Speak. I'll say nothing."

Rebecca hesitated, then said, "My father was involved in a dangerous scheme. He was dealing covertly with His Majesty Philip the Second of Spain—"

"God's blood!" Shakespeare blurted out. It was his turn to pace. "Your father deals secretly with the *Spanish*?"

"It's not what it seems!"

"But what it *appears*, Becca. A Spanish . . . Jew who has secret trade with England's foe. He should be torn apart limb by limb if it were known!"

"I know," Rebecca said. Once again her eyes began to fill with tears. "But it's not as you say. Father is *not* a traitor!"

"Then what was his business with Spain?"

"Business of the *heart*. My father was trying to free our people from the tryannies of the Inquisition. He was paying off His Majesty to close his eyes to the people we smuggle out of his land."

"Secret Jews?" Shakespeare said.

"Aye, conversos like me. Converted Christians who practiced the old customs. Conversos who were previously warned by the Holy See to cease the ancient ways. These conversos, when caught, are considered *relapsos* and condemned to the stake."

"Jews," Shakespeare repeated.

"Yes, Jews," Rebecca said. "We're people, Willy. And like the baptized, we feel pain and scream when tortured."

Shakespeare winced at the well-placed barb. He said, "I pray you to refrain from harsh speech . . . though I've given you reason."

"I feel so *alone*."

"And I've done nothing to comfort you," Shakespeare said softly. "I'm so . . . surprised, Becca. There hasn't been a Jew in the Isle for over three hundred years. . . . But pay me no heed. You stand in front of the drawn arrow, and tis cruel of me to quarrel with you. What can I do for my sweet Rebecca?"

She dried her eyes on her shirtsleeve and quickly said, "There lived in our house a certain weasel named Manuel de Andrada—

an evil churl, a known liar and traitor. He was a spy for Don Antonio—the Pretender to the Throne of Portugal. He was in Don Antonio's service when he met my father—my family. My father was Don Antonio's physician. My father—*as well as England*—supported the Pretender in his attempted coup to free Portugal from Spain. Being a true and loyal man, Father continued supporting the Pretender even *after* the revolt failed—until Don Antonio had become completely daft, a lunatic muttering plots of revenge against the world.''

''Your father supported the overthrow of Philip in Portugal. Yet now he deals with Philip.''

''Gold is an excellent maker of truces,'' said Rebecca. ''My father first supported Don Antonio because the Pretender's mother, Yolanda Gomez, was a Jewish conversa. Our people had hoped that some tolerance toward our beliefs would follow once Don Antonio wore the royal crown. But it never came to pass.''

''Go on,'' said Shakespeare.

''Three weeks ago,'' Rebecca said, ''this cellar rat, de Andrada, defected from our household and departed for places and sanctuaries unknown. Methinks he sold family secrets to Essex—my father's bitterest enemy. Lord Essex has wanted my father's throat for many, many months, solely because Father opposes his War Party.''

''Spain doesn't understand kindness, only its enemies' strengths as witnessed by the Armada.''

''If Essex has his way, he shall lead England into war with Spain, costly battles that will strip the crown of its treasury—and all for his *own* glory. And if I may be so bold to speak, the lord has his own eye on *Her* Majesty—the crown itself. My father opposes war. He wants a stable England, a peaceful England—''

''And he wants to continue his negotiations with Philip for Jews, which is impossible if the state is at open war?''

Rebecca folded her arms across her chest. ''I don't expect you to understand the gravity of his work, but at least know this. My father is *not* an agent for Philip! He is a faithful subject of the crown! His arrest—a creation of Essex—will be proven malicious as well as false.''

''Then what need have you of me?''

''You must help me save Miguel.''

She took a deep breath, then explained to him the mission. How her family paid Philip to turn his back on Jews—*relapsos*—stowed in ships docked in Spanish land, Jews subject to the Inquisition. The *relapsos* were condemned to death, the mission their only chance of survival.

Rebecca said in a shrill voice, ''Oh my sweet Will, if you

knew of the Holy See and its atrocities! How these *relapsos* suffer—women and children as well! My grandam, blessed am I to have such a goodly grandam, spent her teens in a blackened dungeon—raped, beaten, burned, drowned with water because she held different beliefs, because she didn't eat the flesh of swine! Because she changed the linens on Friday! And for what?''

"Calm—"

"I will not be calm! Can't you see the horrors of which I speak!''

"Hush! The thunder of your voice shall put us both in danger.''

Rebecca burst into tears, melting into Shakespeare's open arms.

"You're overcome with grief,'' he said quietly.

"I have no time for grief.'' But she sobbed as if grief were all she possessed. "I want my father!'' she wailed.

"Catch the rhythm of your breath, Becca. You'll become lightheaded if you gasp waves of choppy sea.''

"I love thee,'' Rebecca cried out.

Shakespeare took her hand and kissed it. "I know well of torture, Becca. I pray, continue when you're able.''

Rebecca wiped her salty cheeks. In a slow voice she explained to Shakespeare how the ships bearing the stowaways would sometimes dock in England. Once here, her family would aid those smuggled aboard. Miguel would steal onto the ships, present the stowaways with citizens' papers that allowed them to live legally as Jews in the Low Countries.

"The papers were legal?'' Shakespeare asked.

"Some were legal. When we couldn't afford to buy them— Amsterdam often charged us exorbitant prices—my aunt, my mother, my cousins . . . and I would forge them.''

Shakespeare shook his head. "Why are you telling me this?''

"Miguel has not returned from his latest assignment,'' Rebecca exclaimed. "I would have thought nothing of it—the length of his delay is not extraordinary—but since the arrest of my father, I'm worried that de Andrada has sold him to the Spanish. If Miguel is caught, he'll be brought to trial in Spain under the jurisdiction of the Holy See. They'll *torture* him to death . . . like the Star Chamber.'' She shuddered. "I can't bear . . . my God, I am weak without him!''

She started crying again, great tides of mournful sobs. At the mentioning of the Star Chamber, Shakespeare knew that though she talked of Miguel, her thoughts were with her father. At least with her betrothed, she could *do* something on his behalf. With her father she was pitifully helpless, her heart imprisoned with the man who had sired her. Filial love—a more powerful mover than the winds of heaven.

"Sweet lady of my heart," Shakespeare said. "What dost thou want of me?"

"My cousins, Thomas and Dunstan, are on their way to Portsmouth to ascertain Miguel's whereabouts. An hour after they left, I found a note amongst Miguel's clothing, a scrap of paper with scribbling on it. Miguel often writes himself notes . . . lists. He's very exacting. I found this one, along with several others, hidden in a doublet he left at my father's home. But that's irrelevant. What is important is that it mentioned the location of the ship. It was docked at Dover. Not Portsmouth, *Dover.*"

Rebecca grabbed her head. "I feel faint."

"Sit," Shakespeare ordered.

Rebecca complied. She said, "The plans must have been changed at the last minute and someone neglected to inform my cousins. I must meet up with them and tell them to go to Dover. But Willy, I'm weak, so scared to travel alone, afraid not for myself, but that I'll fail to reach them, fail to reach Miguel and cause my betrothed harm. I need help, William. I need you to accompany me until I find my cousins. My uncles and brother are with my father; Miguel's father is frantic with worry. My God, poor, poor Hector!"

Rebecca buried her head in her hands.

Shakespeare sighed, rubbed his chin. "You carry no bags, Becca. What preparations have you made for such an arduous journey?"

Rebecca knocked her forehead with her fist. "What an idiot God has made this stupid woman!"

"Worry not," said Shakespeare. "I have all of what we require—completely packed and bundled, as the Fates would have it. Enough for just one to the North, but enough for two to travel the road south to Dover. How many horses did you bring?"

"Only one. A fine mare. She's hidden outside the wall near Ludgate in a thick copse. I have her firmly tied and muzzled. I pray no one has discovered her."

"We shall share her," Shakespeare said. "How did you get through into the city? The gates close at nightfall."

"England would do well to patch her armor. Many a crawl space dots her wall."

Shakespeare dressed quickly. He threw Rebecca some rags and told her to tie them around the soles of her boots.

"Why?"

"They will muffle your steps."

She nodded. When she was done, Shakespeare threw the bags over his shoulder.

"Leave us go," he said.

33

T he night was moonless and cold. Rebecca shivered underneath her frieze cloak and wished she had dressed her head in a thicker hat. But at least her legs were warm, housed in double-knitted woolen hose. She flexed her gloved fingers, which had stiffened in the chill, covered her mouth and blew warm air onto her hands and nose. Shakespeare lit a small candle, the flame highlighting his profile in orange. Wisps of hot breath curled about his nose and mouth.

"Do you know the way back to your horse?" he whispered.

"Aye."

"You're certain?"

"Absolutely."

"How did you avoid the watchmen and the rogues?"

"Good hap."

He took her hand and said, "Lead me."

"I came by way of the Cheape," she said. "The gap in the wall lies between Newgate and Ludgate. I suggest we bypass Paul's. Too many vagabonds lie in wait."

Their bootsteps were silent as they tiptoed past darkened buildings that occasionally winked the flicker of a rush candle, past boarded-up booths and shops and dusky taverns whose dim light escaped through red lattice sashes. Their eyes were of little use, their ears their best defense, listening for sounds that could mean attack or arrest.

"Where did you learn to muffle your steps with rags?" Rebecca asked.

"I was a clever boy."

"A thief?"

"No," he whispered. "Just a child who couldn't sleep at night . . . I hear something."

Rebecca listened.

"An owl," they said in unison, looking upward.

It rested on the peak of a thatched roof, as still as the eaves upon which it sat. Its hood was marbled with brown and white, its eyes carved from onyx. Shakespeare and Rebecca exchanged glances. Owls were evil omens. The bird hooted again, blinked, then spread its massive wings and flew away, hopefully taking its bad luck with it.

"This way," Rebecca said.

They walked a few more minutes in silence. Shakespeare stopped suddenly.

"I hear something," he said.

"What?" Rebecca asked. "I hear nothing."

"Muffled steps—like our own."

"Where?"

"Quick, over here," Shakespeare said, jerking her behind the thick trunk of an oak. He blew out the candle and they held their breath.

There were three of them afoot—robbers dressed in coal black. Shakespeare's eye caught the glint of a foot-long dagger one of them gripped in his hand. The trio passed the tree without a second glance.

Rebecca let out a gush of air.

"My God, that was close," she said.

"It was." Shakespeare relit his candle. "Which way now, m'lady?"

Rebecca whispered, "I can't walk, I'm shaking too hard. I'm so scared."

"You're dressed as a man, think like one as well. Though the dark frightens the piss from your body, admit it not."

Rebecca smiled. She inhaled deeply and said, "This way."

They walked another half mile. Rebecca felt her body being drawn to his. She inched closer until she was under the protective tent of his arm.

"I'm sorry I bid you adieu so abruptly," she whispered. "Without explanation. Twas a cruel thing to do. But I did it for family loyalty."

"It was best," Shakespeare said. "For my family loyalty as well."

"Did you summer with your wife and children?"

Shakespeare suddenly found himself swallowing back tears. "No."

Rebecca heard sorrow in his voice and became quiet.

So dark, so still, so silent.

A minute later she seized his arm and brought him to a halt. "Listen," she whispered. "The growl of a wild animal."

Shakespeare answered. "I hear it, too, though the sound is weak in ferocity."

"What shall we do?"

"Circumvent the noise. Can you lead us another way?"

"I'll try, but I might become confused in the dark."

Shakespeare paused, then said, "The growl has disappeared. I don't hear it anymore."

"Perhaps the beast has left," suggested Rebecca. "No. Wait. Now I hear the growling once more, louder than before."

"Wait here," Shakespeare said.

"Where are you going?"

"Just do as I say."

Shakespeare walked a few paces forward, stopped, then motioned her with his hand to approach.

"Regard the centurion responsible for our city's safety."

A constable lay sleeping atop a pile of soft dirt, his thick cloak draped across his body, his hat over his eyes and nose. The neck of an empty bottle was clutched in his right hand, his breath escaping from the rim of his hat like smoke from the closed door of a burning room.

"How deeply I shall sleep at night knowing that London is protected by such honorable hands." Rebecca pulled Shakespeare forward. "Come. We're almost there."

Fifteen tense minutes later they were on their hands and knees, crawling through a three-foot hole in the great city wall. Once on the other side, Rebecca leaped with happiness, took Shakespeare's hand and ran with him to the thick underbrush where her horse was hidden.

She was still there.

Blessed be to God.

Shakespeare loaded the bags onto the horse. Rebecca mounted first, and he sat in back of her. With a firm jerk of the reins they rode off.

Rebecca felt his arms around her, guiding the horse with expertise. She immediately felt her heart slowing, her breathing become steady. They rode the first half hour in silence, both trying desperately to second-guess the direction of Rebecca's cousins, listening for the beats of horses riding in tandem. They trotted through the open countryside, away from the houses and booths, far from the shops and taverns and churches. The vast landscape was filled with never-ending fields of grass and shrub sporadically interrupted by nestings of twisted oak. In the distance shadowed hills rose in the sky like rain clouds.

Alone.

After an hour of riding, the early morning moon had begun its ascent. Shakespeare used Diana's light for guidance.

Rebecca spoke first.

"How is it that your bags were prepared for journey?"

"I was planning to go elsewhere."

"To the North?"

"Aye."

"Harry Whitman?"

"Aye."

Rebecca asked what had happened with Whitman since they had last spoken. Shakespeare explained that much had happened but the news was best left for another time. Again, she asked him what had caused him to become so thin and pale. Shakespeare remained evasive and she didn't press the issue. It was all she could do to keep herself calm. Ten minutes later Shakespeare said,

"You love your betrothed deeply."

Rebecca turned around and nodded. "Not as a woman loves a man, but as a sister loves her brother."

"Much sisterly love you show."

Rebecca sighed, faced forward.

Shakespeare said, "Not the time for the green monster to appear, I know."

Rebecca said, "You've no cause to be jealous of Miguel."

They rode in silence for the next hour. Shakespeare kicked the horse's flanks, urging her to quicken her pace. Finally, he summoned up the nerve to ask the question that had been plaguing him.

"Would I have had cause to be jealous of Miguel's brother?"

Rebecca heard the doubt in his voice. "I did love him," she said. "But never have I loved anyone as I love thee."

"How I love thee," Shakespeare whispered. "Pray, my love. Tell me how your first lover died?"

Rebecca swallowed. She explained how it was Raphael who had first performed Miguel's work. The Spanish somehow intercepted him, sent him to the tribunals for being a *relapso*.

"Our entire family has been tried in effigy in Iberia. We've all been sentenced to die on the stake."

Rebecca began to shed silent tears.

"They have told me that Raphael martyred himself, stabbed his heart with his dagger before the galleon docked, thus sparing his body the ungodly acts of the Holy See. I think they told me tales to make me feel lighter of heart. . . . I know not the truth. I care not to know."

"Whom did you bury that day in the cemetery, then?"

"Some corpse with no kin, dead from the plague. Upon his death, my father snatched the fouled body from Bartholomew's and assigned to him a certificate of death bearing Raphael's name. My fiancé's loss was the gain of a bubo-riddled pauper. At least someone received a proper burial."

Shakespeare guided the horse to the right, over a field of wet mud. The animal slowed, dragged down by the thick muck. Shakespeare pressed the mare forward until once again they rode on firm ground—acres of land made silvery in the moonlight.

Enemies, Shakespeare thought. Everybody had them whether they be overt or hidden—a soldier's sword at your throat, a madman's knife in your back. Foes, plotting and planning destruction of one another, each with his own agenda. Putting prices on human heads as if they were beef cattle. Shakespeare hugged Rebecca and said,

"I'm truly sorry for your loss."

She started to speak, but her voice cracked. She tried again. "I know—"

"Listen," Shakespeare interrupted.

Hoofbeats.

Shakespeare pulled the horse to the left, dug his heels into the animal's side and sent her flying. Her haunches were fluid, shiny and damp, her tongue protruding, her mane streaming in the wind of her gallop.

Rebecca pointed to two small outlines moving in the night.

"Over there," she shouted.

Shakespeare cracked the reins and the animal raced with all its heart.

"It's them!" Rebecca shouted, joyously. "Dunstan! Thomas!"

The outlines kept going.

"Faster, you mother of a whore," Shakespeare muttered to the horse.

"Dunstan!" Rebecca screamed. "Tommy!"

The outlines stopped.

"It's Becca!" she shouted.

Her cousins turned around and waved.

"Becca," they shouted back. "What news?"

"God is with us," Rebecca said, crying.

"God is with us," Shakespeare repeated. "Whose god it is, I know not. But some god is with us."

34

Dunstan glared at Shakespeare. He said, "I cannot believe this!"

Rebecca said, "Dunstan, I—"

"What are you doing here, Becca?" asked Thomas.

"Miguel did not go to Portsmouth."

Dunstan glowered at her, at Shakespeare.

"He knows about our bloodline, cousin," said Rebecca. "I had to tell him."

Dunstan buried his head in his hands. "Your father should have ripped out your throat with his surgery knives!"

Shakespeare started to speak, but Rebecca silenced him with a squeeze on his arm.

"I had no choice," Rebecca explained. "I needed someone to ride with me, and Mother and I decided that telling Shakespeare—"

"Since when does your *mother* make decisions?" Dunstan said.

"Since my *father* was *arrested* and there is no male in our household capable of making them."

"And this was indeed a decision obviously made by a female," Dunstan said.

"Dunstan," Rebecca started out. She was barely suppressing her rage. "Shakespeare was kind enough to see to my safety despite the perils to his own welfare. You should be showering him with gratitude, not contempt."

"I thank you for protecting my cousin from harm's way," Thomas said to Shakespeare. To Rebecca he said, "Why do you say that Miguel went to Dover?"

Shakily, Rebecca handed Thomas the note.

Thomas opened his purse and pulled out his tinder box, steel and flint. Rubbing steel upon flint, he produced the spark, lit a small strip of tinder, and illuminated the paper.

"What does it say?" Dunstan asked.

"That the ship is docked in Dover," Thomas replied.

"Miguel's hand?" Dunstan inquired.

"Of course it's Miguel's hand!" Rebecca snapped. "Do you think I'd risk traveling the open road to bring you a *forgery*?"

"I think, Becca, that your judgment is seriously flawed," Dunstan said.

"It's Miguel's hand," Thomas said. He brought the flame to the corner of the paper and reduced it to ashes. To Shakespeare he said, "See to it that my cousin returns safely to the confines of her home. You have my thanksgiving in advance, and upon our return to London I'll see to it that you're handsomely compensated—"

"There's no need," Shakespeare said.

"The man boasts pride," Dunstan sneered.

Thomas glared at his brother. Such behavior was contrary to their breeding.

"I want to come with you," Rebecca said to her cousins. Before they could protest, she explained, "If circumstances necessitate your boarding the ship, who is going to keep watch over the horses?"

"We shall leave them with a trustworthy innkeeper," Dunstan said.

"Trustworthy innkeeper?" Rebecca replied.

"Mayhap *you'll* have the good fortune to find the rare breed, sir," said Shakespeare to Dunstan. "It's like searching for truffles. One must be a pig to sniff them out."

Dunstan's eyes narrowed, his hand gripped the hilt of his sword. Rebecca saw her cousin's anger and quickly asked,

"What if Miguel or any of the stowaways are hurt? Who is going to provide them with aid?"

"There are doctors in Dover, Becca," Thomas said.

"And how do you explain who Miguel is? Who the stowaways are? And what you're doing in Dover?"

The brothers were silent.

"I shall not be so meddlesome as to try and do a man's toil," Rebecca said. "I've learned my lesson well. But there are things that I *can* do to free you from menial labor so that you may perform your task clear-headed."

"I'll stay with her in Dover," said Shakespeare. "I've come this far already."

"And *this*, sirrah, is as far as you shall go," Dunstan said.

Thomas said, "If Becca is to come with us, she'll need protection."

Dunstan's eyes filled with disdain. "Protection from *him*?"

"Aye," Rebecca answered. "Protection from someone who faints not at the sight of fresh blood."

Dunstan turned red with fury. Thomas said,

"Hold your tongue, Becca." He turned to Dunstan and said, "He has brought her thus far to safety—"

"Tis unthinkable that he should travel with us!" cried Dunstan.

"I already know everything damaging to you and your cause," Shakespeare said. "Your available options are to trust me or to slay me."

"I vote for the latter," said Dunstan.

"Apologize to him!" ordered Rebecca.

Dunstan sidled his horse close to hers. He smiled and said, "Apologize?" He broke into gales of laughter.

"You're a pig," Rebecca said.

Dunstan stopped laughing and suddenly slapped her. "Know thy place, woman."

Again Shakespeare felt his anger being silenced by Rebecca squeezing his arm. Ordinarily he would have ignored her warning, but after his last encounter with her family, he thought it best if she handled the situation. Rebecca locked eyes with Dunstan, then slapped him back.

There was a moment of silence.

Dunstan slapped her again, drew blood from the corner of her mouth. To Thomas he said, "Let us be off."

Rebecca hissed to Dunstan, "You hypocritical, jealous son of a bitch bastard—"

"Becca," Thomas warned. "Respect!"

"You'd rather endanger Miguel . . ." Rebecca continued, "endanger my *father—everything* that we've worked for—than receive help from a goodly man who has won my affections. You miserable, self-serving—"

"Enough!" Thomas shouted.

"Nay, brother." Dunstan smiled tightly. "The wench is amusing."

"You burn from my constant refusal to bed you," Rebecca said, wiping the blood on her shirtsleeve.

Dunstan chuckled, regarded the rings on his fingers. "How does one burn from the refusal of a whore?"

"So would know the whorefucker who's incapable of properly bedding his own wife."

Dunstan's eyes turned murderous. Even Shakespeare was shocked.

"Stow your filthy mouth," Thomas barked at her. But the corners of his mouth crept upward. Diplomatically, he rode in between Dunstan's and Rebecca's horses, separating them physically. "Keep your hatred at home, Becca."

He led Dunstan aside and whispered, "Let us trust Shakespeare. At least for now. He's an able-bodied man and could prove to be of much assistance.''

"As if he'd fight for a pack of 'filthy' Jews.''

"He'd fight for Becca, that's obvious. Possibly for us by extension. The odds against the Spanish are not favorable to us, brother. Let us not turn away two strong arms and a swinging sword.''

"I'll murder that bitch—''

"Leave her in peace, Dunstan. You pester her constantly.''

"Tis none of your affair.''

"She no longer belongs to you! Accept it!''

Dunstan exploded. "Am I to take orders from a beardless child!'' He slapped his younger brother across the face.

Thomas grabbed his brother and placed a dagger at his neck. "Keep your hands off me, brother,'' he whispered.

Dunstan pushed the dagger away. "When Father dies, the entire estate is entrusted to his elder son. Remember that.''

"I piss on you.''

Dunstan sighed. "Such brotherly affection we demonstrate to the stranger, Thomas. Put the dagger away. My pardons for my insult.''

Thomas paused a moment, then slipped the dagger back in his belt. "My apologies for my insolence.''

"If you want the player along, take him. But I'll have nothing to do with that . . . that *flea*. Fleas are meant to be squashed.''

"Fleas can also bite.''

"Welladay, then. *You* use his puny bite. I want nothing to do with him—or her, save to wring her little neck!''

Thomas rode back to Shakespeare. He said, "If you are willing to aid us, I shall forever remain in your debt.''

"Your debt, like your coins, are not necessary, sir,'' Shakespeare said. "I expect nothing in return except civility—for me and Becca.''

"Done,'' Thomas said. "Now what is the best way to get to Dover?''

Shakespeare said, "By my compass and calculations, we're at the eastern end of Sussex approaching Midherst.''

Thomas said, "Dover is due east . . . My God, how much time we've lost. Dunstan!'' he called out. "Come hither, I pray. We need to coordinate.''

Reluctantly, Dunstan pulled his stallion over to the huddle. "What?'' he asked.

"We need to find the most expedient route to Dover,'' Thomas explained.

The most direct path was heavily wooded, but the southern route would take them out of their way. The north required too much retracing of steps. After much debate it was decided that they should ride through the forest. The path: Grinsted to Grombebridge through the middle of Kent, passing through Denham, Wye, finally to Dover.

"How long do you think it will take us?" Shakespeare asked.

Dunstan started to say something, but his eyes went to Rebecca and he held his tongue. Gods, even dressed as a man she was a siren.

"Sixty to eighty miles out," Thomas thought out loud. "Another day and a half. Dawn is upon us. We'll travel throughout the day. Hopefully, nightfall should find us around or about Denham. We'll find an inn there."

"Becca," said Dunstan. "Now that you are among kinsmen, it is proper that you ride with one of us."

Rebecca didn't respond.

"A truce, cousin," Dunstan said.

Rebecca looked at Shakespeare. He whispered, "Go for the sake of peace. We have your betrothed's life to think about."

"You're a wise man, Willy."

She dismounted her horse. Dunstan jumped off his steed and extended a hand to help her up. She glared at the outstretched hand and moved her eyes with purpose up to Thomas. The younger brother smiled, flattered that for once Rebecca was asking him who she should ride with. Though he would have loved to ride with her, to ensure family harmony he jerked his head toward Dunstan and rode to Shakespeare's side. Rebecca snubbed Dunstan's offer of help and mounted the horse by herself.

"I'll lead," said Thomas.

"Well it is," Dunstan said. At least he'd pulled her away from *him*. "Well it is." A few minutes into the ride he leaned forward and lowered his mouth to her ear. "Art thou cold?"

"Never again address me in familiar voice."

"You're shivering. I have an extra blanket as part of my belongings."

"I want nothing of yours."

"So coldly you speak, Becca. You know how your words wound me."

"Words, as wounds, draw no blood," she said, touching her swollen lip.

"Aye, but the cuts run deeper, all bleeding internal."

"How does one bleed from bloodless veins?"

"Ah, bloodless because they're filled with ichor."

"Filled with muck."

"I love thee."

Rebecca laughed. "Do you know what you've become, cousin? *Old.* Though your belly is hard and your legs are strong, you've turned venal, cranky, malicious, and lecherous. You've not yet reached the middle age of thirty yet you act characteristically of old men in their forties and fifties. What has *happened* to you?"

"Ask instead what has happened to my wife."

"Grace has borne you five children. She is entitled to a cushion of fat around her belly."

"I find it repulsive."

"So take on a mistress—discreetly. Grace expects such sport from a man of your stature. What she expects not, nor deserves, is your goatish eye, your frantic bedding of every lower-class wench that lifts her skirt."

"You'll understand what if feels like once you're wedded to Miguel—to be married to a man whom you find lacking."

"'Tis the other way around. He has much to please the eye. It is *he* who finds *me* wanting. Just please God let us get to that state."

"Who will warm your feet when your bed turns cold at night?"

"Not you."

"I know that," Dunstan said. "What I don't understand is why. My love for you hasn't changed. It's your feelings that have grown so icy. Why?"

Rebecca didn't answer.

"*Why*, Becca? It's ripping out my heart."

Rebecca said softly, "I grew up, Dunstan. . . . Try to understand, people change when they reach adulthood."

He didn't answer her, and she felt his sadness in his silence. But there was nothing she could do for him. And other things weighed heavier upon her mind. She asked,

"What will happen to Father?"

Dunstan felt his belly suddenly tighten, his stomach burn in its juices. "Don't worry. We'll buy his freedom."

But his voice betrayed his lack of confidence.

She bit her lip and held back the tears.

Dunstan said, "So far as we could ascertain, neither Essex nor his spy master has definite proof of our dealings with the Spanish. He has acted solely on de Andrada's word."

"Where is the verminous scum?"

"De Gama, our Iberian spy, told us that he now resides in Amsterdam."

"Does de Andrada know of 'David'?"

"I suspect he does. How much I'm not certain. Speaking of what the enemy knows, exactly what does Shakespeare know?"

"He knows not of David."

"Welladay," Dunstan mocked. "The lady shows discretion."

"Your tongue is not the flesh of wit, Dunstan, merely acid."

"What a mouth you have."

"I had to confess our mission to him. I told you that."

"Your mother told you to tell him?"

"Mother told me to take Miguel's note to you. If I couldn't do it alone, she told me to take Shakespeare for protection."

"I cannot believe that your mother told you to trust a Gentile."

"I made a choice. The proper one, I say. I listened to my heart."

"The heart is a foul organ."

Rebecca shook her head. "It's an instrument most sweet if played by nimble fingers."

The road turned muddy, forcing the horses to slow their pace, the terrain dense with foliage as clusters of trees and brush thickened the grassy hillside. Nighttime shadows had begun to disappear as hints of dawn lightened the sky. But the air remained cold and Rebecca shivered. Dunstan wrapped her in his arms. She didn't fight him off. Instead she took the reins of the horse and gave them a firm pull. "We're falling behind Thomas and Shakespeare."

"They seemed to be deeply engaged in conversation. Perhaps they moan their mutual lack of facial hair."

"You taunt with no purpose, Dunstan," Rebecca said. "One time you'll bite hard into meat and find your teeth breaking on a bone."

"My oh my."

"Your brother is decent. And Shakespeare's a most goodly and gentle man. Completely undeserving of the poison you gave him."

Dunstan said nothing.

A moment later he said, "He's almost *thirty*, Becca."

"Twenty-nine. Your age, if I'm not mistaken."

"His head is practically smooth—"

"You exaggerate."

"He's bald, Becca, and the hair on his chin equally as scant. What do you *see* in him?"

She paused, then said, "A poet's eternity."

Rebecca dreamed in the cradle of Dunstan's arms, the steady beats of the horse's hooves rocking her to sleep. Her mind was dark at first, then came the images—chains, racks, stocks, pilliwinks, whips. Her father's body suspended from a noose, his face purpled and smooth, as shiny as an eggplant, his limbs being hacked from their sockets with cleavers—blood bursting with each whack of the ax.

Then came the screams. Once they started, they wouldn't stop.

Shakespeare and Thomas galloped over to Dunstan.

"What's wrong?" Shakespeare asked. "Is she hurt?"

"She's having a nightmare," Dunstan said, firmly shaking her shoulders. "I seem not able to rouse her."

"The events have proven too much for her," Shakespeare said, dismounting.

"Becca, wake up," pleaded Dunstan.

"Hand her to me," Shakespeare said to Dunstan.

Dunstan gripped her waist and swung her off the saddle, her arms and legs flailing about. Shakespeare gently lowered her to the ground. Dunstan dismounted.

She moaned, "My God, no, no, no!"

"Wake up, Becca," Dunstan shouted, holding her face in his hands. He'd turned pale. "Wake up, damn it!"

"What did you say to her to upset her?" Thomas said.

"Nothing," Dunstan said, eyes darting between Thomas and Shakespeare. "She was well before she fell asleep."

"I'll get some wine," Thomas said.

Shakespeare rocked her in his arms as she wailed.

Thomas handed Shakespeare his gourd.

"Drink, my love." Shakespeare brought the mouthpiece to her lips. "Let the wine wash away the poison from your mind."

"Stop!" she groaned. "I beg you to stop! Have mercy on his soul."

"Becca," Thomas said, gently slapping her face. "My God, what'll we do?"

Again Shakespeare brought the gourd to her mouth. He whispered, "Drink, sweet lady of my heart. How I love thee."

Rebecca stopped screaming.

"Drink."

Her eyes opened.

"Praise be God," Shakespeare said. "Good morrow, Becca. Catch your breath. You're safe."

She felt herself panting, and inhaled deeply. The air was bracing, scented with spicy aromatics from decaying foliage—a whiff of chilled incense.

"Dunstan?" she called out.

"I'm here, Becca," he said, kneeling at her side. He stretched out his arms and she slid into his embrace. He smiled smugly at Shakespeare.

Rebecca hugged Dunstan tightly.

"Calm, my sweet," said Dunstan. He stroked her hair.

"What time is it?"

"Nearly two in the afternoon."

"What happened to the dawn? The morning?"

"You've been asleep, my little one."

She suddenly bolted up. "Willy?"

"Here," Shakespeare said.

She broke away from Dunstan and jumped into Shakespeare's arms, buried her head in his chest. It was Shakespeare's turn to grin. Dunstan frowned, then despite himself, let out a laugh. Shakespeare joined him. He said,

"Two cocks preening and pecking for the hen."

"Ah, but what a hen!" Dunstan said.

Rebecca looked up at Shakespeare, at her surroundings. They sat in a glade—a circular clearing surrounded by mossy green yews and boxwoods, tall skeletal beeches and the twisted boughs of leafless oaks. The smell of winter, the rustle of wind, the distant sounds of woodland denizens scampering through the fallen leaves. Bright parallel rays of light crisscrossed through the branches and spotlighted the ground—a lattice of sunbeams.

"My God," Rebecca whispered. "I'm so confused."

Shakespeare offered her the gourd once more. She took a sip of icy, sweet wine, felt it soothe her parched throat.

"I'll tie the horses," said Thomas. "The dinner hour has long since past. Time we've taken a stomach."

"My sweet Will," she said. Her voice was breathy. "You're still here."

"Of course I'm here."

"I dreamt you'd deserted me because I was a Jew—"

"I'm here, Becca."

Thomas offered her a slab of salted beef. She shook her head.

"You must eat," insisted Dunstan. "You'll need your strength for the ordeal to come."

Rebecca took the meat, nibbled on the corner. It was full of pepper and made her tongue tingle. She took the gourd and gulped a healthy swallow of wine.

"Not too much at one time," Shakespeare said. Then he whispered, "Or hast thou forgotten thy limitations in the art of quaffing?"

She smiled and snuggled deeper in Shakespeare's grasp, played with his wispy mustache. "How good it is to be awake," she said. "What a horrible dream I had."

Dunstan said, "You've been under much tension—"

"I dreamt that Father was arrested," she interrupted him. "Tortured by screaming mobs of . . ." Her voice trailed off. "Isn't that absurd!"

The men said nothing, eyed each other.

Thomas finally said, "Drink, Becca."

"Isn't it?" she said with desperation.

"Isn't it what, Becca?" asked Dunstan.

"Absurd! Absurd! Absurd that Father, the Queen's *confidant* and physician, was arrested!"

Her voice was filled with pain. No one answered, and the silence became suffocating. Tears suddenly poured over Rebecca's lower eyelids, overflowed onto her cheeks.

Once they started, they couldn't stop.

35

𝕿he journey to Dover proved speedy and uneventful—a brief stopover in Denham at the Oxtail Inn, six hours of blissful sleep, then back on the highways. Head bowed low, Rebecca said little for the duration of the ride, never initiating conversation, responding to questions with one-word answers or small shrugs. No amount of cheer, teasing, or cajoling could cast light upon her darkened mood. Her eyes remained fixed on the road, dull and sunken, her mouth was slack, her lips ashen and chapped from exposure. Her hands were always cold and trembled slightly.

"Are you sure you're well?" Dunstan had repeatedly asked.

A nod.

"Shakespeare could take you home if the journey is too strenuous for you."

A shrug.

Then nothing.

It drove Dunstan mad. Rebecca had many facets to her character, but never a still tongue. He grew tired of speaking, hearing his own voice ring in his ears, and after hours of endless one-way conversations, he gave up and rode with Thomas and the player. He quarreled constantly with his brother, with Shakespeare as well. The player wasn't an evil sort, but his presence was an intrusion, an *insult*. Dunstan resented his quick wit, the facility of his verbal riposte. The player never complained, ate sparingly, drank moderately, and happily shared his provisions with the brothers. Dunstan hated the man's honesty and didn't trust him a whit. But more than anything, he resented Rebecca's love for him.

But even Shakespeare, with all his clever words, had failed to bring a smile to Rebecca's lips. She sank deeper and deeper, struggling to keep afloat in a dark foreboding sea of gloom. Only once had she surfaced for air—reached out for Dunstan's hand. She allowed him to squeeze the delicate fingers housed in warm, woolen gloves, allowed him to kiss the back of her hand. Even though Dunstan realized he was playing the beggar, the starving mutt groveling at her feet, he still found solace in her gesture.

By the noon hour they reached the southeast corner of England—Invaders Gate to Britain—a small snip of land with a thousand-year history of marauding. First were the Celts; they were overtaken, slaughtered by mighty Caesar and his legions. The Romans camped the land for four hundred years. When the Empire fell to ashes, so did its outposts. The troops were brought home, making way for hordes of Angles and Saxons. Then came the Vikings to plunder, then the Normans. Each new inhabitant frantically threw up defenses, armories of the land—stone walls piled upon older stone fortifications. Henry the Eighth brought in the cannons that poised the coastline, the barrels pointing outward—hundreds of black eyes looking down upon diamond-studded sea.

But God, in His infinite power, had provided His land with the finest of shields. The cliffs of Dover sprang from the loamy coast as if planted from Olympian seed—a cloud-high treacherous wall of undulating oyster-colored rock. The Almighty's wondrous sculpture, blinding white as it reflected the rays of midday sun. Rebecca squinted, her eyes watering fiercely from gaping at the rock. Riding atop the cliffs, she had felt inordinately large. But now, trudging through sand, an ant at the foot of the mountains, never had she been so aware of her insignificance.

Thomas halted his horse and signaled for the others to stop as well. He pointed upward and said,

"There's an inn called the Flounder about two miles yonder." He had to shout above the roar of tide. Sea spray stung his nostrils. "They'll stable the horses for us at a halfpence each per night. As I recall, a room lets for a shilling sixpence, not including board. You two ride there with Becca and get her settled while I assess the situation with Miguel. As soon as I know something, I'll report back. If you don't hear from me for . . . let us say, four hours, come out and search."

Shakespeare nodded. Dunstan said to Rebecca, "Don't leave the room once we've departed, not even to eat. We've packed your bag with much to fill your stomach."

"Too much," Rebecca said. "I'll not eat half of what you've given me. Mayhap you'd be better off taking some of the food. Strenuous work can make a man grow ravenous."

"Take all that we've packed," Thomas said. "We don't know

how long we'll be gone. Better you should be provided for excessively than to grow hungry awaiting our return."

"And don't speak in your natural voice, Becca," Dunstan said. "It's higher pitched than that of a proper man."

Shakespeare said, "If you must converse, speak in a raspy whisper. Claim you have a chill in your throat."

"I'll be a convincing man," Rebecca said. She felt herself coming to life.

"Check on the horses regularly," Thomas said.

Rebecca said, "Don't worry about me or the animals. Just find Miguel."

Thomas said, "I'm off to locate Miguel's galleon. I'll meet you at the Flounder as soon as I can. Then we shall make our plans."

So fine it was to settle, Rebecca thought as she dropped her bags onto the floor of their rented chamber. The cell was large but unadorned—bare plaster walls, a fireplace fashioned from hewn stone, two floor-candle sconces, and a straw mattress on a poster bed. To the left of the bed was a rough-cut wood trestle table on which rested an hourglass, a folded woolen blanket, a bowl, and a pitcher of water. All the basics. The floor held clean rushes, Rebecca noted with pleasure, enough room for all of them to sleep comfortably. A fire had been started inside the hearth, and the air inside was as dry and warm as a clay oven. Without speaking, she stretched out in front of the fire and fell into a deep sleep.

She awoke an hour later, according to the hourglass. The others were sleeping soundly—Shakespeare at her left, Dunstan on the bed, snoring. Thomas hadn't returned. She closed her eyes and horrible images began to dance in her brain. She woke up a half hour later drenched in sweat, stood and began to pace.

Where was Thomas?

She marched back and forth, each step fueling her with fear. She paced for an hour, until she had grown mad with worry, until Dunstan thought her legs would cave in.

"Sit down, Becca," he said sleepily. "You're bothering me."

She paid him no heed, and regarded Shakespeare curled up in front of the fire. She thought he was asleep, but he suddenly opened his eyes. He smiled at her, stretched out his hand.

"Do sit, my love," he said. "You're tiring your legs, and all your pacing will have no effect on the outcome."

She said, "I cannot wait any longer."

"You may not have to," Dunstan said. "I hear footsteps. Shakespeare, get the door."

A moment later a winded Thomas burst into the room.

"What news, cousin?" asked Becca.

"Let him first catch his breath," Shakespeare said.

"Becca, get him a pot of ale," Dunstan ordered. To his brother he said, "Pray, rest on the bed."

Thomas shook his head. He held his stomach and continued to pant. Finally he said, "The *San Pedro* cast off early this morning back to Genoa. Not a sign of Miguel or any of the stowaways anywhere . . ."

Dear God, Rebecca thought. The worst has happened. She rummaged through the bags, found a gourd filled with ale and gave it to Thomas. Nodding appreciation, he gulped, then said,

"I found Miguel's horse, stabled not quite a mile from here. The innkeeper who let him space said he'd last spoken to Miguel three days ago. At that time he was well."

"You are certain he's on the ship?" Dunstan asked.

"Where else *could* he be?" Thomas answered.

"He could have been murdered by the Spanish and dumped asea," Dunstan said.

Rebecca gasped.

Shakespeare said, "Let's be positive. Assume he's alive, but a prisoner."

"My assumption," Thomas said. He felt his lungs slowing down, fatigue seeping into his bones. "We must go after Miguel. But no ships awaiting to cast off are headed in the direction of the *San Pedro*. And no boats available to hire either."

"What, then?" asked Dunstan.

Three months ago the thought would have never entered Shakespeare's brain. But three months ago he would have never considered himself a capable cheat, an expert thief and a convincing liar. Three months ago Shakespeare had been imprisoned by a madman. He'd come away a different person. He said,

"The solution is simple. Pirate a boat."

The others looked at him.

He shrugged, then added, "At night. Less chance of being caught."

"A possibility," Thomas said.

Dunstan had turned green at the thought. He said, "We're going to catch a galleon with what? A rowboat? A cog?"

"David killed Goliath with a slingshot," Rebecca said.

"Thank you, cousin, for that inspirational message," Dunstan said.

"What ails you, Dunstan?" Shakespeare said to him. "Is your stomach ill-suited for the rhythm of the sea?"

Thomas smiled.

"It's 'sir' to you, player," Dunstan snapped. "And my stomach is cast as a true man's. Nothing affects my appetite."

"Except fear," Thomas muttered.

"Go fuck thyself," Dunstan said to his brother.

"Then why do you hesitate?" Rebecca asked Dunstan.

Dunstan paused, then said, "Better one dead than four."

Thomas turned red with fury. "Miguel would do nothing less for you."

"Miguel is a more honorable person than I," said Dunstan.

"I'll go with you and Shakespeare, Thomas," Rebecca said. "Dunstan can keep watch over the horses—arm's distance from harm's grip."

Dunstan ignored her. "Hold your peace, all of you. I never said I wouldn't join you in your foolish quest. I merely pointed out a distinct possibility."

"Still, I should accompany you," Rebecca insisted. "I'll keep the boat safely anchored and manned while you board the galleon. Why should you waste the arms of a needed fighter to tend ship?"

"What do you know about sailing?" Thomas said.

"Nothing," Rebecca said. "Ergo, you have much to teach me and little time to do it. Are we to pass minutes arguing or are we to save our brother?"

Thomas turned to Shakespeare. "Know you the workings of a cutter?"

"A bit," said Shakespeare. "Fore is to the front, aft is to the rear, and the topmast points straight up."

"Welladay," Dunstan muttered.

Shakespeare said, "Kidnap the captain of the ship you steal. Force him at knifepoint to your destination."

"The man talks with greased lips," said Dunstan. "As if words make action."

Shakespeare turned on him. "Stow the insults, *Sir* Dunstan. I've nothing to gain from this, and much to lose. If you want me along, so be it. I'll do it for Becca's sake. But keep thy knightly tongue knotted."

Before Dunstan could speak, Thomas said, "Calm, I pray everyone. Calm for *Miguel's* sake."

Dunstan glared at his younger brother but said nothing.

Thomas pulled out his dagger and flipped it in the air. He caught it by the handle and said, "We accept your help, Shakespeare. We accept it and need it." He cleared his throat. "There is a fine fishing boat docked not more than four miles from this point. It's called the *Good Bounty*—a medium-sized cutter. It could be sailed by three hard-working men, if someone could guide us."

"Who's the captain of the boat?" Shakespeare asked.

"A white-haired jack named Nathaniel Krabbey," Thomas

said. "An old wight of forty. Obese, fond of eating, dicing, spirits, and women." He glanced at Rebecca and arched his eyebrows. "What impressed me about the vessel was its compactness—designed to race at high winds, yet sufficiently bottom heavy to withstand choppy waves. And a large hatch, when emptied of fish, that is perfectly suited for hiding stowaways."

Dunstan groaned. Thomas continued,

"No doubt the ship is guarded at night. But probably not by more than a half-dozen men."

"The numbers are still poor," Dunstan said. "A hue and a cry and we are done in."

"We have the element of surprise," Shakespeare said.

Dunstan cursed the player's boldness—his damn bravery. Thomas began to clean his nails with the point of his stylus.

"Does the captain keep watch over the ship at night?" Dunstan asked.

"No," Thomas said. "Too busy boozing at the local tavern."

Dunstan said, "So even if the three of us could overtake the watchmen and commandeer the ship, the captain still remains on land. How do we get him on the ship to guide us?"

Thomas's lips formed a sly smile. "As I said, Krabbey is fond of women. . . ."

Rebecca smiled back and nodded.

"No," said Shakespeare and Dunstan at the same time.

"Uncle will kill you," Dunstan said.

"If Uncle were to find out," Thomas retorted.

At the mention of her father, Rebecca became grave. Her cheeks flushed with purpose of mission, her eyes glittering like polished silver. She said, "Get me the clothing of a punk. Then leave the captain to me." She tossed off her cap, unpinned her hair, and shook out folds of jet-black velvet.

Thomas said to Dunstan, "Pick up your eyes, brother. They've fallen out of their sockets."

Dunstan closed his mouth and swallowed. He stammered out, "Where are we to find such clothing?"

Shakespeare was amazed how devious his mind had become, at how easy it was to sink morally. But now was not the time to ponder ethics. A life hinged on their cleverness. He said, "Get me a crome and a hook. I'll angle in some duds as they dry on the bushes."

Dunstan said, "And how is it that our player has learned how to hook clothing?"

Shakespeare said, "I've known some knavish men in my life."

A sly bitch in heat, thought Krabbey. As angelic as the heavens yet as real as earth.

He looped his hands around his overhang of belly and pushed it upward, hoping that the fat would magically transform itself to chest muscles. When that failed to occur, he dropped his stomach and let it jiggle loose around his middle.

Yet the bitch still stared at him, licked her lips and smiled.

Her attention amazed him. He was not a youthful man anymore. His hair had turned white, his skin, once so firm, had become as slack as a beached whale's. Now it seemed only hags looked at him with lust. But this one was not only young but incredibly beautiful. That face, those eyes, those large mounds of teat spilling out of her bodice. He could almost see her nipples—aye, he could make out a dash of pink.

He felt a stiffening below and was embarrassed by it. He, a red-blooded English captain of the seas who had fucked more wenches than he could count, should act like a virgin schoolboy.

Maybe it was her dress. She wore his favorite color—red, bright red like blood, with sleeves of black. A meal for the gods, a feast for him. He could imagine her honey pot—moist, warm and sweet, sweet, sweet.

She kept smiling at him, God be praised. He didn't know why and didn't care. The sting was attacking him furiously and he felt himself about to explode in his breeches. God in heaven, what noble deed had he done in his life to find *her*.

A pissant cuss—a mariner half his age—approached the wench. She shook her head and waved him away, but the churl was persistent. He placed a coin upon the tabletop. She pushed it aside and went back to her beer. The drooling jack added another two pence to the pile. She shook her head no.

Krabbey cleared his throat, approached her table. "Away with you, lad," he said to the young sailor.

The girl added, "I've found my escort for the evening, dog. Be gone."

The sailor picked up his coins. "Piss off, punk," he said as he left.

"Piss off yourself," answered the girl.

"Go fuck a horse," the young man muttered.

She laughed. Gods, her voice was lovely.

"Whatcha be drinking, girl?" asked Krabbey.

"What does it look like, man," she answered.

Krabbey swallowed hard, holding himself back. "Can I buy ye another tankard of beer?" he asked.

"No."

"A bit of grub, mayhap?"

"No."

"What then?" Krabbey said, trying to refrain himself from ripping her clothes to shreds.

"How much you got in your bung?" the girl answered.

Krabbey reached into his purse and pulled up a shilling held between shaking fingers. The girl took it, bit it, and slipped it in between those luscious pillows.

"You a captain?" she asked.

Krabbey nodded.

"You got a boat?"

Again he nodded, faster than the first time.

"Let's do it on the boat. I like the waves. Gives me rhythm."

Krabbey bolted upward, knocking over his chair. He squeezed her hand, perhaps a bit too tight. She seemed to wince. He pulled her up, hearing hoots and hollers as he dragged her out the door.

"Faster, wench," he said, yanking her along. "Afore I spend in my breeches."

As Krabbey led the slattern toward his boat, he congratulated himself. How well he played the gentleman, masking the animal urge by not pushing her behind a bush and fucking her right there.

Rebecca thought he'd dislodge her arm from its socket. Dear God, he was revolting! But at least the fresh, cold air brought a tingle to her cheeks. The tavern had been a muckheap stinking of urine, vomit, and the newest vice—foul-smelling tobacco smoke.

Gods, her dress was tight—the only thing Shakespeare had been able to filch was clothing much too small. The seams were ripping under the captain's tugs. Then the uncouth lout had stepped on her foot. As if the ill-fitting shoes weren't doing enough damage. Her feet were cramped and sore.

Finally they reached dock, the deck of *Good Bounty* swaying with the tempo of the tides. He jumped aboard, extended his hand to help her. Strange, Krabbey thought, no member of the watch was on deck.

And then he felt something hard upon his head. He was confused, looked upward thinking something must have fallen on him, the wind must have blown forth—

Then nothingness.

"You pisshead!" Krabbey shouted once the gag was removed. "You rotting piece of turd! I'll see you in the stocks for this—your ballocks cut off and shoved down your throat! Your head on the bridge! Where are my men? The devil with you whoever the hell are you!"

The man didn't answer, only walked away and closed the door to the hatch, leaving Krabbey in darkness. But the captain knew where he was—companion hole, aft side of his cutter. A rope was at his feet, the nets behind him. He knew every single inch of his ship. The hatch reeked from his recent herring catch—a good one that was. The air about him was cold and damp, and his nearly frozen hands and feet seared with pain as he tried to loosen the binds around them. But it was to no avail. Whoever tied him up had done a good job.

Then the bitch appeared. Krabbey was about to spit in her face until she gently kissed his forehead.

Krabbey felt a stirring below. It rose from the dead as if powered by a force of its own.

"I'm placing a towel soaked in cool water upon your head," she said. "Twill soothe the wound."

"Who are you?"

"Not a stew," the girl answered.

Krabbey looked down at his breeches. "But Master Will awaits your attention," he said.

Rebecca regarded his erect penis. She smiled and loosened the binds around his wrist.

"Better?" she asked.

Krabbey said, "G'wan, girlie. Touch it. It won't bite."

"You perform a noble deed, good captain. God shall reward you for this."

"How 'bout you providing a noble reward?"

"A slice of salted beef?" the bitch asked. "I'll feed it to you."

He didn't want to eat. He wanted to spit in her face, kill her, *fuck* her. *God's sointes, what a beautiful wench.*

"Eat," she ordered him.

Krabbey bit off a corner of the meat and swallowed it whole. She also brought a gourd of ale to his lips. Krabbey took a gulp and asked,

"Where are you taking me and my boat, whore? And what the devil happened to my crew?"

"Drink more, Captain," the girl insisted.

Krabbey complied, unable to resist the lilt in the girl's throat.

In walked the man who had removed the gag. He said, "I see our captain is being well fed."

"Yes," said the girl. She and the man locked eyes. He nodded imperceptively and she left the hatch.

"You piece of dog shit! Where is my crew!" screamed Krabbey.

"Calm, man."

Krabbey spit at him.

"Your breath is foul," said the man.

Krabbey spit again.

This time the man ignored the insult. He said, "Lo be me to

tell you most distressing news, but your faithful crew has deserted the ship as if it were sinking. Which, thanks be to God, it is not.''

Krabbey was puzzled.

The man said, ''I paid them off. Gave them lots of silver and told them to revel with cards and dice while I kept their watch over the ship. The only condition—no questions asked. Twas a proposition they evidently found hard to resist.''

''Mealy bastards,'' Krabbey groaned. He looked at the man, his eyes as blue as the white shark's and equally as cold. ''What the fuck do you want of me?'' he asked.

The blue eyes broke into a smile. ''Your expertise, sir.''

The man explained his purpose. Krabbey knew it had to be a trick. Still, he remained curious.

''And I will be compensated?'' he asked suspiciously.

''Generously,'' answered the man. ''If the mission is successful. If not, we'll all be dead. Then the money will matter not, will it?''

Krabbey frowned. ''And what if you cause damage to my *Bounty*?''

''*Generously* compensated, my good man.''

Krabbey liked the emphasis on the word generously. He asked, ''The girl as part of my compensation?''

''No.''

''The whore is your wife?''

''She's no whore.''

''But she is your wife?''

Shakespeare didn't answer. The less said the better.

Krabbey grinned columns of cracked, brown teeth. ''Ifin she was mine, I'd care not who she'd fucked. Just as long as I was included in her long list of cocks.''

Shakespeare remained silent, impassive.

Krabbey snarled, spat on the floor. ''Why didn't you just ask me to let you my ship?''

''Would you have let it to me?''

The captain broke into peals of laughter. ''Not a chance, you son of a bitch.''

Shakespeare shrugged.

Krabbey asked, ''How am I to helm my vessel if you keep me locked up in this pisshole stinking of fish?''

''It's your boat, Captain. You breathe its vapors daily.''

''I can't man the boat from the hatch,'' Krabbey said.

''I'll bring you on deck.''

''And am I to man the ship with my hands behind my back, you prig?'' asked Krabbey.

''Rewards do have their price, sir.'' The blue eyes twinkled.

"*Big* rewards."

"*Very* big," Shakespeare assured him. "Know that your instructions will be followed to the letter."

Shakespeare told him what he wanted. Krabbey swore him to the Devil, then told him what to do.

Dunstan yanked on the halyards, hoisting up the starsail. His back felt a pull of tension, a sharp stab of pain with each draw of the rope. Though cold black gusts of wind had seeped into his bones, he sweated profusely and gasped for breath. A shot of foam sprayed his clothes, dusting his clothes and face with salty mist. He coughed. Lungs of a gallant, he thought, ill-suited for common labor.

A moment later the tautness in his arms was partially relieved by another set of limbs helping him with the riggings. Dunstan turned to Shakespeare and asked,

"And how is our mighty helmsman of the sea?"

"What?" asked Shakespeare.

"The captain," Dunstan shouted over turbulent waves. "How does he fare?" He drew the lines aft, the rope cutting into his palms.

"Quiet finally, the foul-mouthed churl," Shakespeare yelled back. "Though I suppose he has good reason for his spleenish mood. Watch, if you can, how quickly dissipates his bile once the sparkle of gold hits his eye."

"Gold has medicinal powers," Dunstan shouted.

"I've got a bit of good news," Shakespeare said.

"What is it?"

"Inside the hatch lie other things besides fish."

"Go on," Dunstan said.

"Six pistols and three calivers," said Shakespeare.

Dunstan broke into a grin.

"Your brother was most displeased by the discovery," said Shakespeare. "He claimed that true men fight with swords not firearms."

Dunstan smirked and said, "Tommy is entitled to his weapon of defense. I'm entitled to mine."

The boat suddenly lurched portside as white-tipped waves splashed water onto the deck. Shakespeare lunged for the shroud to the masthead and pulled it tightly, keeping the boat upright. The staysail boom swung outward. Dunstan grabbed it, was dragged forward and tripped over his boots. Clumsy was his footwork, but at least he prevented the boom from knocking over the player. Shakespeare offered him a hand, hoisted him upward.

"Many thanks," Dunstan said. The last wave had thoroughly

soaked the soles of his boots. His feet felt like ice. "What's Krabbey doing with firearms?"

"Perhaps he's selling them to the highest bidder," said Shakespeare.

"A smuggler?" asked Dunstan.

"Or a pirate," Shakespeare said. "The man is less than honest, and fishermen are notorious for hauling in booty that doesn't swim."

"What do you know about pistols?" Dunstan asked.

"Not much," Shakespeare said. "You?"

Dunstan shook his head.

Shakespeare said, "The hand-held firearms are noted for being unreliable. They'll just as soon fire backward as forward."

"Ah, but if they do what they're smithed to do . . ."

Shakespeare completed the sentence. "If they work, your enemy is dead." Spray stung his eyes as the boat bounced upon the waves—a small star in a restless black sky. Shakespeare tightened the rigging and stabilized the boom. He said, "The biggest obstacle is how to dry out the gunpowder."

"All of it is wet?" Dunstan asked.

"Every bit."

"Mayhap Becca can blow on it. She's full of hot air."

Shakespeare said nothing. Dunstan felt himself go red with shame.

"Where is Becca?" Dunstan asked softly.

"What?"

"Where's Becca?" he repeated, shouting as loud as he could.

"Singing Krabbey to sleep," Shakespeare said. "I placed the blindfold back upon the old fart's eyes. The moon has risen, highlighting our faces. I didn't want him seeing yours or your brother's. The less men he can identify, the better."

The wind blasted the bellows of their shirtsleeves, cracking them like whips. Shakespeare tented his eyes with extended fingers upon his brow.

Dunstan said, "How far are we from the galleon?"

"Don't know," Shakespeare said. "But Krabbey thinks the cutter is making good time."

"The winds are strong and skittish." Dunstan held the lines with one hand, his stomach with the other. "So are the waves."

"All the better," Shakespeare yelled. "Calm air is the archenemy of the mainsail. Krabbey told me to pull the riggings aft. It will keep the jib upright."

Dunstan tugged on the lines. How his muscles ached.

"You have need of anything else?" Shakespeare asked. "Dry hose, perhaps?"

Though Dunstan's were soaked, he answered, "Mine are dry enough."

Shakespeare asked, "Where is your brother?"

"Opposite side." Dunstan's voice was hoarse from screaming, raw from the blow of cold wind. "At the stern, near the companionway, manning the boom gallows."

"I'll see if I can be of service to him. There shall we continue our discussion of the merits and detriments of pistols."

Dunstan smiled, then grew serious. "How fares Becca?" he asked. "Does she talk with you much?"

"She's stingy with her words, altogether miserly with her thoughts." Shakespeare hesitated, then said, "I fear she is as unstable as the water upon which we sail. May God keep her strong."

"And safe and warm."

"Amen," answered Shakespeare.

The men bowed their heads piously, then eyed each other. The two of them, alone, battling the vagaries of the enemy Neptune, each one dependent on the other for survival. An alliance at last? Slowly, they smiled at one another.

Self-righteous bastard, thought Dunstan.

Machiavellian prick, thought Shakespeare.

36

R ebecca's eyes opened suddenly. She was awakened not by sound nor touch nor bad dreams, but by an intangible aura that told her something of significance was about to occur.

She'd been resting at the rear of the ship, her back against a pile of nets, a bag full of clothes resting in her lap. Her face felt numb, her fingers stiff. Since she was alone, she slipped out of her punk costume and dressed in mariner's garb. Though chilled, the clothes were roomy and *dry,* thanks be to God. She double-gloved her hands, wrapped a cloak and two blankets around her shoulders, and attempted to stand. It was a balancing act accomplished in pitch black. Every time she tried to upright herself, the boat would rock and she'd fall down—a terrible feeling to be unable to walk. She crawled about on hands and knees, her fingers scratching at the wet deck like a cat without claws, her eyes incapable of penetrating the shroud of icy darkness. Needing help, Rebecca almost called out for Shakespeare. Then she remembered: no *real* names, nothing that could link them with the pirating of the boat. She shouted out "Arden," Shakespeare's mother's maiden name, and waited for him to respond. After a minute which seemed like an hour, she heard approaching footsteps.

"Annie!" answered a voice. It was Dunstan's.

"Aye," said Rebecca, on her knees. "I need help standing afoot."

"I'm coming."

"Where's Arden?" she yelled, trying to be heard over the tide.

"Wait a moment," Dunstan said.

A few feet beyond her eyes Rebecca could make out Dunstan's figure, his profile and extended hand. She reached out and he pulled her upward. The boat reeled portside and she careened into Dunstan's chest. He embraced her tightly.

Dunstan said, "Gods, you're warm and dry."

"And you're *wet*," Rebecca said, squirming in his grip.

Dunstan released her. "Sorry," he said.

She could see her cousin clearly now. His teeth were chattering. Salty spray had frozen to slivers of ice that coated his mustache. Rebecca held his face, brought his cheek to her mouth and kissed him softly. For a moment her warm lips stuck to his skin.

"Take a blanket, Dunstan," Rebecca said. "I have two."

Dunstan shook his head. "The blanket is *dry*. Save it for necessity."

"Did you bring a change of clothes amongst your provisions?"

Dunstan nodded. "Several sets."

"You must get out of these—"

Dunstan brought his fingers to her lips. "Worry not about me. Just keep yourself warm, eh?"

"Where's Shakespeare?"

"Watching Krabbey steer the ship." His voice had become harsh. Rebecca ignored his tone.

"Anything new?"

"Krabbey claimed he *smells* something."

"What means that?" asked Rebecca.

"I don't know. I don't speak to the man directly," Dunstan said. "Tommy and I are hidden from the churl's eyes. Shakespeare says that Krabbey insists he *smells* something in the air— the Spanish ship."

Rebecca nodded in agreement. "I *smell* it as well. The stink of the Spanish jolted me awake."

Dunstan said, "All I smell is rotting fish."

The boat swayed upward and the sea threw handfuls of water onto their clothing.

"I must get back to my position afore this whole craft is capsized," Dunstan said. "I'll help you walk to Shakespeare if that's what you desire."

Rebecca was seized with sudden fright, instantly aware of the peril that faced them—a gnawing, raw horror that Miguel had braved and overcome for the sake of their trapped brethren. What was Miguel feeling now? Was he as frightened as she? Was he even alive? And Raphael. What thoughts had filled his head as death bore down upon him? With effort she emptied her mind of horrible images and regarded her trembling cousin. He had not the skill of the fence as Thomas did, nor the bravery of Shakespeare. He was just a man—a man with faults, aye—but nonetheless he knew the animal of fear as she did and was ready to fight it. She hugged Dunstan with an intensity he'd never felt before. He returned her embrace, knowing the reason behind it.

"Don't worry, Becca," he said softly. "My life has been good."

"Watch well your moves, Dunstan," she said.

Dunstan pulled a gleaming firearm out from his cloak. "I shall."

"Where did you find the pistol?" Rebecca asked, dropping her arms to her sides.

"Krabbey had a half dozen lying around the hatch. Better booty than fish, eh? It would be a sin to let them go to waste."

"You know nothing of firearms, Dunstan. You've never battled in war."

"I'll 'prentice on the job," he answered tightly. "I need a service from you."

"Speak."

"The gunpowder is wet. All three of us have been too occupied to find a way to dry it out—"

"I'll take care of it. Where are the boxes?"

"Shakespeare's hidden them somewhere," Dunstan said.

"Then take me to him, to Krabbey as well."

"Aye," answered Dunstan. "Let's go smell a galleon."

"Who is this pissant cuss?" Krabbey said when he saw Rebecca dressed as a man. The captain broke into laughter. "A lad to make merry with when the wench is too busy fucking others?"

Shakespeare said nothing.

"I could use a little making merry," said Krabbey, straining the leather straps that bound his wrists and ankles. "If I can't have the whore, how about the lad?"

Shakespeare said, "Leave your prick in peace and concentrate on finding the galleon."

Rebecca was propelled forward by a sudden wave and tumbled to her knees. Shakespeare helped her up and she grabbed the masthead for support. Bringing her mouth to Shakespeare's ear, she asked him about the gunpowder. He whispered back its location.

"Are you able to walk there without help?" he asked.

"I'll help the lad," said Krabbey. "All he has to do is bend over and I'll help him but good." The captain let out an evil laugh. " 'Course when I'm done helping him, he won't be able to walk too good."

Shakespeare said, "Your tongue holds more muck than the jakes of Paris."

"Piss off," Krabbey said. He made kissing noises to Rebecca. "Come here, lad, and I'll show you what it's like to be a boy on the high seas."

Rebecca ignored him. Her eyes turned to the sea as the captain continued swearing. Then she saw it and gasped.

The galleon grew out of the shimmering fog and displaced the sea—the most awesome craft she'd ever witnessed. A thousand tons of ship with a mast that reached the moon. It held three open decks, two tiers of guns on the lower decks and a third tier on her half deck and forecastle. There must have been two or three decks below as well. Muzzles peeked out from every porthole and above the ramparts like pins in a cushion. Sheet upon sheet of billowy sail blocked out the sky. Scores of oars pushed away the sea, moving the hulk forward. It was impossible to make out each crew member, but there had to be hundreds of men aboard.

"Holy Mother of God!" Krabbey cried, open-mouthed.

Shakespeare felt a sudden sharp pain in his lungs. His knees began to shake. He turned to Krabbey and said, "You did your toil well, Captain. May God grant us the strength to do our job with equal skill."

Quickly, Shakespeare slipped the blindfold over Krabbey's eyes. He said to Rebecca, "Get your cousins. I need help in bringing this corpulent body to the hatch."

Rebecca did as told then sat under the mainsail of the ship to dry the gunpowder. She threw a tarp over her head and prayed it would prevent dampness from seeping in and frustrating her efforts. The tinder was mercifully dry, the spark of the flint rock strong. It was skillful business. The warmth of the flame was needed to dry the powder, but too much heat would cause an explosion. Still, it was her duty to perform her task well, and she knew she would succeed.

All three men were needed to lift Krabbey into the hatch. The captain kicked, spat, and let out inarticulate curses muffled by the gag in his mouth. With Krabbey safely locked away, the men immediately put their plan into action. The English flag was lowered, the Spanish flag raised upon the *Good Bounty* masthead. Dunstan tore open their bags and handed out the clothes of the Spanish seafarers. Quickly, they began to dress.

Dunstan said to Shakespeare, "Remember! You're not to utter a sound, having had your vocal cords severed in battle."

Shakespeare nodded and showed Dunstan the scar about his neck—a self-inflicted scratch. He hoped it looked convincing.

Thomas pulled up knee-high breeches and said, "Well done, Shakespeare. I like how you did all those little nicks. As if you were sliced by a careless hand."

"I was," Shakespeare said. "My own. I'm not very steady without a looking glass."

Dunstan said, "Looks all the more genuine that way."

Shakespeare wrapped his neck in a dirty scarf. He said, "You're certain you're familiar with the Spanish language—"

"Fluent," Dunstan said.

"Fluent enough to fool a native?" asked Shakespeare.

"Spanish and Portuguese are our native tongues," Thomas said. "The languages are the least of our troubles."

Dunstan threw on a jerkin. He was the first one completely dressed. He said, "Very quickly, let me summarize our plan. The names—I am Domingo, Thomas is Tomas, and Shakespeare is Guillermo. Best it is to keep them as close to our real forenames as possible. We are three brothers, Spanish mariners who—thanks be to the Almighty—escaped from the fierce hands of the English devils. We battled bravely, but alas, our carrack was split and sunk by enemy fire. All we were able to keep from our boat was the Spanish flag." He rubbed his gloved hands together rapidly. "What next? What next?"

"Calm," Thomas said, checking his rapier. He slid it back into its hilt.

Dunstan continued their story: "We were incarcerated by the English Drake—*el Draque*—but blessed Jesu showed us mercy and we escaped from the foul Isle in a fishing boat."

Thomas said, "You speak to the enemy first, Dunstan. You're the oldest and look the part."

Dunstan frowned but held his tongue. No sense in vanity at a time as this. He muttered, "Where is Becca with the dry powder?"

Thomas sneered, "You're not really going to use . . . guns, are you?"

"Aye," Dunstan said. "We need as much protection as God and man can give us. Regard the size of that vessel, brother. . . . Dear God . . ."

Dunstan began praying in a language Shakespeare didn't recognize. Then he remembered. They were Jews, they spoke to their God in Hebrew. Shakespeare began to say a few prayers of his own. Five minutes later he pulled a pistol from his breeches, offered it to Thomas and said,

"Take the pistol, Thomas. Dunstan is right. You cannot be overarmed."

Thomas stared at the thick slab of metal, the arced barrel. He shook his head. "Twill weigh down my breeches."

"Take it," Dunstan ordered. "As your older brother I am responsible for your welfare—"

Thomas waved him off and took the pistol. "Anything is better than hearing your lectures."

"There's Becca," Shakespeare said. He staggered over to her, grabbed her hand and walked her to the others.

Rebecca said, "I could only dry a small amount of powder on such short notice."

"Whatever you have is more than we had before," Shakespeare said.

The boat lurched forward.

"God's blood!" she swore. "Doesn't the sea ever tire of kicking its heels?"

"The winds are not nearly as strong as they were an hour ago," Thomas remarked. "I can speak without shouting."

"Give me what you have, Becca," ordered Dunstan. "We must get to our station or the boat will sink." He looked ahead at the approaching galleon. "Marry, what was an armed ship— flying the Spanish flag—doing in England's port?"

Thomas said, "It flew the Italian flag while docked in Dover. Or so they told me."

Dunstan said, "Well, now she flies the Spanish flag—the two-faced fiends!" He turned to Rebecca. "The powder, mistress."

Rebecca handed them each a small packet. "I've oiled the leather. It should prevent moisture from seeping inside the pouch."

"We're best off loading the guns now," Dunstan said.

"And risk shooting off my ballocks?" Thomas said. "Go ahead, brother. I'll wait."

Dunstan thought a moment, then stowed the powder in his jerkin. "I'll wait as well. No sense being intemperate."

Shakespeare filled a pistol with gunpowder and gave it, as well as a dagger, to Rebecca. He said, "Watch well the captain. And don't believe a word the cur tells you. Whatever you do, do not free him unless we tarry so long you have no other option."

"You'll need the pistol more than I," Rebecca said.

"I have one in my breeches, Becca," Shakespeare said. He clasped her hands with his. "A kiss for luck, wench."

Rebecca threw her arms around Shakespeare and kissed him passionately. Dunstan turned his head aside. Strange it was to feel monstrously jealous at this moment, but he couldn't help himself. Rebecca broke away from Shakespeare's lips, quickly kissed her cousins on the cheek. She stared at the men for a moment, standing at the tip of the boat, their tattered clothing flapping in the wind. Shakespeare waved his hand in the air.

"Go before they see you," he shouted to Rebecca.

She nodded, crawled inside the hatch with Krabbey and shut the door. She could smell his foul breath, yet the presence of another was somehow comforting. She rested against the slimy walls and closed her eyes in prayer. She heard Thomas yell for the men to take their positions.

"Cut to the starboard side, next to the forecastle," Thomas ordered as he pulled the riggings portside. The boat began to sail toward the galleon—a flea attacking the bear. The *Bounty* rocked and swayed, but swiftly floated to its desired position. A few minutes later, shouting could be heard from the massive ship. Faces began to form—hundreds of them, staring over the ramparts.

"Help me drop anchor," Thomas commanded his brother in Spanish. A minute later the boat lurched forward, strained against the pull of the waves.

A voice from the galleon yelled, *"Amico o nemico?"* Friend or enemy?

Dunstan approached the side of the boat. His throat was dry, his hands shook. Never had he felt such fear, but never had he such an opportunity to overcome it.

"Amico o nemico?" the voice asked again.

Still trembling, Dunstan wondered if he should continue the conversation in Italian or switch to Spanish?

The voice screamed a third time. *"Amico o nemico? Rispondi ad alta voce o rischi di perdere la testa!"*

"Come on, Dunstan," Thomas whispered to himself. He and Shakespeare were crouching behind the boom, hidden by the mainsail. "For once, darken your damn liver."

Finally Dunstan stammered out, *"Hablo Español."*

"Che?"

"Hablo Español," Dunstan screamed at last. Relief it was to

find his vocal cords! He crossed himself and screamed out praises in Spanish to the Almighty for redemption.

There was a conference on the ship. Dunstan waited, his heart beating swiftly and strongly, filling his body with its frantic rhythm.

A voice yelled from the galleon, *"Amigo o enemigo?"*

Dunstan shouted back, *"Nosotros elevamos la bandera del Rey, de La Majestad!"*

"Quien es usted?" demanded the voice.

Dunstan shouted, *"El marinero de la flota de La Majestad, atacan a los malignos Ingleses de mal corazon—el Draque. Nosotros manejamos el bote robado y escapamos. Pero antes no turimos en nuestras manos la bandera Espanola."*

"Como se llamo el buque?"

"Que?" asked Dunstan, not hearing the question.

"El nombre del buque en el cual navegaron?" asked the voice.

The name of the Spanish boat upon which they had sailed? Invent one, dolt. Just keep talking.

"La Santa Catalina."

"Y como es el nombre del bote Ingles?"

Dunstan's thoughts raced. The English boat that grappled and boarded them . . . He said, "The *High Adventure*."

Shakespeare noted that Dunstan spoke the English name in a perfect Spanish accent. A good player he was.

The voice asked Dunstan, *"Como se llama? Como se llaman vuestra tripulacion?"*

"Rodriguez," Dunstan answered back. *"Somos tres hermanos. Me llamo Domingo. . . ."* He wildly waved the others to come to him. *"Aqui estan mis hermanos. Se llaman Tomas y Guillermo."* The trio of "brothers" stood side by side, looking upward to the ship. They could hear rumblings above. The minutes moved slowly. Finally Dunstan whispered,

"What do you think?"

"As fine a performance as I've ever seen," Shakespeare said. "How did you come by the name Rodriguez?"

"'Tis my grandam's maiden name," Dunstan said. "A salty wench she once was, full of spit and fire, as Becca is now. The old woman's head has gone foggy of late."

There was no response from the galleon. By now they could make out the men—bearded faces swathed in chewed-up clothing. Arms moving like thousands of wriggling worms. The blinding flash of metal hilts. A drone of deep voices spitting out curses.

"A God's sointes," Thomas muttered, staring at the warship in front of them, "what are they talking about?"

"What if they board the *Bounty*?" asked Dunstan.

Shakespeare said, "It would be difficult to send men down here. We're so much lower than their ship. I think they'll tow the *Bounty*—like a spare pinnace—and ransack her when they disembark."

More men appeared. God Almighty, how many hundreds were there? Or rather, thousands?

"Look," Shakespeare said. "Up to the right."

The men raised their heads. A rope had been thrown over the rampart and tumbled down to the deck. There it stood, suspended from the galleon, a sinewy brown piece of hemp cord as lethal as the bite of an asp. Thomas took the rope and tied it to the masthead of the *Bounty*. A second rope followed a moment later.

"I'll go up first," Dunstan said. "They already know my voice. Wait a moment before you come up, Tommy. I'll speak with them casually. If I ascertain that they mean to give us aid and comfort, I'll do nothing. If I see they desire us harm, I'll wave you off." Dunstan secured the cord to his stomach and pulled the knot tightly. "Wish me good fortune and much hap, Tommy."

The brothers embraced.

37

It had been twenty hours since Shakespeare had uttered a sound. He understood some Italian but very little Spanish, and since the Ames brothers spoke only Spanish, he was not only the mute brother, but the dumb one as well. But he had to give the brothers credit. Whatever they said must have been thoroughly convincing. They'd been taken in and treated well, having been fed typical sea fare—mealy biscuits and rancid salt beef—and allowed to sleep unguarded and unmolested.

He lay in an empty hatch as black as tar, feeling the gentle motion of the sea. What had been choppy waves in a fishing boat were nothing more than ripples kissing the keel of the galleon. The hole was a decent size, enough room for him to lie down as long as he bent his legs. The space had once stored spirits, and the wet, wooden walls smelled like a distillery. Tiny droplets of broken bottle glass sprinkled the floor.

God in heaven, what was he doing here? Miles away from his family, away from his work and London—with these *Jews*. But he was with Rebecca as well. Poor girl—holed up with that vile Krabbey, hiding in the hatch of the *Bounty*. The boat was being towed by the galleon, and he hoped that the waves weren't too hard on her stomach.

Dear Becca. His Jewess, an enchanting Levantine beauty, forbidden to him as a Christian. To his absolute surprise, that now excited him rather than repelled him. But it wasn't the only reason he'd come along. Something about what these Jews were doing felt righteous. Though Shakespeare would never understand the mulish will of the unbaptized, neither could he fathom the cruelty of the Inquisition.

Shakespeare heard footsteps and feigned sleep. A moment later the trapdoor to the hole was opened and a body dropped down, then the door was closed. Shakespeare felt a strong tap on his shoulder.

"What cheer have you?" a voice whispered.

Dunstan's voice, Shakespeare thought, the words English. Still, it could be someone masking as the Ames brother. Shakespeare didn't answer, pretended to snore.

"Rouse, Shakespeare," Dunstan said, shaking him slightly. He lit a piece of tinder wood that gave off a tiny flicker of light. "We've serious business to discuss."

Shakespeare rolled over and pointed to his throat.

"Tis me, Sir Dunstan," the brother said. "Would I converse with you in English, if we were in the company of the Spanish?"

Shakespeare regarded the silhouette, recognized the profile. He said, "One cannot be too sure who is the trickster and who is the dupe. What news have you?"

"We must execute our attack soon," Dunstan said. "We're a day away from Brussels."

"Have you found Miguel's location?" Shakespeare asked.

"We've skulked about the ship for four hours and have found nothing," Dunstan said. "The ship is immense. Three decks above, three below, hundreds of hatches and cabins and holes. Hundreds of seamen as well. No one took notice of us. And no one has leaked a word about the capture of an Englishman or the finding of stowaways. I don't think they know about Miguel."

"The captain of the ship must know," Shakespeare said.

"Yes."

"Then we must get him alone," Shakespeare said.

"Tommy's very thought."

"What time is it?"

"Two in the morning," Dunstan said.

Sunrise four hours away, Shakespeare thought. Without the cover of darkness, the work would be that much harder.

There was a long silence. Finally, Dunstan asked,

"Have you any ideas?"

"No."

Dunstan said, "Thomas thinks the only way to get to the captain is to overcome him by force."

Shakespeare said, "And if the struggle is heard?"

Dunstan drew his finger across his throat and made a rasping sound.

"Yet I see no other alternative," said Shakespeare. "Where's Thomas?"

"Guarding the entrance to the hatch as we speak."

"Have you two devised a plan?" Shakespeare asked.

"Rudiments," Dunstan said. "We're open to suggestion."

"Pray, let me hear you out."

Dunstan told him the scheme. An hour later Shakespeare and Dunstan knocked on the door to the hatch and Thomas dropped inside the hole. Another thirty minutes passed before they felt ready to begin.

"Yer pisshead mate ain't comin' back, lad," Krabbey said to Rebecca. "It's been over a day, and you haven't heard a fart from him. He's as good as dead, and so will we be if you stay like a horse's ass and do nothing but shit."

Rebecca said nothing. Dear Providence, it was cold in the hole. To be stuck with this foul-mouthed churl. But at least she was safe for the moment. Krabbey was tied up and the Spaniards hadn't detected their presence.

Krabbey said, "Yer as stupid as yer tight-arsed friend. All he'll be getting you is yer head in the stocks and yer ears burned off. What's he to you anyway?"

Rebecca remained silent.

"You ever had a wench, lad?" Krabbey asked. He arched his eyebrows and snickered. "Not some old cock like your mate diddling your thing, but a real wench, boy. With big teats and a honey pot dripping with love juices. A nice big home for yer throbbin' will, eh?"

She smiled.

"You like the sound of that one, eh?" Krabbey continued. "I can get a wench for you, laddy. I can get you a dozen wenches with whole teeth and big arses. The kind that are plump and white till you squeeze 'em. Then they turn all pink and pretty."

Rebecca didn't react.

"But I can't do nothin', laddy, unless you untie me hands and feet from this chair. . . . Otherwise, boy, me and you and me boat are gonna sink. Or worse, boy. We'll be in the hands of the Devil himself. The Spanish with their racks and stocks and water tortures. Me boy, that's pain!''

Rebecca lowered her head.

''We could escape, lad,'' Krabbey went on. ''We could cut the rope and sail back to mighty England. I could handle the *Bounty* all by meself. But I can't do nothin' if me hands and feet are tied to this blasted chair.''

Silence.

''What do you say, laddy? How 'bout it? You and me on the high seas.'' Krabbey paused and licked his lips, trying to spur his brain to fire. With renewed enthusiasm, he said, ''We'll be *partners*, boy. I'm the captain and you . . . you'll be the first mate. I do lots of other business, lad. 'Nough callin' you lad. Tell me whatcha call yerself, boy?''

Rebecca didn't answer.

Krabbey kept talking. ''I haul in lots of booty for certain rich gentlemen. I could teach you how to fight with a dagger. I could learn you how to shoot a caliver. Blow yer enemy to dust. Pow . . . heh, heh, heh.''

Krabbey looked at Rebecca and stopped laughing. He said, ''They be paying me well, those gentlemen. They'd be paying you goodly, too, if you was me *partner*.''

More silence.

''What do you say? You and me! Partners! Reelin' in the booty. Fuckin' all the pretty wenches till they're sore and beggin' us to stop. 'Course they love to beg. Don't you be fooled by that. Always get yer money's worth, that's what I always say. And beware of the poxed ones lest they be givin' yer will more than a goodly ride. What do you say, m'laddy?''

Rebecca walked over to the captain, stood over him. She picked up the rag that Shakespeare had used for a gag and stuffed it in Krabbey's mouth. Then she sat back down and tried to catnap.

They'd been crouching behind the rope deck for an hour. Dunstan forced himself steady, his knees ready to fold, yet Tommy and Shakespeare were as still as granite. How could they remain motionless without wincing in pain?

Dunstan shifted his weight, again, and Thomas shushed him, again.

They waited. Thomas's eye went to Captain Mundo at the helm of the ship. He was standing twenty feet away under a small roof of wood that protected him from the elements, drinking from a pot. Behind him were his first mate and navigator, both sipping from a gourd, discussing something, pointing to a map pinned at their left, the tidal roars drowning out any hope of hearing their words. Thomas brushed his hair out of his face and cursed the wind. It was blowing at full force again, the cold seeping under his clothes and skin, and it was a feat not to shiver. But he was determined not to expend any unnecessary energy. He glanced at the rapier resting against his leg, then looked back to Mundo—a dark devil with a black beard and olive skin. The enemy captain carried in his belt a falchion. Good for slicing off heads, but unwieldly and slow—easy to take him down. Mundo had a smashed nose and was missing three fingers. But he still had a prick and eventually he'd have to use it to piss.

Thomas's stiff fingers wrapped around the hilt of his dagger. A gift for you, you whoreson—for the death of Raphael, for the torture of all the others held prisoners by the Inquisition, for the death of all his fellow Englishmen fighting in wars, battles that Thomas was barred from joining because his help was needed in the trade company.

To the devil with the business, thought Thomas. This was how a man became a man, not by counting coins in a purse. He looked at Shakespeare, at his brother squirming on his knees. Gods, if he'd known Dunstan would make so much noise, he would have left him down in the boat with Becca. The player and he could save Miguel . . . he could save Miguel alone. All it took was confidence and skill of the fence. And Dunstan had neither.

Cursed am I, thought Thomas. Born without a proper beard, born after Dunstan, thereby being reduced to the status of the *younger* brother. He reflected upon his hap for another moment then asked for God's forgiveness. At least he had the good fortune to live to his majority. Not like the two brothers born between Dunstan and him. Isaac dead at seven from the plague—death so mighty, so swift, his skin never erupted into telltale buboes. Edward, dead at age ten, every inch of his body riddled with pox.

"Does the man have a barrel for a bladder?" Dunstan whispered.

Thomas bade him quiet.

"The Devil take you," Dunstan said, squirming.

Thomas whispered, "Be still, for God sakes."

Shakespeare shushed them both.

A minute passed.

"We've been gone too long from the hatch," Dunstan said. "What if they bring us food then discover us missing?"

"Then go back to the hatch, brother," Thomas whispered back. "That's obviously where you belong."

Shakespeare tapped them both on the shoulder and brought his finger to his lips. A few minutes later he whispered, ''Even if we were discovered missing, it would take them hours to search a ship this well-sized.''

''The scum comes,'' Thomas said.

Mundo gave the helm over to the first mate. The navigator remained deep in study of the map.

''Must have been the last pot that did him in.'' Dunstan smiled.

The captain stood atop the rampart and undid his breeches.

''Let him piss first,'' Dunstan said. ''If we scare him, he'll douse us.''

''Move quietly,'' Thomas whispered. ''We mustn't attract attention.''

Mundo finished urinating and reattached his codpiece. A split second later he was struggling in a pair of powerful arms. A hand was clamped over his mouth and nose, a dagger was at his throat.

''The Englishman,'' the voice said in rapid Spanish. ''Where is he? And whisper else it will be your last sound.''

Mundo continued to squirm, attempted to bite the meaty palm that was suffocating him.

''Where is the Englishman?'' the voice repeated. ''Do you know about the Englishman?''

Mundo nodded his head rapidly.

''Where is he?''

The palm was partially released. Mundo attempted to cry out, but the hand was slapped back over his mouth.

''You son of a bitch!'' the voice hissed.

The dagger plunged in and out of Mundo's shoulder. The pain seared through his body.

''Try again, señor,'' said the voice, calmly this time. ''Where is the Englishman?''

Again the hand yielded a little air. Mundo sucked in a mouthful and answered him truthfully.

''You believe him?'' said the voice in English.

Mundo felt himself go limp. The stranded mariners! Disguised Englishmen! *El Diablo Draque!* He croaked out, ''*Es la verdad!* Zee trute!''

''Zee trute, zee trute,'' mocked Dunstan.

Thomas eased the knife against Mundo's throat and looked at his brother and Shakespeare.

''What should we do with him?'' he asked.

''Tarry not in your decision,'' Dunstan said, firming up his grip on the captain's arm. ''He's a strong one.''

''Ask him if the Englishman is dead,'' said Shakespeare.

Thomas asked, *"Esta muerto el Ingles?"*

"No! Yo juro que no! Juro que el Ingles vive!"

"He swears the Englishman lives," Dunstan said to Shakespeare.

"Como se llama el Ingles?" asked Thomas.

"No se," said Mundo. *"El Ingles no me dice nada!"*

"What next, men?" asked Dunstan.

"Es la verdad?" Thomas asked Mundo again.

"Si, es la verdad!"

"We'd better do something quickly," Shakespeare said. "No piss takes this long."

"Aye," Thomas said. In one fluid motion he slit Mundo's throat. Blood poured over Thomas's hand and arm and over the captain's body. Mundo tried to gurgle out words but provided only bloody bubbles. The captain slumped into Thomas's arms.

Thomas took the sword from the dead man's belt and fastened it to his own hilt. He said, "Help me lift him and don't let the feet drag. We'll throw him overboard twenty feet down, where there's a lot of noise from the turbulence."

Shakespeare took Mundo's feet, but Dunstan froze where he stood.

Thomas slapped him soundly across the face. "Get hold of your wits, man."

Dunstan didn't react.

"Go," Shakespeare urged Thomas. He held the captain's feet with on hand and dragged Dunstan along with the other.

Well hidden from public view, Thomas quickly spotted a piece of iron scrap metal and tied it to Mundo's feet with loose twine. A minute later the body fell unnoticed to its watery gravesite.

"This way," Thomas said, leading the others. Dunstan lagged behind.

Shakespeare whispered to Thomas, "What are we going to do with your brother? He's worse than a woman."

Dunstan overheard the barb. "I'm well," he said shakily. "In sooth, I'm well. Leave us to go. I'm well now."

They quickly descended to the bottom deck. It was dark and dank, reeking with the sour odors of illness, mold, and sweat. They stood at the entrance to the central passageway. Feeding off the hallway—like a river with its tributaries—were the doors to the cabins and hatches. The passageway was barely illuminated by the small flames from rush candles and filled with noise. Sounds echoed against the wooden walls—an unsettling mixture of drunken shouts, slamming doors, raucous laughter, and unhealthy groans in Italian, Portuguese, and Spanish. Whittled mariners staggered about, going in one cabin, out the other.

"Where's Miguel?" Shakespeare whispered.

"Mundo said he was hidden in the bottom deck, third or fourth hole to the left of the first mate's cabin," Thomas answered back. "The whoreson captain was mumbling."

"Where's the first mate's cabin?" Dunstan asked.

"Damned if I know," Thomas said. "I think Mundo said it had a blue door and some sort of red insignia—"

"You killed him too soon," Dunstan said. "You should have waited—"

"Stow it," Thomas barked. "Get a liver, man."

"Let's try this way." Shakespeare pointed.

"Someone's coming," Dunstan said. "Act casual."

They strolled down the passageway, the brothers speaking lower-class Spanish, and the sailors passed the Englishmen without a second glance. They blended in as smoothly as a blackbird in pitch. As soon as the mariners were gone, Dunstan felt his knees buckle under his weight. Maybe it was the stench, the fear, the leaden air pressing down on his lungs. He became light-headed and had to stop a moment. Thomas offered him a hand, but Dunstan slapped it away.

"I'm well," Dunstan said. "Truly, I'm well. Go."

They began to check hatches, constantly glancing behind their backs to see if anyone was looking. Sometimes a mariner would smile at them, engage them in drunken conversation. Shakespeare was surprised at how easily Thomas played the role of the seaman. The beardless boy would have been an excellent player. And he was fleet-footed as well, quickly moving from one hatch to another whenever he had a moment of privacy. He opened a hatch that held crates of wine, broke off the neck on one of the bottles.

"Make a bowl with your hands, brother," he said.

Dunstan brought his trembling palms together into a slight concavity. Thomas splashed the wine into his brother's hands, a wave of it spilling onto the wooden floor.

"Drink," Thomas ordered.

Dunstan complied.

Thomas poured him another handful. "Again."

Dunstan greedily lapped up the wine, snatched the bottle from Thomas's hands and poured the spirits directly into his mouth. He felt his strength returning and said, "Aye, such sweet succor."

"Not too much," Thomas said. He offered the bottle to Shakespeare, who drank the leftovers.

When they finished the bottle, Thomas broke open a second and poured it over his head, shaking out the wet strands of blond hair like a soaked puppy. Shakespeare and Dunstan doused themselves as well. It cooled them off for the moment, small relief from the stifling heat that clogged the bottom deck.

"We'd better go," Shakespeare said, drying his face with his shirtsleeve. "Before we forget for whom we came."

"Aye," said Dunstan. He was walking upright now.

They found another store laden with green-staved barrels full of maggoty meat. Another glance around, another smile for a boozed mariner, an invitation to drink was offered. Thomas declined gracefully. Alone at last, he checked another hatch. This one emitted a detectable stench ten feet away. Thomas held his nose and opened the door a crack. A funnel of black flies swirled from the hole. Thomas swatted them away.

"God, that *stinks*!" Dunstan said.

"Rotted flesh," said Shakespeare.

Thomas lit a piece of tinder and peered inside—gray oblong-shaped lumps of flesh dusted with rice-size maggots. "My God!" he moaned, backing away. He closed the door to the hole.

"Dear Almighty, the stowaways," Dunstan said weakly.

"Must have been," Thomas said.

Shakespeare asked, "Is Miguel among the dead?"

Thomas was about to look, but he suddenly espied a sailor walking toward them. He leaned back against the walls and loudly cursed Dunstan in drunken Spanish. Dunstan cursed back as Shakespeare pretended to bring up dry heaves. The mariner lolled past them without notice. A moment later he disappeared into a cabin. Alone once again, they all took deep breaths and held their noses.

Thomas opened the door and poked around with the tip of his sword. A minute later he slammed the door shut and said, "As far as I could ascertain, there were three—all men. None are Miguel."

"Thank God!" Dunstan said.

"Come." Shakespeare prodded them along. "Captain Mundo's absence is bound to be noticed soon."

"Ye gods, it's foul down here," Dunstan said.

They continued down the passageway, opening holes and hatches, hoping to get lucky. Shakespeare was walking quickly and suddenly tripped. A body lay in the middle of the dimly lit passageway, alive and besotted. He moaned out an obscenity, rolled over and fell back asleep.

Another hatch. The unsuccessful effort was followed by a string of curses. They continued on, passed a group of sailors speaking Italian.

"*Buona sera,*" one of them said.

Thomas returned the greeting. "This way," he whispered.

On to the next hatch, this one storing leaky bags of mealy biscuit flour. Pyramid-shaped piles had spilled onto the floor, bugs wriggling in and out of the white powder like fleas in a sand dune. The smell of sweat thickened, the stale air hot and humid. Shakespeare could feel perspiration dripping from his forehead. Ten minutes later he heard shouting above—frantic shouting.

"They're looking for Mundo," Shakespeare said.

"Move," Thomas said.

Two more hatches—nothing! Then Shakespeare saw a blue door! A red cross painted across the front panel—the first mate's cabin. Thomas counted until he reached the fourth hole to the left, then tried to open the trapdoor. He yanked it several times before he realized it was padlocked.

"Damn!" he swore. He took out his dagger and began stabbing the planks of rotted wood. A few splintered strips were pried loose, but the hatch door remained fixed and impenetrable. Sweat soaked his brow and cheeks.

The commotion above the deck intensified as the search for Mundo heightened. Thank God, the news hadn't hit the bottom deck yet, Thomas thought. So little time remained. He pulled out Mundo's falchion from his hilt and began to slice at the door.

"Wait!" Dunstan said. "Stop!" He pulled out the pistol from his breeches. "Didn't I tell you that this would be useful?"

"Stow the lectures, Dunstan," Shakespeare said. "Shoot off the lock."

"Pray God the noise attracts no undue attention," Thomas said.

Shakespeare said, "Shoot it!"

Dunstan quickly stuffed the powder into the powder pan, squinted and aimed. Dear God, let the priming explode forward and not in his hands. He squeezed the cock and the pistol spat fire. Immediately Dunstan dropped the gun. God, it was hot! He flapped his burning palms in the air. Thomas threw open the door.

The young man was stuffed inside, bound and gagged, but his eyes were uncovered and wide with relief. On his lap sat two children—a toddler girl and a boy not more than eight—the little ones bound but only loosely gagged. At their side lay a young woman. Her mouth was open, her hair matted, her legs bent and contorted. Dead.

Thomas pulled the children and Miguel out of the hatch. Miguel's clothes were torn, his beard and hair covered with lice and grease. Quickly, Thomas unknotted the binds, then drew Mundo's falchion from his belt and handed it to Miguel. The two men embraced.

"You're well?" Thomas asked. "Your arms are still strong."

"Aye," Miguel answered. "They've yet to torture me."

Dunstan took the little girl into his arms and cooed reassuring words in her ear.

"Let's go," said Shakespeare.

"We must take the body," Miguel said.

Dunstan said, "Impossible. We'll be fortunate if we escape whole."

"A quick prayer then," Miguel insisted. "It's their mother—"

"We can pray as we walk, *casually*," Thomas said. "Dunstan, hide the girl as best you can. The boy is old enough to be a sea lad. He can walk in plain view." He gave a final look to the beaten female body. "How'd she die?"

"The children, Tommy!" Dunstan said.

"They speak no English," Miguel said. "She was raped to death." He turned to the boy and said, *"Puedes caminar solo, Pedro?"*

"Si," answered Pedro.

Miguel said, *"Estas seguro de ser fuerte lo suficiente?"*

"Si."

"Muy fuerte, eh?" Dunstan said, tousling Pedro's hair. The little boy looked up at him and smiled. Dunstan took his hand. The men began to stroll back to the *Bounty*.

Miguel said a quick Hebrew prayer as they walked toward the stairs. He heard the commotion above him and asked what it was all about.

"They're searching for Captain Mundo," said Thomas. He quickly explained what had happened, how they came aboard, how they killed Mundo. Miguel nodded, amazed at how clever they had been.

"What's the little girl's name?" Dunstan asked Miguel.

"Reina," Miguel said. "Someone's coming. They might see the girl. Over here!"

They ducked behind a whitewashed wooden trunk. A group of Italians gripping daggers ran down the passageway swearing revenge for their missing captain.

"Vengan!" Miguel said. *"Yo pienso que—"* He looked at Shakespeare and switched his directions to English.

Dunstan said to Miguel, "He's a friend of Becca's—"

"I *know* who he is," interrupted Miguel. "Becca and I have no secrets. This way, to the left. The steps are close at hand!"

They went thirty yards to the left. The hallway dead-ended to the door of the galley. Pungent odors and greasy steam oozed out the cracks around the door.

"Two days of darkness have muddled my sense of direction," Miguel said. "Go back the way we came!"

''Let's speed it up!'' Dunstan said.

Miguel said to Shakespeare as they ran, ''You and your aid are my welcome guests. I thank you for coming, whatever your reasons are.''

''A long tale,'' Shakespeare answered. He took a deep breath, surprised by how quickly his nose had acclimated to the stench of piss and death.

''Aha!'' Miguel said. ''I know where I am now! This way'' He turned to Thomas and asked, ''What's our plan of escape?''

Thomas said, ''We have a boat, and its kidnapped English captain as well. They are both in tow, tied to the forecastle. All we have to do is get to it.''

Dunstan said, ''Marry, do you hear all that shouting?''

Reina buried her face in Dunstan's shoulders. The little girl's hair was dirty and sticky with sweat and dried blood, but the blond tresses still curled tightly. Dunstan kissed the crown of her head and hid her as best as he could under the crook of his arm.

Hundreds of men were emptying the cabins. With all the noise and motion, no gave paid attention to the four disguised Englishmen.

Miguel asked, ''Who did me in? De Andrada?''

''Yes,'' Thomas answered. ''How did you know?''

''The Spanish were expecting me,'' Miguel said. ''Tush, a welcoming party they gave me! The men were tortured in front of my eyes. Then came the rape of the children's mother.''

Shakespeare asked, ''Why were you spared?''

''The Inquisition desires the exclusive merriment of my torture. By law, the seamen must return me to the auspices of the Holy See—to reconcile me to the Church before I die. I've already been sentenced to burn.'' Miguel smiled. ''A hopeless case I am, being both a Jew and a bug— At last! Steps!''

They climbed the stairs. The action up one deck was frenzied. Men carrying torches, searching for Mundo, for clues that could lead to his whereabouts. In the distance Dunstan heard the word blood being screamed. He said in English,

''They've discovered the site where we killed him.''

''Walk with purpose,'' Thomas said. ''Act like we're looking for the captain.''

They hadn't gone more than five yards before they were halted by a thickly built man with heavy arms. His beard was black, his eyes pale blue. Miguel noticed powder stains on his fingertips. A gunner. Thinking quickly, Thomas and Shakespeare blocked Dunstan and the girl from the gunner's view.

The Spaniard said to Miguel, ''You look like shit.''

"I've been ill," Miguel answered back in perfect Spanish. "My first day without fever. Have you found the captain yet?"

The gunner shook his head. "I've checked this area thoroughly. The captain's not here. Go on the orlop and search down there."

Without a pause, Miguel lied, "We just came from the bottom deck. They sent us up here."

"Who did?"

"Diego," Miguel said.

"Which Diego?" asked the sailor.

"The fat one," Miguel said.

"Ah, Diego Cortez," said the gunner. "He has pudding in his head. Go back downstairs and look over the area again."

"Si." Miguel turned to the others. "Come."

"God damn him!" Dunstan said as they descended the stairs.

"We'll wait a moment here," Miguel said. "Then we'll return back to the middle deck."

"God's blood, it's hot in this pisshole," Dunstan said, shifting Reina's weight under his cape.

"You carry a load," Miguel said. "Give her to me."

Dunstan started to hand her to Miguel, but the little girl clutched him. "It's well to leave it as is," Dunstan said.

They waited several minutes in silence. Thomas said, "Let's try again." Again they climbed the stairs. Greeting them at the top of the platform was the same gunner. Again he frowned.

"What are you *doing* here?"

This time Miguel and Shakespeare hid Dunstan.

Thomas said, "The fat one sent us back up!"

"The captain's not here!" the gunner insisted.

"Tell Cortez that!" Thomas said. "He sends us up, you send us down—"

"Do I know you?" the gunner said, staring suspiciously at Thomas.

"Si! Of course you know me! Tomas! We were seafaring mates on His Majesty's Armada in August of 'eighty-eight."

"The *San Martin*?" asked the gunner.

"Si," Thomas said. "Under Diego Flores de Valdes. Together we battled for His Majesty, the King, and the true religion." Thomas squinted his eyes in insult. "You remember me not, eh?"

"Many men sailed on the noble flota," the gunner said, reddening with embarrassment.

Thomas said, "Remember the explosion of the *San Salvador*? We witnessed it together. What did you say to me? Something about the Devil-worshiping Drake in our midst?"

"Si," said the gunner excitedly. "I said, 'The enemy has penetrated our ranks and sabotaged our own boats.' "

"Si," said Thomas, "that was it. Curse it be to Drake!"

The gunner nodded solemnly. "Wait here," he instructed. "I'll go talk with Cortez."

"Si," said Thomas.

As soon as the gunner was out of sight, Miguel said, "This way!"

With lightning speed they climbed six flights of stairs and reached the uppermost deck of the galleon. The wind was fierce, the tides rocky. Spray showered their faces, cooled off their burning skin. Hundreds of seamen were flitting about the ship, buzzing and running without purpose—like bees confused by smoke. Thomas stood on the stern of the deck, looking through the chaos. Opposite him was the highest elevation of the ship— the galleon's forecastle peeking up through the swarm of panic-driven flesh. He said,

"Our boat is tied across the deck—"

"Listen!" Dunstan said. "They've discovered *us* missing! They speak of the stranded Spanish mariners!"

They began to run through the crowds to the forecastle, drawing in lungfuls of air, pushing through hordes of war-lusting men. The ship was mass confusion, total alarm. Groups of mariners finally noticed the Englishmen shoving and racing and began to yell to them, curse them. A fat Spanish sailor shouted halt, blocked Miguel's way with his sword. Without pausing, Miguel drew his falchion, gripped the handle with both hands, and swung it across the mariner's throat. Blood spurted and splattered onto Miguel's jerkin. The sailor's eyes froze in horror, remained that way even as his head dangled from his neck like a bud on a bent stalk.

From under Dunstan's cloak Reina began to cry. A knife flew over Miguel's head. Shakespeare drew his sword and slammed it against an airborne dagger headed for his heart. But God was with them and they managed to reach the forecastle. Thomas screamed, "Slide down the rope," but it was too late. Someone had cut the tackle that held the *Bounty* to the galleon. Shakespeare saw the line drop into the water, saw the fishing boat drift away.

"Rebecca," Shakespeare whispered.

Dunstan barked to Pedro to climb upon his back. Dunstan felt spindly arms wrap around his neck, thin legs encircle his waist. He was carrying both children, their lives in his hands. Heavy, heavy weight more precious by pound than gold.

Thomas swung blindly at the mob of mariners. "To the taffrail!" he shrieked. "The sea is our only refuge."

A rapier pierced Thomas's thigh and slashed downward, ripping through the muscle. Thomas swore, pivoted, and thrust his sword forward. The blade sank into a thick cushion of Spanish belly fat. Thomas yanked the sword out of the dead man's stomach and pulled the embedded rapier out of his leg. He tried to run but stumbled to the ground.

"I can't walk!" he shouted, tears running down his face.

Miguel looped his arm around Thomas's waist and dragged him forward to the edge of the galleon. Threads of morning light were peeking over the horizon as a thin plate of gold began to spread over the ocean. But directly below the galleon was a boiling witches' brew of inky black, waves crashing against the side of the big ship. Shakespeare gripped Miguel's shoulder, wished him good fortune, then pushed him and Thomas overboard. He pulled Pedro off Dunstan's back, gripping him tightly, and yelled at Dunstan to jump.

The winds howled as they plummeted downward, a volley of daggers whistling past their faces, descending upon them like locusts. One second, two seconds, three seconds . . . they plunged into a bath of ice, the vapor of life sucked out of their lungs as chilled ocean brine streamed into their mouths and noses. Midnight waters swirled about their bodies, towing them downward. Shakespeare clutched Pedro with one hand, flailed upward with the other. Thomas held back his cries of agony as salt invaded the open gash in his leg. He kicked furiously, out of rhythm, trying to surface, blowing bubbles out of his nose and mouth, his chest aching with the need for air. His hair danced about his face, thin strands as light as the web of a spider. His cheeks grew fat with air, his eyes burned from the sting of the ocean.

Dunstan and Reina were the first to surface. He sputtered and coughed, spitting out lungfuls of seawater. The little girl was still in his arms, but gasping and retching. Dunstan held her as high as he could and rapped her firmly on her back between her shoulder blades. Reina coughed out gulps of ocean and began to cry.

Thank God!

A cannonball plunged a hundred yards in front of him, drenching his face.

"Thomas!" Dunstan screamed. "Miguel!"

Shakespeare surfaced a second later with the boy. Dunstan dog-paddled over to him and slapped him on the back. Shakespeare gasped and vomited forth saltwater.

"The boy . . . ." Shakespeare said between breaths. "Not breathing . . ."

"Push in on his stomach," Dunstan said. He held Reina's head above water as he paddled.

Gently, Shakespeare pressed Pedro's belly. Water trickled out from the boy's gullet, but his chest remained motionless.

Thomas's head broke through the waves. In his arms was Miguel, as limp as the wet clothing he wore. Thomas cleared his lungs and shouted, "Something . . . wrong . . . with Miguel!"

"Is he breathing?" Dunstan screamed back.

"Aye," Thomas said, inhaling deeply. "Yes . . . but a dagger . . . into his back—" Thomas broke into a series of coughs. "The poniard's handle broke off . . . is . . . near his spine! He cannot move his legs!"

"Put him on his back and hold his neck," Dunstan said panting. "He knows how to float—praised be the Almighty! Our boat! Beccaaaa!"

Shakespeare caught sight of the *Bounty* as he paddled against the waves, keeping the boy's head above water. Thank God for the Avon River, all those summers he'd spent swimming. He took a deep breath and blew warm air between the boy's lips.

Another cannonball belched forth from the galleon and fell a few feet from the *Bounty*. The impact lifted the keel of the boat out of the water.

"Rebecca!" Dunstan screamed.

Shakespeare looked up. "My God!" he cried. Water crashed down upon him. After the shower had cleared, Shakespeare saw the *Bounty* again—intact, moving toward them with lightning speed. God save Captain Krabbey!

"Becca!" Thomas shouted. His lungs hurt, his nearly numb legs were two lead weights sucking his torso down under. So cold, but at least it dulled the pain from his leg wound. A wave crest broke upon them, pushing Thomas and Miguel under. They resurfaced, coughing, greedy for air.

Dunstan screamed, "Becca!"

Shakespeare felt his limbs harden with cold. The boy lay flaccid in his arm. Again Shakespeare blew into the small mouth. No response.

"Breathe!" he ordered the lifeless body. "Breathe, damn it, breathe." He pushed the boy's stomach in and a small rill of water leaked out. Again he exhaled into the mouth.

"The boy?" Dunstan shouted to Shakespeare.

"Nothing," Shakespeare answered. He was panting, nearly out of breath himself. "Breathe," he pleaded with Pedro.

Another cannonball looped into the ocean, perilously close to them and to the *Bounty*. Dunstan held his breath and gripped Reina as the reaction wave sucked them into the churning waters. Shakespeare surfaced first. Pedro was ashen, his mouth slack, his eyes rolled back in their sockets. Shakespeare inhaled and blew air into Pedro's water-logged gullet. The sky reverberated with the booms of muskets, was choked with the acrid smoke of gunpowder.

No response.

The boy was dead.

The *Bounty* dodged cannonballs as it forded the choppy waves.

"Becca!" screamed Dunstan. "Oh God, I prithee, help us!" His own salty tears mingled with the spray of the ocean. He placed Reina on his shoulder and tried to keep afloat.

"Breathe," yelled Shakespeare to Pedro. "Please God, breathe!" The boy was so cold to the touch. Shakespeare began to shiver violently.

"I'm sinking!" shouted Thomas. "My leg . . . I can't hold Miguel!"

"Release me, then," begged Miguel. "Save yourself!"

Thomas felt himself being dragged under, yet he refused to loosen his hold on Miguel.

"Let me go!" Miguel shouted, crying. "We'll both die if you don't."

"Wait!" Shakespeare said, still clutching Pedro. He tried to swim to Thomas. He was shaking with chill. "I'm coming to you."

The *Bounty* neared Dunstan, sprayed him with water.

"Rebecca!" he screamed again.

A rope was thrown overboard. Dunstan paddled frantically in its direction. A cannonball soared over his head, nicked the boat, then dropped into the sea. The waves reacted. When they resurfaced, Dunstan began to sob as he swam, arm and hand extended to the line, fingertips brushing against the fibers of the rope.

Hailstones of musketfire hit the sea.

Weeping, Dunstan clutched the line and Reina as Krabbey and Rebecca tugged on the other end. Slowly Dunstan felt himself rising out of the water, his clothes raining atop the ocean's surface. They pulled him onto the front of the deck, where he and the girl collapsed.

Rebecca's first instinct was to run to them, but Krabbey held her back.

"Never mind about them!" he shouted. "Get the others. Pull the rigging aft, damn you, whore! I'm a thief and a smuggler, but an Englishman as well, and I'll be God damned if I lose one of my own to the bastard Spanish whoresons!" Krabbey held aloft his caliver and fired it into the air!

"Motherfuckers!" he screamed up to the galleon. He was red-faced and shirtless, his belly studded with goose bumps from the wind. But the chilly air did little to cool the heat of his blood. He was burning with the thrill of war.

Dunstan slowly rose to his feet. "What can I do?" he gasped.

"Help the whore pull the lines!" yelled Krabbey. His muscles were bulging with tension. "Hurry you up, you yellow-livered weakling! There are Englishmen down there, and I'm no deserter of my countrymen!"

Dunstan took the line to the mainsail and pulled it forward.

"I see Shakespeare!" Rebecca shouted. "Miguel, Thomas as well!"

"Throw them the line, wench!" Krabbey screamed, and laughed. "Ye bastards!" he said, shaking his fist at the galleon. "I'll see ye in Hell, stinkin' Papists! But at least I lived well while I lived!" Krabbey spat a glob of phlegm into the air.

Shakespeare grabbed Miguel and helped Thomas grip the rigging with one hand, Pedro with the other. Dunstan and Krabbey tugged on the line until the boy and Thomas were pulled to safety.

"Now for the last of us," Dunstan exclaimed, throwing the rope overboard once again. "God saved us!"

Krabbey kicked Thomas in the bottom. "Grab the rope, ye limp-prick son of a bitch, and help us pull up the others."

"But the boy . . . needs air."

"He's dead, you dolt, and you're among the breathin'. Get going!"

Thomas crawled over to the line on his hands and good leg and gripped the rope.

A cannonball flew over the stern of the ship and landed a few feet from the deck, splashing buckets of water into the boat's bilge.

"Pull, you fucking women!" Krabbey screamed. "Pull, pull!"

Slowly—too slowly—the line lifted, hoisting Shakespeare and Miguel upward. Shakespeare lost his grip and fell back into the ocean.

"Gods, I'd better go in after them," Dunstan said.

"Hold yer ballocks, fool," Krabbey said. "We don't need another body weighing down our muscles. Stay here and work!"

Shakespeare and Miguel resurfaced, pale and weak. Again the player grabbed the rope. His hands were scraped raw from the coarse hemp fibers. The air was a spray of gunpowder, enveloping them like a thick gray blanket. Shakespeare locked his arm under Miguel's neck and firmed up his grip upon the rope.

"Got it?" screamed Krabbey.

"Again," yelled Shakespeare. His chest hurt. He couldn't stop shaking.

"Pull!" Krabbey ordered. "Stay with it, man, stay with it!"

Shakespeare clutched the rope as hard as he could, held on to Miguel until he was sure he was choking him. A few feet more . . . Shakespeare felt his hand weakening, his muscles losing strength.

"A little bit more," Rebecca shouted to Shakespeare. Her hair was plastered onto her face, stuffed in her mouth. Her jerkin was soaked, her hands bleeding. "A little bit more, Willy, and we've got you both."

One final tug and Shakespeare and Miguel tumbled aboard the *Bounty*. Rebecca burst into tears. Krabbey laughed and yanked on the halyard.

"Fuck you in the arse!" he yelled to the galleon. "And ye idol-worshiping Pope's arse too!"

"What's wrong with Miguel?" Rebecca cried.

"Knife in the back," Thomas said, crawling toward them.

Rebecca gasped. "Your leg, Tommy—"

"I breathe," Thomas said. "Tend to Miguel and the girl!"

Rebecca looked at the little girl at the front of the boat. She sat huddled, her knees against her chest, her shoulders hunched forward, thumb in mouth. Rebecca wanted to comfort her, until her eyes went back to Miguel. He lay next to the girl, as inert as stone. Immediately Rebecca went to work, running to retrieve blankets, stumbling over her feet with each rock of the boat. Upon her return she began to strip Miguel of his wet clothes, singing soft lullabies to him. He grabbed her hand, squeezed it with strength that belied his condition, and begged her not to let him die. Rebecca swore she would not, her voice strong and sure. But she had her doubts. Miguel was white, making horrible sucking noises with each inhalation.

Thomas crawled over to Shakespeare, dragging his injured leg. "I'll hold the boom. Go find another spot to man."

"He's dead," Shakespeare whispered, still trembling.

"Who?"

"The boy," Shakespeare said. Tears ran down his cheeks. "I couldn't save him. He lies on the deck . . . dead."

Thomas sat on the deck and took the boom from the player. He shrugged helplessly.

Krabbey shouted to Shakespeare, "Get your arse over here, ye land chicken, and help me with the boom! The galleon is closing in, starboard side. We have to get the hell out of here!"

Shakespeare ran to Krabbey's side, holding the sails for support against the unrelenting sea.

The winds were hellish, but in Krabbey's hands they became a divine gift from God. The Spanish galleon, propelled by oars, was ponderous and clumsy. The *Bounty* with its sails was a fast-flying wench, and under Krabbey's command she was able to outmaneuver the Iberian dowager at every turn. Though the *Bounty*'s sides were riddled with musket shot, no lethal damage was done to her body.

An hour later the galleon was nothing more than a fierce memory, as mighty, yet as intangible, as the roar of the tide.

38

𝕿he first thing Krabbey did when out of harm's way was to lower the Spanish flag and hoist England's atop the masthead. By noon the *Good Bounty* was cursed with a becalmed sea, the winds nothing more than baby's breath, the waves small wrinkles in a sheet of sage-green glass. They were a day away from English soil, but if the winds didn't shift, the voyage might take them twice as long. But Krabbey didn't dwell on "what ifs." He took advantage of the respite and surveyed the damage done to his boat, each nick reported to Dunstan and Shakespeare with much exaggeration and a string of obscenities. But Dunstan, still reeling from the aftermath of his escape, was too drained to protest the captain's absurd assessments. He'd pay for all necessary repairs, for the captain's time and skill as well. Just as long as they arrived home safely.

An hour passed, the sea remained quiet. Dunstan napped in the sunshine at the front of the boat, Reina snuggled in his arms. His dreams were nightmares of disemboweled flesh, of a shrouded little boy crumpled in the hatch. He was jolted awake by an imagined scream, his heart beating wildly. Reina sighed and nestled deeper into the cradle of his embrace. Dunstan kissed the crown of the little girl's head and tried to steady his own breathing.

Thomas had been tending the stern of the ship, but the quietness afforded him a chance to sleep. He drifted off then awoke suddenly with fever, his wounded leg swollen to twice its natural size. Rebecca had done a fine job stitching the wound, yet it throbbed worse than when the flesh had been exposed to the air. Thomas forced himself to sit, then tried to stand, but fell. Cursing, his throat clogged with tears of pain, he lay back down. He debated hobbling over to Shakespeare, offering to help the player repair the ripped sails and frayed cordage, but decided against it. Soon Krabbey would have need of him. Best to rest as much as he could while the sea was peaceful.

Miguel slept groggily under the protection of the mainsail, his body alternating between bouts of chills and burning fever. Rebecca sat by him, having been awake for over twenty-four hours—dressing wounds, preparing syrups and poultices from supplies she had carried when they initially boarded the *Bounty*. Her lids drooped, her body ached, but she pressed on. How often she had seen her father languishing in the same condition that was overtaking her now, yet even as he complained, he had never compromised his obligations to his patients.

Krabbey approached Rebecca as she ministered to Miguel. She had set out fresh blankets atop the companionway hatch, laid Miguel on his stomach under the shade of the mainsail. The blade of the broken dagger was completely swallowed up by the flesh of Miguel's back. How deep the point sat, how close it was to his spine, Rebecca couldn't tell without opening him up. She prayed the seas would remain gentle, that her betrothed would be jostled as little as possible. The captain glanced at the man's ashen face, then at her.

"He's lost," he said. "Ye'd best pay attention to the one with the gash in his leg afore he's lost as well."

"Speak not like that in front of him," Rebecca whispered.

"He's as good as dead, wench," Krabbey insisted. "He don'na understand a word I speak."

Rebecca said nothing, wiped beads of perspiration off Miguel's brow. Krabbey regarded her face—suffused with exhaustion yet beautiful. He felt himself grow hard, his stare turning to a leer.

"You gonna give me just due, girlie?" he asked.

"I'll pay for the whore of your choice, Captain," Rebecca offered. "A fair bargain."

"Don'na want a whore," Krabbey continued. "I coulda taken you by force, wench, once you undid me binds. You know that."

Rebecca didn't answer.

"Ach," Krabbey said, waving his hand in disgust. "Krabbey never begged for wenches and he ain't gonna start now."

Rebecca said, "I'm deeply indebted to you for my life, Captain. For the lives of my kinsmen as well. You could have deserted us, your fellow countrymen. Instead you proved yourself to be a true Englishman—a man of valor."

Krabbey laughed, slapped her back at the compliment. "Yer pissass cousins'll pay dearly for their lives." He leaned over Rebecca's shoulder, his foul breath and body odor assaulting her nostrils even in the open air. He said, "Between you and me, girlie, I might be tempted to say that yer men did me service."

"Aye?" Rebecca asked.

Krabbey nodded. He took her hand, brought it to his groin and squeezed her fingers around his erect penis.

"Feel that good, me little whore," Krabbey said. "Ifin they don't feel like that, send 'em home to mama."

"I shall remember such wise words." She struggled to extricate her fingers but to no avail. Krabbey grinned, then finally released her hand. He lay back on the deck and stared at the sky of woolly gray clouds.

"Been a while since I seen a maiden blushin'." Krabbey snickered. He inhaled deeply then said, "The smell of the Spaniard makes a true Englishman go hot, his blood boil with ire but his cock bulge with excitement. Aye, m'lassie, this morning were not the first time I tasted the victory over the Papist bastards!" He turned to Rebecca. "Excusin' my language if you ain't no whore."

"You fought under Drake?"

"Three times, girlie," Krabbey said. "I earned my sea legs proper. I was aboard the *Victory* when Drake attacked the rear-guard wing of the mealy-assed Armada. I was under Howard when we sailed, our spirits high with the chance of drinkin' Papist blood. Then comes around the *San Juan de Portugal* to meet us in battle. I'll tell you that ship was bigger and mightier than the one we just escaped from. A heavy bastard with rows and rows of guns, over a thousand tons of weight and at least six, seven hundred evil-drooling Catholics ready to grapple and board our ship, burn us at the stake and offer our ashes in their idol worship. Man, I could tell ye, lass, that I was aching for the kill, but I'll tell ye the truth when I say that we all pissed in our breeches when we saw the size of that galleon. We braced ourselves for a hot fight."

Krabbey laughed.

"So in comes the *San Juan* ready to attack, and the rest of the Armada just sailed on, leavin' Captain Recalde at the helm of the *San Juan* fightin' a solo battle. They were a sight to spit at, wench. Drake closed the range to three hundred yards of the Spanish galleon and pounded the shit out of Recalde with our long guns and culverins. Finally the rest of the bastard Papist fleet realized that they'd left the *San Juan* out to die, and sent in *Grangrin* to drive Drake away. But by that time Recalde learned faster than a virgin in a vaulting school that Drake could maul the flota whenever we wished and without retaliation."

Krabbey grabbed his groin again. "The smell of the sea infected me blood, girlie. I knew I'd never return to me former labor as a tinker. I went out to battle again with Drake in 'eighty-nine, under Norris this time.''

"The revolt of Don Antonio, aye?" Rebecca said.

"Aye, the Pretender. Ach, stinkin' Papists, all of them! Portuguese as well as Spaniards. No wonder we were wiped from the seas. We should have been fightin' against the Catholics, not with 'em, even if they were fighting each other. Philip, Don Antonio, they're the same to me—ass-fucking bugger Papists!''

Miguel moaned. Rebecca stroked his burning cheek and sighed heavily. Quickly, she began to mix a medicinal paste of garlic, flour, and stale beer to bring down Miguel's fever.

"Who's this one to ye?" Krabbey asked her.

Rebecca said, "My betrothed.''

Krabbey looked confused. "Then who's your whole-bodied baldy repairing the sails?'' he asked, pointing to Shakespeare.

Rebecca sighed. Too difficult to explain. "Another cousin,'' she answered.

"Ye with the dying one's child?'' Krabbey inquired.

"Why do you ask?'' Rebecca answered.

"The boy'll be a corpse in your arms before we sight land, lassie,'' Krabbey said. "Ifin you be with his babe, I'd be willin' to make ye honest and take the bastard as my own. I got lots of silver, girlie, and can be buying you fine clothes and goodly trinkets. I'm over forty-two and don't have much time left in this world. All me possessions would be goin' to you when I die. A goodly bargain, mistress, ifin you could put up with a whoreson like meself for a few years.''

Rebecca was touched. She said, "I'm not with child, Captain. And by my troth, my betrothed will not die. But I thank you for your kind offering.''

The winds began to kick up, filling the previously slackened sails with air. At last, thought Rebecca. Motion. Krabbey rose.

"The winds call me to my helm, and I got me business to do,'' he said. "The clouds'll be asquallin' afore I can spit. I won't go frettin' none over your stubbornness. Me proposal was just a thought.'' He grabbed his groin again. "By tomorrow night, I pledge you that it won't be goin' hungry.''

Rebecca bowed her head demurely, waited until Krabbey was gone before she looked up again. She would have laughed to herself had not Miguel shivered violently in her arms.

As the *Bounty* came in to dock at Dover, Rebecca held back tears. Her land! Her country! The steel sky, the pelting rain suddenly seemed not gloomy but glorious, renewing. When the boat was anchored, she stood a moment upon the deck, shivering, her arms wrapped tightly about her chest, breathing in English air. Shakespeare came up from behind, threw a cloak around her shoulders and handed her Reina. Rebecca covered the little girl and ran for the protection of an overhang. Fifteen minutes later Shakespeare reemerged with Thomas, who supported himself with two iron bars for walking sticks. His movements were slow, methodical, and painful. Rebecca noticed he winced with each step, but he refused more than once to accept help from Shakespeare. The two of them made their way over to Rebecca and Reina.

Shakespeare said, "Dunstan and I will stay with Miguel on the *Bounty*. Your betrothed sleeps deeply, and I think it unwise to wake him. Best if you take your cousin and the girl back to the Flounder, and we'll join you as soon as we're able to move Miguel."

Rebecca nodded, then regarded Thomas struggling with the sticks. She said, "We should get a hackney—"

"Rubbish!" Thomas cried out. "It'll harden my leg muscles to walk."

"Tommy, I—"

"Let's go!" Thomas commanded her. "I said I'm well."

Rebecca knew by her cousin's tone that she had no choice but to listen.

It took them an hour to trudge to their rented chamber—mercifully prepared, the hearth ablaze. Thomas fell onto the bed. His face had hardened from two days at sea, his skin no longer held a youthful blush. His cheeks were chapped and rough, his eyes sunken and old.

Rebecca removed the little girl's wet clothing, wrapped her in a blanket and set her by the fireplace. Reina curled into a ball, stuck her thumb in her mouth and fell asleep. Rebecca approached Thomas and began to strip him of his shredded clothing. In a flash he was on top of her, his chest weighing heavily on her body, his hands under her doublet. Rebecca froze with shock. He clamped his lips over hers, then as abruptly as he came upon her, he pulled his mouth away.

"Pray, Becca," he whispered. "Get me a whore."

She whispered she would.

"And flasks of port," Thomas added. He removed his hands from Rebecca's breasts and held her cheeks. "Anything to distract me from the pain in my leg."

Rebecca embraced her cousin, brought his head down to her chest. "Poor Tommy." She stroked his cheek. "Need you further help in removing your clothes?"

He shook his head and rolled off her. "I only have need of a stew and stupor."

* * *

Thomas was noisy, the whore even more boisterous, but Rebecca could have slept through it all had her mind been at peace. But her thoughts were with Miguel, with her father as well. She lay stretched out on the floor, her back to the fireplace, Reina in her arms. With an exasperated sigh, she brought the blanket over her head.

Across the room the whore laughed.

Shut up! Rebecca thought. God, just shut up!

Again the whore let out peals of raucous laughter, then said something lewd to Thomas. The trull had an irritating squeaky voice! Rebecca stuck her fingers in her ears and cursed her throbbing head. She could feel the pounding of her heart in her brain through her fingertips. *Thump, thump, thump, thump, thump*, each beat fireworks inside her head.

Again the whore squealed like a sow. Thomas was giggling now, speaking in a slurred voice. Rebecca wrapped Reina in the blanket, then stood up and glared at the stew.

"Out!" she shouted, pointing to the door.

The whore made a face to Thomas. "What's sticking in *her* craw?"

There it was! That tinny voice again!

Rebecca marched over to the bed and pulled the whore from the sheets. The room stunk of sweat and spilled seed.

"Get your clothes on and leave!" Rebecca ordered her.

"You're naked," Thomas said to his cousin.

"Go to sleep, Tommy," Rebecca said sourly. She pulled a chemise over the whore's body.

"I can dress myself!" the trull protested.

"Not fast enough!" Rebecca answered, slapping a bodice onto the whore's chest.

"What'd *I* do?" the whore said. She began to whine.

"I've never seen you naked," Thomas said, grinning stupidly at Rebecca.

"Your brother is very good," the whore squeaked out.

"I rejoice with the knowledge that he hath pleased you," Rebecca said, lacing up the last of the trull's points. She pushed the whore out the door.

"Go to sleep," she repeated.

He flung off the sheets and patted the mattress. "Come to me."

Rebecca ignored him and slipped on her chemise. The room was dark except for the dwindling fire that flickered in the hearth. She placed a log on the flame and lit the rush candles in the wall sconces, wondering what was taking the others so long.

Thomas said, "Pour me another tankard. Then come and join me. I have need of company."

"You have need of sleep." But she dutifully opened another bottle and gave it to Thomas. She pulled back the sheets, picked up a candle and examined his wounded leg.

Thomas grew serious. "How does it fare?" he asked.

Eventually she said, "No evidence of gangrenous tissue. I do believe that you will be whole-bodied in no time."

Thomas smiled with relief.

"The pain is bad?" she asked.

"This scratch? Bah!"

Rebecca stood and began to pace.

"Sit with me," Thomas bade her.

"I cannot stay still. My mind is too preoccupied. I'm going back to the boat. I find this uncertainty maddening."

"No," Thomas protested.

"I'll be but a half hour at the most. Reina's asleep."

"What will you wear? Your clothes are soaked."

"No matter. It rains furiously outside. Even dry clothing would become sopping wet in a matter of minutes."

"Don't leave, Becca. Wait another hour. Perhaps they'll be along shortly."

Rebecca paused. "A half hour," she said.

"A half hour, then," Thomas said. "Sit with me."

She shook her head and lay down next to Reina.

"The floor is hard," Thomas said.

"I'm comfortable. I'll keep guard over the little one."

"You avoid me."

Rebecca didn't answer. Fifteen minutes later she sat up and listened. "I hear someone coming. Dear God, let it be them." She ran to open the door.

Shakespeare entered, holding Miguel over his shoulders. Dunstan cradled the lifeless Pedro in his arms and carried their provisions on his back. The men were dripping wet, as if they were watercolors bleeding on canvas.

Rebecca said, "Let me help you out of your clothes!"

Thomas shifted to one side and Shakespeare gently placed Miguel on the bed, facedown. Rebecca knelt by her betrothed's side. He was a breath away from death.

Dunstan placed the little boy's body in the corner of the room then dropped the bags onto the floor. Shakespeare stripped naked then dressed quickly. The new clothes were limp, damp with moisture, yet they felt warm upon his chilled skin. He said,

"Krabbey awaits us downstairs for cheery company and supper. We dare not displease the good captain. Do you want to go down or should I?"

Dunstan pulled off sopping breeches. He said, "You go. Make

sure the fire in his stomach is well doused. And buy him a whore. I'll join the two of you in a few minutes.''

Shakespeare nodded and left.

"Get me my vials, cousin," Rebecca said to Dunstan. Her voice was weak with dispair. "I'll see what I can prepare for Miguel."

Dunstan stood and sniffed. His head began to pound, his hands began to shake. Anger blurred his vision, dulled his reasoning. He took a deep breath and calmly asked Rebecca, "Why does this room smell like a brothel? And pray, cousin, *what* do you wear under your chemise?"

Rebecca glared back at him, angered by the insinuation.

"What has passed in this room?" Dunstan asked.

Stupid ass, she thought. Impetuous fool, always seeing the worst in people because he was such a woodcock himself.

She said, "My potions, I pray you, Dunstan."

"What were the two of you doing?" Dunstan asked menacingly.

Rebecca shrieked, "Ask your brother, if your curiosity is so overwhelming."

Dunstan burned with hatred. He grabbed Rebecca by the hair and ripped her chemise from her body. "You whore." He slapped her across the face several times in succession. "You dirty, disgusting whore!"

"Dunstan!" Thomas interjected. "God's blood, you ass, what are you doing!"

Dunstan shouted, "You've been fucking my brother!" He slapped her again and shoved her into the wall. Rebecca slumped to the floor and moaned. Reina began to cry.

"And *fornicating* in front of the child, yet?" Dunstan screamed. He fell on top of Rebecca and began to choke her, felt himself squeezing the life out of her pretty little throat. Just desserts, the worthless slut! And to think he had ever *loved* her.

Rebecca was turning purple, clawing at his hands. Dunstan didn't even feel the gouges she raked into his skin. Only a moment later did he realize Thomas's arm was looped around his neck, forcing him to release her. Rebecca held her throat and rolled about the floor, sucking up air.

"Are you *moonstruck*!" Thomas cried. "Stop it!"

"Let me go!" Dunstan screamed, thrashing about in Thomas's arms. He managed to pull out his dagger. "I'll kill her! And you as well if you get in my way!"

"Stop fighting me, damn you!" Thomas yelled. "I bedded a whore up here! A *whore*, Dunstan, not Becca! Becca found me a whore! I *asked* her to find me one! She's been doing nothing but worrying about your welfare! She would have gone back to the boat had I not stopped her!''

Dunstan stopped struggling and dropped his dagger. His head began to spin. Thomas loosened his grip.

"I *did not bed* her," Thomas said. "She *did not bed* me. I had a *whore*! Understand?''

"Let go of me!'' Dunstan ordered.

"Swear you'll not lay—''

"Let me go,'' Dunstan said wearily. "I've regained my wits.''

Thomas hesitated, then released Dunstan from his hold. He limped over to Rebecca. Her face was puffy, cuts had surfaced upon her brow and lips. Her nose was bloody. She was breathing easier now, and wiped her nose with the back of her hand.

"Do you need help?'' Thomas asked.

"No.'' Her voice was barely audible. "Pray, go comfort the child.''

Thomas wiped tears from Rebecca's face with his fingertips, his eyes filled with pity and guilt. "Let me help you to your feet.''

Rebecca insisted, "Go to Reina.'' She crawled over to the bags and began rummaging through them for her vials, pulling out several jars. She slipped on another chemise, then walked shakily back to Miguel and knelt beside him.

"I need more light, Dunstan,'' she said.

Dunstan brought her the candle and regarded her face. The left eye was red and swollen. He felt his stomach buck with self-revulsion.

Rebecca wiped her bloodied hands on her chemise. She said, "I need water. I cannot work with sticky hands.''

"Aye,'' Dunstan said.

After Rebecca washed her hands, she examined Miguel's wound. It was closed shut and topped with a hard node of green pus. Laudable pus, the Gentiles called it, a sign of healing. But Grandmama had taught her that it was a river of death. To break the skin, to send the pus into the blood was as harmful as breathing evil vapors.

Radiating from the swelling beneath the skin were spiderwebs of green lines. She dabbed Miguel's brow, then held his face in her hands. His complexion was wan and pasty, his breath sour. His hands were as hard and cold as ice. She pried apart his chilled, dry lips and forced some poppy syrup into his mouth. Miguel sputtered and coughed out the first sip, but was able to swallow the second and third.

His body was heavy with bad humors. Rebecca knew she'd have to cut him open and remove the blade from his back. She ordered Dunstan to go down and fetch Shakespeare, as he would

need help in holding Miguel down. She also told him to scrounge
up knives from the inn's kitchen.

"If the scullery maids and cooks be penurious, offer them a
groat or two," she said. "That should increase their generosity
immensely."

Dunstan nodded.

"Oh, and get an ice pick," Rebecca added, "and a whetstone
as well. And a needle and thread."

Dunstan stared at her, his feet unable to move.

Rebecca said, "Go, go! Make haste! Every second counts!"

Dunstan still hesitated. He said, "Becca, I—"

"Stow you, Dunstan," Rebecca said sharply. "Just do as I
say. For *once*."

Dunstan sighed and shut the door behind him. Rebecca closed
her eyes and prayed to God for strength, fortitude to do what
her father had done every day since he'd become a doctor, what
she knew her grandam could do with her eyes closed. She was
such a weak woman. Please God, the Creator of miracles, give
her the will to do her duty. After she finished her personal en-
treaties, she began what Jews always do when death has its sucker
under the wretched's skin. She began to recite *tehilim*—the
psalms of King David—by rote.

39

"God's Sointes!" Shakespeare exclaimed when he saw her.
Her face! It had been whole just a moment ago.
"What happened? Troth, your eye—"

"I'm well," Rebecca said flatly. "I stumbled and hit the floor
in a rather ungainly manner. The eye is not beautiful but it's
functional. I see clearly."

Shakespeare looked at her, then at Thomas—his face expres-
sionless. Shakespeare stammered, "We should summon another
surgery doctor. Rebecca cannot—"

Rebecca interrupted, assuring him it was not necessary.
Though Shakespeare knew she was lying, he did not press her
for the truth.

He embraced her tightly and whispered, "I love thee."

"By my life, I love thee," Rebecca said, hugging him back. "I'm scared, Willy. What if Miguel dies under my hand?"

"He won't." Shakespeare studied her face. It was bruised, as if someone had slapped her repeatedly. The skin around her throat held the imprints of fingertips. He looked at Thomas again. This time the younger knight avoided his gaze and lowered his head.

Shakespeare felt himself go hot, rigid with anger. He squeezed his hands into fists, then looked at Rebecca.

"Thou wert whole when I left thee with thy cousins. Only Thomas or Dunstan could have done this to thee, and I warrant the guilty one stands not in this room. . . . I'll kill him."

Rebecca knew he meant it. She said, "This is not the time."

Shakespeare didn't answer right away. He breathed slowly, trying to control his rage. Finally he said. "Retribution is a well-seasoned actor who knows his proper time and place. If peace be possible, peace thou shalt have—for now." He kissed her forehead and held her hands. "Miguel shall *not* die, Rebecca. These fingers shall be as crocheting hooks, knotting up the unraveling caused by the bastard Spanish. I've witnessed thy magical needlepoint on Thomas, my love. Indeed, thou art a wizard—making that which was rent once again inseamed. Thou hast no need of hap, Becca, as thou possesses God-granted skill."

Rebecca squeezed his hands and lay her head on his chest. His words, so soothing. How she loved him.

Dunstan came into the room, bearing an assortment of blades, towels, and a whetstone. He instantly noticed Shakespeare's murderous eye and dropped the knives, a cleaver nicking the tip of his boot.

"Oaf," Shakespeare said. "Pick them up."

Dunstan sneaked a furtive glance at Rebecca, at Thomas, who sat cuddling Reina on the floor. All were averting their eyes. Dunstan swallowed, straightened his spine and said to Shakespeare, "Remember thy place—"

Shakespeare sprang. He clamped his arm around Dunstan's neck and held a dagger at his throat.

"You live at the insistence of your cousin. Do you understand what I am saying?" Shakespeare whispered.

Dunstan said to Thomas, "Wilt thou allow this stranger a hand upon thy brother?"

Thomas turned away. Shakespeare compressed his arm around Dunstan's throat, who began to cough.

"Let him go, Shakespeare," Thomas finally said.

Shakespeare eased the pressure and said, "If ever a wee scratch finds its way upon your cousin, you're a dead man."

"To the Devil!" Dunstan answered.

Shakespeare said, "I've not explained myself sufficiently to thee."

Dunstan said nothing.

"Answer me!" Shakespeare shouted.

"I have ears, man!" Dunstan said. "I hear you speak. Let me go."

Shakespeare released him with a shove. Dunstan stumbled to the floor. He rose slowly, then bent over Thomas and spat in his face.

Thomas wiped the glob of phlegm from his cheek and said, "Had Rebecca been my wife, I would have killed you for what you'd done. Shakespeare showed commendable restraint."

"You'll not have a penny of inheritance!" Dunstan shouted.

"I shit on your money!" Thomas shouted back.

Rebecca said, "Spare the strife, for Miguel's sake. We've no time to lose on useless bickering. Dunstan, pick up the knives and wash them clean."

There was an awkward silence, then Reina began to cry. Thomas rocked her in his arms, tried to coo the child back to sleep but the more he talked, the more distraught the little girl became.

Shakespeare said, "Like lepers, we fall apart piece by piece."

"Sing to her in her Spanish," Dunstan suggested.

Thomas crooned an old Spanish lullaby, one that his mother had sung to him. His voice was melodious and deep and instantly quieted the little girl. Rebecca sighed and began picking up the knives herself. It took her about thirty minutes to set up for the basics—boil the water by placing a kettle in the hearth, then washing the knives. She asked Thomas to vacate the bed and lay clean sheets upon it. Holding the little girl in his arms, Thomas limped over to the fireplace, refusing help from his brother or Shakespeare. Warm and swathed in soft blankets, he rocked the little girl to sleep. Hopefully, she'd stay deep in slumber and Miguel's screams would not wake and scare her.

After the knives had been rinsed with boiling water, Rebecca sorted through the blades. A fish-gutting knife looked sharp enough for the job. And the tongs would make a good clamp. Two paring knives looked passable. She held them against the light in the fireplace and studied the blades, sorely missing her father's surgery knives with their fine-honed edges and their solid ivory handles.

She said, "I'll have to sharpen these. Where's the whetstone, Dunstan?"

"Here." Dunstan leaned over her shoulder, whispered, "I beg your forgiveness."

Rebecca said, "On my grave, never! May your death be slow and painful, your soul be sent to purgatory. May God not grant you redemption and may your eternity be spent in Hell."

Dunstan said, "Tis your spleen and not your heart that talks."

Though inwardly livid, Rebecca replied calmly, "I should have bedded your brother. At least he was able to rise when the occasion presented itself. But we shall not speak of such items, eh?" She paused, then stated, "These marks upon my brow, Dunstan, were made by the frustrated soldier who had arrived at many a battlesite without a pike."

Dunstan stiffened with embarrassment and anger but controlled himself.

Rebecca shrugged. She picked up a knife and meticulously began to sharpen it, a stroke against the whetstone, a check of the angulation against the light. When she had finished with one blade, she went on to the next one. When all the knives were honed to her satisfaction, she spread them out at the foot of the bed along with the towels and strips of cloth, two large bowls of fresh water, and the needle and catgut thread. She washed her hands in one of the bowls, muttered last minute prayers, then said out loud,

"Dunstan, you hold Miguel's feet. You'll also be in charge of passing me my tools." Rebecca turned to Shakespeare. "You hold his arms and my light." She handed him the candlestick. "Be sure to keep the flame over the wound, else I'll see not where I'm cutting. Best to kneel at the head of the bed. Keep Miguel's head cradled between your knees and thighs. Secure his wrists with one hand, the candlestick with the other."

Shakespeare did as she instructed. Rebecca repositioned Shakespeare's hand in the air.

"Hold the light here. Like this. Don't move. Don't drip tallow on him. Don't get in the way of my field of vision. And keep Miguel firmly anchored no matter how strenuous his movements be. One slip and he'll not walk again."

Shakespeare and Dunstan nodded.

Rebecca said, "God give me strength and judgment."

Picking up a clean towel, she covered the green nodule of pus, then lifted a knife and placed the blade against Miguel's skin. She'd shaped the blade's edge razor thin. A fine job, thanks be to God. A well-honed instrument cuts cleanly and quickly. Rebecca positioned herself comfortably and incised the skin. Miguel came alive, jerking in the men's grips, howling in pain.

"Hold him, damn it," Rebecca cursed, deepening the cut.

Miguel screamed, panted.

"I need a towel," Rebecca said to Dunstan.

"Which one?" Dunstan asked.

"Any of them, you woodcock, just give me one. The cut has filled with blood and I can't see beyond my initial incision!"

Dunstan offered her a small one, and Rebecca snatched it from his hands. She dabbed the wound, deepened and widened the cut. Miguel sobbed.

"Keep breathing," Rebecca said. "Shakespeare, wipe his brow."

Rebecca asked for a bigger knife, enlarged the site. Miguel was exhaling rapidly, out of control.

"Breathe with him, Shakespeare," she ordered. "Exhale, inhale, exhale . . . slow it down, Willy. Inhale, exhale. Keep that rhythm. Inhale, exhale . . . Clutch the bedsheets, Miguel. Curse, my love! Just keep breathing. Inhale, exhale."

Rebecca dried the blood, began to slice into the fascia and underlying muscle. She told herself: *at all cost, avoid lancing the green boil.* She covered it with a rag and began to probe for the broken dagger blade.

More blood. Rebecca blotted it away.

"Inhale, Miguel," Shakespeare ordered. "Exhale."

Miguel continued screaming. Rebecca said, "Dunstan, cover his mouth with a rag. He'll become faint if you don't *and* someone will hear us. Breathe slower, Miguel," Rebecca said. "Slow it down. Clutch the bedsheets, my love. Thou will be well, I swear it on my grave. Inhale, exhale . . . The light, Shakespeare." She jerked his hand and moved the candlestick directly over the open skin. "Keep it there! Dunstan, another rag!"

"Aye," answered Dunstan, reaching over to grab a towel.

"Keep Miguel immobilized, damn you!"

"I can't hand your surgery tools and hold his legs!" Dunstan protested. By Pythagoras, he thought, she has been infused with her father's spirit."

He offered her the rag. She grabbed it and snarled,

"You're worthless!" Again she soaked up the blood from the wound. Now the exploration. Gods, how could Miguel be so pale yet so full of blood! She probed with the ice pick, felt a hard surface embedded in a layer of tissue. She brought the tip of the pick against the surface and scratched. Metal to metal. Thank God! She'd located the snapped blade.

Dunstan noticed that Rebecca had broken into a smile.

"We're through?" he asked.

She shook her head. "Just do what you've been requested to do and molest me not with questions! Hold the light closer to the cut, Willy." She blotted the blood from the wound and began to strip away tissue from the buried blade. Miguel groaned, screamed, bucked. Dunstan gripped his legs and held fast, his brow wet from exertion. Shakespeare's arm began to shake, having been suspended in air for over ten minutes.

Miguel screamed as he felt his flesh ripped apart. His fingernails tore at the mattress. He buried his head against Shakespeare's upper thigh. Another stab of agony. He chomped down onto something—flesh—Shakespeare's flesh. The player gasped but kept the light steady.

"What happened?" Rebecca asked, not taking her eyes off her work.

"Miguel just bit me," Shakespeare said through clenched teeth. "No matter."

Rebecca sopped up more blood with a clean towel. All of the blade was nearly exposed, yet the most difficult part of the surgery was yet to come. The tip of the blade lay periously close to the gray nerve column. Rebecca took a deep breath and began to tease the remaining shreds of flesh away from the blade.

A section of the spine was exposed, glistening white sheets of nerve.

Steady! Delicately! She often heard her father mutter those words to himself. Dear God, her father! Think not about that now!

Concentrate!

A piece of tissue had coursed its way around the tip of the broken blade. Long and sinewy. Not tissue. A tendon? A nerve? A blood vessel? Elastic, shiny. A nerve. But leading where? She asked for the tongs, used them as a clamp to hold back tissue from the surgery site. Miguel howled.

Rebecca felt her head begin to spin, the sickly sweet smell of blood overwhelming her nostrils. She closed her eyes and envisioned an intense sky of crimson. Reopening them, she took a deep breath. The same sky assaulted her vision.

Calm! Steady!

She took the ice pick and looped it around the nerve, tried to stretch it over the tip of the dagger.

Too short. No success.

Another approach.

From the top.

She dried the cut with a clean towel and began to peel away the broken blade from Miguel's tissue. Shakespeare held his breath. Slowly, the blade loosened from the fascia and muscle. Inch by inch. Yet the tip of the blade remained stubbornly fixed to Miguel's flesh, the nerve encircling the blade.

Damn!

Rebecca cleared her throat, her eyes and head throbbing. Miguel was whimpering, his breathing shallow and choppy. Again she retracted the nerve, eased away bits of flesh from the blade. So close to his spine. God help her.

The tip would not budge.

Miguel was growing paler by the second, his breaths nothing more than pitiful puffs.

No choice!

Rebecca picked up a knife and cut the nerve. Quickly, she dislodged the rest of the broken dagger blade and removed it from Miguel's back. Shakespeare and Dunstan let out audible moans of relief.

"That's it," Rebecca said wearily. She dried the wound and doused it with a special potion formulated by her grandam. Miguel cried with agony when she applied it gently to the open sore. Rebecca examined the tissue and reapplied the potion.

"Almost done, my love," she said to Miguel.

Minutes later Rebecca was sewing up the ripped seam of skin, each stitch tiny and done with precision.

"You don't tent the wound?" Shakespeare asked.

"No." Rebecca rolled her eyes. The Gentile surgeons placed cloth inside the incision site to allow scarring to take place. But Grandmama's way was to mend the skin together as if it were torn material. Her father learned the procedure from the old woman, and his wounds always healed the cleanest of any doctor in London.

After she'd finished the stitching, she coated the incision site with a salve she'd prepared on Krabbey's ship, then dabbed Miguel's forehead with a rag. She said to her betrothed, "You'll recover faster than a peregrine's flight."

His breathing was still very weak.

Rebecca opened a vial and said, "Miguelito, chew on this. It's moldy cheese."

Miguel's lids fluttered, opened for a second, then closed.

"Grandmama swears by it. It wards off the evil vapors that invade the weakened body," Rebecca said.

Miguel didn't respond.

Rebecca placed a small bit of blue cheese in his mouth. His cheeks were hot, burning with fever. "If thou art too weak to chew, allow it to melt in thy mouth. Twill serve the same purpose."

Miguel nodded almost imperceptibly. The cutting and probing upon his body had ended, and he allowed the poppy syrup Rebecca had administered to overcome him. He fell asleep.

Rebecca rinsed and dried the knives. She ordered Dunstan to take the knives back to the inn's kitchen.

"Now?" Dunstan asked.

"Yes, now," Rebecca said. "They'll want them for the gentlemen's dinners tomorrow."

Dunstan gathered the supplies and slammed the door shut.

"Bastard," Rebecca muttered. Marry, the room stank. Blood, sweat, seed, urine. Miguel had pissed on the sheet. But she said nothing. She looked at Shakespeare, at Thomas.

"Do you need some poppy syrup for your leg?" she asked her cousin.

Only sleep, was Thomas's answer. He placed Reina on the floor, stretched out and closed his eyes. Rebecca began to apply salve to the cuts above her eyes.

"I'll do that for you," Shakespeare said, taking the salve.

"Much thanks," Rebecca said.

"Are your cuts tolerable?" Shakespeare asked.

"Aye, they're tolerable," she answered. "It's hard to discern between pain and exhaustion." She glanced down at Reina. The little girl had curled into a ball.

"She has the proper idea," Shakespeare said. "We'll all do better in the morning."

Rebecca covered the child's exposed shoulders and kissed her good night.

Shakespeare dropped to the floor in front of the hearth. Rebecca smiled at him, cocked her head to the left. Shakespeare felt his heartbeat quicken. Rebecca's lips were puffy, her eyes as well, yet the look she gave him sent shivers down his spine.

He said, "Come, my lady. Let me give thee sweet succor."

Rebecca blew out all the candles and fell into Shakespeare's arms.

Dunstan returned a few minutes later, aching with weariness. But once he saw Rebecca with Shakespeare, he became revitalized with jealousy. Yet he could say nothing, do nothing, even as Rebecca boldly caught his eye and smiled. He lowered his sore body onto the floor, next to the child, and forced himself to stay awake until he was sure that Becca and the player had fallen asleep, that nothing beyond kisses had passed between them. Only when he heard them breathe rhythmically did he let slumber's soothing arms rock him into blackness.

40

Blessed be God, Miguel was strong and young and his fever broke within twenty-four hours. Two days later, able to sit upright as long as he wasn't required to move, Miguel insisted that they head back for London. Pedro needed to be buried religiously, alongside the other conversos. Rebecca implored him to rest, explaining that the young boy's body could be brought home by Thomas and Dunstan while she and Shakespeare waited for him to recover. Miguel wouldn't hear of it. Three days later, at dawn, they began their long journey back to London.

The unrelenting rain made the first part of travel ponderous. The horses moved tentatively, faltering at each yank of the reins. The paved roads were heavily pocked, the cracks overflowing with mud and slush. The nautical tarpaulin they'd purchased from Krabbey kept Miguel and the little girl dry, Rebecca thanked God for that, but she and the others had no protection from the unmitigating downpour. Wet, cold, stiff, they plodded through the rain, their bodies parting the sheets of water like curtains.

In the afternoon the rain let up slightly—enough to make out the vast gray landscape before them. The highways remained treacherous—rivers of mud. The horses sloshed through the dirty water, the muck splashing onto the men's boots and hose. A few pools proved deeper than had been thought. Once it was necessary for Dunstan and Shakespeare to dismount and pull Rebecca's stallion out of knee-deep sludge.

Onward.

Nightfall.

Another inn.

The morning on the road again, the weather had grown worse. Cold winds nipped at their faces, bit the tips of their noses. Rebecca shivered until her body gave up and allowed the chill to invade her bones, feeling as if she'd been dipped in icy starch.

Reina constantly cried for her mother, her father. Dunstan comforted the little girl, sang her Spanish songs of his youth. Rebecca thought of her own parents, prayed that her father had been released and was home safe, that he was worrying about her instead of the other way around. Her father had not been a paradigm of patience when she was a child, always quick with the reprimand and the back of his hand. Yet, more than anyone, it had been he who had noticed her achievements, who had bestowed upon her lavish praise when she had accomplished something of value.

Mother had been more balanced. She was kind, but had been heavily involved with Father's business, occupied with running a household that seemed always in a state of flux. Jews coming in and out, traveling to the Low Countries, to Mytilene, to the Rhineland and the New World. Never time to answer Rebecca's questions. Never, never time for play.

Nurses had been strict—lessons in needlepoint and music, instructions on how to maintain the stillroom and the knot garden. Her tutor, John Cherry, had been a nervous twit, leaving her to learn most of her Latin and handwriting on her own. There had been Emmanuel, her oldest brother, and he'd eased the boredom by telling her tales, but he had died too soon, leaving Mother behind a barrier of sadness. Sarah Lopez had retreated inward, giving Rebecca occasional wistful smiles as she related to her bits and pieces of the old ways in Spain—the old religion.

Everybody always on the go.

Twas Grandmama who had comforted her when she had skinned her knee, when Benjamin had hit her, when her father had slapped her, when Mother hadn't had the will or the time to utter proper words of solace.

Rebecca ached from cold and fatigue, but it was loneliness that lay so heavily on her heart. She missed her family, missed her home. Then she thought, how much more so did this little orphaned girl miss her home and family. Rebecca needed to be strong, and knew that she would be. Witnessing the mission firsthand had changed her. Her hands, just like the men's, had been needed for survival. And just like the men's, they, too, had become cut and blistered as they'd pulled upon rigging. They and God had also saved Miguel's life. Rebecca had gone from observer to participator. And a small toddler and her dead little brother had taught her the word sacrifice.

She prayed. With God's help, tomorrow would find them home.

They reached Holborn the following nightfall. Upon their entrance into the Lopez manor, Rebecca's mother fell to the floor and prostrated herself. Martino rushed to his mistress's side and eased her back into her chair.

Rebecca knelt before her mother, let her head rest in her lap. She glanced up at the worn face, shocked by the rapid deterioration in Mother's normally fastidious appearance. Her gray strands were greasy and loose, carelessly streaming out of her coif and bun. Her nightgown was dirty, spotted with food stains, as if she hadn't dressed in days. Her breath was foul, her nails dirty. Her face was chalky white. She seemed so frail. Rebecca hugged her mother's knees and cried. How much pain had *she* suffered these past few weeks?

Sarah covered her face and wept out, "God be praised, I thought I'd never see any of you again!"

"Amen," they responded.

Sarah allowed herself no more than a moment's worth of crying. Uncovering her face, she dried her tears and went to work. She summoned blue-gowned chamberlains, grooms, footmen, scullions, handmaidens—dozens of servants in all. Ride into London and retrieve a doctor for Sir Thomas and Master Miguel, as they are in need of medical care! Make up the toilet! Light the fireplaces and dress the travelers with clean clothes! Prepare a supper of fresh victuals! Take the child and set up a nursery!

Dunstan gave Reina to a young handmaiden who looked to be no more than fourteen—a dark-skinned beauty, probably a Morosca. Famished, but not for food, Dunstan whispered in the maiden's ear that he'd join her and the baby in a moment. The girl's skin reddened behind her ears.

Sarah barked more orders to Martino, demanding that he supervise the chores with a watchful eye. Make sure everything was done perfectly.

"By your will, mistress." Martino hurried off.

Sarah commanded, "All of you, upstairs!"

Dunstan felt a sudden hollowness. Something wasn't correct. *Sarah* was giving the orders. His stomach began to churn. "What news, dear Aunt," he inquired anxiously.

Rebecca lifted her head and asked, "Has Father—"

"No news yet, children," Sarah said, twirling Rebecca's wet hair in her fingers. She lifted her daughter's face and kissed her cheek. "Lord Burghley's men were here yesterday, sifting through Father's papers, searching for evidence of God-knows-what. Of course, I'd hidden—"

Sarah looked at Shakespeare and smiled demurely—a smile he'd seen before on her daughter's face. Sarah cleared her throat, then said, "Of course, I preferred to remain hidden from the ordeal and witnessed not their quest for . . . whatever. Uncle Solomon and Cousin Jacob arrived early this morning from Mytilene and await with Benjamin at Burghley's house, where Father is under arrest. We all pray that the matter will be handled with much expedience at court tomorrow. Now, upstairs all of you, lest you wish ague upon your haggard bodies! The chamberlains await you with dry clothing. Go!''

As the rest of the men started for the staircase, Rebecca said, "A minute more in your hands, Mother."

"Becca, you must dress or you'll catch your death."

"Just a minute, I pray you. I've missed you so much!"

Sarah couldn't hold back the tears. She cried as she stroked her daughter's wet head, still cradled in her lap. She was so proud of her and told her so.

Rebecca said, "I only did what was expected of me."

Sarah was taken aback. Rebecca's voice had become as grave as her own. What had happened to her little girl? Sadly, Sarah knew the answer.

"Mother?" Rebecca said.

"Yes, daughter."

Rebecca's eyes began to water. "The little girl's brother . . . He was not as fortunate as we were." Her voice dropped to a whisper. "His body is outside, wrapped in sheets. . . . I think it proper that we tend to the matter as soon as possible."

Sarah sighed and nodded. "Go upstairs, Becca. I'll take care of it. I've buried many a child in my day."

"And while the men make merry with food and drink, they've saddled you with an old woman?" the hag asked Rebecca. The old woman was in bed, propped up with pillows, holding her granddaughter tightly in her arms.

Rebecca answered, "They invited me to join them for supper and I chose to be with you, to tell you my tale personally. However, if you remain unpleasant, I'll leave for company of better cheer."

"Bah," scoffed the old woman, squeezing Rebecca harder. "If I meet not your approval, find the door."

"I love you, Grandmama," Rebecca said.

"I suppose I love you as well. I've no choice. You're the only one who still converses with me."

"If you wouldn't act so moonstruck—"

"I am moonstruck!"

Rebecca smiled, then grew quiet. The old woman knew that she was thinking about her father. The hag had thought about him as well. She sighed, knowing that she couldn't say anything to comfort her granddaughter.

"Now you have experienced firsthand your father's travails," Grandmama said.

"Yes." Rebecca turned to her. "Do you ever wonder if we've done more harm than good in trying to smuggle Jews out of Spain? Had we not interfered, Pedro would have been alive. Yes, he would have been taken into a Catholic family and raised in the Papist religion, but he would have been counted among the living."

"They would have made him a priest," Grandmama said.

"A living priest," Rebecca argued.

"Then someone would have found out his origins—the child of *relapsos*—and he would have been rooted out. Brought before the tribunal of the Holy See. They would have tried him, condemned him, tortured him, then murdered him before a crowd of cheering olive-skinned bastards. Is any cruelty too strong for the Iberian Papists and their blackhearted forked-tongued Bourbon prince? God knew what was best when He plucked the child from this earth, rest be to his ashes."

Rebecca said, "Even with all the torture, Grandmama, you lived. . . . You . . . *lived.*"

"Yes, child, I lived. And I suppose I'm glad I did. A burden it is to make choices for our children. We're not perfect specimens, we make mistakes. Had the boy's mother known what was in store for him, she might not have opted for escape. But in the end, Becca, is it we who choose or God? Pedro's fate, our fate, is God's will."

"I envy your faith, as strong as the hands of Samson." Rebecca snuggled deep into her grandam's bosom. "How did *you* keep loving a God who'd condemned you to torture?"

"I didn't always love Him. There were times when I was certain that God had forsaken me. But in the end I was remembered by the true Master of the universe."

Rebecca paused, then asked, "Pray, how *did* you escape the dungeons?"

"I never escaped the dungeons."

Rebecca waited for more.

"A moment while I recollect my thoughts." The old woman closed her eyes, trying to visualize a memory interred decades ago. "I am back there now. Dark. Foreboding with the smell of the wretched and the dead. God have mercy upon their souls."

The hag moaned.

"When the torture failed to elicit the wanted response, the Inquisitor ordered me back to jail to await my final punishment."

Back to despair, she thought, back to hopelessness.

"My cell had been a box. I could not stand. I could not lie down. But I could sit if I hunched my shoulders in a certain manner."

"Dear God—"

"Terrible it was. Rats and vermin were my constant companions." The old woman could feel them even now, upon her skin, licking her sores, gnawing her fingers and toes. The memory made her shiver. "But the rats were the least of my troubles. The guards were the true beasts. Taking advantage of a young girl whenever they wished, not a drop of decency in the toadish pack. If there lives such an animal as 'Christian kindness,' I've yet to pet it."

Rebecca lowered her head and thought of Shakespeare. He had been more than kind, he'd been her savior, a saint. But she didn't say anything. She noticed Grandmama was shaking.

"You're cold," Rebecca said. She rose and threw well-seasoned wood into the hearth. The flames crackled, burst into sparks and let off a gush of warmth. She sat back down at her grandmother's bedside.

"Thank you, girl," the crone said.

"Can you continue?"

"I must. You must know my history." The old woman hesitated, then said, "Among the beasts there was this man named Alberto Ramires. Not human, but not as foul as the rest. He fulfilled his needs with my body, but at least was gentle about it.

"'Twas a miracle that you married after such treatment."

"I swore not to wed. As you have done many times."

Rebecca said nothing.

Grandmama smiled. "A vow sworn by the young is as good as broken. You'll marry. And you'll have children. More bairns than I had, if God be with you. Whereas your parents are your legacy, your children are your future. And so it was that through a child I had a future."

"How so?"

"Alberto Ramires had a wife, six daughters as healthy as breeding mares and a sickly son named Jaime. The boy was cursed with fevers, chills, a poor appetite, and bones so soft you could mold them around your throat for a chin piece. But the lad was the light of his father's heart, as most sons are. Your father is most unusual, treating you exceptionally well for a girl."

Grandmama stroked Rebecca's cheek.

"But Ramires was the more ordinary Spanish padre. The sun rose and set on little Jaime, and every time the boy became ill, which was often, Ramires would become mad with fright. Now, he knew that I was learned in the Levantine practices of medicine. That I, as a Jewess, knew secret arts passed down from mother to daughter . . . or from grandmother to granddaughter. Whenever the child was afflicted with an illness, Ramires came to me."

"And you gave him your secrets after what he'd done to you!"

"Aye."

"I would have spat in his face!"

"And you would have erred, Becca. What good would have passed had I killed the child by withholding my secrets?"

Rebecca was silent.

"You would have done it as well," the hag went on. "I gave Ramires our remedies. Ground cow hooves for the boy's bones, salts for the fevers—"

Rebecca added, "And cheese mold."

"He was hesitant, but I convinced him. The child lived through many a difficult bout of illness because of my potions. And in the end, God, in his infinite mercy, showed me kindness—*Jewish* kindness."

Rebecca smiled.

The old woman said, "God chose the moment of my destruction to show the rotten Papist his supremacy!"

The hag went on to explain how Spain and Portugal back then were still separate countries, how Portugal was anxious to imitate their Spanish cousins and set up tribunals. In 1540 the Portuguese Holy See finally met with success. Grandmama held the honor of being the first Portuguese Jew sentenced to be torched to death.

Grandmama said, "I was determined to die the way I had sworn to live—a Jewess. I cursed the Inquisitor General—a foul snake named Don Henrique, with a beak for a nose. I wished him to the Devil, would have shat on him if they'd allowed me the opportunity. I refused their stinking salvation and their hateful false god—some woodworker nailed to a cross—and they refused me mercy. They tied me to the *quemadero*—the stake—and Queen Catalina herself lit the pyre under my feet."

Grandmama paused to catch her wind. Rebecca held her breath.

"The flames began to rise, enveloping me in smoke. The pain . . . Ah, how could I speak to you of the agony!"

"Grandmama, perhaps we should stop—"

The old woman shook her head. "I remember screaming, my roasting flesh being burnt off my feet. I called out God's name! It was as if an angel put the word in my mouth. I saw my soul leave my body. I saw it wrestle with an angel, Rebecca, so help me I swear it! Then I must have fainted. Upon my awakening, I found myself gasping for breath, lying in a man's arms."

"Ramires!" Rebecca said. "He saved you!"

"Yes. He'd hid me in his house. His wife bandaged my feet, gave me oil for my lungs—they had been badly burnt."

"And that's not Christian kindness?" Rebecca said.

Grandmama laughed. "There's no such animal, I tell you. Ramires wasn't being kind to me. He *needed* me. He'd been my sentry the day I was chosen to be consumed by the conflagration, and had arranged to guard me for his own purposes. As the Almighty would have it, his son fell ghostly ill the day before the auto-da-fé and he wanted my arts. So when the smoke was thick, he unloosened my binds, wrapped me in burlap, and threw me to a waiting servant. In my place a live goat was sacrificed.''

"This happened in front of the Inquisitor's eyes?'' Rebecca asked incredulously.

The old woman began to choke with laughter. "In front of the Inquisitor . . . and the King and his piggy queen . . . and thousands of stinking Portuguese Papists! I wish I would have been awake to enjoy it!''

The hag doubled over with laughter that turned into spasmodic coughs. Rebecca gave her a sharp rap on the back.

"I cannot fathom such a feat,'' she said.

"My granddaughter,'' the crone said, wiping away tears from her eyes, "there is no way to describe how heavy was the air, how putrid and repulsive was the stench of burning flesh. If wizards can make themselves disappear behind their cloaks, if pigs can learn to count, if beggars can foretell the future with divine fits, how much easier is it to snatch a woman behind a blanket of smoke and fog! Who would have assumed so bold, so unexpected an act?''

Grandmama paused. "Now ponder this, granddaughter. Had I been reconciled to the Church, they would have been 'merciful' and garroted me before reducing my body to ashes. Ramires wouldn't have had his chance to save me. But because I chose to die as a Jewess, God—blessed is He who has the power to restore Job—was merciful and let me live as a private, unmolested Jewess . . . of sorts.''

"If you call having your feet burnt away—to be left in life a cripple—merciful.''

"There are diverse qualities of mercy, young mistress.''

"I still cannot imagine how Ramires stole you away in front of all those watchful eyes.''

"He had accomplices.''

"Ah, he had help.''

"Aye,'' said the crone. "Ramires knew what was required to operate so brazen a task. Later I found out that he'd bribed other sentries to secure their aid.''

"And they agreed?''

"I'm here to attest to the success of Ramires's scheme. I was removed from the pyre, with nothing for feet save bones, and brought to the Señora Ramires. As I lay recovering from burnt lungs and feet, I mixed salves, medicines, potions, drugs, brought the child again back to health. My life depended on it.''

How many times had Ramires told her that if the child died, so would his nurse.

The old woman said, "Had Ramires been discovered harboring me, his whole family would have been murdered."

"He risked his entire family to save his son?" Rebecca said. "Yes."

"That was most intemperate," Rebecca said.

"Wait until you have children, my granddaughter. Perhaps then you'd not be so quick to condemn."

Rebecca hugged her grandmother fiercely. "I thank God for what I consider to be Ramires's poor judgment."

"You'll crush my bones, you stupid girl," the old woman said. "Off of my body."

Rebecca released her.

Grandmama continued her story. How Ramires kept her hidden for well over a year, until his son had grown robust. Then her presence was no longer needed. Ramires couldn't just turn her loose. The Holy See might have found her and learned of the details of her escape. Instead, Ramires packed the hag into a crate, went out into the countryside, and sold her to a brothel.

Grandmama said, "At least as a whore I was not required to stand."

"Oh Grandmama! How dreadful!"

"Not as dreadful as the dungeon. I used to thank God every morning for allowing me to see sunshine."

"I love you," Rebecca said, squeezing the old woman's hand.

"Don't you get mushy on me, mistress. I loathe sentimental tripe!"

"Oh, shut up, you bony old harpy!" Rebecca answered. She felt an encroaching yawn and stifled it. The need for rest had suddenly seeped into her body, but she had to hear more. "Tell me the rest of your tale. How'd you get to England?"

"By being well-spirited in bed."

"Grandmama!"

The old woman explained that she'd been nice to a certain man and he'd gotten word to her relatives. They'd bought her freedom, sent her to Turkey, and found her a husband—a crookback missing one eye.

Grandmama said, "My husband David could not function as a man, yet he was my godsend." The old woman's eyes filled with tears. "My daughters, Rebecca! He found my babies. Brought them back to me! I will always worship him for that!" The old woman started to cry.

Rebecca was taken aback. Never had she seen her grandmother so suddenly emotional. Rebecca rocked the fragile body. "What . . . what babies?"

"Your mother and aunt . . . My babies were taken from me. In the brothel . . . I had become pregnant . . . twice. They took them away from me. Ah, the pain was so much worse than the fire that had eaten my flesh. . . ."

The hag nearly collapsed with sorrow.

Rebecca said, "Stop—"

"No," said Grandmama. "Someone must know the truth before I die. I have told no one, not your mother, not your aunt. I was afraid they would have hated me."

"No, Grandmama. Never!"

"Daughters of a whore, their fathers unknown . . ."

"They love you!"

"How I loved them, my babies! Nothing else mattered to me. And they were ripped from my breast!"

"I pray you, stop these horrid memories!"

"No, Becca, painful memories they are, but not horrid. You must know. I cannot die in peace until I've unburdened my soul."

Rebecca nodded for her to go on. The old woman stammered out how her husband David was deformed but wealthy. He used his money for good, searched for three years, until he found her babies. They'd been used as slaves by a wealthy couple in Braga, had been beaten when they worked too slow.

"Aunt Maria was six when she was brought to me," the hag said. "Your mother was four."

Rebecca was stunned. "Mother never told me."

"Mother was too young to remember, thank God. Aunt Maria still possesses one or two dark shadows of her childhood, but actually recalls very little. Blessed is time. How mercifully it heals." Grandmama wiped her eyes. "Maria responded readily to her Christian forename, and I continued to call her that. Your mother was such a quiet, scared little girl. She didn't seem to care about her peasant name—Concepcion—so I named her Sarah, our first matriarch."

"Sarah is a beautiful name," Rebecca said.

"I thought so." The old woman sighed. "Those days were different, Becca. Darker. We had no organized smuggling as we have now. At that time twas easier for me to move back into Portugal than to smuggle the girls *out*. The sentries at the dock were very wary of children leaving the country—almost a sure sign that a Jew was trying to escape and taking their children with them."

Grandmama resumed her tale. After she was smuggled back into Portugal, she assumed many names to avoid detection by the Holy See, moved at least a dozen times. Luckily, their constant relocations didn't arouse a great deal of suspicion, because her husband had been a merchant and traveled a lot.

The old woman said, "But the need of a continual watchful eye proved to be very exhausting. My life almost collapsed when your stepgrandfather died. I . . . I didn't see how we could go on."

Rebecca held the old woman's trembling hand, kissed it gently.

"Maria was twelve," Grandmama continued. "She'd almost reached her majority, thank God. Both she and your mother were beautiful girls. Twas easy to find them proper husbands—men who still retained the old ways. Through Uncle Solomon, I was able to marry Maria to Uncle Jorge.

"*Your* mother was our first step into the business of smuggling Jews. Through Uncle Solomon, your father expressed a desire to marry my Sarah. I agreed. We packed your mother in a crate and shipped her out to England, right under King John's nose. Twice we were almost caught at the docks. Yet we continued undeterred. Thank God, we were successful. Next, Roderigo and Jorge conducted my safe passage out of the country. Twas an ordeal, as I couldn't walk. Jorge had to carry me to the docks on his back! He slipped me onto the boat, stowed me in a hatch in the deep hours of the night."

"Blessed be God, you made it."

"Yes. And once I was secure in England under your father's wing, Jorge and Maria escaped to the Isle. Thanks be to the Holy One, we are now all together! Your father and Uncle Jorge had sworn to help others, if God would help them in their efforts—a vow they had taken and had *kept*, at great expense. But God shall see them through these difficult times."

"Amen," Rebecca answered. She thought about her father's arrest, but the pain was too intense. Pushing the thought out of her mind, she knitted her brows in confusion. "How old was mother when she married?"

"Ten," said Grandmama.

"Ten?"

"Your father didn't touch her until she was fourteen. A promise he made to me and Uncle Solomon. Though Mother be his legal wife before the state and God, Father was an honest man. Ach, your father, *my* son-of-marriage, has his peculiarities. But never will I speak ill of him who has treated my daughter as a princess."

Rebecca's eyes began to mist.

Grandmama said, "Now, you've heard your history. Go and get some sleep."

"Shall I sleep with you?"

The old woman shook her head. "I'm like the wolf. I thrive

in solitude. Go upstairs to your bed. Say *tehilim* for your father's release.''

''I have,'' Rebecca said. ''Many times.''

''Say them again.''

Rebecca rose, emotionally drained and physically exhausted, overwhelmed by her grandam's revelations. She was the granddaughter of a woman she worshiped, but also the granddaughter of a whore, her mother's paternal bloodline a blank page. Rebecca wiped the old woman's forehead with her sleeve. The hag slumped in her bed and said,

''Let me rest, girl. Perhaps tonight I'll find eternal peace.''

''Grandmama, don't—''

''Sha, girl. I was never afraid of dying. Twas living that always caused me fright.''

41

A nightmare had jolted Rebecca awake.

Miguel was dead.

The night winds and rains were furious and unforgiving. Icy drafts leaked through the windows and doors of the Lopez manor, emitting deep moans throughout its black hallways. Teeth chattering, Rebecca drew her shawl tightly around her nightdress and cupped her hand around the waning flame of her candlestick. The house seemed ghostly, and fear pricked her skin. But it was idiotic to feel afraid. She'd witnessed more peril in the last few days than most men had experienced in a lifetime. Yet here she was in her own home, safe, out of harm's grasping fingers, and she couldn't ward off her demons.

She hurried to Miguel's chambers, and to her relief, her betrothed was peacefully asleep, his chest rising and lowering in steady rhythm, his brow dry and cool. His father Hector sat slumped in a chair, head back and mouth open. Hector's superior attendant, Elija, kept watch over both of them. He told Rebecca that Hector had fallen asleep about an hour ago, after Miguel had awakened with enough strength to eat and drink aqua vitae. Rebecca asked about the young master's medicines and Elija assured her that Miguel had taken all of them per her directions.

Rebecca observed Miguel for an hour, absorbing his sweet slumber as if it were her own. After her nerves had steadied, she trudged back down the long hall to her quarters. A few feet from her bedchamber a sudden gust of wind extinguished her candle. Rebecca groped her way to her door, shutting it quietly and bolting the latch. Though her cell was as dark as mud, her nighttime vision was sufficiently acute to make out the oblong shape under her counterpane.

A body.

She gasped and covered her mouth, yet the shape reacted not to the noise, remaining still. As her eyes further adjusted, she gradually recognized the form, the sleeping face.

Shakespeare.

Rebecca smiled. She let her shawl fall to the floor and placed the candlestick upon a table. Tiptoeing to her bed, she lay her hand gently upon his shoulder. Her touch seemed magical. He began to unfold, blossoming like a flower in the sun. His eyes opened and his lips curved upward in a dazzling smile.

Through the window blue veins of lightning arched across the sky. Thunder crackled a moment later. Rebecca hugged her shoulders.

"I bid thee welcome to my tent," Shakespeare said, holding open the covers. "Let me be thy sheik."

Rebecca buried herself in his arms. Shakespeare's skin was hot and damp and warmed her own chilled flesh even through her nightdress. Her fingertips danced upon his naked arms and chest, upon the defined relief of his muscles. A flash of heat burst through her body as powerful as the lightning outside.

Shakespeare gently lay her onto her back and lifted the hem of her gown to her waist. He lowered his body onto hers and wedged his thick legs between her slender limbs. He kicked off the blankets and felt for her breast, but his hands caressed only cloth.

"Need you all this wrapping?" he whispered, tugging her nightdress upward.

Rebecca shook her head.

Shakespeare raised her gown over her head, tossed it aside, then lay his head upon her large, soft breasts. Rebecca arched her neck backward and moaned as she ran her fingers through his hair, stroked his neck and back. Shakespeare nibbled her flesh, kissed her nipples, sucked them, gently bit them. His hands reached up to her face and lips. Rebecca kissed the fingers, then lightly licked them one by one. Tears welled up in her eyes and streamed down her cheek. Shakespeare felt them drip upon his hand and looked at her.

"Why dost thou weep?" he asked softly. "Do I offend thy chastity with my advances?"

"Thou knowest my virtue has been blackened by dishonesty."

"To me thou art as honest as any maiden that lives."

"Tell me thy will," Rebecca whispered.

"To be thy Will," Shakespeare answered.

Rebecca smiled. "Aye. Thou are my Will."

Shakespeare said, "And thy will shall be as mine."

"Nay, not as hard as thine," Rebecca said.

Shakespeare laughed at the pun, softly kissed her cheek.

Rebecca said, "My sweet William, play not with me like other false lovers."

"Is my love for thee so shallow, expressed solely under covers?"

"My will from other men has suffered much taint."

"My will from thy will can suffer no more restraint."

"Aye, is it only burning lust that binds thy love to me?"

"Hot flames first held the lock, tis true, but thy love now holds the key."

"And thou shall feel the same when dawn doth shine her light?"

"As morning blossoms its petals of gold, shall my love grow in its might."

"Everything my hand hath touched has brought upon it strife."

"Yet by that hand thy betrothed breathes and shall live to call thee wife."

"If my father's mishap should pass to thee and bring thee ill, I'd die."

Shakespeare smiled. He said, "Far be it me to cause the death of a delicate butterfly. Kiss me, maiden."

Rebecca brought his mouth onto hers, then gently bit his lips. She said, "I speak with deadly earnest, Willy. My father's situation is grave, can bring us to our graves. For the sake of thine own sweet neck, thou knowest it's best if thou knowest me not."

"Thou fled not from *my* dangers, my love. Remember how close the knife was to *thy* heart?"

Rebecca thought back to that night, the black shadow poised above her, the point of a gleaming dagger perched over her chest. She shuddered.

"Tell me what thou desires, Becca," said Shakespeare. "By my will, it shall be done."

Rebecca lowered his head back onto her chest. Together they toasted imaginary glasses, drank the nectar of earthly delights.

* * *

Shakespeare awoke screaming. He jerked himself into a sitting position and panted like a hound after the chase. Rebecca sat up and hugged him from behind.

"What is it?" she whispered.

He shook his head, trying to slow his breathing. Dawn had cracked through a rain-streaked sky. The wrath of the winds hadn't seemed to dwindle with the light of the sun. Rebecca looked at her hourglass. Gods, it was after six. How late she'd slept. Sound and sweet had been her dreams. Not so for her lover—her *true* lover.

"What is it?" Rebecca repeated. "What demons have fouled thy precious sleep?"

Shakespeare swallowed dryly. "Too much blood," he said. "Too much death!" He ran his hands over his face, then exhaled into his palms. "I dreamt of fountains of blood. Of scarlet rivers emptying into an ocean of crimson. Twas as if Israel's God had smitten His fury upon England as He'd done in Egypt, and had turned its waters red."

And more . . .

Harry had been in the dream, drowning in a pool of red.
Help me. Help me.

Mackering throwing Shakespeare down a well filled with blood, closing the lid, leaving him wading in eternal blackness.

"Only a dream," Rebecca said, rubbing his shoulders. She kissed the nape of his neck. "Only a dream."

"Though my nightmares live solely in the cells of my brain, they are reality, Becca. My ghastly images are as tangible to me as if they existed in the flesh."

"Thou must tell thyself over and over that what thou seest is fantasy."

"I cannot allow myself to distinguish between fantasy and what is earthly. To do that would be to destroy what I am. No, those horrors that invaded my sleep are now a part of me—as real as thine own sweet arms. Yet there are ways of exorcising devilish spirits without denying their existence."

"Tell me."

"To destroy he who has infused them inside my head."

"What does thou meanest?" Rebecca said. "It were the evil Spanish who had planted such naughty seeds in the field of thy brain. Dost thou intend to destroy the nation?"

"The Spanish?" Shakespeare let out a hollow laugh. "Ah, the bastard Spanish. No, my sweet Becca. Those aboard the galleon were not the Devil's disciples—just men serving their ship, their captain, their country. I hold no ill will toward them, though they be responsible for a little boy who died in my arms. No, the Spanish have not placed Hell inside me. But there lives another, an asp that lies in wait, ready to strike the guileless when least expected. A man who woos evil by raping the honest. By my troth, shall he live until my vengeance with Harry is completed. Then by my hands shall he die.''

''Which man?''

''A man who had uncovered my nakedness—stripped from me time and dignity. Time can never be repaid, yet I could have forgiven him the days I've lost. But he stole from me with relish the fragile feather called manhood. He confined me to darkness, wished my body and spirit to wither and rot. Only the nourishment of a fruitful mind kept me alive. And I survived—but *not* unscathed. Fiendish dreams do haunt me, evil visions surround me. For these sufferings shall the wolverine pay with his life.''

''Whose life?'' Rebecca asked. He seemed to be talking as much to himself as to her. ''Willy, what dost thou mean?''

Shakespeare was silent. Rebecca saw the muscles of his jaw tighten. His hands were clenched into fists.

She asked, ''Willy, what happened to thee this past summer? Who has made thee taste such bitter herbs?''

Shakespeare said nothing.

''Tell me!'' she begged. ''Is it Mackering?''

Shakespeare suddenly turned around and kissed her lips. ''Dress quickly,'' he said. ''I hear thy mother bidding thee a good morrow.''

''Thou dismisseth me as if I were some scullery maid!'' Rebecca said.

Shakespeare closed his eyes and brought her hand to his lips. ''I love thee,'' he said.

Rebecca sighed. ''I love thee too.'' She nuzzled his neck with her nose and kissed him lightly, gently prodding his sides with her fingertips. Shakespeare laughed.

''I'm easily tickled,'' he said. ''Stop that.''

Rebecca continued. Shakespeare pushed her down onto her back and pinned her arms at her side.

''Make thy move, wench,'' he said.

Rebecca knitted her brow a moment. ''Thou hast forced me to take drastic measures, Shakespeare.''

''Aye?''

''Aye.''

''What?'' he asked.

''I'll have to employ my feet!''

She swung her legs upward and tried to knee him in the belly, but he avoided her blow. Straddling her body, he pinioned her legs against the mattress with his own.

Rebecca squirmed in his grasp, trying to free her hands. ''Let me go,'' she said.

Shakespeare said, "First, make thy requests with lordly respect."

"Let me go!" Rebecca said.

Surprised by the harshness in her voice, Shakespeare released her. Rebecca wriggled out from under him, sat up and rubbed her wrists.

"Did I hurt thee?" he asked, concerned.

Rebecca shook her head. "No. I greatly mislike being restrained."

"I see that," Shakespeare answered. "My apologies. I was toying with thee. I meant no harm."

There was injury in his voice. Rebecca held his hand and answered, "I know. It's just that . . ." She waved him off.

"Tell me," Shakespeare said.

"I hate being weak," Rebecca said. "I loathe being at the mercy of those stronger than I, depending on their good graces for my freedom." She looked at Shakespeare. "I've spoiled the playfulness of thy mood. *My* apologies."

Shakespeare turned away and said, "I left my clothes in the spare bedchamber—where I was to have slept last night."

"I'll get them," Rebecca said. She paused, then said, "I don't know the dreadful deed that Mackering had imposed unto thee, but I am sorry thou suffered at his hands, Will."

"I thank thee for thy sympathy," Shakespeare said.

Rebecca opened her arms and they held each other in a soothing embrace. She asked, "Did Mackering kill Harry?"

Rebecca felt instant tension in her lover's body. Shakespeare remained motionless for a moment, then slowly shook his head. "I don't think so. But the uprightman had much to do with my mentor's death. And so I shall have much to do with his."

42

Had Essex the power, he would have strangled the bitch. Her Royal Highness—a vicious old harpy with sour breath. She sat upon her throne as snug and smug as a roosting hen. The room was small, cold air leaking through the shutters. Wind dusted his forehead, rushes blew about his boots. But Essex was hot. Standing before the Queen, he could feel pools of perspiration under his doublet, the starch of his collar wet and sticky. He felt as taut as a bowstring yet he dared not take his eyes off Elizabeth. That would enrage her further.

He sneaked a sidelong glance at Robert Cecil. The fawning woodcock—kneeling by the throne as still as a turd, the hump of his back almost level with the top of his head. He was as deformed in mind as he was in body. A malevolent gnome he was, the puny crookback, cast from his father's mold—stupid, slow, plodding, a damn Puritan. And that ever-so-smug smile plastered upon his lips. How Essex wished he could smash Cecil's face to bloody pulp. Nay, fists were for commoners. A rapier up the hole of his arse! And another down his throat! Skewered like a pig in an open pit. If the bitch would stop her railing, if she'd just leave the two of them alone—

"Devereaux, I'm talking to you!" Elizabeth screamed.

"Twould take a deaf man not to hear you, madam," Essex said.

Elizabeth bolted from her throne and yelled, "Then I must have my loyal and trusted physician, Dr. Lopez, examine your ears, as you seem not to attend to the words I speak! And kneel before your Queen lest I reprimand you for showing disrespect to your God-given monarch!"

Essex felt himself go even hotter. Lowering the shin of his left leg behind him, he extended his right leg in front of him, bent at the knee, foot flat on the floor. He cringed at the thought of his staff waiting motionless by the door, watching his debasement. How could she do this to him, *her favorite*, in front of his servants!

Cecil stifled a smile and regarded the Queen's pet. Essex was simmering, his cheeks as red as his hair. The Earl's dark eyes oozed with ire, his long but womanish beard dotted with spittle. His round nose was pink and wet, the pores open, the nostrils flaring. The starch of his collar was now running down his back. All in all, the young lord's appearance was anything but noble.

The more the Queen ranted, the easier Cecil breathed. They were two of a kind, Essex and the Queen—sanguinous cousins—red-hot hair and red-hot temperament. Yet this time the Queen was on *his* side, even though it was for the wrong reason. Cecil couldn't understand Her Grace's loyalty to this lowly Jew of a doctor, but anything he could use to give himself and Father the upper hand over Essex was well worth pursuing. So, allies with the Jew he and Father would be. Allies until Lopez's political currency had been devalued to nothing.

Elizabeth sat back down. She said, "Where is he now?"

"Who?" Essex asked.

"Lopez, you dolt!"

"He's still with my father at Burghley House, madam," said Cecil.

Elizabeth smiled at Essex. "I mention my doctor's name and you flinch, Devereaux. Why is that?"

A witch, thought Essex, just like her mother. She must have eyes in the back of her wig. Aye, the name Lopez enraged him. The man was a mite, yet for some ungodly reason the doggish Jew found favor with Her Grace. The beaked-nosed mutt and the steel-cunted bitch—what a duo they made. Arf, arf. And de Andrada! How he wished he could find *that* worm and crush him!

Dr. Lopez's house is full of treasonous evidence, de Andrada had assured him. Yet when they searched—

"Unplug your ears, Devereaux!" screamed Elizabeth. "Your mistress speaks!"

Essex could no longer hold his tongue. "Madam, you rebuke me in front of my loyal staff, in front of those that hold me in esteem—"

"So much the pity for them that they have such poor judgment!" Elizabeth smoothed the stomacher of her gown. "You, Lord Essex, are a rash and temerarious youth! How dare you insult the honor of my trusted physician, Dr. Lopez, thereby insulting my honor as well!"

Essex bit his lip, then said, "I was informed by trustworthy servants that madam's physician was conducting matters of malice—"

"Madam," Cecil said. "If I may be so bold to interrupt Lord Essex—"

Elizabeth said, "Spare the wind, Cecil, and make your point!"

"We have conducted an extensive search of Dr. Lopez's manor in Holborn. No matters of malice nor any writing of intelligence have been found in his home—"

Essex said, "The Jewish doctor—"

"Lopez was baptized, Essex," the Queen interrupted him. "He attends state's services on the sabbath. He is a good English Protestant."

A false Protestant, Essex thought. But something in the Queen's voice told him not to press the issue. He said, "Lopez lets a cell in the city—at Mountjoy's Inn, where he is said to conduct business of a secretive nature."

"Lord Burghley's men searched his cell at Mountjoy's as well," Cecil said. "Aye, his business was most personal, madam. We found trinkets and toys belonging to various young ladies—none of whom were his wife. If Dr. Lopez be guilty of sedition because of this deceit, then almost all the noblemen of court should be arrested for treason!"

"Enough of that, Cecil," Elizabeth said. "You need not cast aspersions upon the faithful and true lords to prove your point."

"My apologies, madam—"

"Yes, yes," the Queen said, brushing Cecil off. "What say you to that, Devereaux? Shall we hang and quarter my faithful servant because his codpiece isn't exclusively reserved for his wife? I've been told that *your* codpiece is like your arguments. Both suffer from loose points."

Essex boiled over with anger. "I had the man arrested not because of his diverse mistresses, but because he posed harm to Your Grace!"

"And what harm is that, Essex?" Elizabeth said. "Your men made their own search of the man's house. No secret papers were found upon the premises."

"He deals with the King of Spain, madam!" Essex bellowed. "Philip, King of Castile, your sworn enemy!"

"Bah," Elizabeth scoffed. "His Majesty is old, with brains as runny as his bowel movements—that's not to infer that the Papist is harmless. Indeed not! But methinks the green monster of jealousy shines deeply in your eyes, Devereaux. How many times have you come to me hoping to win favor in my heart by relating to me rumors concerning the Papist monarch?"

The Queen laughed out loud.

"Haven't you looked like an ass, dear lord, when I reported to you that Lopez had told me the selfsame rumors two days earlier. Your sources are slower of pace and dimmer of wit than those of my doctor."

Essex clenched his fists. "I still proclaim the man a spy!"

"No one is interested in your proclamations. Least of all Your Grace," said Elizabeth. "You mislike Lopez because he pleases me. Yes, he's a drooling dog to be sure, but amusing. And the man has useful relatives throughout the world, Devereaux. That pleases me greatly."

Essex said, "Madam, if you'll permit me to explain—"

"Your explanations thus far have done anything but explain," said the Queen. "Open your ears and listen. You might even learn a trick or two." Elizabeth walked across the hall and stood in front of the hearth.

"It's frosty in here," said Elizabeth. "Cecil, I grant you the honor of warming Your Grace by stoking the fire."

"By your will, madam," Cecil said, picking up a poker.

Essex started to rise. Elizabeth shouted out, "Stay where you are. Have I given you permission to stand?"

Essex turned scarlet.

Elizabeth said, "You loathe Dr. Lopez, Robert, because he advocates peace with Spain and stability for the English treasury.

You, however, crave glory in a Spanish war and money from my purse strings. Well, young lord, you'll have neither until you learn the meaning of the word temperance!"

The Queen turned to Cecil and said, "Nothing has been proven against my servant, Dr. Lopez. He is to be released immediately!"

"As you desire, madam."

"'Tis what *justice* desires," Elizabeth said. "You do know the meaning of that word, do you not, Lord Essex?"

Essex could no longer contain his fury. He stood and turned his back to the Queen.

"I haven't dismissed you, Devereaux."

"Aye, you haven't," Essex said. "I've dismissed myself." He stomped out of the room and slammed the door behind him. His servants stood at the doorway, trembling with fear. Elizabeth shooed them away and they quickly exited the hall.

Elizabeth sighed. "What am I going to do with him, Cecil? The young lord needs a weathervane, as he possesses much misdirected wind. I fear that someday he'll find his neck on the block."

Only savvy prevented Cecil from smiling.

Rebecca stirred the mush, then fed a spoonful to Miguel. He immediately spit it out and demanded meat.

"Meat isn't good for your stomach," Rebecca explained.

Miguel said, "How can you feed me such vile victuals? Get me something edible. If not meat, fowl or fish."

"Miguel," Rebecca said, "this is a special preparation that will promote healing—"

"It's slop!" Miguel answered angrily. "You're to be my wife. Act dutiful and get me real food!"

Rebecca shrugged off his harsh tongue. Five days ago they had been equals—fighting side by side. Now, suddenly, he'd become her *master*, she his nursemaid. He'd changed since the beginning of the mission, having become prone to fits of temper even before their harrowing experience. He had turned as moody as his brother. Ye gods, was her beloved friend, her *confidant*, turning into a prig like Dunstan? Was this her lot in life? To be the wife of a prig, and one who fancied men at that?

Miguel noticed Rebecca's tired expression and softened his tone. "This muck is unpalatable, Becca," he said. "Taste it."

"I have," she said.

"Well, I can't stomach it," he said crossly.

"Very well. I'll bring you something else."

Rebecca stood, but Miguel took her hand and held her back. Kissing it softly, he said, "I'm not hungry anyway."

"You must eat, Miguel," Rebecca said. "Your father hopes that you'll be well enough to make a brief appearance at the festivities tonight."

"Come down to the hall, carried—or in a wheeled chair—like an invalid?" Miguel said incredulously.

"The chair is only temporary," Rebecca said. "You'll be able to walk soon."

Miguel knocked the bowl out of Rebecca's hand. "I'd rather die than present myself a cripple! Tell my father that I'm sore with pain and temper and I'll have nothing to do with any banquet. Though God knows the extent of my gratitude concerning your father's freedom."

"By your wishes," Rebecca said.

They sat in silence.

Miguel squirmed, then announced, "Becca, I am born with a curse. The Almighty knows I've tried, but I cannot change. Though my head tells me to love women, my body keeps pulling me to men. That's not to imply I cannot function as a man. I've had diverse women—"

"Miguel, let's not discuss this now," Rebecca said.

"I love you as a sister," Miguel said, ignoring her. "You understand my needs, I understand yours, Becca."

"Rest," Rebecca said. "We'll talk about this when you're stronger."

"I've much strength!"

"I know. All I meant to say was—"

Miguel blurted out, "You didn't sleep alone last night."

Rebecca felt her body stiffen. So that was the reason for this conversation. Yes, Miguel understood her womanly needs as long as they weren't acted upon.

"So?" she said coldly.

"You cannot slap me in the face, Becca!" Miguel exclaimed. "You cannot embarrass me in front of servants and staff! How much I'd suffer if such indiscretion should come to my father's ears! Is this your idea of being a goodly wife?"

"I never asked to be married!" she cried. "I never *wanted* to marry—not to you, or even your brother for that matter. But no one was ever interested in what I wanted!" Her voice suddenly wilted. "All I desire is peace. What do you *want* from me? To shut out my womanhood at eighteen?"

Miguel sank back into his propped pillows, feeling sapped and short of breath. Stabs of pain shot through his back and sides. "I feel hot," he said.

Rebecca felt his forehead. Miguel had refused to eat his medicinal mush and the fever had returned. She excused herself, returned ten minutes later with a leather pouch full of ice and placed it on his forehead.

"Where's Shakespeare?" Miguel asked.

"Tenacity has always been your strongpoint," Rebecca said. "Shakespeare's been holed up in the North Chamber since dawn, writing . . . something. I've invited him to stay for Father's homecoming."

"And he accepted the invitation?"

"Yes." Rebecca looked Miguel in the eye. "Shakespeare fought with us, side by side. He deserves to partake in the banqueting. Tomorrow he returns to his rented room within the walls of London."

Miguel said, "You still love him, don't you?"

Rebecca felt a sudden rush of emotion. With a trembling voice she answered, "With all my heart."

"And he loves you?"

"He says as much."

"And you believe him?"

Rebecca said, "Miguelito, his words are gold."

"Yes," Miguel said. "They're beautiful, but are they solid?"

"They're true," Rebecca answered.

Miguel sighed. Who was this player anyway? A middle-aged, balding nothing, who was married to boot. How could he resist a dazzling young woman like Rebecca—a woman of superior rank? But the player was brave, no denying that. Daft as well. Lovestruck! Why else would he fight for Jews? Miguel knew he couldn't protest Rebecca's dalliances with the player, because he had nothing to offer her in return. But he was still her betrothed. One day he would be her husband.

He said, "As your future master, I've two demands."

"Speak," Rebecca said.

"One, don't dally with the player under the roof of our home. Two, give me at least *one* legitimate heir—a son we both know is mine. I can provide your womb with ample seed, Becca. *Younger* seed."

Rebecca felt her cheeks go hot.

"Agreed?" Miguel asked.

"You ask me as if I had a choice," Rebecca said.

"As my wife, you don't have any option but to obey me." Miguel squeezed her hand. "But as my dearest friend, I beg this of you."

Rebecca smiled.

Miguel was a wonderful man, so much kinder to her than those in the past who had ached for her body. She kissed him and swore that she would honor his requests.

Miguel hugged his pillow with his left hand. "Becca?" he asked.

"What?"

"When will I be able to move my right arm? It feels completely dead."

Rebecca felt her body begin to shake. She knew she'd have to tell him, but that didn't make this moment any less dreadful. To make matters worse, Miguel was right-handed. Rebecca picked up the limb and curled the fingers into a fist. The muscles underneath were still full and tight. "Try to move your fingers."

"I *have* tried, Becca," Miguel said exasperatedly. "Many times. How long will this last?"

She bent the limb at the elbow, scratched the underside of the forearm. "Can you feel my nails?"

"No."

She scratched another spot.

"No, nothing," Miguel said. "I tell you the arm is dead. When will it heal?"

Rebecca rotated his arm at the shoulder joint. She asked Miguel to repeat the motion, which he did.

He said impatiently, "My shoulder is well . . . except for the limitations of the stitches in the back. It's my *arm*, Becca."

She ran her hands over her face, then said, "Miguelito, certain nerves had to be cut when I removed the blade from thy back."

"How long will it take for them to mend?" Miguel asked.

Rebecca felt tears coming down her cheeks. Very softly she said, "Nerves do not mend, Miguel."

Miguel's head jolted up. "What!" he whispered.

"Nerve tissue is very delicate—"

"My arm is to remain lifeless forever?" Miguel said, breathing rapidly.

"Calm yourself—"

"Cannot a master surgeon repair the damage? Sew the nerve together again?"

Rebecca wiped her cheeks with her fingers, then laid her hands on his shoulders. "No," she whispered. "I'm so sorry. Perhaps another more skilled than I could have done better."

Miguel felt weak. The room spun before him. He closed his eyes but still felt himself spinning, flying through the air. He remembered the feel of the dagger sinking into his back. He gasped as he envisioned Thomas breaking through the water's surface, Thomas's flailing arm pushing the poniard deeper into his spine.

Miguel became dizzy, nauseated. He couldn't talk.

"I'm sorry, Miguel," Rebecca cried. "Please forgive me. I'm so very sorry."

Miguel reached out for her hand and listened to her sob. His own weeping was silent.

43

Sarah Lopez had personally supervised every detail of the homecoming. She'd stood side by side with Cook, sweating in the kitchen, peering over his shoulder, sampling his dishes. The meats were undercooked, Sarah complained. Back into the oven, she ordered. The lettuce was wilting, she railed on. The scullery maids had been careless and had left the leaves in hot air! More sweets! Does not the master enjoy gingerbread as well as sugar cakes? More comfits! More marmalades!

The mistress of the manor was equally as demanding with the doctor's personal body servant, Martino, with the chamberlains, the footmen, the grooms. Boil the water for the bath now! Sarah insisted. A goodly mistress dare not let her master wait even a second for a good, hot soak! Kindle the fire. Lay out the doctor's clothes. Prepare his turnspit, his toilet!

Rebecca spent most of her time tending to Miguel and keeping out of her mother's way. She had tried to talk to Shakespeare, to catch him alone, but it seemed a pair of eyes were always upon her; Dunstan's, her mother's, Hector's. Wherever she walked, lay people or staff watched her—men and women with wagging tongues.

Do no dishonor to thy husband.

Yet Rebecca hurt to see her lover and was determined to meet with him alone to exchange vows of love and passion.

The opportunity came shortly after three of the clock. Miguel was asleep. Rebecca tiptoed out of his chambers, down the hall to the guest closet. Shakespeare answered her knock immediately and pulled her into the room, into his arms. They kissed passionately. Shakespeare abruptly broke it off.

"I cannot stay here past tonight," Shakespeare said. "I'm an unwelcome guest. At best, I'm tolerated by thy kinsmen with thinly veiled contempt, at worst, I'm glared at with open hostility."

"I love thee," Rebecca said.

"I love thee as well," Shakespeare said. "Let us flee to the

Continent together! To France, to Genoa, to Venice, Becca. I speak Italian and they will welcome my talents as a bookwriter—''

"I cannot."

"Thou can do whatever thou wishes."

"I need time."

"Time for what?" Shakespeare asked.

"Miguel still mends. I must care for him."

"Thou told me that he's past death's clutches."

"Yes, but—"

He grabbed her shoulders. "Come with me!"

"My family . . ." Rebecca faltered. "I have to think about this, Willy."

Shakespeare snapped back, "They sell thee as if thou wert merchandise. Dunstan offered me money if I'd leave thee forever. *Pounds*, Becca, not pennies, not shillings . . . *pounds*!"

"I'll kill him," Rebecca swore.

"Yes, my lover," Shakespeare said. "Kill him with action. Come with me!" He hugged her. "Come with me."

"I'm a Jewess, Will," Rebecca whispered.

"Thou art a lawful Christian," Shakespeare said. "Thou wast baptized."

Rebecca shook her head.

Shakespeare sighed. "No matter. Together we'll both be baptized—anointed into the Church of Rome. What difference does it make how we worship, as long as we're together?"

Rebecca said, "What of thy wife and children?"

Shakespeare whispered venemously, "Why dost thou lay stepping-stones in front of a blind man? I love thee and thought thou felt the same."

"I do—"

"But not enough," Shakespeare said.

"Thou asks me to become a Papist," Rebecca said. "Dost thou lovest me enough to become a Jew?"

Shakespeare stared at her. "Why would thou wish such a curse upon me? A Jewess, thou art, but thy soul shall be saved by me, thy Christian husband!"

"I don't want a Christian husband," Rebecca said. "I want no husband at all!"

She gasped the minute the words were out of her mouth. Shakespeare dropped his arms to his sides.

"Then what am I to thee?" he asked. "A toy to be petted and fondled until novelty erodes and passion is spent? Am I then to be tossed aside?"

"No, Will," Rebecca protested.

"I'm willing to give up everything I own for thee," Shakespeare said. "Wilt thou do as much?"

"I don't know . . . you must give me time to think."

"How much time? An hour? A day? A year?"

"A year," Rebecca said.

"After thou hast married Miguel, eh? And I noticed thou hast addressed me with a you. Is our intimacy dead?"

"No . . . marry, I cannot think clearly." Rebecca's head began to pound. "Give me until the end of the year. It's only six weeks away."

"And what magic shall come to pass then?"

"Will, I pray you—I mean I prithee, I *beg* thee, give me time. Thou hast asked me to give up my family, my religion—"

"I give up my family and religion, my land and language as well. Gods, I *postponed* my revenge on the Devil for thee—"

"Settle thy revenge," Rebecca said. "Thou'll not sleep until thy revenge is complete!"

"Providence has ordained that I shall have my vengeance," Shakespeare said. "But thee . . . I feel our hearts beating further out of rhythm with each minute that passes."

Rebecca said, "I pray, give us six weeks."

"No," Shakespeare said. "The moment is now. This minute! Once thou art ensnared into the bosom of thy family, I've lost the battle."

Her sweet, sweet William. She couldn't bear the thought of losing him. Of going through life without his touch. She said, "I will do whatever thou desires. But I beseech thee. Let me see my father one more time."

"Then tonight thou'll come away with me?"

Rebecca bit her lip. She couldn't let him go. Her body needed him as sure as it needed blood. He was her sustenance, her vapors of life. What heaven it would be to wake up in his arms. She was consumed by his love, and her brain was beyond its reasonable wits. She exhaled, then rapidly nodded.

"Swear it!" Shakespeare said. "Swear thou'll come with me. Swear by thy God."

"I'll swear it by *thy* God," she answered. "Very soon to be *my* God."

Shakespeare paused, then said, "Well, then, swear by my God—*our* God."

Rebecca pledged her troth in the name of Jesu Cristo.

The Great Hall of Roderigo's house greeted him like the arms of a lover. Its walls were covered in brightly hued arras work, its stone floors covered with sweet rushes sprinkled with aromatic herbs. Torches and candles were lit from every wall sconce. The night was dreary, cold and wet, but the fire in the hearth burned as never before. *Warmth.* He'd forgotten its feel.

Looking around, Roderigo tried to get oriented. His family, attired in their finest clothes, was lined up in front of the dais, waiting to greet him. Three dozen servants, scrubbed shiny, stood nervously at two long trestle tables, waiting for him to be seated at the place of honor—at the dais, in the middle seat. His chair was as big as a throne. Yes, he was king of this house, but he felt as awkward as a commoner. How long had he been imprisoned in Burghley House? A week, they had told him. It felt like a month.

Rebecca anxiously awaited her father's entrance. Never had she seen him looking more haggard. Deep folds of flesh underlined his eyes, his beard seemed to have grayed overnight, his walk had become stooped and old. His fur-lined physician's robe hung on his thinner frame. She held her tears in check and waited patiently as Roderigo greeted those who stood in line before her. Uncle Jorge, Uncle Solomon. Hector Nuñoz, who made excuses for Miguel's absence. Roderigo said he understood and would minister to Miguel as soon as the festivities were over.

Next, Roderigo greeted Benjamin and his nephews—Dunstan, Thomas, Cousin Jacob, and Enoch, Uncle Solomon's son.

Then the women. Her mother bowed before her master, openly crying. Roderigo gently chided her for her emotional outburst. But there was kindness in his scolding. The quiver in his voice only made Sarah cry harder. Then Roderigo dutifully kissed his sister-in-law Maria, Dunstan's wife Grace, Thomas's wife Leah, and patted their children on the head. The last in line was Reina. Roderigo inquired who she was, and after Dunstan explained, Roderigo picked her up and kissed her forehead. Dunstan announced that she had been adopted by his family, and Roderigo commended him for his generosity.

Absent was Grandmama. With a cursory question, Roderigo dutifully asked about his mother-in-law. She was ill but sent her love, Sarah told him.

Roderigo cast his eyes upon his daughter. Rebecca kneeled before her father, but Roderigo lifted her upward and took her into his arms, hugging her as tightly as his strength would allow.

"Dear God," he cried. "I quaked with fear at the thought of dying. Yet worse was the thought that I'd never see you again."

Rebecca whispered, "I love you, Father."

Roderigo continued embracing her, rocked her in his arms.

Shakespeare witnessed the reunion with the staff of the kitchen—at the request of Rebecca's family.

That's not to say we don't appreciate your service, Sir George Ames had said. *But we must explain your presence to Dr. Lopez, and as we will not have adequate time to properly—*

Shakespeare had cut him off, saying he understood.

Sir George had offered him money.

Shakespeare had refused. He now wondered whether it was a wise decision. His pockets were nearly empty after sending Anne his money, the theaters were bolted shut, and he hadn't received funds for his writing from his patron, Lord Southampton. Had Shakespeare accepted the converso's money, at least he would have walked away with *something* tonight. For as he looked at Rebecca in her father's arms, he knew that her troth would never come to pass.

44

Shakespeare listened as Rebecca made her excuses, unmoved by her pleas, tears, and promises. They stood just inside the front entrance to the manor house, speaking in hushed tones, Rebecca holding his sleeve and hoping that this meager physical joining would keep him by her side. She begged for some more time. Six weeks at the most. She was obligated to Miguel until his recovery was complete. Her father would be devastated if she left so soon after his terrible ordeal. She just wanted a little more time with her grandam.

When she finished her impassioned speech, he simply shrugged, pulled away from her, stuck his hands in the pockets of his jerkin and closed the door behind him. Rebecca cursed and followed him out into blackness, down the estate's arcade, oblivious to the winds and to the freezing rain that sprayed her woolen nightgown.

"Don't leave now," she implored. "It's three hours until sunrise. At least wait till the crow of the cock."

"The gates of the city will be open by the time I walk the distance," Shakespeare said.

"I'll come to thee this afternoon," Rebecca said.

"No."

"Tomorrow, then," she said.

"No."

"When?"

Shakespeare reached the end of the colonnade and adjusted his hat. Stepping into the courtyard, he was assaulted by downpour.

"When can I see thee?" Rebecca repeated, walking into the open space. She didn't flinch even as water showered her face and nightclothing. Angrily, she brushed wet strands of hair from her eyes.

"When can I see thee?" she repeated, following him.

"Farewell, Rebecca," Shakespeare said. "I wish you good hap."

Rebecca grabbed his arm. "I *will* elope with thee, my love, but I need time. Just grant me a little extra time."

"Take as much time as you require," Shakespeare said.

"I'll meet thee today, at two of the clock at the corner of Old Jewry near Gresham's mansion."

"You may do as you wish," Shakespeare said. "'Tis no concern of mine."

"Willy—"

"You'll catch ague if you remain unprotected in such cold, mistress."

"The outside chill is but a balmy breeze compared to the ice of thy heart," Rebecca said.

Shakespeare said, "I pray you, release my arm."

"I'll come to thy closet *directly*," Rebecca said. "At two. Swear to me that thou wilt receive me."

"No."

"William, please!" she said, shivering. "Just give me a chance to explain. Then if thou desires to cut me out of thy life, I'll not object."

"Let go of my arm."

"Promise me."

"Promise you what, mistress?" Shakespeare said.

"I'll be in the city at two." Rebecca steadied her voice. "Please, I beg thee, let me come to thee and explain my position."

"Your position is clear, Rebecca," Shakespeare said. "It couldn't be clearer."

Rebecca yanked her hair and stamped her foot in a puddle, splashing mud and water up into her nightdress. Shakespeare noticed her feet were bare. She began to cry.

"Go back inside, Becca," he said tenderly. "Please."

"Then swear thou'll meet me at thy closet at two," Rebecca said.

Shakespeare paused. It was useless to argue with her. She was as tenacious as a bulldog. He agreed to meet her. She made him swear it.

"At two, then." Rebecca smiled as she trembled. "Thou'll be there waiting for me?"

"Aye."

"Thou swore it."

"I know."

"And thou shalt keep thy pledge?"

"Aye," Shakespeare said.

"I love thee, Will," Rebecca said.

Shakespeare stroked her damask cheek and said, "Back into the house, m'lady."

"I love thee," Rebecca repeated.

Shakespeare swatted her bottom. "Go."

Rebecca wiped away tears and rainwater from her face and headed back to the manor. Shakespeare wondered whether she *really* believed he'd keep his pledge.

By the dinner hour he was well fed, packed, and penniless. He'd taken "The Rape of Lucrece" off to William Jaggard for printing, allowing plenty of time for the Stationer's office to register it by the upcoming spring. In Shakespeare's leather pouch was a copy of the poem for Southampton. If hap be sweet, the earl would be moved to tears, so emotionally swept away by the poetry that he couldn't help but part with some gold coins for its writer.

After the success of *Venus and Adonis*, Shakespeare's friends had been astonished that he didn't abandon the stage and acting in favor of writing pamphlets. But Shakespeare understood the whims of public taste, that his writings could suddenly lose popular appeal and he'd be left destitute. The life of an actor and bookwriter was, in its own curious way, more stable. Plays could be written quickly and altered just as fast. They could be made timely by simply inserting a reference to a current topic. More important, the fellowship, if successful, was financially independent—not at the mercy of a benefactor's purse strings.

Shakespeare was confident that the earl would find the dedication of "Lucrece" to his liking and would enjoy the poem as well. If Southampton was as generous as he'd been in the past, Shakespeare would have the means for a merry Christmas with his family—a big yule log, presents for the children, and pots of ale for wassail. Christmas with his loved ones—his parents, Anne's parents, the children.

And to think he'd been ready to give it all up for a Jewess. Aye, he'd been correct the first time he'd laid eyes upon Rebecca. She was a witch.

Yet, strangely, he wished her no harm. All he wanted to do was forget her, to distance himself from the perfume of her body, from her silken touch. . . .

Shivers trailed down his spine.

Maybe in another lifetime.

His schedule: first Southampton, then Christmas with the family, then on to Brithall—to Henley manor house.

Talk to the priest, Mackering had told him.

Harry, the Catholic—a man as faceted as a royal jewel.

Shakespeare threw his bag over his shoulder.

Rebecca had waylaid him once. But no more. He didn't feel even a tinge of remorse at breaking his pledge. Hadn't she broken her troths countless times?

Shakespeare closed and locked the door of his closet, leaving behind no note of explanation. Rebecca was a clever wench. She'd read the unwritten lines.

45

𝕴t was not the Christmas Shakespeare had imagined.

Its beginnings had been promising. Anne had been delighted with her Christmas present—three sovereigns wrapped in gaily colored paper. She'd even kissed him spontaneously, loved him wickedly the night of his return. Yet the longer he stayed in Warwick, the more he felt like a stranger in his own house. Anne's business never seemed to pertain to him. When he tried to talk to her about domestic concerns—the condition of the house, the health of their parents, Hamnet's schooling—Shakespeare sensed a note of impatience in his wife's voice. She seemed even *less* interested in what had happened to him in London since his last home visit.

Their dialogues were soon steeped in cold silence.

The morning after Twelfth Night, Shakespeare was on the road to Brithall.

Travel was slow, but the inns were warm. He was able to afford the best, thanks to Southampton's generosity—more money than conceived in his most fanciful dreams. His pockets and purse jangled pleasantly as he rode. Rich with coins, poor with love.

By the time he arrived up North, freezing rain had turned to snow and sleet, muddy trails covered with strips of gray ice. Winter had fallen upon the country, draping the mountains, hills, and grasslands with yards of folded white velvet. The air had been mercifully calm on his trek upward, the winds stinging cold but gentle. Aye, the snow fell constantly, but it was as if Providence had chosen to tickle the landscape this January rather than to pummel it.

He reached the outskirts of Brithall on January ninth, shortly before the supper hour. It took him another ten minutes of riding through open snow drifts before the manor came into view. Riding up to the gatehouse, he pulled his horse to a stop, reached inside his bag and pulled out the personal letter of reference from Margaret Whitman. Though Shakespeare had spoken briefly with the lord of the manor, Viscount Henley, on his first trip up North, he'd not met the priest. The letter assured the lord that Shakespeare was trustworthy and would defend the secrecy of the Jesuit with his life. Shakespeare wondered whether that was true, but hopefully he'd never be forced to prove the boastful words. He placed the letter back in his cloak. The parchment was of poor quality, and if left too long in the cold, would freeze and crack.

Shakespeare studied the manor. On his last visit he'd been so engrossed in the house's magnificent gardens that he scarcely looked at the building itself. But now, with the rest of the land covered with white, Brithall stood out like a full moon against a black sky. Beyond the gatehouse was a gravel courtyard, then the entrance arch to the manor. On either side of the arch sat a hexagonal tower several stories high, ringed with leaded-glass windows. The peaks of the towers were embellished with rich plaster molding, cast in a rose and hawk motif—the Henley crest. On either side of the towers were square walls of cut stone. The left wing of the manor house seemed a bit larger than the right— no doubt it held the Great Hall—and ended in another tower fashioned like the pair flanking the arch.

Shakespeare waited to be halted by the guards at the gatehouse, and when no one came to greet him, he rode through the courtyard up to the front of the manor. He dismounted and knocked on the arched door—a solid piece of wood crisscrossed with iron—a door that should have been part of a fortified castle rather than a manor house. Unless, of course, the manor house concealed a priest . . .

It took five minutes before a footman opened the door. Shakespeare introduced himself, presented Margaret's letter, and then was left in the cold, waiting to see if Lord Henley would bid him welcome or send him away.

Another few minutes passed before the door was opened again by Robert Whitman, Viscount Henley himself. He was a man of dominating physical appearance—tall, swarthy, and solid. Nothing about him was subtle, a portrait created in dark, brooding oils rather than pastel watercolors. His beard was long and pomaded, his eyes tarry black. He nodded recognition, threw open the door and stood aside from the threshold, allowing Shakespeare to step inside. With a snap of his fingers Henley had his servants removing Shakespeare's cloak and gloves and brushing off his boots. A groom was dispatched to take care of Shakespeare's horse.

"We were just about to take supper," Henley said, his voice loud and deep. "I'll have one of the servers set a plate for you upon the dais."

Shakespeare was about to protest, but Henley cut him off.

"Come, good man. The ride up here must have been treacherous."

Shakespeare said, "Aye, but blessed be the Almighty, no storms did arise. And the inns of England are the finest in the world."

"God save the Queen," said Henley.

"God save the Queen," repeated Shakespeare. He stopped walking and pulled out a wrapped package. "If your lordship will allow me the honor, in humble gratitude I offer you a small trinket—a toy unworthy to be housed with such finery that your worship possesses."

Henley took the package, unwrapped it, and inspected it. It was a silver plate of sterling, heavy, and richly engraved. Henley knew it had cost the player well over what he could afford, yet he accepted the plate as if it were a bauble, thanking Shakespeare in a cool, detached voice. Any large display of gratitude would be ignoble, considering their differing classes. Still, Henley was impressed that the actor had taken such care in his selection of a gift. Harry had been correct in his assessment of his young apprentice. Long ago he'd said that Shakespeare was a man of unusual wit and taste. A clever man, not to be taken lightly. He knew much . . . too much.

"Shall we proceed?" Henley said.

"After your lordship," Shakespeare said.

"Well, then." Henley took the lead. "Come."

Shakespeare followed Henley into the Great Hall—as he'd guessed, in the left wing of the house. The stone walls rose fifty feet, the ceiling timbered and beamed with coarse slabs of dark-stained oak. Upon the walls hung selected weapons from the family armor. The dais, resting against the eastern side of the room, had a direct view of the open floor pit. Rotating on the spit—the broach—was a boar, its dripping fat feeding the crackling flames below. The smell of grease and fresh-cooked meat sent Shakespeare's belly astorming. It had been almost a full day since he'd taken a stomach. On the other side of the pit were two rows of trestle tables flanked by benches. On them sat the staff of Brithall, waiting for their lord to take his seat.

Henley kept his servants squirming as he introduced Shakespeare to his wife, Lady Henley, and his three daughters—Mistress Jane, Mistress Anne, and Mistress Gertrude. They were beautiful girls—blond like their mother, with deep blue eyes. Their bosoms were full, their skin ivory white. Shakespeare bowed deeply, and sensed immediately that the two younger ones held disdain for him. Not only was he not nobility, he wasn't even landed gentry. Yet the eldest daughter, Jane, had a gleam in her eye as she extended her hand for Shakespeare to kiss. Her fingers were soft and warm.

Shakespeare withdrew his lips quicker than protocol dictated, for he didn't want to give Mistress Jane nor Lord Henley any unwarranted ideas. Yet as hap would have it, he was placed next to Mistress Jane at the left end of the dais.

Finally Lord Henley sat down and the first course of fowl was served. Shakespeare's silver plate was piled high with moorcock and turnip, pigeon stuffed with figs, roasted goose, whole quail boiled in wine and plums, leek and pheasant coated with cinnamon, ginger, and honey. Accompanying the first course were pies of mincemeat, cheese tarts, spinach tarts, and bowls of fresh greens and wildflowers.

Shakespeare picked up his knife and cut the flesh of the birds into tiny bits. He was careful to avoid scratching the metal. He'd only eaten off fine sterling plates twice in his life, and the first time had been a disaster. He'd been completely unaware that silver was as soft as butter compared to pewter. He was determined not to make the same error twice.

Even though he was starved, manners prevented him from eating hurriedly. With measured pacing, he picked up pieces of meat with his fingers and put them in his mouth one at a time. He kept his eyes focused away from the damsel at his right. Yet he felt the warmth of her breath, smelled the perfume of her pomander.

The aroma of the girl made him ache for Rebecca. Gods, would the Jewess ever leave his mind in peace?

Mistress Jane had said something to him, but he didn't hear her. He begged her pardon for not hearing her the first time, feeling like a crude peasant. He knew what his characters would say in an uncomfortable situation such as this one—he could make *them* witty and charming at will. Yet when he was forced to live out the scenes of his mind, he felt like Moses—as if his tongue had been burned with coal, rendering him slow of speech.

"I asked if you were enjoying your meal," Mistress Jane repeated.

"The food is splendid," Shakespeare answered, head down.

"It usually is on Thursday," Jane said. "It's the night my lord father hosts grievances from the servants. Tis the only night of the week we're forced to sup in the Great Hall with the staff, instead of eating in our *private* dining hall." She smiled, leaned over and whispered, "My lord father thinks a grand banquet and succulent victuals makes the servants soft of heart and stomach, less likely to give him troubles."

Shakespeare nodded dutifully, and tried to concentrate on his food. Yet he felt Jane's eyes upon him.

"Does the strategy work?" he asked quietly.

"Beg your pardon?"

"Are the servants happier with a satisfied stomach?"

"I suppose so," Jane answered. "My lord father gets little uprising from the lower class. He and Mother run the household very sensibly."

Shakespeare returned his attention to his food.

"Have you been here before?" asked Jane. "Your face . . . I've seen it."

"Aye," he said. "I visited about six months ago."

"Yes, I recall you clearly now. You strolled the gardens with Father."

"Aye."

"About the same time as Cousin Harry's death."

Shakespeare said nothing.

"Did you know my lord father's cousin?" Jane asked.

"Yes. I knew him well," Shakespeare said. "How well did you know him?"

"Harry?" Jane smiled. Her eyebrows arched. "He'd been visiting Brithall since . . . before I was born."

"And," Shakespeare prodded.

"And that's all." Again the sly smile. "He was a bit of a cad. A harmless man, but Father never left us alone together. Just to make certain that our silly games were kept as such."

"What kind of silly games?" Shakespeare asked casually.

"Oh, tag and football and wrestling. Lots of play wrestling."

Shakespeare didn't answer.

"How close were you to Harry?" Jane asked.

"We were very dear to each other. As dear as—" He hesitated, then said, "As dear as cousins."

Jane pushed around the food on her plate with her knife. "Did he ever mention me?"

"He always spoke fondly of his beautiful cousins up North," Shakespeare lied.

Jane smiled again. "Did you ever meet Harry's wife?"

Her words were meant to display an air of casualness, but

Shakespeare detected a note of tension. Jealousy. He pretended not to hear. Jane didn't pursue the discussion.

"A pity he died so horridly," she said.

"A great loss it was."

"How do you think he died?"

"I wish I knew, mistress," Shakespeare said. He noticed an icy stare from Lady Henley and quickly turned his head away from Jane's. A moment later he felt the young girl's leg brush against his. Moving his leg to the left would cause him to sit in an awkward position, yet he felt he had to do something to discourage her advances. But what? A minute later her hand was upon his knee. Shakespeare felt himself go hot. Inconspicuously, he slipped his hand under the table, picked up hers and returned it to her lap. She slumped back into her chair and pouted. Her expression held anger tinged with emotional hurt.

The two of them ate in stony silence. Shakespeare managed to catch her eye and gave her a disarming smile. She smiled back, then coyly returned her attention to her food. A smart one she was, he thought. One rejection from a commoner was enough. She'd not have another.

"You're very isolated up here," Shakespeare noted.

"Quite," answered Jane.

"You must have few visitors to Brithall, mistress," Shakespeare said.

"Very few," said Jane wryly.

After the meal Shakespeare was forced to sit through hours of complaints. One by one the servants approached their lord, telling him their problems, hurts, and slights.

One scullion complained that a server was too much a prankster, purposely trying to trip him whenever he carried hot caldrons of pottage. The server denied the charges emphatically, claiming the scullion was angry with him because he, the server, had won the heart of the scullion's wench—a buttery maid. The maid denied having anything to do with either of the boys, insisting she'd rather join a cloister than to have unmarried fucking with men. Lady Henley blushed at the ungodly language. The girls giggled. Shakespeare held back laughter himself. Lord Henley rebuked both servants, settling the affair with a stern lecture and the extraction of a promise for peace between Christians.

It took almost two hours for all the grievances to be aired. Then came the accountings of the land. How many cows had given birth the past week? How much food were the sheep consuming, now that most of their land was covered with snow? How were their coats of wool growing? How many eggs were the chickens laying? Would the soil be adequately prepared for crops come the spring?

Some of Lord Henley's tenant farmers presented themselves. A few gave their lord coinage for their rent. One pleaded with him for an extension on his rent, saying that his wife and child took suddenly ill. He hadn't had a chance to work that week for his money. Lord Henley was a merciful man and gave the farmer another week to come up with his rent money.

The farmer wept with appreciation, heaping benediction after benediction upon his most gracious landlord.

It was deep into the night—almost nine of the clock—before all the problems were sorted out. At the conclusion of the dealings, Lord Henley stood. He, his family, and Shakespeare left the Great Hall, and the others returned to their household positions. It was time to bed for the night, but Henley was restless. Something was on the player's mind, and he aimed to find out what it was. Just the two of them. Alone. He asked Shakespeare to join him for a stroll in the long gallery and the player accepted the invitation. Henley led him back through the entry arch and up the spiral staircase to the second floor of the right tower.

The long gallery was sixty feet in length, fifteen feet in width, illuminated by torches resting in wall sconces. The walls were fashioned of smooth plaster and upon them hung the portraits of the family—past and present. A three-sectioned mullion window on the right allowed an excellent view of full-moon-lit orchards, now frozen over with snow. The left wall held three Norman arched windows—the old shutters recently glazed over, Henley announced. It made for less draft in the winter.

Henley pointed to each portrait and introduced the ancestor to Shakespeare. The Whitman family had originally come to England at the time of the Norman invasion. They'd been elevated to nobility—the Viscount Henley—during the reign of Henry the Second, Brithall granted to them as a reward from the king for their support in the Becket affair. Their great-great-grandfather was fluent in French and Italian as well as English and Latin, and insisted that the family head carry on this tradition.

"I speak them all," the lord said proudly.

"Truly remarkable," said Shakespeare.

"This portrait," said Henley. "This was my father's brother, Lord Chesterfield." The painting flickered in the muted orange light. "I speak no ill of my own father when I say this, but my uncle was quite an influence on me. Both of my uncles were."

"Have you a portrait of your other uncle?" Shakespeare asked.

A pinch of pink arose in Henley's cheeks.

"No," he said. "Not at the present time."

Viscount Henley quickly went on to explain that Lord Chesterfield was Harry's father. Harry had been the fifth of seven sons, and there had been four girls as well. Harry had been a wayward boy and caused his lord father a great deal of grief.

"There is no predicting how children will turn out," Henley said.

Shakespeare agreed.

Henley suddenly turned on him, "And just what was your passionate connection with my cousin?"

"He was my mentor," Shakespeare answered without pause. "He was my friend."

"And that's *all*?"

Shakespeare was puzzled by Henley's acid tone. "I don't know what you mean, m'lord."

Henley sighed and said, "He was a thorn in my uncle's side."

"Harry was a rare breed of animal," Shakespeare said. "He had his wild side. But I loved him."

"Why did you come up here?"

"I came to give my friend eternal rest. That cannot come to pass unless his murderer is apprehended."

"Just what are you implying?" asked Henley.

"Nothing," Shakespeare said. Once again he explained that he was simply trying to retrace Harry's last steps.

"And what do you hope to find now that you found not the first time you were up here?"

"An overlooked clue, mayhap."

"Have you discovered one?"

"Not yet, m'lord."

Henley took a step forward and started to pace the gallery again. He said, "Harry used to visit me and my family every year for two weeks right before Mayday. I allowed him to keep visiting Brithall out of tradition. My father had always been kind to Harry even though he'd known well Harry's . . . shortcomings as nobility. He never rose past his station. . . . As a matter of fact, he regressed!"

Shakespeare said nothing.

"So be it," Henley said. His voice had become louder and full of tension. "I'm not responsible for the sins of my kin. As children, Harry and I got on well, as adults, we were of differing rank and wanted nothing to do with each other. Yet the visits here served some purpose for him, else he would have stopped coming altogether."

Shakespeare held his breath. "Perhaps it was the priest," he suggested.

Henley looked him square in the eye, the flames highlighting his dark pupils—pools of smoldering coal. After reading Margaret Whitman's letter, he'd been expecting the topic and was prepared for it. "I beg your pardon," he said.

Shakespeare held the viscount's eyes.

"The priest that you house, m'lord," he said.

"We have no priest here," Henley said. "We follow the Church of the land—the religion of the state."

"I need to speak with him, m'lord."

"Speak with whom?"

"With Fra Silvera."

"I know of no such person, man," said Henley. His voice was even, his expression fixed as if cast in stone.

"I desire you and your household no ills, your worship," said Shakespeare. "But it is necessary for me to converse with Fra Silvera. It is my firm belief that he holds some deep knowledge of your kinsman's death."

"We have no such person here," Henley repeated angrily, and turned his back on the player.

"If I were an agent of the Queen," said Shakespeare, "would I find no such man if I looked behind one of the fireplaces? Or perhaps I should look under the staircases. Or for a trapdoor up in the attic—"

"Are you an agent of the Queen?" Henley asked.

Shakespeare shook his head.

Henley spun around, stared at him with rage. "What do you want from us? Money? Land? An upwardly social marriage to one of my daughters?"

"No—"

"I saw how you looked at Mistress Jane."

"Twas your daughter who advanced upon me."

Henley suddenly looked defeated. "I repeat. What do you want?"

"To speak with Fra Silvera," Shakespeare said. "That's all. Once I've spoken with him and satisfied my curiosity that he had nothing to do with Harry's murder—"

"And if we had this imaginary Fra, and if he had something to do with Harry's murder, then what? Would you have him reported to the authorities, have us all arrested and hung, my lands confiscated, my servants sent out penniless to fend for themselves?"

Shakespeare paused. He'd never considered the consequences of his actions. He assured Henley that the secret would forever remain inside Brithall. But the lord was dubious, angry, and scared.

"I spoke with you the first time you were up here, Shakespeare," said Henley. "I gave you my time, told you as best I could remember what Harry did in the weeks he was here. I told you he came and left here in good health. Now you intrude upon my gracious hospitality and threaten to report me to authorities—''

"I have not threatened you, m'lord," said Shakespeare. "But I need to speak with the priest. Secrets between him and Harry may reveal to me something about the murder."

"A priest would never reveal secrets told to him by another man. He follows laws higher than the laws of the land."

"I'm aware of that," Shakespeare said. "But perhaps some things were not told to him within the sanctity of confession."

"And if I refuse?" said Henley. "If I deny that there is a priest in this house? Then what?"

Shakespeare thought before speaking. Finally he said, "I pray you, m'lord. Allow the dead to rest in peace. Harry's soul will not be laid to sleep until the circumstances of his demise are fully disclosed. You owe your kinsman perpetual rest, your worship."

Henley remained motionless for a minute, then slowly nodded his head. As a Catholic the viscount would never damn his cousin to perpetual restlessness. He'd have to account for his actions later on in *his* afterlife. He instructed Shakespeare to wait in the long gallery, as he needed to be alone for a minute.

Henley started to walk away, then stopped and turned to Shakespeare. He said, "You must have loved him dearly."

"I did."

"Harry spoke kindly of you as well," Henley said. "He admired your wit. What *was* he to you?"

"He acted my father when I first came to London. He was a great teacher, a most generous person with time and money."

"Generous to a fault," said Henley. "He squandered his inheritance as quickly as he received it. Of late he was constantly short of money."

Shakespeare said nothing. Harry had extracted good coinage from the fellowship, but apparently it hadn't been enough. Money goes fast if a body is involved in extortion and gambling.

Henley said, "Oddly, Harry never asked me for money until three years ago. After that his need for money became insatiable. He borrowed no less than one hundred pounds from me the last time he was here."

"One hundred *pounds*!"

"Yes."

"Dear Providence, where did that money go? It wasn't upon him when his body was discovered?"

"The highwaymen probably took it," said Henley.

"But they left him several shillings in his pockets."

"Perhaps the few shillings were overlooked."

"Perhaps." Shakespeare shook his head. "One hundred pounds! And this habit of borrowing was recent?"

Henley said, "Three years ago. I remember it clearly, because I was so surprised. Up to that point Harry had never wanted anything from me, certainly not my money. He'd been red-faced when he'd made the request."

"Have you known Harry to gamble?" Shakespeare asked.

Henley shook his head no, then neither spoke. Henley knew Shakespeare wouldn't give up. The balding mule meant to talk to the priest—dear God, he even knew the father's name—and he wouldn't leave until he did. Henley wanted him out of his life, and the sooner the better. A minute passed in silence, then Henley smiled bleakly, feeling like a sparrow caught in a cap. He said,

"Wait here, Shakespeare. I'll see if I can find your imaginary Fra Silvera. If such a person is willing to speak with you, I'll not object."

46

The outside chapel formed a ninety-degree angle with the east wing of Brithall. It was built from fieldstone—small, pebbly rocks instead of large, hewn blocks—yet its walls, Henley told Shakespeare, were as thick as those of a fortified castle. There was a grace to the building, its intricately carved door arched harmoniously with its windows. The panes of leaded glass were glazed as clear as springwater. The church seemed to rise endlessly into the full-mooned sky, peaking so high that the top of the spire was obliterated by the night fog and clouds. The interior, Henley lectured, could hold hundreds of people for worship, sufficient pew space for any guests that the family might entertain, including the Queen and her retinue.

Yet Shakespeare knew the chapel was nothing but a showpiece. There was another spot, a place well hidden from view, where true prayer took place.

Henley pursed his lips and blew out frigid air. Nothing was going to dissuade him from taking his nightly stroll, not the weather, not Shakespeare. He noticed the player trembling with cold, but shrugged it off. Let the man learn how to live with the elements. A bit of frostbite was not fatal . . . if only it were. One sure way to get rid of this man who knew too much. As it was, Henley had no choice but to appease him. Let him converse with the Fra, and hopefully that would be the end of his visits. Only when the viscount's *own* toes and fingers tingled painfully did he suggest they finish the walk.

Shakespeare answered him with a dutiful, "Whatever you wish, m'lord." He flexed his fingers, trying to bring blood to the near-frozen tissue. His hands were numb, on their way to frostbite, but mercifully not quite there yet. His toes were warmer—only pain and no numbness. Rubbing his hands together, he thought Henley a malevolent prig.

The viscount led Shakespeare around the chapel, then back to the far west tower. Once inside he picked a lit torch from a wall sconce and motioned for Shakespeare to follow him upward. The spiral staircase was low—Shakespeare had to crouch—the stone of the steps smooth with wear. The stairs ended at the archway of the heraldry hall. Swords were hung in circular formation, the tips converging to a center point as if the blades were petals on a metallic flower. Family crests were positioned between the sword daisies. Full suits of armor stood around the room, invisible guards propped up by wires and sticks. Yet in the dimness they looked menacing and impenetrable. Henley walked hurriedly through the hall—no more lectures about ancestry—to its far end, and opened a small door.

Hands and feet still aching from the cold, Shakespeare followed him into a small guest closet. The cell barely accommodated a mattress and a table upon which were a pitcher and basin for washing. The stone walls were flat and unadorned, but the east wall did hold an *immaculately* clean hearth, too large for the size of the room. On the left side of the fireplace were piles of well-dried logs; the right side held pokers, andirons, and a large pail of ashes.

Henley put the torch in an empty sconce and dropped to his hands and knees. He crawled into the fireplace box and pushed on its back wall. The panel instantly yielded to his touch, and he crawled through the hearth. Shakespeare suddenly realized the purpose of the bucket of soot. If the Queen's agents ever stormed the house, a family member would simply pour the ashes over the hearth and make it appear as if blazing fires had been burnt upon it for centuries. Shakespeare went down on his knees and followed Henley.

The other side of the fireplace held England's past— pre-Reformation—before King Henry the Eighth's desire for a son had altered the course of a nation. The chapel was tiny, no more than a single bench in front of an apse. On either side of the vestibule were two small stained-glass windows obscured from outside view by evergreen trees. One showed Christ on the cross, the other was the Virgin, her head tilted upward, palms pressed together in holy supplication. The scenes were eerily backlit by the blue-white moonbeams, making the glass appear as if it had been plated with silver. The altar and its raised pulpit were haloed with the twinkling of several dozen orange flames, religious candles lit for the Saints, for the Virgin—relics of a bygone age. At the top of the wall hung the gilt crucifix, what Puritans would have denounced as a toy of idol worship. Resting upon the pulpit were the communion plate and a gold chalice.

Shakespeare felt no righteous indignation at the sight of the icons—the candles, the containers of the Eucharist, and the crucifix. He felt strangely moved. Catholicism was the mother of Protestantism, and even if her offspring were rebellious, they should acknowledge from whence they came.

Henley crossed himself and meditated for a few moments in silence. Shakespeare remained on his knees, feeling clumsy, not knowing if he should pray or if prayer here constituted treason. He clasped his hands together and closed his eyes, picturing the Queen's agents suddenly raiding the room, dragging him away to be burnt alive for heresy and sedition.

Yet there was an aura of holiness and peace about the room. Shakespeare had sensed it the moment he crawled through the space. It comforted him like the cradle of the Madonna's arms.

Finally Lord Henley lit a candle and crawled out of the church, leaving Shakespeare alone in the silence with nothing but his thoughts.

He wondered where the Jesuit was. Hiding outside? In one of the suits of armor he'd seen in the heraldry hall? Five minutes passed. Shakespeare began to feel dizzy. The walls seemed to move in the flickering light, appeared to close in on him.

Only his imagination.

His mind suddenly shifted to thoughts of imprisonment, to a box of darkness where his hands and feet were bound. Though the room was a chilled crypt, droplets of perspiration fell off his forehead and nose. The air became choked with the acrid smell of tallow. He stood, hit his head, then fell back on his knees. He pushed on the panel that led to the fireplace of the chamber. It was tightly bolted into place.

Calm he told himself. *Calm.*

A minute later a stone in the chapel was pushed outward and a shriveled man, wrapped in a brown robe, crawled out like some oversized rodent. He held a lighted candlestick.

Shakespeare sighed with relief, angry that his imagination had sparked so uncontrollably.

Fra Silvera was old—much older than even Shakespeare had
imagined. But it made sense when he thought about it. Harry,
thirty-nine at the time of his demise, had known the Fra since
boyhood. The Jesuit had to be at least sixty. He looked to be in
his eighties. Living thirty-odd years without daylight, in constant
fear of being discovered and burned, could age a man faster than
nature's wear and tear. His face was partially shadowed by a
cowl, but what Shakespeare could make out was wrinkled and
pale, like a crumpled parchment. His hands were thin, the skin
stretched over the bones, translucent and hued bluish pink. Placing the candlestick by his side, the Jesuit knelt in front of the
altar and removed his cowl. He was bald except for a thick ring
of silver hair at the base of his scalp. The denuded crown looked
like a pink skullcap.

Shakespeare made no attempt to speak with Silvera. There
was a rhythm to the man's movements, an order. To upset it was
to court disaster. He remained on his knees watching the priest's
profile as he prayed. Fra Silvera's lips moved but no sound came
out. Shakespeare saw his cheeks, dampened by a sudden out-
pouring of tears. They came in torrents, then stopped as abruptly
as they'd started. Still kneeling, Silvera turned his head to Shakespeare, motioning him to come forward.

Shakespeare stood and hit his head again. If he crouched uncomfortably, he could remain on his feet. The only alternatives
were sitting upon the bench, which he'd not been invited to do,
or to kneel once again. Shakespeare remained upright, his shoulders stooped.

Silvera said, "Help me to my feet, my son."

His voice was no stronger than a whisper. Shakespeare gently
lifted the priest. The man stood no higher than a crookbacked
gnome, his head easily clearing the ceiling by five or six inches.
Silvera motioned for Shakespeare to sit on a bench, and the
player gratefully complied.

"You want to open old wounds," Fra Silvera said. "Why?"

Shakespeare stared at the old man. Something about him consumed his powers of speech. Shakespeare stuttered out, "Harry
was my friend."

"And you do this for all your friends?"

"Only those who've been murdered," Shakespeare answered.

"And how many has that been?" Silvera challenged.

"Harry's the first, thanks be to Providence."

Silvera looked him in the eye. For the first time Shakespeare
could see him full-faced. His eyes were narrow, with a perpetual, cynical squint. His mouth was thin and hard, his nose narrow and red-tipped, his chin fixed and stubborn. A man who
carried anger like a dagger.

"How close were you to Harry?" Silvera asked.

"He was my mentor," Shakespeare said. "I loved him as a father."

"And how else did you love him?"

Shakespeare felt his heart beating. "I loved him as a friend, as a brother."

"And?"

Shakespeare stared at Silvera, stymied by the question. Silvera waved him off. He said, "So you want to avenge Harry's death because he was your friend."

"His soul visited me, Father," said Shakespeare. "Or at least something visited me."

"Tell me about it."

Shakespeare related to him the dreams, the bump on the back of his head, and finally, his altercations with his fiendish creature in black.

Silvera said, "And this creature advised you to cease your inquiries into Harry's death?"

"Aye."

"Yet you persisted."

"The *real* ghost of Harry Whitman still visits me in my dreams. He begs for my help. I dare not damn Harry's soul to eternal unrest."

"If his soul is indeed so condemned."

"I feel he will not be laid in peace until we know the circumstances that led to his murder," Shakespeare said.

Silvera suddenly boomed: "And you are wiser than God! If God in his infinite wisdom saw fit to leave Harry's death unchallenged by man and nature, who are *you* to do otherwise!"

Shakespeare hesitated, then said, "Perhaps I was sent by God to do Harry's bidding."

Silvera's eyes widened. "Are you implying that you're an *agent* of God?"

"No, Father—"

"How dare you attempt to correct what should be left to the hands of God!"

The little man's rage was fearsome, his voice echoing loudly in the small room.

Like Harry's voice. Though a dwarf, the Jesuit's lungs operated at full capacity. Shakespeare said nothing. Silvera drummed his fingers together.

"You are a heretic!" he announced.

Shakespeare remained silent.

"Though I suppose that's no fault of yours," Silvera said as an afterthought. "You were raised by heretical parents and brought up in a church riddled with hypocrisy as well as heresy.

But know, son, that you are a heretic and will account to God because of it.'' Silvera sat down next to Shakespeare. ''But I can help you, my son. I can bring you back to the true light and faith. You must rise up against the false faith and its false ruler, the Queen of—''

''Was Harry a heretic?'' Shakespeare interrupted. He was not about to engage the Jesuit in a conversation that constituted treason.

Silvera shook his head, tears welled up in his eyes. ''Never,'' the old man said in a hushed voice. *''Never!''*

''He kept his Catholic beliefs well hidden,'' Shakespeare said. ''His superficial beliefs, the ones that he espoused to the fellowship seemed almost . . . dare I say it, atheistic.''

''You did not know the true Henry Whitman,'' Silvera said. He made it sound like an accusation.

''Then teach me about him,'' Shakespeare said.

''Why should I?'' answered the priest stubbornly. ''Who are you to him? To me?''

''Mayhap I could tell you a side of Harry to which *you* were not privy,'' said Shakespeare.

''I was his father,'' said Silvera. ''I knew all sides of Harry.''

Shakespeare paused. The way Silvera had said *father* made the player wonder whether the monk had meant it spiritually or physically.

''He told me a great deal about you, Shakespeare,'' said Silvera. ''He said he loved you.''

''I loved him as well.''

''How well?'' Silvera asked.

Shakespeare didn't answer right away. Henley had asked a similar question. The meaning of their inquiries slowly came to him. He said, ''Our love was purely spiritual, Father.''

Silvera dropped to his knees, crossed himself, and muttered a slew of Latin. Though not fluent in the language, Shakespeare could make out words of thanksgiving to the Almighty for making Harry pure.

Shakespeare had never noticed an Italianate inclination in Whitman. Though Harry drank often at Bull's with Marlowe, it seemed natural that the most formidable player of the times would discuss topics with the most sought-after bookwriter. Yet Harry was a private man and could have concealed a lover from him.

Studying the Jesuit, Shakespeare pondered the priest's powerful reaction to the fact that Shakespeare was not Harry's lover. A reaction of extreme relief, like a wife verifying the faithfulness of her husband. Had Harry been the priest's lover? Many a Jesuit had been known to bugger a young novice.

Silvera had stopped mumbling to himself. Shakespeare waited for him to speak. A quarter hour must have passed. Finally Shakespeare said,

"Tell me Harry's history as a boy. Lord Henley seemed to think him rebellious."

Silvera glared at him with fiery black eyes. He snarled and shouted, "Harry rebellious? Harry was the most sincere of the crop of them."

"Who're *them*?" Shakespeare asked.

"Why do you want to know?" Silvera asked again.

"His past may give me a deeply hidden clue that will explain his demise," Shakespeare said.

"I doubt it," said the Jesuit. "Still, I am grateful, in a certain aspect, that you've returned to Brithall. You've eased my mind. As far as I'm concerned, Harry Whitman had not engaged in mortal sin."

"Buggery?"

"Aye. There had been fiendish rumors about him spread around town."

"Hemsdale?" Shakespeare asked.

"Yes."

"Spread by whom?"

"By those who spit in God's face. By those who knew the Whitmans before the Reformation—knew that they'd been staunch supporters of the true faith! The muck was no doubt flung by the heretics, the followers of Calvin, Ridley, Latimer, and—dare I say such a blasphemous name—*Luther.*"

"Who in specific?" Shakespeare asked.

"I know not," Silvera said. "Harry told me that certain people thought him a buggerer. He assured me this was not so. In sooth, his problems were just the opposite. He had a weakness for women. But that didn't bother me. His wife and he were not married in the true faith, so I thought of Harry as being unmarried all his life, his children as bastards. Yet when he spoke of you . . . the love in his heart . . . I confess to God that I wavered in my faith of the boy."

Shakespeare thought of Margaret, how she was suffering to raise Harry's seven children, the ones Silvera so easily dismissed as bastards. Anger shot through his heart, yet he kept his temper. Calmly, he asked again who had spread the buggery rumors, and again Silvera denied knowing the answer. Shakespeare asked the priest if he knew Edgar Chambers.

"The hostler?" Silvera said. "I know of *his* nature. Twould not surprise me that *he* buggered, the filth! I've met the weasel several times when I've ventured out to the burg in one of my many disguises." Silvera laughed. "I'm quite the player myself.

I've acted the beggar, the baker, a chimney sweep. . . . Heaven knows, I'm short enough to be one—''

"Did Harry and you ever talk about Chambers?" Shakespeare interrupted.

"Not at all. Harry never mentioned the snake in the grass. Never.''

"What about George Mackering?''

Silvera shook his head.

"How about a whor—a wench who'd been known to dally—''

"I know nothing about Harry's sport.''

Shakespeare wanted to ask him what the two of them had done every two weeks in May for the last forty years, but restrained himself. The Jesuit greatly misliked being interrogated. Instead he asked the priest to talk about Harry as a child.

"It is impossible to understand Harry unless you understand the family.''

"Tell me about the family, then.''

Silvera shook his head. "They are still among the living, my son.''

"They have trusted me with their deepest secret, namely your presence at Brithall.''

"That was their decision. If it were up to me, I'd shout my existence to that witch of a queen. But Henley is fond of his neck. I hold my peace out of respect for him.''

"I will *never* betray you, Father," Shakespeare said. "If I am so misinformed about Harry, educate me.''

Silvera stared at the player, his eyes still as hard as flint. "A moment," he said. "I must pray." He closed his eyes and lowered his head.

A minute later he said, "I suppose the family history has been gossiped about for years. I'll tell you what is—or could be—common knowledge.''

"I thank you, Father," said Shakespeare.

"When I first came to England . . . twas after fat Henry had cursed himself by marrying that whore Nan Bullen—''

"After the Reformation," Shakespeare said.

"Have it your way," Silvera said disgustedly. "You'll all burn in Hell.''

"My apologies for interrupting you," said Shakespeare. "I pray you, go on.''

Silvera described for Shakespeare the Whitmans. There had been three brothers, the eldest being George, Viscount Henley, heir to Brithall, Lord Robert's father. He was the domineering one—shorter than the others, but he made up for his less than overwhelming physical stature by an astute mind and industrious labors.

"Robert Whitman is a tall man," Shakespeare noted.

The Jesuit nodded as if Shakespeare had just learned catechism. He said, "He resembles Harry's father—Lord Chesterfield, Isaac Whitman, Baron of Rochbury."

The priest explained that Chesterfield was the youngest and tallest of the brothers. And he married a very tall, handsome woman, the type of girl that most men would be afraid to touch. But not Isaac Whitman. The girl's father had been very rich and well connected, a distant relative to the virtuous Queen Mary. Upon Isaac Whitman's engagement to the lady, the Queen raised him to peerage and he became Lord Chesterfield. Once a lord, Chesterfield dutifully impregnated his wife—and a variety of mistresses.

"A charming man," Silvera said.

"Harry was very charming," said Shakespeare.

"Isaac was the most bewitching of Whitman's sons," agreed the priest. "In sooth, Chesterfield's enchantment came back to haunt him in the likes of Harry."

"What about the middle brother?" Shakespeare asked.

"Ignatius Whitman—the spiritualist of the family. He became Lord Bartley upon his marriage to Beatrice Lennox—a very plain girl but well titled. Bartley was quiet and contemplative. The brothers were superficially staunch supporters of the new faith. King Henry demanded the support of his subjects upon the pain of death. But inside, like many, the brothers remained true Catholics. They raised their children secretly in the ways of the true religion."

Shakespeare asked about Lord Bartley since Henley had made mention of Bartley's influence upon him.

"Ah," said the priest. "My gracious Lord Bartley. He, more than the others, found it intolerable to hide his true beliefs. He is now known as Fra Domingo."

"He became a Jesuit," said Shakespeare.

"Twas a most rewarding day for our order!"

Silvera smiled widely, his eyes shone brightly for a moment, then darkened as if a cloud passed over them. Then he told Shakespeare the sad tale. When the boy-king, Edward the Sixth, found out that Bartley had become a Catholic, he confiscated Bartley's lands and stripped the family of its crest. Bartley's eldest son was hung for heresy. Five years later some of Bartley's lands were returned to his wife by the good Queen Mary. The Queen also knighted the second son, but the Bartleys never returned to their former state of wealth and prestige.

Shakespeare digested the history, noting how everything was beginning to piece together. No wonder there was no picture of the Jesuit in the long gallery. To have a portrait of a Catholic priest hung in a public place was to admit a kindredship with a traitor.

He thought a moment, then said, "Yet with all the dishonor, Bartley left a major impression on his nephew—the current Viscount Henley."

"Bartley left a bigger impression on his grandnephew, Master Harry Whitman."

Shakespeare asked how so.

The priest said, "Harry was much impressed with Bartley's integrity, the strength of his conviction, his refusal to submit to hypocrisy. Harry was indeed a child of the true faith. Now, as I've stated, Lord Chesterfield, Harry's father, was overtly a staunch follower of the false faith, a supporter of the Queen and her Church."

Shakespeare noted the disdain in his voice when he mentioned the Queen.

"But twas Harry who truly felt the calling."

Shakespeare was baffled. Nothing about Harry had ever suggested a calling.

Silvera continued, "He wanted to become a true priest—a Jesuit priest. Not what the Queen calls priests—men who marry, who scoff at the holy language of Latin, who fornicate with women they call their wives—and *worse*, believe it not to be sin. Harry wanted to be a true Jesuit. Like me. Like his uncle, Lord Bartley."

The priest put his hand to his heart and continued:

"Harry's father, Lord Chesterfield, was fearful that what had happened to Bartley would happen to his branch of the family if Harry were sent to Rome. Lord Chesterfield had used his charm wisely. It had earned him lands—rich lands. He wasn't keen on the idea of being reduced to a pauper. Harry didn't understand what he saw as sheer hypocrisy, and became a rebellious son, despising his father, I regret to say. Harry was deeply resentful that his father refused to send him to Rome and sought out ways of revenge against him. He spat on his bloodline, he fornicated with his father's mistresses and other lowly women . . . marry, he even wed a commoner, the daughter of a false priest, irony of ironies. But the most shameful thing he did was to become a public embarrassment to his family."

"By becoming an actor," Shakespeare said.

"Yes," Silvera said. "Disgraceful!"

"Yet he retained his Papist ties—"

"He retained his ties to the *true* religion," Silvera corrected. "Yes, in his heart Master Henry Whitman, the prodigal son of Lord Chesterfield, was still a priest."

Harry had acted anything but priestlike, Shakespeare thought.

He closed his eyes and pictured Whitman, carousing with women and drinking with ne'er-do-wells. Then the tortured voice shot through his ears.

My father failed me. My God failed me.

You're the man I wanted to be . . . a man of honesty.

Silvera cleared his throat loudly and Shakespeare opened his eyes.

"Am I boring you to slumber?"

"I apologize, Father," said Shakespeare. "It's been a most exhausting day, but that's no excuse for such unmannerly behavior. I pray you, continue. I'll be more diligent."

The Jesuit seemed mollified, and finished up the family history. Viscount Henley, George Whitman, was the richest brother of the clan, since as the eldest son he was the heir to all his father's lands. After the Catholic uprising of 'sixty-nine, when it was life-threatening to harbor a priest, Henley had decisions to make. The priest could be smuggled back to Rome or stay hidden in England and continue to be the spiritual leader of the three families. Henley decided to hide the Jesuit, and his son Robert—the current Lord Henley—carried on his father's commitment. Fra Silvera ended by saying that Harry, badly in need of spiritual healing, had seen him for confession, two weeks every year for the last twenty years.

The priest wiped tears from his eyes. "I cannot believe he's actually gone from the mortal world, Shakespeare. I loved him. My dear, dear son."

Shakespeare let him weep for a minute, then asked softly, "Your son in spirit alone?"

The Jesuit looked at him with red-rimmed eyes. "Harry told you?"

Shakespeare shook his head. "Simply a well-placed guess."

Numbly, Silvera said, "I was once a handsome man, my son, not the ancient . . . skeletal . . . wretch you witness now. Women found me desirable, more so *because* I was a priest. I committed a very vile sin when I was young, and from sin can only come tragedy. I've prayed to God: let my body shrivel, my heinous appetites be gone, so that He would enter my heart forever. And Jesu Cristo, in His infinite mercy, has answered my prayers. He has made me old and weak, molded a shrunken dwarf out of a once strong and able-bodied man. May my body become even more hideous as my spirit fills with enlightenment, *in nomine Patris et Filius et Spiritus Sancti.*"

The Jesuit crossed himself and fell upon the floor weeping with grief.

Shakespeare waited patiently and contemplated. Harry's behavior was easier explained in light of the priest's confession.

Harry had somehow found out that he was Silvera's bastard son. Yet he hadn't seemed to despise his mother for her deception. Perhaps because his father was such a cocksman, Harry felt his mother had justification. Whatever the reasons were, Harry and the priest formed emotional and spiritual bonds. In every sense of the word, the priest had been Harry's true father.

Silvera returned to his knees and whispered, "My son's death was the will of God, His retribution for my most hideous sin."

"*Did* Harry know?" Shakespeare asked.

Silvera said, "I never told him, and I don't think his mother did. But somehow he knew." The Jesuit suddenly pounded on the back of the fireplace panel.

"Your time is up!" he announced.

The panel opened. Henley escorted Shakespeare out of the chapel.

47

It was nearly two in the morning before Rebecca sank into her feather mattress. The fatigue she felt was all-encompassing, the kind of weariness that gripped and squeezed and encumbered the sweet dust of sleep. Her stomach quivered with waves of nausea. Her head throbbed so badly that her pillow seemed as solid as a bar of iron. Her limbs ached and her vision was blurred. Yet her physical discomfort was easily tolerated compared to the pain in her heart. And nowhere was she more acutely aware of her nagging loss than when she lay alone in darkness.

It had been three weeks since she'd last seen him. They would have been in Venice by now. Perhaps they would have gone down to the southern Italian states—Naples or Sicily—with a troupe, until the winter was over. In the late afternoon she'd bask in the strong sun of Tyrrhenia while Willy sat under a veranda writing playbooks of comic conceit or history. They'd eat citrus picked from sweet-smelling orchards, pluck piquant grapes from emerald vineyards, nibble on fresh cheeses, sip fine sherries.

She turned onto her left side and groaned, wiping tears away from her eyes, willing herself back to the present. Outside, freezing rain pounded furiously against the slate roof. She had strained a back muscle yesterday. Rebecca wondered what she'd done to pull it. It must have been when she held the shoulders of the barrister with the melon-sized growth in his stomach. Marry, it was *huge*, but encapsulated. He'd survive if blood poisoning didn't do him in. What was his name? Folly? No, of course not. Twas Foley. He'd fought like a tiger, struggling against the restraints even before her father had taken a knife to him. She heard her father's voice in her head.

For God's sake, hold him tighter, woman!

Rebecca had gripped him with all her strength. The armpits of her sleeves were soaked. It hadn't been enough.

Tighter, girl! Roderigo had screamed. *Use your whole body, Becca, not just your arms!*

It was then that she felt a sudden sharp pain in her side. But she had done her duty. Her father had been able to begin the surgery.

Her father's work seemed endless. The list of patients grew longer as the winter progressed. The daylight hours were spent ministering to the sick at St. Bartholomew's, followed by an infinite amount of home visits. In the past Rebecca had begged to come along. But since Father's release, it had become routine for her to accompany him—to assist him. He had an endless need for her companionship, and after what he'd gone through, she dared not displease him.

When they were together, he expected her to work—preparing salves and poultices, spoon-feeding medicines and drugs to the feeble, holding the hands of the mortally infirm, cradling babies as they died in her arms, restraining surgery patients. As hard as she worked, her father's labors were even more stressful—his hands washed as often in blood as in water. Death was a constant companion, life as fragile as spider's silk. Yet despite the raw and demanding days, her father's tongue lashings and an occasional slap, a tacit understanding grew between them, and with it came a stronger bond of love.

Their daily toils were finished once they reached home. But the night brought on a new set of chores and obligations. After a quick supper, Roderigo met with the other men of the family. Then the whisperings began. Plans to save the Iberian conversos were birthed, along with new names, secret letters, code words, different agents. Whisper, whisper whenever the staff was out of earshot.

Who would take over for Miguel? Rebecca had asked her mother.

They'll find someone, Sarah had answered. *Keep your voice down!*

Who? We've hardly any able-bodied men left. Dunstan is too old, which only leaves Ben, and he's— Rebecca had stopped herself. Ben *was* too slow-witted. Everyone knew it. But no need to rub salt in a wound.

Sarah went back to her work. But Rebecca heard the name de Gama—their Spanish connection—surface in the whisperings. He seemed the logical heir apparent to Miguel's luckless throne. The entire family worked with an urgency as if time were a dream, destined to end.

After supper Rebecca tended to Miguel. Their nuptials, originally scheduled for February, had been postponed, giving Miguel as much time as he needed to convalesce. Together they strolled the gardens when the rain and snow fell lightly, Rebecca surprised at how gracefully he walked, albeit with a noticeable limp. It was learning to use his left hand that gave him troubles. She coached him as he wrote. It was a humiliating experience for him. His letters were wobbly, his sentences illegible. Sometimes he accidentally ripped the paper with the tip of his quill. Once he spilled ink over his hose. Often he tongue-lashed Rebecca, blaming her for his failures. She took his temper in stride and pushed him to continue, even as she saw tears of frustration well up in his eyes.

She worked Miguel to the point of exhaustion. When she knew she could take him no further, she whispered the daily prayer to him, kissed him good night, then hurried to the stillroom to make the medicines for the next day. Sometimes she met her mother there. They'd talk as they squinted in the dim light of flickering rush candles, grinding leaves to powders, blending salts with syrups. Usually her mother spent her daylight hours tending to household business, supervising the staff (the kitchen alone took up hours), making sure the stock of food wasn't depleted too rapidly, sewing and embroidering, accounting of the household expenses, and sending servants to market when weather permitted. Rebecca began to notice knots in her mother's hands, a pastiness in a complexion that once had been smooth and rosy. Often she would hug her mother ferociously, then worry that she had broken the woman's bones. Sarah would simply smile.

Rebecca turned onto her back. The clattering upon the roof intensified until the house seemed to shake under the downpour. Lightning exploded through the sky, followed quickly by a tremulant clap of thunder. Her brain was an ensemble of irritating buzzes. Her eyelids suddenly fluttered, one leg twitched. She felt as if a demon were burrowing inside her body, and it scared her.

Dear Grandmama gave her solace. Rebecca prepared her

morning toilet, then breakfasted with the old woman. She loved the sweet nectar of mead and brewis—bread saturated with gravy, which required no teeth to eat. But with each new wintry day the old woman seemed to be withering away. She couldn't walk anymore, even with her walking sticks. Rebecca had to feed her, bathe her, and change her sheets often because the old woman had lost control of her bladder. Rebecca was worried. But when she voiced her concerns to her mother, Sarah just shrugged philosophically. There was nothing either one could do for her except make her final days comfortable.

Final days? Rebecca had asked. *What do you mean by final days?*

Sarah had answered, *My mother is old. She has already cheated death.*

When Rebecca didn't immediately respond, Sarah kissed her daughter gently and said, *You've been a most dutiful granddaughter, Becca. May your daughters be as dutiful to me.*

There were questions that begged to be asked, but Rebecca knew that none would be answered to her satisfaction. She suffered in silence, doting upon Grandmama whenever time permitted.

Rebecca knew she was doing goodly work, helping her father, mother, grandmother, and future husband. She knew she was doing God's bidding, becoming industrious, instead of petulant and idle, using her hours wisely, not selfishly. But her slavish devotion to duty did nothing to rid her of a shattered hole in her chest.

She loved her Will, wanted him, missed him with a painful longing. Three times she stole away and rushed to his cell. She knew he'd left for travel three weeks ago—his neighbor told her that—but she kept hoping he might have returned.

Fruitless hopes.

She *had* meant to leave with him, to convert to his God. But something intangible, something incredibly strong, held her back. Rebecca thought of her ancestral rituals—the prayers, the fasts, the food prohibitions that the family secretly followed. Their refusal to eat pork, slaughtering their own chickens and cows. The secret sabbaths.

It's your legacy, Grandmama had once told her. *You observe the same laws that our matriarchs—Sarah, your mother's namesake; Rebecca, your namesake; Rachel and Leah, God willing, your future daughters' names—observed fifteen hundred years ago, when God still spoke to us through prophets. And you will ensure a legacy for your children, Becca.*

Though she laughed and loved with her heart, she lived by her blood. Her ancestors: sacrificing, dying for *Kiddish*

Hashem—for the holy name of God. Hundreds of thousands of them. Yet the people of Israel, the Jews, persisted as a nation. Babylonia had tried to erase them. Babylonia had disappeared as a people, a nation. Rome tried to murder her people. Rome—gone. Greece failed, Persia as well. And so would Spain. So would any nation that tried to eradicate God's chosen. He would never let it come to pass. She believed that with all her heart, with all her soul, and with all her might.

Shma Yisroel . . .

Am Yisroel Chai—the people of Israel live.

Fifteen hundred years was a long time, and she was too much a Jewess to let her children's legacy be washed down the river. Though she ached for Shakespeare, it was duty before love.

48

Shakespeare slept badly. He dreamt of dwarfish priests, of Rebecca masked as the Virgin, of Harry nailed to a cross. There was a foreboding miasma in the air, a suffocating vapor that spoke to Shakespeare of danger—both close at hand and distant. He awoke before dawn, lit a candlestick and kindled a fire in the hearth. Brithall had many guest chambers. His was situated with a window facing east. After washing from a basin of near-frozen water and dressing quickly, Shakespeare leaned against the chilled stone wall and watched the sunrise. The night had given way to daylight, the wintry landscape turning from a darker to a lighter shade of gray as the hidden sun broke through the horizon.

An hour later Shakespeare was offering his final words of appreciation to his host, his speech stuffed with overflowing hyperbole. Henley insisted that the player drink a tankard of ale before departing. Shakespeare complied while a groom fetched his horse, and he was on the road before seven.

The snowdrifts were deep, the air bitter. Shakespeare's hands felt frozen an hour into the ride. He wondered if he could make it to Hemsdale before dark. Unlike his springtime trip, sleeping outdoors was no longer an option. Henley had given him a circuitous route, one that required an overnight stay at an inn called the White Hart. Ordinarily Shakespeare would have traveled the more direct route—one that required passage over steep hills and treacherous crags. But not in such a climate. Shakespeare was determined but not daft.

Back he rode, retracing Whitman's last steps. Harry hadn't lodged at the White Hart, Henley was sure of that. Which meant that Harry had to have traveled from Brithall to Hemsdale using the more dangerous but faster route—the path due directly south. Which meant he conceivably could have met the stew whom Shakespeare had bedded in the bilberry bushes. What was her name? Cat, the alderman had said. Her forename was Catherine.

But the whore claimed not to have known Harry.

But the alderman said she was a liar and Harry regularly passed through Hemsdale. And Harry was fond of women. If no decent wench would bed him, a strumpet would suit him well. But the Jesuit had said there was gossip about Harry having Italianate sexual proclivities. In Hemsdale, did Harry play with men?

Chambers. He was a sly one. He'd spoken nervously of Harry. Mayhap Harry was killed not because he was a Papist but because of a lover's spat between him and Chambers.

Tomorrow he'd speak with Chambers. Perhaps the innkeeper would help him, perhaps he'd be mulish and say nothing.

And maybe the innkeeper had nothing whatsoever to do with Harry's death. Perhaps Harry had been a random victim slaughtered by a greedy highwayman. Or cut down by the blood-lusting hand of an anti-Papist fanatic. Or the sacrificial lamb of some madman's demented mind.

Shakespeare shook his head in confusion.

Another hour passed. The icy winds had finally calmed and the air lost its painful bite. The sky was tufted with silver clouds. At noon honey-colored beams broke through the gray skies, pillars of shimmering gold streaming to earth. The blinding snow reflected and scattered the sunlight back into the sky and atop the snowdrifts. The day held about it a virginal freshness, a sweet, clean smell. Even Shakespeare's horse seemed to sense a change. It had become less sluggish, less winded. Shakespeare burst into song, the echoes so sustained that he could almost sing harmony with himself.

God was everyone. God was everything. God was all around.

The following day was steeped in violence, the weather refusing to clear until early afternoon. Shakespeare had bedded down at the White Hart and left around one of the clock, his stomach full, his bones warmed. The air was so choked with mist, Shakespeare could barely see ten feet ahead. But thanks be to Providence, his sense of direction was good. He reached the area outlying Hemsdale shortly before dark.

In the springtime the dreary burg had been livened by the hawking tunes, the colorful stalls on the streets, lute music and young maidens dancing. But draped in the coarse, dark fabric of winter, the town looked to be in mourning. The streets were deserted, the houses seemed to shiver in the cold. Shakespeare rode a few feet down the main road. The houses faded into the darkness, their presence hinted at by an occasional flicker of a rush candle leaking through warped wooden shutters.

Shakespeare noticed the red lattice of a tavern. He dismounted, went inside and looked around. The alehouse was dark and foul-smelling, with air that made the skin itch. It had been a while since the floor rushes had been changed. They had turned dirty, were coated with grease and God only knew what else. Huddled groups of drinkers sat in corners, buxom wenches upon their knees. Shakespeare felt inside his doublet for his dagger. It rested comfortably at his side. If hap be sweet, by his side it would stay. He spied a tapster—a man so fat as to be round—and walked up to him.

"Where can a man stable his horse for the night?" Shakespeare asked.

"Twopence for the horse, twopence for a bucket of feed."

Shakespeare nodded. "How about bedding for myself?"

"On the floor," the tapster said. "At two in the morn, after all the paying men have left. Twopence for that too."

"The man's not interested in your hospitality, Rupert," interrupted a familiar voice. Shakespeare recognized it instantly. He turned around and at a well-shadowed table spotted Alderman Fottingham highlighted by the blaze of the hearth. He sat about three feet from the table's edge—his girth had grown to enormous proportions. He wore a black robe trimmed with ermine, and his beard was longer than ever. Fottingham waved Shakespeare over.

"I knew you'd come back," he said. His deep voice hadn't changed a whit. "I just wondered what took you so long. Come join me, if you will."

"I must stable my horse," said Shakespeare.

"Rupert," Fottingham said to the tapster, "take the horse outside and stable it for my good cousin, Shakespeare. He is my guest."

The tapster nodded, then snarled when the alderman had turned his head away.

"Man's as fat as a distended bull's bladder, is he not?" Fottingham whispered. He patted his own rotund belly. "I should pass judgment, eh?"

Shakespeare laughed.

"What shall you drink?" asked the alderman.

"Ale for starts."

Fottingham pushed his tankard in front of Shakespeare's face. "Drink," he ordered.

"I couldn't—"

"Drink, boy," insisted Fottingham. "I've had more than enough." He dried his upper lip on his sleeve. "If I drink any more, I'll float home. It displeases my wife when I'm over-bloated."

Shakespeare brought the tankard to his mouth.

"So, what have you found out about your friend, Harry Whitman?" Fottingham asked, his cheeks flushed.

Shakespeare was surprised by the alderman's directness—no doubt due to excessive drinking. He answered, "I found out that Edgar Chambers is a liar."

"I could have told you that, if that is indeed the sole reason you came up here. And in such ungodly weather? Poor boy! Drink, drink. Warm your stomach."

Shakespeare took a large quaff of ale and asked, "Why do *you* say Chambers is a liar?"

"Why is the sun yellow? Why is a clear sky blue? It is because it *is*. Tis the will of God. Chambers is a liar because he is a liar. Everybody knows that."

Shakespeare paused a moment, wondering why the alderman hadn't told him that during his first trip up North. Fottingham was a strange animal—jovial, hospitable, helpful. But something about his eyes told Shakespeare that he had yet to play all his cards.

Fottingham noticed Shakespeare was quiet and added, "Aye, Chambers is a liar and a braggart. But he's harmless."

Shakespeare didn't think that was true, but now was not the time to challenge the alderman. He said, "Some ungodly talk has been written here, with Harry the unwitting protagonist."

The alderman picked up a pewter pitcher and refilled Shakespeare's tankard. "Tongues do flap indiscriminately," he said.

"Which tongues?" Shakespeare asked.

"Everyone," said Fottingham. "Gossip is the mainstay of small burgs."

"What *words* do they flap?" Shakespeare asked.

"That Harry was . . . how do I say this delicately . . ."

"That Harry was a buggerer," said Shakespeare.

Fottingham laughed. "Where is the poetry of your language, Shakespeare?"

"There is a time for poetry and a time to speak plainly. From what *I* knew of Harry, the gossip's not true. Who started the evil rumor?"

"I know not."

Shakespeare said, "Aye, the gossip monger is an anonymous writer. From whose lips did *you* hear those words?"

"It was last year. I don't remember."

"Why would a burg invent tales about a man it hardly knew?" asked Shakespeare.

"All small burgs are afeared of the Londoner. He's a natural subject of gossip. And Harry, though not intrusive, was known to have read a bawdy piece of poetry now and then at the Fishhead. He made many a man laugh—a marvelous comedian he was—so unlike the man I saw on stage six years ago. A tragic figure he played back then."

"Harry was a great player. He could become anyone."

The alderman thought for a moment, then said, "Yet he remained skillfully private about his personal life. So fanciful minds here filled in the blank space."

"Did you see any seeds of truth in this weed of a rumor?"

"No," Fottingham admitted.

"Why did Harry choose to stay at the Fishhead Inn, when Hemsdale has its own fine inn?"

The alderman shrugged.

"Were Harry and Chambers . . ." Shakespeare paused. "Were they known to be friendly to each other?"

Fottingham smiled. "I don't know, Shakespeare. Edgar has been known to partake of the local whores here, but that doesn't mean he couldn't be doing other things privately."

"Did Harry ever dally with a local whore? Mayhap with that whore who is also a notorious liar. The one that I had."

"Remind me again which one you had. All stews are notorious liars."

Shakespeare described the whore. He wanted Fottingham to mention the name.

"That sounds like Bess."

"That wasn't her name," Shakespeare said.

"Maybe it was Cat."

"That was it," said Shakespeare.

"Aye, Cat's a wily little thing." Fottingham thought a moment. "She lies for the fun of it. Whitman might have dallied with her, though you'll never know by asking her. I never saw them together. Then again, I don't go around spying on people."

Shakespeare said, "Of course you don't—" He stopped talking when he saw it. Out of the corner of his eye. A shadow exiting the tavern. Black and ominous. His muscles tightened, his heart raced. A blink and it was gone. Disappeared. Dematerialized. A poof of smoke blown away by wind. He bolted up, needing to follow it, but Fottingham grabbed his arm and held him back.

"What is it?" the alderman asked.

"Did you see that!"

"What?"

"That man who just left?"

"No."

"That shadow! That man! Who was he?"

"Shhh," the alderman said. "Calm down."

Shakespeare suddenly realized he was shouting. Eyes were upon him. He felt a jolt of heat sizzle through his body.

"Sit down," Fottingham said quietly.

"I . . ." Shakespeare lowered his voice. "I must follow that man."

"There was no man, Shakespeare," said Fottingham. "Sit down."

"No," Shakespeare said. "No. I must leave."

"Very well. Come to my house, then." The alderman asked for their capes, gloves, and scarves. Once they were in hand, the two of them left. The nighttime had turned the air unbearably icy, yet it felt soothing on Shakespeare's burning forehead.

The two men mounted their horses and rode to the alderman's house. A serving man took their coats and led them into a hall warmed by a burning fire. The room was sparsely furnished— six chairs and a wooden table that held steaming pots of cider. A chamberlain lit the floor sconce, and shadows flickered against the tapestries on the walls. Fottingham offered Shakespeare a chair and asked,

"What has been happening to you in London?"

Shakespeare told him the story of the phantasmal man in black and a ruffian named George Mackering.

"And you think you just saw this specter or man?"

Shakespeare nodded.

"Could it have been this cur Mackering?" asked the alderman.

"I don't think so, as he already passed on his chance to kill me. I think he hopes that I'll lead him to Harry's killer."

"A man like Mackering could find the killer himself."

"Maybe," said Shakespeare. "But Mackering is a very visible man. Easy to spot, easy to hide from."

"In sooth," said Fottingham. "Why's Mackering interested in Harry's killer?"

Shakespeare paused, wondering if he was talking too freely. Yet there seemed no point in hiding the truth. It shouldn't surprise anyone that Mackering was an extortionist on top of his other nefarious activities. Shakespeare explained that Harry had been paying the uprightman money to keep secrets.

Fottingham bit his lip, stroked his beard. He asked, "Is Harry a Papist? His uncle was a Jesuit, you know."

"I didn't know," Shakespeare lied.

Fottingham took a gulp of cider. "Are the Henleys Papists? They are rumored to be."

"And Harry was rumored to be a buggerer," said Shakespeare. "We know what rumors are worth."

"True," said Fottingham. "What was Harry's secret, then?"

"I don't know," Shakespeare continued lying. He heard Harry's booming voice in his head.

An actor must be such an adroit liar that even should his wife catch him fucking a wench, he could convince her otherwise.

What lies could he tell her? Shakespeare had asked, laughing.

Why, that she was seeing things, of course . . . or the poor girl had just fainted and you were just giving her air.

Through her legs?

No one ever said acting wasn't challenging, Shakespeare!

Letting go of the memory, Shakespeare steered the discussion back to Chambers. He asked the alderman if the hostler were capable of murder.

Fottingham said, "If the rewards were high enough. As you may well remember, Chambers is fond of money." The alderman paused. "Yet why would he risk his life knowing that Harry's death would incur Mackering's wrath?"

Shakespeare conceded the point. But somebody did Harry in. And most likely he wasn't murdered by highway robbers. Harry had no money on him worth protecting. He'd gambled—or given—most of it away to Mackering.

Fottingham fidgeted in his chair, rocking his meaty buttocks over the hard wooden seat. His face was beet red, his nose protruded with veins. Shakespeare knew his host was tired, and didn't want to overstay his welcome. But when he rose to leave, Fottingham insisted that he spend the night. The alderman walked him to the guest chambers, and just as Shakespeare was about to close the door, Fottingham asked him who he thought his specter was.

Shakespeare hesitated a moment, then said, "A man who nobody notices."

"That wouldn't be Chambers," said Fottingham.

"No," said Shakespeare. "I would have noticed *him.* But it could be someone who was paid by Chambers. Someone whose presence is always around us but we never notice. Someone as common as dirt."

Someone like a beggar, he thought. Or someone like a whore.

* * *

The next morning was again marked by blizzards. It wasn't until late afternoon that Providence's wrath had abated. Shakespeare thanked the alderman and headed out to the Fishhead Inn.

Upon his arrival, dozens of men stood about the front door of the public house. Another dozen had gathered around the enormous walnut sign of the carved fish. As Shakespeare rode up to the door, an expensively dressed man waved him away. He wore a thick velvet doublet under an ermine-lined cape and looked like an older version of Chambers. He sprouted the same ginger hair but thinner, the same pinched features, but the skin held a wrinkle or two. Shakespeare imagined that he was Edgar Chambers's brother.

"We're closed," he shouted.

Shakespeare stopped and dismounted. "What's the problem?"

"There is a suitable inn in Hemsdale not more than two hours' ride from here. It's called the Grouse—"

"I'm well aware of Hemsdale," said Shakespeare. "I just came from there."

"Are you going south?" asked the tapster.

"Aye."

"Then five miles following the main road there is an inn called the Portwater."

"Good, good," said Shakespeare. "I'll lodge there. What about all these other men? Are they staying here?"

"Yes. They've already paid for their lodging."

"Cannot I pay as well?"

"No," said the man firmly. "The magistrate will not allow any new gentlemen in the inn today."

"Why?"

The caped man rubbed his gloved hands together. "There has been a terrible incident," he said quietly. "Just simply dreadful. My brother . . . the innkeeper has been murdered."

Though shocked, Shakespeare's face registered nothing. He looked about the crowd of men for a familiar face. To his eye they were all strangers. Yet shadows were notorious for hiding in small places.

"Edgar Chambers was your younger brother?" Shakespeare asked.

"Yes." The man looked at Shakespeare suspiciously. "How did you know?"

"You look like him. I've met your brother. I've stayed here before."

"I don't remember you."

"It was only once," Shakespeare said. "A long time ago."

Chambers seemed satisfied with the explanation.

"This is just terrible." His voice was bordering on hysterical passion. "An incident such as this one can drive away business for years. I should have known better than to let Edgar handle such responsibility. You can't do anything well unless you do it yourself, you know. Edgar was notorious for getting himself into trouble. And I, famous for always having to pull him out of the muck—" Chambers suddenly clutched his arms. "My God, what am I saying? My God! My God!"

Shakespeare patted him on the shoulder. "When was he killed?" he asked.

"I know not the time exactly. It *had* to be during the night. Which means it had to be one of these so-called gentlemen or their staff, damn them!"

"It could have been someone from Hemsdale who stopped in for a meal."

"True," Chambers conceded. "I just hope they find the murderer soon. A killer on the loose does nothing for business."

"When was your brother discovered?" Shakespeare asked.

"Edgar was usually up by six," Chambers said. "When he still hadn't come into the dining room by seven, I went to his room. It was locked. I took out my own key . . . oh God, it was awful!" He buried his face in his hands. "Lying in all that blood." His hands began to shake.

Shakespeare gave him a minute to calm down. Then he asked, "By any chance was he visited by a whore?"

Chambers blanched white with fear. "Who are you?"

"Why do you ask?"

"Where were *you* last night?"

"I had the privilege of being a guest of Alderman Fottingham. I slept at his house."

The answer softened Chambers's previously wary face.

"He was visited by a whore, then?" Shakespeare asked.

"Aye," said Chambers.

"Who?"

"A whore named Catherine Bollingham. She was known about Hemsdale as Cat."

"You're sure?" asked Shakespeare.

"Positively," answered Chambers. "She's with him now. Lying in the same pool of blood. As dead as he."

49

It was the third tooth de Andrada had lost since Christmas. But at least this one had fallen out naturally—from rot—rather than being punched out by Essex's men.

He stood hunched over the fireplace, a frayed brown blanket of coarse wool over his shoulders. He closed his eyes and thought of Spain—Malaga, so mild in the winters. Amsterdam was a God-forsaken city as cold as fish eyes. Her houses were narrower than reeds, the canals stank of garbage, and the language was an abomination. People here spit when they spoke. De Andrada began to shiver. He rubbed his hands together and warmed them over a kettle hanging inside a tiny fireplace.

Spain was but a faraway dream as long as Philip sat on the throne. The wrinkled old fart of a king would never forgive him for his part in the rebellion of Don Antonio. No matter that the Spanish whoreson had forgiven the rabid wolf Lopez. The witch doctor had money, and that was all that mattered to Philip. Money! It bought the old king furs to warm his brittle bones, soft food for his toothless mouth, young whores to suck his withered stick.

The thought of that old wretch pawing nubile bodies made de Andrada sick with disgust.

Spain and his homeland, Portugal, were lost for the moment. But England was not such a distant revel. The great Isle had more than its share of luscious maidens with their gleaming cornflower eyes and wavy, golden hair. The thought of fair wenches caused de Andrada's skin to prick with excitement. England was almost within his grasp if he could get the witch doctor done in.

If . . .

Gods in heaven, how he had mucked it up the first time! He had been so sure he had sufficient evidence against Lopez—the secret cell in Mountjoy's Inn, and Nan, the chambermaid, who claimed that Lopez kept secret writings in his desk. Who knew that the doctor maintained the sequestered closet just for his whores? And no letters or seditious correspondence from Philip had been found anywhere—not in Lopez's home, not in the house of Sir George Ames as well.

The news had not sat well with Essex.

De Andrada shuddered as he remembered the men Essex's secret spy master, Antony Bacon, had sent from England to visit him in Amsterdam. Two of them. The larger one had a jaw as big as a serving bowl, hands the size of saddles. His fingers were twisted, the knuckles like balls of iron. He cracked them constantly.

"We are men of the most esteemed Earl of Essex, Master de Andrada," the big-jawed man introduced himself.

Crack!

Big Jaw continued, "Our lord—your lord as well—is in good health but is rather displeased."

Crunch!

"What desires m'lord?" asked de Andrada, shaking. As if he didn't know. "Whatever it is, twill be my honor to do his bidding!"

Big Jaw smiled.

Pop!

The other one was smaller, but thicker with muscle. His face was so fat that his eyes looked like two currants set in bread dough. The currants held de Andrada with an evil stare.

Calmly, they told what had happened in England.

"Your lord Essex much disliked the Queen's rebuking," said Big Jaw.

Crack!

"M'lord Essex does not like to play the fool for the doggish Jew's delight!" the fat face with the currant eyes said.

Big Jaw added: "M'lord is much ired, as Her Majesty chose to reprove him in front of his servants. Her voice was far from modulated, and other courtiers have since been known to glance at our lord with bemused scorn."

Snap!

"What plans have you to change the situation to the good of your lord Essex, Master de Andrada?" said Fat Face.

He quaked as they spoke, sniveled as they began to bang their fists into their fleshy palms.

De Andrada croaked out. "I pray you, tell Lord Essex that I'll rectify the situation forthwith, I swear. I still know much, I still have many spies—"

"We need evidence, Master de Andrada," Fat Face said. "Secret letters and documents. People who will speak of Lopez's treachery against the throne of England. The Queen's bench needs evidence to prosecute!"

De Andrada answered, "I swear on behalf of the Almighty I'll bring you evidence!"

"Soon," said Big Jaw.

Pop!

"Very soon," said Fat Face. "His lordship expects to hear from you by the twentieth of January."

And then they beat him to a bloody pulp.

He'd recovered quickly and went to work. He contacted every single whore in the dock areas of Holland—every strumpet who had seen and serviced ships of the Englishman. Perhaps over the years they had seen something lurking in the shadows at night— a well-hidden transaction of money followed by stowaways being sneaked off the ships. If one whore had seen just one suspicious-looking thing . . .

If . . .

De Andrada's diligence had paid off. At the start of the second week in January he met up with a twig of a blond whore who spoke of a good-looking but odd man. He was Portuguese and kept to himself, never succumbed to her advances. The stew thought at first the odd man to be a buggerer, but he never went with the boys either. He spent most of his time scribbling notes to himself, walking amongst the incoming ships. And he always appeared at night.

"He was friendly, though," she said to de Andrada as an afterthought.

"Why do you say that?"

"He waved at me, winked at me. I think he wanted me sore, but some wights are a little . . . ." She shrugged her bony shoulders.

"What else was strange about him?"

"That's all, man," the whore said, smiling with brown teeth. "Just the way he skulked around the ships at night. I thought him a thief, I did."

"Mayhap he was."

"Mayhap," said the whore.

"Did he skulk around all the boats?" de Andrada asked.

"Only the English."

De Andrada had no choice but to lay down a plan and hope. With a few coins—stews came cheap—he enticed the whore into partnership.

The night came. With friendly banter the stew distracted the Portuguese. De Andrada sneaked up from behind, slipped a sack over the man's head and hit him with a stick. When the man was completely out, the whore acted as lookout while de Andrada dragged him to a secluded spot under the pilings of a canal and rummaged through his pockets and purse. The man had six gold

coins of Levantine currency and a letter that identified him as
Gomez D'Avila.

De Andrada rummaged deeper into his pockets and found a
mysterious communication—a letter written to David and signed
by Francisco de Torres.

De Andrada had no idea who Francisco de Torres was, but
knew that David was the witch doctor's connection in the Low
Countries. It was safe to reason that this Gomez D'Avila was,
in fact, David.

The letter spoke cryptically of deliveries of pearls, musk, and
amber for His Worship.

> *The bearer will inform Your Worship in what price your pearls*
> *are held. I will advise Your Worship presently of the uttermost*
> *penny that will be given for them, and crave what order you will*
> *have set down for the conveyance of the money and wherein you*
> *would have it employed. Also, this bearer shall tell you in what*
> *resolution we rested about a little musk and amber, the which I*
> *determined to buy.*

His Worship was, of course, King Philip.

D'Avila was coming back to life. De Andrada hit him again,
stuffed the gold coins and letter in his own doublet and ran back
to his closet.

Under the flickering light of a rush candle de Andrada reread
the letter. He had two weeks to formulate a plan of attack.

Who under God was Francisco de Torres? Never had the name
been mentioned in Lopez's household, and never had Nan, the
bitch chambermaid, spoken of him.

Assume, de Andrada thought—for the moment at least—that
Francisco de Torres was a man in the secret employ of Lopez.
Or better still, that de Torres was a false name for the witch
doctor himself. The witch doctor had written the enigmatic letter
to his agent David, now identified as Gomez D'Avila.

A very good start.

David was to deliver the letter to His Worship, Philip.

But what did the letter mean?

Pearls, musk, and amber. The commodities, de Andrada
knew, were code words for Jews under the auspices of the Inquisition—pearls meaning Spanish Jews, musk and amber referring to the Portuguese. From what de Andrada could tell, the
cryptic letter asked Philip for the price to buy the Jews freedom.

Lopez, the witch doctor, a present-day Moses, redeeming his
people from an Iberian pharaoh. Once Lopez had redeemed *him*
from the Tower—a long time ago in another lifetime, before the

doctor had turned evil and mistrusted his loyal servant, de Andrada.

The spineless cur. The dog! The wolf, rat, swine, snake . . .

De Andrada halted his string of curses and returned his concentration to the letter. The correspondence showed that Lopez had secret dealings with His Majesty, but that alone did not imply sedition. Essex wanted Lopez hung for treason, would be happy with nothing less.

That being the case, de Andrada would have to instill new meaning to the code words.

What could Lopez deliver to the Spanish king that would constitute treason?

Secret documents.

Where would Lopez obtain sensitive state secrets?

De Andrada thought and thought but came up with nothing. He discarded the idea that Lopez was delivering secret documents to the King.

What seditious service could Lopez carry out for the King of Spain?

After an hour of ruminating, trying to invent something plausible, de Andrada suddenly slapped his forehead. It had been before his eyes all the time yet he'd been too shortsighted to see it.

Lopez, the poisoner! Lopez, the expert with Indian acacia and henbane! Lopez, the doctor of Don Antonio, who would have poisoned his master while under his service! Lopez, the devil who had tried to poison him!

Ideas swarmed inside de Andrada's skull.

Pearls, then, would be a code word for Her Majesty! Amber and musk, for England's most prized possession—her navy. The tale could be very simple. For money, Lopez had promised the King of Spain that he would poison his mistress, Elizabeth Tudor, and arrange to destroy her navy. The former was the easier task, as Lopez was her trusted physician. The latter was more difficult, but money could buy many of England's secret Papists. For additional ducats Lopez would arrange for the burning and splitting of England's ships. Hadn't Philip been seeking a way to destroy England's navy after his own Armada's humiliating defeat?

Beautiful! Plausible! If only he could convince *Essex* of his lies! The lord was a rash youth, steeped in hatred for Lopez. Perhaps it wouldn't take much connivance after all.

De Andrada formulated his treachery:

Item one: Lopez was working for Philip. Even the Queen knew that the doctor had had past correspondence with the King of Spain.

Always blend veracity with fabrication.

Item two: Lopez had offered to poison the Queen and burn her ships for payment. Hadn't Roderigo offered to poison other sovereigns—such as Don Antonio for King Philip? Again, a basis of truth.

Item three: Logic would then dictate that Lopez would also poison the Queen if Philip paid accordingly. Lopez, the secret Jew, would do anything for his brethren. Everyone knew that Jews—even those scheming Jews who professed to be Protestant—worshiped not God but money.

But evidence! He needed *evidence*!

He had the letter. What else? De Andrada snapped his fingers. Gods, the lies were coalescing like fat atop beef broth.

Item four: De Andrada knew that Lopez's daughter had in her possession a certain ring—a large ruby surrounded by diamonds—a ring from the old treasury of Spain. Lopez had explained worriedly to his brother-in-law, Sir George, that he had given it to the Queen, but Elizabeth had returned it to Rebecca for some unknown reason. Lopez had been quite distraught that day.

It could be used against us, Lopez had whispered to Ames. *A ring from the old treasury in our hands can seem very suspicious to the wrong set of eyes.*

Then sell it hence, Ames had replied.

But what if the Queen calls Rebecca back to court and she wears it not, Roderigo had countered. *Her Majesty will be most displeased.*

In the end they had decided to keep the ring.

Evidence! And seasoned subtly with pinches of truth.

De Andrada would claim that the ring was Philip's initial payment to Lopez for the gruesome task of poisoning his mistress, Elizabeth Tudor. More recompense would come once the job was successfully completed.

Yes, yes!

The ring was given to Lopez as payment. But Lopez was a clever man and had given it to the Queen as a gift, showing him to be a man capable of much duplicity. But Her Majesty, the Queen, was too acute for the cunning Jew! She discovered its origins and gave it back to Rebecca at first opportunity.

Brilliant!

Twas unimportant what the code words of the letter actually meant, why the ring was in Rebecca's possession. All that was necessary was that de Andrada persuade Essex.

The letter. He read it again. It went on to speak of Esteban Ferreira de Gama—the former Spanish smuggler of Jews—as the purveyor of the goods.

Was de Gama the new English connection now that Miguel Nuñoz was a cripple? Had to be.

If de Gama could be persuaded to bear false witness against Lopez, to say that the witch doctor was working for His Majesty against Her Majesty . . .

What would seduce de Gama to lie?

Not money, surely. The man was too much the gentleman to ruin his good name for gold. Not women as well. He was as faithful to his *esposa* as a lapdog—the stupid dolt.

Torture was the only alternative. Using the proper techniques, twas possible to get a man to say anything. De Andrada would request that Essex arrest de Gama at once, claiming he was Lopez's accomplice. Then the skill of the torturers would take over and de Gama would confess Lopez's evil plans.

De Andrada formulated his ideas on paper, then wrote a coherent letter to Essex. He ended the correspondence with:

> *All these actions must be employed with utmost haste lest grievous harm fall upon England's Gloriana, her most virtuous and chaste Queen.*

De Andrada dispatched the letter immediately to Essex through Big Jaw with the cracked knuckles, bypassing the lord's own spy master, Antony Bacon. All that done, he finally allowed himself the luxury of sleep. When he awoke, his room was gray and cold. He lit a fire and hung a kettle over the flames, noticing a minute later that another tooth had fallen out of his decayed mouth. It lay on the floor among the rushes like a pitted pebble. Yet it bothered him not.

He had *evidence*—letter, ring, and a witness who, under torture, would testify against the witch doctor. Soon all of it would be resting in Lord Essex's hands.

If Essex swallowed his lies, he would be back in England in a month—speaking a language that didn't sound like guttural retching, in a warm bed under Lord Essex's protection, his stomach full, his member plunging into the soft folds of a young wench—maybe even a virgin. Lopez would be hung as a traitor, his family destroyed.

Quickly, he posted the letter. If only Essex would believe such bald lies.

If only . . .

Essex sat upright in his desk chair and fingered the correspondence as if it were a string of rosary beads. The natural warm oil of his hands was smudging the exterior ink and melting the seal of the wax—de Andrada's seal. Essex's eyes peered across his desktop, his malevolent stare landing upon Big Albert. The giant-jawed servant dropped his eyes and squirmed under his lord's scrutiny.

"And de Andrada had told you that the evidence was indisputable?" Essex said, leaning forward, elbow on his desk.

"Aye, m'lord," said Albert. "He used the word indisputable."

"Has he informed you of the contents of the letter?" Essex asked.

"Why no, m'lord," said Albert. "Did you want him to?"

Essex picked up a silver bowl of ale and threw it at his servant. It whacked Albert in the stomach and drenched his gown and face. The servant didn't flinch.

Essex said, "Of course I don't want you to know the contents of the letter, you stupid dolt. I just wonder whether the weasel told you things that should have been kept secret."

"He told me nothing, m'lord," answered Albert.

"Save that the contents of this letter hold indisputable evidence against Dr. Roderigo Lopez."

"Aye," said Albert.

"Sit," Essex said, pointing to a stool in the corner.

Albert obeyed. Essex walked over to the main hearth of the library and stoked the fire. His lodgings at Whitehall Palace were the largest of any nobility. His library was wood-paneled, the ceiling fresco overleafed with gold and silver. Others had to be satisfied with wee cells that barely had enough space for a desk and globe. But his was a huge chamber. It easily accommodated all of his books, two gold floor sconces three feet in diameter, a pair of marble statues dedicated to him by some peasant artist from the Royal Academy, three desks, two fireplaces, four globes, and an assortment of tables and chairs. In addition to the library, Essex's quarters contained a comfortably sized sleeping chamber—its walls covered with silk arras—a separate wash and tub closet, two guest cells, and ample room for his staff.

Splendid lodgings reserved for the Queen's favorite.

The bitch had softened her anger against him, and he was once again a person to be reckoned with at court. Yet he felt that others laughed at him behind his back. *Little pet Essex being scolded by his schoolmaster*—say, rather, *schoolmistress*. Gods, how he wished he could strangle them all—those well-fed, clean-faced asses who brayed.

They also laughed when Elizabeth had commanded him back home from the Spanish front. Though Essex carried himself proudly, always attired himself in the finest of dress and armed himself with the best of swords, others had snickered that he was naught but a castrated peacock displaying wounded feathers.

Lopez among them.

Marry, he'd love to kill the bastard dog of a Jew.

He sat back down at his desk and once again fingered the letter. With one fluid motion he broke the seal and pulled out the papers.

He read de Andrada's letter.

He read Lopez's letter to David.

He reread de Andrada's letter, then studied all the correspondence carefully.

He frowned.

"Indisputable?" he muttered.

He took his quill, dipped it in the inkwell and began to scribble some notes as he reread de Andrada's letter.

He put down his quill and rubbed his chin.

"Maybe," he whispered.

He reread Lopez's letter to D'Avila and raised his eyes.

Once again he began to scribble notes.

"Maybe," he repeated. Louder. "Though I strongly doubt the verity of the weasel's words, his implications might work indeed." He clapped his hands together and studied the letters for an hour, scribbling notes, tearing them up, sighing, laughing, scowling. Finally he stabbed the quill into its holder, sat back and closed his eyes. He sat so quietly that his servant thought him asleep.

"M'lord?" Albert whispered.

"Quiet, you fool," answered Essex without opening his eyes. "I'm thinking."

Albert retreated back to the wall. Ten minutes later Essex opened his eyes and dipped his quill in a silver pot of ink. On the finest parchment he addressed a letter to his spy master. With confidence he wrote to Antony Bacon,

> *In haste, this morning, I have discovered a most dangerous and desperate treason. The point of conspiracy was Her Majesty's death. The executioner should have been Dr. Lopez, the manner poison.*

He sealed the letter, then regarded Albert, quaking in the corner.

"Dispatch this immediately to Master Bacon in Eton, Albert."

Albert bolted up. "With assurity, m'lord."

"I need not remind you of what discretion is required in this task."

"No, m'lord. Not at all."

"Well, then! Go!"

Albert left. Essex sat back in his chair. He smiled.

50

A week had passed since Fottingham last saw Shakespeare. Yet he wasn't at all surprised when the player, carrying a leather bag upon his back, showed up at the threshold of his door.

"Back to London?" Fottingham asked.

Shakespeare nodded.

"Come in a moment," boomed the alderman. "You've plenty of daylight left. My house is warm, my fare is plentiful and pleasing to the stomach. I was just about to dine. Do stay and tell me what you've discovered about Chambers's murder this past week. Then I'll tell you the whisperings about town."

Shakespeare had just come to say good-bye, as good manners dictated. Yet the possibility of learning more drew him like bait. Realizing he'd probably have to give information to receive some in return, he weighed his decision. Curiosity won out. He said, "My horse stands uncovered outside. It's raining heavily."

"I'll have one of the servants stable it," said Fottingham. "Come in."

Shakespeare said thank you, then entered the alderman's home and dropped his bag on the floor. Fottingham called out the order to a blue-gowned boy, then said to Shakespeare,

"This is the second time in a week that you have mentioned your horse's needs before your own. Care about animals, do you?"

"I've an affinity for dumb beasts."

"Don't we all?" said Fottingham.

Shakespeare smiled and said, "Harry Whitman hired me as stable boy for the fellowship when I first came to London. I was not overly familiar with the finer points of grooming, but I learned very quickly."

Shakespeare thought back to his first visit with Harry. Whitman could have called his bluff immediately. But he hadn't. Not until years later did he admit he'd known Shakespeare had been lying. It had been one of those frequent times where Harry's drinking had turned him boisterous and unstable. It was hard to take him seriously.

You didn't know a damn thing about horses when I took you on, did you, Willy?

Whitman slapped Shakespeare on the back loudly. The thwack caused men in the alehouse to turn around and laugh.

Not a whit, Shakespeare said softly.

Harry let out a series of raucous guffaws. *You little cellar rat of a liar.*

If you suspected me of lying, why did you hire me?

You looked able-bodied enough to do the job.

Why did you hire me, Harry?

Aw, what the devil. I admit it. It was the book. Most of the writing was . . . How shall I put this?

Whitman held his nose with one hand, fanned away imaginary fumes with the other. He burst into laughter.

It wasn't that foul, Shakespeare said.

It was rot! Harry announced to anyone who had been listening. *But!* He had held his finger in the air. *But it contained two fine soliloquies, Willy. Two beautiful soliloquies. I'd never read anything quite so moving.*

Harry suddenly grew sentimental. There was moisture in his eyes. Had Shakespeare not escorted him out of the alehouse, he would surely have cried.

A week later, when Harry was sober, Shakespeare asked him the same question.

Whitman gave him a sad smile.

I have a soft heart for dreamers and you were as fresh as they come. Aye, I did recognize your talent. But I would have welcomed you even had you been a simpleton. Willy, my son, I know what it's like to live with thwarted desires.

Shakespeare heard the alderman talking.

". . . long have you had the horse?" Fottingham said.

"The horse?" Shakespeare said. "It isn't mine. Just a hackney. But it has served me well."

"Sit," the alderman repeated.

"Thank you, I will," said Shakespeare.

Fottingham poured him a pot of beer. "Tell me what you know about Chambers."

"He and the whore were murdered in the middle of the night," Shakespeare said. "The girl was dealt with swiftly—her throat was slashed, her heart by a single stab of a dagger. Chambers was stabbed repeatedly. His throat was also slashed."

Fottingham paled. "God in heaven! Where have you learned such horrible detail?"

"I told the magistrate that I was an eminent physician from London," said Shakespeare. "He allowed me to examine the bodies. I even signed papers certifying them dead."

Fottingham stared at him.

Shakespeare drank the pot of beer and said, "I'm quite well regarded as an actor."

"You *signed* death papers?"

"They asked me to perform the honors," said Shakespeare. "Besides, the cause of demise was obvious."

Fottingham said thoughtfully, "I suppose it was. Was any murder weapon found?"

Shakespeare shook his head no.

Fottingham asked, "Did not *someone* hear them cry out at night?"

"Not a single gentleman claims to have heard a sound," Shakespeare said. "Chambers's cell was at the end of a long hallway. Besides, I think the murderer immediately slashed their throats. It prevented them from screaming for help—"

"My God!"

"Horrible," Shakespeare agreed.

"Yet," Fottingham said, "the murderer appears to have escaped without punishment."

"God witnessed the deed," Shakespeare said.

Fottingham thought about that.

"What have you heard about town?" Shakespeare asked.

Before the alderman could answer, a servant entered the room and lay on the table a tray holding two stuffed chickens. The birds were ample and would make a satisfactory dinner, but Shakespeare compared the plate to the copious platters of meat the alderman had served him last spring. Wintertimes were hard up here, food supplies scarce. Shakespeare knew the alderman was sharing his dinner with him and appreciated the act of kindness. He thanked him for such mouth-watering fare. Fottingham smiled, tore off the left leg of a bird and took a bite.

"Be not shy, Willy." His mouth was stuffed with meat. "Take."

Shakespeare amputated the chicken's other leg. Before he ate, he asked, "What winds of gossip do the townspeople blow?"

"Chambers had many foes," said Fottingham, still chewing.

"Aye? Who?"

"Myself, for instance," said the alderman. "I owed him not a small sum."

Shakespeare didn't react.

Fottingham said, "Aye, you're a fine player, Willy. Not a hair in your brow did you raise, but I know you must consider me a suspicious man in this whole affair. I knew you were in town. I knew you intended to visit Chambers. Perhaps while you slept soundly in my house I stealthily tiptoed down to the Fishhead and did Chambers and the stew in, rendering my debt to that slimy eel null and void.''

The conversation was to be a game of wits. Shakespeare countered, ''You'd murder for ten pounds six shillings?''

The alderman smiled slyly. ''I knew you were a clever fellow.'' He broke the bird in half. Oatmeal stuffing tumbled onto the platter. Fottingham picked up a fistful with his fingers and gorged himself. ''How'd you find out?'' he mumbled.

''Many about town paid money to Chambers,'' Shakespeare said.

''How'd you find out about *me*?''

''I talked to Chambers's brother Edmund. He showed me Edgar's secret accounting ledgers.''

''Why would Edmund do that?''

Shakespeare rubbed his thumb back and forth against his fingertips.

''The Chambers brothers are easily bought,'' Fottingham said. He looked at Shakespeare. ''Can you be bought as well?''

''Do you want to buy me?'' Shakespeare asked.

Fottingham chuckled nervously. ''No,'' he said.

''I can be bought,'' Shakespeare said, ''but not for money.''

''For love?''

''For a certain love I'd act the ass. For a certain love I've *been* an ass.''

''In sooth?'' said Fottingham.

''Yes,'' Shakespeare said. ''But asses are beasts of burden, and lest I become an ass and a burdensome beast, I'll keep my words sweet and succinct. Why did you borrow money from the innkeeper?''

Fottingham said, ''A personal affair.''

They ate for a moment without speaking. Shakespeare said,

''Mayhap I should rephrase my question? Why was the innkeeper extorting money from you?''

Fottingham stopped chewing. He resumed mastication a moment later, then swallowed his mouthful in a big, dry gulp. He coughed. Shakespeare hit him on the back.

''What makes you think I was a victim of extortion?'' Fottingham sputtered out.

''Chambers was wrestling money from diverse people.''

''Who else?''

''Harry Whitman, for one.''

''Who else?''

''My lips are sealed,'' Shakespeare said. ''However, Edmund's may be pried open for the right price.''

The alderman coughed up a bolus of food, spit it onto the floor and managed a sickly smile. Shakespeare had spilled his information. Now he expected the alderman to pay in kind. He asked,

"What dirt did Chambers—Edgar Chambers—have on you?"

Fottingham sighed, knowing that the player would discover his secrets eventually. It might as well come from him.

"I am a member of the Queen's Church," Fottingham whispered. "I have lived and shall die a Protestant. But up here . . . some years ago . . . and on occasion even to this day, I have housed some cousins of my family. . . . Some were very old men and women who still remembered when King Henry the Eighth was called the Defender of the Faith. . . . Do you understand what I'm saying, Shakespeare?"

"Chambers knew you had sporadically hidden Papists," Shakespeare said softly. "He started asking you for money two, maybe three years ago to keep your secrets hushed."

Fottingham nodded. He was sweating now. He said, "I've asked you this before, Shakespeare, but I'll ask you again. Was Whitman a Papist?"

Shakespeare sighed. The alderman had confided treasonous secrets. Shakespeare felt it wise to give him something in exchange. He admitted Whitman's Catholicism, and Fottingham let out an audible sigh and felt it was safe to proceed. He explained that Hemsdale was like numerous northern burgs in the country, that there were many who were Protestant in their worship, Catholics in their hearts. There were also many who'd welcome Chambers's death.

"Edmund showed me a list of no less than twenty names," Shakespeare said. "Edgar Chambers would have been a rich man had he not been a gambler."

That stopped Fottingham for a moment. "Chambers was a gambler?"

Shakespeare nodded. "The money was scarcely held by the innkeeper. Once it touched his fingers, he was merely a conduit, linking the rivers of his victims' purses and a certain ruffian's pocket."

Fottingham said, "I've never seen Chambers dice."

"Edmund informed me that his brother diced in private. Edgar had also accrued enormous debts."

Shakespeare explained how Edgar Chambers's dicing habit was a logical assumption. Why else would George Mackering himself be this far north, away from his own haunts in London, unless there was substantial gain to be made? Mackering must have sent a few men up here a couple of years ago. They must have reported back what a perfect gull Chambers had been.

When Mackering first arrived, Chambers hadn't known him from the hundreds of other gentlemen who'd spent the night in his hostel drinking and dicing. But Mackering knew Chambers, knew he was a fine coney, as greedy as he was dishonest—the perfect combination. Mackering began to dice regularly with Chambers—as often as every month, according to the ledgers. Only after his debts mounted did Chambers discover with whom he was playing—that Mackering was not a simple gentleman and was not likely to forgive debts. The innkeeper began needing money badly. Shakespeare surmised he began his extortion scheme then.

The alderman said nothing.

Shakespeare told him, "You knew Chambers was extorting others for their Catholic beliefs when I first visited Hemsdale, didn't you?"

Fottingham squirmed in his chair. "I suspected I wasn't alone."

Shakespeare let him squirm. It was all part of the contest of wills—how much do you reveal, how much do you trust? He steered the conversation back to Harry and asked the alderman if he'd known that Harry had been an extortion victim from the beginning.

Fottingham turned red and wiped his damp forehead with his robe sleeve. "I swear to you, Shakespeare, I barely knew Harry Whitman. Aye, maybe I suspected he was a Papist, as I knew his uncle had been a Jesuit priest, but I swear I didn't know that Chambers had embedded his stinger in your friend. I merely thought that Whitman had come up here on a yearly pilgrimage to visit his kinsmen, to escape the grime and loneliness of London."

"Even after Harry was murdered you didn't suspect that Chambers had anything to do with it?" Shakespeare asked.

"No one in this town had been murdered, yet many had been victims of extortion." Fottingham was flustered, acting like a trapped animal. He stammered out, "What . . . what do you want me to say? What should I have *done*? Made unfounded accusations that Chambers was Harry's murderer? I directed *you* to him. I thought that was enough!"

Shakespeare paused a moment, realizing he was attacking the wrong person.

"It was, Master Fottingham," Shakespeare said quietly. "It was. I failed to ask Edgar Chambers the proper questions, and now I'm embarrassed by my incompetence."

Fottingham took a deep breath and let it out slowly. He did it again and seemed to calm down.

"Chambers's death is no surprise," the alderman said. "The

town spoke ill of him, many had wished him dead. Who would want to kill Whitman is your riddle.''

Shakespeare was silent.

Fottingham crossed and uncrossed his legs. He said, ''Mayhap Whitman was tired of paying the weasel. Perhaps he announced his intentions to Chambers and an accidental but most disastrous exchange occurred.''

''Chambers killed Whitman?'' said Shakespeare dubiously.

Fottingham nodded eagerly.

A bit too eagerly. Shakespeare knew the assumption was absurd. Hours before he died, Harry himself had diced with Mackering in a desperate attempt for money. Harry would not have needed money to pay off Chambers if he were going to speak his mind once and for all. Besides, a confrontation might inspire Chambers to talk to the wrong people. That could have meant death for Harry's kinsmen, certain death for the Jesuit. Harry would never have chanced it.

Mackering. He'd caught a healthy group of coneys in Hemsdale. Lots here would have need of extra pence to pay off Chambers. Gambling would be seen as a viable and quick solution.

In one respect Fottingham was correct. The question was not who killed Chambers. The correct query was who killed Whitman. Shakespeare had his suspicions, but he kept them to himself.

The alderman stopped nodding and cast his eyes upon the floor. He had been drained of all his joviality. It was useless to keep badgering him. Shakespeare didn't believe he'd been involved in Harry's death, and that's all that mattered to him at the moment.

''I must be off,'' he announced. ''I cannot repay you for your kindness, Master Fottingham. You have been a gentleman beyond compare, have heaped upon me, without bound, too much graciousness.''

Fottingham waved him off, saying that his house was open to the player any time. He hesitated, then added in a whisper, ''I don't know who did Chambers in. I swear to you, Shakespeare, I don't know. But if I knew who he was, I'd kiss him. If it be Mackering, then the ruffian has a warm bed in my house.''

Shakespeare didn't reply.

''Do you think that Chambers killed Whitman?'' Fottingham asked.

Shakespeare shrugged. Fottingham didn't press him. He was very grateful to see the player off.

The sky had reduced its downpour to simple rain. The country lanes had become rushing brooks and Shakespeare was soaked to the bone. No matter. His stomach was full and he was making good time. He had been riding south for two hours and would probably reach the next inn—the Portwater—by nightfall.

He felt certain of one thing. Chambers's murder was connected to Harry's. Someone had waited until Shakespeare had revisited the North to do Chambers in. As for the stew, maybe she was part of it. Or maybe she'd been in the wrong place at the wrong time.

Only two people here knew that Shakespeare had meant to question the innkeeper—Fottingham and the Jesuit, Silvera. He had not mentioned Chambers to any of the Henleys, nor to anyone else in town.

One possibility was that Chambers had been killed by Fottingham. The alderman, upon talking to Shakespeare in the alehouse, had felt his grave secret was about to be uncovered. By killing Chambers he rid himself of an extortionist and protected his confidences. But Shakespeare had his doubts about Fottingham cast as a murderer. The hospitable alderman seemed appalled as Shakespeare described the murder, genuinely horrified. Fottingham just didn't seem like a heartless killer.

A second possibility: Chambers had been killed by Silvera. After Shakespeare had questioned the Jesuit, Silvera assumed that Chambers was the murderer of his true and spiritual son. The priest, consumed with grief, sneaked into town in one of his many disguises and did Chambers in with his own hand. The whore was an unfortunate victim. Or was she? In his religious fanaticism the Jesuit wouldn't mourn the death of a harlot. Perhaps he believed the town gossip and thought the stew a witch.

Thou shalt not suffer a sorceress to live.

There were diverse men who desired Chambers dead. But Shakespeare still had no idea who desired *Harry* murdered, or how the two—or three—slayings were connected.

Mackering was the common thread. Harry was filling the coffers of both Mackering and Chambers. Chambers was dead. So it was back to Mackering and London once again.

Another hour of riding put him in the burg of Cordick at dusk. The town was small and dreary and awash in mud—indistinguishable from Hemsdale. Dusk was an evil witch, as cold and still as death, hooded by shadows—malevolent, vaporous shapes lurking everywhere.

Shadows. They set his nerves tingling. What had he seen in that tavern a week ago? Just a shadow? Or the black beast? Who was he or it? At least Shakespeare knew that shadow wasn't Fottingham—Shakespeare had seen it leave the alehouse as he spoke with the alderman. It had been watching him constantly.

Even as he rode, Shakespeare sensed he was being followed, yet he turned around and saw nothing.

Thick mist was behind him, as amorphic and mutable as the Devil. Shakespeare saw in it the frothy tips of an endless tide, the windblown sails of a stranded ship, the billowing velvet gown of a duchess, a silent, evil specter of night.

A chill swept across his body.

51

The banging on the front door woke up the entire Lopez household. Rebecca sat up in her bed and reached for her candlestick but knocked it over with the back of her hand. Cursing silently, she dropped to the floor and fumbled around on hands and knees.

The pounding grew even louder, muffled voices inside—her parents, the servants. Scampering feet.

"Open up!" demanded a voice. This one from outside the house. "Open up!"

So loud. Rebecca felt herself shaking. The devil with the candlestick!

She stood up, threw her shawl around her nightdress, and stumbled through the darkened gallery, trying to reach the staircase without tripping. She met her mother on the second-floor landing. Sarah was holding a candlestick, the light quivering from the tremble of her hand.

"Go back to sleep," Sarah ordered her daughter.

"Where's Father?" Rebecca asked. "Is he dressing?"

"OPEN THE DOOR!" ordered the voice once again.

"Where's Martino?" cried Rebecca. "Why isn't anyone opening the door?"

"Go back to sleep!" Sarah screamed.

A loud thud shook the house.

"They're breaking the door down, for God's sake!" said Rebecca. "This is absurd! I'll open the—"

Sarah grabbed Rebecca's arm and yanked her away. "You desire to make it easy for that red-haired bastard!"

Rebecca lurched backward as if pushed. It was the first time in her life she had ever heard her mother swear.

Essex, Rebecca thought. What did that self-serving, evil cur want with Father now! "Where's Ben?" she screamed above the pounding.

"He heard them coming and dashed out the back way," Sarah said. "He's off to your uncle. May God show him strength! May the Almighty have mercy on our wretched souls—"

"Oh Mother!" Rebecca started to cry.

"Stop!" Sarah ordered. "Oh, I pray you, daughter, do not do that." Her face contorted; scrunched-up eyes that tried to dam the flood of tears. "Stop!"

The two women hugged as they heard the door crack, splinter into planks of wood. They remained motionless, holding each other tightly as the Queen's men charged through the open embrasure of the door arch. There were a dozen of them, carrying torches and ropes. Swords and daggers swung from belts fastened around their waists.

Rebecca felt her mother go slack. She gripped her soundly, dragged her to a chair resting on the landing and fanned air in her face with her shawl.

"Where is that treasonous dog!" screamed the same voice Rebecca had heard on the outside. She could barely make out his face. Big with a black beard. Or did it only look black in the night?

They were bounding up the steps.

"Where is your father?" demanded the black-bearded man. He said *father* as if it were an obscenity. He was close to her now. She could feel his hot breath, taste his spit. "Where's your father hiding out, girl! I advise you to speak, else you'll be arrested along with the traitor—"

"He's dressing," Sarah answered weakly. "I pray you, let him finish—"

"He's here!" shouted one of the men from the top of the stairs.

"Drag him hence, the filthy dog," ordered Black Beard.

"What are the charges?" Rebecca asked.

"Out of my way, girl!"

Rebecca felt the clip of his strong forearm against her mouth. It caused her teeth to cut through her lip. She held her mouth, then fell to her knees and grabbed Black Beard's robe.

"I pray you, what are—"

Black Beard backhanded her across the face. Rebecca was stunned, her face burning with pain. She crumpled to the floor.

"Not my daughter, I beg you!" her father's voice cried plaintively. "Anything but—"

"Silence!" Black Beard ordered.

Rebecca's head was still ringing. She heard the word treason as the charges were read. Through blurry eyes she saw her father. He was flanked by two of the Queen's guards, each one gripping his arm. Two others were binding his hands behind his back. Roderigo had on his hose and shirt, but no sleeves and shoes. Without thinking, Rebecca stood up and went to fetch his remaining garments and boots, but was quickly stopped by another blow to her face. Again she dropped to her knees, her head an explosion of pinpoint lights.

She heard the faint cries of her father's protests, the sharp sound of flesh against flesh, the sickening crunch of broken bone.

Roderigo howled in pain. He looked at his wife, held out his hand to her, but was pulled away before they could touch. He gave a single glance over his shoulder as they dragged him away. Rebecca was holding her head, crying, the blood of her mouth mixed with tears.

"I love thee, Becca," he shouted to her.

He thought he heard her shout it back. But he wasn't certain.

It was known in the Tower as the Dungeon amongst the Rats. It lay adjacent to the water somewhere beneath the Cradle Tower, a cave twenty feet deep with no light. At high tide the clammy hole became infested with rats seeking shelter.

High tide was approaching. Esteban Ferreira de Gama could feel the icy rocks turn even colder. He could hear occasional squeaks, and whispers of scampering across boulders, make out the glow of red eyes. He could feel sharp paws tickling his ankles, scratching the soles of his feet, and knew it was only the beginning.

He reached upward—dear God, what a supreme effort that was—and tried to pull himself onto a ledge two feet above the floor of the cave. But he was too weak and the rocks were slimy and wet. He fell into a nest of squirming rats, his face burrowing in their dank, wet fur, their mouths licking his nose. De Gama held back a dry heave and stood up, brushing cold, wet noses off his legs.

He tried again, raw fingertips gripping the slippery rocks. One big hoist and he was up, resting uncomfortably on a small algae-covered table. His hands were tucked into the crevices of wet rock and helped support his weight. His still-swollen shoulders were in excruciating pain. His feet dangled a foot away from the floor. Yet for the time being he was safe.

What had he done to deserve *this*?

What did they *want* from him?

He had told them the truth almost immediately. Not all of it, but most of it. He had told them he was aiding the escape of hundreds of Spanish and Portuguese Jews doomed by the Inquisition. He admitted falsifying citizen's papers, giving them to the smuggled so they might live legally in the Low Countries. But that was the extent of his clandestine involvement with Lopez.

He had expected deportation—to be sent back to Spain, or to the New World perhaps. A term of forced servitude in the Queen's army. Or even prison. But never did he expect the rack, this dungeon . . . or worse, what lay ahead. . . .

The rocks became colder, the cave echoed with piercing whistles. De Gama felt as if he were dangling from a gangplank, about to drop into a sea dappled with red dots of light. He dug his hands farther into the cracks between the rocks, scraping his knuckles in the process. A cool, slithery-soft glob of something sucked his fingertips. Startled, he withdrew his fingers.

Lopez! Ye Gods, only an hour on the rack and he had given them *Lopez!* What a coward he was! But it wasn't enough. Essex had wanted more. Much more than de Gama had to give. The lord had wanted to know how Lopez had intended to murder his mistress. De Gama hadn't known to what he was referring.

So they took him to the torture chamber. It was a ten-foot-square stone cell, lit only by a torch hanging in a wall sconce. It smelled of rot and garbage, of human excrement and blood. It was dank and cold, the ceiling covered with cobwebs. They put him on the rack. The frame was six feet long with three rollers of wood within it. His back lay on a middle roller studded with iron teeth. His ankles and wrists were stuffed into tight iron cuffs, his stretched limbs fastened by ropes to rollers at opposite ends. Essex repeated the question: How had Lopez planned to murder his mistress, the Queen?

"I know not what you mean!" de Gama protested.

The beefeaters turned the end rollers a quarter of a revolution. Sharp points of iron dug into de Gama's back. He felt his arms and legs reach their limit; every muscle in his body grew taut.

"Tell me how Lopez plotted to poison the Queen," Essex said calmly.

De Gama frantically explained: "Lopez paid King Philip to look aside on conversos that he smuggled out. He said nothing about a scheme to murder his mistress!"

Essex sighed and nodded to the yeoman warders. Another quarter revolution. Pain! Ripping muscles! Hot joints! *Agony!* He began to breathe rapidly.

"Tell me about the pearls, musk, and amber letter."

De Gama lay there, his body coming apart.

"Tell me about the letter," Essex repeated.

"I know nothing about a letter," de Gama had choked out.

Another eighth turn; his arms were tearing from their sockets. He screamed.

"Wh-What do you *want* to know?" he cried. "I'll say anything."

"Lopez wrote a cryptic letter under the name Francisco de Torres to your agent in Amsterdam, David, did he not?" said Essex.

De Gama nodded. "Yes, yes! Anything you say!"

"In this letter he mentioned pearls, musk, and amber," Essex continued.

"Yes! Oh God, the pain—"

"Lopez asked David to find out the price of pearls, aye?"

"Yes, yes!" howled de Gama. "God in heaven, help me!"

"Loosen the wheel, my good warders," said Essex.

The jailers did as told.

"Better?" Essex asked de Gama.

De Gama nodded.

"What meant Lopez by 'the price of pearls'?" Essex said.

De Gama was breathing more calmly. But agony still pierced his shoulders and inner thighs. He answered, "Pearls were the price of the Spanish Jews. How much Lopez was willing to pay to redeem Spanish Jews . . . Spanish conversos."

Essex looked displeased. "Pearls meant the price charged by Lopez to murder his mistress, Her Majesty!"

"No—"

"Warders! Another turn!"

De Gama screamed.

"Lopez was paid by Philip to murder Her Majesty, the Queen of England!"

"No!"

"Lopez was planning to poison her as he had planned to poison Don Antonio, his former master."

"No!"

"Warders!"

"NOOOOO!"

"Then tell me the truth!" Essex shouted. "Lopez was planning to poison his mistress! *Pearls* was a code word for the Queen!"

"No—"

"Warders, another—"

"NOOO. Aaaahhhh!"

"Lopez was trying to poison the Queen!" Essex screamed. *"Admit it!"*

De Gama felt his head going numb, drool ooze from his mouth. His vision turned black.

"Admit it!" Essex ordered.

Before he fainted, de Gama heard one of Essex's men storm into the chambers and talk excitedly about a ring.

When he woke up, he found himself in the infamous rat dungeon. Last night had been horrible. He hadn't known what to expect. But now he was prepared.

He hoped.

The rocks turned still colder. The red sea of eyes thickened. A wave of seawater was encroaching upon his feet. The rodents were climbing atop one another, feverishly trying to escape the water that had covered the floor of the cave. Wriggling little crimson pinpoints, smelling of disease and scum. The stink of muck from the Thames saturated the cave. The stench was overwhelming, yet de Gama could not even hold his nose. He needed his hands to support him upon the ledge. The rats were entering the dungeon in droves now. Eyes upon eyes, building their own quivering tower of rodent bodies, their tower of evil in a cave underneath a tower of evil.

They were a finger span away from the soles of his feet.

The grating whisper of tiny paws clawing fuzzy bodies. His nostrils became congested with rat fur, his eyes watered, his ears reverberated with high-pitched squeals. The rocks reached their final level of chill. De Gama felt a wet nose brush against his little toe, a paw tickle his heel.

He shook them off, kicked them away, but it was only temporary. Soon came another wave, another wet nose, and another, and another.

He kicked his legs furiously, but there were too many of them. They were climbing too fast. He closed his eyes, clenched his jaw, and waited for the tide to recede.

De Gama was screaming with delirium when the jail warders brought him into the torture chamber the second time. Most of his clothes had been eaten away, leaving the converso dressed in tatters that barely covered his chest and groin. His once-thick frame had turned pitifully limp. His cheeks were gaunt, covered with a sickly pallor. The skin of his body was raw and red and covered with rat and flea bites.

He eyed the rack and went berserk—screaming, sobbing, his arms and legs flailing about.

But this time the jailers passed up the frame of torture and let him stand in the corner unmolested.

What horrors awaited him this time?

Essex entered the chamber and gave de Gama a stern glance. The prisoner knew by the look in the lord's eyes that the rack had just been the appetizer to a full-course banquet. My God let him live through it all. Please don't let him die. He began to pray:

> Shma Yisroel, Adonai Elohenu, Adonai Ehad.
> God have mercy upon my soul!
> God have mercy upon my soul!
> God have mercy upon my soul!
> God have mercy upon my soul . . .

"Have you visited the daughter lately?" Essex said blithely to de Gama. "The Scavenger's Daughter, that is. Let me introduce you to her."

De Gama kept praying. Essex smiled, strolled over to a stone wall and patted an implement of iron hanging upon a large hook.

"It appears harmless does it not?" Essex said.

De Gama stopped his supplication to the Almighty and glanced at the instrument. It resembled a set of four-foot-long tongs. And it did appear harmless. But at first glance the rack seemed nothing more than a set of rollers. Whatever this was, it was not something commonly used in the chambers in Spain. The Spanish had their own devices—the ropes, the water jugs, fire . . .

All of them had been used on de Gama. He'd been so strong back then, withholding names regardless of the agony. And God had rewarded his silence by letting him live. He'd been sentenced to burn at the auto-da-fé in Toledo and would have died if Teresa Roderiguez hadn't saved him. She'd been sent to him by the Almighty for being strong. Now, as surely as an angel of life had saved him for his fortitude, so would an angel of death strike him for his weakness. But he couldn't stand any more pain.

Essex said, "Let me explain to you, de Gama, how our good English Daughter works. Or better yet, let me demonstrate—"

"No," de Gama whispered.

"No?" Essex asked.

De Gama began to pant.

"Have you something to tell me about Dr. Roderigo Lopez?" Essex said.

"I . . ." de Gama tried.

"Yes?"

"I . . . I know nothing about his scheme to poison the Queen."

Essex slapped de Gama across the face. "Insolent mule!" The lord turned to the warders. "Place him in the—"

"No!" De Gama cried.

"Place him in the Scavenger's Daughter!"

The top part of the tongs were recessed to go around de Ga-

ma's neck. His palms were forced together, his lower legs pushed
to his thighs, the thighs to the belly, all locked into position with
two iron cramps. He lay on his back, compressed like a dead
fetus after a miscarriage.

"Tell me about Lopez's pearls, musk, and amber letter," Essex began.

De Gama tried to talk calmly. But his voice was nothing more
than a hoarse whisper. He said, "*Pearls* was Lopez's code word
for Spanish Jews—"

"Warders, tighten the cramps."

The tips of de Gama's fingers and toes turned red from the
pressure.

Essex repeated, "Señor Esteban de Gama, tell me about Lopez's pearls, musk, and amber letter."

"It—" De Gama stopped and tried to think.

Tell him what he wants to hear!

"It was written by Lopez," de Gama started out. "He used
the name Francisco de Torres."

"Good," Essex said. "Very good."

"It was written to David, Lopez's agent in the Low Countries."

"Go on."

"I . . . I pray you, m'lord, loosen the cramps," de Gama
implored. He began to cry.

Blood had leaked out through his fingertips.

Essex said, "If you cooperate and confess freely, we will take
you out of that ungodly device, señor."

"I'll confess!" de Gama sputtered out. "Anything, I'll confess!"

"My good warder," Essex said, "go fetch an official recorder
incontinently."

"Right away, m'lord," said the beefeater.

"What do you wish to confess?" asked Essex innocently.

"The letter."

"Yes, yes. You shall tell me about the letter."

"I beg you, m'lord," said de Gama. "Loosen the cramps."

"In a moment."

"Please—"

"I said in a moment," Essex said testily.

De Gama began to pray. Ten minutes later a scribe entered
the cell. He carried a stool, a board, a quill, a scroll of parchment, and around his neck, an inkhorn. The man was as small
as a boy and moved very slowly. He looked around the chamber,
waiting for his eyes to adjust to the darkness.

"Tarry not, I beg you," de Gama said. "I'll—"

"Quiet!" ordered Essex.

Blood began to ooze from de Gama's toes.

The scribe placed the stool under the light of the torch. Methodically, he removed the inkhorn from around his neck and uncapped it.

De Gama began to feel dizzy. Essex noticed the glassy look in the prisoner's eyes.

"Hurry up, you fool," Essex said.

The scribe unrolled the parchment and placed it against the board.

"I cannot last much longer," de Gama pleaded.

"Loosen the cramps," Essex said.

De Gama felt the dizziness fading.

"Ready, m'lord," announced the scribe. His voice was a frog's croak.

"Speak!" Essex ordered de Gama. "Tell me about the pearls, musk, and amber letter!"

De Gama repeated, "It was written by Lopez—"

"*Which* Lopez?"

"Dr. Roderigo Lopez," said de Gama.

Essex clarified, "The physician-in-ordinary to Her Majesty, the Queen."

"Slower, slower," requested the scribe.

Essex paused a moment, then repeated the statement.

"The very one," said de Gama.

"Go on."

De Gama said, "The letter was written by Dr. Lopez—using the name Francisco de Torres—to his agent David in the Low Countries."

"Slower, slower," repeated the scribe.

Essex sighed, waited for the nod of the scribe to continue.

"What was David supposed to do with the letter?"

"Slower, slower," repeated the scribe.

"Speak slowly," Essex ordered de Gama.

De Gama enunciated, "David was to give it to the King of Spain. Philip the Second."

"And what did the letter mention?"

"The cost of pearls, musk, and amber," de Gama answered. Though still in pain, he was calmer now.

"Was Lopez intending to buy pearls, musk, and amber from King Philip?"

"Slower, slower," said the scribe.

"Write faster, you muck-filled jack!" Essex shouted. "As you can see, the rack is empty, waiting for a man who does not perform his function adequately."

The scribe blanched, nodded, and began to scribble as fast as he could. Essex repeated,

"Was Lopez intending to buy pearls, musk, and amber from King Philip?"

"No, m'lord."

"No?"

"No, m'lord."

"Then what was meant by the words pearls, amber, and musk?"

"They are code words, Your Worship."

"Code words?"

"Yes."

"Lopez's secret code words?"

"Yes, Your Lordship."

"What did Lopez mean by these code words?"

"*Pearls* was a code word for Spanish Jews—"

"Strike that," Essex said angrily to the scribe. "Warders, tighten the cramps!"

"No, no!" screamed de Gama. "I erred."

Essex held out the palm of his hand, signaling the beefeaters to stop. "Oh?"

"I forgot," de Gama pleaded.

"Aye, to err is human," said Essex. "What meant the code word *pearls*?"

De Gama said, "It meant . . . poison?"

Essex shook his head and mouthed the word queen.

"*Pearls* was a code word for queen," de Gama whined.

Essex smiled. "Very good." He turned to the scribe and said, "Did you get that down, you old turd?"

"Certainly, Your Worship," croaked the scribe.

"What was Lopez going to do to the pearls?" Essex asked.

De Gama felt his bowels about to burst and said so.

"Shit on the floor!" Essex said dismissively. "What was Lopez going to do to his mistress, the Queen?"

De Gama tightened the muscles of his anus. God, his body was about to collapse, the pressure was still too much. His guts churned in acid. He couldn't hold them anymore and defecated upon the floor.

Essex wrinkled his nose in disgust and repeated the question.

"Dr. Lopez was planning to . . . scheming to poison the Queen," de Gama whispered.

He saw Essex grin.

That was it! He had said it! Lopez was doomed. De Gama's confession signed not only the doctor's death warrant, but his own as well. Anything, *anything* but torture!

"At whose behest was Lopez planning to poison the Queen?"

De Gama felt like fainting. He looked quizzically into Essex's eyes. The lord mouthed the word Philip. In a hushed voice de Gama said,

"Lopez was planning . . . ach . . . to poison . . . my head . . ."

"Go on," ordered Essex.

"Poison . . . the Queen at King . . . Philip's behest."

"Was Philip to pay him for his act?" Essex asked, then nodded yes.

"Yes," said de Gama.

"Was the initial payment to Lopez this ring that was in the possession of his daughter, Rebecca?" Essex held up the ring and again nodded yes.

De Gama had never seen the ring before. But he answered yes.

"Do you have that all on parchment, Master Scrivener?" Essex asked gaily.

"Yes, m'lord."

"My good yeomen warders, please release Señor de Gama from the Daughter."

As soon as the cramps were off, de Gama collapsed upon the cool floorstones and wept.

"Now, now," Essex chided. "You must sign the confession, *señor*, if you expect mercy."

The prisoner scribbled his signature across the parchment.

"You confessed the deed very well," complimented Lord Essex. "Very well indeed. Of course, you'll be hung, as you were an accomplice to Lopez's heinous plot. But in exchange for your free confession, I'll guarantee you a swift death. In addition, while you wait for your demise I'll have you placed in a suitable chamber, señor. One tall enough for a man to stand and long enough for a man to lay his body—if his knees are kept slightly bent. A cell with a fag of fresh straw for a pillow and a torch for light and warmth. A dry cell with very few rats. No window, though, I'm afraid."

De Gama sobbed with relief.

52

Rebecca's eyes peered over the top of her prayer book just long enough to see it was Benjamin who'd walked into her chamber. Without acknowledging her brother, she finished the benediction of silent devotion—the *amidah*. Grandmama had taught it to her when she was knee high, said it with her every day as if it were a special game between the two of them. Rebecca hadn't even known what the words meant until she reached twelve. How long ago was that? Only six years?

"I was about to go back to her." Rebecca closed the book. "How's she been in my absence?" She regarded her brother now. He was worn out. Eyes that hadn't held peaceful sleep for centuries.

"Grandmama slept for an hour," Benjamin answered. "She woke up a minute ago and asked for you."

"I shouldn't have left—"

"You needed rest," Benjamin insisted.

There was a tremble in his voice. His eyes were mirrors reflecting her visage. She was as battered as he. She buried her face in her hands and cried.

"Not now, Becca," Ben whispered. "Not now."

Rebecca continued sobbing. "Oh Ben! I'm such a wretched disappointment to everyone! And now both she and Father are being ripped away from me before I can make amends."

She expected to hear her brother's berating. Instead, he put an arm around her shoulders.

"*You're* a disappointment?" Benjamin said. "Rebecca, I'm the *definition* of the word. You should have had my body. My maleness was wasted on me. Or maybe it's your mind that is wasted on you. Either way, Providence has played a nasty game."

Rebecca didn't answer him, but she stopped crying.

Benjamin kissed his sister's cheek. "Since I was not born with natural cleverness, I reasoned that all I had to do was work harder. I practiced fencing more than any man in Oxford, yet remained mediocre. I studied music and still my voice cracks when I sing. Dancing? Not a clod, but nowhere near the grace of a gazelle. And then there was my attempt to conquer the art of medicine. I saw it all in Father's eyes—all my errors, my bungling. He never had to speak a word." He shrugged his shoulders in acceptance. "I was born one step above the commoner and there I shall remain, destined to be forgotten as soon as met."

"That's not true!" Rebecca said.

Benjamin laughed bitterly. "I would have been well had Emmanuel—the family's *rightful* heir—lived. With a son as clever as he, Father would not have noticed me. But I was all the poor man had left. And now he shall . . . he shall die . . . knowing the progeny he's left behind is an abysmal failure."

Benjamin's eyes had become wet. It was Rebecca's turn to comfort.

Her family—crumbling like stale bread. Father, locked away in the Tower. It made her faint whenever she allowed herself to think about it. Grandmama. Aye, she was old, but somehow Rebecca had always believed she'd live forever. Now the dear woman had finally tired of life.

Thomas with his limp.

Miguel with his dead arm.

Only Dunstan and Benjamin remained able-bodied, but both were crippled in the brain. Benjamin by his commonness, Dunstan by haunting nightmares of drowning, of blood and gore. Often he cried in his wife's arms. Once he even cried in Rebecca's—babbling about his sons drowned in the open seas, begging her forgiveness for choking her. Pathetic. Yet Rebecca had hugged him tightly, the same way she held her brother now.

Once she had held Shakespeare that tightly. But that, too, had become nothing but the past. A minute later Benjamin pulled away and clasped her shoulders. He said,

"Go to her now."

Rebecca heard the urgency in his voice. Life was slipping away too fast . . . too easily.

"I'm back, Mother," Rebecca said. "Go rest."

Sarah turned her head away from the old woman and mouthed *Father?* to Rebecca.

Rebecca shook her head. No news had come.

Sarah seemed to wither. She dropped her mother's hand and stood up, allowing Rebecca to take her place at the old woman's bedside. Rebecca sat upon the stool and stroked her grandam's forehead. It was hot and dry.

Sarah squeezed her daughter's shoulders and left the room. Grandmama was swathed in sheets. Only her head and one tiny hand were visible. Her once-thick hair had become white wisps covering a crusted scalp. Her eyes were sunken, yet the light in them remained stubbornly alive. Rebecca tried to look cheerful, but moisture clogged her own eyes.

"None of that," the old woman said. Her voice was as clear as daylight. "Too much of life to feel sorrowful about dying, girl. . . . I welcome death . . . like a bride greets her groom."

"Don't say that," Rebecca whispered. Tears tumbled down her cheeks.

"I've been tortured, Becca," said the hag. "Dragged down . . . drowned . . . burned . . . made a whore." Her breaths had become shallow. "Faith kept me afloat . . . faith in our God . . . your God, I pray."

Grandmama tried to raise her hand to dry Rebecca's tears but dropped it in exhaustion. Rebecca picked it up and kissed it.

"Rest."

Grandmama ignored her. She wheezed, "Merciful God . . . He knows I cannot live to witness another—" She stopped herself. She wanted to say "another execution," but couldn't bear the agony it would cause Rebecca. "Cannot live anymore," she said. "Life's too painful."

The old woman moaned. "I've been a burden to you, girl—"

"You speak nonsense—"

"What you passed up for me—"

"Hush now," Rebecca said. "I've passed up nothing. A maid at court? And what would I have done there? Served an ill-tempered old chrony with lecherous designs—idling away hours giggling and gossiping with silly girls who preen like peacocks? Nay, Grandmama. You were a convenient excuse. I should be thanking you!"

Grandmama spoke in a whisper, "Not . . . court."

"Oh Grandmama!" Rebecca wept. "You've done so much for *me*! Instructed me in the ancient arts of our ancestral mother, Miriam. Taught me how to mix special potions and drugs known only to our people. Your knowledge made Father distinguished here in London. *Your* knowledge! Information he did not learn at his studies at the university."

"I've . . . held you back," the hag said.

"Stop talking," Rebecca chided her. She felt her grandam's forehead. It was wet now, covered with tiny droplets of sweat. She wiped it with her sleeve. "You're tiring yourself—"

"Little breath I have, girl," said Grandmama. Her eyelids fluttered. "Must say my piece."

Her voice sounded distant, as if it had already left her body. She looked so frail, all the fight gone. Only the gleam in her eyes was left. A moment later that dulled.

My God, she's fading away! Rebecca said, "Say your piece."

In the same distant voice the old woman said, "Faith . . . it
kept me alive . . . defiant. Worked well—" She broke into a
series of weak coughs.

"Sleep," Rebecca ordered.

"Come closer," Grandmama whispered.

Rebecca leaned in.

"Listen," the old woman said. "Faith is what . . . *I* needed.
Is it what *you* need?"

Rebecca was confused.

"My sweet little Becca," the old woman cried out. "I've been
so *blind*! . . . Forced you to believe in my God . . . You loved
me and obeyed me . . . left behind your heart. Did I sell you
lies, girl?"

"No," Rebecca insisted. "You're weak with illness and age,
Grandmama. You've never lied to me—"

"I don't *feel* God, Becca!" Grandmama coughed again. "Almost dead, and do not *feel* Him! Maybe this is it. Nothing . . .
then what will become of me?"

Grandmama was weeping with fear.

"God will be there for you," Rebecca said, squeezing the
bony hand. "He'll embrace you with open arms—"

The old woman sobbed, "Don't want to live . . . but . . .
frightened of death. My entire life . . . Not God's destiny . . .
merely bad hap."

Rebecca lay her head upon the old woman's chest and embraced her. The hag was her baby bird who'd fallen from its
nest. Small bones, a rapid heartbeat, her chest heaving with
fright.

"You're part of God's destiny," Rebecca insisted. "And
you've earned eternity in Heaven, Grandmama. Tis your reward
for remaining steadfast in your faith. Now drink some watered
wine."

The old woman was too weak to argue. She allowed Rebecca
to bring the cool, metal goblet to her lips. Most of the spirits
dribbled out of the corner of the hag's mouth. Tenderly, Rebecca
dabbed the hot lips. She tried to give the old woman more, but
Grandmama turned her head.

"Becca . . ."

"Yes?"

"This life . . . it's all we have."

"No, my sweet grandmama," Rebecca assured her. "You'll
have your Heaven."

The old woman smiled. "Maybe, maybe not. What if we're
. . . like the animals. Does a cow have Heaven?"

"You're not a cow, Grandmama."

"Horses?"

"Man is not an animal."

"I've felt man's . . . lust of flesh . . . food and blood. We've much in common."

"God created man on a different day. He created us in His image. He made us rulers of Heaven and earth—*haaretz ve hashamayim.*"

"Hear me out," Grandmama whispered. "Our only life, *if* we are as . . . animals . . . disintegrated to dust when dead . . . Then . . . I've led you astray, girl. . . . Made you choose a God . . . You lost a chance to love."

Rebecca felt a dry lump in her throat. This time the tears came not from sadness for Grandmama, but for the man she had lost. The hag squeezed her hand.

"Go back to him if you want to," she whispered. "If you need to. If you think I'm right . . . that we're . . . animals. Go back. Hope . . . it's not too late."

"Shakespeare," said Rebecca.

"Aye, Shakespeare." Grandmama closed her eyes. She seemed at peace. She brought Rebecca's hand to her wet cheek. "It must be . . . your decision. Not mine."

"Only God knows how much I love you," Rebecca said.

The old woman smiled weakly, then coughed up blood. Rebecca covered a gasp with the back of her hand.

"Grandmama, you must drink—"

"No," Grandmama whispered. "Listen, Becca. Love him . . . if you must. Let him love you. Hard times . . . terrible ordeals face you, girl."

The old woman coughed again, weaker this time. She said in a hushed voice, "Mayhap you . . . need *love* to see you through. . . . Just as I needed faith." She turned her head away from Rebecca. "So much suffering," she cried. "For you . . . your mother . . . your brother. Be strong for them. Give my name to your daughter . . . and grab all the happiness you can, girl."

The snow had stopped falling but the winds were still strong. Shakespeare knelt before the white-dusted grave and stuck a sprig of greens into the ground against the headstone. The leaves flapped in the draft until the bundle finally blew away. Shakespeare watched the greens tumble against the drifts until they were lost in the mist.

"Can you hear me, Harry?" he asked the mound of snow. "If you can, visit me tonight and tell me how you died, you son of a bitch."

Shakespeare recalled one wintry night as he walked Harry home.

I'm dying, my friend, I'm dying.

You're just drunk, Shakespeare had said.

Nay, I'm dying. The world has become black.

It's night.

Harry suddenly turned to him, his nose bright red. *Remember me when I'm gone.*

Harry had begun to sway. Shakespeare looped an arm around him and propped him up.

Could I ever forget you?

Harry suddenly grabbed his hand and kissed it with emotion. *Remember me, Willy. You're the only man I know with the decency to keep this promise.*

Shakespeare had felt a swell in his heart. *I shan't ever forget you, Harry.*

Swear it!

I swear.

Now Shakespeare wept openly. He was exhausted, cold, lonely, and wasn't any closer to finding Harry's murderer than he'd been when he left London a month ago.

Go home, he told himself. Go home and write. Create a man more wretched than yourself.

He stood up and brushed the snow off his cape, determined to put the past behind. But it was not to be.

He felt his knees buckle, his heart pound. His teeth began to chatter loudly.

Rebecca!

Standing not more than ten yards away from him.

A ghost?

No. It was she. In the flesh.

Life's a whimsical fiend!

Shakespeare dropped to his knees and hoped that she didn't see him.

She appeared to not notice anything. Through a swirl of white and gray Shakespeare saw that she was weeping. She was a different person than the enchantress he'd spied the first time at the cemetery. She seemed smaller, completely broken. Then Shakespeare remembered that, so long ago, she had not really buried anyone she loved. This morrow was very different.

Shakespeare shivered and waited for the funeral procession to pass Harry's grave. Thomas was limping badly. Miguel had recovered and was walking as straight as any able-bodied man. Yet his right arm dangled lifelessly at his side. Rebecca's mother, supported by her son, was sobbing.

God in Heaven, who in her family had died—or had been captured this time? He regarded the Jews, then his eyes widened.

Where was the *doctor*?

The doctor had *died*?

He was an old man.

Yet he'd appeared healthy.

Plague could reduce a man to ashes in a day. The evil vapors of the disease were still strong in London.

Shakespeare realized that he was visible. He covered his mouth with his gloves, turned his head aside and pretended to cough, but Dunstan noticed him anyway. Shakespeare expected a vile lour, even a glob of spit, but to his surprise, Dunstan immediately stopped Rebecca and moved his head in Shakespeare's direction.

Rebecca looked up. Her eyes were as swollen and red as boiled cranberries. She whispered something to Dunstan. He nodded, joined their kinsmen and proceeded to the gravesite without her.

Shakespeare waited for the funeral train to blur into the fog, then he locked eyes with her. The wind had loosened her hair, blowing it over her face like a veil, the cold having turned her cheeks rosy. She looked as unreal as the first time he'd seen her. One blink and she'd be gone. Slowly, Shakespeare stood and approached her.

"You've yet to return to London," Rebecca said. Her voice was choked with tears.

"Yes," Shakespeare said. "How'd you know that?"

"I stopped by your cell yesterday and again talked to your neighbor. She said you hadn't come back from your trip to Warwick."

"I wasn't at Warwick. . . . Well, I was, but not the whole time." His mouth felt stuffed with cotton. He was trembling and it wasn't from cold. "I was up North."

"Then you don't know, do you."

"'Tis your father whom you bury?" he asked.

Rebecca shook her head and said, "My father is alive, imprisoned once again. This time he's in the Tower. Today we inter my grandam."

Shakespeare was about to reply with the usual words of condolences but Rebecca's eyes stopped him, reminded him how close she and the old woman had been. At that moment he understood that words couldn't express how deeply he felt her pain. A minute of awkward silence passed, one of the few times in his life when Shakespeare felt at a loss for words—a foreigner who did not speak the language of the country. Rebecca seemed to sense his reticence and spoke up.

"She died very peacefully. In her sleep."

"Blessed be the Almighty for that." Shakespeare held out his hands to her. "I'm so sorry—"

"Do you believe in God?" Rebecca asked.

Shakespeare was taken aback by the force of the question, by the abrupt, clear tone of her voice. He dropped his hands to his sides and answered yes.

Rebecca said, "Then your God would have my grandam condemned to Hell, as she was not baptized."

Shakespeare didn't answer.

"No matter," Rebecca said. "In sooth, I hope there is a God. And I hope He is neither judgmental like Moses's God—my God—nor as interested in forcing his beliefs upon others as Jesu—your God. In sooth, I hope God, unlike those made in His image, is kind and loving."

"And forgiving?"

"Aye," Rebecca said. "And forgiving as well."

Shakespeare dropped to his knees and kissed her gloved hand. She stroked his pink cheek, then brought him to his feet.

Shakespeare said, "Thou art my weakness. A poison so sweet that it is Heaven to die with thy venom on my lips."

"I'll not cause thee any more grief, I swear!" Rebecca said. "Once again, I offer myself to thee."

They embraced. Rebecca allowed herself to go limp, to melt into his arms. It was the first time she permitted herself to share her grief with another. He was her pillow, molding himself for her comfort, offering warmth and softness in a hard, cold world. How she loved him.

Shakespeare whispered, "Tell me, what can I do to help thee?"

She hugged him tightly and said, "I must return to my family. My heart mourns for my grandam." She began to cry. "My God, Will, how I loved that woman. What will I do without her?"

Shakespeare was silent. His arms, not his words, would give her the solace she needed. A moment later he felt her stiffen.

"Thou knowest what she would say if she were alive?" Rebecca said.

"What?"

"'Tis a waste of time to wail the dead. Concentrate on the living."

"A rarity," Shakespeare said. "A wise woman."

Rebecca pulled away from him. She was a bale of confusion. Tears in her eyes one moment, a lethal look of action the next. She said with animation, "In which tower my father is imprisoned, I know not. Communication between him and family is forbidden. But I do know he lies somewhere in that vile prison, Will. Help me find him."

Shakespeare was stunned. "What dost thou propose? We hire

a boatman, cross the guarded moat, and stealthily make our way through the stone walls of the Tower?''

"I don't know how. Simply that I must see him!"

"Thou might as well steal thy way into the Queen's bedchamber."

Rebecca thought a moment. "Mayhap we shall do that instead. Does she not present herself before her loyal subjects?"

Shakespeare rolled his eyes and said, "Becca, I—"

Rebecca quieted him with an icy kiss on the lips. She said, "I must return to my family. We shall discuss this tomorrow. I'll come by thy closet at eleven?"

"I'll not sleep in anticipation," Shakespeare said.

"And thou wilt *be* there this time?"

"Most definitely," Shakespeare said. "I was moonstruck to leave thee the first time."

"Tomorrow, then," Rebecca said.

Shakespeare nodded, thinking: Tomorrow it will be, if a deathly shadow stays hidden in its murky swamp and the Queen's men leave thy kinsmen in peace. So much had come between them, most of it still unresolved.

Reluctantly they parted ways.

53

The following morning Shakespeare tried to write. He'd awakened before six and, according to his sand glass, had been scribbling for three hours. All he had to show for it was a floor littered with crumpled paper. His hand began to ache, his middle finger heavily ink-stained.

The Devil with it!

He cleaned his quill and capped the inkpot. He paced and stoked the fire. Rebecca was consuming him, robbing him of the empty mind he needed for creativity. His mind was agog with impressions of her, his skin tingling at the thought of their reunited flesh. She seared his brain, scorching from it all images but her.

When she did show up at his closet—at eleven, as promised— she was costumed as a boy and in a state of panic.

"They've scheduled his *trial*!" she said. "He's actually going to *trial*! My brother just found— God in heaven, they don't even have evidence—just hearsay, rumors, gossip! . . . My uncle's there now. . . . It's all based on mere conjecture and some babbling he made no doubt under . . . under *torture*." She seemed to choke on the last word. "The slimy bastards! May they rot in Hell. May that toad Essex burn, nay, be tortured and burned! And even that would be too kind for him."

Shakespeare waited for her to stop ranting, waited for the tears to come.

She began to pace. "I cannot believe this!" she screamed. She kicked his pallet. The straw exploded with dust. "He never planned ill against the Queen. He's been nothing but her loyal subject! Aye, maybe he's used his position a time or two to request favors. And who has not? Has the bastard, Essex, not used his title and charm to beguile the Queen to do *his* bidding? God will get the ambitious son of a bitch. God will get him! If there is a God . . . Of course there's a God! *Thou* thinkest there is a God, correct?"

"With absolute certainty," said Shakespeare.

"Yes," agreed Rebecca. "There is a God, and He will save my father, will He not?"

Shakespeare asked, "When is your father scheduled to be tried?"

The words he spoke hit her with sudden reality. Her face contorted in a mixture of anger and terror. She said, "The twenty-eighth of February."

"Come," Shakespeare said, holding open his arms.

She fell against his chest and cried.

"I must see the Queen," she said, her speech muffled. Her lips were pressed against his shirt. "I must see her. How can I see her? If only I had listened to Father in the first place. I would have been at court. I would have been in Her Majesty's favor, and Essex would never have dreamed up such lies. God, I hate everyone. I cannot . . . I cannot stand these evil political games. . . . Now I understand why Grandmama was so grateful to die."

She bit her lip and wiped her face. "I hate everyone! Not thee, of course. Nor my mother. Just everyone."

Shakespeare hushed her. "Lay upon my pallet."

He eased her down onto the mattress. She sneezed.

"It's been some time since the cell has been dusted," Shakespeare said.

Rebecca blew her nose into a silk handkerchief—one that Raphael had given her. Marry, did everything she treasure dissolve into ghosts? She sneezed again. "It's the straw," she said.

"I haven't changed it yet."

She stared at the ceiling. Shakespeare held her hand.

"I must see the Queen," Rebecca said. "Have you any way to get to her? You've a reputation as a clever writer. Cannot you write her something magnificent so that her heart must summon you in appreciation? I have it—a love poem!"

Shakespeare said, "If it were that easy, she could set London ablaze with the paper that would fill her chambers. Not a writer in the country would hesitate to bestow amorous words unto his queen."

"But can they write as you do?"

"Her Majesty does not need another fawning dedication of love. Her Majesty likes to be entertained. She enjoys a well-placed pun along with a well-placed kick in the rear. She enjoys laughing."

"Then write her a comedy!" Rebecca said. "Oh, never mind. I see the futility of what I speak."

Shakespeare wasn't sure whether she meant the futility of her plan or the futility of getting him to cooperate. Either way, she dropped the issue. She tugged on her cap.

"God's blood, what am I to do?"

"The trial is in two weeks," Shakespeare said. "Perhaps it is best if we do nothing until we know its outcome."

"*No!* Once condemned, my father has no choice but to . . . to die." Rebecca felt short of breath. "Oh my God! I cannot bear this alone . . . without her. Marry, I miss my grandam. *She* would have known what to do!"

"I have not the wisdom of the old woman," said Shakespeare. "But I am here for thee. Thou art positive he'll be condemned?"

"That weasel lord will be satisfied at nothing less."

Shakespeare lay down next to her and said, "Tell me the evidence they have against your father."

Rebecca hesitated, then in a rush of words told him all she knew—de Gama's coded letter to King Philip, de Gama's testimony under torture, her ring, a jewel from the old treasury of Spain.

"Twas a gift to Her Majesty, for God's sake! A gift! How could that have been *payment* for the nefarious deed of which my father has been accused if he gave it to the Queen?"

Shakespeare agreed with her.

"Thou knowest what that asp Essex claimed?"

"What?"

"That my father gave it to Her Majesty with dishonest intent! That he knew how the queen adores trinkets—it's a trinket at one *hundred* pounds—and was trying to ingratiate himself with Her Majesty."

"'Tis hardly unusual for a subject to give his queen a gift."

"Exactly! But Essex claims it was payment, and my father, knowing that it was a link between him and King Philip, purposely gave it to the Queen to rid himself of that link. Are those thoughts of logic, I ask?"

"No."

"So thou seest how fallacious the charges are."

"But what about the letter?" Shakespeare asked. He stuck a tress of black hair back inside her cap. "You say the words mean one thing, Essex says they mean another."

"But he has no proof!"

"Save de Gama's testimony."

"But that was said under torture!"

Shakespeare didn't respond. He knew of many men who had been convicted and executed upon much less evidence of malice. Rebecca turned her head and faced him. She saw the defeat in his eyes. Her anger began to abate. It was replaced with hopelessness. Shakespeare felt his heart sink with hers.

"Rebecca," he said. "We cannot do a thing before the trial. It comes too fast."

"He will be arraigned, tried, and sentenced to die." Her voice was flat. "I have had nightmares about it. I have seen him suffer. Was God preparing me, Will?"

He hugged her tightly.

"He's gone from me," she said. "Just like everybody I have ever loved."

"I'm here, my sweet lover."

"For how long?"

"For as long as thou desirest me, as long as thou needest me."

She snuggled against his chest and heard her grandam's voice. *Mayhap you need love to see you through. . . .*

A rarity. A wise *woman*. A wise person regardless of what was between her legs.

Shakespeare said, "Rebecca, I don't want to indulge you in fantasy but . . ." He paused.

"But what?" she said, raising her head.

"'Tis the Queen's fashion to make an appearance before her subjects around Lent—a splendid progression. During such time she has been known to bestow a good word upon the commoner. Mayhap . . . just mayhap our hap will be sweet and we'll be able to approach her then."

Rebecca suddenly brightened. "Do you think it possible?"

Shakespeare was cautious. "It's possible."

"My God! Shakespeare, you are brilliant! A man far more clever than a man of letters."

"I'm not saying it will happen but—"

"Oh no!" Rebecca said. She turned morose.

"What is it?"

"My father will have been sentenced by then!"

"The Queen has granted pardons in the past."

"Not for treason!"

It was the truth, thought Shakespeare. "Perhaps we can get a stay of execu—a stay. Procure enough time for the Queen to review the case against thy father."

"We have to buy time," Rebecca said. "The longer he lives, the longer we have to prove the charges false."

"Yes," Shakespeare said.

"Thou will help me?"

"In any way I can."

She embraced him. "I love thee. Dost thou lovest me?"

"Aye."

"Will thou lovest me now and forever?"

"Aye." Shakespeare held her and said, "Let us start with the now and work our way to the forever."

For the first time in months Rebecca smiled. "Tis a long road to forever, Will."

She placed his hand upon her chest. Shakespeare traced the swells of her bosom with his fingertips. Unbuttoning her doublet and shirt, he liberated a breast and kissed the erect nipple.

"In sooth," Shakespeare said. "Forever is a long road. But how merry we will be traveling to our destination."

Their lovemaking was rough and frantic, bursting forth with pent-up passion. They held no desire to tantalize and tease, they had no patience. Only a burning craving to finish so they could start over again. The sand in the glass slipped away yet time stood still. They had loved but a second. Their minds, their desires, ached for more, more, more but their bodies begged them to stop. They fell asleep entangled about one another—hot and sweaty, pulsating with sensation that bordered on pain. They could have slept for hours had fortune allowed. But it did not.

They were awakened by the shattering of glass. A cold draft suddenly gushed through Shakespeare's closet, extinguishing the glowing cinders—remnants of the fire that had warmed them as they loved. It was Shakespeare who assimilated the circumstances first. Someone had smashed his window.

"Stay down," he ordered Rebecca.

The room was nearly dark, but still contained enough light for the eye to see objects in muted color. Shakespeare grabbed his dagger and quickly slipped on a pair of hose and a shirt, cursing as he tied the points.

"What is it?" whispered Rebecca.

Shakespeare didn't answer her. He brushed away the pieces of broken glass and crept about on his belly. He saw the telltale dagger. It was the same type of crude blade that the beast had used against them in the past. Dangling from its handle was a rock. A strong arm had hurled it through the window, a wickedly determined strong arm.

Rebecca saw him holding the dagger, examining the blade. Her blood froze with fear.

"Where is he?" she managed to say.

Shakespeare boldly stood and glared out the window. People, shadows, shades of gray. He could have been any of them. Shadows blend easily into dusk.

"Probably gone," Shakespeare announced.

"He tried to kill you again."

"No," Shakespeare said. "This was a warning, a theatrical ploy meant for my benefit." He faced Rebecca. "He had left me in peace for a while. No doubt he knew that Mackering had captured me. Maybe he thought that Mackering had killed me. Then I reappeared up North and he realized I was still among the living, still on the hunt for my mentor's murderer. He followed me back to London. And this time he means to do me final harm."

"It doesn't make sense, Willy," Rebecca said. "He wouldn't *warn* you. He'd just sneak up and *kill* you."

"He *wants* me to know, Rebecca. He wants me to quake with fright, to turn my head at every sudden sound. My tension amuses him."

He began to pace, thinking: Mackering had enjoyed playing tricks with his brains. Maybe the shadow was Mackering all the while, the ruffian planting false trails for play before a final trap was set.

Rebecca asked in a shaky voice, "What is going on?"

Shakespeare shot the offending dagger at the wall. The blade sank into the soft-planked cedar, the rock swinging from its handle.

"I do not know," he said. *"I . . . do . . . not . . . know!"*

With sudden rage he marched over to the wall and pulled the knife free. He stabbed the wood siding over and over, each stick of the blade punctuated by a strangled scream.

"Calm, Willy," Rebecca begged. "Calm."

He kept stabbing.

Rebecca walked over to him and touched his shoulder. He whirled around, eyes wild with fury. He threw the dagger across the room, kicked the wall, cursed and stomped.

Someone was knocking on his door. He didn't care. He picked

up his trestle table and threw it against the wall. It crashed and came apart, falling to the floor in three pieces. Fruit skittered across the floor, rolled about like bowling balls.

"Willy, stop!" Rebecca pleaded. She didn't approach him this time. She dared not get in his way.

He saw his dagger, picked it up, then plunged it into his pallet. Ripped the fabric into shreds. Straw flew about the room like a windstorm. When his mattress was destroyed, he screamed and kicked the wall again.

The knocking on his door became banging. A female voice yelling from the outside. Rebecca was shouting too.

The devil with it!

He spied his desk as if he'd never seen it before. As if it were an enemy to be annihilated. With a single swoop of his arm he swept his quills and inkpot onto the floor and jumped on them. The spilt ink was immediately soaked up by the rushes, turning them black. He grabbed his desk. Lifted it into the air.

"Stop it!" Rebecca screamed. "STOP IT!"

He paused a minute, took in her words. He looked at her. She was staring at him, terrified. He was holding his desk. What in Heaven's name was he doing with his desk of nine stones in his arms? The weight drew his arms downward. He dropped the desk and it fell to the floor with a thud.

The pounding upon his door continued.

"What in the devil is going on!" screamed a raspy feminine voice. His landlady—Inus Meadhead. Meathead, Shakespeare called her behind her back.

"It's nothing!" Shakespeare shouted. "Nothing at all. Go back to your cell and my apologies for the racket."

"I heard a heap of caterwauling, Willy," Inus said harshly. "Who you got in there with ye?"

"Mind your own business, buswife!" Shakespeare roared.

"Up yours, you bald woodcock!" Inus screamed back. Her footsteps receded and were followed by a slamming door.

Shakespeare kicked the wall again. He was panting.

Rebecca stared at him, at the room.

Shakespeare nudged the black rushes with his toe. He said, "The straw needed changing anyway."

"Art thou well?" she asked.

"A moment of madness was all," he said. "I'm well . . . I think."

"Sit down," Rebecca said.

Shakespeare didn't move.

"Marry, what a mess!" Rebecca said.

Shakespeare ran his fingers through his hair—what little he had left. Bald woodcock! The old harpy! His eyes fell upon

Rebecca. She was still naked, her skin studded with goose bumps.

Gods, she was delectable.

She broke into a shy smile, her eyes settled below his waist. Shakespeare stared at his bulging hose.

"Troth, I thought not I had it in me," he said.

"How I wish I had it in me," Rebecca retorted.

Shakespeare laughed. Quickly, he gathered a pile of straw and covered it with a blanket.

"Suitable?" he asked.

Rebecca pushed away grisly thoughts of her father's imprisonment.

Grab all the happiness you can, girl.

"Twill do," she said.

He jumped onto the pile and held out his arms. Rebecca lay down beside him, still shivering with cold. He placed her on her back. Within moments he was on top of her, pounding at her. Gods, she was sore. The ends of the straw had poked through the blanket and were scratching her back. But she didn't say a word about it. She was content.

54

For an instant Roderigo Lopez understood nothing of what was being said. Then he remembered: they're speaking in English. So disoriented he was, his thoughts had slipped into his childhood tongue of Portuguese. Happier years.

Roderigo forced himself back to the present. He was at Guild-hall—a Norman stone edifice, the seat of English justice. Countless trials had been held here. But this was *his* arraignment. The walls of the chamber seemed inordinately tall, the coffered ceiling monstrously broad. From a three-by-five cell to this. Life was on a grander scale. People were bigger, noises louder, the sunlight intensely bright—he'd been squinting since they took him out of the Tower. They'd transferred him in daylight. *Daylight!* He'd forgotten what that was.

The Tower—how long had he been confined there? If today was the twenty-eighth of February, he'd been locked up for nearly six weeks.

Rebecca! Sarah! Benjamin—his only living son. He wept when he thought about him. Sarah and Rebecca were strong. But the boy—*his* boy! God keep him.

An auto-da-fé in England. Spitting as they tortured him, spitting the word Jewdog. The thumbscrews, the rack. He screamed. Yes, yes, whatever you say. Yes, stop the torture. Stop the pain!

He signed the confession. The one that Sir Edward Coke, the Solicitor General, held in his hand. Soon Coke would show it to the commission; it was a damning piece of evidence. The trial was a formality. Lopez had been officially condemned the minute his shaky hand had scratched his signature across that piece of parchment. But Roderigo knew that with an enemy as determined as Essex, he'd been condemned long before his arrest.

A Special Commission had been called to try him—not one of mere gentlemen, but of peers. They sat in two rows of chairs facing each other, a twenty-foot space separating the rows. It was occupied by a low table on which rested the "evidence" as well as Coke's notes. Coke was positioned at one end of the table: he, Lopez, at the opposite end, heavily guarded. No spectators, no witnesses, no advocates on his behalf, no family members for support. Just him and the men who would execute judgment upon him.

Execute him.

The commission. All were present except the old man—William Cecil. His crookback son Robert was there. He sat next to Essex, who held a gleeful smirk. On the other side of Essex was the Lord Mayor of London, Sir John Spencer. Who was the man to his right? The Chancellor of the Exchequer. What was his name? Sir John something. The surname was Fort something. Something with a Q-U-E or a C-U-E in it. A dozen other lords as well. There were London's sheriffs—Robert Lee and Thomas Benet. The official recorder, a sergeant of arms, a bailiff. They were wearing their robes. Why wasn't he, Lopez, wearing his? Why was he costumed as a prisoner? He'd done nothing criminal.

Roderigo knew the answer only too well—it was all Essex's doing. The doctor's defiant eyes confronted Essex's smiling orbs, then rested upon Coke.

The Solicitor General was ready to present his official opening speech. An aggressive, ambitious man, he resembled a bird of prey—a beakish nose, a feathery beard, the deep-set colorless eyes. He smoothed his robe with his fingertips, adjusting his mortarboard cap. He cleared his throat, silencing all noise in the chamber. All eyes were upon him. He addressed the commission in a booming voice.

Roderigo listened to the charges levied against him.

Muck.

All was muck.

Coke, acting in behalf of the Queen's bench, began to establish King Philip as England's most fearsome enemy—a foe with whom Roderigo had been conspiring. No matter that Roderigo's schemes with the Spanish monarch had caused no trouble for England. Collusion with the enemy was grounds for treason.

Grounds for his death.

Coke rambled on and on. Roderigo managed to glean from the florid speech that he was being tried for two capital offenses: attempting to take the blood of the Virgin Queen by poison, and attempting to set England's ships afire on Philip's behalf. Consistent with what he'd been forced to confess under torture. His hands began to shake. Quickly, he clasped them together. He'd not show fear, he *swore* he wouldn't, even as Coke's words pierced his skin like poisonous barbs.

Coke pointed to Lopez, announced his name with contempt. Lopez tried to plant his feet firmly upon the ground, but the chair was too high and only his toes reached the floor. *God in Heaven, he prayed, let me put up a good face. Permit not the commissioners to see a Jew cower at their feet.*

Coke said, "This . . . man who calls himself a doctor, a perjured murderer, worse than Judas himself, undertook the poisoning, a plot more wicked, dangerous, and detestable than can be imagined."

The commissioners' heads were nodding in agreement. Roderigo was done in. The challenge: Would he maintain his dignity or fall upon his face and weep for mercy?

Coke continued to roar, "He was Her Majesty's sworn servant, graced and advanced with princely favors."

Dear God, help me be strong.

". . . used in special places of credit, permitted access to her person . . ."

Shma Yisroel, Adonai Elohenu, Adonai Ehad.

". . . not so suspected, especially by Her Majesty."

So cold! Light of head. Clouded vision. Pray don't let me faint as a weak woman!

". . . Lopez made a bargain with the King of Spain and the price was agreed upon . . ."

Faith! As Daniel was cast into the lion's den and kept his faith, so will I.

". . . the fact only deferred until payment of the money was assured. The letter of credit for his assurance was sent, but before it came into the doctor's hands, God most wonderfully and miraculously revealed and prevented it."

Bladder suddenly full, bowels about to explode. How could that be? They haven't fed me more than a half cup of solids in three weeks.

"It is my intent," Coke said, "to prove to the commission that Lopez is guilty of the crimes of which I have spoken. Guilty of aiding and abetting the sworn enemy of England, King Philip of Spain. Guilty of trying to poison his mistress, the great Queen of England. Guilty of trying to destroy her navy with poison fireworks. And guilty of committing all these atrocious deeds not for religious conviction, but for advancing his own personal wealth."

Coke had stopped speaking. The sudden stillness was worse than the orated lies.

What came next in their unholy plans?

Coke went over to the evidence table, his footsteps measured. He picked up a faded piece of parchment and said: "I hold in my hand a letter from Emmanuel de Andrada—a former courier for the Spanish government. The letter was addressed to Spain's agent, Bernadino de Mendoza, and was intended for the eyes of the King of Spain himself. Note this is indeed Emmanuel de Andrada's seal."

Dear God, Roderigo had forgotten about that incident—words he'd uttered to de Andrada at the height of Don Antonio's defeat, in the heat of frustration. Lopez had been so eager to make amends with Philip—to save Jews—that he had said he might do *anything* to Don Antonio that His Majesty desired. And it was the *anything* that was now being interpreted as *poisoning*. De Andrada had written down his impetuous words, had sent them to Philip through Mendoza. The letter was intercepted and de Andrada had ended up in the Tower. Only Lopez's intervention and his pleas to the Queen had kept de Andrada's neck whole. To think he had actually saved that worm's life!

The Solicitor General handed the letter to Essex.

"If m'lord will be so gracious as to pass the evidence around. Here is the translation of the Portuguese text." Coke handed Essex a second piece of paper. "The arraignment took as long as it did because so much of the evidence is written in Portuguese—Lopez's native tongue—and not in mother English."

Essex looked at the letter, immediately recognized de Andrada's writing and smiled.

Coke said, "Master Recorder, let it be stated that the letter confirms Dr. Lopez's willingness to do service to the King of Spain." Coke bellowed out, "The text proves beyond doubt that Lopez was guilty of item one—aiding and abetting the King of Spain."

A faint buzz was heard through Guildhall as the commissioners conferred with one another. Coke waited several minutes, then quieted the men down. Continuing his case, he said,

"Let it also be stated that the same letter shows Lopez's willingness to poison Don Antonio, his *former* master, if the King of Spain so desires it. If in the past Lopez had been amenable to poisoning one master for the King of Spain, would he not oblige Philip and poison another master? I will soon show Lopez guilty of charge two—intent to poison the Queen!"

Roderigo couldn't contain his anger. He rose from his chair and shouted, "Those are *de Andrada's* words to de Mendoza! Not *mine!*"

"Guards will restrain the prisoner," the Lord Mayor of London demanded.

"But—"

"Quiet!" demanded Coke.

Lopez sat back into his chair. *Let them have their venal game. Just let it be over. Let me be strong.*

Coke continued his lies, smiling as he spoke. Roderigo groaned inwardly. Unbearable it was to hear such treachery and not be able to respond to it.

Coke said, "We have clearly demonstrated that Dr. Lopez has been willing in the past to poison his master—provided that the King of Spain requests it and pays for it."

No! Lopez wanted to shout. But he restrained himself, and managed to look at Essex. The bastard's moment of triumph. But one day, God—Roderigo's God, the God of Justice—would call upon the earl to account for his sins. *Midah keneged midah*—the way one lives is the way one dies. Essex will get his. Roderigo felt a sudden calm.

Coke waited until the letter was back on the evidence table. He picked up the next insidious document. "This letter was intercepted by our own Lord Essex's spies in the Low Countries."

De Andrada's words—as deadly as a murder weapon. Roderigo tried to convince himself: *God will see me through.*

Coke handed the letter to Essex. Coke said, "Notice the signature. Though the name be Francisco de Torres, the writing is identical to Dr. Lopez's hand. And also notice the purposely obscured language. Pearls? Since when has Spain become an international marketplace for the trade of *pearls*?"

Coke glared at Lopez. He demanded, "Just what do those words mean, Dr. Lopez?"

All heads had turned in Roderigo's direction.

"Am I to speak?" he asked.

"Only if thy mouth has something of importance to say," Essex sneered. "Which I doubt."

Restrained laughter was heard.

"Go on, I say," prodded Coke. "What meant you to the King of Spain when you asked him for the price of pearls?"

Roderigo chose his words. To admit the truth, that pearls meant the price of redeeming Jews, would brand his family as those of the full Mosaic faith. Only true, believing brethren would risk their lives to save one another. Being labeled as practicing Jews would mean deportation for his family—or possibly death, if the commission wanted to prove a larger conspiracy.

Roderigo said, "In the New Lands—" He stopped, noticed he was whispering. He started over in a clear voice. "In the New Lands the King of Spain had come suddenly upon a sea rich with pearl oysters. I was interested in acquiring a load—"

"Come, come," scoffed Essex. "Are we expected to *believe* this?"

"It's the truth," Roderigo said.

"He lies in his doggish throat!" Essex exclaimed. "Even now he tries to save his neck. But it is too late!"

The Lord Mayor of London touched Essex's shoulder, bidding him to quiet. The earl became quiet, an angry sneer upon his lips.

Coke said, "Is this commission to believe that you were paying the King of Spain for pearls?"

Roderigo nodded.

"Where did these pearls come from?" Coke inquired.

"An undisclosed sea in the New Lands," Roderigo said.

Essex blurted out, "Under torture you have tried to convince us that the word pearls meant Jews. That you were saving Jews, yet you deny that now!"

"Yes," Roderigo said.

"Why would you say under torture that the word pearls meant Jews?" Coke asked Roderigo.

Roderigo felt his tongue cleave to the roof of his mouth. Had he really uttered those words?

"This vile Jew," Essex said, pointing, "was no doubt plotting with his kinsmen, other secret Jews, as well as Philip, in the murder of Her Majesty."

"I am a member of England's Church," Roderigo managed to say.

The statement was met with laughter.

"Let us not veer off the mark," Coke said. "Everyone knows that Lopez is a secret Jew and is only a member of the Church of our land to prevent deportation—"

"That is not true!" Lopez said.

"Ye villainous dog!" Essex said. "Blessed be Jesus Christ that you hid your devilish practices, as mere deportation would have been a slap in the face of justice. You shall die the death of a traitor!''

Again the Lord Mayor hushed Essex. Coke was irritated with the interruption, but Essex didn't care. He was flushed with delight.

Coke went on, ''If *pearls* simply meant pearls, how do you explain this *ring*, Doctor?''

He held up a ruby and diamond ring—the one Roderigo had given to Her Majesty.

The one Her Majesty had given back to Rebecca.

''Was it not given to you by the King of Spain?'' Coke said.

Lopez was slow to respond. Eventually he said, ''The ring was—''

''Answer the question—yes or no! Was the ring given to you by the King of Spain?''

Roderigo spoke with dignity, ''Yes, it was.''

Coke said, ''Why would the King of Spain give *you* a valuable piece of jewelry? If you desire to purchase pearls from His Majesty, should not *you* be the one to offer him such payment?''

Lopez was silent.

''Why *did* the King of Spain pay you with a ring from his treasury?'' Coke pressed.

''He did not pay me.''

''Then what was the true purpose of the ring?'' asked Coke.

''It was given—'' Lopez cleared his throat. ''It was given to me by the King of Spain. I was to give it to Her Majesty as a token of friendship.''

''A token of friendship?'' Coke said in disbelief. ''The King of Spain giving our great Gloriana, our Virgin Queen, a token of friendship?''

It sounded absurd even to Lopez. He felt imbalanced, as if inflicted with falling sickness.

Coke asked, ''Is that what you told Her Majesty when you gave her the ring?''

Lopez didn't answer.

''Is this what you told Her Majesty when you presented the gift to her?''

''No,'' Lopez whispered.

''Did you tell Her Majesty from whom you obtained the ring?''

''No.''

''And why was that?''

''Because I doubted that Her Majesty would accept the ring . . . if she knew from whence it came.''

''Then why did you give Her Majesty the ring?'' Coke asked.

''His Majesty wanted it in her hands, not mine,'' Lopez answered. ''I simply served as his intermediary.''

"And we are to believe this?"

Lopez was silent.

"And we are to believe this?" Coke repeated. He now addressed the commission. "I have a more likely explanation—one suggested by Emmanuel de Andrada's letter to Lord Essex. The King of Spain gave you the ring as an initial payment for poisoning your mistress! The word pearls does not refer to pearls. Nor does it refer to Jews. . . . Nay, not at all. It refers to the price of poisoning the Queen, does it not?"

"No!" Lopez protested.

"Musk and amber refers to the price of burning Her Majesty's ships!"

"Never!"

"Yet you have stated that those words mean exactly that, Dr. Lopez," Coke continued. "You have signed a confession that says as much!"

"Signed it as I lay stretched upon the rack!" Lopez retorted.

Essex could not contain himself. He said, "Ye vile Jew *confessed* it, yet now you belie yourself and say you did it only to save yourself from a racking. As the Lord is my sole witness, you know this to be untrue! Judgment of guilt shall pass against you to the applause of the world!"

Coke added, "You signed the confession, Dr. Lopez! And others will show it to be the truth! The ring was initial payment for the poisoning of your mistress and burning her ships—*guilty* of item two, intent to poison the Queen, guilty of item three, intent to burn her ships!"

"Untrue!" Lopez yelled.

But he could not be heard over the clapping of the commissioners' hands.

Coke orated, "A clever wolf you are, Lopez. You knew how damaging it would be to have a ring from the King of Spain in your possession. So with devious intent you gave the ring to your mistress and hid its origins."

"No," Lopez insisted.

"Then why did you give it to the Queen?"

"The King of Spain wanted Her Majesty to have it."

"Then how did it get back into your hands, Doctor?"

Lopez said, "It was given to my daughter by Her Majesty the Queen."

Coke said, "Her Majesty gave it back to your daughter when she found out from whence it came, did she not?"

"I know not," Lopez said. "Only that Her Majesty gave it to my daughter."

"To give back to you."

"No," Roderigo said stubbornly. "It was given to my daughter as a gift."

Coke said, "Maybe it was given to your daughter because she, too, was involved with this nefarious plot."

Roderigo turned white. He cried, "NO!"

"Hadn't she visited the Queen with you on more than one occasion?"

They were trying to implicate Rebecca. Dear God, dear God, help me.

"Rebecca knew nothing—"

"Then admit it, Jew. The ring was given back to *you* because it came from the sworn enemy of England."

"Yes, yes," Roderigo said. *Anything, please God, so long as they don't touch Rebecca.*

"You lied when you said it was given to your daughter, did you not? It was given back to you personally when the Queen found out its origins?"

Roderigo said yes, he had lied.

"He admits his perjury!" Coke said to the commission. "Only the threat of his daughter's neck forces him to confess the truth. In sooth, the King of Spain gave it to Dr. Lopez as payment for a certain service that the doctor was to perform for him—that service being the poisoning of your mistress, the Queen, and the burning of her ships. Guilty, guilty, guilty!"

Roderigo lowered his head and stared at the floor.

"The man is a murderer," Coke accused. "A notorious liar, a wolf dressed up as a man of medicine. And more, as we shall hear!"

He called in the witness against the accused.

Roderigo saw Esteban Ferreira de Gama enter the chambers. He was skeletal, his eyes feral, mad. They had treated him very badly. He must have gone through much torture before he agreed to play the witness against him. Roderigo's heart held no anger against him. Instead it was sated with pity.

They sat him near Essex. The red-haired lord glared at him malevolently, but de Gama didn't flinch. Only when the tortured man sneaked a sidelong glance at Roderigo did he begin to cry.

"Shall you tell your story?" Coke said to de Gama.

De Gama was sobbing.

"Shall I read you your confession?" Coke said. He didn't bother to wait for an answer, read out loud the document signed by de Gama while under torture. Midway through the recital de Gama peeked at Roderigo. The doctor caught de Gama's eyes and gave him a reassuring nod.

You did what you had to do, I understand.

It made de Gama weep all the more.

When Coke had finished reading the indictment, he said to Roderigo, "Is this not the very story that you yourself admitted? The very confession you made and signed?"

"I suppose I did say something like that. Under torture."

"I shall remind you of your exact words, Doctor," Coke said with an air of triumph. He read aloud Roderigo's confession, then handed it to the Lord Mayor to pass around to the other commissioners.

Coke said to Roderigo, "The commission has now heard the very confession in which you expressed your willingness to do heinous and treasonous service for the King of Spain."

Lopez didn't answer. There was nothing left to do but acquiesce. Though the case was built upon lies, it had been organized carefully. They had it all—de Andrada's old letter stating that Lopez was willing to do service for the King of Spain, Lopez's letter to Gomez D'Avila—the agent David, in the Low Countries—stating that Lopez was willing to do more business with the King of Spain. Obscure code words that could be interpreted in any manner the reader of the letter desired. A ring that was given to him by Philip. A witness to corroborate their lies, his own statement corroborating de Gama's forced falsehoods.

Had Lopez been a member of the commission, he would have condemned himself.

Coke made a few cursory closing remarks—most of them insults to Roderigo's character—a vile, contemptuous villain, a currish Jew not worthy to breathe the air of the English. The commissioners took the vote. One by one they pronounced him guilty. Unanimous.

Roderigo was asked if he wanted to say anything in his defense. What could he say that wouldn't be met with disbelief, with jeers and derision? He accepted the verdict with stoic resignation. It was useless to do otherwise. He did not apologize. He did not beg for mercy. His only statement to the commission was that his family—his wife and children, his in-laws, his nephews—had known nothing of his deceit. Suffer not the innocent for the sins of the father, he stated.

Silence followed Roderigo's pleas, then Coke stood and motioned the commissioners to stand as well. Held firmly by armed guards, Roderigo was led out of the chambers, led back to the Tower to await his execution.

55

$\mathbf{L}$ ike a fiend, Rebecca paced.
  Her father, guilty of treason, of trying to poison the Queen!

As if the verdict were a surprise. The trial had been a mockery.

She muttered a string of curses in Portuguese and kicked the door. Shakespeare looked up from his writing desk. He'd almost burned his tallow dry. Gods, he was tired. Through dim light he could make out the lines on his hourglass—four in the morning.

"Go to sleep, Becca," he said. "Close thine eyes and dream."

"About what?" she answered. "My father's execution?"

Shakespeare regarded the piece of paper before him. He crumpled it and threw it down on the floor. His nerves were taut, his stomach churned. His mind was as thick as a bucket of mud.

"I'm sorry," he managed to say. "I wish there was something I could do for thee. I feel useless."

Rebecca picked up an apple from his trestle table and threw it against the wall. It was soft and fell to the floor, oozing mush. Ye Gods, Shakespeare thought. He'd just finished repairing all the damage *he'd* done during his fit of madness and now *she* was going to undo it all again.

"The bastards," Rebecca snarled. "Foul toads, each and every one of them."

"Shh," Shakespeare said. "The walls are thin."

She stopped pacing, weak with fatigue. She spoke haltingly. "We cannot leave our doorstep without someone calling us vile names . . . without someone spitting at our feet. They gather outside our house all day. They throw garbage over the walls . . . hurl rocks at the windows. . . . It's horrible!"

Her legs could no longer support her weight. She sank onto Shakespeare's pallet—newly sewn, stuffed with sweet straw. He stood up from his table, waded through piles of discarded papers crushed into balls and lay down beside her.

"Night is my true ally," she whispered. "Darkness is a lover. I am hidden. I can breathe freely."

463

Shakespeare asked, "What can I do for thee?"

"Nothing," Rebecca said, turning her back to him. "Nothing at all. We live in constant fear, Will. Much like thee with thy murderous shadow, except that all of England is out to do us in. My brother is particularly vulnerable. I worry for his life."

"Perhaps he should leave the country for a while."

"And desert Father?" She rolled over and faced him. "He'd never do that. Do you not recall Benjamin's loyalty the night thou called my father a whoremonger?"

"Too clearly," Shakespeare said. The boy had been frothing with rage. "Cannot your mother leave at least? Surely the strain is too much for her."

"She'll not leave until Father is freed . . . or laid in his grave."

Rebecca turned to him and stroked his cheek. "Oh my honeyed lover . . . if it were found out by certain people that thou hast befriended me—a Jewess, daughter of a traitor—"

Shakespeare placed his fingers on her lips. Rebecca kissed them softly, then nestled his hand between her breasts. She said,

"I must return to my house before daybreak. I must not be fragile in front of Mother. I must be strong."

"Stay," Shakespeare said, wrapping his arms around her. "Just a moment longer. Then I'll walk thee home."

Rebecca closed her eyes, finding comfort in the cradle of his embrace. So sweet, so kind. He was everything to her, seeing her through these days of madness. Her rock, her redeemer. He had even offered to run away with her once again, thereby tainting himself forever. Of course, she had refused. Never would she permanently inflict her woes upon him. Yet she knew that had he left her alone, she would surely have perished.

Rebecca said, "Thou hast yet to write anything acceptable?"

"Nothing that would move a queen to pardon thy father," Shakespeare said. "I've failed thee—"

"Stop," Rebecca said. "What about what thou hast tossed on the floor?"

"Words unworthy for a monarch."

"We have no time for vanity or perfection, sweet William. *Anything* is better than nothing."

"Regard what I've written, if it will make thee lighter of spirit," Shakespeare said, sweeping his arms over the floor. "But I confess that my mind has been a barren womb." He regarded her with profound sadness. "I'm sorry."

Rebecca felt a lump of despair in her chest. She said, "If I can get through the crowds, and if I can squeeze through the guards, and if I can manage to capture the Queen's attention, and if I am allowed to speak without immediate arrest . . .

What . . ." She felt tears well up in her eyes. "What am I to say to Her Majesty, Willy?"

Shakespeare ran his hands over her face. He sighed. "Let's see what I've thrown away. Perhaps I can play around with the words. . . ." Rebecca was about to rise from the pallet. Shakespeare said, "No, no. Rest, my love, while thou hast peace and opportunity."

"I love thee."

"I love thee too." Shakespeare stood, picked up some balls of paper and smoothed them out. He read to himself and muttered, "This is dreadful . . . this equally as much. This is a bald embarrassment—"

Rebecca interrupted, "I believe thee not. Hand them to me."

Shakespeare continued uncrumpling the paper. With reluctance, he finally handed her a sample of his attempts. He glanced over her shoulder as she eyed his writing.

"This was the best of my feeble efforts," he said nervously.

Rebecca read out loud,

> The quality of mercy is not strain'd
> As gentle rain, it falls from heaven
> Upon the place beneath: it is twice blest;
> It blesseth him that gives and him that takes:
> 'Tis mightiest in the mightiest: it becomes
> a throned prince superior than his crown . . ."

She stood up and stared at him.

"It's still in foul form," Shakespeare explained.

She read the rest of it and said, "How could thou cast this aside like . . . like *muck*?"

"Something's lacking."

"Nothing's lacking. It's *perfect*. So deeply it will move Her Majesty to mercy. It has brevity of thought, clarity of purpose, elegance—"

"It's void of passion, Rebecca," Shakespeare said.

"Thou hast rocks in thy head," she said, throwing her arms around him. She crushed her lips to his. "I must memorize these words at once."

"Not yet. Let me amend—"

"Nothing needs amending."

"Small things, Rebecca," he said. "The order of subject-verb, the choice of words . . . It's hard to explain. The rhythm is unbalanced."

"Thou could true up the scales of justice on thy words, so balanced they are."

Shakespeare was still not satisfied. He said. ''The lines are well constructed if one intends to recite them in a play—a lawyer orating on behalf of his client. But a daughter pleading for her father's life—''

''Thou speakest nonsense!'' Rebecca said. ''My God, Will, I'll never be able to intone such beautiful words. They shall fall out of my mouth like rotten teeth.''

''Nothing coming out of that mouth could ever be rotten. Let me work with the words, Becca—''

''Oh Willy, even if we could get something that pleases thee, how shall I speak before a queen? I've never addressed anyone, let alone a monarch.''

''Well,'' Shakespeare said, ''I'm not the player that Richard Burbage is, that Harry Whitman was, but I've had experience performing before a hostile audience.''

''Then teach me all thou knowest,'' Rebecca said.

Shakespeare said he would.

Crowds! Bodies upon bodies! Like maggots in rotten meat the people undulated and pushed to catch a glimpse of their monarch.

The royal progression departed from the palace at Greenwich, the Queen scheduled to travel to Lord Burghley's residence in Theobald. The military escort was small but brilliantly displayed. The halberdiers in brightly colored livery—scarlet sleeves and jerkin, black hat, cinnamon hose with yellow panes, black shoes adorned with a velvet red. They were followed by ranks of pikemen and musket bearers—the finest of England's soldiers. The military men were matched in numbers by a great cortege of mounted lords and ladies—a stunning show of exquisite dress. Yards and yards of embroidered velvet and silk flowed over glistening flanks of superior horses—bays, brindles, black and white stallions.

Lord Essex was in his full glory. As Master of the Horse, he had presented London a spellbinding progression. He led the retinue toward its first destination—a waterworks display upon the Thames, the first of the new year. Up until a week ago the Master of the Revels had not been sure the program was feasible, as much of the Thames was still caked with ice. But unseasonably warm March weather had sent the river flowing once again.

Elizabeth was in bright humor over the fortuitous weather. She sat behind a silk curtain in a gilded coach, pulled by six white horses. From time to time she'd draw back the curtain and wave a perfumed glove embroidered in gold thread at her subjects. As she did this, the cannons boomed, the people roared:

Long live Eliza!
Long live Eliza!

Elizabeth, the Virgin Queen. She had a lover named England, and nowhere had been consummated a more passionate affair. Her subjects, thousands of them gathered under gray skies, sang Gloriana's praises.

> *Eliza is a fairest queen*
>   *That ever trod upon this green.*
> *Eliza's eyes are blessed stars*
>   *Inducing peace, subduing wars:*
> *Eliza's hand is crystal bright:*
>   *Her words are balm, her looks are light:*
> *Eliza's breast is that fair hill*
>   *Where virtue dwells and sacred skill.*
> *O blessèd be each day and hour*
>   *Where sweet Eliza builds her bower . . .*

The Queen rested upon a velvet seat and gleefully listened to the adulation of her people. She held in her hands a bouquet of two dozen roses, the stems void of thorns, their perfume pleasantly scenting the inside of the coach. Whimsically, Elizabeth plucked a rose, drew the curtain and tossed the flower to the cheering masses.

A goodly crowd, she thought. Essex had put on a grand retinue. She reminded herself to reward him if he maintained good behavior and kept his temper under control. What did she see in him? His rashness made for a very exciting man but an exceedingly poor statesman. But for the time being he was safe in his position. As Master of the Horse he could do little damage. As long as he didn't reach beyond his capabilities, his position in court would be assured.

Elizabeth heard commotion outside the coach—her sentries commanding someone away. Twas not an unusual request. There was always some simpleton who wished a gracious word from his queen. It was her duty to bestow upon him cheer.

"Hold!" she ordered her coachman. "Stay the good person," she commanded.

The royal coach horses were immediately jerked to a stop. The progression was halted.

Elizabeth drew back the curtain and leaned forward, expecting to see a day laborer garbed in a simple jerkin and galley slops. Such audacity and lack of manner was expected from one of the lower class. Instead the Queen was stunned to see Lopez's daughter. This was not appropriate behavior for a gentlewoman, even one whose father sat in the Tower awaiting death! Yet Elizabeth saw the desperation in the girl's eyes. The girl dropped to her knees, muddying her fine skirt of green silk. Her breasts were beautifully framed by a bodice of rose damask embroidered with silver thread. The Queen remembered their downy softness, recalled the soft curves of her body. Her black hair was neatly pinned, but that night it had been long and loose. Elizabeth recalled the warmth of the girl's hands—beautiful they were, graced with slender fingers.

But now the gloveless hands shook with cold, her fingers raw and unadorned. The child was not wearing the ring she had given her. Then Elizabeth remembered: it had been evidence used to convict her father. Elizabeth sighed. What Coke had said was true. She had returned the ring to the girl when Essex had told her that the jewel was from the Spanish king.

Essex rode over to the coach. "What means this delay?" he yelled to the coachman.

"I commanded it," Elizabeth said.

Essex eyed Rebecca, knee deep in mud. "Who is the girl?"

"I believe it is my former physician's daughter," said the Queen. "Am I correct?"

"As always, Your Grace," Rebecca said. Her voice was small. Her eyes darted momentarily to Essex's. His were filled with bitter hatred, but well matched by Rebecca's own rage. Slowly, Rebecca grew bold enough to look at her queen.

Nine months ago Rebecca had lain with a woman weakened by fever, her body frail and small. But now she saw the power, the fortitude—the great equalizer that could raise the commoner to nobility, that could lower the sword of the executioner. Her Majesty's face radiated absolute command, the royal eyes scrutinizing her: Was she properly dressed? Was she showing proper reverence? Had she displayed sufficient humility before her queen?

"Do you wish her removed?" Essex asked, containing his anger.

"If I had wanted her removed, I would have commanded her gone," Elizabeth answered. She said to Rebecca: "Is it your intent to speak on behalf of your convicted father?"

Rebecca cleared her throat and managed to whisper, "If my audacity is tolerated by Your Grace."

"It is tolerated," said Elizabeth. Her eyes began to sparkle. "Speak."

Rebecca paused, her mind in a state of panic.

Shakespeare's words. They were gone from her head.

All the careful planning—how to intonate, how to enunciate, how to project without sounding like a blowhole—all of it had vanished. She sneaked a quick look over her shoulder. Willy was still there, frantically mouthing something to her. She didn't comprehend a word of it.

Great God's wounds! she thought. What now?

"Your most holy Grace . . ." she began. She paused, then spoke her heart: "I am nothing, a lowly yet devout servant of Your Majesty, born of humble birth and as devoid of peerage as a dung monger. I have naught to offer you, nothing to entice you to listen to my pleas. It is wholly presumptious of me to *beg* of you an audience. Yet as a daughter sired by a loyal subject of the crown, a girl whose father has been unjustly accused of most heinous treason, I beseech Your Excellence to lend me your ear.

"What cause have I to speak on behalf of my father? Yes, blood binds tightly the noose of filial devotion, making us children ready tapsters anxious to pour as soon as our parents sip. Yet no offspring can condone—all offspring must condemn—those who seek to tarnish the golden crown ordained by God. Tis a crime of humanity to do less. Yet I stand before you, most good and divine Queen, I stand before God and state that my father, Roderigo Lopez, is your true servant and bred no ill to the crown, no harm to mighty England.

"What are my father's iniquities? If love of his fellow brethren be a felony, then yes, my father is a criminal. If the milk of human kindness is foul posset, I say yes, again, my father is a fiend. If liberating those unjustly sentenced to death is wrong, then let my father be hung. But if the quality of mercy springs from the wells of Your Grace's soul, know that my father played out his deeds with a pure and tender heart.

"Facts do state that my father erred in judgment, executed decisions without benefit of your most excellent royal counsel. Yes, his plans were ill-conceived, ill-advised. And I know that Your Majesty must mete out punishment for this infraction. But to say that my father acted with malice, with a desire to endanger his queen and country, is to speak falsely. I pray Your Majesty, armed Athene and divine ruler of this land, consider my father's crimes, but consider also the reasons why they were committed. Yes, my cries afoul come from daughterly obligation, but they leap out from my heart as well.

"I beg Your Majesty's forgiveness for my impudence."

Rebecca fell to the ground.

The Queen stared at her prostrated at the base of the royal coach. She raised an eyebrow, then said to Rebecca, "If your father did nothing else, he sired a most dutiful and eloquent daughter. Essex! Give Mistress Lopez a helping hand. She will ride with me to Burghley House."

Essex stared at the Queen in disbelief.

"Come, come," Elizabeth said. "Off your horse and help her now. Lest you want to give Mistress Lopez your own horse and go afoot."

Essex felt his body go hot, felt his head about to explode.

Control, he managed to whisper under his breath. Slowly, he dismounted and extended his hand to Rebecca. She grabbed it, then squeezed it with all her might, hoping his rings would cut into his skin. She thought she saw him wince, but the expression dissipated so quickly she couldn't be sure.

She looked over her shoulder. Willy was still there. Smiling. He brought his fingers to his lips and blew air upon the tips. A kiss . . .

One step up and into the coach.

Rebecca, muddy gown and all, was face to face with Her Royal Highness, Elizabeth Tudor, Queen of England.

56

Riding with the Queen was like being trapped with a brooding tiger. It was hard to act invisible, but Rebecca did as best she could. She dared not speak to Her Highness, but couldn't help chancing a quick glance. The Queen was wearing a gown of pure white, the topcoat of her bodice beaded with freshwater pearls. The royal wig was weaved with jewels and sparkled whenever Her Majesty turned her head. During most of the progression Rebecca sat straight-spined and stared left at the drawn curtain—the barrier that separated the coach and the outside world. It was red velvet worn bald at the hem. Strange, the details noticed from up close.

The bumpy ride, the fatigue, the emotional strain—all were descending upon her. She ached with exhaustion and fought to keep her eyes open. Nonetheless, she found her lids shutting, her head slumping forward. A minute later she realized that she was dozing and snapped her eyes open. The Queen was staring at her. Red-faced, Rebecca sat up and returned her eyes to the curtain.

Invisible.

The crowd outside cheered as loud as a thunderstorm, the noise crescendoing every time Her Majesty opened the curtain and waved a rose. The carriage wheels sloshed through mud puddles for another twenty minutes before Her Majesty halted it. This time it was for a day laborer who wished a good word for his daughter. The Queen extended her hand through the side panel and placed it upon a towheaded lass of five. She blessed the girl, her good parents, and all the good people of England.

With a pull of the reins, the coach resumed its progress.

Once again Rebecca felt the heat of royal eyes upon her. She sneaked another glance at the Queen. There was anger in the black orbs, a smoldering glare that sent a shiver down Rebecca's spine.

What was displeasing Her Majesty now? Rebecca thought hard, noticing the Queen's hands brush against her ear. The gesture was repeated.

My earrings, thought Rebecca.

The royal lobes were adorned with pearl drops surrounded by diamonds. Rebecca's ears were also bejeweled with pearls and diamonds, and her pearls were not only bigger than Elizabeth's, but of more perfect symmetry and superior luster. Special earrings—a family heirloom loaned to her by Aunt Maria for this occasion.

With a shaking hand, Rebecca removed the earrings. She asked for permission to speak, and the Queen granted her request.

"I have been of unclear head of late." Laying the earrings in her open palm, Rebecca offered them to the Queen. "I pray madam to forgive my stupidity. These are from my fam—" She thought again. "These are but a humble gift from me to Your Majesty."

The Queen regarded Rebecca. She took off her own earrings and dropped them in Rebecca's hand.

"Which of the two sets is the superior?" Elizabeth asked.

A game. If Rebecca answered hers were better, she would be insulting the royal jewels. If she lied and said the Queen's were the fairer earrings, she would show herself to be just another sycophant.

Rebecca said, "I am not worthy to offer an opinion."

"Offer one anyway," pressed the Queen.

Rebecca hesitated, then scrutinized the earrings as if she were giving the Queen's question serious consideration. She finally answered, "As madam well knows, bigger isn't always better."

Elizabeth laughed, then said, "But sometimes it is." She slipped Rebecca's earrings on and, retrieving her earrings from Rebecca's palm, dropped them in her purse. "I accept your gift."

"Thank you, madam."

The Queen drew back her curtain once more, waved to the crowd. Another half hour of riding in silence. Finally the coach stopped for the first of its two destinations. Elizabeth peered through the crack of the curtain and regarded the throne that the Master of the Revels had set up for the waterworks display. The chair was gold, the seat and back padded with purple velvet. It was placed under a canopy decorated with vines and flowers—adequate protection if the rains returned. Elizabeth pulled out a looking glass from her purse and adjusted the crown atop her auburn wig. Neat and precise. She dropped the glass back in her purse and waited. A minute later Essex opened the door to her coach. He extended one hand to his queen and placed the other arm around her small waist. Gracefully, he swept her out of the coach, then closed the carriage door behind her.

Rebecca sat without moving a muscle.

She heard the Master of the Revels, Sir Edward Tilney, greet the Queen with all the expected lavish praise: The great and wise Virgin Queen, she was the mightiest prince among princes, how stunning was her gown, how brightly jeweled was her hair, how fortunate he was to have an opportunity to put on this show for her.

In a charmingly gay voice the Queen answered in Italian: Your lips are brown from eating shit.

The Master of the Revels cooed with delight at what he mistakenly perceived to be a compliment.

Rebecca couldn't help herself. She giggled, then covered her mouth when she heard no laughter coming from the outside. She could only guess that no one else had understood the Queen's words. Sir Edward heaped more flummery upon his royal mistress and bade her to her throne.

"A minute," Elizabeth answered, extending her gloved hand for Sir Edward to kiss it.

He was dismissed.

The Queen gave a hard rap on the door and said, "Open up."

Rebecca swung open the carriage doors. Elizabeth climbed in, shut them tight and drew the curtains. The woman was in her sixties but was as light on her feet as a crane.

Royal eyes fell upon Rebecca, stern and hard. Elizabeth said, "I shall have to watch my words around you."

Rebecca felt her heart bang against her chest.

"What other languages do you understand?" asked the Queen. "Besides Italian . . . and Portuguese and Spanish. No doubt you understand those quite well."

Rebecca nodded.

"What else?" pressed the Queen.

"A bit of German," Rebecca whispered.

"And?"

"Some Arabic from my father's medical books."

"And?"

"A wee crumb of French."

"Do you speak Chinese, the language of Cathay?" Elizabeth asked.

"No madam."

"Ignoramus." The Queen's eyes were dancing now. "Have you a good, solid working knowledge of Latin?"

"Not as poor as some, not nearly as well-versed as Your Majesty."

Elizabeth studied her. She said, "Write me a speech in Latin. I have to address a group of scholars tonight and I haven't had time to write one myself. Make it long, make it complicated, make it exceedingly tedious and boring. I want to test the attention span of England's educated."

"As you will, madam."

"I am going, now, to watch a pageant of waterworks. If the gunpowder is dry, it is my understanding that Sir Edward has planned a surprise fireworks display for me as well. You stay here and write my speech." She looked at the mud stains on Rebecca's gown. "I'll have one of my ladies bring you a suitable dress. Bright blue pleases me. Twould compliment your coloring."

"A perfect choice," Rebecca said.

Elizabeth paused. "I should have insisted that you become one of my maids. I would have had great use for your linguistic talents. Events past might never have occurred with you in court. Now, of course, it's too late."

Rebecca lowered her head and fought back tears.

Elizabeth furrowed her brow and asked, "And how is your aged grandam?"

Rebecca jerked her head to attention. Then she remembered: Grandmama had been her excuse for not accepting the position at court.

Grandmama. Rebecca had ritually washed the wasted body. She could still feel the delicate bones, the texture of cold, sagging skin . . .

Do not cry!

"Dead, madam," Rebecca answered.

"Dead?"

"Yes, Your Majesty. It happened around the same time as my father's arrest."

"You've hit upon quite a streak of misfortune." Elizabeth thought for a moment, then said, "You will come with me to Burghley House. We'll have an opportunity to speak in privacy. Then, I suppose, you'll be anxious to return to your mother."

"If it pleases madam."

"I'm not certain it does please madam, but you'll have my permission to leave." She kicked open the door, clipping Essex in the ear. He held the side of his head and bit back pain. The Queen howled with laughter.

"Not very subtle, Devereaux," she said. "Would Lord Essex be so kind as to do service for his queen?"

Essex extended his hand, and Elizabeth stepped out of the carriage. She thwacked him on his sore ear with the back of her hand.

"How dare you eavesdrop!"

Essex didn't answer.

"Retrieve a quill, ink, and paper for Mistress Rebecca," the Queen told him. "Then join me for the pageant. You may sit at the foot of my throne." She pinched his cheek playfully. "I need a handsomely dressed lapdog."

With utmost care Rebecca drew back the curtain and peeked outside. The Queen had left Essex standing alone. The lord's cheeks were bright red. He was clenching his fists.

The night had passed the witching hour before Rebecca was finally settled in Burghley House. Her cell, a small chamber off of the guest quarters, barely accommodated a bed and a hearth. She lay upon the mattress and closed her eyes.

The Queen had been pleased with the speech Rebecca had written. She'd promised to speak with her tomorrow, at five in the morning.

What would Her Majesty say?

Don't expect miracles.

Don't expect miracles.

Don't expect miracles. . . .

Rebecca did not sleep at all. At four-fifteen she lit her candlestick and dressed quickly. The corset prepared by the queen's maids fit perfectly around her waist but was too tight for her bosom. She looked as if she were holding her breath. No matter. The Queen would probably think it quite suitable. Besides, she had more important things on her mind than her dress.

At quarter to five a knock sounded at her door.

Her hair was knotted and held in place by gold and ivory combs. She would offer them to the Queen. With what else could she entice the monarch to mercy?

Snowbird perhaps. Father had often said the gyrfalcon was the envy of every eye—

The knock repeated itself louder.

She was trembling as she opened the door. A pair of sentries dressed in the Queen's livery—one with a black beard, the other clean-shaven—greeted her. They stepped aside and allowed Rebecca to cross the threshold, then led her down a dark foyer toward the Queen's lodgings.

Halfway to the royal chambers the clean-shaven sentry stopped and sent the other guard away on an errand. He walked with Rebecca a few feet, then pulled her into a dark corner. She noticed his hands were shaking. She thought the man odd. He said, "I must search you for weapons."

"Weapons?"

"Have you a dagger hidden in your skirt, mistress?"

"No—"

"Reflecting upon your parentage, your word is not trustworthy, Mistress Rebecca Lopez. I take every precaution to protect my queen."

"But—"

"What are you hiding, Jewess?"

"Nothing—"

"Then why do you falter?"

"I—"

He pushed Rebecca down, fell upon her and clamped his palm over her mouth. Freeing one hand, he pulled out a dagger from his jacket and held it in front of her eyes.

"You were hiding *this* in your skirt, were you not?"

Rebecca shook her head emphatically, rigid with terror.

"I say you were!" said the sentry.

"No," Rebecca mumbled out.

"Shut up!" the sentry whispered. He began to undo his hose and codpiece.

Dear God, Rebecca thought. She blinked back tears and struggled in his grip.

"Stop it!" the guard hissed. "Stop squirming or I'll kill you."

Rebecca forced her body to go slack. He smiled, showing a mouth missing front teeth. His breath was foul.

"That's better," he said. "If you fight me . . ." He was lifting her skirt up. "If you utter a sound, I shall say I found this dagger hidden in your dress and, just like your doggish father, you desired harm against your queen. Do you understand me?"

Rebecca nodded, tried to remain passive, but there was something so evil about his touch. She couldn't help herself. She bit his hand and cried out.

He was momentarily stunned. Rebecca screamed again. Recovering, the sentry slapped his hands over her nose and mouth, but the noise had attracted attention. In seconds they were surrounded by torches. The clean-shaven sentry quickly stood and frantically tried to retie his points.

"She was going to kill Her Majesty," he explained, his fingers entwined with string. "I found a dagger—"

"You found what?" interrupted a low-pitched female voice.

The sentry looked up, then dropped to his knees.

The Queen cast her eyes upon Rebecca curled into a tiny ball, then upon the guard. "You found what?" she repeated.

"A d-d-dagger, Your Majesty," stuttered the sentry.

"Are you saying that *this* girl was armed with a dagger?"

The sentry nodded. His hose and codpiece were tied messily, his shirttail hung out of his doublet.

"Are you implying that the girl meant to do harm to her queen?"

"Yes . . . Yes, exactly, Your Majesty."

Elizabeth said nothing.

"Here . . ." The guard held up the dagger. "Here is the weapon, Your Highness."

Elizabeth's eyes shifted from his face, to his codpiece, to Rebecca lying on the floor. Her skirt was still hiked over her knees. The Queen returned her eyes to the sentry.

"And why would she desire me harm?" Elizabeth continued.

The sentry felt his voice strings constrict. He whispered hoarsely, "Her father is a traitor."

"And that is your explanation?" the Queen queried.

"Yes . . . I mean, Your Highness . . ." The sentry's bladder exploded and warm, wet liquid drenched his hose. "She was following her father's orders—"

"She's not had contact with her father in three months," said Elizabeth. "Are you telling me that this girl—whose father's life rests in *my* hands—desired *me* willful malice?"

The sentry nodded, but weakly. He realized the futility of his argument.

The Queen kept staring at him.

"Oh merciful Jesu!" he cried out.

Elizabeth said to the guard on her right, "Bring the girl into my chambers."

Rebecca felt herself lifted to her feet. She waited a moment to catch her breath, smoothed out her skirt and dried her tears upon her gloves. One of the combs had fallen out of her hair. She picked it up, repinned a tress of loose hair, then allowed herself to be led away.

Elizabeth hadn't taken her eyes off the sentry. She stared at him for a minute, two minutes, four minutes, until the man was a heap of quivering gel and admitted his lies. Yes, he had tried to have his way with the girl. But only to teach her a lesson. She was of treasonous stock. He begged for mercy, pleaded for the sake of his wife and children. Elizabeth remained as cool as soapstone. When the man had finished his begging, he began to pray. Elizabeth grew weary of the performance.

Finally she said to no guard in particular, "Take him to New-gate." She walked several steps, then added, "Have him hanged."

Rebecca managed to regain superficial composure by the time the Queen and her ladies entered the Privy Chambers. The room, built for Elizabeth, was fifty feet in length, sixty feet high, the coffers of its ceiling leafed with gold. Intricate arras work was displayed not only on the walls, but covered the floor as well. The Queen promenaded across the chamber, her women following her like a bridal train, sat down in her throne and motioned Rebecca forward. Feeling as soiled as muck, Rebecca carefully tried to avoid stepping on the tapestries—an impossible task—and her tiptoed dance made Elizabeth smile. Rebecca stopped ten feet from the royal throne and began her deep curtsy of reverence. Elizabeth pointed to a velvet pillow at her feet and told her to sit. She sent her female attendants away, leaving only two guards posted at the door. Rebecca lowered herself onto the cushion, her bluebell-colored skirt encircling her like a pool of springwater.

"Men are animals," Elizabeth said. "My stepmother's husband tried to have his way with me when I was your age." She clucked her tongue. "He was beheaded."

Rebecca knew she was referring to Thomas Seymour but said nothing. She removed the combs and wordlessly offered them to Elizabeth. The Queen inspected them and nodded approval.

"Your earrings, your combs . . . If you continue, you'll soon find yourself with naught but a chemise." Elizabeth plucked a stone from her jeweled wig. It was an emerald. She picked off three more, then handed them all to Rebecca.

"I couldn't accept—"

"Nonsense," argued Elizabeth. "Of course you can. You can and will do everything I request of you, and I'm requesting you to take these. Go on . . . before I change my mind. I'm known to be sudden in my moods. God's wounds, girl, take advantage of my good humor."

Rebecca took the jewels and thanked her profusely. Elizabeth stood, stepped over Rebecca's feet then strolled around the chambers. Dawn was creeping through the mullioned windows, throwing a checkerboard of light upon floor tapestries. The walls underneath the arras work were draped with red damask cloth, the royal crest embroidered in silver, gold, and blue. Elizabeth ordered one of the guards to extinguish the wall torches.

"Have you eaten?" she asked.

"No, madam."

"Are you hungry?"

"My stomach is accustomed to waiting until dinner for food."

The response pleased Elizabeth. She faced Rebecca and said, "Your father's foolishness is unfathomable. Simply incomprehensible. That he was corresponding with the King of Spain there is no doubt, child. And that he was involved in personal negotiations with His Majesty without my knowledge, again that is fact."

"Yes, madam."

"The question is, for what purpose."

Rebecca didn't answer.

"I do not take lightly my signature that condemns a man to death, and I *have* signed your father's death warrant— You're shivering. Would you like a blanket?"

"It is not necessary, madam."

"As you will." Elizabeth stood up again. "I am deeply perturbed. I cannot ignore the evidence against your father. He did present me a ring and hid its origins for reasons unbeknownst to me. Yet even though I signed the warrant and handed it to a cheering parliament, I hesitate to release him from the Tower and send him to death. I must ask myself why."

She walked over to the window and peered into a steely sky. "Do I believe he is guilty of consorting with the enemy? There is no question the answer to this is yes. Do I believe he wished me malice . . . I know not. How would he have benefited from my demise?"

She waited for an answer.

Rebecca said, "My father would have gained nothing."

"Money, from His Majesty Philip?"

"No godly creature would dare compare mere coins to the heavenly graces that madam has bestowed upon us."

Elizabeth smiled. "In sooth, why *was* he corresponding with His Majesty?"

Rebecca took a deep breath and said, "He was paying His Majesty to redeem those condemned to the atrocities of the *Catholic* Inquisition."

"Did he redeem some secret Jews as well?"

"Mayhap among the doomed were secret Jews."

Elizabeth began to pace. Her eyes were deep in reflection, very troubled. "Your father is a fool," she repeated. "Why didn't he come to me?"

"He should have done so."

"A fool," she said. "A stupid, idiotic dolt." She turned to Rebecca and said, "But an excellent physician. For eight years under his care I have lived in good health. Yet the Queen's bench has convicted him of treachery, the good people of England demanded his limbs on the gates of Tyburn. What was I to do but sign the warrant?''

Rebecca knew this question was rhetorical. She said, "Her Majesty rules with truth and justice as her armed companions.''

Rebecca's answer added to the old woman's burden. The Queen said, "I shall stay his execution scheduled for April and reflect upon the situation.''

"Thank you, madam," Rebecca answered. Her lower lip was trembling.

Elizabeth added, "I suppose Ferreira de Gama's execution must be stayed as well. One goes with the other.'' She turned to Rebecca and said, "As long as Roderigo remains in the Tower under *my* auspices, he will be safe. If for any reason he is taken from the Tower, he is at the hands of the law and will be executed. I will double the watch upon him to make certain no attempts are made to remove him from his cell.''

Rebecca prostrated herself before the Queen and wept openly.

"Come, come, child," Elizabeth chided. "Dignity.''

Quickly, Rebecca dried her eyes and waited for the Queen to speak.

"You may leave," Elizabeth said.

"Madam?''

"Dear God, what is it now, girl? No fawning words of praise, I hope.''

"I pray you, madam, have I the right to entertain a glimmer of hope that my family might be allowed visitation privileges while Her Majesty conducts most burdensome judgment?''

"You want to see your father?'' Elizabeth said.

"Yes, madam. My mother and brother as well—''

"Stop," Elizabeth said. "You may see your father. Only *you*. You shall carry his wishes—if he has any—to your kinsmen. I'll not allow anyone else to see him.''

"Yes, madam. Thank you, madam.''

"You may leave," Elizabeth said. "Someone will take you back to London.''

Rebecca departed before the Queen could undergo another shift of mood.

57

Rebecca heard the cry of the watchman. It was an hour past midnight, and she lay in Shakespeare's arms, wide awake, resentful that her lover was sleeping so soundly. But why shouldn't he sleep? It wasn't *his* father locked in the Tower, Father's fate wasn't held in *his* hands. She sighed out loud.

"What is it?" Shakespeare asked, not bothering to open his eyes.

"Go back to sleep."

Shakespeare didn't say the obvious, that it was impossible to sleep with her fidgeting and moaning. "Becca, my love, talk to me. Unburden thy soul."

"Why should thou suffer my ills?"

"Pray, talk to me," Shakespeare repeated.

"No," Rebecca said. "Thou should speak to me. Get my mind off of my woes, off of tomorrow and the Tower. Gods, Willy, what will I say to Father?"

"Speak as thou didst with the Queen, Becca. Speak thy heart." Shakespeare laughed to himself.

"What strikes thee as merry?" Rebecca asked.

Shakespeare said, "Strange what flashes in the mind at times like these. I hear Harry lecturing to me, 'Suit the action to the word, the word to the action!' Harry was always giving me bits of advice, especially when he was drunk." He kissed her softly. "I hope I'm not waxing pompous with thee."

Rebecca smiled and shook her head no. She said, "Speak to me of Harry's murder."

"God's sointes, Becca—"

"Twill take my mind off tomorrow."

Shakespeare exhaled, rolled onto his back. He was fully awake now. Speak of Harry's murder? What was there to talk about? He wasn't any closer to the solution than he'd been eight months ago and it frightened him. Shakespeare's father in London—Harry Whitman—the man who'd cared for him in the big city, had nurtured his acting and bookwriting talents. Whitman's soul wandering eternity, unable to find rest until the murderer was caught.

Think, he screamed to himself. Think! You're not trying hard enough!

Rebecca asked, "What is it?"

"What is what?"

"Thou hast become silent."

"Nothing," Shakespeare said. He noticed his abrupt tone of voice and immediately added, "I love thee."

"I love thee too."

"Dost thou?"

"Oh, Will, how could thou believe otherwise?"

"Then why dost thou refuse to come away with me?"

"My shame would brand thee as traitor. Never would I allow that."

"It matters not to me."

"Aye, but it matters to me. Think of thy son. Is such shame what thou desires for him?"

Shakespeare turned onto his stomach. His pallet was lumpy and it irritated him. He said, "If we were to flee to Venice—"

"I will not become a Catholic," Rebecca said flatly.

Shakespeare said, "If thou refuses my God, I will follow thy God."

"Become a *Jew*?"

Shakespeare said, "Has not a Jew eyes, has not a Jew hands? If I tickle this Jewess, does not she laugh?" He dug his hands into Rebecca's ribs.

"Stop it," Rebecca said, giggling.

"Has not a Jew affections, passions?"

"This Jewess does."

"Then so shall I."

"Never." Rebecca turned to Shakespeare and said, "Becoming a Jew, my love, would be thy ruin, I regret to say."

"Will I be of different form once I pronounce allegiance to thy God? Will I suddenly be bereft of my writing skills, of my acting talents?"

"William," Rebecca said. "In Venice the Jews live in a ghetto."

Shakespeare felt his stomach sink. He'd forgotten about that. The Jews, confined behind gates—no Christians entered the ghetto, and the Jews did not come out. No plays were performed behind the iron gates. The city of Rome was the same way.

"Our union is impossible," Rebecca said. "We must accept our fate—"

"What about Padua?" Shakespeare asked hopefully. "There, Jews are known to live with Christians—"

"Only a matter of time," Rebecca said. "No, Willy. Even if thou would convert of thy own free will, I wouldn't run away with thee. To be a Jew is a burden—aye, a burden I have accepted. But I refuse to imprison thee to such a hard existence.''

Shakespeare secretly felt relieved, then cursed his cowardice. Would he really have converted had Rebecca said yes? He doubted the veracity of his own words and hated himself for it. He hugged Rebecca, kissed the nape of her neck. Of the two of them, she was the stronger, the more clever. Had she devoted her energies to finding Harry's murderer, the fiend would have been tried and convicted by now, his corpse nothing more than ashes in Smithfield. Shakespeare felt Rebecca's body relaxing in his arms. He held her in silence, and soon her breathing became slow and steady. Maybe it was his willingness to become a Jew that suddenly gave her peace. Whatever it was, Shakespeare was grateful that she'd finally fallen asleep.

He was too alert to try sleeping. His thoughts turned to Harry, to his murder—over and over. Mackering, Chambers, Fottingham, Lord Henley, the Jesuit who was Harry's true father, the stew Catherine—Cat. Harry's wife Margaret, who wore her bitterness like armor. Individually they all had separate identities, separate characters. But together they were like a spinning color wheel—the result was dead white.

He tossed them around in his brain. Just white, white, and more white. Then he stopped suddenly. His logic was all befuddled. Start from the beginning of the first trip up North. *Everyone* he conversed with, down to the most insignificant tapster he'd met on the road to Brithall. . . .

No, start with his conversation with Margaret at the funeral.

Could Margaret have killed her husband?

Shakespeare considered the possibility. It seemed absurd—Harry's death was the reason for her hapless condition. Yet Harry had been a less than ideal husband. His carousing had left Margaret keeping company with time and loneliness. Like Anne . . .

He shooed away the melancholy thought.

What about the innkeepers he'd met on his first trip up North? He reflected a moment, trying to awaken his dormant memory. They had told him nothing of significance. Harry had told bawdy poetry. He had departed without incident.

His mind began to drift . . . .

The first stop at Brithall. Who had he spoken to there? Lord Henley. No, hadn't he met a guard at the gatehouse first?

Maybe the guard was a lookout for the Jesuit. Maybe he'd *told* the Jesuit someone was at Brithall asking questions about Harry.

Maybe.

Had he mentioned Harry Whitman to the guard?

Gods, it was so long ago.

The Jesuit. Why would he kill his son?

Then there was Lord Henley. What reason could he have to kill Harry?

Shakespeare thought.

Perhaps Harry had finally decided to follow his calling as a Catholic priest, exposing the family as Papist. Henley had panicked and killed his cousin in a heated argument.

Yet nothing in Harry's most recent behavior had indicated any impending change.

Shakespeare yawned.

On to Hemsdale.

Alderman Fottingham.

Another yawn.

Then Chambers.

So tired.

No, wait . . . The stew. The stew had been before Fottingham and Chambers.

Catherine the stew, in the bilberry bushes. Now she was dead.

The stew.

Then the trip into Hemsdale.

The maidens dancing in the street.

Who had he seen before the stew?

The bilberry bushes.

Who had been after the stew?

The hawkers on the street.

The mongers . . .

A costermonger . . .

A pear . . .

He was overcome by sleep. His dreams were restless. His dreams were revealing.

The Thames was crusted with oil and muck, the water reeking of garbage. Rebecca's stomach was knotted, and the green soup upon which she sailed did little to calm her nerves. At least the waves were gentle, blessed be God. And Shakespeare was with her—she had requested that he be the one to accompany her. His hand stroked hers and she feasted on his touch like a ravenous dog. At first her family had protested the player's presence, but it had been Miguel who had insisted she be allowed to take him along. She needed his comfort, his love, and it was unwise to upset her in any way. She was their last hope.

The waterman rowed at an agonizingly slow pace. Faster, she wanted to cry out, but she said nothing. She drew her cape tightly around her neck and snuggled against Shakespeare's chest. Mist coated her face and dampened her hair. She was warm yet she shivered.

What would she say to Father?

She might not even have enough time to speak freely; she had a dozen messages to deliver from the family—her mother's love, news about the Ames Trade Company, her brother's ambitions, Miguel's commerce. With help from Uncle Solomon, Miguel had entered the competitive, mercantile world of the cloth trade. A thousand bells ringing in her head at once. She held in her lap a bag of woolens. Perhaps she'd spend the entire time dressing Father in proper clothes. First the shirt, then the hose, then the socks. Thick socks, triple-knitted. She was muttering to herself. Shakespeare asked her what was wrong.

"Nothing," she answered. "Nothing at all."

He held her tightly and said, "Worry not. God is with thee."

Rebecca didn't answer.

"I wish thee good fortune, beautiful mistress. Thou deservest fair fate."

Rebecca mouthed a thank-you. Suddenly she had lost her voice.

The tip of the White Tower peeked through the fog. How far were they now? A mile? A hundred feet? Rebecca felt Shakespeare tighten his grip on her hands. Develin Tower, Beauchamp Tower, Bell Tower . . . the Middle Tower—the foot entrance to the great fortress.

Rebecca trembled, looked at Shakespeare. He seemed composed, yet on second glance his calmness was a facade. It made Rebecca all the more nervous.

A boat manned by three yeomen warders ordered them to stop. They asked for Rebecca by name, they knew her business. A fat warder boarded their boat, almost tipping it over, and held out his hand to Rebecca.

"I love thee," Shakespeare repeated.

"I love thee too," Rebecca said. She picked up the sack that held her father's clothes, but a fat man confiscated it.

"It's warm clothing for her father," Shakespeare explained.

The warder rummaged through the bag and pulled out a blanket. He eyed it, then nodded greedy approval. He wrapped it around his shoulders.

Shakespeare explained, "The man is freezing in prison—"

"The man deserves his neck in a noose!" answered the warder. His voice was deep, ominous. "He's a traitor. And if ye be his kin, so are ye of treacherous blood."

Rebecca squeezed Shakespeare's arm, urging him to cease his protests. It was impossible to prevent the man from stealing. The warder pulled out the hose and held them up to his waist. Too small, he mumbled, stuffing them back in the sack. Disgusted, he examined the shirt, sleeves, and robe, none of which pleased him. He stuffed the clothing back in the sack and shoved it in Rebecca's face.

Rebecca studied his features. If she ever had the opportunity, she'd report the pig to the Queen. He offered her a hand to help her into the boat, his flesh like chilled dough. She turned to Shakespeare.

"Go," he whispered.

She nodded and boarded the boat. As they rowed her toward the Tower, away from Shakespeare, Rebecca blew her lover a kiss good-bye—a kiss he returned in kind. She watched him fade into the ashen expanse of fog and sea.

Gone.

What stood before her were hostile walls—a place of no escape. She reminded herself that she was just a visitor, but the thought only deepened the pain of her father's bondage.

Gods, let this be over.

She saw the arch of Traitor's Gate flanked by the Tower wharf. The top half was semicircular steel lattice, iron spikes welded to the bottom of the cross-bar. The doors of the gate were open, greeting her like the jaws of a dragon. The waterman rowed quickly through the gate, past St. Thomas's Tower, until the boat pulled alongside a staircase.

Time to exit to dry land. Rebecca was dizzy, her feet numb as she stepped on the solid ground. Her brain started to hum and black sparkles appeared before her eyes. She felt herself falling but was caught by a yeoman warder before she hit the ground. The beefeater was young and anxious. His blue eyes seemed refreshingly honest.

"Are you well, mistress?" he asked. "You're ghastly white."

"My feet . . ." Rebecca mumbled. "Twas a cold ride on the river this morning." A trickle of sweat ran down her face. She mopped it off with a kerchief and took a deep breath.

"Ye almost fainted," said the fat warder—a swine, he was. *Her* blanket had been stuffed into his livery coat. Yet he was so obese it hardly showed.

"Best ye rest," said the blue-eyed warder. "The ride was quite cold."

"I'm well now," Rebecca answered.

"Can you walk?" asked the blue-eyed warder.

A third guard—a short man with a skimpy beard—grunted at them to hurry it up.

"Yes, we must hurry." Rebecca shook her feet, trying to bring the blood back to her toes. She laughed nervously. "There. I think I'm ready to chance it on my own."

The warder released her from his arms. Rebecca stood and took tentative steps up the stairs to a cobblestone pathway. The fat warder had no patience with her slow-footedness and urged her along with a shove. The mortar between the cobblestones was pocked and rough. The heel of her shoe had loosened and she tripped. Again it was the blue-eyed yeoman who helped her to her feet.

"I'm terribly clumsy this morrow," Rebecca said, almost in tears.

"Speed it up!" ordered the wispy-bearded warder. He was already five paces ahead of her.

The blue-eyed guard took Rebecca's hand. "Hang on to me, mistress. I'll make sure you don't fall again."

"Thank you," whispered Rebecca.

They hurried her along. Rebecca tried to get her bearings. The Thames was to her right, so they must be heading east, on the outer bailey. To her left was the inner wall, the inner curtain of the Tower complex. The stones were blackened with time but the buildings seemed as solid as if erected yesterday. Cross-shaped loopholes were carved into the wall every fifty paces, the battlement crenellated. Everything about the place was hard, dense, impenetrable.

Rebecca felt light-headed. Mercifully, a waft of foul-smelling sea assaulted her nostrils, bringing instant clarity into her brain. She was entrenched in fear but forced herself onward.

"Where resides my father?" she managed to ask.

"Ye'll find out soon enough," answered the fat warder.

The men walked faster. The stones beneath Rebecca's feet seemed like stumbling blocks and she fought to keep her balance.

"Come along, girl," ordered the piggy guard. He smiled and added, "Stay too long and we'll be throwing *you* in the Tower as well."

Rebecca looked to the blue-eyed warder for comfort. He squeezed her arm and smiled. His eyes. They reminded Rebecca of Shakespeare.

They approached a large tower near the eastern end of the fortress. "That's Lanthorn Tower, is it not?" Rebecca said to the warder by her side.

"Aye, mistress."

"Is my father there?" she asked.

"Nay, mistress, the next one over—"

"Quiet!" ordered the pig.

"She'll find out in a minute, sir," said the blue-eyed warder. He turned to Rebecca and said, "Your father's imprisoned on the second floor of the Salt Tower. His cell is spacious. He was moved there not more than a week ago on the Queen's orders."

"God save the Queen," Rebecca said.

"God save the Queen," the yeomen warders replied in single voice.

The Salt Tower rose from the southeast corner of the fortress, a three-quarter cylinder of stone, the remaining quarter filled by a square turret that housed the spiral staircase. The stairs were so narrow that Rebecca could not place both feet on the step at the same time. She concentrated on her footwork, tried not to fall. The walls were an irregular patchwork of solid rock coated with dirt and streaked with chalky limestone deposits. Midway between the first and second floors the stairwell widened to allow for a deep hole between the wall of the turret and the staircase—a privy, stinking with recent use. The air was chilled, the walls freezing to the touch. The three warders took Rebecca as far as the second landing. There she was met by three other beefeaters. The two sets of guards exchanged greetings, then the first trio left.

The warder in charge this time was older, his face scored by wrinkles. His expression was blank, but his voice was kind as he told Rebecca to wait a moment. He fished out a ring of keys, then opened the cell door.

Roderigo was sitting at a small desk, a sheet of paper, an inkpot and a quill before him.

Rebecca whispered, "Father."

There was no response.

She approached him and saw that the ink was dry, the paper blank.

"Father," she repeated.

Roderigo's first thought was his ears had deceived him, his eyes were playing tricks. A vision, an angel, a goddess. No, better. His daughter! His Becca! He felt the tears come down in torrents and could do nothing to stop them. They rained upon his paper. Weakened by shock, he dropped his head in the enclosure of his arms and sobbed upon his desk. Rebecca rushed to him and embraced his back.

The warder shut the door and took up post inside the cell. "You've a half hour, mistress," he said.

Rebecca raised her head and said thank you. "Father," she whispered.

Roderigo kept crying.

"Father," said Rebecca, "we haven't much time and I have a great deal to tell you—"

"You're going to have to speak louder, mistress," said the beefeater. His voice was firm.

Rebecca apologized and forced her father to stand. His legs seemed wobbly. He needed exercise. At least the cell was quite spacious, thanks be to Her Majesty. Five wall faces, each one containing a splayed arrow loop within an arched embrasure. A desk, a writing chair, a small fireplace, fresh straw on the floor. No privy. He was probably taken to the one in the stairwell. . . .

"Let's take a walk," Rebecca said.

Roderigo jerked his head up. "I am freed?"

"No," Rebecca said. She felt sick to her stomach. "Let's take a walk around your closet—"

"My prison," Roderigo said flatly.

Rebecca slipped her arm under her father's. Gods, he'd become so thin and pale. His beard, once full and rich with color, had turned completely white and brittle.

"Are you warm enough, Father?" she asked. "I brought you clothes."

"Clothes?"

"Yes, clothes," she said. "Warm clothes. Woolens, thick hose—"

"Clothes?" Roderigo repeated.

Rebecca held back tears. "Let us walk for a while," she said. "Get blood into the legs."

She gripped her father and led him around the cell, each step taken with great care.

After a few moments he said, "I'm tired."

"Yes," Rebecca said. "Pray, Father, sit down in your chair and I shall dress you properly. Do they feed you well?"

Roderigo allowed himself to be seated. He said nothing. Without warning he started to cry again. Rebecca dried his cheeks, then wiped her own eyes. She was completely unprepared for such deterioration. She undid his points. His garments were filthy, the smell so malodorous that she had to turn her head away as she pulled them off. Her father had always been so fastidiously clean. His disintegration was ripping out her heart.

Let me be strong, she prayed. Do not cry in front of him. She thought of something to say, then remembered the warder. She dare not speak of the Queen's contemplations. Anything could be misinterpreted as treason.

She said, "I shall tell you about the family—"

"Louder," reminded the warder.

Rebecca raised her voice. "Mother sends her love." She took off his old stockings and immediately noticed open blisters upon the white skin of his calves. "What are these?" she asked.

"Burns," Roderigo said.

"The sores must be treated—"

Her father broke into frightening laughter. Rebecca forced herself to breathe smoothly. Without speaking she ran her fingers through the pomade of her hair and covered the sores with the grease. Slowly, she slipped the woolen hose over his legs. Roderigo didn't even wince.

"Mother sends her love." She continued to dress him. "Dear me, I've already said that, haven't I. . . . Miguel is well. His right arm is dead, but he has mastered the quill with his left. He and Uncle Solomon have had correspondence. Cousin Jacob has been in England—also conversing with Miguel. I fear that Miguel is about to enter the world of mercantilism at their behest—cloth trading, I think, as I heard a great deal about the silk route."

Roderigo said nothing.

Cheerfully, Rebecca went on, "Dunstan and Thomas have been talking to Uncle Solomon as well." She looked at the guard. He seemed alert, yet utterly bored. "The company is planning to expand its efforts into the New World—*if* Uncle Solomon can get another charter in the Levant. Thomas is in Turkey now with Leah—they're staying at her father's villa—but he's due back in a week." She waited for any kind of reaction from her father but received none. He was worse than Grandmama—at least her mind had been sharp to the end.

Dear God, *help* him.

"Benjamin is going to Padua—"

"When?" asked Roderigo.

A *reaction*! Blessed is God!

"Not immediately," Rebecca said. "After this unfortunate incident is cleared up and your good name is restored."

Roderigo was silent. A strange smile formed upon his lips.

"Anyway, Padua has not yet confined the—confined certain people behind gates, as other Italian states do. Uncle Jorge has a cousin named Benzoni who resides in the city. His son studies at the university there . . . under Galileo Galilei, the famous mathematician. Surely you must have studied some of his works, Father."

Roderigo didn't answer.

Rebecca sighed. Her father seemed to crawl back into his shell.

She tried again. "Benjamin . . . Benjamin was invited to spend some time at the Benzoni villa. . . . Actually, Ben's Italian has become quite educated. He's studying Greek as well, Father. You'd be quite proud of him."

Lowering his head, Roderigo began to cry again, his bony chin sinking into the hairless skin of his chest.

"Oh Father!" Rebecca exclaimed. "We all love you so much. Not a minute passes where you're not on all of our minds. We'll overcome this mishap, I swear we will!'

"Fifteen more minutes, mistress," said the warder.

"What about Grandmama?" Roderigo asked suddenly.

"Grandmama?" Rebecca said weakly. "Then you don't . . . Of course, how could you know."

Roderigo looked at her expectantly.

Rebecca said, "She died, Father. My God, I'm sorry to tell you this . . . three weeks ago today."

Roderigo was slow to react. Finally he said, "She was a great woman when she was your age." He paused, then said, "Her name was Teresa Roderiguez, you know."

"Yes—"

"She had quite a story to tell," Roderigo said with emphasis. "Did she ever tell you the story about her as Teresa Roderiguez?"

"The story of her life?"

Roderigo began to address her in rapid Portuguese. The warder sprung to his feet, struck Roderigo across the face.

"English only!" he ordered.

Roderigo seemed unaffected by the beefeater's slap.

"My honest apologies, my good warder," Rebecca said. "My father was simply reminiscing about more pleasant times— childhood memories."

"I care not, as long as he does it in English."

"By your will, sir," Rebecca said. She turned to Roderigo. "You must speak English, Father."

Dejected, Roderigo said nothing. The beefeater returned to his position at the door.

"Grandmama's name was Teresa Roderiguez, yes," said Rebecca carefully. She dressed her father in a clean shirt and sleeves.

"*Teresa,*" Roderigo enunciated. "Think of your grandmama as Teresa. As a young girl in a foreign country." He whispered, "About to be burnt."

"Louder," demanded the warder.

"Of course, sir," Rebecca told the guard. Still confused, she finished with her father's points. Suddenly her brain came alive. Her head began to buzz, her heart thumped in her chest. "You must speak up when you talk to me, Father," she said to Roderigo as she winked. "The good yeoman warder must be able to hear our conversation."

Roderigo grinned, his smile conspiratorial.

"Teresa Roderiguez was a remarkable woman," Rebecca said. "Very brave, and God was with her. So shall God be with you, Father . . . in the same way!"

Roderigo nodded rapidly.

"Your time is up, mistress," said the guard.

"Yes." Rebecca stood. "I will think of Teresa, Father."

"Aye," Roderigo said, his hands clinging to her gown. "Think of Teresa."

"I will." She hugged and kissed him good-bye, and his hands released her dress.

Roderigo whispered in her ear, "Even as I hang, Becca."

"Come along," ordered the yeoman.

Rebecca blew him a kiss as the door was slammed then locked behind her. She stood for a moment, until a guard gently prodded her along. As she walked back, she thought about what Father had told her. She knew she had to save him, and Father, through well-staged moonstruck ramblings, had told her how. A windstorm of schemes and plans blew in her mind. Visions of corpses and grave diggers.

58

Another stay of execution, the Lopez hanging rescheduled sometime after Mayday. It gave the conversos more time to implement their plans. Rebecca told no one, not even Shakespeare, yet he knew something was brewing. Rebecca had become preoccupied. Begging for understanding, she rarely came to his closet. Shakespeare didn't challenge her; her father's life was at stake. Besides, he'd become involved in his own plots of revenge.

The conversos kept close watch over their homes during the Easter season. They prayed for peace yet remained vigilant. The period of Lent through Palm Sunday was always dangerous for those of Jewish extraction because of its association with the holiday of Passover—the Feast of the Unleavened Bread. For centuries Christians had mistakenly believed Passover a time when Jews killed Christian babies and drank their blood. This year was especially dangerous because Roderigo—the *Jewish* doctor—sat in the Tower, accused of trying to poison the Queen. Though the crowds outside the Lopez estate had been dispersed by order of Her Majesty, the morality plays could instigate sudden mob riots and impulsive sacking.

The conversos prepared for their secret holiday with extreme caution.

All the household valuables were hidden. Once that was done, the women began their secret work in the wee hours of the morning, when the staff was still asleep. The kitchen was scrubbed. Then came the preparation of the matzoh. Unleavened flour and water were mixed into dough, patted into flat circles, and baked in beehive clay ovens for no longer than eighteen minutes. Though matzoh would be the only bread allowed to the conversos during the eight-day holiday, it would be eaten clandestinely.

The first evening of Passover came. The conversos waited until the staff had gone to bed, then gathered in Roderigo's closet. In secrecy they quickly read the Haggadah—the story of God's redemption of the Jews in Egypt. Before they retired for the night, Rebecca placed two wine goblets on Roderigo's desk— one for the prophet Elijah, the other in honor of her father. She beseeched God: by His mercy who redeemed all the Jews, let another Jew be redeemed.

The holidays came and went and the conversos breathed a sigh of relief. Another spring without incident. The days passed hurriedly. Mayday was only weeks away. Plans were discussed, schemes solidified.

Finally, on St. George's Day, Rebecca quickly donned the garb of a young gent and found a few blessed idle hours for a walk into town. Her body tingled with expectation. It had been almost a month since she'd seen Shakespeare. Though London was convalescing from two years of plague, this year was proving to be healthier. Only five outbreaks of Black Death in a week, and each one contained rapidly. The air smelled clean, the cisterns yielded sweet water. Yet the wards of St. Bartholomew's Hospital were still packed with wretched souls, other diseases clamoring for the throne of death as the plague abdicated. Rebecca wondered how the hospital was getting on without Father. Did his enemies ever stop to realize how many lives could have been saved had Father not been cruelly imprisoned? She spat upon their memories as she walked on.

Today London was buzzing with merriment. Lads and lasses flirting, little boys scaring off little girls with loud boos and horrid-looking masks. Tonight would be a time of mummeries— masked plays and dances by the light of the bonfires. Bells and music. Strolling troubadors plucking their lutes, singing songs of spring and young love. Tonight the city streets would be packed with people reveling, drinking themselves blind.

The graveyards would be empty.

She hurried through Cheapside toward Shakespeare's closet. He should be in good humor, thought Rebecca. The Master of the Revels had announced that the theaters would open soon after Whitsunday. She ran to his tenement and knocked on his door.

No answer.

She knocked again.

Nothing.

She sat in front of his door, dozed off and woke up when she heard the bellman cry out the time. Three-thirty.

With disappointment her constant companion, she left his closet.

The midnight bonfires set London aglow; the graveyard was as black as pitch. Thomas lit a piece of tinder, a glowing orange star in an endless inky sky. He pulled the black hood off his head and motioned for the others to do the same. He said to Rebecca:

"What was the man's name?"

"Joseph Gladstone," she whispered. "He died of a foul heart. He was sixty-two, the same height and stature—"

"Even as a corpse?" Dunstan asked. "Death eats away the body."

"Death was very quick," Rebecca said. "I saw him at the hospital on Tuesday, and he was dead by Thursday. The resemblance was remarkable. Besides, once we drench the corpse in blood, no one will know the difference. All they'll see is red—"

A low wail filled the air.

"What was that?" Rebecca whispered.

"Just an owl," said Benjamin. He hugged his sister protectively.

Miguel said, "Go on, Becca."

The noise repeated itself.

"Are you certain?" she asked Benjamin.

A bat darted across the expanse of charcoal sky. The hooting stopped and a huge shadow soared after the winged mammal.

"There," Thomas said. "You see? Just an owl after his supper."

Rebecca's eyes darted about. The sky was moonless; the leafless trees stood like cadaverous watchmen about the graveyard. The air was rich with the perfume of newly budding vegetation, but the earth reeked of death.

"Dear God," said Rebecca.

"Shall I stay with you while the others dig?" offered Miguel. He took her hand.

Rebecca shook her head. "I'm well." She kissed his hand, his lifeless hand as well.

"You're certain?" Benjamin asked her.

"Quite certain, Ben. Thank you."

Miguel asked her, "Have you any idea where this Gladstone's body is buried?"

Rebecca breathed deeply and looked around. In the daytime the graveyard hadn't seemed so large, but tonight it was enormous. Acres of tombstones, a garden of the dead. She pointed to the far corner of the cemetery. "I followed the funeral party out here yesterday. I think he's buried somewhere over there."

"You'll keep watch here?" Thomas said.

"Aye," Rebecca said. "Go."

Miguel asked, "Are you certain you're well? You're as pale as a—"

"Don't say it!" Dunstan said.

"I'm well," Rebecca insisted. "Go with God's speed!"

The men, black-shrouded and carrying shovels, quickly made their way to the other side of the graveyard.

"I feel like a monk in this dress," complained Dunstan.

"Act like one who has taken a vow of silence," Thomas replied.

"If you wouldn't be limping so badly, we would have made better time," Dunstan said.

"If you would have fought like a true man, I wouldn't be limping at all!" Thomas said.

"Stop it, both of you," Benjamin said.

"You're one to speak harshly," Dunstan said. "You weren't even there!"

"It was not my desire to stay in London," retorted Ben. "'Twas *your* father who requested my attendance."

"And that stopped you, eh?" Thomas sneered.

Miguel broke in, "I was there and I say to all of you, stop it! And for God's sake, keep your voices down. Roderigo's life is in extreme jeopardy, and you're all chattering like magpies. Find the grave, Tommy."

Thomas passed the light over the tombstones. "Pickerson, Oldham, Bartley, Chatterton, Bingham . . . Glaston was the name?"

"Gladstone," the other three answered in unison.

"Gladstone, Gladstone."

"Light the torch, Tommy," suggested Miguel. "Shine it on the ground and look for freshly dug earth."

"Someone will see us," said Benjamin.

"And if we don't find the plot soon, someone is sure to see us as well," Miguel said.

Thomas brought the burning tinder to the head of the torch and set it on fire.

"Ah, a beacon," announced Dunstan.

"Shh," said Miguel.

"Over there," Benjamin said, pointing to a mound of newly packed dirt.

"Good, good," said Thomas.

They hurried to the spot and began digging. They had just started their labors when Rebecca gave the signal whistle.

"The Devil!" said Miguel.

"Quickly, douse the light," Dunstan said. "We've got company."

Thomas extinguished the flames of the torch. They all lay flat, bellies on the ground.

"The watchman?" Benjamin whispered.

"Let's pray not," answered Dunstan.

Two men carrying lanterns stood not more than one hundred feet from them.

"Grave robbers," said Dunstan. He stood up. "We've nothing to fear from them."

The other men stood. The two ghouls stopped walking. Thomas relit the torch and approached them.

"State your business, men," he said.

"Looks like our business be the same as yers," answered one of the grave diggers, eyeing their shovels. He was tall and thin with a huge nose and a thick crop of black hair. His companion was short and dumpy with a broad nose and saucer-shaped eyes.

"We were here first," Dunstan said.

The big-nose one said, "Aye, but all the society knows that this graveyard belongs to the master."

"I'm of superior class than ye," said Dunstan, pointing to his chest. "And I say get out of here."

Big Nose answered back, "Ye'd not be talking so stronglike ifin it was the master here himself, that'd be the truth, aye?" He turned to his companion.

"That'd be the truth," chirped the dumpy one.

"And the master won't be merry to find ye here, that'd be the truth, huh?" said Big Nose.

"That'd be the truth," said Dumpy.

Thomas drew his sword. "*This* is the only truth I know, good-fellows." He placed the tip of the sword against the bob in Big Nose's throat. "Know you this bit of warning?"

Big Nose nodded.

"And you?" Thomas said, looking down at Dumpy.

"That'd be the truth," answered Dumpy.

"Your master is George Mackering?" asked Thomas.

Big Nose nodded. "Can ye be removin' that point from me neck?"

Thomas said, "Tell your master he will be compensated for his losses."

"Who ye be?" asked Big Nose.

"The only one who can challenge George Mackering in a

duel,'' Thomas answered, drawing the blade across Big Nose's neck. A thin line of red appeared. ''Got that?''

Big Nose jumped back and clutched his throat. He gasped.

Thomas lowered the point of his blade until it touched Big Nose's groin. ''Got that, I asked?'' he repeated.

Big Nose nodded.

''And you?'' Thomas asked Dumpy.

''That'd be—''

''Get out of here, both of you,'' ordered Thomas.

When they were gone, Miguel laughed. ''Such audacity. Using *our* chosen graveyard!''

Benjamin joined in, ''Men with much gall.''

''One would think them Gauls,'' said Dunstan.

Miguel was the first to resume digging. Ten minutes later the coffin was unearthed.

''Who holds the sack?'' asked Miguel.

A bat dove at Dunstan. He waved his arm in the air, made contact with the animal and slapped it. The bat flew across the graveyard.

''Good show,'' Benjamin said.

''Naturally,'' Dunstan said. He turned to Miguel. ''I have the sack.'' He unfolded a piece of burlap. ''Who's going to do the honors and open up the coffin?''

''Step aside,'' Thomas said. He drove his dagger into the wood, twisted and tore the planks apart, piece by piece.

''Tush, that stinks!'' Miguel said, covering his nose.

Dunstan held open the sack. ''Heave the old boy in.'' Thomas looked at Miguel. Miguel looked back at Benjamin. Sighing, Benjamin took a deep breath, then looped his arms around the corpse.

''Troth!'' he exclaimed. ''He's heavy as well as putrid.''

''Dead weight,'' Dunstan said, and laughed.

''Give me a hand,'' Ben said.

Thomas took hold of the feet and the two of them dropped the body into the bag. Dunstan gathered the neck of the sack and closed it with rope.

Thomas said, ''Let's fill this grave and get the hell out of here.''

''I greatly mislike graveyards,'' said Dunstan, shoveling dirt back onto the empty coffin.

''As opposed to the rest of us, who adore them,'' said Thomas.

''I mind them not,'' Miguel answered.

''Why is that?'' asked Benjamin.

''I think of who is here and who is not and with great merriment count myself as one who is not. I thank Providence daily that it was only my arm that died during the frightful ordeal.''

Quickly, they filled the grave. Benjamin hoisted the sack over his shoulder. He said, "Let's hope the body preserves until needed. Rebecca will coat it with ointment to retard its spoilage. She also suggested we rebury it in our property. The cool ground will enhance its preservation."

"A repulsive idea," said Dunstan.

"Have you a better one, brother?" asked Thomas.

Dunstan didn't answer.

They interred the body in a heavily wooded spot on the outskirts of the converso common property. In deference to the man's religion, Rebecca marked the spot with a simple cross.

59

While England slept, Rebecca and her mother fashioned material into liveries of the Queen's guard. As they cut, basted, and stitched by firelight, they spoke of things past and present. They mourned the loss of Grandmama, they prayed for Roderigo's release. They fantasized about future times, better times. After their nightly toils ended, they curled up in Rebecca's bed and passed the remainder of the night writing correspondence, jotting notes into diaries, or reading. They became moles, craving the darkness, loathing the light, burying dawn's ugly truths by sleeping during the day.

But tonight Sarah Lopez was uncommonly tired. She lay in bed stroking Rebecca's hair, watching her daughter read. She leaned her head against Rebecca's shoulder and fell asleep. Her dreams were of fairer times, when all her children had been alive. Bittersweet reveries that brought tears to her eyes even as she slept. She was awakened suddenly by a thud upon the window.

Startled, Sarah asked Rebecca, "What was that?"

"I don't know." Rebecca picked up the candlestick and swung her legs over the mattress. She stood up and peered out the window. "My God, it's Willy. . . . I'll be right back."

"Oh Becca, don't leave me!" Sarah cried. She clamped her hands over her mouth. "I didn't mean that."

"I'll be right back, Mother," Rebecca said. "I'm not leaving you."

"I didn't mean that," Sarah insisted. "I didn't mean that . . . I don't want to be a burden to you."

"You're not a burden, Mother," Rebecca said.

"I never wanted to do to you what Grandmama did to me . . . . God forgive me, I shouldn't have said that either." Sarah began to weep. "I . . . I just can't bear this pain by myself."

Rebecca hugged her mother. "I love you," she said. "You've always been my rock of strength."

"But now it is I who suck strength from you." Sarah dried her tears. "And so it was with Grandmama, God rest her soul. She was so strong, then suddenly I was her nursemaid. My sweet daughter, you don't know the burden of caring for an aged parent—"

"I know the joy of loving an old woman I called my grandam." Rebecca kissed her. "You shall be as she. And you'll never be a burden to me."

"I've become so dependent on you since Father . . ." Sarah's voice trailed off.

"Soon Miguel and I will marry," Rebecca said. "We'll always take care of you."

"And what about him?" Sarah said, pointing to the window.

Rebecca's throat tightened. She shrugged and muttered something about duty.

"You love Shakespeare," Sarah said. "You should be with him. Oh Becca, you deserve happiness, but I'm so afraid to be alone."

"I'll always be here for you," Rebecca said. "As will Benjamin."

The mention of her son seemed to calm Sarah immediately.

"Aye," she said. "Benjamin. He's changed much in the past three months. He's become his father's son . . . stronger in character, I think. Did you know he invited me to come with him to Padua. Naturally I refused, but—"

Sarah stopped. Such silly chatter. She clasped her shaking hands and said, "Go see what your Shakespeare wants."

"I love you, Mother."

"Go," Sarah whispered. "Please."

Rebecca pulled a shawl over her shoulders, rushed downstairs, and opened the door to the gardens. He was waiting for her in the gazebo. They embraced. Shakespeare picked her up and twirled her in the air.

"Blessed God, it's been ages!" Rebecca kissed his lips. "Where have you *been*?"

"Warwick."

Rebecca stiffened. She asked, "How does thy family fare?"

"Thy gray eyes have turned green," he said, smiling. "You

flatter me, mistress." He hugged her again, stroked her as he held her. "My love for my children does not diminish my consuming love for thee, beautiful lady."

Rebecca was suddenly ashamed of herself. Of course he should adore his children. She'd think him less of a man if he didn't. "Then thy children are well," she said with genuine interest.

"Aye," Shakespeare said. "Well they are, and older as well."

There was something disquieting about his voice, something that scared her. Rebecca gripped his hands and asked, "What is it, Willy? Why the sudden trip to Warwick?"

"I longed to see my children," he answered. "Five months is a long time to be away from them. My elder daughter is ten, almost of marriageable age. And my son has become such a handsome lad—bigger than his father ever was." The pride in his eyes shone through the dark. "Time's a constant drummer, though it seems to beat too slowly when we're young, too fast when we're old. We ripen and then we rot. Once I wanted immortality. I longed to have my words widely read and revered like those of Robert Greene—remembered from generation to generation. Now I realize that will never happen and I'm content to let my immortality live on through my children. If God permits thee good hap, have many children, Rebecca."

Shakespeare paused, then said, "I know the hour is ungodly. But I wanted to see thee before the cock's crow, thy face framed with swirling mist that kisses thee with its jeweled droplets. It's the way I choose to remember thee."

Rebecca's lip began to tremble. Such finality in his voice. She said, "Why settle for my memory if thou havest me in the flesh?"

He smiled cryptically and sadly. "It might be a while before I see thee again."

Rebecca's heart began to crack. "Does . . . thy family call thee home for good?"

Shakespeare hugged her tightly. "No, my sweet. Thou art my home."

"Then what is it?"

"Ask me no more questions, Becca."

Questions, Rebecca thought. He's the one that had asked too many questions. And now he was in danger. Rebecca blurted out, "It has something to do with Harry's murder—"

"No more questions—"

"Thou hast found him!"

"No."

"Thou liest, Willy—"

"Becca, I prithee—"

"Thou knowest who the villain is and mean to pursue him, maybe even meet him come this morn. I'm coming with thee."

"No!"

"Yes!"

"Never!"

"Ah, thou admit I speak the truth!"

"I admit nothing," he said with anger. But his ire was directed more at himself than at her. He shouldn't have come to say good-bye, he knew she would figure it out and she had. But there was that chance that something would happen to him, that he'd die without seeing her one last time. And he couldn't bear the thought.

"Willy, let me help thee," she begged.

"No—"

"Please!"

"Help me by staying out of my way, Becca. Help me with thy prayers—"

"Prayers? Dear God, who is this fiend?" Rebecca became defiant. "I'm coming with thee."

For her own safety, Shakespeare had no choice but to leave her and walk away.

"Willy," she shouted, running after him. "Art thou going to allow me to walk with thee in my nightdress?"

"Rebecca—"

"Just listen to me for a moment," Rebecca said. "Let me come with thee—"

Shakespeare began once again to leave.

"Just wait a moment," Rebecca insisted, hanging onto his sleeve. He dragged her as he walked. She shouted, "Aye, Shakespeare, I give up! Thou art the victor. I'll not accompany thee. But *stop* for a second. I want to give thee something before thou leavest."

"What?"

"Wilt thou quit walking?" Rebecca asked. "My hand is cramped from squeezing thine arm."

Shakespeare pried her fingers from his wrist and said, "I must go, Becca. And thou cannot come with me."

"But—"

Shakespeare said. "Becca, three people, one of them a girl your age, have died. This is not play adventure—"

"Neither was rescuing Miguel, Willy."

"Thou art an incredibly brave woman and a superior swordsman—swordswoman. I will not debate that. But now is the time to think of thy father! He needs thee so much. His life depends on thee."

Rebecca had no answer. The gravity of what Shakespeare said

left her speechless. Her father *did* need her. What if she were to die? What would become of Father? Of Mother? But Shakespeare needed her as well. She felt it in her heart. Torn. Always torn between love and duty. But for once the former would win out. She kept her thoughts to herself and said,

"Wilt thou wait but a minute here? I want to give thee something for good luck—my own personal charm for thee."

Shakespeare thought, then nodded slowly. "Hurry."

Rebecca rushed in the house and quickly informed her mother that Shakespeare needed her for an emergency. Sarah didn't question her daughter and Rebecca didn't bother to clarify the situation. There wasn't enough time. She gave Sarah a peck on the cheek, then quickly changed into her brother's clothes.

As hap would have it, the men were at Hector Nuñoz's house discussing the trade company's expansion into the Levant. Benjamin would spend the night there in the guest quarters. Rebecca kept her eye upon the window at all times. Shakespeare was keeping his word, still waiting for her. After all this time he was still so naive. Did he really think she would desert him? Once dressed, she stuck two daggers in her belt and held Ben's rapier in her hand. It wasn't as fine a weapon as Thomas's blade—there was no way she could sneak into her cousin's house and retrieve it now that Leah was back in England—but it would serve Shakespeare better than the one he carried. She threw her nightdress over her costume, her shawl over her nightdress, and ran back outside.

"Here," Rebecca said, presenting him with Ben's sword.

Shakespeare noticed the initials B.L. carved into the handle. "Whose is this?"

"Take it!" Rebecca insisted. "It will bring thee good hap."

Shakespeare took the blade and gave Rebecca his weapon in return. He moved to embrace her, but Rebecca backed away.

"Go," she said. She didn't want him to feel the blades under her gown. "Go, so thou may come back to me soon."

"A kiss?" Shakespeare asked.

"I will die from longing if I kiss thy lips." She pretended to cry. "Just go."

Die from longing? Rebecca? Shakespeare was puzzled. He said, "I love thee, Becca. Know that. I love thee!"

"Away with thee!"

Not a kiss good-bye, not even a hug? Shakespeare knew she was up to something. But he left because dawn was advancing faster than he was. After he had climbed the wall, Rebecca yanked off her dressing gown.

Allez! she told herself. *Vite!*

She followed him quietly, skulking behind brush, darting for cover of trees so he couldn't see her even when he glanced over his shoulder, which was often. His walk was brisk and tense, his body rigid. Yet his footsteps hardly made a sound—a faint shuffle in the dirt. He was a man with a mission.

A small crescent of moon floated in and out of an endless swirl of fog. The air was still and smelled of spring, of life about to bloom. Rebecca watched Shakespeare crawl through a hole in the city wall and enter London. She counted to twenty then dropped to her knees and crept through the same spot. Once inside, she swept her eyes over the empty streets but couldn't see Shakespeare anywhere. Just the city: so dark, so quiet. Not a lighted window in sight. Her heart began to race. Suddenly a hand was clamped over her mouth, a dagger was at her throat. Terror gripped her bowels and gut.

"See how easy it is to die?" Shakespeare asked her. "One slash and it's over. It's that easy! I saw Thomas do that to a man without losing the rhythm of his breath." He loosened his grip on her and she squirmed out of his hold.

"Damn thee!" Rebecca said.

"I'll walk thee back home."

"Damn thee, damn thee, damn thee!"

Shakespeare took her arm and pushed her to her knees. "Crawl under the wall."

"No."

"Thou desirest me dead?"

"Stop it!"

Shakespeare said, "Rebecca, I cannot concentrate on him and thee at the same time! I have good reasons for wanting thee gone!" He exhaled and sat down on the ground. "Let's go home." He tried to act calm. "Now, eh?"

Rebecca didn't budge.

"Mulish girl!" Shakespeare growled. "Thou'll be my death!" He stood up and began to pace.

Rebecca stood and said, "I'll hide so he'll see me not. . . . Who is he anyway?"

Shakespeare sighed. He knew Rebecca's tenacity by now. She'd press and press and he'd finally relent. He might as well tell her and save them both time and effort.

"A kiss, first," he said.

She embraced him tightly, pressed her lips against his. His breath—so warm and sweet. She kissed him several times then forced herself out of his arms.

"Who is he?" she repeated.

Shakespeare said, "His name is Edward Mann—a moonstruck Puritan driven mad by the death of three wives. I encountered him on my first trip up North and he was of such little consequence that I forgot about him. But then his voice sounded in my dreams. A gravelly voice that I had heard several times before: the night the ghost appeared in my closet, the day we dueled . . . there was a Puritan preaching atop a box, damning everyone who was betting on us—''

"I remember him!" Rebecca said. "He was dressed solely in black—thy black shadow!"

"Aye, Puritans love black," Shakespeare said. "He was also in London the day I took thee to the Mermaid. Thou laughed in his face—''

"Yes! Yes!" Rebecca said. "He was going on about sinners and repentance."

Shakespeare nodded.

"How could we have missed him!" Rebecca said.

"How could *I* have missed him!" Shakespeare said. "I saw him three separate times yet never pieced together the face—or the voice—until the dream. Old Scottish daggers he threw at me. Mann spoke in a common accent of the English northerner, yet he told me to repent before the gloaming. *Gloaming!* He must be of Scottish blood, he must have crossed the border frequently. That's where he came upon the daggers. And Puritanism is strong amongst the Scots. It seems so clear now that it must be he."

"What did he have against Harry?"

"I'll answer thy question with a question," Shakespeare said. "How wast thou dressed on our excursion to the Mermaid?" Shakespeare didn't wait for her response. "Dressed as thou art garbed at this moment. As a man . . . And that's why he attacked thee.

"Harry was a good soul but loose of tongue when he drank in gross excess. There must have been a night when he had become exceedingly drunk and dallied with a certain whore—a stew named Cat. In his stupor he suddenly became weepy—I've seen him in that state diverse times. He started declaring to the whore his love for a certain man, a priest—''

Rebecca broke in, "I know. Harry was a Catholic and this Puritan, Mann, hated those of the Papist religion—''

"No, no, no," Shakespeare said. "Aye, Mann detested Harry because he was a secret Catholic. But half the town of Hemsdale is composed of secret Catholics. That's why Mann preaches there. He's trying to make them repent for their evil, idolatrous ways. If he killed Harry for being a Catholic, he would have killed many more a long time before."

"Why, then?" Rebecca asked.

Shakespeare said, "Harry must have drunkenly confessed to the stew that he and the priest were bound in a special way that went beyond the usual spiritual father-son relationship. Cat misunderstood Harry's love for the priest. She thought that Harry had lain with him, and told the entire town rumors to that effect. In fact, what Harry had meant was that the priest and he were father and son by blood.''

''*What?*'' Rebecca whispered.

''It's the truth. The Jesuit's own lips told me as much.''

''Harry was a bastard?''

Shakespeare nodded. ''For all the world to see, Harry was the legitimate son of Lord Chesterfield. But only his mother knows for sure, eh?'' Shakespeare leaned against the wall. ''But Mann didn't kill Harry because he was a bastard. Mann killed Harry because he mistakenly thought that Harry had lain with the priest, that Harry was a buggerer. To lay with a whore is a sin, but to lay with a man is a grievous sin punishable by death.''

Rebecca curled up against Shakespeare's chest. ''Then Mann thought thou wast a buggerer as well, because I was with thee dressed as a man—a boy, actually.''

''Yes,'' Shakespeare said. ''The first few times, Mann merely wanted to cease my inquiries about Harry—to warn me away from him. The dagger at the duel, the bump on my head in the middle of the night—nothing mortal. But after he saw me making merry with thee, he wanted us both killed—according to God's law.''

''Then what of Mackering and the murdered innkeeper?'' Rebecca asked.

''Both were extorting money from Harry.''

''To keep the Jesuit's presense at Brithall a secret from the authorities.''

''Aye.''

''Then why did Mann kill Chambers and the stew? Was Chambers a buggerer as well?''

''I think not,'' Shakespeare said. ''No, not at all. Chambers wanted me out of the way for his own selfish reasons. He didn't want me learning the affairs of a small town—his source of extortion income. But the innkeeper was too cowardly to do the work himself. He sent me to Mackering, figuring the uprightman would do me in. But for some reason Mackering did not kill me.''

Shakespeare hesitated a moment, then said, ''I don't think Mann killed the stew and Chambers. The Puritan hated the stew, thought her a witch. Biblically speaking, he was justified in killing her. But Chambers? The man was a user of whores, an extortionist, but I've never seen it written that thou shalt not suffer the extortionist to live. Mann is a fanatic. In his own twisted thinking he could not commit a murder without a biblical passage to support him.''

"Then who killed Chambers and the stew?"

"There are only two people left who might have done such a thing. An alderman in Hemsdale named Fottingham or the uprightman himself—George Mackering. What Fottingham did or didn't do is of no concern to me. I interest myself in Harry's murderer only. But Mackering and I still have things to settle between us."

"What kind of things?"

Shakespeare didn't answer. He looked up at St. Paul's Cathedral, its spire rising and disappearing into the fog. Dawn would be upon the city soon, the sun piercing through the gloom, highlighting the east side of the church's Gothic tower in gold.

"That's where I'm going," Shakespeare said. "Mann will be right outside the churchyard soon, standing on a wooden box, ready to preach doom and destruction to all who pass lest they repent."

"How dost thou know?"

"He was there yesterday, many days before yesterday as well. He was at that spot the day I walked with thee to the Mermaid." Shakespeare bent down and picked up a rock. He threw it over the wall. "It's his spot, and he'll be there today. But so will I." He turned to Rebecca, his eyes as hard as granite. "Now I will walk thee home."

She returned his own stare with a determined look of her own. "I will not go back unless thou forcibly carries me home. Even then I will fight thee all the way!"

Shakespeare grabbed her shoulders. "Stay away!" he ordered. "I cannot do what I must with thee in my way."

"Still I shall remain," Rebecca said.

They were locked in icy combat. Shakespeare knew he couldn't convince her by logic. Dear God, she was stubborn. He considered tying her up and carrying her home. Or he could carry her across the city and lock her in his closet.

He never had the opportunity to do either.

A black figure bearing a wooden crate was approaching them. Shakespeare tensed. He straightened his posture and waited, his hand resting upon the hilt of his sword.

"This is thy last chance to get thee gone," he whispered frantically. "Under the wall, Becca."

"I'm staying by thee, Willy."

Shakespeare pushed her out of the way and stepped toward the figure. He shouted, "Ho, Mann! So we meet again. Not as the cowardly killer desires, but rather face to face."

Still walking toward Shakespeare, the figure emitted a horrible, rasping sound. "If I would have wanted ye dead, I could have killed ye many times over, evil player. I was just toying with ye brain—which I must say is less than clever.''

"Aye, you've a point," Shakespeare said. "You might wonder what took me so long to name you Harry's slayer."

"I might," said Mann, his face hidden under the hood of a sackcloth robe. "Then again, I might not." He laughed. "I saw ye looking at me yesterday, sinner, with ye filthy eyes. Did ye think ye could play me for a fool!"

He looked at Rebecca and spat, then turned back to Shakespeare. "Ye are as wretched as ye muck-filled sinner in Hell, Harry Whitman. I tried to warn ye when I saw ye with the whore named Cat. Ye were following his filthy ways—first the whores, next boys. But ye listened not and became an abominator just as he."

"Harry was not a buggerer," Shakespeare said. "And neither am I. But even if we were, tis not up to you to execute God's judgment."

"Whitman was an abominator *and* an idolator. The latter, God will punish. But tis I who must eradicate the former sin. I am the hands of God."

Shakespeare said, "Never had Harry lain with his priest."

Mann smiled, his eyes burning with an unholy anger. "Not the priest, may the Jesuit rot in hell. The uprightman."

Shakespeare paused, then said, *"Mackering?"*

"Aye, accursed Mackering," Mann said. "And though he be strong, he, too, shall feel the wrath of God upon him. The worst is saved for last. So it be, player, that ye sinner, Whitman, was an abominator and so are ye." Mann cocked his head in Rebecca's direction. "What is this filthy toy with which ye dally?"

Before Rebecca could speak, Shakespeare interrupted. "Tis not of your concern."

"All abominators are my concern. I am the hand of God!"

"I'm a woman," Rebecca said, removing her cap. Hair tumbled down her shoulders, across her back.

The Puritan was momentarily stunned. "Ye and the Jewgirl are the *same* person?"

"Apparently so," Rebecca said.

"Daughter of a traitor!" Mann said with renewed hatred. "Ye must die as well!" The Puritan reached into his black robe and withdrew a rapier. The metal reflected the first hint of daylight, and the glare blinded Rebecca. She squinted and Mann charged. Shakespeare drew his sword, caught Mann's rapier, and used his free hand to push her away.

"Run, Becca!" he screamed. "Run, damn thee!"

But she remained welded to the ground.

Mann shouted, "God's fury upon ye, sinners one and all!"

He pulled out a dagger and parried Shakespeare's stoccata. Shakespeare saw Mann's blade thrusting toward his groin and tried to parry, but Mann deceived the blade and quickly aimed his point toward Shakespeare's chest. Shakespeare's dagger was barely able to catch the rapier before it skewered his heart.

Mann advanced.

"Prepare to meet the Devil," the Puritan shouted as he pushed Shakespeare against the wall. Shakespeare tried to sidestep past Mann's left hand, but the Puritan was too quick. His footwork was lightning. Mann feigned a thrust to the right, then slashed against Shakespeare's left arm as the player attempted to parry with his dagger. Shakespeare's flesh burned, his arm was warm and wet. He feigned an attack to Mann's left, lunged, then double-deceived Mann's blade until the Puritan was forced to yield several inches of space between the wall and his right side. Shakespeare took advantage of the gap and slipped around Mann, but not without consequence. The Puritan's dagger nicked his shoulder.

Rebecca pulled out her sword. Mann saw her out of the corner of his eye. He retreated, giving Shakespeare room to advance, but strategically placed the player between himself and Rebecca. Too late, Shakespeare realized what Mann was doing.

"Get out of here!" he screamed to Rebecca. "The dog is an expert with a sword!"

Mann smiled at the acknowledgment, then charged Shakespeare. A brilliant move. Shakespeare couldn't retreat or step out of the way—Rebecca was positioned behind him, ready to receive the fatal blow of the rapier. Shakespeare parried with his dagger, but Mann deceived the block. Shakespeare stumbled forward and Mann seized his opportunity. With a single sweep of his rapier he knocked the blade out of Shakespeare's grip and placed the tip of his rapier against Shakespeare's throat.

"Drop the dagger!" Mann ordered.

Shakespeare gripped the dagger so hard that his knuckles turned white. He felt the tip of Mann's sword break his skin.

"Do it, Willy!" screamed Rebecca. "Drop the dagger, for God's sake!"

"Listen to ye whore," Mann said, grinning.

"Get out of here!" Shakespeare pleaded with Rebecca.

Mann said, "Ye move an inch, whore, and ye love is dead where ye stand. Now ye be a good girl and drop all ye weapons on the ground now. I know ye have three."

Rebecca obeyed. Mann kicked the blades away.

"Drop the dagger, sinner," Mann repeated.

"Do it, William," begged Rebecca.

Shakespeare loosened his grip and the dagger clinked upon the ground.

Mann laughed. "Now I have ye two where I want ye." He pushed Shakespeare back against Rebecca, Rebecca back against the wall. "Like Phineas I'll kill the adulterer and the fornicatress with one sword!" Mann's lips curved upward into a crazed smile. He licked his lips. Dawn held enough light to capture the Puritan's pinched features, the flat look in his mad eyes.

"Don't even think about moving, Shakespeare," he said. "I'm faster than ye. Know that well."

"I know it," said Shakespeare. Sweat was pouring off his brow.

"My hands are not my hands, but instruments of God," Mann preached. "I am an instrument of God. He has made me the *most* nimble of fencers, nimbler than ye foul sinner in evil, Whitman . . . though I must confess, the abominator put up more of a duel than ye."

"He was a better swordsman than I," Shakespeare said.

"Ah, but *I* was better than *he*. Whitman felt the rage of my blows, of God's blows. Twas God who gave me such skills of the fence. God is my shepherd!"

Mann's eyes suddenly widened. His mouth opened in surprise. He dropped his rapier, coughed and sucked in air. The fiendish smile slowly dropped from his lips. Wordlessly, he fell forward, blood leaking from his nose and mouth. Shakespeare stepped backward and watched Mann slump to the ground, a dagger in his back.

Rebecca cried out, her shrieks echoing against the silence.

A moment later a low voice intoned, "Second nimblest swordsman. And I'll not praise God for *my* skills!"

Shakespeare looked up, still confused.

"Never let it be said that the master isn't merciful," Mackering said, laughing. He walked over to Mann, pulled the dagger from the Puritan's back and kicked the body. "Imagine that muck heap thinking he could best me in swordplay!"

So it was as Shakespeare thought. Mackering had ordered him followed since his release, the thief just waiting for him to find Harry's murderer. One of Mackering's slaves must have seen Shakespeare dueling with Mann, must have reported it to the master. Mackering must have hurried to the scene.

Mackering wanted to know who the murderer was but had been too lazy to do the work himself. The bastard was a cuckoo laying its eggs in others' hard-built nests. Even though the uprightman had saved his life, Shakespeare regarded him with contempt. But Mackering didn't seem to notice. He held out Mann's dagger to Shakespeare and said,

"For your efforts."

"Give me my sword," Shakespeare said quietly.

Mackering threw the Puritan's dagger over his shoulder, looped his toe under Shakespeare's weapon and kicked it over to him. The player caught it by the handle.

Mackering's eyes darkened, as if they had finally registered the hatred in Shakespeare's eyes. He said, "You shouldn't be challenging me, Willyboy. I have nothing against you." He licked his lips. "In sooth, you could please me greatly."

"As Harry pleased you?" Shakespeare said.

"Aye, Harry was a great pleaser," Mackering said.

Shakespeare studied the wicked face, the dead eyes, the flat, yellow hair that hooded his brow, the bloodless lips that had turned upward in a lopsided smile. Mackering was twice the swordsman Shakespeare could ever be. Logic told Shakespeare to cower before him, to make peace for his neck. He, more than anyone, had known Mackering's villainous way. But as it had been months ago, Shakespeare refused to be broken by evil. Childish thinking he knew, as good does not always triumph over bad. Yet Shakespeare had to believe that this time it would.

"You are more hateful than this lump of turd," he said, toeing Mann's dead body. "Chambers was extorting money from Harry, promising to keep quiet about the priest. You were extorting from Harry as well."

"In a manner of speaking," Mackering said.

"You extorted not money from Harry, but his body. You thought Harry a buggerer. You thought he had lain with his priest—"

"I regret to tell you, Willyboy, but he did. The whole town knew it."

"As in Sodom and Gomorrah, the whole town was in error. The priest wasn't Harry's lover, he was Harry's father—his father by blood."

Mackering looked sharply at Shakespeare.

"Aye," Shakespeare said. "Harry was no buggerer. Yet, loving his father as he did, Harry permitted you to debase him so you wouldn't report the Jesuit to the authorities."

Mackering said, "Harry enjoyed it. He held me in great esteem."

"Behind your back he spat in your face," Shakespeare lied. "Aye, he told me what you had done to him. He trusted me, loved me as much as he loathed you, Mackering. He mocked the size of your member—"

Mackering said, "You rile me, Willyboy—"

"Is that what you called Harry, Mackering? Harryboy?"

Mackering tensed. Quietly, he said, "Is it your intention to duel for your friend's honor, Willyboy? You'll lose if you take me on. You haven't a chance on earth—nor in Heaven and Hell. I'm more skilled at the fence than Mann, and you dueled so clumsily with him, Willyboy.'' He suddenly turned to Rebecca. ''Get out of here, girly, lest you want to see your lover die. And tell your cousins to keep out of my graveyards!''

Rebecca remained where she stood.

Mackering said, ''Your choice, my sweet wench. In sooth, I could take you both as a pair. Wouldn't that be fun?'' He looked at Shakespeare. ''If you keep your mouth shut and do what I desire, you may live, Willy. Think about it. I'll give you things. I give all my little toys things. I gave Harry money, lots of money to pay off Chambers, whereupon Chambers gave the money back to me.''

Mackering sneered. ''But the greedy little pig wanted more. Poor Harry had to start borrowing from his relatives. Then I found out that that priggish swine Chambers was holding back on me. Gads, he had become a bloody nuisance!''

''But you didn't murder Chambers for that reason,'' Shakespeare said. ''He was giving you much gold and silver, and you would never cut off a source of revenue.''

Mackering smiled, bemused. ''Then why did I murder him?''

''You murdered the stew,'' Shakespeare said. ''Chambers just happened to be present. Since my release you've had me followed. When my trail finally led back to the North, *you* shadowed me. Twas you and not Mann in the tavern where Fottingham and I drank.''

Mackering kept smiling, yet Shakespeare knew he was listening to every word he spoke.

Shakespeare continued, ''You murdered Cat because she knew that you'd lain with men. And you knew I meant to speak with Cat. Yes, I understand it all now. Harry must have told her your pleasures.'' He added the lie, ''Just as he told *me*. And Heaven forbid it be known that the great Mackering, the *fiercesome* uprightman, the world's greatest *cocksman*, stiffens well for wenches but even greater for *men*.''

Mackering's smile disappeared. ''You use words well, Shakespeare. Too well. Your mouth is not to be trusted.'' He drew his sword, brought it to his forehead and saluted. He opened his arms, exposing his chest. ''Come get me, Willyboy.''

Shakespeare charged. Mackering blocked. Then the game began. Shakespeare executed an attack, only to have Mackering outmaneuver him. Shakespeare lunged, but Mackering was always slightly out of reach. Mackering. Always laughing! Always sneering! Shakespeare knew the uprightman was toying with him. No matter how fast he moved, Mackering was quicker. No matter how brilliant his attacks were, Mackering's were superior. It was only a matter of time.

Shakespeare charged, his sword pointed toward Mackering's shoulder. Mackering easily parried and threatened Shakespeare with a head cut. Shakespeare blocked the attack with his dagger.

His legs were giving way.

He tried to lunge, tripped and fell forward onto his knees. Mackering let out a belly laugh. Swaggering over, he held out his hand to Shakespeare.

Shakespeare regarded the helpful hand, knew what it implied. He recalled what Mackering had done to him, fingered the handle of his dagger, and suddenly plunged it into the proffered palm and pulled it out. Mackering howled in pain. His nostrils flared with rage, his cheeks turned crimson. He choked out,

"That was a very foolish thing to do, Willy." Yanking off his sleeve, he wrapped it around the bloody flesh. "The hour is getting on. Soon the city will be alive. Since you insist on remaining obstinate despite my good nature, I see I have no choice but to kill you."

This time Shakespeare saw the murderous look in Mackering's eyes. And so did Rebecca. On her belly, she slithered out of Mackering's sight and grabbed the first thing that made contact with her hand—a dagger.

Mackering smiled at Shakespeare and said, "I greatly like to see before me a man on his knees." He drew his sword. "Drop the dagger, Willyboy. I desire not a sudden poke in my privates."

Shakespeare didn't move.

"Drop the dagger." Mackering extended his blade toward Shakespeare's heart. "Drop the dagger, wee Willy. Or not only will you die, but the girl as well." Mackering's eyes swiftly darted to his right and left.

"I'm behind you, Mackering," Rebecca whispered.

"Nooooo!" Shakespeare shouted.

Mackering whipped his head around just in time to see the dagger sink into the soft flesh of his throat. Rebecca drove the blade forward and twisted, felt it break through the soft bones that surround the windpipe. She pushed until it would go no farther. Mackering dropped his sword and stumbled forward, his hands around the hilt of the stylus, attempting to dislodge it from his neck. He moaned, gurgled blood. It spilled down his chest, coating the tips of his blond hair in scarlet. He convulsed, the green eyes twitching.

Shakespeare stood up and watched Mackering frantically trying to yank the dagger out. In a last desperate attempt, the uprightman reached behind his head and tried to push the blade out from the back end, succeeding only in impaling his injured hand on the dagger point.

Shakespeare walked over to Mackering, placed his hands on the uprightman's chest and pushed him down.

"Good morrow, *Georgieboy*," he said.

Mackering lay still at Shakespeare's feet, the muddy, pea-green orbs now rolled back so only the whites were visible.

"Oh my God!" Rebecca groaned. "Oh my God, oh my God, oh my God!" She placed her hand over her mouth. "I'm going to be sick."

Shakespeare quickly snatched up as many weapons as he could and said, "Through the wall!"

"I'm going to be sick!" Rebecca wailed.

Shakespeare pushed her down, shoved her through the wall. He followed, and once on the other side, watched her vomit.

"We must get home," Shakespeare said.

"They'll come for me!" Rebecca said, gasping. She dropped onto her stomach and clutched the wet earth. "They'll charge me with murder—"

"Listen to me!" Shakespeare pulled her to her feet. She lost her balance, felt her head go black.

"Up, damn thee!" Shakespeare slapped her across the face. "Listen to me!"

"I'll hang." Rebecca sobbed. "I'll hang, I'll hang, I'll hang—"

"No one will ever know!" Shakespeare said. "No one saw thee. No one saw me!"

She sucked in her breath, shuddered and retched. When the heave passed, she said in a small voice,

"Thou art certain?"

"Quite!" Shakespeare tried to bring Rebecca to her feet. "We must get home, Becca! Soon the roads will be clogged with people. Walk! I prithee, my love, walk! Walk for me!"

But her knees buckled.

Shakespeare hoisted her over his healthy shoulder and began to run. His breath was short, his legs weak.

"The dagger!" Rebecca suddenly screamed. "They'll trace me through the dagger—it's Benjamin's! It has his initials on it. My God, Willy, what will I do?" She sobbed. "They'll come for him, they'll come for me. I'll hang, I'll hang, I'll hang with my father!" Her body shook wildly, her arms flailed about.

"Stop fighting me, damn it!" Shakespeare screamed. He could no longer carry her. His injured arm was too weak, his shoulder too sore. His back gave out and he was forced to lower her to the ground. She dropped onto her stomach and writhed about like a snake in agony.

Shakespeare looped his hands under her arms and pulled her up.

"Becca, we're covered in blood. We must keep going! We've got to get out of these clothes!"

"They'll find me through the dagger!" she cried.

"I'll go back and get it!" Shakespeare said. "But thou must go home now—"

"Don't leave me!"

"Becca, listen—"

"Don't leave me!" Rebecca screamed.

"Stow thee, damn it!" Shakespeare screamed back and slapped her.

Rebecca reeled backward but quieted.

Blessed silence. Shakespeare took a deep breath and withdrew the weapons from his belt. He held them up to the dawn's light and said, "There is thy brother's dagger. . . . wait. I have two of them, in fact."

"I brought two," Rebecca said.

"Then I have them both. . . . Here is thy brother's sword. And here are all of my weapons, God be praised."

Rebecca said nothing, listened to her panting breaths. She covered her mouth.

"Thou must . . ." Shakespeare exhaled and took another deep breath. "Thou must have killed Mackering with Mann's dagger. Picture it, Rebecca. Mackering and Mann—the sinner and the redeemer—locked in a hand-to-hand combat to the death. Mann's dagger aimed at Mackering's throat. Mackering frees an arm and loops it around Mann's body. At the same instant that Mann plunges his blade into Mackering's neck, Mackering stabs Mann in the back. They killed each other, Becca! Repeat it! They killed each other!"

Rebecca looked at Shakespeare, confused.

"They killed *each other*! Say it!" Shakespeare commanded.

"They killed each other."

"Yes. And no one will know differently, *if* no one sees us drenched in blood. Dawn is upon us. People are up. They will see us covered in blood, Becca. They will see my wounds." Shakespeare stuffed the weapons back in his belt. "We've got to get to thy house."

"Wounds?" Rebecca looked at Shakespeare and gasped. "My God, thy shoulder and arm—"

"These scratches are far from mortal inflictions, but they're bloody," Shakespeare said. "Even the most doltish watchmen would notice them. We've got to get *home*, Becca, *home*! We must burn these clothes. Give me thy hand. Canst thou walk now?"

"Aye."

Shakespeare muttered "merciful God" and took her hand.
They began the walk to the Lopez estate. A minute later they
broke into a run and didn't stop until they were at the gatehouse.
Minutes later they stripped naked and bathed clean, their clothes
turning to ashes in the Great Hall's fireplace.

60

Mackering dead.
        The news was shouted about Paul's, spread from stall
to stall at the Cheape.
Killed by a fanatic Puritan.
London's sentiment: good riddance.
For many reasons Shakespeare and Rebecca felt it best if they
lived apart. The Lopez estate had been besieged by gawkers and
hecklers since Roderigo's arrest. If just one person had seen
them running away, connected them to Mackering's murder, dire
consequences would result. As much as Rebecca's heart wanted
him to stay, her wits warned her of what could happen if he
remained at the Lopez manor house.
Tearfully they went their separate ways—during the day.
Shakespeare went back to his closet, Rebecca visited him in the
deepest hours of the night. She traveled alone, unguarded by her
brother or cousins or Miguel, but she no longer felt the fear that
once had plagued her solo treks. She'd become inured to nighttime shadows, apathetic to drunken laughter, to echoing shrieks.
Armed with Miguel's rapier, she knew she could defend herself,
knew she must and would survive.
Shakespeare's lovemaking was nourishment for her troubled
soul, balm for muscles made tight from family obligations. Rebecca's days were filled with endless demands, minute details,
each one necessary for the plan to work. One couldn't forget
anything. Anything! But she would not complain—not to her
lover, not even to herself. There was work to be done. Lots of
work.
And so little time.

* * *

Shakespeare had put off the visit, his mind trying to think up the proper words. But they wouldn't come. Finally, four days after Mackering's death, he forced his feet into Margaret Whitman's tenement. Harry's story was not an easy tale to tell. Selecting his words carefully, Shakespeare recounted the story, awkwardly informing Margaret of all she needed to know but leaving out certain facts that he thought would upset her. Margaret's reaction was strange. Though it had been her idea to find her husband's murderer, she no longer appeared interested in his story or its bloody conclusion.

"It's late," was all she said.

Margaret had become old and bony, the skin underneath her chin hanging like a turkey wattle. Her eyes were as dull as scratched glass. Her hands held red, raw fingers, her knuckles were misshapen nodes. Shakespeare took her hand and kissed the dry, scaly skin. He asked if there were anything else she wanted to know, and Margaret shook her head.

"Then I'll be going," Shakespeare responded.

As he stood to leave, Margaret called his name.

"Aye?" Shakespeare answered.

"Times have been good to you, Willy?" she asked.

"I've been well," he responded.

She paused, looked down at her feet. "Have you any spare coins, then?"

Without speaking, Shakespeare handed her a sovereign.

She didn't bother to thank him as she closed the door behind him.

Returning to his closet, he felt melancholy. He lit a fire and gazed out of his window, hoping he might see Rebecca. Though charcoal skies had hodded Londontown, it was too early for her to visit. A nightingale began her sweet song, the composition immediately plagiarized by a mockingbird. Shakespeare's eyes fixed on the empty street below. Life was a black page written in invisible ink, a tale all told, just waiting to be deciphered. He thought of Harry, of his unrestrained drunken laughter, of his weeping—sad melodies intoned by a righteous man who had never fulfilled his earthly dreams.

Shakespeare peered out the window for over an hour, then lay upon his pallet and closed his eyes.

Dreams haunted his wits. Disturbing reveries made suddenly sweet by a mellifluous voice from Heaven singing him words of gratitude.

Sweet dreams, my friend. Sweet dreams and may God bless.

He slept in peace.

61

hakespeare arose the next morning at dawn, fresh and whole, but lonely. There had been no shadows, no nightmares, but no Rebecca either. Diamonds of sunlight dappled the rushes of his floor. He dressed quickly and set out to the Lopez house, hoping her absence wasn't an evil portent.

But it was.

A large crowd had gathered on the front lawn of the Lopez estate in Holborn, more people than usual. Shakespeare pushed his way through the mass but was stopped at the gatehouse by one of the Queen's men, a short man with a serious expression. He held a halberd.

"Back," ordered the guard.

"What news?" Shakespeare asked.

The halberdier ignored him. Shakespeare started to step forward but was blocked by the spear.

"I said back!" snapped the guard.

Shakespeare pivoted and repeated the question to the person directly behind him—a fair-complexioned commoner wearing a black cloak.

"They arrested the whole lot of them," the commoner explained.

Shakespeare turned ashen.

"Looks like they're all going to the gallows." The commoner snickered. "Justice is served, the filthy Jews."

"When?" Shakespeare said.

"Sir?"

"When?" Shakespeare repeated, shouting this time. "When were they arrested?"

"I know not," the commoner said. "Why are you shouting at me, sir?"

Shakespeare didn't answer.

A young gentleman standing to Shakespeare's right said, "I heard the Queen's men came last night. Cleared them out before dawn."

The commoner wiped his nose on his cloak and said, "They already hung the first one at dawn."

"Hung?" Shakespeare asked. "Who was hung?"

"Not the dog Lopez," answered the gentleman. "The other dog, Lopez's conspirator."

"De Gama," the commoner said.

"Yes," the gentleman said. "De Gama. They hung him at six in the morning. Lopez is next, tomorrow at dawn. That should be a goodly one. . . . God save the Queen."

Shakespeare felt his heart hammering. He asked, "Where is the family now?"

"Which family?" asked the commoner.

"The others who were arrested!" Shakespeare said. "Are they at Westminster?"

The gentleman shrugged, then stared at him suspiciously. "What are they to you?"

"Aye," said the commoner. "Why are you so interested in the family? Are you one of *them*?"

Shakespeare looked down at the ground, then raised his head and faced two sets of hostile eyes.

"No," he said. "I'm not."

The gentleman said, "Thank God for your most fortunate hap, my goodfellow."

"I'm not family," Shakespeare said. "But as God is my witness, I should have been."

He turned on his heels and left them gaping.

After making frantic inquiries that took up the greater part of the afternoon, he discovered that all the converso community had *not* been arrested. They'd been expelled from their homes during the night, all their property and land confiscated by the crown. A clerk at Westminster had said the Jews were to be deported, but his knowledge had been scant with details.

Good Queen Eliza, Shakespeare ruminated with sadness. Rebecca had much gratitude in her heart for her ruler, her father's temporary redeemer. But all of Eliza's kind feelings for Rebecca, all of her doubts about Lopez's guilt, could not prevent her from bending to the will of her people. Two stays of execution were all that could be tolerated. Ever since Lopez's trial at Guildhall, England had demanded a traitor's execution at Tyburn for the hapless doctor.

Lopez must be hung, the masses had cried. *He was a conjurer and a poisoner. He was a Spaniard at heart, plotting with the fiendish Philip against the great Gloriana. He was a wolfish Jew.*

The Queen had signed Lopez's death warrant long ago. Now her people were demanding that she make good on her promise.

But though the doctor might be guilty of his crime, the daughter was not! Shakespeare was determined to save his lover. He

searched the city for Rebecca. A fruitless effort since no one
knew for certain where the Jews had gone.

At least she was well hidden, wherever she was.

Thank God.

He returned to his closet at sundown, exhausted from his travails.

Lopez's execution. Tomorrow at dawn.

They would be there. Shakespeare would be there as well.

Maybe he'd see her again.

Maybe not.

He slumped into his desk chair, grabbed air, opened his fists.
Nothing. Gone.

A Sisyphean love. Forever doomed. Rebecca . . . a painful
memory.

He closed his eyes and thought of her. Of their bodies entwined under soft, warm sheets, of honeyed kisses and velvet
embraces.

It had been so real yesterday, but now it was just a dream.
Yesterday was far away.

Deep melancholia seeped into his bones, stabbed his heart.
Yet a tiny speck of light managed to shine through his blackened
soul. Maybe he would find her. Maybe he could see her again,
talk to her, hold her.

Maybe.

Just maybe.

62

Ｔhe mob had been congregating in the streets before dawn.
Roderigo heard the shouts and curses before streaks of
sunlight penetrated the cold, sour air of the prison. He was re-
citing the *Shma* when the guards opened the door to his cell. He
continued praying as they tied his hands around his back, refusing to stop even as he was pushed down the staircase of the Salt
Tower. He fell on his side, was kicked in the ribs by a beefeater,
then pulled to his feet and dragged to a boat docked at Traitor's
Gate.

Shma Yisroel, Adonai Elohenu, Adonai Ehad.

The essence of the religion for which he lived. For which he was about to die.

Hear oh Israel, the Lord is our God, the Lord is one.

Our God.

Adonai.

He boarded the boat that carried him west to Tyburn. It docked ten minutes later. Heavily guarded, Roderigo was taken off the boat and walked to a wheeled cart.

The guards opened rank, and rotted food was thrown in Roderigo's face.

He hardly noticed, his body and soul still immersed in prayer.

The guards bound his feet, then placed him supine upon a burlap sling attached to the back of the cart. They bound him onto the sling.

Roderigo kept praying.

Did Adonai hear his prayers? he wondered.

Did He hear his prayers even as the sling was dragged upon the ground?

As mud splattered upon his face? As he was pelted with slop?

As his bare feet were scraped against the cobblestones and turned bloody raw?

As his head was smashed against the ground, as rocks were hurled at his brow, as his ribs were bruised by swift kicks?

Amid all the curses and pain, did Adonai hear his prayers?

A dog ran up beside him, growling, baring its teeth. A moment later sharp canine fangs sank into his shoulders. The spectators cheered. The guards waited a moment before shooing the heroic beast away.

Somebody exclaimed that the dog was now infected with the blood of a Jew and should be killed.

Another agreed.

People shouted,

Curse the Jewdevil!

Poisoner!

Slayer!

The Devil's creature!

God be thanked, Essex had caught the Devil.

God save the Queen!

More slop dumped; this time in Roderigo's eyes. Burning, burning.

Eyes open, eyes closed. The same nightmare.

He thought of Teresa's tale, how her faith had saved her from burning in the pyre.

Shma Yisroel . . .

The cart continued its trail westward.

Out of the city of London.

Into Westminster.
More people.
More pain.
More stink.
To the gallows of Tyburn.
Roderigo continued to pray, his faith stronger than ever.

The site was black with people pushing, shoving, shouting, cursing. Rotten smells: everything around Tyburn stunk of decay and death. Shakespeare sat upon a rise overlooking the field. He'd been looking for Rebecca for an hour, but all he could see were ugly faces lusting for blood.

None of the Lopez family was there. At least, none stood by the gallows.

Where were they? Surely they had not abandoned their kinsman during his most desperate hour of need.

Shakespeare continued to search the mob with his eyes.

Spectators were still arriving. Executions drew big audiences. But this one was exceptionally large considering the condemned was not nobility. They had come out in droves because it had been discovered that Lopez was a secret Jew.

A secret Jew, his daughter a secret Jewess. It didn't matter to Shakespeare. He loved her still. He had to touch her again. He ached for her—his gut burning with the agony of loss.

Where *was* she?

Where were any of them? Her brother? Her cousins and uncle?

His eyes scanned the crowd once again, then fixed upon a familiar face—black and shiny. Lopez's blackamoor servant Martino, standing near the gallows, holding a burlap bag. Was he the only one?

The crowd roared. Shakespeare knew that the condemned man's cart was coming through the gates of Tyburn. The black-hooded executioner suddenly appeared to the right of the gallows, then climbed six steps up to the raw oak platform. He waited, ax in hand.

Everyone waiting.

Where were Rebecca's kinsmen? Where was *she*?

The crowd parted, making way for the cart. The mob grew riotous. More of the Queen's men were sent in to quiet the unruly masses.

The cart stopped: a swarm of bodies descended upon it, only to be repelled by sentries' pikes and halberds. Protecting the hapless doctor from being torn limb by limb . . . before the appointed moment.

Shakespeare felt sick. Evil air—murderous vapors.

Roderigo stood, bloodied and stooped. Flanked by guards, he

was pushed up the platform steps. To his right were the gallows, a hemp rope ending in a noose swinging from the rafters. To his left stood the executioner. Not a single inch of Tyburn's field was visible, so packed it was with human flesh.

"Quiet!" the executioner ordered the audience. "The man must be allowed to speak and be heard!"

But the noise would not abate. The crowd inched toward the platform, ready to pounce upon the battered doctor. The sentries closed their ranks around him.

"Quiet!" shouted the executioner once again.

The guards lifted their arms, made menacing gestures to the crowd until the noise reduced to a low-pitched hum.

"Speak," the executioner ordered.

Roderigo looked around. He whispered the *Shma* to himself.

"Louder!" commanded the executioner.

Roderigo prayed silently to God, prayed that Rebecca had known what he tried to tell her that day. He suddenly spotted Martino's black face and smiled inwardly.

Rebecca had known! She had to have known!

It gave him strength.

"I am innocent," Roderigo whispered.

"Louder!" ordered the axman.

"I am innocent!"

The crowd jeered. Garbage was hurled at the platform.

"The man has a right to his last words!" shouted the executioner. "Let him speak!"

Roderigo felt his throat constrict. He knew what *he* had to do. Causing confusion was his only hope. Confusion had been Teresa's salvation.

Create a riot! Say the outrageous!

"I loved my mistress!" Roderigo shouted.

An immediate chorus of hisses and boos drowned him out.

"Silence I say!" screamed the executioner. "The man is entitled to speak his last words!"

Again the crowd quieted.

"I loved my mistress!" Roderigo screamed. "I loved her more than . . . than Jesus Christ!"

A burst of derisive laughter obliterated Roderigo's last words. The angry mob advanced toward the platform, and the executioner knew he could no longer retain order. He quickly slipped Roderigo's head through the noose and hoisted the doctor upward. Roderigo felt the rope tighten around his neck, felt the breath being squeezed out of his body.

Adonai . . .

Shakespeare saw the executioner cut Roderigo down. The doctor's body was limp; any facial skin not covered by white beard

522   *Faye Kellerman*

was purple and puffy. Yet it was obvious that the man was still breathing. His chest was still moving.

Shakespeare turned his head, unable to watch the final destruction of the traitor. Yet some invisible force willed his eyes back to the gallows. He had to observe the barbaric rite to its conclusion.

The audience was wild, crazed with a desire to see blood.

So crowded was the platform that the executioner had disappeared from sight. Waves of people pushed forward as guards shoved them off, Roderigo lost in the multitudes. Finally Shakespeare saw the executioner reappear amidst the pandemonium, his ax held high. The blade swung down with a mighty blow.

A bloodied arm was raised in the air.

Shakespeare felt hot, bitter bile rise in his throat.

Another bloodied arm was hoisted upward, shreds of scarlet flesh dangling from the shoulder socket, the fingers clenched in a fist.

Done to the man whilst he lived.

Shakespeare held back a dry heave.

The leg—hairy, dyed crimson.

The crowd went berserk.

Shakespeare vomited.

The last leg.

God have mercy!

Three guards carried the severed limbs and tied them upon the gates—a warning to any man contemplating treasonous activity.

Shakespeare saw another guard drop the head and torso into a burlap bag, then looked away from the defilement. His eyes passed over the spot where Martino had been standing. The blackamoor was gone.

The executioner was walking away, the ax dripping with red ooze slung over his shoulder.

The black-hooded executioner . . . His walk was odd.

He limped.

He *limped*.

A familiar limp.

Another guard stood watch over the bag containing Lopez's remains. He held a halberd in his left hand; his right hand dangled lifelessly by his side. Still another sentry was positioned to his left, black-bearded but pale.

Where was *she*?

Shakespeare looked out across the field. On the other side he saw a draper and boy apprentice pushing a cart piled high with burlap away from the bestial packs. The apprentice was costumed for the part—worn brown jerkin, yellow hose, scuffed black boots, and brown cap.

Yet his walk was strange, measured, overly careful . . . and triumphant. All too familiar—those contours, those delectable curves.

For all the world to see, Roderigo Lopez's limbs hung from the gates of Tyburn.

But Shakespeare knew otherwise.

God was merciful!

He longed to run to her, to take flight and scoop her up like a hawk claiming its prey. But he remained motionless. The discovery of her disguise would be fatal to everyone. He had no choice but to let her go . . . forever.

With wet eyes he watched the draper and his apprentice recede until they vanished from eyesight, then he turned around and walked away.

He didn't look back.

63

The envelope was wrinkled and yellow and smelled of seawater. The ink had bled into the paper, but the smudged handwriting was as precious to Shakespeare as gold. He ripped open the letter.

Dear William,

Thank God my letter reached thee, my love. Our hearts now may speak. I first wrote thee as soon as I was able, but alas we are both at the mercy of ships which sail unbearably slow for lovers apart. I eagerly scrawled these rambling words to thee as soon as I received thy response to my first letter. By the time I held thy glorious words in my hand, they were already three months old. So much time will have passed before thou receivest this letter.

Seven months since I've seen thee. Yet I picture thy face as clearly as the last time I saw thee, the last time I held thee—at my bedchamber. No, I was not at Tyburn that dreadful day dressed as a boy apprentice. How could I possibly have saved my father's life? And how could thou entertainst such wild fancy? Thou saw-

est with thine own fair eyes my poor father's fate hung upon the gates.

Shakespeare paused. Her father's *fate* hung upon the gates. But another's limbs. Yet if Rebecca had reason for keeping her father's miraculous rescue a secret from him, so be it. He read on.

> *My father still lives so vibrantly in my heart. And another lives inside of me. I'm pregnant, my sweet Willy. My only regret is that the child is not thine. I prayed that our last encounter might have brought forth a permanent bond of our love, but it was not to pass. Yet even though the child is not of thy blood, I feel it is of thy soul.*

Not his. In all the times they had loved, his seed had died within her. Yet it was Miguel, performing his husbandly duties to his new wife with perfunctory interest, who had given her womb vitality.

He felt an illogical rage at Miguel, at his own worthless member. Three with Anne, none with the one he loved, the one he worshiped. He bit his thumbnail and continued reading.

> *I am four and a half months pregnant as of the date of the letter.*

Seven months by now.

> *I look as though I've swallowed a melon. My womb is as hard as a melon as well, yet it is vibrant with life. I feel the ever-so-slight tickling of his kicks. Thou wilt note that I use the masculine pronoun. I think the baby a boy, and if this indeed is so, I should like to name him William.*

Shakespeare smiled.

> *Miguel was not pleased by my choice of forename, but if the past be an indicator of things to come, I will prevail over my husband's objections. Miguel, I've discovered, has no armory against my tears. My husband is such a sweet man. I've been so volatile of late, my weeping and my laughter come at strange and awkward times and for no reason whatsoever. My mother claims she, too, acted strangely every time she was with child.*

The next line was heavily crossed out. The sentence started with the word *My*. Shakespeare squinted and tried to read what

Rebecca had so strongly deleted. He flipped the letter over and felt the bold strokes with his fingertips. No doubt about it. The word *my* was followed by the word *father*. He couldn't decipher anything else. Whatever the sentence had said, it was now lost to him.

He read on:

> *I thank God thou art spared my spells and my vicious tongue as well. Miguel is tolerant of my moodiness but will have none of my sarcasm. He scolds me when I become waspish but has yet to hit me, though I've deserved a bit of a reminder on more than one occasion. He is truly a gentle man, a most worthy husband. Yet our marriage bed is no warmer now than it was on the night we were wed. How could it be when he is repulsed by my body and I am repulsed by anyone other than thee?*
>
> *I never realized what love was until I met thee. My love for thee keeps me awake at night, dreaming during the day. I am never free from thee—thou holdest me in bondage yet thou art my ultimate liberator. I think of thee and only then am I happy. There are no words to describe my loneliness. Merciful God has tried to keep me occupied by giving my womb life, but even that which daily expands my belly cannot replace the emptiness in my heart.*
>
> *I hear my*

Another cross out, the word husband inserted above the top of the sentence.

> *I hear my husband calling me. I'll leave thee by saying that my life as a Jewess in the Levant has been blessed. It is not always easy—is anything simple?—but it has its rich rewards. The rewards, however, do not fill up the space left by thine absence.*
>
> *Dream of me, Willy.*
>
> *Rebecca*

Shakespeare wrote back.

> *My dearest Becca,*
>
> *I write rapidly because Cuthbert Burbage is coming to drag me away. We are in the midst of rehearsing* A Comedy of Errors—*a book I'd written several years ago. It pleases the nobility—a play of amusement for Twelfth Night, which is naught but a month away.*
>
> *I weep with joy at thy womb brimming with life. May thy fruit be healthy and lusty and a source of constant happiness.*
>
> *My sweet Becca, thou knowest I am a madman without thee. I have slept nightly with thy first letter in my hand, so much so that*

the fibers of the parchment have weakened and shredded from the sweat of my palm. I care not. As long as I hold something written by thine own sweet hand, I feel closer to thee.

Thou requestest me to dream of thee, as if I were able to dream of anyone else. My mind is blinded with thine image, especially at night, when the blackened mist delights in naughty tricks. I see thee standing beside my pallet. I jump out of bed and reach to embrace thee, discovering too quickly that dark hours have played once again the conjurer. I weep when I realize that I hold nothing.

I need to hold thee.

There was a banging on his door. Cuthbert. Damn. Shakespeare quickly wrote.

I am a wretched man without thee.

"Shakespeare?" Cuthbert called from outside.

I must leave thee now. I will write thee a longer letter tonight. I love thee. If it be suited to thy needs, I will come to visit thee in springtime—

"Shakespeare!" Cuthbert pounded the door. "Where the devil are you?"

"A minute," Shakespeare shouted. "I'm getting dressed."

"Let me in first."

"A minute!"

Love me as I love thee.

Forever thine,
Will

Postal service beyond England's shores was sporadic at best, depending on the vagaries of weather and merchant shipping. The next letter took half a year to arrive. London was drenched in rain, and Shakespeare found the envelope floating in a small puddle outside the door of his closet. He looked upward and his eyes were assaulted by droplets of dirty water.

Leaky roof: his luck, it was right outside his door. The last windstorm had blown off some of the roof's shingles, and no one had bothered to replace them. At least the *inside* of his cell was relatively dry.

He picked up the letter, opened the door to his closet, and placed the envelope upon his table. It took ten minutes for the fire to burn the bitter cold from the air. He stood in front of the hearth and rubbed his hands, exhaling warm breath onto his fingers and nose.

Her seal.

Carefully, he picked up the envelope and tried to dry it out with the heat of the fire. After a half hour of careful drying, Shakespeare noticed the handwriting.

Different.

Rebecca's seal, but not her handwriting.

He wanted to tear open the letter but knew that the paper was still too damp to read.

He held the letter in front of the fire for another fifteen minutes, watched the paper yellow with heat, the ink fade. The writing was still legible, but quite faint.

He opened the slightly moist envelope. The paper inside was damp, stuck to the side of the envelope. With utmost care Shakespeare liberated the letter from its casing.

Too wet to read, but not too wet to notice that it, too, hadn't been penned by Rebecca's hand.

He held it to the fire. The words . . . impossible to read unless he unfolded the paper.

More drying.

More waiting.

Slowly, Shakespeare straightened the first crease.

The ink was smeared, but the words were readable.

The second fold was undone.

One single page. A short note.

He held it up to the light and read,

Dear William Shakespeare,

He turned the letter over. The signature at the bottom said Miguel.

Bastard.

He was forbidding Rebecca to write to him.

Bastard.

Shakespeare read as best he could:

I write this letter out of duty to my wife—a promise I made to her. I will be brief.

The baby came at eight and a half months—a goodly-sized healthy girl with rosy coloring and a strong set of lungs. Everything appeared to be progressing very smoothly, mayhap in retrospect too smoothly. Rebecca's labor was quick and her milk came in three days later, on time. Tis when she encountered her first fever.

Shakespeare paused.

Fever.

He read on,

> *Childbed fever. They say it happens to many women. But that makes no difference when it happens to your wife. I need not elaborate. Let us say that God was merciful and swift and she suffered very little. The fever was strong, and she was deep asleep long before she died—*

Shakespeare's eyes suddenly blurred. He slumped to the floor and forced himself to finish the letter.

> *The child is in fine form. Her name is Teresa Hannah. A lovely girl, she resembles Becca except for her eyes. They are the palest of blue—*

Pale eyes. Shakespeare began to cry.

> *This letter is a deathbed promise I made to her. It is not my desire to cause you pain, only to do what has been requested of me. Rebecca also wanted me to tell you that if you desire to write a book for her, do not write about her. On that point she was firm. Instead, pen a work that will pay homage to her dishonored father. A book about a man hated and spat upon, a man wronged because he was a Jew.*

> *Miguel*

Shakespeare dropped the letter in his lap and watched the flames of the fire sprint from log to log. A sharp crackle followed by an upward stream of glowing embers. His chest hurt, a deep untendable wound. He sat staring at the fire for what seemed to be hours.

The room became cold and dark. He shivered until his muscles ached, but he didn't feel the pain.

He no longer felt anything.

She'd been lost to him months ago. But the arrival of Miguel's letter had smothered his last breath of hope.

All of it, finally dead.

He held the letter in his hand, suddenly crumpled it and threw it on top of the smoldering log. The paper caught fire, turning from yellow to brown then black. A brief flash of light soared through the hearth, then died into ashes.

From dust to dust.

Shakespeare stood up, lit his candlestick and sat at his desk. He took out his quill and a blank piece of paper.

Gone.

She had been lost to him years ago, the day she'd been conceived from Jewish stock.

The room was an icy midnight crypt, the only light the flame of his candle. He sat until the first flickers of dawn broke through his window. The rain had let up.

Write a story. Pay homage to her father.

Write a story about a Jew.

Write.

Anything but this pain, this unrelenting pain.

Write anything. Just write.

Dry-eyed, he picked up his quill and scratched,

In sooth, I know not why I am so sad. . . .

Historical Summary

Doctor Roderigo Lopez lived from 1525 to 1594. A Portuguese converso, he was educated at Salamanca in Spain and settled in London during the early reign of Queen Elizabeth I. He rose to professional prominence by becoming a member of the College of Physicians and was the first house physician at St. Bartholomew's Hospital. He obtained the patronage of the Earl of Leicester and went on to become Lord Leicester's house doctor. But his most significant advancement came in 1586 when he was appointed physician-in-ordinary to the Queen. He was married to a Portuguese conversa named Sarah and was known to have at least one son and several daughters. Lopez's brother-in-law, Jorge Anoz, had a son named Dunstan Ames, and Solomon Aben Ayesh, the Duke of Mylitene, was related to Lopez by marriage. An interesting note: Aben Ayesh remained on good terms with the Queen even after Lopez's execution.

In 1589, on behalf of his patrons Leicester and Walsingham, Dr. Lopez presented Don Antonio's cause to Queen Elizabeth. The Queen consented to aid Don Antonio's bid for the Portuguese crown by sending English forces—headed by Sir John Norris and Sir Francis Drake—to the Iberian shores. This invasion to liberate Portugal from Spanish rule ended in dismal failure, leaving Lopez with much to explain to Her Majesty. Eventually, he found his way back into royal favor, and a year after England's military defeat, he broke off with Don Antonio. Lopez then began working covertly with King Philip of Spain for peace between his nation and Spain.

Lopez had also worked closely with Manuel de Andrada in furthering the cause of Don Antonio. It was de Andrada who gave Lopez the indicting ruby and diamond ring in 1591. Lopez did offer it to the Queen, and she refused to take it, perhaps after learning about its origins. Meanwhile, de Andrada had shown himself to be an untrustworthy man, not only to his former master Don Antonio, but to England as well. Eventually Lord

Burghley placed de Andrada under house arrest in Lopez's home in 1592. But a year later, de Andrada escaped to the Low Countries, never to be heard from again. It was de Andrada who first suggested Lopez's willingness to poison Don Antonio for King Philip of Spain. But the veracity of this indictment remains in doubt.

Nevertheless, Lopez was arrested in January 1594, accused of plotting to poison the Queen and planning to destroy and burn England's warships. Lord Essex was the driving wind behind Lopez's arrest, levying treasonous charges against Lopez in a letter written to his spymaster, Antony Bacon. Lopez was tried at Guildhall, the evidence against him a ring given to him by the King of Spain, correspondence written by de Andrada that mentioned Lopez's willingness to poison Don Antonio for King Philip, and a mysterious letter that spoke of the purchase price of pearls, musk, and amber. These cryptic words were eventually interpreted by the trial committee. Pearls meant Lopez's price for poisoning the Queen, the musk and amber, the price of burning the ships. Dr. Lopez was hung and quartered at Tyburn in June 1594.

In all probability, Lopez was innocent of the charges against him. However, correspondence with the King of Spain showed Lopez to have been a shrewd negotiator, a keen politician, and an expert in the methods of poisoning. As for Lord Essex, his political ambitions finally proved too much for Elizabeth. He was found guilty of treason and beheaded in February 1601.

The Lopez case attracted the attention of England's masses and its anti-Jewish ramifications captured the interest of London's playwrights. Many Shakespearean scholars believe Dr. Lopez was the prototype for Shylock in *The Merchant of Venice*. It has even been suggested that Shylock's traditional red beard emanated from Richard Burbage's personal knowledge of Dr. Lopez's appearance. (They both had been in the service of the Earl of Leicester.) *The Merchant of Venice* has been carefully scanned for allusions to Lopez and some have been found. For example: Act IV, scene i, lines 130-140, contains references to Shylock as a wolf. In Latin, wolf is Lupes, hence Lopez. Similarly, the name of Shylock's chief rival is Antonio. Does this refer to Don Antonio, Lopez's enemy at the time of his execution? If allusions are looked for, allusions will be found. Only Shakespeare knew what he had in mind.

THE RITUAL BATH

Someone declares unholy war on the holiest of places when the quiet, ordered world of a yeshiva is shattered by an unspeakable crime: a woman is brutally raped as she returns from the *mikvah,* the bathhouse where women perform their cleansing ritual. Detective Peter Decker of the LAPD is relieved to find Rina Lazarus there as a witness. But as the trail grows cold, Decker and Rina grow closer—until a sudden horrific revelation threatens to tear them apart.

SACRED AND PROFANE

LAPD detective Peter Decker is camping in the California foothills with two young friends—sons of the beautiful, beguiling Jewish widow Rina Lazarus—when the older boy stumbles upon a horrifying sight: two charred human skeletons. Suddenly Decker is plunged into a deadly case of murder.

MILK AND HONEY

While Rina Lazarus is out of town wrestling with Peter Decker's marriage proposal, Peter comes across a strange sight: a two-year-old child covered in blood and bee stings crawling around a housing complex. By the time Rina comes back to town, Peter's obsessed with the case—especially when he stumbles onto a grisly quadruple murder.

DAY OF ATONEMENT

Peter Decker and Rina Lazarus, honeymooning in Brooklyn during the Jewish High Holidays, are drawn into the search for a runaway Orthodox Jewish teenage boy. But Peter, whose specialty is finding runaways, is a stranger in this close-knit community, and it's tough to get anyone to open up—until he discovers a dangerous link between the boy and the outside world. . . .

FALSE PROPHET

Rina Lazarus is six months pregnant and miserable, while her husband, LAPD detective Peter Decker, has his hands full with the assault and rape of Lilah Brecht, a celebrity spa owner. After one of Lilah's family members is murdered, Peter begins to suspect that she and her family are keeping secrets from him. . . .

GRIEVOUS SIN

Peter and Rina, with a newborn baby girl, are concerned that budget cutbacks have left the Los Angeles hospital a security nightmare. When a baby is kidnapped and a respected nurse vanishes along with her, Peter pursues a twisted path of hospital politics and misplaced passions that will bring him face-to-face with the most grievous sin.

by FAYE KELLERMAN